D1783803

Bloody Thorn
~ Book One of the Thorn Trilogy ~
2nd Edition

By
Sarahbeth Lazic

Bloody Thorn ~ Book One of the Thorn Trilogy
A Thorn Publication
Copyright © 2014 by Sarahbeth Lazic - 2nd edition

SELazic@aol.com
ISBN-13: 978-1507739518
ISBN-10: 1507739516

Cover and internal art designs © to:
Cover image by Sandrine Tsong Hoan © eagielts@gmail.com
Cover layout by Mavrosh Illustrations © mavrosh@yahoo.de

Dedication
~ ~ ~ ~

To my dear friend Debbie. For all the support and love you have shown not only to me but to my boys, I thank you! You are always a sturdy and constant support (even though we're both held together by a lick, stick, and a promise). With endless thanks and hugs, I dedicate not only Bloody Thorn but the entire Thorn series to you. You have done more than I could ever ask of you. Thank you for allowing me the use of Jamie!

May your kitchen be forever stocked with jars of delicious jam. One day, our dream of having our little writers' cottage by the sea will be granted! Because, let's face it, by the time we're finished with all of our books, we'll need someplace to go where we can live out our lives in our happy corners, giggling devious giggles.

In Thanks
~ ~ ~ ~

I want to thank my wonderful and artistically brilliant friend Mavrosh for the time she donated to constructing the cover. I appreciate all the time and work you have done, not only in the creation of this cover but also the cover to Warlock. Thank you for double checking my German, and thank you for allowing my imagination to run crazy through your art gallery where I find endless hours of inspiration.

Thank you to the delightful Eagiel for coming through in the last minute to create such a beautiful cover image! Your work is not only stunning but captures the beauty and the essence of this book. I owe you a great thanks for your quick work and your kindness.

~

*A*llow me the pleasure of introducing myself. *My name is Daniel Rhys Thorn, a humble businessman, dedicated art historian, and restorer of archeological artifacts and relics. And I am creature born from a mythical world; a creature who lives within your darkest imagination.*

I am a Lamia.

I am a vampire.

They say that my kind was born from a curse, a strike of vengeance against a few men of arrogant nature who dared question the order of the Gods. In an act of divine punishment, the ancient Gods and Goddesses ordered the Fates to alter the destinies of these men and their families.

The world was a much different place when the Roman Empire declared its supremacy. Arrogance and ignorance ran freely through the concept of man - through cities and across lands. To question the Gods was an act done out of desperation or intoxication.

The true reason as to why these few men questioned the narcissistic Deities is still unknown, and will forever remain a secret. All that is known is that the Fates descended down upon these families and spinning their curse that came in the form of a violent and deadly plague. Many members of these families died within one night. Others were spared but forced to live on with the horrid consequences of their foolishness.

Those who survived that brutal and cold plague became the carriers of the curse, holding within their body the genetic malfunction that would carry on the Gods' mockery in the form of the Proprietas , or as we call it, the Trait. In this Trait, a genetic mutation, the birth of our race is formed. Humanus become the carriers of the Proprietas, passing along the Trait through their breeding. When a child is born, that infant may have the Trait and either become a carrier or a Lamia - the cursed.

Lamia are what humans consider to be vampires. However, we are nothing like the figures seen in movies and on the television or read in books. Those 'vampires' are generic figments of human imaginations, nothing close to the true monster known as a Lamia. Only a human containing the Proprietas can be altered into a Lamia through the act known as the Creare and with the aid of the Mordĕre - the vampire's bite.

In many fandoms, this change is romanticized for the publics' pleasure. But in truth, the Creare is a cruel and violent change that effects the human body on a molecular level, changing physical systems and genetic coding. A Humanus holding the Trait can be changed by being drained to the last drop of their blood through feeding - the Edĕre. When the mortal is dead, the Lamia must infuse his or her Sanguis, blood, into the human's body by any means necessary so that the Key within the Lamia's blood can activate the Trait, reanimating the human and rebirthing that individual into a Lamia.

The process is dreadful, and the human going through the change can experience unimaginable pain and torment during the process. Some humans live. Some do not. Luckily, and by some heavenly gift, humans who survive the Creare do not remember the particulars of their change. They simply wake up to a new life and a new world void of human warmth and compassion - a world created for the dead and haunted by the living.

Over the centuries, those direct descendants of the original families began to create organized institutions of Lamia who contain the same genetic traits passed down through their lineage. We call these institutions, Familia. Each Familia produce Lamia and Humanus that obtain certain talents and skills that are passed on through human offspring and that can be activated by a Lamia with similar skills and talents. Some Familia breed Lamia who have excelled in Ars Magica, sorcery and other forms of magic. Other Familia pride themselves on being able to control all of the Coercêre. There are also Familia who produce exceptionally skilled warriors. My Familia is one such Familia of unimaginable machines of battle - the Drasus.

While we are considered 'vampires', we are far from the historical and mythological creatures who have taken over the media world. Yes, we are dead - to a degree - but no, we're not blood addicted zombies of any form. Between you and me, I'm rather exhausted from battling those decaying hunks of reanimated bodies. Though the curse from long ago has retarded the abilities for our bodies to function properly, we do need to breathe and feed in order for our bodies and our organs to operate. Oxygen is needed for our brains to function and for our hearts to beat, though on a greatly decreased scale. Our blood also turns cold, and our senses and strengths increase. Our brains are able to function at over seventy-five percent capacity. Just imagine the powers and abilities that are opened to us.

Then again, I look at my twin and cannot help but think that the seventy-five percent must have missed him somehow. He runs into walls with a nightlight on. Don't tell him I stated that, please.

As to the concept of feeding from humans and the need to consume blood, much of this is true. Our bodies do not break down organic or chemical nutrients as well as the human body does, and so we need to replace many nutrients with fresh blood from a living human or animal. Though I would rather prefer feeding from a human than a cow. How very ironic since I still do enjoy a fine steak tartar from time to time.

We can consume foods and drinks that are of the finest components or of the most basic, organic, and all natural ingredients. Chemical derivatives, GMOs, and additives are not very kind to our systems. And alcohol, narcotics, tobacco, heavy carbs, caffeine, and sugars can send our systems into shock whether or not we consumed these products directly or fed off of a human who had partook in a little too much of one or more of these addictive pleasures. Then again, I always enjoy sitting at a little street side café in Paris or in Rome while taking pleasure in the night with a fine espresso. Though I suffer greatly the next day if I overindulge. There is nothing so amusing and so painful to watch than a Lamia acting upon a caffeine or sugar buzz. The migraines can be intolerable, and I speak from personal experience.

Though my world can be distant, lonely, empty, and quite often overrun with cruelties and danger, my life is not without splendor, comfort, and kindness. Lamia can choose to retain our humanity or become the monsters that our Daemon's demand us to be. The choice is always up to us. Some of my kind turn quickly to the allure of power and control that our internal Daemon promises. Others, like me, strive to live a life filled with as many human pleasures that remind us of our once short-lived mortality.

I, and my two brothers, grew up in an English village on the border of Wales and England with our mother and father, the late Eduard and Vivian Thorn. I was born in 1904 alongside my twin brother and a number of years after the birth of Kain. I have seen both the creation of modern society and the corruption of modern greed. I have seen many whom I love die, and I have met many who have gifted me with the reminder that humans are, in fact, a stronger race than mine.

We Lamia are within the shadows - watching and waiting - always. You do not know who we are, yet you pass us upon the streets and sit next to us upon the busses, always at night...always. We can hear your heart, and we can hear your thoughts.

Fear us, for we are death.

- *Daniel Rhys Thorn*

~ ~ ~ ~

The late nights of the London springtime seemed to be filled with more cold rain and heavy fog than in the previous years. Though it seemed that each and every night came with heavy rains falling from above, the streets were never empty. Tourists and locals alike were out and about visiting the local pubs, restaurants, theaters, sightseeing locations, and clubs. One such club had claimed its title as the hottest new music club along lower Thames Street from the moment it opened.

In the early spring, the Crucible had opened in a renovated gothic church that had once been condemned to demolition on London's south side along the Thames River. The old church had been brought back to life with accents of flaming torches, iron gates of imposing black, flagstone walkways lined by ancient trees, and tall brick walls dotted with ivy and spiked guards circling the property. At the massive front doors of the church, two medieval gargoyles loomed high above the crowds, watching all who awaited entry with their glowing red eyes radiating life. Behind the gothic structure resided a four-hundred year old cemetery that had also been revitalized, cleaned and restored, thus allowing those buried within a restful state of peace, safe from the destruction of modern-times and the endless lines of guests that came and went from the property.

The Crucible was a Receptaculum, a sanctuary for the darker kind that loomed within the shadows of London. Here, within the old walls, the Lamia of London could seek safety while enjoying entertainment away from hunters and the horrors that lingered around every corner. Not only was the old church the resting place of the dead but the living place for the undead.

The last week of Maius was just about over when life, for some, would take a new direction while the life of others would be snuffed out by events that would be considered impossible, yet fated to occur. The doors to the Crucible had been opened to the public for yet another busy night, and from outside, music could be heard thumping loudly from within and colored lights could be seen fluctuating from behind the magnificent Catherine window in time to the heavy rhythm coming from the live band. Upon this night the club was a breathing entity of streaming life from the souls that came and went from its belly.

Outside the massive ebony doors, lines of people waited entry, moving slowly but steadily past security. And though there was a steady rain trickling down from above, club-goers didn't seem to care for the excitement of the atmosphere was a drug to them, calling to those who were waiting to have a taste of euphoria.

~ ~ ~ ~

"**I** promise, this will be fun!" Joyce Scott called in loud anticipation as she tugged her cousin forwards in line.

Regan Scott groaned in agitation as she stumbled forwards, pulled off balance by Joyce's tugging. She was having second thoughts about coming to this place after looking up to the massive church that sent cold, uneasy shivers throughout her body.

"This place is creepy," she whimpered with a faint chuckle of uncertainty in her voice. The cathedral looked like it belonged in a theme park meant to scare people for entertainment, certainly not a place that she would ever want to visit.

"What do you mean? This place is awesome! I've been waiting to get in here since it opened," laughed Joyce in her bright, English toned voice. "And you're coming with me whether or not you like it. I told you I'd take you out for your birthday during your visit, and so I shall keep my promise!"

Joyce was speaking of Regan's visit from America for the duration of the summer. The two had plans to travel across the U.K., but first Joyce was going to take Regan to the Crucible for her twenty-first birthday. A bash it would be, she proclaimed! Regan wasn't so sure.

As Regan took another step in line, she ran her eyes to the front doors that were guarded by two bouncers and a young woman dressed in heavy Goth who was taking money, scanning identification cards, and stamping hands. When it was their turn to get their hands stamped and pay entry, Regan actually hesitated in handing over her I.D. She only did so after Joyce threatened to tear it from her hand. Once they were allowed to enter, Regan felt a wave of doom press down upon her.

"You can com'an go as ya want fer tonight,' said one of the brute bouncers as he waved the two forwards, 'bu' ya will 'ave ta 'ave yer hand checked ta get back in. Is that clear?"

7

"Will do!" screamed Joyce, pulling her cousin towards the sound of the thundering music.

Once inside, the two girls forced their way through the heavily crowded building, keeping clear of the dance floor and the sea of bodies dancing wildly to the band's song. The music was so loud that Regan felt her head pounding within seconds, and she made a mental note to check her hearing upon departure. Wincing, she looked up to the neon lights high upon the ceiling that were flashing and spinning from iron catwalks circling the dance floor. A touch of dizziness took her, so Regan turned her attention to visually exploring her surroundings.

At the Aspe, behind the original altar, was a large metal stage rising out of the Ambulatory where a band was raging over the laughter and talk of the crowd. The Choir area had been replaced with marble flooring and was now a magnificent dance floor where bodies moved and writhed. Tables and chairs dotted the open Naïve, and along each side of the Aisles were leather bound booths and more tables. Instead of beautiful stained-glass windows depicting religious scenery, there were colored windows showing mythological scenes, erotic creatures and naked women coiling about each other in raw embraces.

Along one wall stretched an ornate bar with a glass mirrored wall lined with illuminated bottles of liquors, all different colors and of the finest quality. And behind the bar were a number of high-class bartenders working quickly to hand out bottles and drinks to both patrons and wait-staff who would rush off into the crowd. Along the East End of the church was an iron walkway stretching above the crowds and secured by heavy iron chains. All about the walls were burning torches and iron made chandeliers. The place was done up like some medieval dungeon, and for some inborn reason that terrified Regan.

"This place gives me the creeps!" When her worried call to her cousin went unanswered, she added, "I can't even hear myself think!"

Joyce spun about with her arms in the air. "Oh hush!" she yelled. "Will you just enjoy yourself?"

"What? What did you say?" The American cupped a hand to her ear as if mocking the inability to hear her cousin. "I can't hear you. I think somebody turned the music up a little too loud."

"You know what?" Joyce snickered, grabbing her cousin's hand and pulling her towards the crowded bar. "I think you need a drink!"

"No," Regan snapped in panic. "I need to know where the closest fire exits are! If there's a fire, we're all dead! I need to know where they're located so I can get my butt out first and all of these weird people can burn to a crisp thanks to their alcoholic induced happiness!"

"Girl, you must be fun on an airplane!" Joyce huffed in agitation then stopped and turned to face her cousin with her hands planted to her hips. "I suppose you'd also like to know what escape plan the staff have incase Godzilla comes to crash the party?

Regan blinked her dark, chocolate eyes at the question. She only thought for a moment before a bright smile took her lips and she nodded her head. She replied joyfully, "Yes! That would be wonderful. Do you think they have their emergency plans on a text download or maybe an app?"

8

"Ugh! You're hopeless!" The English girl rolled her bright, green eyes and tossed her arms up in the air. "You need to learn to relax. Now come on. One drink never hurt anybody!"

The grin Joyce had upon her lips only made her cousin groan. She shoved Regan forwards and shouted, "Onward, my friend! We drink!"

"I'm doomed!"

~ ~ ~ ~

"**W**e are making millions!" laughed an excited young man with short, pumpkin dyed hair. He was hanging over the bar while starring out at the sea of thumping life. "We've only been open for three months and we're the number one club in London for those three months in a row!"

Alasdair Baird grinned, in utter delight, laughed, and clapped his hands upon the bar top. His beautiful amber colored eyes, speckled with tiny flecks of black, danced with enjoyment and excitement - flashing with silver when caught in a ray of stray light.

Seated upon one of the leather bar-stools across from Alasdair was another young man of equal age to his own, mid-twenties, or so it seemed. He was dressed in full gothic style from the black fishnet shirt across his slender chest to the leather pants that were bound low to his hips by a thick belt of royal blue that oddly matched the long highlights of metallic blue to his black hair. His flesh was pale, like the other man's, yet his eyes were an unnatural iced blue due to the theatrical contact lenses he wore.

Rhain Connal Thorn cast a grin towards his friend. "It's beyond brilliant, mate,' he commented in his smooth accent of upper-class British, 'within the first two months this place has paid for itself - in double."

"How much did this place cost us anyway?" Asked Alasdair out of curiosity. "Eighty thousand pounds or so?"

"Fifty thousand for the church," answered, in correction, a young woman of perfected beauty from next to him. She was clothed from neck to floor in a gorgeous leather jumper that cuddled her tightly held breasts together in a white blouse, and her long hair of sleek ebony fell delicately about her features that were too flawless to be true. She offered the two men a sweet smile with long lashes batting playfully over slender, olive green eyes.

"Fifty?" Alasdair blinked his eyes towards Philomena Damasippus. "That's it? We paid fifty thousand pounds for an old cathedral? Why did I think it cost eighty?"

Philomena, just as pale as he, gave a nod as she sipped what looked to be a thick Bloody Mary. Phil licked her lips as a warm shiver trailed her body to the taste and sensation of the drink. "You and Rhain spent close to eighty on the restoration after the purchase of the building, the grounds, and the cemetery," she explained with a rather sassy grin settling her hair and while flipping her long dark hair of silken ebony.

9

Alasdair snorted with a slight grunt when strands of her hair slapped against his face. He swatted her hair away. "Can you believe those corporate pricks wanted to tear this place down? What a pity. Bunch of fat bastards with more money falling out of their pockets than they can count. All piss and no wind, that's for sure," he said with a laugh and a slight shake of his head that let his short cut, dual colored hair skim across his sharp nose, hailing to his Roman decent. "We saved this old place and turned it into a money pig. We'll be rich, mate."

"When it comes to profit and possibilities, I don't fuck around." Rhain grinned, looking to his friend. He too shared the same excitement he saw mirrored within his associate's eyes. With a deep groan, he stretched his arms up and over his head then laced fingers within his black hair. "It's all about the business and giving the people what they want."

"It's still too loud," spoke a smooth, male voice from behind the trio.

The three turned about to observe an individual who came walking from the crowd. He was tall, at least 6'2", and with a slender frame clothed in a thick dress-coat of black over a neat pair of trousers and a tucked, buttoned shirt of white. As the other three, the man's skin was pale and a flash of silver could be seen glinting within his ebony eyes when touched by a stray flash of light. He was beautiful, in an effeminate sort of way, with his sleek black hair drawn back into a tight bind at the base of his neck, falling free down the middle of his back.

Rhain groaned dryly, tipping his head to the side when he heard the voice belonging to his brother. In fact, the new comer was more than just his brother but his identical twin, Daniel Rhys Thorn. Besides their difference in attire and hair styles, the two men looked exactly the same with their lean bodies and their tight bone structure. Even their voices were the same.

Rhain grumbled under his breath, "Look what the cat dragged in - my second half."

Daniel arched a slender, perfected brow. He said nothing as he stepped behind the bar and away from any prying hands. How many times his backside had been groped as he walked through this club on a busy night...well, he'd long lost count.

"What do you want, mate, an orchestra? Or maybe you'd like us to find some hip boy band to prance around on the stage while all the young birds in the club throw their bras at them?" Alasdair cast Daniel a playful wink. "We all know who would be at the front of the stage to be the first to toss her knickers." The Veneficus nudged his head towards the only female within the group of friends.

Philomena huffed, pouting out her scarlet-red lips. "You're such a bastard, Alasdair."

Rhain shuddered, his face twisting into a look of disgust. "Are you insane?" he snapped to Alasdair. "I don't want my club overrun with teenage fangirls. All their bloody squealing..."

"Hormones rampaging..."

Rhain pointed to Phil who had spoken up. "You, hush up. You had hormones once, you know."

10

Phil giggled, sticking her tongue out at him. "Yeah,' she laughed, 'decades ago, which for your information was before the age of the boy bands. Can you imagine what a boy band would've looked like back when I was young? That's a frightening picture."

Alasdair grinned to the second Thorn twin who stood at the bar next to his brother. "Maybe that's what Daniel here would appreciate, a boy band dancing around to Mozart or singing Ode to Joy."

"That would be nice. A little Bach would do these kids well. They lack culture anyway, and such musical perfection is better than this depressing crap they love listening to." Daniel Thorn chuckled as he poured himself a glass of dark red liquid from an old bottle that was upon the bar among the friends. He shook his head, slowly sending thin strands of ebony to dance along his back. "It's amazing what passes for music these days."

"Face it, Frater, this is what makes profit. We give these kids what they want," Rhain said towards his twin.

As close as the brothers were to being identical twins, they were equally as far apart. Many commented on how Daniel's kindness showed through his effeminate features while Rhain had more devious features. While Daniel held a more professional and clean appearance, Rhain preferred throwing on anything that he found clean in his closet - or on the floor. The more chains on a garment the better, the darker the leather the better, and the more holes and fades the better. Rhain was his own personal stylist while Daniel hired a professional stylist. If Daniel didn't remind his brother to shave once in a while, Rhain would be looking more like old man winter - in grunge.

"Thorn Inc. makes money through art, history, and culture, Frater,' Daniel corrected with a soft smile, 'this club of yours gives youth their addictions so they may be able to face their disorganized and crumbling world. Most of your patrons can't even remember where they parked their cars once they leave this place. Those who come to the galleries of Thorn Inc. leave with a sense of beauty and enlightenment after viewing artifacts and artwork that are centuries old."

Rhain stuck out his tongue. "Who wants to see dusty old pieces of pottery?"

"Nerds."

Rhain barked out a laugh, jabbing Alasdair with his elbow. The orange haired Warlock gave a wicked grin.

Daniel narrowed his eyes over the glass he raised to his lips. "And what do your patrons view here?"

"Our toilets as they throw up the liquor they've drowned themselves in," answered Alasdair in cheeky honesty.

"Nice asses?" added Rhain with a waggle of his brows.

"Hot guys?" Philomena giggled, and her interest was perked as a handsome, male patron just happened to pass by her. She smiled a sassy smile and he smiled in return. "Oh, yes, so many to view."

Daniel rolled his black eyes with a slow shake of his head. "A money maker the Crucible may be,' he said with another drink, 'but it is nothing more."

Phil smiled towards her friend with an almost loving expression. "So it may be, Daniel, but the young, the hip, and those who have money burning holes in their pockets demand places such as this. They want the music, they want the drinks, and they want the hot bodies."

"And our bathrooms," Alasdair added with a chuckle under his breath.

Rhain grinned as Phil bopped the Warlock on the back of the head, then he slid his gaze to his brother. "She's right. Money talks, and what the money wants we shall give. It's all about marketing and finding a business that makes profit for the owners."

Rhain gave a pat to his brother's back. "The modern world desires and demands places such as the Crucible, Frater. History and culture aren't bad things. You have your own subculture that embraces the old world and the artifacts that come from those dead cultures, but your world and my world are completely different. So why not tap into the demand and make a nice size pocket off of it? Supply and demand, that's business 101. You should understand that concept as well as any of us, brother."

"That sounds very much like exploitation to me," muttered Daniel, taking a long draw of his drink. He licked the red stain of liquid from his lips then continued, "At least in the world of art restoration there is no feeding our clients drugs and alcohol to keep them happy and sedated."

"Oh?" Rhain shifted to sit up in his chair and turned to his brother with an arm draped over the back and with a scowl to his handsome mouth. "You give them artifacts and you give them donation banquets and their names highlighted in every financial and museum magazine around the world. Both of our patrons get some satisfaction for their desires, but what we provide them is different to the business. You have your addicted patrons just as we have ours. So stick it, mate."

Daniel gave his twin a droll stare then turned his attention away.

"Bah!" exclaimed Alasdair, clapping Daniel upon the shoulder. "Will you two knock it off? Seriously, if you want to fluff your feathers over whose business is better then go into the back and beat each other to a pulp. The one who doesn't end up on the floor bleeding to death wins."

The sound of something crashing behind the small group drew instant attention. They all turned about to look into the gathered crowd at the tables in a corner where some girl was shrieking over her drunk boyfriend spilling his drink on her. She was furious, but the guy and his two mates were more amused over her fussing and anger than the incident. When she slapped the boyfriend, his drunk friends turned their laughter at him.

Then the first swing was made. Instantly, two bouncers were upon the men to break up the fight before the testosterone and alcohol transferred over to the other male patrons who had perhaps also enjoyed a few too many drinks.

Rhain snorted. He didn't move an inch. And why should he? He paid his bouncers well to do their jobs and they did their jobs to perfection. And so they should, considering they were just like he, his brother, and the other two - Lamia. The bouncers could overpower any brute no matter how much alcohol or drugs had been consumed.

12

"Well, that's rather bothersome," Alasdair breathed out with a shake of his head.

Philomena giggled softly as the girl continued to screech insults as the group was escorted out of the church and off the property. No doubt they would be given a clear warning that they were banned from the club for a month. The rules of behavior for the Crucible were as clear as they were harsh. And Rhain made sure the laws of his club were followed by Lamia and Humanus alike.

With the incident handled and the patrons returning to their entertainment, the group turned back to their own conversation. Rhain eyed his brother cautiously, waiting for Daniel to jump on him about how the incident was related exactly to his argument on how the Crucible was only adding to such deplorable human behavior. Daniel, pointedly, ignored that glare as he adjusted the lapels of his long, fine coat. However, after a few seconds the weight of Rhain's stare crawled under his skin. He turned his head just slightly, and their eyes locked.

"Go on then. Say it," Rhain muttered with his arms crossing to his thin chest.

"Say what?" Daniel inquired in his calm, collected voice even as loud as it was over the thumping music.

Alasdair couldn't help but grin as he looked between the twins. "He's expecting you to scold him."

Phil laughed as she wagged a finger towards Rhain. "Bad you for not being psychic and foretelling that fight."

Rhain snapped his glare towards her causing the woman to shut her mouth and slip closer to Alasdair's side. He then returned his eyes to his brother. "You want to tell me how my club adds to the drinking and the drug use of my guests."

Daniel tipped his head with a slender brow arching. "Would you give them drugs if they demanded such? You already supply them with plenty of liquor."

"Daniel,' chortled Rhain at his twin's concerned question, 'that's an unfair question. We would never jeopardize the Crucible for any illegal crap. We're not fools. This place is for entertainment, not death."

Phil laughed brightly as she rested her head upon Rhain's shoulder. "He's right. Other clubs might allow drug use but not this place. Our staff keep a close eye out for any sign of drug use or illegal sales."

Daniel shook his head and took another drink. "You think you have taken every precaution to keep out illegal activities?" He snorted while adding under his breath, "Impossible."

Alasdair jerked his head towards the marked security guards then to the cameras placed high above on the metal catwalk and in every corner of the building. "We've taken every precaution."

Daniel followed the pointing. True, his brother and Alasdair certainly seemed to have taken every precaution in the security personnel and the camera system that loomed over the club, but the illegal activities could, and would, always find a way through the doors. Though he could argue with his brother till the moon falls from the sky, in the end, there would be no solid

13

outcome other than his brother bickering with him till the next century.

Rhain smirked as he saw in Daniel's eyes the dismissal of the discussion. His twin was always one to prefer tension to disperse rather than dealing with growing agitation. Rhain, on the other hand, preferred a head on and very heated confrontation, which was to him more entertainment than anything else.

"I don't think I've ever seen you so agitated, Daniel," Philomena mentioned with a delicate frown upon her painted lips. "Are you okay?"

Daniel nodded and thought back to his involvement with the club. Before the club opened, Daniel had been mostly a supporter on the side. He wasn't one who enjoyed being within the establishment when the doors were open and the activity was pounding in his eardrums - like it was at this very moment. He was a silent partner in his brother's interests no matter what. After all, they were twins, and their blood was thicker than the nectar of the Gods.

Rhain chuckled at Phil's coddling of his brother. "Daniel doesn't like this type of social setting. He'd rather be at home in his bed with his earphones in his ears while some dead musician makes the mean world go away."

Phil giggled, slapping at her friend's shoulder.

Daniel cast a glare to his twin then looked across the crowd, muttering as he raised his glass to his lips. "In truth, I wouldn't mind that one damn bit. It's better than having my eardrums blown for the rest of my undead life."

"I hate to break it to you, my friend,' Alasdair laughed, reaching over the bar to pat Daniel on the cheek, 'but even if your eardrums were blown, they'd heal in a few hours."

Daniel shook his head as he finished off his drink. He couldn't help but smirk and slap his friend's hand away. "All of you can stay here and let your little brain cells pop from this accosting music. I believe I will retire for the evening. After all, this is my one night off this week so I plan on enjoying the evening as much as possible. I would rather enjoy the night with some of those dead composers you mock than with you three."

He flashed a charming smile to them all. "No offense…"

Rhain huffed. He slumped back down into his bar seat. "Go fuck yourself, Daniel."

"None taken, mate." Alasdair laughed. "Half the time I don't want to be around myself!"

Philomena pouted to Daniel. She didn't have to say a word as he stepped to her with his warm smile touching his handsome, gentle features. He bent to kiss her cheek. "Always a pleasure, Philomena. Don't let these two get you into any trouble."

Rhain gave a kick to his twin's backside, giving a push into the crowd. "Get your boring ass out of my club, Daniel. You're tainting its style." But before Daniel could slip into the thrones of bodies, Rhain called out, "Tell Kain I'll get the finances ready by tomorrow."

Daniel waved a hand then disappeared from sight.

14

~ ~ ~ ~

"Alright,' Joyce giggled as she and her cousin stepped up for their turn at the bar, 'what will it be?"

Amused panic touched Regan's features as she gazed upon the hundreds of bottles, all unique unto themselves, lining the glass mirror behind the bar. She then turned her eyes to a drink menu glowing from a tablet built into the bar top. It all confused her. She couldn't even pronounce some of the names etched into the glass containers or on the digital menu.

"How the hell should I know? I've never had any alcohol before. Do you think they have diet coke?" she asked with a flip of a wrist. "What the hell, I'm feeling feisty. Maybe I will ask to have it with a slice of lemon."

A look of horror took Joyce, and she feigned a gasp with her mouth open. "You need to get out more!" she laughed while turning to wave frantically towards the bar tender.

Her waving caught the attention of a particularly handsome bartender, and he returned a nod of acknowledgment. With a look of anticipated hunger and curiosity, Joyce leaned against the bar while she examined the fancy bottles of various liquors and mixes before looking to the digital menu. "I wonder which one I should try first. They all look so fancy and expensive."

Regan frowned. She looked from the bottles to her cousin with a scowl setting upon her lips. "I don't want any of them."

"What?" Joyce balked, glaring to Regan. "Oh, come on! You just turned twenty-one. Live a little and try something. I'm sure they have a drink here that's not going to kill you on first sip."

"No thanks." Regan shuddered with a shake of her head that sent thick waves of dark silk about her shoulders. "I can't even stand the smell of liquor, so I doubt I could handle even a sip of the gentlest drink they have."

"Fine then,' Joyce huffed, waving her cousin's scowl away, 'maybe they have some Kool-Aid for you."

"What can I get you ladies?" inquired the bartender when he came up to serve them, placing two red napkins upon the glossy bar top.

Joyce grinned to the tender, flashing him her sassy smile in an attempt to charm and sway the man. "My cousin here just turned twenty-one the other day, so I am taking her out to her first club. What do you suggest for breaking her in?"

"Joyce," Regan moaned, humiliated at her cousin's choice of words.

The bartender, with streaks of sandy-blonde falling before his gaze, flashed a grin at the other girl. She was cute, for fresh blood - young and innocent. "Birthday girl, huh?"

"Yes!" Joyce beamed and shoved Regan forwards. But then she huffed sweetly and grumbled, "Though, she's not really into liquor. So, do you have any Kool-Aid?"

"I'm going to kill you," Regan hissed, giving her cousin a shove away from her.

Joyce laughed.

"I got just the thing, and no, it's not Kool-Aid." The bartender smirked then stepped away.

He headed further down the bar where the owners of the club were seated. "Excuse me," he spoke up with a grin to them as he reached under the bar for a small box of baby-pink velvet decorated with a cross of silver stitched onto the fabric.

All three Lamia turned their attention. "Hey, Cultor,' Rhain spoke up, leaning slightly as his bar manager bent beneath the bar top, 'need something?"

"We have a birthday girl who has just turned twenty-one," he told the group who were looking at him with curiosity marking their features. Once he explained his reasons for bothering them, Rhain and Alasdair turned their attention to the crowd.

"Twenty-one you say?" Alasdair peeked around the other employees behind the bar and down to the far end. "Which one is she?" With his attention dancing among the many women coming and going around the bar, Philomena cuffed him on the back of the head. He yelped and snapped his amber eyes, flecked with darkness, right to her. "What the hell was that for?"

She waggled a finger to him. "It's not polite to stare."

"Sure it is, when there's a miniskirt involved." The Veneficus purred, waggling his brows in suggestion. He didn't hide the trail of his unique eyes down her luscious form. "Which, I shall point out, would look rather nice upon you, my dear."

Phil squeaked. She smacked the Sorcerer, gently, then pointed a finger right against his sharp nose as she turned a sweet and overly pouting pout to Rhain. "Did you hear what he just said?"

"No,' Rhain replied with his attention still focused down the bar, 'just like I didn't see your assault upon him in my presence."

Philomena narrowed her eyes, anger crackling within the metallic shine that flashed amongst the deep green. She hissed at both men then muttered under her breath, "I didn't hit him that hard."

"Which one is she?" Rhain asked Cultor.

"The young woman in the pink blouse. See her? She has long, dark hair that's wavy. She's next to the girl with the blonde hair,' Cultor frowned then sighed, hanging his head,' who is currently doing the chicken dance."

Philomena laughed brightly. "Look at her! Whoever thought of dancing the chicken dance to Crazy Stacy?" She spoke of the current heavy metal band blaring and pounding their song out from the stage. The crowd seemed to really be enthralled with this new, local band of all girls who, of course, were clad in leather and looking to have stepped from a BDSM video than anything else.

"I see her! Ah, she's a cutie." Alasdair grinned.

Rhain tipped himself back in his seat so he could get a look at the Humanus. He cocked his head to the side then smirked looking to Alasdair. "She's not bad. But who goes out to the clubs wearing a blouse like that?"

Philomena huffed as she linked an arm with Rhain's giving a tug to get his attention back on her. "She doesn't look to be the traditional club goer, does she?"

16

Cultor chuckled.

"She looks like a stuck up tart."

Rhain ignored Phil and her want for his attention as he studied the two girls down the bar. The one in the pink blouse was trying to hide her head as the other girl was now imitating the Y.M.C.A. His body shuddered as he glanced back to Cultor. "Give her and her friend a drink on the house along with her gift."

"Sure thing." Cultor gave a nod to his two bosses and their friend before he turned away.

"Ask her name. Will you, Vincent?" Rhain called.

"Yes, sir!"

When he returned to where the young women were seated, he placed the small box before the birthday girl. The young woman blinked her rich eyes, looking to the box then up to him with an expression of 'what the hell is this' written across her features. Vincent Cultor smiled to her and answered her confusion. "A gift from the owners," he began to explain. "It's tradition to give something special to a birthday girl, especially on her twenty-first birthday."

He clapped his hands together as if to get their attention. "Now, what can I get you girls to drink?"

"Nothing too expensive, that's for sure." Joyce sighed with a pout.

"Nothing too alcoholic, please." Regan added.

Cultor chuckled to the blonde, "First drinks are on the house, even a soda if you wish."

Regan smiled from the bartender's gentle reassurance of her preference for no alcohol. "Well, it is my birthday. I should treat myself. Do you have something a little fancier than a coke?"

"I can make you something special." He winked to her then to the other. "And for you?"

"Well, since the drinks are free, something damn good to start this night off with a bang!" Joyce flailed her arms about dramatically.

Cultor tried to keep his smile upon his lips. By the way this girl was acting he was becoming worried that one sip of alcohol would put her over the edge. "Coming up."

Joyce nudged Regan when the guy turned away. "Open it, Regan. Go on!"

"I don't know," Regan said while turning the small box within her hands. "I feel awkward."

"You are awkward." Her cousin huffed as she made a grab for it. "Here, if you won't open it, then I will!"

Regan snatched the box away with a scowl and a swat to her cousin's hand. "I don't recall it being your birthday."

Pulling her hand back with a gasp as if she had been touched by fire, Joyce glared. "Then open it."

Regan grumbled under her breath as she took up the box, twisting it within her fingers. The lid came off with simple ease and inside, buried in soft, white paper, was a silver chain with a beautiful silver cross accented by a pink agate in the center. Regan stared at the pendant as it slowly turned above her palm. The chain itself was thin, definitely designed with the ladies in mind as the links were delicate and slender. The silver metal of both the pendant and the chain shined within the bright lights above. Turning the cross over within her palm, Regan noticed 'The Crucible – 2014' inscribed within the metal.

"Oh my," breathed Joyce in awe as she looked to the necklace. "Is that real?"

"I have no idea. If this is real, I'd hate to know how much it cost." Regan frowned as she let the chain pool to her palm over the pendant. "Why would the bartender give me this?"

"I don't know."

Regan glanced up just as the bartender returned with their drinks. He placed before her a tall glass filled with something pink that bubbled ever so delicately and was finished with a slice of watermelon on the rim. "What's this?" she asked, lifting the glass. The scent drifted from the popping bubbles to tickle her nose with a touch of watermelon and strawberry.

"A spritzer of my own creation,' Cultor replied with a wink, 'sprite with some nonalcoholic strawberry Champaign and a touch of organic watermelon juice."

Regan took a sip and mewed in pure ecstasy. "This is fantastic!" She popped the watermelon piece into her mouth.

Joyce pouted to Cultor. "And mine?"

Once again Cultor had to force a smile to his features. He didn't like greedy girls, and though this one tried to play sweet and coy, he could taste the narcissism seeping from her. He set before her a martini glass that had a dual colored drink within it. The lower half had a copper tone to it while the upper portion was clear with little bubbles drifting up from the bottom.

He grinned and said with pride, "The Apple Slut."

Obviously, Joyce didn't pick up on the name or the fact that Cultor had picked that specific drink out because of the title. She took up the drink to take a long sip. A shiver ran her spine to the shots of vodka mixed with a fruity, sour taste. She could taste the sprite, but the sour notes puckered her lips.

"This is awesome! I'm going to want another!" she squealed before taking another sip and then another.

Regan winced while watching Joyce attack her drink. She sighed with a little shake of her head before offering the bartender an appreciative smile. "Thank you very much."

"You're welcome. Anything else I can get for you girls? We have a bar menu if you'd like to see it. Good ol' traditional pup grub."

"Yes!" Joyce cried out, raising an arm. "I am in the mood for something deliciously greasy. What about you, Regan? Are you hungry?"

"A little."

"Regan?" Cultor repeated with a smirk to his lips. "Is that your name?"

The American gave a nod. "Yes, it is. I'm Regan Scott."

"She's my cousin visiting from America," Joyce added.

"Can I ask,' Regan presented the chain and cross, 'who gave this to me?"

The man smiled then pointed towards the far end of the bar. "The two gents at the end. The one with the orange hair is Alasdair Baird, and the one with the blue highlights is Rhain Thorn. They own the club. As I said before, it's their tradition to give a gift to any birthday girl who visits their establishment."

"Really?" Regan turned her eyes down to the pendant.

"I'm cute," purred Joyce, pointing to herself. "Can't I have one too?" She batted her lashes and pursed out her lips.

Cultor rolled his eyes. "Come back on your birthday and you'll get one then."

"I can't take this," Regan explained, reaching to unclasp it.

Her cousin snapped in shock, "What?"

The bartender shook his head. "Of course you can. Your twenty-first birthday is a special day. Keep it." Cultor gave a nod of his head then turned away.

The two girls watched him head back down the bar to the group he had pointed out.

"I feel really awkward now." Regan whimpered as she locked eyes with the young man who had the black hair streaked with blue. A cold shiver ran along her skin so she pulled her eyes away to once again look down to the pendant. "I'm not sure I can accept this. Maybe I should call him back and return this to the owners."

"Enough, Regan." Joyce swatted Regan's hand from the pendant. "It's a gift. Why not enjoy it?"

"Maybe I should go thank them."

Joyce glanced down the bar to where the bartender was still speaking to the two owners and an unknown and unnamed woman. "I'd leave it alone. I doubt the owners want to be bothered. Let's just enjoy ourselves and these amazing drinks!" Speaking of which, Joyce picked up her glass to take a nice, long sip.

Regan wasn't so fast returning to her drink. She continued to watch the group at the end of the bar while playing with the pendant. Why would the owners want to give her something? After all, she wasn't anybody amazing or stunning, rich or obviously social like many of the club-goers who surrounded her. She was just Regan Scott, a college student visiting from Chicago. She was a fish out of water in this club, and the longer she stayed within the church's old walls the more uncomfortable she became.

~ ~ ~ ~

Leaving the two girls, Cultor returned to his employers with the answer to Rhain's inquiry. "Her name is Regan Scott, an American visiting."

"Fresh international Sanguis." Alasdair grinned. "I can tell you one thing, mate,' he chuckled with a sneaky glance tossed to his business partner, 'some new blood in here comes with some fresh air."

Rhain rolled his eyes at the Warlock's sweet tooth for international blood. "Did you give her the gift?"

Cultor gave a nod and replied, "I did. She was rather apprehensive at first, said she didn't deserve it and couldn't take it."

"Aaww. That's sweet," Phil muttered with a sarcastic tone to her voice. "What woman would turn down a gift from the owners of this club? There are women waiting in line who would give the last drop of their blood for one of those necklaces."

"Not every woman is like you and half of the women in this club tonight, Phil." Rhain shook his head.

Though he had known Philomena for a number of decades now, had claimed her as a friend, she could only be explained as a 'hard keep'. She was expensive to maintain, and her last lover tossed her aside after she threw a fit that a twenty-thousand pound ring wasn't enough for her Christmas gift.

"I think this girl might be the first humble female who has visited the club in a long time," chuckled the Veneficus in passing comment.

Phil frowned while glancing between her friends. She huffed softly. "What are you two talking about? I'm humble."

Alasdair regarded his friend with a sympathetic smile upon his handsome, unique features of Roman ancestry. "Dear, don't take this wrong, but you haven't known humble since the day of your Nasei."

Rhain barked out a laugh. "Come on, Alasdair. Phil has her moments of humbleness and humility - once every decade or so."

Phil scrunched her overly pretty features, and shadowed in her green eyes - behind the dangerous glare - was a cloud of anger twisting and twirling. She may be an 'air-head', as Alasdair liked to call her, but she was far from stupid and not an object of jests. She knew what Rhain had said was a point against her character. Through the cloudiness of self-centered narcissism, realization came to her that Alasdair and Rhain had taken far too many cheap 'shots' at her tonight. She frowned then slammed her glass down to the bar top.

Both men jerked as glass shattered, shooting across the bar top.

"What the bloody hell?" barked Rhain as he jumped up, snarling, while looking down to the dark splatter of drink that now stained his expensive shirt. Rage coiled hotly within his eyes as his lips pulled back exposing a hint of fangs. "Phil! Are you daft? You owe me a shirt, woman!"

Alasdair, who was quieter on his reaction, glared daggers to Phil as he picked up pieces of shattered glass. His concern was more for the crowd closest to them, whom had paused in their enjoyment to stare at them. What they saw was some girl throwing a fit at him and Rhain, the owners of the club and two of the wealthiest young men in London. Fucking hell, this would all hit the media outlets across the U.K. by morning.

Philomena grabbed her purse from the bar top, consequentially sending more shards of glass dancing to the floor. "I've had enough of you two making fun of me tonight. Enough! Do you hear me?"

Alasdair looked to Rhain who was looking to him - confused and dumbfounded. Both men shrugged, and that shrug only fueled Phil's anger. She clenched her hands, stomped a foot, and made a sound that only an animal could make. "Go to hell! Both of you!" she screeched at them.

20

"What in bloody hell was that all about?" inquired the Veneficus to his friend as he delicately brushed a clean bar cloth to the stain upon his shirt.

Rhain shook his head as he began to sweep glass into his hand. "I don't get women, Alasdair. One moment they're perfectly fine then the next they're clawing at you, screaming at you, and throwing things at you."

"Is everything alright?" inquired Cultor upon his appearance at their side to clean up the glass and spilled drink with a heavy frown.

Alasdair cast the bar manager a sly grin. "Phil couldn't handle my overwhelming charm."

"Was that it?" Cultor chuckled. "I swore she was telling you both to go to hell."

Rhain grunted, unamused at the event. "She had a Philomena moment, Cultor. Nothing to worry about."

The bar manager gave a knowing nod. The woman was known for her sudden outbursts of drama that were mostly done to obtain attention or if she felt the attention she was getting was not to her desire. Phil could be sweet and she could be gentle, but more than often she was as narcissistic and self-loving as many of their kind could be.

"Cultor? Do we have anything to get stains out of clothing?"

"Yes,' answered Vincent, pointing to a door at the end of the bar, 'if you go into the laundry room there is a shelf above the washer. There should be a tube of blue jell. Just press the top down onto the stain, rub it in, and then put your shirt into the washer on gentle with just cold water."

Alasdair sighed, looking down to his shirt. "Another shirt ruined by that woman." He grumbled sourly as he stared at the darkened fabric. "She owes me ten shirts now."

"Grab one out of my closet," Rhain told his friend with a smirk. In the past six months Phil had thrown several drinks at Alasdair for one reason or another.

"Thanks."

"Maybe I need to be a bit harder with Phil," Rhain thought out loud as he and Cultor continued to clean up the bar while Alasdair departed. "She's getting too comfortable on the idea, that because she's a friend of ours, she can take too many liberties in her expectations of us and our club."

Cultor nodded. "It's not really my place to comment."

"Sure it is. You've been working here since we opened and you're a Servus to my own Familia, the Drasus. That makes your thoughts on what happens in my club important. You're my bar manager, Cultor, and a damn good friend."

Vincent Cultor smirked as he dumped a palm full of glass into the garbage bin beneath the bar then swept a few fingers through his unevenly cut, sandy-blonde hair. "You really want my advice?" He leaned back to the counter behind him with his hands placed to the bar top.

Rhain nodded.

"Well,' he began to say, 'Phil is a little hot headed. She takes everything far too seriously, especially if a situation has to do with her. You're right. She does seem to think that she deserves to be involved in the everyday functions of the club because she knows both you and Alasdair."

21

He motioned a hand towards his employer. "She really has no stake in the club, does she?"

"No." Rhain shook his head as he finally stood from his chair to step about the bar. He needed a drink, so he took a bottle out of a key locked mini fridge of black beneath the bar, opened the cork, and poured a thin, bubbling liquid of red into a wine glass. "She's never been invited to participate in any part of the construction, development or business decision. Sometimes I think she holds that against us because both Daniel and Jamie were involved."

"True, but they did most of the serious restoration work. For free, I might add."

Rhain balked and stared with wide eyes at Vincent. "For free?" He snorted as if the very idea was preposterous. "Do you know much I spent on espresso and lattes and scones for those two? I probably paid for the rent on that coffee shop across the street for a bloody year!"

Cultor chuckled softly and shook his head in amusement. "They also took up your cause with the British Historical Society on obtaining the rights and license to turn this place into the club. Hell,' Cultor laughed deeply, 'how many days did Jamie spend on his back high on some scaffolding with a tiny brush in his hand while staring at these old ceilings?"

Rhain grunted a grunt that bordered on pouting and said, "I don't care what that boy says, his eyes are not permanently crossed."

Clearing his voice, and thinking to change the subject off Alasdair's mortal cousin, Cultor inquired quietly, "Remind me, Phil has done what exactly in either the creation or the promotion of the club?"

Rhain shrugged. "She was at the opening of the Crucible. I guess that in her warped mind that makes her somehow my watchdog."

"Your stalker, you mean," said Cultor under his breath.

Rhain arched a brow. "What was that?"

Vincent shrugged in reply.

Rhain ran a hand through his hair. "I swear, that girl thinks she's the star of this entire show. Fuck that shit. I'm the damn star!"

'You're a spoiled Drasus, Rhain,' Cultor thought in his mind. After a quick cough, he cleared his thoughts and went on to say, "She's attaching herself to the status and wealth of the club, just as she's attached herself to you and Alasdair because of your statuses in the London spotlight and in your Familia."

Cultor shook his head as he began to tap his fingers to the bar top. "You three have known each other for decades now, but friendship is just friendship and people are still people, even if they are Lamia. Philomena will always have her personality and her traits that she had before her Nasei. My bet, she's still as self-centered now as she was before her Creare."

"I can't allow her to continue to violate my trust and the laws of this establishment that all employees and guests must accept by throwing tantrums in my club, Cultor." Rhain turned to face his bar manager. "Four fits in the last month and a half is too many. Three times she's broken glasses, and I can count on both hands how many times she's caused a disturbance with my patrons."

"One time,' he raised a single finger to indicate one, 'she got into the face of another girl because she thought that girl was hitting on me. Who gives a flying fuck if some human wants to hit on me? She shouldn't. Girls hit on me left and right - every night - but I don't even pay attention."

Cultor couldn't help but smirk a little. Rhain not caring that some pretty thing was hitting on him was like Daniel not caring that there was a speck of dust on an old vase. There were plenty of times Rhain had taken a pretty girl, or two, to his office for a private introduction. His enjoyment of the female flesh wasn't a secret among the waves of women who came and went through the doors of the old church. However, most were fools in thinking he would actually keep the numbers they pushed at him, hoping upon hope that he would call upon them. He never called. Cultor couldn't count how many times one of these girls returned, heartbroken, to scream at him about breaking her heart, desperately pleading with him that they were to be together - forever. Or so that is what the women thought before they were thrown out of the club and sent home to cry in their humiliation till the liquor and their desperate lust wore off.

Cultor took in a dry and flat breath, expelling it in a slow sigh. "Then maybe she does need to be put into her place, not in any negative way of course."

Rhain waved a hand and nodded thoughtfully. "You're right. She needs to know where she stands and that there are consequences for her behavior."

Cultor couldn't agree more. "There is that consideration. The Crucible is a Receptaculum to our kind, and there are rules that need to be followed and obeyed. I've worried sometimes, given a chance, Phil may cross the line."

"She's crossed that line already, twice over." Rhain took a long draw of the Sanguis he was nursing, the little bubbles of added Champaign tickling his throat. "I can't have any one, even a friend of mine, threaten the regulations of my license. I won't have the Crucible taken away because of a hissy fit."

Cultor chuckled as his tight body pushed away from the bar. "You'll make the right decision. Now, if you excuse me, I have customers to see to and employees to bitch at."

Rhain nodded, and as Cultor began to walk away, he called to his bar manager, "Hey!"

Vincent stopped, glancing back with a brow arched.

"Thanks for all your work. This place couldn't function properly without you behind the bar."

Cultor smirked and gave a two fingered solute before he went to service once more.

23

~ ~ ~ ~

By the time Philomena stormed out of the doors, the dark and cloudy heavens opened allowing a heavy trickle of chilled rain to tumble down. The Lamia growled as she felt the drops pelt into her hair and down her face.

'*Of course. This always happens to me,'* she muttered within her mind as she tucked her arms tightly around herself. Her eyes swept the ocean of people waiting to gain entrance and curled her lips in disgust. Stupid fools - they would wait in Armageddon to get into this club. Muttering a curse, she fished her car keys out of her small purse then proceeded through the courtyard.

She was in such a sullen mood that even the staff on the grounds avoided her. Gods how she despised this time of year, Tempus Vernum - spring. Her mood was so dark that if anyone spoke to her, she might just snap and not with just words. But when she heard a familiar voice call out to her, her angered attention slipped. Phil stopped, glancing to the side, and looked towards a small alcove within the massive stone and iron twisted wall. There she saw Daniel and Mark Crossman, the security manager, standing beneath an overgrown tree, seeking shelter from the rain beneath the tree's thick branches. Daniel was waving her over, so she complied with a soft sigh. At least she wouldn't mind speaking to him since he was always kind to her. Daniel never belittled her, made fun of her, or questioned her thoughts or decisions. He was a respectful and honorable Lamia. Such a pity he was married to his work.

"Phil? What are you doing out here?" asked Daniel as his friend came beneath the tree. He frowned upon seeing her pale skin pinkened from the touch of cold raindrops that skimmed along her features to slink across her clothes. Even her hair was stuck against her cheeks. However, what he saw within her green eyes was more than agitation at the rain but a shadow of dancing anger.

"I'm leaving," she bit back, trying hard to keep from snapping at her friend.

Mark drew in a drag from his cigarette as he gazed to the Lamia. "Is everything alright?" he asked in his deep, Welsh voice as he tipped his head to blow out a ring of smoke.

Turning her eyes to Mark, Phil scowled. He wasn't like Rhain or Alasdair or even Daniel. He was a Servus, a human employed within the Lamia world, and an alright sort of fellow - for a mortal. The only Servus she tolerated within the club was Cultor, and only because the man had saved Rhain's life decades prior. Vincent also carried the trait within his blood, and that made him important to the Drasus Familia, and to Rhain. Mark's blood, however, was vacant of the Trait and that made him nothing of importance - at least to her.

Pity Phil had to play nice with Mark due to his connection with the Drasus. She really didn't like the man, but Rhain liked the guy and was protective of any member of his Familia. Though the Damasippus and the Drasus held a truce, there had been very volatile waters between the two Familia for centuries. Both had struggled to claim London as their financial territory, but sadly, the Drasus won the battle. The Drasus Familia was now one of the most powerful and influential Familia in the United Kingdom, not to mention one of the wealthiest across Europe. In London, the Drasus Familia was known as the Regio Familia. In other words, the Drasus held all the political and financial power within London, and having such power and influence came with great benefits and allies within the Concilium of the Republica of England.

Philomena offered a thin smile to the two men, as well as a dainty shrug of her shoulders. "I'm bored."

Bored? Mark and Daniel exchanged knowing looks. In code, bored - when spoken by Phil - meant that she had been annoyed or ignored. Mark sighed as he took another draw of his cigarette.

It was Daniel who spoke up, questioning her on what had occurred. "Should I ask what happened, or would you prefer I walk into the club and chastise my brother?"

It was obvious that he knew Rhain was the culprit to Phil's bad mood. Then again, Alasdair could also be a qualified perpetrator if his tightly controlled buttons had been pushed long and hard enough, which Phil did have the talent and history of doing.

The rage Philomena continued to stir within her gut instantly simmered to Daniel's sincere offering. She chuckled, reaching out to pat his arm but didn't directly take her touch off the sleeve of his coat. "That's very sweet of you, Daniel, but beating Rhain won't do any good. He'll just be an ass tomorrow."

Daniel arched a slender black brow. He wouldn't go that far as to physically assault his twin. He took offense in thinking that Phil would automatically assume he would go rushing into Rhain's club and attack him in her defense. No. Daniel was the pacifist, Rhain was the abuser, and Kain was the referee. Those were the roles of the three brothers in the Thorn family.

Daniel glanced down to Philomena's hand that sat gently upon his arm. He then looked to Mark who rolled his bright, blue eyes. They both knew her subtle, yet dangerous, games.

Daniel smiled to her and gave her hand a comforting pat. "So, tell me, what did those two do?"

Here came the over dramatized pout.

Philomena's lips pouted out and her fluttering lashes dusted her high cheekbones. She was all drama with crocodile tears and the teeth to go along with them. "I'm exhausted from their constant sarcasm directed towards me. Do they really need to be so cruel?"

"So honest?" Mark muttered under his breath. He knew Philomena heard him as she shot flames of rage towards him.

Daniel chuckled and gave a pat to her hand once more that drew her attention back to him. Her eyes quickly went from rage to tenderness with a touch of admiration. "Don't pay attention to Rhain and Alasdair, Phil. You've known them for decades, four to be exact, and they have always treated you like a little sister. That includes sarcasm with a touch of big brother attitude."

25

Phil's features fell, and the admiration trickled away as her lips turned down to a little frown. They considered her a little sister to be teased and poked at? Daniel couldn't be right, could he? She had hoped that Alasdair and Rhain considered her a friend, perhaps more than a friend with feelings neither one had come to understand. Their teases and play were all in the name of flirtatious fun, not sibling bullying. She certainly didn't see either of them as a brother. How could she when her nights were filled with erotic dreams involving one or the other and at times…both?

To hear from Daniel that his twin saw her as only a sister was a brutal and cold strike to her character, her image, and her soul. Philomena prided herself on her sexual image, and in her mind she was the dream of every male, mortal or immortal. Rhain Thorn, luckily, was on the top of her list to snag. She couldn't give up till she had him at her side. He would raise her status not only within her Familia but within the Lamia community across the U.K. Her Regulus would speak of her with such pride that her name would become an icon.

Daniel's words stung her, stung her deeply.

Suddenly, a voice came over the Nextel that Mark had attached to his belt. His name was being called by one of his bouncers requiring assistance with a belligerent male inside. "If you'll excuse me, I'm being called off to duty."

Daniel gave a nod. "It was nice to see you again, Mark."

"Same here," replied the Servus before he gave a polite and respectful nod to Phil. "Good evening, Miss. Damasippus."

Philomena paid little attention to the mortal as he headed back into the church. Her eyes were still locked to Daniel. She asked sadly, "Do they really hate me so much?"

The Lamia blinked his black eyes at her question and a soft smile touched his lips as he cupped her cheek in his cool hand. "They don't hate you, not at all." Dipping his head, Daniel placed a kiss upon her forehead. "Don't worry yourself with them, Phil. Go home and take the remains of the night easy then have a good rest in the day. You deserve some quiet time to yourself."

Wait, was Daniel brushing her off? Her eyes narrowed beneath thick lashes as she searched his handsome features for an answer. If he was trying to shove her away, like Rhain and Alasdair had, Phil swore she would leave all three bleeding. Nobody tossed her aside as if she meant nothing to them. Even though he kissed her forehead, she couldn't help but feel as if she was becoming nothing more than a shadow slowly being pulled into the dark background.

"Maybe you're right," she sighed with a heavy breath.

"Are you driving home?"

"Yes."

"Then drive carefully, alright?"

She gave a tight, fake smile. "Don't worry about me, Daniel,' she chuckled dryly, 'I'll get home in one piece."

26

Phil leaned up to kiss his cheek then turned into the crowd. She left Daniel staring at her with concern. By this time, Philomena wanted nothing more than to leave. The rain was starting to increase as she walked down the short distance to the open car park behind the church where her expensive Mercedes was parked within a security fence next to Rhain and Alasdair's cars.

Within minutes, Phil was speeding away from the vibrant church with a sense of mixed relief and dread. She didn't like leaving the boys alone. They couldn't take care of themselves if she wasn't there to remind them of their Ps and Qs. Besides, Rhain and Alasdair needed her.

They would always need her.

~2~

There is a world that is far outside the reach of mortals - a world filled with monsters and nightmares. This world is not for the living, not for the innocent nor for the kind, and not for the gentle or the pure. To thrive in this world one must become the monster and the nightmare or face the destruction of their terrified soul. There is nothing but red coating the moon, dripping life over the night sky that rules my kind. We are forever locked within Nox's tight hold, never again to feel the warm kiss of the sun upon our cursed flesh.

This modern world is not the world I was born into. The world I live in now is full of constant nightmares. From the moment I wake at the coming of dusk to the moment my eyes close at sunrise, my mind is tormented by the cruelty and the coldness that surrounds me. I don't understand why I cannot adapt, as my brothers have done, after a century of living in the world that borders life and death, humanity and monsters. Rhain functions without skipping a beat. He embraces all opportunities that the Lamia world and societies can give to us. Even Kain, my eldest brother, has embraced this life with little discomfort.

While my brothers hold the night and the future close, I continue to embrace the day and the past. Even my life revolves around the study and the regeneration of art from time and cultures long past. I refuse to let the beauty of history, both the vibrant cultures and the turmoil of the life, drift away into the shadows that have embraced us all.

I don't see myself, my life, changing or growing if I continue to molt within my lab. My life is never ending, though I'm still not sure how wonderful a gift my limited immortality is. I have seen friends, employees, and clients grow old, mortal and immortal, and pass on. And though I miss those who have passed, I also envy them. Rhain embraces this immortality and the incredible abilities that have been passed down to us by the ancestors of our Familia with enthusiasm and open arms, often pushing the limits of our supposed immortality to the breaking point. I, however, cannot help but wonder if life has more meaning to a person when they know that every second of every night brings them closer to their demise.

Mortals seem to take every act, every interaction, and every moment as if their next breath would be their last. We Lamia know that tomorrow, the next day, the next year, the next decade, and the next century will not be our last. Perhaps that's why the idea that every breath being precious isn't a concept that is truly embraced by my kind.

I refuse to let time and life slip me by. If I am to live this long life to its fullest, then I will treat every night and every moment with great caution and care. I will embrace those whom I love and thank them with all my heart for making my life worth living.

-   Daniel Rhys Thorn

~ ~ ~ ~

The drinks did not last long, and though Joyce ordered a few more for herself, Regan was content sipping her first, casually, while watching her cousin dance not too far away. The longer she stayed within the club, the quicker unease came upon her. As the hours passed, and pass they did, more and more visitors filled the old church, crowding into every nook and cranny they could squeeze themselves into. After being bumped a few times, and a hand groping at her bottom, Regan was ready to return to Joyce's flat.

Her cousin, on the other hand, wasn't about to leave.

Cultor had been nice enough to get her an aspirin and a cup of tea when she mentioned a headache developing. He informed her that if the headache increased, and her cousin didn't wish to leave, he could get her a cab back to her place. She declined, indicating that she couldn't leave without Joyce. If worse came to worse, Cultor said he'd speak to the owners about letting her rest in the office. He wouldn't take no for an answer. After all, her safety, along with the safety of every guest, was the highest priority of the owners and the staff. In the end, she promised to let him know if her headache turned into a migraine.

After a few cups of soothing tea, Cultor returned to check on Regan. "Are you feeling any better?" he asked.

Regan smiled and nodded. "Yes, thank you. The aspirin helped, but I think I might step out and get some fresh air. Is that allowed? Can I get back in?"

"Of course. You got your hand stamped on entry didn't you?"

She raised her right hand. "Yes."

He nodded. "That's your ticket back into the club. If you start to feel worse, let one of the staff at the door know and you'll be shown in. If your headache becomes debilitating, have one of the staff come and get me - no other. Understand?"

Again she nodded. "I will. Thank you again."

As she stepped away from the bar Cultor called to her, "Don't leave the property! If something happens to you, the owners will be liable!"

"I'll make sure to stick around. Besides, where would I go?" She gave him a wave. "I don't live in this country."

Regan left the club to meet a tumble of steady rain. The chilled drops cascaded down to the cobblestones creating a beautiful but ghostly fog that drifted and coiled lovingly around the legs of those outside. Smiling softly, she raised her head to the soothing rain allowing the cool drops to comfort her overheated forehead. The air itself was crisp and scented with the smell of London - pollutants and rain. For a short while she walked about the grounds of the cathedral, breathing deeply the fog thickened air. In spending only a few minutes out of the church, Regan's pained head began to ease and the knot that had formed within her skull began to loosen. Finally, she was feeling some respite from the club's overwhelming environment.

29

Turning a corner of the church, she came face to face with the walled cemetery. Stepping closer to the massive gates of iron, she tried to look through the thin bars as well as she could. This sort of graveyard would be perfect for a creepy horror movie with its old trees growing amongst the graves and along the property that was outlined with the continuation of the massive wall topped with iron spikes. With the fog rolling over and between the dotting graves, tombs, and sarcophagi, she was certain that this cemetery was haunted. It gave her the chills and entranced her all at once. From where she was, and from what she could see, the graves looked to be very old. Time had not been so kind to many of the markers. Some had sunken into the earth, some had broken in different pieces or chipped, and some were covered in thick grass and moss.

Looming like spectral shadows within the rolling mist were a few eerie statues, but to Regan, any statue was creepy in a graveyard. There was one in particular in the center of the cemetery that stood about ten feet tall and was a carved depiction of a cloaked and hooded figure with its arms stretched outwards and with bony fingers reaching out from beneath the drape of long, stone sleeves. There was no face to the figure, only a shadow that sank into the crevice of the hood where a face should have been carved.

A chill danced along Regan's spine, as she stared at that statue, bringing with it an unnatural feeling that somebody had just walked over her grave, ironic since she was staring at a cemetery. She felt as if there were eyes viewing her from the darkness, not from behind her or around her but in front of her as if peeking out from behind the old tombstones or from the shadows that clung to the aboveground sarcophagi. No longer did Regan gaze upon the hauntingly old cemetery with a sense of wonder but of building distress. Her hands upon the lower gate turned white. Somebody, or something, was watching her.

Gathering her strength and willpower, Regan forced herself to release the bar she had been holding so she could back away. Once she had steadied herself, she walked to the front of the church as quickly as she could only to discover that the sensation of being watched turned into a sensation of being followed. Twenty minutes was plenty of time to get fresh air and for her headache to calm. Wasn't it?

A frown pulled her lips when she was faced with forcing her way through the crowd so she could get to the front doors. It took some skill for her to wiggle her way through the horde, but she managed and soon was standing in the line to get back inside. However, waiting in line was just as irritating as it had been earlier. More and more people were getting rowdy and loud, pushing and jerking about in their disgruntled excitement. Just as she took her next step somebody behind her pushed forwards, throwing her off balance when the back of her shoe slid off her heel.

"Ow!" she snapped, jumping a bit so she could pull her shoe back on. By accident alone she found herself stumbling directly against the back of the man in front of her.

The guy behind her apologized for bumping her, but the man in front turned sharply around with a hard scowl upon his chiseled features. "Wha' appened?" he grunted with a slow growl pressing up from his broad throat. His words were thickened with a heaviness to his English accent that made his question difficult for Regan to understand.

"I'm sorry. I didn't mean to bump you, but I got pushed and my shoe came off..." stuttered Regan, stopping with a draw of breath when the man, in his early thirties and rather scruffy looking, spread a slow grin to his face.

He was at least half a body taller than her, and with his broad height, he had to bend forwards when he looked to her, his muscular body looming over her with a dense presence. He pulled a long drag from his cigarette as he openly eyed her, making her shiver and obviously enjoying doing so.

"An' ya just 'appen ta come fallen right inta ma arms, ey girl?"

A hard shiver ran through Regan's body as the used ash from his cigarette illuminated his flesh in an eerie light, and when the smoke coiled about his face, speckles of silver flashed within his pale, green eyes. The shadows upon his chiseled face danced for a moment as a lock of his dark, wavy brown hair fell forwards to trail along his jaw.

Regan took an instinctual step back. "I didn't mean any harm. I tripped."

Her reply didn't thrill the man as he flicked his glowing cigarette butt to the ground. When she stepped back, he took a step forwards - leering at her. "Aint I gunna ge' an apology? Ya hurt ma back."

"I said I was sorry," she sputtered with a crack in her voice.

"Aww, now ain' tha' sweet?" he purred with a slow trail of his tongue to his smirking lips. "Sweet lil thing like ya all by ya 'self, huh?"

"I'm not by myself. If you'll excuse me, I need to speak to one of the staff members at the doors." When she went to step around him, he reached out and grabbed her wrist with such speed that she startled. "Let go!" Regan yelled, but her cry was drowned out by the music and voices that surrounded her.

"No' until I get wha' I wan, girl," he purred slowly and with a waft of smoky breath.

"And what is that? My knee connecting with your groin?" muttered Regan, pulling harshly on his grasp.

The man's devious grin darkened. "Naw, bu' some other par' of ya would be nice."

"Let go before I call security!"

"Like they could hear ya."

He was right. The music and the voices were so loud that nobody would notice her calling for help, and if they did, she hardly thought they would care. After all, who would want to mess with this man? He stood at least 6'3" with a body built as if he lived and breathed his gym on a daily basis. He was frightening, especially to her.

Regan swallowed a lump of growing panic and whimpered beneath the heavy gaze of the leering man.

~ ~ ~ ~

Daniel had been heading to the street when his keen hearing caught the panic stricken call of a woman amongst the crowd. The cry halted his steps, turning his eyes to sweep through the crowd, and by chance he caught the flash of a silver cross about the neck of a woman who was in the brutal hold of a Lamia - David Servilii. A growl pushed against his thin pressed lips upon recognition of the particular Lamia who, by order of Rhain, was not permitted on or near the property. Narrowing his black eyes, Daniel pushed through the crowd with determined and dexterous strides.

When he arrived upon the scene, he saw that David had the girl's wrist in a tight grip causing her youthful face to contort in fear as she struggled and cursed. Coming right behind the young woman, Daniel cast a dangerous glare towards the Lamia, and in a voice that was cold and threatening, he snapped, "Release her!"

Regan froze to the sudden command that sent chills crackling through her body. She saw the roughian glance over her head, and when Regan turned to peek over her shoulder to see who he was looking to, she saw a young and handsome man looking very displeased. His hands were stuffed into the pockets of his fine over coat, and his face, pale and attractive, held no look of amusement within his dark eyes that were narrowed dangerously from behind a few stray strands of lengthy ebony.

"David Servilii." Daniel shook his head. "What a surprise to see you here considering your banishment from the property. What are you doing here, you fool?"

The other man, now christened David, smirked and released Regan's wrist with a faint shove. "Enjoy'n myself, Sucker."

The force of the shove sent Regan stumbling right into the arms of the longhaired stranger, who caught her by pressing a gentle yet firm hand to her back. "That's not the answer I wanted to hear," he muttered in a suave voice caressed with a gentle accent.

Regan glanced back over her shoulder just as the young man looked down. Their eyes met and he offered her a comforting smile. His eyes, as dark as the night around her, seemed to soften and glisten with a silvery shine as a random light fell into his vision. He then looked towards the other man and the danger and harshness appeared within his etched gaze once more.

"Com'on, mate," David grumbled while cocking his head to the side and with his arms opening in placation. "We were jus' hav'n a bi'o' fun." He chuckled and cast his eyes towards Regan as a suggestive and rather lewd smile coiled his lips. "Weren't we, girl?"

She recoiled with a huff. "We certainly were not." She glanced to the man behind her with a heavy scowl. "I accidentally bumped into him when the guy behind me pushed me in line. My shoe came off causing me to stumble. That's all." She jabbed a finger towards the brute. "He's taking this way out proportion. I did apologize to him and tried to get out of line but he grabbed me."

32

David hissed, "Shu'it bitch." He moved to raise his hand but another hand snapped out to catch his wrist.

Regan yelped. The move was so quick that she didn't see the arm come about her shoulder. She did, however, see discomfort flash across David's face when the popping of the bones within his wrist could be heard as they were crushed.

"Control yourself," growled the stranger. "After all, you were ordered not to step foot onto this property after the last little bit of fun you had. Must I remind you of my brother's proclamation?"

David's green eyes narrowed and a slow grin spread his thick lips. "Ya be'er let go of me, mate, or I'll scream. You wouldn' wanna cause a scene over this cunt, would ya?"

"Watch your language." A flash of dangerous warning shot through the man's black eyes as he slowly released David's wrist. Yet, he inclined his head in what appeared to be a conceding apology. "You're right, David. We wouldn't want any laws broken here. How ironic considering you have a history of breaking many laws at will. Speaking of which, you have already broken a law by coming here." Lifting a finger, the stranger wagged the lean digit with an added tsk - tsk to each motion. "I'm afraid I am going to have to ask you to leave, or another offense will be added to your long list of belligerent activities here upon the Crucible property."

David coiled his lips with a low growl. "Fine," he hissed with a snap of his teeth, and with a shove, he pushed between the two, purposely forcing Regan away. He didn't say a word but marched past the gate of the Crucible and out on to the busy street.

When he was gone, Regan sighed. She was shaking after her run in with the man. The intensity of the moment wouldn't be removed from her mind by a hot soak in the tub, nor would the sensation of the man's touch be removed by a loofa scrubbing. "Thank you," she said in exhale, looking up to the dark eyes of her savior; he smiled softly to her. "Who was that man?"

"Only a local trouble maker. He shows himself here every so often to see if he can cause trouble. Are you alright? Did he hurt you?" he asked with his eyes drifting across her face. Carefully, he reached to take the wrist that she was favoring only to shake his head in displeasure upon noticing her red and irritated wrist. There was a bruise already developing, and the sight of the discolored and puffy skin drew a throaty rumble of disapproval from Daniel.

"A little," Regan replied with a sigh as she rubbed her wrist.

Daniel's keen vision caught sight of the silver chain and cross that was set about the young woman's throat, confirming his quick suspicions. The young woman that David had assaulted was the birthday girl that Cultor had mentioned earlier. Leave it to the Proscriptus to ruin a birthday.

"I see that my brother and his friend gave you their little gift." He gently tapped the pink agate in the center of the pendant. "I suppose a happy birthday is in order."

"Huh?" Regan looked down to the cross. "Your brother gave me this?"

"Yes. He and his orange haired cohort own this place. Forgive me for not introducing myself. I am Daniel Thorn. You must be,' he paused in thought then nodded, 'Regan Scott. Am I correct?"

Daniel, so that was his name. He looked like a Daniel with his gentle features, dark eyes, and long black hair. She had never known a guy with such long hair and oddly found the style very attractive. "I am. Look, I'm really sorry for all the trouble I've caused. I just came out for some fresh air and was trying to get back to my cousin."

She groaned, pressing hand against her forehead. "Great, my head is pounding again."

Daniel frowned with his brows knitting together. "Are you sure you're alright? Can I call a cab for you?"

"Thank you, but no. My cousin's inside, and I told the bar manager that I would be back."

"Cultor?"

She nodded. "Maybe he has another aspirin tucked away somewhere."

Daniel clicked his tongue to the roof of his mouth then pressed the back of his palm to her forehead. He could feel the burning heat of her pulse pounding erratically.

The instant his touch was upon her, Regan felt a cooling sensation spread throughout her aching nerves. Her eyes closed with a sigh of relief. She didn't know what he did, but when the instant coolness of his touch fell against her flesh the pain began to subside. When he drew his hand away, she smiled to him in appreciation.

"Thank you."

Daniel inclined his head to her with a stray lock of ebony drifting against a cheek.

"Again, I'm sorry about all of his. That man took an accident very personally."

"David takes everything personally," Daniel chuckled. "Why don't I give you an escort back inside? I'm sure Cultor can make you some tea, and I think there's another aspirin somewhere in the nurse's station. I can find you one."

A twist of discomfort flickered upon her face. "I guess I should go back in. Although, I am not really all that fond of clubs. The loud music and the drinks bother me, not to mention all the rude people. It's not really my idea of a place to celebrate my birthday."

"If I may ask, then why are you here if you're not enjoying the invigorating environment?"

Giving a deep sigh, the young woman cast an annoyed glance to the front doors of the club. "It was my cousin's idea. She's wanted to come here since the club opened, and since I'm here visiting for the summer she decided my birthday would give her the perfect excuse to wait in line."

With a sly smirk, Regan leaned closer to Daniel with a hand outlining her lips as if to whisper secretly, "Personally? I would rather be at home with a nice glass of wine, some pasta, and a good scary movie."

34

Daniel smirked. "That sounds like many of my nights." He shrugged his slender shoulders then glanced to the church. "To tell you the truth, this really is not my idea of an entertaining evening either." Daniel frowned and added sympathetically, "I'm sorry your birthday was ruined."

Regan waved a hand to him, dismissing his apology. "Wouldn't be the first time," she told him with an amused flash to her eyes. "In fact, I think my seventh birthday was the worst. My parents decided to have a pony there for pony rides, but they hired Taco the psycho pony." Regan shuddered at the horrible memory. "That thing got loose and ran amuck in the backyard knocking over everything and eating my cake. Anybody who came near him, including his owner, was bitten and kicked at. I think I was in therapy for that."

Daniel laughed an honest laugh at the image her words danced through his mind.

She frowned with a shake of her head. "It was horrible."

Twisting his lips in thought, and with a stray glance across the street, he noticed the coffee house he often occasioned while waiting for the club to close. There were a few people still within its dim lights, but for the most part it was quiet.

He looked back to her as a sly and charming smile took his handsome mouth. "How about I try to make up for David and your evening? Would you like to have a cup of coffee with me and get away from the pounding music and rude people for a little while?" He nudged his chin across the street.

Regan followed his motion. Oh, a coffee house! She smiled brightly and with excitement. "That would be lovely!"

Daniel offered her his arm. "Shall we?"

Regan fell beneath his dark gaze and a warm caress trailed its way along her skin. She felt her heart skip a few beats, and taking his arm, the two stepped away from the crowd.

~ ~ ~ ~

"What would you like?" Daniel asked Regan as she peered upon the board highlighting specialty coffees, hot coco, teas, and sweet treats.

"Everything sounds too tempting,' breathed Regan as she tapped fingers to the pastry case. Her eyes scanned each and every treat with hunger. "I would love a coffee. I've had so much tea since I've gotten here that my stomach is swimming in a pot or two."

"Can I make a suggestion?"

"Of course!"

Smiling, he flicked a lean finger towards the board. "They have a mocha coffee with Mexican chocolate that has a subtle but warm touch of spice to it. It would be very warm on a chilly and wet night like this."

The suggested drink sounded absolutely wonderful, mostly because she loved anything that had chocolate in it. Who could go wrong with chocolate? "That sounds perfect."

35

"Miss?" Daniel motioned to one of the girls working behind the counter. "I'll have a tall latte, hot, with almond milk and she will have a tall, hot Aztec."

"Of course," giggled the employee with a very flirtatious smile to Daniel. "Anything else I can get for you?"

"Would you like anything else, Regan?"

"Oh, I'm not sure," she replied with a soft blush to her cheeks, but then he leaned closer to her and that blush scorched her skin. She nipped her lower lip as he pointed over her shoulder to the display case and to a cinnamon, apple scone that was obviously screaming her name.

"How about a scone? You can't come to England and not drown yourself in scones. Would you share one with me?"

Oh Heavens, his aftershave heated her insides. Loving the smell of exotic spices, Regan instantly fell victim to the hypnotic and tantalizing caress of his cologne that reminded her of the smells of a Middle Eastern bazaar. She found herself closing her eyes and leaning to him.

"Regan?"

Daniel's voice, curiously asking her name, brought her attention back from the luscious scent of his cologne. He was smirking at her with friendly amusement touching to his features. All she could do was smile to him before looking back to the case. "Oh, yes. That scone does look delectable."

"Then get it."

"Alright. I'll take that cinnamon, apple scone as well," she told the employee only to frown when she noticed the young woman staring at Daniel - blatantly ignoring her request. "Excuse me? I would also like that scone."

The young woman scowled with a glance to Regan then quickly looked back to Daniel. "Would there be anything else for you, sir?"

Regan sighed.

Hearing the sigh, Daniel narrowed his eyes towards the employee. He wasn't a fool. He saw the flutter of her eyes and the pursing of her lips. He was used to such attention, and quite frankly, he was getting tired of it. The overly dramatic and flirtatious play from the young woman turned his stomach. Not only did he despise desperate women, but he also disliked women who were openly rude and arrogant, much like this woman appeared to be.

With the employee ignoring Regan, Daniel was growing agitated. He cleared his voice. "Yes. She,' he motioned to Regan next to him, 'would like one of the cinnamon, apple scones. I am sure you heard her."

The flirtatious eyes and the pouting smile turned instantly to a pout and a glare. The moment the handsome man disregarded her advances and forced her attention to the American next to him, her politeness turned sour. With an air of flippancy, the employee looked to Regan. "Fine." With that grunted, she turned about to prepare their order.

"I bet you get a lot of that, don't you?" Regan asked.

He tipped his head. "A lot of what?"

"Women giving you puppy eyes. You know, flirting with you."

The Lamia chuckled with a slight shrug of his shoulders. "I used to enjoy the attention, but now I have grown weary of the emptiness within the attention. I don't fancy such advances anymore. I've never been the type of man to pay attention to desperate women who pine for my affection. My brother is the twin who enjoys that."

After paying for their order, Daniel nodded to her and smoothly changed the direction of the personal topic. "Let's find a table. Our order will be brought to us." He scanned the area, then upon noticing the rain had stopped, suggested the two sit outside and enjoy the fresh air in hopes that her headache continued to diminish. Once the two had decided upon a table set off to the side, they settled down to wait for their order.

"You know,' Regan stated with a dreamy sigh, 'I always have been attracted to England, especially London. There's a magical feeling to this city."

Daniel nodded in agreement. "There is an ancient power that resides across England. After all, the land here is very old, even the land beneath these streets. London has a soul of its own, an old soul that still breathes deep from within the Earth. Perhaps you're feeling that ancient soul calling to you."

She arched a brow, looking back to him as he spoke. His words sent a little shiver through her as if there was truth in what he had said. She smiled to him. "Perhaps."

The two looked up when a waitress came with their order. She set their coffees and the pastry down to the table then disappeared into the café.

Regan frowned to him. "How much do I owe for this?"

Daniel waved off her question, replying with a sly but handsome grin, "Consider this a minor birthday gift."

She shook her head but then, with a cool gust of wet wind, Regan's entire body shuddered from head to toe. Every muscle contracted to the chill that swept through her. Seeing the hard shudder, Daniel stood from his chair while sweeping off his coat that he draped over her shoulders. Even though the material would be missing much of the heat radiated from a human body, it would at least offer her protection from the chilled elements. Being a Lamia, his body didn't respond to the change of temperature as a human's body did.

"Thank you." Regan drew the fine coat closer about her shoulders then took the first sip of her tantalizing coffee. "This coffee is wonderful," she mewed, taking another sip of the spiced brew.

"How is your headache?"

Regan's chocolate-brown eyes blinked as if his question had come out of nowhere. Headache? She tipped her head as her mind searched for an answer, but then she chuckled. "It's gone. I guess your touch is magic."

"Perhaps it is," Daniel whispered over the rim of his coffee cup as he took a slow, small sip.

"So, how long did it take for your brother and his friend to repair the old church? It's massive. I'm sure it took a long time." Regan sipped her spiced mocha while trying to find a topic for simple conversation. At the same time, she was very curious how a church, condemned to destruction, became one of the hottest clubs in London.

"That's an interesting question. They didn't do anything to fix up the old place, per say," chuckled Daniel as he shook his head. Leaning back a bit, he shifted to gain comfort as he placed one hand to the table top while the other kept his coffee close to his lips. "Sure, they purchased the building and the property but they did little in the restoration process let alone dealing with the London Historical Society to get the permission needed to remodel the church into a nightclub."

Regan winced. "I'm sure that was rather difficult. In the States, historical societies don't look kindly on people revamping historical buildings for much of anything but a museum."

"That's how it goes here as well. Luckily,' he smirked, 'I have vast connections through the different historical and cultural societies about England. With the financial grants that my department donates yearly to museums, schools, and historical societies, the London Historical Society was willing to look the other way in granting Rhain the licenses needed for his venture."

"It does pay to have a name."

Daniel smiled with a conceding nod.

"If I may ask, who did the restorations? I saw some before and after pictures stuck in a corner of the church. The process must have been very delicate."

"Again, I lent my skills and Alasdair's cousin stepped in to help. Jamie Baird is a well-known architectural restoration expert and architect in Britain. With my aid on the cleaning and restoring of the art and the artifacts, Jamie helped with the physical reconstruction of the building and the foundation. We also helped in the location of burial documents to try and find the identities of those buried within the church and the cemetery."

Regan blew out a soft whistle. "You're an artist then?"

"I dabble." Smirking, Daniel took a quick sip of his coffee, allowing the liquid to warm his insides.

"That sounds very impressive." Regan gave him a cheeky grin then said with pride, "I can draw a straight line."

Daniel laughed softly and took a piece of the scone. "Tell me about yourself, Regan. What are you doing here in London?"

"There's not much to tell really. I'm just about to start my junior year at college studying nothing of importance. I live in a western suburb of Chicago, a little town called Elburn, where my family owns a decent size horse stable."

"Your family owns a riding stable?"

She nodded. "Yes. It's not too big, about thirty horses or so are stabled there. We have a good size property so we host some shows for the locals throughout the year. I grew up on the farm so I've been around horse, the show circuit, and the pony club scene my entire life."

"Then we have more in common with our lives than you think. My brothers and I were raised on a small farm in a quaint countryside village set on the border of England and Wales. It was a small place, but beautiful none the less."

"Is it still there?"

38

"I'm not sure. It's been a long time since I've bothered to check on the old place, memories you know."

Regan's smile brightened. "And you had horses?"

"A few for the farm work, but there was a rather nasty pony that had a personal grudge against Rhain. From the start, Rhain and that pony had it out for each other. Rhain's still afraid of horses, especially Shetland ponies."

Regan chuckled softly, giving a knowing nod. "Those ponies can be nasty. I speak from experience."

"The Taco incident?"

Regan shuddered. "It was horrific."

Daniel chuckled. "I believe you mentioned that you are here visiting your cousin."

"Yes."

"And what are your plans?"

"We had plans of doing some minor traveling, but I'm not sure if that will happen. I would love to see some horse shows, but Joyce isn't very fond of horses. She's more interested other forms of entertainment, which is why we're here tonight."

"Which you're not too keen on."

"Not at all."

"There is a lot more to London than nightclubs."

"Exactly," she breathed out with a smile. "I hope I get the chance to explore a castle or two. Then again, I would give anything to see some remains of the Roman settlements."

"How long will you be staying?"

"A month."

"That is plenty of time to see some sites in and around the city."

"But not to see everything."

Daniel smiled. "No. For that you would need…"

"A lifetime."

Daniel nodded in agreement. "Yes, a lifetime."

Two and a half hours passed and the two were still discussing random topics of their lives and their interests. Regan was fascinated to learn more of Thorn Inc. and was eager to know more about Daniel Thorn himself. She asked every question she could think of on his travels to exotic destinations and his adventures digging around archeological sites in Egypt, Asia, Italy, and Greece.

As their conversations, and the time, went on they both discovered that many of their hobbies and interests went hand-in-hand. They liked the same music, the same movies, and had similar tastes in cuisine. They also shared a deep rooted passion for traveling, as well as an enjoyment of museums and historical sites.

The longer they talked, the faster Daniel found himself entranced by the Humanus. She was filled with humorous stories of her childhood that were accompanied by the most amusing hand signs and facial expressions, entertaining analogies of world events, and a rather comical view on philosophies.

"So,' she said with a little smile of curiosity, 'can you tell me more of the old church?"

"Well,' Daniel licked his lips as he leaned back in his chair with a side glance tossed to the club, 'the Crucible was Rhain and Alasdair's obsession for many years. They had worked with the concept for a while before the church came on the market. Honestly, I never expected their creation to get off the ground, and when they did purchase the church, I was rather surprised."

"Surprised?"

Daniel chuckled softly as he ran a fingertip about the rim of his coffee mug. "Rhain has a very creative imagination, but not all of his creative ideas come to fruition."

"But it seems that the Crucible has done very well for itself. Rhain and his business partner must be very proud."

Daniel accepted her compliment for his twin with a respectful nod of his head. "They are very proud of their money child."

"How long did it take for the restoration to be completed?"

After taking a slow, dry breath of London air, Daniel explained how hard the venture had been to start, not to mention all of the problems associated with the reconstruction of the old property that smacked all involved: foundation problems, cracks in the structure and the walls, a minor flood in the crypts, and a sewer leakage that ran beneath a section of the cemetery. Thankfully all the problems were handled correctly and quickly.

He told her that when the business and conversion plans were announced to the public that many were very upset with the preconception that the sacred grounds would be destroyed. Regan agreed that destroying the cemetery would have brought a lot of resentment towards the two owners, yet Daniel assured her that his brother and Alasdair had never put any of the dead in jeopardy. Not a single body or soul had been removed from their ordained resting place, and that seemed to appease the public. The local businesses never complained either since the late night crowd brought an increase in pay to their shops and restaurants, especially this little café.

"And you and Jamie did all that work by yourselves?"

"Of course. That's our profession after all - overseeing the restoration of antiques, artifacts, and historical buildings."

"Tell me more about your company. It all sounds very fascinating to an individual who is artistically challenged, like me." She leaned forwards with a bright and curious grin.

"Very well. I am the head of the restoration department, or so it says on my office door, so it was only fitting that I aid my brother and his pumpkin haired friend in their efforts to give new life to the Crucible."

Regan's features brightened as she listened to his quick explanation. So, he was an art lover and owned his own business? Those two facts only added to his charm and her genuine appreciation for him. "And what of Jamie?"

"Ah,' he chuckled with a quick lick of his lips, 'Jamie is a Scotsman from Edinburgh. He's known as one of the go-to guys for wealthy property buyers and owners who have some dusty, old castle or country cottage that needs restoration. He's a brilliant architect and fancies himself an architectural engineer and restorer. I, on the other hand, am a humble art nerd."

Regan laughed softly.

Daniel chuckled and went on to say, "Jamie and I worked tediously and tirelessly for months making sure every crack of plaster and every chip of wood was restored and the paintings and windows repaired. We also saw to the repairs of the crypts and graves both on the inside and outside of the church." Daniel shook his head slowly and brushed at a lock of his hair away from his face that had fallen forwards. "There were many nights when Jamie and I would retire to this café for a coffee and scone while my twin and his cousin fought over some minor conflict of interests. If I remember correctly, a hammer or two had been thrown and somebody got their pride kicked."

Or their ass, but he wasn't about to say such a crude word in front of a young lady.

Regan smirked, and her cheeks darkened with a soft blush. "Forgive me for saying, but you're making yourself sound very intelligent and charming."

Daniel arched a black brow over a sparkling eye then laughed brightly, amused at her playful jibe. "Perhaps I am. I can't help being so. After all, I really am proud of the work Jamie and I executed on behalf of the church and its two owners."

"Well, you both did an amazing job. I think I was more impressed by the historical past of the cathedral itself than the club."

Daniel raised his coffee mug and offered a nod of his head. "And that, my dear, is a wonderful compliment. I shall pass it along to Jamie." After a draw of his coffee, he went on to ask Regan about her courses in study and her college experience.

She shook her head then smiled to him. "You don't want to hear about my trivial and boring education. I'm not studying anything fancy, mostly the required subjects to get them out of the way before I settle on a specific major. I guess I have too many interests."

"Picking an educational discipline is not an easy task."

She nodded her head in agreement. "Not at all, however, I'm sure that sooner or later some light bulb will come on in my head and I'll pick something."

"And what of your family?"

"As I said, my family owns a stable." A soft and warm smile of sentiment touched Regan's face. She settled back in her chair to raise her eyes to the handsome man before her. "My father operates the stables now with a few hired hands, and I come home on weekends and holidays to see the horses, visit friends, and check up on my father."

"And your mother?"

A shadow of discomfort fell over her eyes and she sighed turning her eyes to her coffee cup. "My mother was killed in a car accident a few years ago. It's just my father and me now."

41

Tipping his head, Daniel offered her a sincere and apologetic frown. "I'm sorry for your loss. It's not easy losing our parents. I know that personally as both of mine passed away when Rhain and I were not but ten or so."

Regan looked back to him with a tender expression of shock. "You lost both of your parents?" He nodded and she whispered, "How tragic. I'm so sorry."

Daniel offered a dismissive wave of a hand and a soft smile. "It was many years ago. Like your mother, an accident took my parents at the same time."

"How did you manage? I mean, you and your brothers seem to have done incredibly well for yourselves, going through university and operating businesses on an international scale. That's very impressive."

Daniel smiled at her lovely compliment. "Kain was in university here in London when our parents passed away. He sold the family farm and used the money to purchase a small flat in the city for us all. We moved here with him and he cared for us, seeing to our needs as well as he could. Our parents had a trust fund that put Rhain and I through university when we came to age."

"Kain did a wonderful job raising you both. It must have been difficult for him."

Daniel smiled fondly and gave a solemn nod. "He did his best."

Taking a breath, she turned her attention out to the street and the lively cathedral. When she looked back to him, she inquired about his company. "Tell me more about your company. I'm very curious as to how somebody who is so young can operate such a massive construct."

Daniel chuckled with a playful roll of his eyes. "It is not too difficult. I only operate one of the departments. Kain is the one who handles the rest."

Regan leaned forwards to place an elbow atop the table and her chin to an upturned palm. "Tell me more, art nerd."

Daniel's face brightened at the term she used to identify him and laughed with a handsome smile parting his equally handsome mouth. When his laughter simmered into a chuckle, he went into his explanation. "Thorn Incorporated supports the restoration and repairs of private art collections owned by private art collectors, museums, and investors. We work with international museums and art communities by donating money for archeological preservation and restoration, as well as donating funds every year to select schools across the world that are lacking in modern equipment and finances for their art programs."

Regan blinked her eyes - stunned. "That sounds like a massive company."

"We are growing every year."

"And your other brother doesn't work for the family business?"

"No," Daniel breathed out through a smirk. "Fortunately, Rhain keeps his business interests to his humble club. He doesn't know a pencil from a pen. Thorn Inc. works rather well without him, and we all seem to like that balance."

"Well, your life certainly outshines my own." Taking another bite of scone, Regan chewed upon the piece before taking a longer sip of her coffee. "And you run the entire company with your older brother?"

Grinning, he leaned forwards with his elbows setting atop the table and his fingers lacing beneath his chin. "Not all of it. I am the head of the preservation department that oversees the restoration and cleaning of pieces that come to us. My department also sees to repairing damages such as weather damage, fire damage, water damage, and so forth."

"And you are the one in charge of all of that?"

"Indeed I am. I oversee all of the pieces that come to be cataloged and cared for, distributed and returned. I do have eight employees who work for me."

"Only eight?"

Daniel flashed a handsome grin. "I'm very picky on who is allowed to work for me and who is allowed to handle the priceless creations of art that we work on."

Regan breathed out a whistle. "I can imagine. You must see amazing works of art."

"Many."

"And do you travel for your company?"

He nodded. "I do, when time permits. I have contacts, clients, and connections with minor restoration artists and companies across the globe. I also work with archeological institutions and governments, both local and international."

"That sounds like a lot of stress."

Daniel's smile was genuine and proud. "It is very stressful, but I do what I must."

"And you still find time to visit your brother's club?"

He chuckled a very deep and warm chuckle. "Somebody has to keep my twin from burning down the neighborhood."

"Wouldn't his business partner handle that?"

Daniel laughed openly as he leaned back in his chair. "Hardly. Give those two a match and they'll put something to flame."

Regan chuckled. "And what position does Kain hold?"

"Kain claims to be the CEO. He manages the dirty bits of the business such as finances, grants, and company politics. Most of his time is spent staring at stocks and intimidating every soul who works for us. He's very talented at that, intimidating people."

"You must love your job."

Daniel gave a sheepish smile. "My work is a passion of mine. I can't tell you what it feels like to hold a piece of sculpture in my hands that was created hundreds if not thousands of years ago. People think that life is intimidating and fragile, but to me…what we create with our own hands is fragile and priceless - precious."

When he saw Regan grinning to him from over the rim of her coffee, a glimpse of white teeth nipping upon her lower lip in amusement, Daniel chuckled in embarrassment. "Forgive me. It's not often I have somebody interested in my work who doesn't know me personally. It's very refreshing"

Regan snickered to the delicate touch of embarrassment that danced across his youthful face. "I find it odd that you and your brothers seem so different from each other, almost as if you're all from different worlds. You from a world of sophistication, beauty, and history, your twin from a world of social excitement surrounded by both modern conveniences and historical references, and your eldest brother stuck in the middle somewhere."

Regan frowned at her words, and her features scrunched as if she was trying to understand exactly what she just stated. "That didn't quite make sense. It sounded better in my head."

Daniel laughed and waved off her confusion and her concern with a flick of fingers. "I believe I understood the concept of what you said, and you're right. My twin and I are from different worlds even though we came from the same womb. Rhain isn't the type to delve into the world of study and exploration as I am. The world he enjoys to romp about in is the underground sub-cultures that London society demands to be fed. He's the type that wants his gratification at the moment, not years down the road and with hours of hard work."

"And what of Kain?"

"He's an enigma. He's neither like Rhain nor like me, but he is like both of us. It's confusing, even to me. After all these years, I'm still trying to figure him out. He changes with the season, but at the same time he's solid like a damn rock." Daniel sighed, shaking his head. "Honestly, if it wasn't for the internet and photos from space, he'd still think the world is flat. Rhain and I used to joke with him about his stubbornness, so one year we bought him a large globe for his office saying that one day he'd figure it all out."

Daniel chuckled with a wicked grin. "He still loathes that globe but can't bring himself to toss it."

Regan sighed dreamily. "I've only known you for an hour and I'm already blown away by your accomplishments and the accomplishments of your brothers. And here I get excited if I pass a simple quiz."

Daniel leaned forwards, observing her as she quietly sipped her coffee. And as he gazed upon her, he found himself becoming more and more entranced by her. He realized that from the moment he looked into Regan's eyes, he felt a pull towards her. So when he saw her fear and the bruise upon her flesh from her run in with David, he felt instant rage explode within him. Daniel had dealt with countless mortals over his long life, but he'd never come across a human so interesting before, especially not a young woman who took his fancy directly and for nothing more than being so simple and not overly projecting a seemingly false image. She captivated him, and that had Daniel tickling with excitement.

He was thoroughly confused with his perception of her, pleasantly confused. Leaning back, Daniel bent one arm upon the back of his chair and stretched the other out before him with fingers running along his cup of coffee that he lifted to his lips. Finishing off his coffee, Daniel raised a finger to the woman across the table and said, "I'm not sure if I should be saying this, but there's something about you, Miss. Scott, that fascinates me."

Regan blinked in surprise. "I fascinate you? I've never had anybody say that about me before." She teased him with a grin. "It was the fact I can draw a line, wasn't it?"

Daniel flashed her a deviously handsome wink. "Perhaps. I have an idea."

"Oh? What's your idea?"

"Next Thursday night an associate of mine is hosting a formal event at his home, invitation only. He is showcasing his collection of Japanese woodblock prints and wall scrolls before the assortment is sent off to museums on tour. I would be honored if you would join me."

Regan looked to him with an expression of bewilderment. "You want to take me to a social event? Why?"

Daniel shrugged while keeping his eyes upon her. "You're here visiting London, so why not enjoy a random moment of culture? Besides, telling your family and friends that you were with Daniel Thorn at an exclusive art exhibition would go a long way."

A little shiver danced along her spine as every excuse flooded her mind. "I don't have a dress." Once those words left her mouth Regan wanted to crawl under the table. She didn't have a dress? Was that the first logical and rational sounding excuse she could come up with? What in hell was wrong with her?

Daniel laughed; his laugh was warm and rich. "We'll find one for you. There are many dress shops around the city. In fact, I know the perfect shop where you can find a dress."

Now that he had the time to get to know Regan, as short as it was, he was not going to let her get away from this invitation. Daniel Rhys Thorn did not take no for an answer, especially when his request involved a beautiful woman who had caught not only his attention but his curious interest.

"Are you sure?" she asked quietly as she nibbled on the inside of a slender cheek. "You don't know me all that well."

"We're getting to know each other."

"You don't know where I live."

"You can give me your address. It's perfectly reasonable to do so."

Regan drew in a deep breath that expanded her lungs. "I don't know where you live."

Daniel grinned, enjoying their little verbal game of tug-of-war. "Knowing where I live is not relevant to this invitation. However, if you really wish to know, I can give you my address."

He added with a charming chuckle, "I would like to have you accompany me. We won't have to stay long, and afterwards I will take you for a night tour of London. What do you say? This event is a once in a life time chance for anyone outside of the artistic community here in London. If you enjoy art and Japanese culture, you wouldn't want to pass this opportunity up."

"Why me?"

"You fascinate me." He smiled to her and covered her slender hand within his; the warmth of her human body trickled from her fingertips to tease his cool palm. "Allow me to treat you to a wonderful evening, Regan. Consider the offer a birthday gift."

45

His eyes watched the show of expressions flittering upon her features: confusion, fright, apprehension, desire and excitement. He looked back to her hand where his fingers danced and played over her knuckles.

"How can I trust you?"

Daniel brought her hand to his lips, and with his eyes locked to her, he spoke softly and in a voice that vibrated from the depth of his soul, "You would be no safer in any other's hands than in mine. I can promise you that."

After a moment of thought, Regan's lips tucked into a soft smile and she gave a little nod. "Alright. I would love to accompany you, Daniel."

"Wonderful! Here,' he took out his wallet and passed her one of his business cards and a small silver pen, 'write me your number so I can call you in a few days to make arrangements with you."

Regan took the card, reading the inscription within her mind: Daniel Rhys Thorn - Restoration Department Head, Thorn Inc. His office number and address were listed upon the card. She scribbled the number to Joyce's flat then handed the card back to him. "I don't have a mobile here, so that number goes to my cousin's apartment."

"That will do fine." Glancing to his watch, Daniel drew in a shallow breath. "I hate to end this wonderful evening so soon, but I have stayed out later than I had expected. I must be getting back to my office. If I'm not there to oversee my employees, they end up hanging from the ceiling as if they've reverted back to apes."

"I'm sorry that I've kept you out so late," Regan stated in apology as she scooted her chair back so she could stand.

"Nonsense." Daniel winked and moved to her side to guide her chair back - an old habit of his gentlemanly ways. "I would stay longer but no one in my family can draw a stick figure so I can't leave my office for too long. I doubt they could try and restore a tinker toy set."

Her chuckle brought a smile to his lips and he offered her his hand. "Allow me to walk you back to the club. I can't leave you sitting here by yourself, now can I?"

Regan raised her eyes to his and found herself captivated by the kindness she saw reflected within a dance of silver sheen. She didn't hesitate to set her hand to his. Daniel guided her to stand then took his coat from her shoulders before they walked back to the club in comfortable silence.

They stopped in the courtyard and faced each other. "I will call you soon, alright?" When she nodded, Daniel leaned down to touch a chaste kiss to her cheek, then he drew back to smile to her. "Till we meet again, have a goodnight and stay safe."

Regan felt a warm rush of heat trickle its way up her spine when he touched the cool kiss to her cheek; his lips felt so soft. "I will." Regan watched Daniel turn and depart the grounds to disappear down the foggy street.

Standing at the gates, she stared in the direction he had departed from. Rain began to trickle down from the sky once again, and only when she felt the wet chill from the droplets seeping into her did she turn back to the club. But then she stopped and looked up to the massive structure and the looming Gargoyles with their burning red eyes. She decided that she wasn't ready to go into the church just yet, so she took to sitting upon a bench next to a small garden where she could see the front doors clearly. There she would wait for Joyce exit so the two could go home.

Till then, she'd sit amongst the magic of London, the caressing fog, and the romantic memories of coffee with Daniel Thorn.

III

Miss. Scott, would you please stop haunting my thoughts - my dreams? At least till later this week. Till then, allow this simple man's mind to settle. Otherwise, I may start hearing your voice seeping out from the cold faces of stone that I stare at every night.

It has only been a few days since we met, and yet you are constantly in my thoughts. I hear a whisper of your name in the corner of my office and think that I will look up and see your radiant smile, but you are not there. You are never there. Though ghosts are not unknown in my world, I prefer to keep my life haunting-free. Perhaps you are a spirit come to tease my soul.

I have known many humans in my long life and not a single one has captivated my thoughts as you have. What magical spell did you put upon me? What captivating allure do you have that causes my mind to distract itself from every task in my night? I would have the answers, Miss. Scott - one way or another.

A week. I must wait a week to ask you these question and for you to grant me the answers that I need in order to rest during the day. Till then, haunt me only in my sleep where my dreams can be more enjoyable than the long minutes of the night.

- *Daniel Rhys Thorn*

~ ~ ~ ~

"Then what happened?"

The next day, Joyce sat cross legged upon Regan's bed within the guest room of the small London flat. Joyce buzzed with excitement as her cousin retold the story of meeting Daniel Thorn for the fifth time. By eleven thirty-two in the morning, and a few hundred cups of coffee later, the fog was starting to lift from Joyce's clogged mind and reality was setting in. The idea that *her* cousin had a date with one of the hottest, young bachelors in London was impossible. Wasn't it? Joyce still couldn't make the connection. In truth, she felt a little upset that Daniel Thorn had found an interest in her simple cousin who wouldn't know Armani from army. Hell, Regan was born in a barn.

Regan, gazing at a dress catalogue, lifted her eyes. Again? Joyce wanted to hear the story again? She sighed then spoke, "Again?"

"Yes, again. And don't skip on the details!"

"Very well,' groaned Regan as she hung her head. "But this is the last time. Daniel was very suave in his actions as he grabbed the guy's wrist, bending his arm right back. I swear he could've broken the man's arm. I mean, this guy was a street punk,' she chuckled, 'you know the type that is all muscle and no brains."

"Pft, I know the type. Did he hurt you?"

"Not too badly. I still have a little bruise, and my wrist's still tender." Regan blushed softly at the memory of Daniel appearing out of nowhere, like a dark knight off his steed. "Mister Thorn took control of the situation directly. David backed off after they tossed some manly threats back and forth. Turns out David is not allowed on the property anyway, so Mister Thorn ordered him to leave and he did."

Joyce sighed dramatically, falling back upon the bed. "That's so romantic!" She breathed a little sigh with a tiny giggle. "Daniel Thorn comes out of nowhere to sweep you off your feet and save you from the ass-hole."

Regan shook her head. "It was nothing that dramatic, Joyce. He was in the right place at the right time. That's all. You're making it out to be more than what it was."

"Right,' grinned Joyce, 'then he invites you to a formal event at some private art party. That doesn't happen every day."

"He was being nice." Regan shrugged.

"He's asked you on a date."

Regan snorted.

Joyce snickered. "I can't believe you hooked up with Daniel Thorn while I was getting drunk!"

"We had coffee together. We weren't 'hooking up," muttered Regan, quoting the air. "I don't think you can term a cup of coffee and a scone a date."

"You two had coffee *together* for almost two hours." Joyce grinned while madly poking her cousin in the hip with her foot. "You still haven't told me what you two talked about."

Regan huffed and delicately brushed back a lock of her chocolaty hair that had fallen forwards from her headband. "Just little things. You know, where he works, what he does, and what I do."

"Boring!" Joyce chimed with a gag. She then grinned as she poked Regan again. "You were out on a date."

"Not a date. We had coffee."

"Whatever,' muttered her cousin, 'you were out on a date with one of the most wanted bachelors in London and you talked about work." Joyce sat up with a look of horror. "Oh, bloody Hell! Don't tell me you told him about your stinky horses."

"For your information he was rather interested in my stinky horses. He was honestly curious about me, including the family stable and my school." She opened her mouth to tell her cousin about Daniel growing up on a farm and retelling the story of Rhain and the pony from Hell, but who was she to give hint of his childhood? The last thing she wanted was for Joyce to tell somebody else and the innocent story getting out to the tabloids only to be twisted for public enjoyment.

Joyce shrugged as she began tossing a pillow up into the air and catching it. "So, what are you going to wear to the party?"

"I don't know." Regan sighed, looking back to the magazine. She had never felt comfortable with dresses, or parties or social events for that matter. Give her breeches and boots and a stable any day over having to dress up and put makeup on. "The last party I went to was my high school graduation party, and I wore jeans. I have no idea what to wear to a formal event."

The pillow was tossed to the floor and forgotten. Joyce crawled up to her cousin's side to look at the magazine through a few locks of her bleached hair. "That one is pretty," she said, pointing to a lovely satin, green gown with golden trim.

"I can't afford any of these." Regan frowned then glanced to Joyce. "I'm going to ruin his evening, aren't I?"

"Don't say that, luv." Joyce turned the next page of the magazine. She gagged when she saw the prices listed. "Where'd you get this? Harrods?"

"I picked it up at a news-stand this morning when I went to get us some pastries."

Suddenly, the phone rang on the desk across the room. Handing over the catalogue, Regan slipped from the bed then walked across the soft carpet to pick up the phone.

"Hello?"

"Miss. Scott?"

"Oh,' she breathed out in a shy gasp, 'hello, Mister Thorn." Regan recognized that smooth, accented voice as it sent chills spreading across her skin.

"Please, call me Daniel. There's no reason to be so formal."

"Alright. Daniel." Regan cheeks flushed hot red.

"Forgive me for calling you so early. My shift has just ended so I thought I would try and reach you before I turn in for some rest."

Joyce snapped her attention upwards at the mention of Daniel Thorn, and the magazine slipped from her hands as she clapped excitedly. "Is it him?" she mouthed with eyes wide.

Regan hushed her cousin with a waving hand. "It's alright. What can I do for you?"

"I was calling to make sure you are still interested on accompanying me to the art exhibit. If you are, I would like to give you the time."

"Of course!" Regan spun about frantically looking around the desk for a pen and paper.

"Then you're still interested?"

"Don't be silly, Daniel. Of course I am." Finally, she found a damn pen and paper.

"Wonderful. The event is next Thursday at nine. I hope that's not too late for you. The host enjoys evening engagements. Is the time acceptable?"

"Sure. That's not late at all. What time should I be ready and where should I meet you?"

50

"I'll come by and pick you up at your place around eight-thirty. I simply need your address"

Regan's heart skipped a few beats and her cheeks turned pink. "Next Thursday at eight-thirty." She scribbled down the information Daniel gave her. "The address is 1840 North Crestward road. Flat C - London."

Daniel repeated the address. *"Very good. Now remember, this event is formal. Have you been able to find a dress?"*

Regan mewed softly as she pressed the phone receiver closer to her ear only to squeak at his question. "A dress?" She snapped a panic filled expression to her cousin.

Joyce picked up the magazine and pointed it to it over and over again, trying not to squeak with excitement.

"No,' Regan said honestly and sadly, 'I have not found one yet. They are so expensive from what I have seen. I'm not sure what I should get or where to go to find something inexpensive that won't look like it's to be worn to a barn dance."

She sighed, "And before you even ask, yes, I've been to a barn dance before and a hootenanny."

On the other end of the line Daniel laughed softly. *"No worries. I know where you can find a dress. Why don't I swing by and pick you up tomorrow evening? I'll take you to the shop I suggested the other night."*

Regan gasped softly, stunned at Daniel's offer. Joyce giggled, wiggling to sit upon her knees. She bounced up and down excitedly. But Regan let out a deep sigh as she leaned back to the desk behind her. "You don't have to go out of your way, Daniel."

Daniel scoffed with a slight, deep huff. *"You are going as my guest, Regan."*

"But you don't need to take me shopping."

"I'm only being a gentleman. Please, don't worry. This is my treat."

"I can't afford much."

"The price will be of no concern. I'll be by the flat around eight tomorrow."

She nodded softly, her eyes fluttering behind dark lashes. "Alright. Tomorrow then."

"Good. Have a good day, Regan."

Regan swallowed a little giggle. "You too." The phone went silent on the other end so Regan slowly put it back upon the receiver.

Joyce laughed brightly. "What did he say? Tell me. Tell me!"

"He wanted to check with me to see if I am still interested in going next Thursday."

Joyce rolled her eyes. "Duh, of course you are going!"

Regan sat down upon the edge of the bed in a daze of happiness and went on to say, "He asked if I have found a dress. I couldn't lie, so I told him no. Well, you heard what I told him."

"I did. What did he say?"

"He said he knows a place where he'll take me to find a dress."

"What did he mean by that?"

Turning to the side, Regan looked to her cousin with a shrug. "He is going to take me shopping tomorrow, and he told me not to worry about the price."

"Oh!" screamed Joyce, slapping her cousin gently on the shoulder, but the slap was strong enough to jerk Regan's shoulders. "He's going to take you shopping? That man could buy you anything you wanted." She mewed dramatically, "That's so romantic."

"Yes, romantic," mewed Regan. In the next moment she felt herself being tugged from the bed.

"Come on! We're going to go and get you some lovely accessories to wear. You're going to need makeup and shoes!" Joyce was off now, rambling as she always did.

At the bedroom door she spun about pointing to her cousin. "I know where you can get your hair done! A friend of mine owns a hair boutique. She'll do a great job! And we can have lunch at an adorable café down the street!"

Regan groaned as she was pulled from the bed then left standing in the hall to stare at her cousin's departing back. Her shoulders slumped with honest confusion on how Joyce could have such incredible excitement and energy after being sick all night with a hangover. Chuckling, and with a helpless shrug, Regan followed after her.

~ ~ ~ ~

Regan was somewhat aware of being pulled around Joyce's neighborhood for the entire day, going to this store then the next store. By the end of the day she couldn't recall what she had purchased even though the bags were sitting on the floor at her feet where she had been staring at them for the last fourteen minutes.

The woman at the hair boutique had been very insightful in showing her how to style her hair in a modern, fresh, but simple style that wouldn't over shine Regan's natural beauty. By the time they got back to the flat, Regan could hardly move. She was so tired that she bid Joyce a goodnight, went to her room, and fell flat upon the bed while Joyce went off to do her nightly Internet cruising.

Sleep didn't come to Regan as quickly as she would've liked. She was so excited to meet with Daniel again that she kept replaying their little coffee 'date' over and over again. When sleep finally knocked her out, the night went way too slow. She kept waking up then falling asleep, waking up then falling asleep, and so on. The next morning she woke up and was jittery, as excited as a school girl

By midafternoon Joyce had woken but was rushing to get herself ready for a previous engagement. She would be gone till late in the afternoon but promised she would be back as fast as she could to help Regan get ready for her engagement. So Regan was left for the rest of the day to keep her mind distracted and to keep active. She cleaned the flat, twice, but the hours still clicked slowly on by till Joyce came home, then the two went right to work.

They ordered Indian from a restaurant down the block and opened a bottle of nice ginger beer while running through all the clothes Regan brought with her and all the clothes hanging in Joyce's massive closets.

While Joyce tried to pair-up a cute outfit for her cousin, Regan took a soothing, hot shower to help calm her nerves. After everything had been tossed out, turned over, and thrown around, Joyce had found a combination of clothes that would fit well with Daniel's suave style.

"This will look good on you." Joyce grinned when Regan stepped from the shower. The Brit held up a black, velvet zip-up jacket hinted with a delicate sweep of mauve, and in her other hand she held a black, pleated skirt. "Classy and sophisticated with just enough leg," purred Joyce, winking to her cousin.

Regan reached out to finger the velvet jacket. "I think this is a little much, or lack thereof. I am not out to seduce him."

Joyce's face fell as she huffed, "Why the hell not? I would."

"I don't want to scare him away." Regan chuckled while rubbing a towel to her wet hair. She sat to a small dressing table to finish drying her hair

"You won't. Regan, luv,' Joyce said, taking up a brush to comb through Regan's hair, 'Daniel Thorn is class mixed with sophisticated sexy. You're not only dressing for the occasion, you're dressing for that hunk of hot man flesh."

"We are going out shopping, not to the theater or a strip club." Regan shook her head as she watched her cousin brush her hair in the mirror. "For all I know we could be going to Wal-Mart."

"Wal-Mart does not have dresses like the one you need. Besides, there is no Wal-Mart around here." Joyce chuckled and said in thought, "I doubt Daniel Thorn would be caught dead in a Wal-Mart. He'll probably take you to someplace where you have to pay big bucks just to breathe the air."

"I hope not. I would feel horrible if he had to pay that much."

"It's his money," said the Brit as she began to braid Regan's hair. "Go with the flow. If he wants to spend the money on you looking beautiful, then let him. Maybe he really does like you. Let him indulge you. You deserve it, for once." Joyce smiled to Regan in the mirror.

"I will not let him buy my attention or my affection."

"He's not buying your affection, Regan. He wants to show you a world that not every person gets to see," said Joyce gently. "Why not see where this goes, huh? Now then, time is wasting." She grinned while leaning over her cousin's shoulder to give a playful and seductive grin. "Let's make your image burn into his imagination."

~ ~ ~ ~

As Regan prepared herself for the evening, so did Daniel. He didn't want to feel excited but there was no helping the quickening beat of his near dead heart.

Daniel thought on the evening as he finished braiding his hair in to a single, thick braid of ebony that fell down his back. He had been involved with many women over his long life, yet none warmed his blood as Regan had done.

Was he crazy? Befriending a human could lead to the danger of that human discovering the Lamia world. The risk was as great as the punishment - death. Could he trust Regan? Then again, why should he be so concerned when he had simply invited her to an art exhibit?

He stared at his pale image reflecting back to him in the full length mirror. Daniel had a long time to build up a wall of excuses as to explain one oddity or another about himself, his life schedules and rituals, and the strange occurrences that surrounded him, but he had to wonder what Regan would think of him. He was much paler than a normal individual, and if one looked close enough under bright light there could be seen the green lines of his veins running beneath his skin. With a tip of his head his eyes flashed with a touch of metallic silver, a trait to the eyes of all Lamia. His attention was pulled from his thoughts when his mobile phone's alarm went off. Time was up. He had to go and collect Regan.

The drive across London was one of relaxation, contemplation, and inner reflection. That was, till his phone rang and he saw the identity of the caller.

"Rhain, I have to ask that you cease this annoyance directly," muttered Daniel. "I am not interested in what the Lumania Familia are bitching about. That Familia is always complaining about one thing or another. Why do you even care what is going on within their dark secrets?"

"That's the point, Frater," Rhain Thorn muttered right back on the other end of the connection, *'that Familia is always up to something. We should be concerned about their dark secrets and their even darker bed-buddies considering they're in league with demons and everything hellish."*

"Why are your knickers in a knot over them anyway?"

"The bastards want to purchase a block of rundown buildings two streets up from the Crucible. So you can see why I'm interested in what they're up to."

"And this is a reason for you to have a panic attack? If they wanted to set up a kindergarten next door, they have the power and the money to do so, not to mention the laws of the mortal world."

"That's not fucking funny and you know it. Those bastards always set up shop where another Familia has developed a profitable business. It's their way of trying to control competition. They're going to try and set up a bigger and better club than mine."

"There's no proof of that."

"Of course there is! Just look at our Familia's financial ventures and investments. You'll see the direct connection!"

Daniel hung his head. He had to give it to Rhain, the guy could create a conspiracy theory out of thin air. "Life is a bitch, is that not what you say, Frater?"

Rhain snorted. *"Did you just swear, brother? You never do that. And you say my knickers are in a knot. What got up your ass and died to put you in a foul mood?"*

"I am not in a foul mood, Rhain, but if you continue on with this pointless argument, you'll be agitating me rather quickly."

"That's a talent of mine, isn't it?"

"Yes. You are very talented at that."

Daniel rolled his dark eyes as his twin continued to complain. To amuse himself, he glanced to the world passing behind the darkly tinted glass of the Audi limo. This night the streets of London seemed to be oddly quiet, especially for a night that came without rain.

"Are you listening to me, Daniel?"

"Of course I am."

"Bull shit,' Rhain growled hotly, *'you haven't heard a word I've said. That's fucking typical of you."*

Daniel gave a dry, airless sigh. "I have heard what you've said, Rhain, but at this moment I have made the choice not to care. I'm rather busy this night, so why don't you go to Kain and bitch to him about the Lumania, hmm?"

Rhain grumbled something inaudible, more than likely a lovely and colorful curse. With a chuckle and a smile Daniel spoke up, "Kain told you to bugger off, didn't he?"

"Shut up," Rhain snarled.

"Very well. I'm hanging up now. I will speak to you when I return."

"Wait! Where are you going? Don't you work tonight?"

"If you paid attention to what is going on inside our company and not in your fantasy world, you would know that I have taken the night off. Now go bother Alasdair. Better yet, go find Phil and let her coddle you for a while. I'm sure she would be very pleased to do so."

"I'm not in the mood for Phil's attentions tonight. So tell me, what's gotten you out of your hole?"

"Nobody of importance to you."

"Nobody?" Rhain didn't miss a beat of his brother's words. *"Who's nobody?"*

Nobody? Did he say that out loud? Daniel released a low growl as he ran a hand down his face. Great, just great. He would never hear the end of that slip up. "If you must know, I am on my way to meet a young lady."

Rhain suddenly exploded in laughter. *"Are you serious? You're going out on a date?"* Then there was a pause as if Rhain was thinking. The tone to his voice changed to one of sarcastic amusement, *"Or, are you picking up one of London's beautiful and talented ladies of the night?"*

"I did not mention anything about a date," Daniel bit out through clenched jaws. How he disliked his brother's irrational reasoning and unending personal questions. "And I would certainly never consider visiting a prostitute."

"You're going to pick up a girl, Daniel. Last time I checked that's considered a date. Is she Lamia? Who is she?"

"She's...not Lamia."

"She's human?" The sound in Rhain's voice was pure shock. *"You're going out with a human? Are you fucking insane? That's against our laws!"*

"Correction,' Daniel snapped with a dangerous growl to his smooth voice, 'there is no law in the Lex that says we cannot interact with mortals as long as we keep our secrets to ourselves. And that is what I intend on doing. I have no intention of breaking any law."

Rhain huffed as his brother shot down his building curiosity.

"Now, if you'll excuse me, I must end this conversation. I will speak with you when I return home."

Before his brother could say another word, Daniel ended the call then slid his mobile into the breast pocket of his blazer. He certainly wasn't looking forwards to returning home so his brother could chew his ear off. His gaze turned back to the streets as the car came to a stop at a red-light. Honestly, why would he care what the Lumania Familia was scheming? That Familia was always twisting their fantasy world about, threatening the sanctity of the Concilium, but nothing ever came of their stupidity or their threats. Yet Rhain seemed to be obsessed with finding out every dark and twisted secret and plan that Familia had, like a damn hobby. Pointless waste of time according to Daniel and Kain, but there was nothing they could do to stop Rhain once he put his mind on a juicy conspiracy theory.

One more street was turned down then the limo stopped at a three story complex of flats. Not bad looking, but he had seen better homes and in better locations. "We are here, sir," the Servus in the front seat said from behind darkly plated, bullet proof glass.

"Thank you, Patrick." Daniel opened the door to exit the vehicle. "Keep the car running, will you?"

"Yes, Mister Thorn."

The night greeted its Filias, its Dark Child, with kisses of crisp air as a touch of wind began to grow. Daniel walked to the front door of the building with his hands in his slacks' pocket. Eight-thirty on the dot and he pressed the button beneath the listed name of Joyce Scott: Flat Number C.

"Yes?" sang a bright voice. It was not Regan's.

Daniel cleared his throat, pulling his silk scarf tighter. "I'm Daniel Thorn, and I have come to pick up Regan. Is she ready?"

The voice on the other end giggled excitedly. "She'll be down in a moment."

Daniel looked back to the car and noticed a few people were walking down the sidewalks, and he also noticed an Indian restaurant not too far away. When the door clicked open, he turned about to see Regan standing in the threshold. The vampire was caught by his own thoughts as he let his eyes wander. She was beautiful wearing a fitted zipper jacket of velvet, a black pleated skirt, silken black stockings, and a pair of shined penny loafers. When he looked to her features, he found himself captivated by her natural beauty and the delicate blush dusting her cheeks.

A quick shake of his mind brought his thoughts back under his control. "You look lovely," he said with a boyish, lop-sided smile.

Regan swept back a loose strand of hair behind a single pierced ear. "Thank you. You look very handsome."

And he did, in a slender blazer of deep black over a red silk shirt tucked into a pair of black trousers. His long hair was braided down his back and pulled back to show his young and gentle face. Joyce was right. He would dress to impress, complete with a silk scarf about his neck and shoulders.

He politely offered her his arm. "Shall we? My car is waiting for us."

"Where are we going?" she asked, taking his arm.

"If you trust me, I will take you wherever your heart desires."

~ ~ ~ ~

Across London sat Cardevior, a small boutique that specialized in designer gowns, formal mostly and expensive. Inside the showroom there were countless gowns on display, each incorporating intricate patterns of sequins and crystals that glistened whenever a touch of light graced them.

Regan cringed inwardly as the car pulled to an easy stop and she saw the incredible gowns presented in the windows. Other shops upon the street were closed up tight but this one still had its lights on even though the sign said closed.

"Are we too late? The sign says closed."

"Don't worry about that." Daniel waited for his drive to step about and open the car door. He then gracefully slipped form the car, stepped about, then open her door with his hand held out in offering. Regan took his hand and stepped out to the curb by his side.

Before they walked to the door, it opened and they were greeted by a middle aged woman of pale complexion and overly dyed, red hair that was pulled in a bun. She smiled to Regan then grinned affectionately to Daniel as if she knew him personally.

"Schatz!" called the woman to Daniel in a voice that was laced with flirty sensuality and a strong German accent.

Regan expected him to release her hand and sweep the beautiful woman into a romantic embrace, but he didn't. Instead, he held Regan's hand and drew her up next to him, closer.

"Guten Abend, Gretchen," said Daniel, smiling to the other woman. "Allow me to introduce you to Regan Scott, the young lady I spoke of on the phone the other day."

Regan prepared herself for an uncomfortable moment of snooty judgment. Gretchen was beyond beautiful, even with the fire engine-red hair, her flawless skin, and her perfect hourglass figure. Regan had known women like her before, judgmental and critical. Surprisingly, however, instead of some haughty remark on Regan's attire, attempt at makeup, or what she thought would be a scoff and a once over on the woman's part, Regan was greeted with a bright smile.

"Of course!" said the woman, sweeping an arm to the store. "Come in and I will find the perfect dress for your lady friend."

The inside of Cardevior was scented heavily with exotic burning oils, lavender and thyme mixed with a touch of sandalwood or sage. There were wine glasses and bottles of wine set upon beautiful tables lined up outside dressing rooms curtained by velvet. Manikins stood about the shop dressed in gowns only Regan's imagination could create. While she looked at some dresses, Daniel seated himself to one of the leather chairs, and before Regan could question him, she was taken by the hand and pulled before a standing, three paneled mirror. Gretchen took her purse from her, sat it down, then stepped back so she could carefully analyzing every curve and inch of Regan's body, even lifting her arms and turning the girl this way and that way.

"She is a beauty, Daniel," the German said with a devious smile and a wicked laugh. "Come, let's try a few things on. We'll leave Daniel here to his imagination - for now."

Daniel scoffed, rolled his eyes, and waved the two off. He folded his hands to his lap as he crossed one knee over the other. He could wait.

Before Regan could say anything, and with one last look towards Daniel, she was pushed into a dressing room. Over the next hour she tried on one gown after another that Gretchen brought her. All were expensive pieces made with fabrics and gems that Regan had never even heard of before. Some of the prices cost more than her paycheck for three years combined, yet Gretchen never asked once what hers or Daniel's price range was.

Finally, Gretchen clapped as she looked to Regan standing in the mirror. "This is it! It's magnificent."

Regan turned about, looking at herself in the mirror. The gown fit her like a glove, perfectly etched upon every curve of her body. The print was an Asian inspired print, looking to belong more on a Geisha than on her, with cherry blossoms upon white and baby-pink silk. The bodice of the gown fell low upon her breasts, giving a little peek of her bosom, then down her hips before flowing outwards in a delicate sweep of blushing silk. With the slender, off the shoulder sleeves, Regan felt intimidated by the exposure of her skin.

"I'm not sure." She sighed while looking to the hand printed label and the price of fifteen-thousand pounds. Her eyes went wide. "Oh, my gosh!"

Gretchen smirked while adjusting a part of the gown in back. "Don't you fret about that price," she chuckled warmly as she swatted Regan's hand away from the tag. "Daniel has agreed to whatever price is printed upon that little piece of paper."

"He can't pay this much, just for one night? Why would he pay this much for me, for a dress?"

The German shrugged her shoulders. "I have never known him to do this before, but I won't deny a special request by him."

"But why would he spend such money on a stranger?" Regan frowned while trailing a finger down her side if just to feel the silk.

Gretchen shrugged again. She obviously did not know either. "Daniel,' she said in thought, 'is a very unique gentleman. His mind still thinks and operates in the old ways. He is a purebred gentleman who views a woman as something special, delicate and beautiful, to be protected from harm with his life, even if she is a stranger. When he sees somebody special, let us say a young woman who really does entice him, he would go to the ends of the Earth to show his appreciation for her. He views you as a gift to him, and in return, he wishes to bestow gifts upon you. There's nothing wrong with that."

She huffed with a roll of her eyes and went on to say with a devious smirk, "If more men thought the way he did towards us women, there'd be a lot less PMS in the world and a lot more romance and erotic pleasures."

"A gift?" Regan starred at her reflection in the mirror. "He views me as a gift?"

Gretchen frowned, reaching out to touch Regan's cheek to turn her eyes. She smiled. "Daniel works hard, my dear girl, and because of such he has a stressful life, very stressful. It is not easy for him to find somebody to spend time with, one who can understand the differences in his unique life inside and outside of his family's company. Personally, I'm very glad he has found a lovely girl like you to take out for an enchanted evening."

Regan blinked, staring into the woman's stunning eyes. Within those bright orbs there was a glint of silver, much like she had seen flash in Daniel's eyes, and David's.

Gretchen smiled a sly smile as she gazed upon the Humanus. "Shall we go show him the gown or would you rather surprise him?"

Regan sucked in a breath with a little nip to her lower lip. Show him or surprise him? "He'll know the price won't he?"

"Of course."

"Then I want to surprise him and look like the price upon the tag."

"Schatz,' cooed Gretchen, 'you already do. But so be it. Come, let's get you out of this so I can pack up the dress. He won't know which one you'll be getting."

While Regan fussed with dress after dress, Daniel's attention had been drawn to a text conversation with Kain as to the reason Rhain was strutting about the house like a damn peacock acting as if he knew something nobody else did. He had just returned a text when the curtain moved and the two women appeared. He smiled to Regan as she held the curtain for Gretchen whose arms were full of gowns.

"Did you find a dress?" he inquired, slipping his smartphone into the breast pocket of his blazer.

"Oh, she did!" Gretchen called as she took the gowns towards the back of the shop. "And let me tell you, you'll…die…when you see her in the gown she decided upon."

Daniel arched a brow to the chosen term his friend used, but when Regan came walking up to him, he shook his running thought away and smiled to her. "Are you sure on your choice?"

She smiled. "I am."

"It'll take a moment for Gretchen to box up your dress, would you like some wine while we wait?" He motioned to one of the bottles.

"No, thank you. I'm not much of a drinker. Daniel,' Regan spoke softly so he would look to her, 'I don't know how I can thank you for this, let alone repay you for your kindness, but I'll have to find a way. It'll take some time but I promise I'll make sure to get some payments to you."

59

Tipping his head, Daniel watched her with an acute eye. He smirked, reaching out to trail a finger along her warm, smooth cheek. "There was no mention of payment, Regan."

She frowned beneath the trailing touch.

"No frowning. If you want to put a price upon this dress, then consider the payment paid in full. You've already agreed to accompany me to the exhibit. What more could I ask for?"

Regan's brows furrowed as she stared up to him. She still didn't understand what was going on, and she certainly couldn't wrap her mind around all that he was offering her. The dress was more than she could ever imagine, and he wasn't even questioning the price of the gown. Just who was this man to go around throwing away money on a dress she would wear once and he would never see again after the exhibit?

"Here we go!" Gretchen walked back with a large, white box in her arms. She smiled to the two as she approached then offered the box to Regan. "Everything you need to wear with the dress is in here. If you have any questions, or need any alterations, you give me a call. My card is in the box too."

"You both have been so nice about this." Regan glanced between the two.

The German smiled, waving a hand. "I only demand a photo of you in this gown for my portfolio of designs. This dress is one of a kind, not another one exists. Agreed?"

Regan's jaw nearly fell from her face. The gown was a one of a kind? Seeing Regan's features turn to shock, and before she could say a word, Daniel touched her shoulder and nodded to Gretchen. "I'll make sure you get one, Gretchen." He stepped to his friend offering a kiss to her cheeks, and she, in return, offered kisses to him. "Dankeschön, Gretchen."

"Wonderful! Now Regan,' she purred, turning to the American, 'enjoy yourself, yes? Let Daniel treat you like the beauty you are. I'm sure we'll be seeing each other again. Now go, I have a shop to close up."

"Ich wünsche Dir eine gute Nacht," said Daniel to his friend, ushering Regan back towards the door.

Gretchen smiled and waved to the two. "Das wünsche ich Dir auch."

The ride back to the flat seemed to be shorter than the ride to the store. Time always flew by when one didn't want a wonderful moment to end. Resting upon Regan's lap was the dress box encased in a gold and silver ribbon and bow. She looked down to the box, fingering the golden fringe upon the bow strands. Next to her, Daniel looked on with concern. She had been silent for a while, seemingly lost within her thoughts.

"What's on your mind?" she heard him inquire.

Regan pulled her thoughts from the box and looked across the seat to Daniel. "Fifteen-thousand pounds for a dress?"

"Is that what it cost?" he asked with a nonchalant shrug of his shoulders.

"But why?"

"I have said why."

"I don't even own a shirt that wasn't purchased off the sales-rack."

Daniel chuckled. "And I have never purchased a shirt from the sales-rack." Sensing her continual unease, Daniel reached over to cover her hand with his. "Please, I insist you accept the dress. Allow me to treat you to something special."

Regan slowly shook her head and a 'tsk' under her breath. "You talk like a romantic."

"I am a romantic."

"We're here, Mr. Thorn," spoke the driver from behind the security glass as the car pulled to a stop outside of Joyce's building. Daniel opened his door, exiting the car, then stepped over to the other side to open the door for her.

The night had grown colder, so when Regan took his offered hand, slipping from the car, she could see her breath as she expelled her first breath of the London night air. Hugging the box tightly to her, she walked next to him and up to the apartment door. Once the door was opened and she was just about step in, Daniel placed his hand over her hand to stop her actions. She blinked, shifting to look to him and saw him smiling to her, but then she felt his lips brush against her cheek, skimming lower to touch a soft kiss to the corner of her soft lips that parted in a tiny little mewl of delight.

Daniel kissed the corner of her sweet lips. He couldn't help himself, and the want to taste her sweet lips pounded blood through his veins. Afraid of her reaction if he did steal a kiss, he settled himself for a timid touch upon her cheek and a shy kiss to the corner of her mouth. That simple act had been plaguing his thoughts since he had met her, the want to kiss her. The thought of how her flesh would taste kept swimming in his mind, taunting him.

This kiss was chaste, sweet and innocent, and she tasted just as he thought she would, like delicate femininity. He caressed her cheek with the back of his hand letting his fingers thread into the silken texture of her hair at the base of her neck. After a moment, Daniel stepped back, lowering his hand, and forcing his passions under his control.

Bloody hell! It was so hard to grasp his control when he saw the blush upon Regan's features, a blush that had colored her cheeks in a delicate shadow of pink. Her beautiful eyes of rich chocolate had clouded over with a shadow of desire, and her lips had parted with the subtle push of breath, a motion of anticipation. Forcing himself to take another step away from her, Daniel smiled and spoke in a voice that held tightness to its accented rumble.

"Thank you for indulging me tonight, Regan. I don't think I could have made it to Thursday without seeing you again."

His touch sent hot shocks of electricity through her body, and she felt a twisting knot grow tighter and tighter within her belly as she stood beneath his dark gaze. It was then she knew that there was something oddly different about this man, something she couldn't put a finger on. Up close, a few inches apart, she could see that there were parts of his physique that were mysteriously feminine yet uniquely attractive - the paleness to his skin, his high cheekbones, and the silver dancing within his black eyes. The longer she stared into those deep eyes of ebony, the faster she was drawn to him with her attraction increasing.

When she finally gained control of herself, Regan whispered, "Thank you for the gown. I hope I don't displease you in it."

"There is no way that you could, Regan. You would look beautiful wearing polka-dot pajamas."

"I have those," she chuckled then proceeded into the hallway where she paused to glance back to him. "Goodnight, Daniel. Thank you again for everything."

The door clicked closed behind her.

Daniel stared at the closed door as her disfigured image disappeared behind the distorted glass and up the stairs. The night had gone well, better than he had imagined. And even with the reservations Regan still had, Daniel was confident that their next meeting would go off without a hitch. He'd make sure of it.

A proud, sly grin coiled Daniel's pale lips and he forced himself to turn away from the door and return to the limo. All the way back to his home the Lamia allowed himself to swim within his ego as his lips tingled from the lingering sensation of Regan's skin. Nothing could ruin this night - nothing.

IV

There is a moment in time when minutes become hours and hours become days; when a moment causes time itself to slow and halt. There comes a point in time when the realm of reality separates from the control of time and we are no longer victims of the wicked play of Chronos. To conquer and to master the laws of time and space can lead us into the clutches of the God of Time, and when we play with Chronos, we play with our fate.

I tempted fate when I left Regan at the doorstep of her flat. I shamefully demanded that Lord Chronos stop time for me so I could share another precious minute with her, to feel her warm human skin and kiss her soft, inviting lips. Yet the God refused me. Do not play with me God of Time, I do not like trickery. In the end, I always get what I want. What I want is more time with Regan, and I shall have my time. This I swear.

Father Time, I wish you to know that I loathe you as much as Rhain loathes leafy green vegetables.

-    *Daniel Rhys Thorn*

~ ~ ~ ~

"So, the Casanova returns."

Daniel groaned at the sound of his twin's mocking voice. The evening had gone so well and ended on such a lovely note that he really had no want for Rhain's inquisition. He turned the question back to Rhain, as he shrugged off his blazer, with his dark eyes narrowing upon the back of a leather chair where the twin's voice emanated from. "Shouldn't you be at your club, Rhain? Or has the difficult concept of work bored you already?"

Rhain arched his body from where he sat in the white painted living-room decorated in the art deco style, including leather and chrome. The dancing, teasing eyes of Rhain Thorn looked over the back of his chair towards his twin walking towards him. "Why the sad face, mate? Did you bite her too hard? It's only your first date with the girl. Isn't it a bit early to start pining over her as if she were your Socia?"

Daniel's hand came forwards to slap Rhain upside the head. "I have no interest in taking her as my lover, and if I did have a consideration of doing so, I would certainly not inform you."

The strike was hard enough to cause Rhain to jump away holding his head and flashing his fangs. "What was that for?"

"You deserved it," Daniel hissed in an oddly calm tone. "Actually, you deserve more. So why are you not at the club? Has the Lumania Familia built that kindergarten yet? Have children already washed in waves through your doors of your club demanding cookies and milk?"

Scowling, Rhain rubbed his sore head. "Piss off."

"Watch your tongue," muttered Daniel under his breath as he looked about, the scarf slipping from about his throat easily as if it were alive. "Where are Kain and Amber?"

"They've been called to a meeting by our Regulus and Senator."

"When will they return?"

Rhain scoffed. "Why should I care?"

"It's our Familia's business, brother. Try to pay attention to what is happening in the dark world around you."

Rhain watched his brother walk down the hall. He smirked and called after him, "Hey! Is it possible that when you and I were born you got the bastard gene and I got the dashingly charming and deviously sexy gene?"

"I do not think so, Rhain. Otherwise, you would have been on the date tonight, not I!" There he went, calling the evening a 'date'. How easily that word slipped right off his tongue.

Daniel shut the door to his room behind him and he sighed to the soft warmth that instantly curled about him from the embers glowing within the ebony carved fire place. After a century of undead life, Daniel still could not get accustomed to being forever chilled. The scarf was tossed to a chair followed soon after by his shirt. He couldn't bring himself to remove his trousers even after he pulled his shoes off and slid the black belt out of the loops. Tiny movements from beneath the bed covers caught his eyes and he shifted the cover so a tiny head peeked out.

"Good evening, Pixie,' the Lamia chuckled as he moved to sit upon the edge of his bed, 'I see you have had an exciting night of sleeping in my bed."

Pixie, Daniel's three year old Teacup Pomeranian of white and brown spots with a tan little heart upon one side, wiggled out from beneath the covers with a quick shake of her body. Delicate little feet carried the petite dog over to her master where she was welcomed to his lap so she could climb up to put her little front paws against his chest. Back and forth, back and forth her curved tail wagged as her master stroked his cool fingers over the arch of her head. He couldn't help but roll his eyes when he saw the pink and white bows in her ears. Amber had taken her to be groomed. Great. His dog was wearing bows.

Daniel moved to lay down upon his bed with Pixie settling herself upon his chest. "I don't suppose you'd like to hear about my night, would you?"

Pixie wagged her tail and gave a tiny little yip.

"I took Regan out tonight to find a dress. She's a unique girl for a mortal." He stroked the Pomeranian's belly. "There's something about her that I can't put my finger on."

Daniel groaned as he slid a hand beneath his head and turned his gaze up to the ceiling. "Do you think there's something wrong with me for wanting to make her happy, a complete stranger? I spent fifteen-thousand pounds on a dress for a girl I hardly know, and I would gladly do it all again just to see the excitement and delight upon her face."

Pixie licked his ear and wagged her tail.

"I can still smell her scent on me." He sighed in remembrance. Her scent, the delicate and subtle touch of spices and flowers, still haunted him.

After a few more moments enjoying his memories of Regan, and Pixie's little licks, he let the darkness encase him. He settled down with fingers lacing behind his head and within the long strands of his ebony hair. His lungs tightened as they were forced to move, inflating and deflating, and soon fell in to a gentle pattern.

How long did he lay lost in his memories while giving in to his imagination? Every thought that passed from his mind was of her, of Regan. Daniel's dark eyes parted open and he frowned as he stared up at the ceiling of his bedroom. He couldn't stay the rest of the night delving into his memories and his desires. He had a department to run and clients to work for. There were countless files awaiting his attention and shelves lined with priceless items needing to be cared for, documented, restored, logged, and then returned to their rightful owners.

Within an hour, he was down in his laboratory carefully brushing and cleaning an ancient mosaic and delving into his work to help keep his mind off of the warm flesh that tasted of vital life. If need be, Daniel would lock himself away in his office with his work till Thursday came around. At least this way Regan would not haunt his mind, or so he hoped.

~ ~ ~ ~

Days came and went till Thursday finally arrived.

Crepasculum had gracefully settled over a clear and beautiful skyline of London. The streets were alive on this cool evening as if the last chill of spring was ending and summer was peeking over the horizon. Daniel had been awake for at least an hour, and with each passing minute his body roused with his muscles and nerves firing back to life. His lips were dry and his lungs stung from lack of movement as the remainder of his rest held tight to his mind. He hated the waking hour. He still felt tired, cold, and dead.

"Ah, you are up early."

Daniel turned to see Amber standing in the doorway of his room. She was a beautiful woman, even in her undead life, who had 'model' written all over her. Her hair was thick and curly with a smooth, golden-chestnut tone and with eyes as green as emeralds and a face to match the world's most beautiful woman.

"Yes," he said to her and grumbled as to why she found it perfectly logical to enter his room without knocking.

"So,' she said, slipping further into his room, 'tonight is your big night. Excited?"

"Of course."

Amber sighed, looking to her Socius' Frater. "I'm happy for you."

"What do I owe the pleasure of you wandering into my room unannounced, hmm?"

The woman offered him an apologetic smile. "I only wanted to wish you luck, Daniel. I've noticed that since you met this girl that you have been a bit touchy. Rhain told Kain of your little attack on him. Lucky for you he said that he will not be pressing any charges. Even Kain has noticed you are more, how should I say,' she shrugged, waving a hand before her, 'preoccupied with this human than you have been with any lover before, human or Lamia. I'm a little worried that you may be getting yourself involved with this mortal too quickly."

"Why? Because she is mortal, a Humanus?" he asked flatly, narrowing his eyes dangerously. He stood from his bed, moving gracefully across the room to his dressing mirror. His hair looked as if it was tied in knots and he needed a shower.

"That could be it," she said with an honestly. "You will be careful, won't you?"

"Of course, Amber. I do not need a pep talk on the rules," he muttered, fumbling in the dark to find his hair brush.

She chuckled, stepping up to him. "I'm sorry, Daniel. I don't want to see you hurt."

He sighed in agitation at her mothering. "Thank you for your concern, but I can handle myself. I am, after all, old enough to know my restrictions and limitations. Though I am still a Filias, I do have a head on my shoulders. Besides,' he said as he began to tug the knots from his long hair, 'there is no romantic interest in her."

Even as those words slid past his lips, he knew they were untrue.

"Very well." Amber gave a nod. She trusted in him as she trusted in his brothers. However, she knew his emotions were tender towards the mortals. Daniel had never lost touch with his Humanitas, his connection to human nature. He still held tenderness, care, consideration, morality, guilt, honor and many other emotions, ideals, and concepts that their kind often abandoned after their Creation, their Creare.

She offered a hug to him and pressed a kiss to his cool cheek. "Do enjoy yourself." She offered a pat to his shoulder as she walked out of his room. "Don't forget to shower."

~ ~ ~ ~

Across London excitement bubbled within the flat belonging to Joyce Scott. While days flew by, the nights seemed to drag on. But the day finally came when Regan would meet Daniel again.

She couldn't sit still, not even while plaiting her hair in beautiful braids down the sides of her head before tucking the ends in loops at the base of her neck. For an hour she had worked on those damn braids even though she had done the same hair style since she was a child, but it seemed today her fingers wouldn't work and her hair was being a bitch. She tried, but failed, to replicate the hair style Joyce's stylist friend tried to teach her. Then again, she had been excited and nervous the entire day since she woke up so she wasn't surprised she was all butter-fingers.

At first it seemed her cousin was just as excited as she was, but as the day progressed Joyce became oddly quiet. By lunch time she had recused herself to her room, and since then Regan could not get her out. When Joyce finally came out to check on Regan, close to the time Daniel was to arrive, she leaned to the door frame with her arms crossed, completely silent, and staring blankly - angrily.

The gown that Daniel bought for Regan was beyond what Joyce thought the man, or any man for that fact, would be willing to pay for. It was beyond stunning and made her feel a sting of jealousy deep within her gut. At first she'd been happy for her dear cousin that she gotten a date with THE Daniel Thorn, but then he took Regan out to purchase a gown that neither cousin could ever afford. And now Regan was going out again with Daniel to view a private art display.

It wasn't fair - it wasn't right.

"How late will you be?" Joyce asked, trying to force a smile upon her lips.

"I'm not really sure, Joyce. You don't have to stay up."

"I have no intention of that."

Regan's features scrunched. The answer came out in a snip of agitated tones. "Are you okay? You've been acting strange today. Are you mad at me?"

Joyce shrugged then blew off her cousin's look of worry with a puff of air. "I think I'm going to go back to the Crucible, find somebody to play with."

Frowning, Regan turned back to the mirror. "Are you sure that's a smart thing to do? I mean, going to that place alone?"

"You're going to have your fun evening, so I'm going to go have mine."

Regan frowned even more. There was malice in Joyce's voice.

That was all Joyce said before she turned away, disappearing into the flat. Regan sighed with her eyes turning down to her lap where her fingers played with the delicate fabric of her long skirt. Why was Joyce disgruntled? Regan couldn't remember doing anything to upset her cousin. Maybe she had spoken about this date and Daniel with too much excitement and that had saddened Joyce. Regan sighed once more then looked to her image. She had to finish her make-up before Daniel arrived. Hopefully, she could do that without smearing lipstick across her face.

To Regan's surprise Joyce returned later. She entered the room and sat upon the bed, sipping a soda. Neither said anything to each other, simply watched one another through the reflection in the mirror. When the silence had gotten the better of Regan, she spoke gently and in apology, "I'm sorry if I've upset you. I didn't mean to."

Smiling, she stood from the vanity to sit at Joyce's side. "I really am sorry, and I do hope you have fun tonight. Maybe you will find somebody."

Joyce snorted. Regan, in Joyce's agitated mind, sounded sarcastic in her comfort, as if making another painful point that she had Daniel and Joyce had nobody. Joyce was close to responding with a cruel and cold comment when the doorbell down the hall rang. Both girls looked to the clock on the wall. Daniel was right on time.

"Looks like your prince charming is here," muttered Joyce. She stood up, departing the room.

Regan shook her head, picked up her delicate evening bag, then followed after Joyce. She expected to have Joyce buzzing the door open but she had seated herself in one of the arm chairs before the TV. Regan winced.

"I'll be going now," she said, draping a cashmere wrap about her bare shoulders. When Joyce didn't reply, she left.

As she walked down the stairs to the front door, Regan came to realize that even if Joyce was feeling jealous, there was no reason why Regan should let her night turn sour just to match her cousin's gloomy mood. Joyce was acting this way so Regan would pity her and either decline the date or be worried about her all night. How selfish. If she allowed her cousin's foul mood to influence her evening, the night would be ruined.

No! That wasn't going to happen. Regan was not going to let Joyce's pissy mood ruin the evening she had been waiting for and the evening Daniel had spent so much money on. This event was a dream for Regan, a dream she would never experience again.

When she came to stand at the door, she took a quivering breath upon seeing the blurred image of Daniel behind the tinted panels of uneven glass. She couldn't let him wait and she certainly couldn't let her nerves get a hold of her, not this night. The last thing she needed was to forget how to use a doorknob.

The moment Regan opened the door her eyes brightened upon seeing Daniel looking so very handsome in a fine, black dress coat as well as a white dress scarf hanging loose about his neck. Beneath the lapels of the closed coat was shown a hint of a blood-red dress shirt. His polished attire ended in a pair of sleek black slacks and a pair of black loafers. Daniel took Regan's breath away, but when she saw that his black hair was actually free this night, caressing down his back but for one strand over a shoulder, her heart actually stopped.

Did Daniel Thorn ever dress down? No, it didn't seem like he did. Daniel was charming. He imbued class and fashion all wrapped up in to one handsome package, but without the ego to tag along.

From his point of view, Regan took his soul away. As he gazed upon her it seemed his entire body went hot and cold at the same time. His mind slid to a stop as he felt every fiber of his being crackle, and he shivered. When they were at Cardevior, he never had the chance to view the gown he had purchased for her. Now he stood completely and utterly stunned, realizing that he had made the right decision to purchase her the gown.

"I'm lost for words," he said in a delicate whisper as he took one of her delicate hands to his lips.

A burning blush raced Regan's cheeks as he kissed her hand. "I'll be honest with you, Daniel, I'm really nervous about tonight."

"Why is that?" He looped her arm about his so they could walk to the waiting limo.

"I'm afraid I'm going to do something stupid like tripping on this long skirt or choking on a drink." She smiled a shaky smile then sighed a nervous giggle. "This is an important evening for you. I wouldn't want to embarrass you."

Daniel chuckled softly as he helped her into the back of the limo. It took a bit of navigating to get the skirt in before he could join her, close the door and send the limo off.

"I promise you, Regan, there is nothing you can do that would ruin this evening even if you think you're going to trip choke on a drink, or get drunk, and bark at the moon." He flashed her a wink. "Come to think of it, I'm sure the man hosting this party would join in if you end up barking at the moon. There is nothing that should worry you. We'll be looking at art pieces - perfectly safe."

"Oh, before I forget."

Regan looked to him, tipping her head as he dug into a compartment of the limo. He offered her a white jewelry box topped with a pink ribbon. "This is for you. I thought I would give you something prettier than flowers."

He offered her the box. "Go ahead, open it."

Regan didn't hesitate. She tugged at the ribbon so she could carefully open the box. Inside lay a stunning diamond tennis bracelet with delicately carved clasps of Welsh gold. "Oh," she breathed softly with a hand set against her chest as she lifted the bracelet out to set upon her palm. "Daniel." She raised her eyes to him in astonishment. "This is too much. I can't possibly...."

He took the bracelet and clasped it about her wrist without breaking his gaze from hers. "Please, I insist. I always thought it proper to give a lady a gift upon a formal invite. It is an expression of gratitude for you accepting my invitation tonight."

"This is too much, especially after the dress." Gazing down to the bracelet, Regan sighed dreamily.

Daniel frowned as he saw a soft yet saddened shadow cross her features. "Did I do something wrong?"

Seeing the concerned look within his eyes, Regan smiled and raised her fingers to gently touch his cool cheek. "No, not at all. Thank you."

That touch swept heat through Daniel's body like a wave of fire. Muscles within his stomach twisted, forming tight knots. Giving a smile, he covered her hand with his so he could press the warmth of her palm as close as he could to his chilled skin.

"Sir, we have arrived."

Daniel reluctantly released her hand as the car pulled to a gentle stop. It took a moment for the driver to leave the car, circle the vehicle, and open Daniel's door allowing him to slide easily out of the car to offer Regan his hand. "Shall we?"

Regan shivered to his handsome grin. There was a look, an unexplained look, deep within Daniel's dark eyes that sent a shiver down her spine. She hesitated till she swallowed her apprehension and offered him her hand then nodded. "Yes, I am"

Daniel, as if feeling her curiosity, smiled down to her. He offered her hand a gentle squeeze of reassurance. "Everything will be fine. Trust me."

Regan nodded to him, taking comfort in his smile of comfort and reassurance as they continued on their walk to the home. Feeling the last bit of her unease drift away, she slipped her arms about his and ever so tenderly hugged his arm. The Lamia glanced down as she did so and smiled fondly.

Regan wasn't prepared for what awaited them upon entering the stunning brown-stone. She thought that an art exhibit would be a quiet and subdued event but she was wrong. Within the home there was a sea of visitors filling every room and every hallway. There were waiters walking around with trays of fancy drinks and little bites of appetizers while photographers and journalists took pictures and interviews of the art critics and well-to-do members of London high society.

"This is incredible."

The Lamia chuckled. "It is a bit overwhelming at first, I must admit, but you do get used to all the pomp and circumstances. We won't stay long. I have something else planned that I know you..."

"Daniel Thorn!" called a bright voice, cutting off Daniel's thought.

Coming towards them was an older man in a tailored suit of deep blue with a silver handkerchief of silk in the blazer's breast pocket. His arms were open in welcoming and upon his handsome features was set a warm and gentle smile accented by the brightness of his blue eyes and his dark grey hair. Regan noticed, like Daniel, this man's skin was pale, almost ashen color, and when his eyes caught a touch of light they danced with silver speckles.

One look to Regan and the man's smile widened. He quickly took her hand to press a kiss to the back of her palm. "Daniel,' he proclaimed in a suave and old-fashioned English accent, 'I am surprised at you for keeping such a beauty like this to yourself. I must be introduced."

"Behave yourself, Theodore," chuckled Daniel as he calmly reached forwards to take Regan's hand away from the other man. Regan blushed, Theodore smirked, and Daniel shook his head.

"Theodore Servilii, allow me to introduce you to Regan Scott. She is visiting from America. Regan, this is Theodore Servilii, one of Europe's most avid collectors of ancient art and artifacts." He then added under his voice, "And one of London's most notorious charmers."

Theodore puffed out his chest at the introduction. "A pleasure, my dear." He waved a hand towards Daniel. "Pay no attention to the boost of my ego granted by our friend here. He only says that since he is the only one I allow to handle my treasures. So,' he beamed, sweeping his arms wide to the many glass cases upon the walls that held secure beautiful rice paper and bamboo wall scrolls, 'what do you think, Daniel? These arrived a few weeks ago from Japan."

70

Daniel drew his gaze over the collection pieces within the first room. His eyes turned intense as he concentrated on one than the others, picking apart the collection. "All of these are authentic?"

"Of course they are." The older man grunted, rolling his eyes. He took offense to such a preposterous question. He folded his arms to his chest. "When have I ever purchased an item that was neither authentic nor younger than two hundred years?"

Daniel's brows furrowed then his lips pulled back to a smile. He chuckled, shook his head then returned to viewing the collection.

Theodore nodded and leaned to whisper to Regan. "He's just jealous that he can't get his hands on these just yet. He's a kid in a candy store right now."

Regan chuckled, watching how intensely Daniel studied the pieces behind the glass security cabinets. He was scrutinizing each little section from one piece to another. "How old are these, Mister Servilii?"

"My dear, they are each centuries old, at least to my simple expertise. Daniel,' he said, stepping forwards to tap his friend upon the shoulder, 'I do want to find out the exact dates on these, for authentication purpose of course. So I have an offer for you, an offer which I know you cannot refuse."

"What are you wanting, Servilii?"

"I am willing to offer you a good sized donation to your department if you are willing to take a few pieces of my collection here to date and catalogue for me pro-bono. I would trust them only in your hands, my good man. Does that tickle your fancy?"

Daniel's dark eyes seemed to brighten then narrowed. "What is the catch?"

Theodore grinned. "I need them back in four weeks so they can travel to the Art Institute of Chicago. There, they shall be the center of attention at a fund raiser for the museum. And you know how much dedication I have to that specific institute and school of art."

Daniel gave a nod. He knew how devoted Theodore was to the Art Institute of Chicago for upon the first day of opening Theodore was there at the dinner that was held in celebration and a few pieces from his medieval armory collection were still on display. They were one of the first donations to the Institute. To this day a few members of the Servilii Familia worked for the museum and the school attached to the Institute.

"I have an agreement with the curator of the Asian art department to loan a few selected pieces to them for a year."

"Then why not have the Institute authenticate and date them, Theodore? You have associates working at the museum."

"My friend,' Theodore chuckled, clapping Daniel on the shoulder, 'because my agreement and trust in you will always outshine the skills and resumes of any other. They can work for the Louvre and I would still only allow you to touch them."

Regan chuckled ever so gently as she covered her lips with a hand. "Now who is stroking whose ego, hm?"

Theodore flashed a grin to her. "This young man is an expert in his field. He has a natural talent! So what about it, Daniel? Think you can complete the work in four weeks?"

"Four weeks is pushing the envelope, Theodore. I already have a line of work waiting for me that has been delayed as it is."

"Come now, Daniel. We both know your skills and your dedication to your work. You can get it done. The payment will be well worth your time, trust me. Besides,' he spoke back to Daniel, 'let your employees work on everything else. I would like your attention upon these works of art."

Daniel frowned. He wasn't pleased with the suggestion of his employees working on the pieces with his name upon the files, but Theodore's offer was very, very tempting. In the end he sighed, "Very well."

"Wonderful!" Theodore gave a hard pat to Daniel's back. "Let's slip into my office and I will give you all the documentation. Regan, my dear,' he purred, turning his attention to Daniel's beautiful guest, 'would you mind if I stole him for a short while? I will return him to you shortly"

Daniel saw a frown of unease touch Regan's lips. "Don't worry," he spoke softly, brushing the back of his fingers down her cheek. "I won't be long. I promise. If you need me,' he pointed down the hall that was to their right, 'this old bat's office is down the hall, second door on the right."

That touch instantly soothed Regan, and she smiled as she leaned to his caress with a nod. "Alright. I'll just wander around."

"Good." He dipped his head to touch a kiss to her cheek then departed with Theodore.

As the two men spoke behind the closed doors of Theodore's office, Regan began to wander the exhibit. As she walked the room, one particular and beautiful work of art drew her to it, a woodblock print of a gray horse, prancing within a forest of bamboo. The animal was incredible, expressing the excitement of being free to run.

"Such an impressive work of art, said a sudden voice laced with a strong Scottish accent from her side.

Tipping her head, she glanced to the right to see a tall, young man with waves of blondeish brown tickling a very handsome face. The man turned to her and smiled brightly, kindly and Regan was surprised to see two different colored eyes, one green and one blue. He motioned a hand to the art case, a hand that held within strong fingers a glass of golden liquid.

"It's not often we see pieces like these out of the museums."

"No, I guess not." She watched as the handsome man leaned forwards, and in the same way that Daniel did, began to study the image.

"Not a single flaw, not a line too thick, or a color bleeding into another."

"Are you an artist?"

The man shrugged his shoulders and the finely tailored jacket of black and thinly woven threads of crimson shifted. He flashed her another charming smile then grinned. "I don't like to boast, but I can draw a straight line if I rather say so myself, lass."

72

Regan couldn't help but chuckle. The man's personality magnetized her and evoked playfulness and benevolence. "You're lucky. I can't draw a straight line, let alone walk one." She sighed and hung her head in shame. "I've tried, but I had to swear on the Bible not to try to draw a line ever again."

The man's eyes sparkled and his attractive mouth pulled back in to an amused smile. "Should I ask why?"

"Something to do with the apocalypse." Regan's smile widened when the Scotsman's warm laughter echoed about the room. A few people stopped to stare at them, but the man's amusement was so contagious that Regan didn't care who glared at them, so she laughed along with him. In fact, she was thankful that he had approached her as his laughter and easy aura comforted her.

The Scotsman gave a tsk and a quick shake of his head. "The apocalypse, ey? I'd hate to see what happens if you ever drew a circle."

"A good smiting by God himself and a court order to never pick up an art tool again."

He was about to take a sip of his drink when her words choked a laugh in his throat. He began to cough and Regan squeaked, quickly patting him on the back till his laughter came forth from his convulsing throat. He looked to her with his dual colored eyes shining and with a bright smile upon his lips.

"Lass, you are a breath of fresh air in this circle of old knobs whose pockets are stuffed more with money than their brains are with a single, solid thought."

Regan winced with a click of her tongue to the roof of her mouth. She glanced about the room looking at the vast variety of men and women all dressed in their finest. She had wondered if many of these guests were wealthy donors and contributors to museums in London.

The gentleman caught her gaze and spoke as if to clear her curiosity. "There is not a man or woman on tonight's guest list who is not seated on some board of directors or contributor list to one art gallery or museum across Europe. They are not only here to offer their support for their colleague but also to bid for any piece of this collection to hang in their own galleries."

He sipped his scotch then muttered under his breath, "Ego suckers, all of them." He went on to add as an elder man strolled by with his nose tipping up in the air and a scrutinizing eye tossed their way, "Don't mind any of them, lass. I doubt they could find their way home from their own driveways."

Regan shrugged her shoulders and drew her shawl a little higher as it had slipped to her elbows. "I'm not one for this type of crowd. I'd rather be at a coffee shop or out for sushi."

"Aye, lass, so would I."

"Then why are you here?"

The man gave a slight arch of his shoulders. "Duty to a higher cause." After taking another sip, he offered the woman at his side his arm. "Care to see more of the pieces?"

"Well, I'm waiting for somebody." Regan pointed over her shoulder with a frown. "I shouldn't go too far."

"Don't worry, you could be half a mile away and Daniel Thorn could still find you."

Regan blinked and tipped her head. "You know Daniel?"

This time, when the man smiled to her, a devious and slightly seductive grin pulled the corner of his lips. "Oh, yes, very well." He held out his hand. "Forgive me for not introducing myself. Jamie Baird."

Regan took his hand and blushed when he raised her hand to his lips for a kiss. "Regan Scott."

"A pleasure to meet you."

Regan's eyes flashed with familiarity at the mention of his name. "Jamie? Oh, yes! Daniel spoke of you when we were having coffee at the café across from the Crucible."

"He did, did he?" Jamie smirked and licked the taste of fine scotch from his lips. "I hope it was nothing embarrassing."

"Not at all. In fact, he spoke highly of you and the time you two spent refurbishing the old church. You both did an amazing job, the church is stunning."

Jamie offered a raise of his glass to her and a nod of his head. "Cheers. I nearly broke my back on the scaffolding one evening when Rhain decided to play earthquake."

Regan chuckled. "Oh, dear."

"So, lass,' grinned Jamie, 'tell me, just what has Daniel Thorn said about me? I'm dying to know."

~ ~ ~ ~

Within Theodore's office, Daniel read carefully over every word and line of the contract he had been given.

"She's a lovely woman, Daniel," Theodore Servilii mentioned as he looked up from his desk with a wicked grin set to his lips.

Daniel, who was seated before the desk and just about to put pen to paper, paused in his writing to look up to his old friend. "What do you mean by that?" he asked with a slight scowl to his lips.

Theodore's grin darkened as did the amusement within his eyes. He saw a look within Daniel's eyes that was laced with possession and mixed with the slight growl that brought a laugh from the older Lamia. He waved a hand before him as if to dismiss Daniel's threatening glare. "I simply meant, for a mortal, she is lovely. She's beautiful and eloquent and innocent. She is the complete package, my friend, or so she seems from my point of view."

Daniel glanced down to the documents as if trying to pass off Theodore's compliments as nothing of great importance. "You're talking as if she is something more than just a human," he muttered under his breath as he began to flip through the pages to sign his name upon the marked lines.

"Is she?" The older Lamia leaned against his desk with his aged eyes were locked upon his younger associate. Theodore was asking, directly, if Daniel knew that Regan was a carrier for the Proprietas, the genetic defect that could create a Lamia.

74

With an irritated sigh, Daniel replied, "How should I know? I'm not my Familia's Consiliator, nor do I plan to stab Regan with a test stick and check her blood."

Theodore arched a brow. He couldn't help but detect a hint of malice within Daniel's voice. He frowned with a heavy, dry sigh. "Are you done?" he inquired gently.

Daniel nodded in silence as he signed his name one last time then handed the paperwork over to Theodore. "Yes. Everything is signed and in order. I expect every piece to be delivered to the lab by the end of the weekend, if possible. Is that acceptable?"

Watching Daniel stand and straighten his coat, Theodore gave a nod as he tucked the papers into a drawer of his desk that locked when closed. "Of course." Then he grinned, pushing from the desk to clap his friend on the shoulder. "Now then, why don't you get back to your lovely lady before some other handsome young man sweeps her off her feet?"

The very idea that another man could be pawing at Regan had Daniel turning upon his heels and marching right from the room. He heard Theodore call his name, but his mind was already set on facing any bastard who even dared touch her. He wasn't expecting Regan's admirer to be the last man he'd expect.

He found Regan in another room and in full conversation with Jamie Baird. He wasn't expecting Jamie to be at the art exhibit, but with the close relationship between the Augur Familia and the Servilii Familia the appearance of the Scotsman was not surprising. It was obvious that Jamie was working his natural charm for when he pointed at something, both he and Regan would laugh. The Lamia was pleased that Regan's aura had calmed and was not so uncomfortable.

Smirking, he crossed the room and said as he approached the pair, "I leave her for a few minutes and come back to find that you have swept her away, Jamie Baird."

Jamie and Regan turned their eyes at Daniel's voice. Regan smiled and Jamie laughed. "'I've told you once, I've told you twice,' the Scotsman chuckled with a finger pointing to Daniel from about the scotch glass in his hand, 'do not leave your woman unattended."

Daniel flashed a dashing grin as he gently set a strong hand to Regan's shoulder, subtly guiding her back to his side. He never took his eyes from Jamie as the man hid his grin behind the rim of his scotch glass. "Was this rogue bothering you, Regan?"

Regan glanced to the Scotsman, who winked at her, then back to Daniel. She raised her chin and said in a little sassy tone, "Not at all. He's been a wonderful gentleman."

"You hear that?" teased Jamie over the rim of his glass. "I'm being a gentleman."

"Did you get the paperwork finished?"

Daniel turned his black eyes down to Regan who had offered the inquiry. He gave a nod. "Everything is in order."

"Paperwork? What paperwork?"

Daniel looked to Jamie. "Servilii has asked that I see to the authentication of his pieces before they are moved to Chicago for display."

Jamie blew out a soft whistle. "That's going to be a large undertaking."

Daniel conquered with a nod.

Jamie clapped him on the shoulder. "Well, you better get on with it. I think I shall find another scotch and drown myself in it before Servilii notices me. I don't need to hear an hour long speech detailing his last meeting with my uncle. I don't know if I could survive another one."

Daniel could sympathize. Maximus Baird, the Augur Familia Regulus and uncle by lineage to Jamie, was never a positive subject to discuss, and once or twice in the past, Daniel had found himself nodding off during a meeting held with the powerful Veneficus.

"Perhaps I should escape while I can, make a run for it."

Daniel flashed a dashing and devious grin towards the Scotsman. "Good luck." He took Regan's hand, giving her a gentle squeeze to draw her attention to him, but then smiled. "I have an idea. There's a late night curry shop a few streets from here. How about we enjoy a simple dinner to end this evening?"

Jamie chuckled. "Curry? At this hour?"

"Or you can stay here and fend for yourself, Jamie." Daniel's dark eyes darkened even more to shadow the curl of a grin to his lips.

Jamie cleared his voice and recovered himself rather smoothly. "Curry sounds bloody good right about now."

Daniel glanced to the mortal at his side. "Would you like a bite, Regan?"

She gave him the warmest smile she could and nodded softly. "What classy evening out at an art exhibition would not be complete without curry?"

Jamie and Daniel laughed, then Jamie swept an arm towards the front doors of the home. "Lead the way, Daniel."

The small group departed the home as quickly as they could without drawing attention from Theodore. They walked down the winding old streets and over a few blocks before arriving at the simple and small restaurant tucked back in a corner of a dead-end. With the hour growing late, there were only a few other patrons enjoying the warmth of luscious curries and other Indian dishes. The restaurant itself was small with less than fifteen tables total, but the authenticity of the environment, with the music and spices lingering in the air, was nothing but spectacular.

The three sat to a table near the front windows and ordered a variety of dishes they could share. For the next three hours, they ate and laughed and ate some more. Daniel and Jamie told Regan of their adventures with Rhain and Alasdair during the restoration of the Crucible. They told her of the time when a sewer line ruptured out in the cemetery and raw 'everything' was shooting at least twenty feet up in the air. They followed that story with another, the night when the crypts flooded due to a water-pipe cracking. Both times had some questionable body parts floating around.

Regan had not laughed so brightly and so strongly in a long while, and it felt good to relax and enjoy the men's humor. The laughter never ceased with the stories and tales told by the men. They had one amusing story after another, and Jamie was not short of poking humor at Daniel and Rhain, the Thorn Twins.

With bellies full of delicious curies, spiced rice, samosas, masalas, and a variety of naan, the three left the restaurant and out to the chilly night that awaited them. The three departed company on the sidewalk while waiting for the limo to arrive. When it did, Daniel helped Regan guide her dress inside before he turned to bid farewell to his friend. She waited patiently as Daniel and Jamie shared an embrace, not a 'bro-hug' as it was called, but a true embrace of friendship.

Once inside the car, Daniel and Regan settled down for the ride back to the flat. He instructed his driver to 'take the long way' back so he could spend a few more lasting minutes with the mortal who was quickly capturing his heart. That's the only way he could explain the hints of emotions and the natural ease he had with Regan, the ability to simply be himself, the humble little art nerd, and not be 'Daniel Thorn' the Lamia - the Inquisitor. At first the closeness had not been noticed by neither he nor Regan. However, now that they were in closed space there was no way he could ignore the level of ease that was forming between them.

A serene quietness had blanketed the car as Regan shifted closer to him, leaning against his side. He welcomed the warmth of her mortal body and draped an arm about her shoulders, drawing her as close as possible. They rode in silence, Regan seemingly drifting to sleep and Daniel staring at the London scenery passing them by. To have a mortal pressed so intimately to him swept buried emotions within Daniel that he hadn't felt for decades. He couldn't remember the last time when he had invited a woman to slip past the layers of defensive walls he had constructed over half a century. True, he had many 'flings' over the years, yet never had he kept a lover for more than two nights. He was too busy with his work and with his Familia to really pay attention to the needs of a lover. When he did find a woman to take to his bed, he rarely invited her back.

Daniel was hardly a disconnected lover to say the least. He was gentle, considerate, giving, and very passionate. Beyond a one or two nightstand, the concept of a relationship was not needed by him, nor was it wanted. But to hold a woman, a mortal woman such as he did now where her warmth and life could be felt deep within his soul, was something he had not felt in a very long time.

That was the cold truth to being a Lamia. Regan was a mortal and he was a child of the undead - a vampire. They were never meant to be.

Daniel frowned. He stared out through the reflective glass of the car to see his image embracing Regan. He saw how she curled and pressed herself to him with a smile so sweet upon her lips. Then there was his image. It was a pale image, slender and unnatural, with his black hair framing a face that would be forever locked within time. Daniel would never age, never grow old, and never fall to human illness.

Regan, on the other hand, would grow old, fall prey to her mortality, and eventually pass on while Daniel would be as he was this moment and thousands of moments before.

He forced his gaze away, closing his eyes, and tightened his arm about the human he held as he pressed his features to her soft hair. *'Please,'* he whispered within his mind, *'if there is a God in Heaven that will listen to me, don't take her away from me just yet. Please.'* Why he spoke that little mental prayer confused him. In such a short amount of time knowing her, Daniel found himself wishing to keep her. But why?

Fate.

Destiny.

Where those the answers?

Impossible.

"Daniel?"

The Lamia's dark eyes slowly drew open when he heard his name whispered upon a sleepy voice. "Yes?" he asked in a hushed and warm whisper.

"Can I say something that would make me sound a little selfish?"

"Of course."

"I don't want this night to end."

"Neither do I, Regan, neither do I."

78

The Predators of my world are creatures born from the imagination of Hell.

Though Demons walk the Earth, seen as shadows to the humans, we Lamia can be monsters that could make a Demon grin with pride. Within us all is a monster, a creature of our own creation that is waiting for a crack in our control so it can slip out and feast upon the succulent innocence that is around us.

Our Daemon, as it is known, is born the moment a Lamia awakens to darkness. Everything dark, everything twisted, and everything cruel and murderous generates the Daemon within us all. Not a single Lamia has ever been created, to my knowledge, without an internal Daemon shadowing their every move and their every thought. It takes time to learn to control this creature, to tune-out its cackles and its suggestive whispers. This monster is perverted in every sense of the word. While many of us fight to contain our Daemons, there are many who embrace the power that is promised them, using their Daemons for their own pleasures. When this happens, Hell steps forth upon mankind's world and nothing but blood can feed it and nothing but death can stop it.

I fear the Demons, the killers, the rapist, and the Daemon-lovers who wander the city around me. I know what they are capable of, so I fear for her safety – Regan's. I never once put care or concern to the threat of these dark souls upon those around me for my brothers and my friends are always aware of their surroundings and of the shadows moving in the darkness. But Regan is mortal. She is unaware of the darkness waiting to snatch up her soul. Yes, I am sure she is aware of the dangers in her own world, but she is ignorant of the true monsters that would do anything for a taste of her innocent flesh and warm blood.

I have never before felt the urge to protect a human. Attaching myself to humans leads only to disappointment and emotional instability. However, I know already that Regan is more to me than a quick moment of mortal enjoyment. Only a short while spent with her and my Soul has made the decision that I must protect her. It is my duty to keep her innocence free from the tainted intentions of the monsters around her, including the Daemon that is inside of me.

-    *Daniel Rhys Thorn*

79

~ ~ ~ ~

Joyce lit her fifth cigarette since arriving at the Crucible. All night, no, for the entire day she had been growing more and more agitated with the idea of her cousin having a splendid night out with one of the most wanted and wealthy bachelors across the U.K. At first, she didn't feel any jealousy over the issue. She was happy that Regan was going to have an amazing evening. One night with Daniel Thorn wasn't something for Joyce to get jealous over. Right?

Her annoyance and jealousy bubbled angrily within her, but why? Joyce had her guys. She had her little black book of numbers on her nightstand filled with the names of willing men, but none of those guys she knew could compare to the Thorn twins.

Why was Regan so damn lucky?

Curling her lip, she tossed her cigarette to the ground, stomping it out with the toe of her healed boot. Joyce huffed as she glanced down to her attire comprised of a black mini skirt, lace stockings ending in calf length boots that laced up tight, as well as a crimson corset beneath a half cut jacket of black leather. Sure the guys slobbered on her, and more than a handful even asked for her number, but they were mostly drunk and not worth her time. Normally, she might just take one of them home, but this night she didn't want any of them. She wanted somebody on the same level as Daniel Thorn. She could go throw herself at Rhain, Daniel's twin brother, but that'd just get her banned from the club. No, Joyce didn't want to come out a desperate fool.

After hours of flirting, dancing, and drinking with anybody she could get close to, she was still not enjoying herself. She'd had enough when some drunken man nearly vomited on her. After that, Joyce pushed through the crowd and out of the church for some fresh air - well, as clean as the air was around the streets of London. Without a thought Joyce lit another cigarette. She slowly breathed in the toxic fumes, delighting in the burning warmth the menthol sent down her body, and out from her pursed lips she blew a puff of curling, minty scented smoke.

"Go' one ta share?"

The gruff voice turned Joyce's attention to a tall man that seemed to her to be in his mid-thirties. His face was sharply boned with a bit of scruff to his jaws, and his pale green eyes seemed friendly enough as they looked upon her past loose bangs of dark hair that was a mixture of black and brown.

"Excuse me?" she asked over the loud music coming from the doors behind her.

The man gave her a charming smile. "The fag." He jerked his chin towards her cigarette.

For a moment she stared at the man, taking in his broad form dressed in blue jeans and a long sleeved t-shirt of red with some inscription coiling around the left arm. "Oh, yeah, sure." She pulled out the pack, popping up a stick that she offered to him. "It's menthol."

"Wha'ever,' he said with a shrug, taking the stick from the pack, 'dun bother me."

A flash from her lighter struck the cigarette for the man. "There you go. Enjoy." With a dismissive hand, Joyce went back to scanning the crowd; she was bored.

The man drew in a lungful of potent, menthol death then blew it away as he watched her features turn dull. He had seen that look so many times, a look of life turn spoiled. "Wha' are ya out' ere for? The party's inside."

Joyce looked him up and down only to settle upon his face with a slender brow arched. "Is that any of your business?"

A sly grin pulled his lips as he tapped the cigarette's ashes onto the pavement at his feet. She was spunky - he liked that. "Ya just dun look like ye're enjoying ye're-self out' ere."

"I wasn't enjoying myself in there either," she muttered, taking a drag from her cigarette.

"Yea,' he licked his lips, 'ya dun look like tha type o' girl who likes this kind o' thing - loud music, drunk 'n' desperate guys, an' piss poor drinks."

Joyce watched him in silence as he moved before her and leaned himself back against the iron fencing set atop the brick wall that blocked off the old cemetery and the entry walk. He was reading her rather well. *Men*, she scoffed with a roll of her eyes. "Yeah, well, what's it to you?"

Such a tongue on this one. He knew he had made a good choice, a piece of fun ass to play with. "Wha'as yer knickers in a bunch?"

"For your information I'm not wearing any knickers," said Joyce, flashing him a sassy smirk. It was true. Beneath that short skirt was nothing but bare flesh.

"Sweet." He smirked, kicking his feet out to cross. "Bu' I still say tha' ye're a bi' snippish."

Joyce shrugged. "I'm here by myself while my cousin goes off to some fancy-ass party with one of the hottest men in the city, so forgive me for not being Mary Miss Etiquette."

"Aww,' he grinned, dragging his eyes slowly along her body when the girl looked away, 'an' she left ya ta yerself?"

"Yeah. She left me for that Daniel guy."

A silvery flash snapped within the man intense, green eyes. Daniel? Did she just say Daniel? He tipped his head, eyeing her intently. "Tha' Daniel guy?"

Joyce rolled her eyes as she groaned loudly, tossing her used cigarette to the stone ground that she smashed with the sharp heel of her boot. "You know, Daniel Thorn? Mister hottie himself with the twin to boot? Yeah, she got a date with him tonight. Bitch."

'Daniel Thorn,' the man repeated the name in his mind. *'Fuck'n 'ell,'* he thought with a laugh, *'this girl really is un'appy.'* She sounded as if her cousin had driven a stake through her heart. "Tell me," he said, blowing out another wisp of smoke. "Yer cousin about yer height with dark, wavy hair? Was here last week probably wit' ya and had a silver cross chain abou' er neck?"

Joyce blinked with a touch of surprise to her face.

That was the only look the man needed. He laughed heartedly into the air then began to shake his head. "I know who yer talk'n abou'. I ran in ta yer cousin last week, her an' tha' pretty boy. He wasn' ta nice ta me."

Joyce snorted. "Yeah, that was her. Gets assaulted by some ass, Daniel comes to the rescue, and now he's treating her like a damn princess."

"Assaulted? Really?" The man's lips curled to dry scowl. He wouldn't call his first introduction to the girl last week as an assault.

Joyce shrugged. "That's what she said."

The man clicked his tongue to the roof of his mouth then ran a hand through his uneven hair. "Fuck, I am bored," he heard her mutter.

"Tell me,' Joyce purred, exploring his tight and powerful body with her open gaze, 'where can a girl find some more exciting entertainment?"

Arching a brow, he looked back to her. She couldn't have spelled sex any better even if she had tried. He tossed the burning cigarette over the cemetery wall without a care. Let it burn the fucking place down, the dead would be better off any way. The girl was not too far away from him so it was easy for him to wrap a powerful arm about her, yanking her roughly against him. His other hand spread large fingers to her tightly clad ass, dragging her hips forwards and between his legs as he spread them for her.

Joyce didn't refuse the embrace as she giggled a playful giggle. Her breath held a tainted touch of sweet liquor and menthol. Like a spell, Joyce's mind toned-out the rest of the world. At this moment she didn't care for anything, or anyone, once she was wrapped within his arms. She only saw his seductive smile and his pale eyes sparkling with silver.

"Wha' da ya have in mind, lass?" he rumbled while leaning forwards so he could take a deep breath of her scent - liquor, smoke, and woman. He felt her tremble.

"I want attention," Joyce growled seductively as she laced both sets of fingers into the stranger's disheveled locks. Her mouth raised to his, forcing her hot tongue past his lips. She could taste the menthol that was left upon his breath and a faint taste of whiskey. She didn't care who he was for he was sex on a chocolate dipped stick, hot and available.

The sudden change in the woman's demeanor didn't bother the stranger. Her instant want for him was all thanks to his natural charm, so he allowed her to take control till he returned her kiss with hungered intensity. Joyce whimpered as he curled his nails into the skirt at the curve of her rump. They kissed, hungrily and heatedly, till he pulled away to lick her flavor from his lips - so sweet.

A dark, twisted grin crossed his lips and he snarled against her lips, "I am 'ere ta serve. Let's go someplace else, puppe'."

Joyce gave a juvenile giggle and purred, "But I don't even know your name."

"David."

~ ~ ~ ~

Joyce never considered that the man she was taking back to her flat could be a monster. She didn't care. It seemed that she couldn't look past the blatantly obvious fact that the man radiated sex - hot, animalistic sex. The ride back in the taxi had her undressing every inch of David's body with her eyes. If it wasn't for the driver glancing back at them every so often, she'd have been on him like desperation on chocolate. The ride was almost too painful for her in having to appease her desires with simply curling to his side with her hands upon him and her lips against his.

Normally, Joyce would've frowned at such forward behavior, acting as if she were an animal in heat, but she couldn't help herself. There was no control within her what-so-ever. She remembered David laughing when she tried desperately to unzip his pants because her fingers kept fumbling.

David had told her to calm down - that they had time - but in her mind Joyce only heard her body demanding more of him. When they finally arrived at the flat, she was scrambling over him to get out and still his laughter rang out through the night as she pulled him towards the front door.

He didn't mind her frantic attention. He hadn't had a hot mortal in a few years, and this mortal was hotter than any other. She was seductive, needy, desperate, and wild. Her mind and her body reacted to his every touch as if her skin burned with sexual want. When the taxi drove off, leaving them alone on the street, David gave in and allowed Joyce a few minutes of ease. She had to have been burning alive with hunger for him.

She was trembling from head to toe as he pushed her against the front door while ravaging her mouth with a moist, searing kiss. The woman moaned against his mouth with her lips molding against his, so he slanted his head to deepen the kiss as his tongue drove into the sweet, hot recesses to drink in every pitiful sound of elation that tore from her. Her hands were on him again, fingers dragging down his shirt in an attempt to tear fabric till they reached his belt. She fumbled once again to get the zipper down, but once she did, Joyce didn't hesitate to slip her devious fingers beneath fabric.

She giggled when she touched bare flesh. There was no fabric between his jeans and his body. Oh, yes, she really liked a man who was willing to go commando in public. Joyce pulled her lips from his to trail a hot line of kisses along his jaw till she found an ear. The moment her lips and teeth closed around the fleshy lobe she heard David release a deep, throaty groan.

Grabbing her hips, David yanked her hard against him causing her fingers to press against his swelling shaft. He was none to gentle as he began to grind himself in her delicate grip, urging her to curl her fingers about his growing length. She wasn't timid or gentle when she figured out what he was wanting, so she wrapped her fingers about his manhood and began to jerk and stroke him roughly. There were times that required romance and seduction but this wasn't one of them.

Deep, heaving gulps of air plunged in and out of his overwhelmed lungs that burned within his chest as his body was forced to compensate for the increase in physical function. The Lamia's body, though considered 'dead', did function much on the same level as a human and would respond to strenuous situations and stimuli. Their hearts would pump faster, pushing their limited reserve of blood through their veins and forcing the small amount of oxygen held within their lungs to the required organs. Their bodies would ignite in response, sending their senses and their desires into overload.

If the body of a Lamia continued to be pushed to its limits, that Lamia could lose control of themselves. When that loss of control occurred, a Lamia could easily slip in their self-control and allow the brutality of their internal Daemon to come out to play a game of ruthless purging of desire upon any that came near. The result, especially upon a human, was nothing more than a nightmare - a homicidal, gory, and bestial nightmare.

Joyce was certainly pushing him. Her teeth tugged upon his flesh wherever they touched, and her kisses ran along his skin while her tongue washed a slick path to follow. Her fingers continued to play him like an instrument, urging him higher and higher to a crescendo, but David couldn't allow that - not yet. With his cold blood pounding in his hears and Joyce's heartbeat screaming at him, he grabbed her hand to rip her fingers from his throbbing flesh. With her other hand taken in his vice like of a grip, he pinned her arms at her sides and pulled back enough so her lips could no longer assault his sensitive flesh.

A grin coiled across his handsome features upon seeing her pout as her blonde hair fell about her face to frame her cheeks and her sultry eyes in waves of shadowy lust. There was a slight blush of color tinting her flesh that he always adored upon human women. The Lamia took a deep, trembling breath as he leaned close to her so he could bury his sharp face against her neck and listen to the beautiful and hypnotic rhythm of her blood flowing violently through her veins.

"Easy, girl."

Joyce whimpered to the feel of his cool breath bathing her skin. She shivered, gasped, and groaned while tipping her head to the side when the sensation of his tongue flicked along her neck. Her body moved, twisting and arching, in an attempt to feel David's hard, male body. Joyce couldn't stop herself. She wasn't thinking rationally as she tried to feel more of him.

David chuckled at her hungered enthusiasm. He took both her wrists in one hand then wrapped his other hand about her throat as he took her mouth in another burning kiss. That kiss sated her, and she eased and moaned sweetly for him. He drew back, flashing a devious grin, while relaxing his grip upon her.

"Open tha door."

Exhaling dramatically, Joyce leaned her head back as a slow chuckle trickled from her smiling lips. "If you say so." Damn it! She could hardly take her eyes away from him so she could fish her keys out of her purse. When she finally had them in her hands, she dangled them playfully before him then turned with a swivel of her hips to unlock the door.

David snorted.

84

It took a few seconds for the door clicked open, but when he moved forward to enter the flat, Joyce blocked his way. The Lamia passed her a quick, harsh look as well as a low, threatening snarl. Nobody, especially a little human, blocked his way.

Joyce ignored him with a passing giggle and mewed while leaning herself sensually against the door frame as she reached out to skip her fingers up along David's chest. "Say please…"

If humans had a limit to their patience, then Lamia had an even shorter amount of patience to work with, especially David. They are creatures of the moment, and many, like him, couldn't care less about the seconds that were to come after the moment at hand. He wanted what was happening now and now only. He curled his lips. Playtime was over.

David grabbed Joyce by the hair, fingers curling within the silken strands so he could drag her forwards. His voice turned low, vibrating through his chest in the form of a harsh growl, "Either ya le' me in now, girl, or ya 'll be goin' ta bed alone wi' noth'n but somethin' plastic stuck between yer legs."

Joyce whimpered to the rough yank and moaned to the splash of cool breath against her hot cheeks. "I'd rather have something hard and hot," she purred as her lips turned to a sly smile. She slipped a hand between their bodies to cup him through his open jeans. "If you know what I mean."

David whispered, grabbing her hand to pull it away, "But yer no' getting' a thing if ya don' move."

With a laugh, Joyce twisted away from him and motioned him inside. "Come on then."

David's lips formed a cold, cruel smile when she turned her back to him. Slowly he shut the door behind him, locking away the outside world and any hope Joyce had…

It wouldn't be long till the spider had the fly.

~ ~ ~

J oyce's naked body, covered in glistening sweat, trembled in hot pleasure.

Her thighs hurt, convulsing wildly as they tightened about David's hard, flexing flanks as she tried desperately to control him. His thrusts were brutal, painful, urgent, and wild as he drove over and over into her body. He had her in his lap, his hard member embedded deep within her quivering form that kept her locked and grinding against him. She was urging him on, harder and harder while begging for more pain - for more pleasure. Tossing her head back, she cried his name in wild ecstasy while clawing at his muscular shoulders with her manicured nails.

David couldn't believe he was enjoying her as much as he was, after all, she was just a human - expendable and replaceable. Yet this superfluous little morsel brought forth his bestial side, his Daemon, and a thrill he hadn't felt for a very long time. He could hardly keep himself from releasing his callousness upon her fragile body, even as her screams for more ricocheted about the room.

The sound of her heart pounding within her chest was a symphony of exotic deviancy, and the tempting flow of her Sanguis a cocktail David salivated to taste. Her hot blood, flowing like a torrent through her body, swirled desire so deep within him that his mind, his rationality, quickly fell into the clutches of his daemon.

For Joyce, the night dragged on from one pleasure filled moment to the next, just the way she liked it. She didn't want this night to end too quickly, not when David was playing her body like a whore on Sunday. From one position to another position he moved her without missing a beat of his erotic rhythm, and not once did she question her trust in him when he dominated her body like a willing slave of sexual bliss.

All she wanted from him was sex, pure animalistic sex - as hard, as deep, and as twisted as she could get. And David was more than happy to provide for her! He didn't mind her clawing at his skin. He didn't mind her biting at him with her teeth, and he certainly didn't mind her demand for more. Every crude word of encouragement that dripped from her lips was another lash of the erotic whip upon his hide, pushing him higher and higher!

He moved her again, pressing her down on her belly before jerking her rump up in the air. He didn't ask if she was ready for him, just drove into her body with a violent surge. Joyce cried out, bucking frantically, as her new found lover repeatedly thrust in and out of her.

"Com' on, puppe', sing fer me," growled David tightly as he gripped her hips in a bruising curl of his deadly fingers and pulled back his lips to show a cruel and pleased grin.

Unable to reply, she pressed her features to the bed so the messed sheets could muffle the scream of her pleasure. She tried so hard to grind herself back against him, wanting to feel the thick base of his shaft rubbing and teasing her trembling flesh, but her temporary lover only laughed at her sexual hopelessness and ran his hands up her back before digging his fingers into her hair. Joyce whined in discomfort when he yanked her head back, drawing her body to arch violently so he could assault a firm, sensitive breast with a hand.

"Is this wha' ya wan'?" he purred hotly and with a deep, violent thrust into her body to punctuate his lewd question.

Joyce's answer was a low whimper of erotic sensuality that broke in to a high pitched cry of pain when he twisted a pert nipple till it flamed red with irritation.

He barked out a laugh of animalistic pride as he grabbed her arms in a grip that would certainly leave bruises come morning. He bowed her body forwards, and with his grip tight, began to assault her body till Joyce submitted to his every twisted pleasure. Only then did David allow her release. Joyce shook from head to toe, and her belly tightened and her sex pulsated about his buried shaft as she screamed to the Heavens.

With every fiber of his being blazing, the Lamia threw back his head and opened his mouth as a demonic sound of pleasure ripped from his throat. Before he could stop himself, he jerked Joyce against him, yanked her head to the side then dug his fangs into her neck. Stupid girl wouldn't know what happened as a surge of sensations washed over her from the pressure of his jaws sending her into a powerful orgasm that tore through her violently.

She was so sweet - too sweet.

David shuddered as he drank the hot, thick blood that flowed from the small puncture wounds. The taste of her Sanguis instantly ignited a part of David's senses that brought a possessive snarl to press against her throat. He could taste that her Sanguis was sweeter than any other human he had ever fed upon. Growling against her neck, David wrapped his arms about her as he continued to thrust into her trembling core, and when he felt her body tightening about him with each pump of his hips, he knew she was close to a second release.

Joyce reached over his shoulder, digging fingers into his hair, as she rocked and bucked against him. She moaned softly and whimpered, "Yes! Oh, yes!"

He drank his full till Joyce gasped and screeched in pleasure, then he released her, tearing his fangs from her flesh! Joyce shrieked and her body spasmed in orgasmic relief as David emptied his dead seed into her quivering womb just before the two fell upon the bed in a pile of slick, trembling flesh.

Minutes later, Joyce fell into a sexual coma, purring and smiling in rapture. David, however, stared at her while reclining next to her and listening to the dulling beats of her heart. He licked her blood from his lips, enjoying the taste of drying blood from the trail that skimmed down his chin. Yeah, there was something different about her blood. His own blood felt alive and hot, scorching through his veins with a sense of excitement.

David had only a few hours till dawn; he couldn't stay. When the first rays of Solis Ortus would begin to creep upon the horizon, David's body would begin to fall into slumber. He couldn't risk Joyce discovering the truth to his identity. He groaned, rolling to his back, as he dragged his hands down his face. That's when his mobile rang, muffled in a pocket of his pants.

He shifted carefully upon the bed, reaching down to his pants that were in a pile on the floor to dig his phone from a pocket then rolled to stand. "What?"

"Where are you?" inquired a calm and deep voice on the other end of the phone.

David groaned in both exhaustion and agitation. He moved away from the bed to one of the windows that over looked the street below. "Doesn' matter. Wha' tha hell do ya wan'?"

"You're late."

"I'm busy."

"That means nothing to me, David. I was expecting you."

Rolling his eyes, the Lamia slid his gaze to where Joyce lay resting upon the bed with her naked body twisted to expose her curved back to him. "I'll be there soon."

"You'll be here...now," growled the voice with a dark threat to the underlined tone.

David smirked. "Wha' if I told ya I 'ave found a pawn ta use in yer game?"

For a few seconds there was silence on the other end of the phone. *"Continue."*

"I met a girl tonight a' tha' damn piss-hole Rhain Thorn owns. Her name is Joyce, an' she's tha cousin ta tha girl Daniel Thorn's tramping about' tha city with tonight."

"Go on."

"From wha' she told me, Daniel an' her cousin are lookin' rather tight."

"Is that so?"

"Yes, sir, it is. An' Joyce isn' ta happy with i'." David leaned against the wall with an arm crossing his naked chest. "Ya said ya want a way ta fuck with them Thorn boys. An' we know tha' Daniel's more susceptible ta his emotions. Ya get wha' I'm sayin'?"

"It is too early to play my hand, David."

"Oh? Well, ya may wanna reconsider tha'."

"Don't get arrogant with me, boy," hissed the voice.

David licked the cruel grin upon his lips. Him? Arrogant? Hardly. He purred darkly, "This girl's blood tastes mighty sweet."

"Sweet? Explain."

"She's got i', mate - tha trait."

"The Proprietas? Are you sure?"

"My taste buds never lie."

"Bring her."

David's lips twisted into a sadistic and inhumane sneer. "Yes, sir."

The phone went silent as David crossed the room. He quickly, silently, got dressed then crawled upon the bed to lean over Joyce. "Wake up, Joyce," he whispered, dragging nails up her body to leave little red lines decorating her skin.

Joyce moaned as her mind was scraped from sleep, and feeling the sharp nip of pain along her skin, she stretched and yawned. Her body hurt in all the right places. How many years had it been since she'd had a good fuck like that? Her orgasms had been so strong and his pumping so hard that she swore she cried herself into oblivion.

"Mmm, that feels so good," she purred before twisting to face her lover. The fact he was dressed brought a frown to her lips. "Don't tell me you've got to get home to your wife or girlfriend now."

David chuckled. "No."

"Then why are you dressed?" Joyce pouted while running a set of fingers up his chest. "You don't have to leave, not just yet," she said suggestively.

"Oh, I'm leavin', puppe', an' yer comin' with me." Cocking his head to the side, David offered her a grin so dark that he saw the warm color in her features drain. In the next moment he had a hand clamped about her mouth, silencing her scream of terror when she saw a flash of fangs descending upon her.

~ ~ ~ ~

"**W**ill you be okay by yourself?" asked Daniel later that night as he and Regan stood outside the front door of Joyce's building. He was generally concerned for her safety since he could detect a whisper upon the breeze that was troubling to him. There was blood on the air that caused his senses to prickle to the metallic taste skimming through his lungs.

Regan smiled and lifted a hand to touch her palm against his cool cheek. He seemed distracted all of a sudden with his features tipped to the delicate night breeze. She watched as he closed his eyes and leaned into her touch. "You worry too much, Daniel," she whispered, pleased to the very subtle nuzzle she felt upon her fingertips. "I'm sure Joyce is home. And if she's not, she should be on her way soon. After all, we're going to a museum tomorrow. She better not be too late."

A coy smirk touched his lips as Daniel pressed his cheek to her palm with the want to feel her warmth for just a little bit longer. "Very well. You have my number if you need me."

Regan nodded and reluctantly drew her hand away. "Thank you again for an evening that was beyond magical." She sighed dreamily, twisting her lips in hopeful thought while turning her gaze shyly to the side. "I know this may sound awfully silly of me, but I hope we can see each other before I leave."

Daniel considered the suggestion and found himself smiling in agreement. "I would very much like to see you before you return to the States. I will call you soon, alright?"

"I look forwards to it." Regan bid him goodnight then turned to open the door, but she paused when she felt a brush of cool fingers skim down her neck. A shiver traced her flesh causing her eyes to flutter closed, but only for a moment. When she turned around, Daniel was there.

He stepped closer to her, threading both hands into her hair to disarm the tight braids that trailed her scalp. He drew her up to him and brought his mouth down to brush a slow, tantalizing kiss to her lips. That faint, delicate little kiss brought a warm quiver to rush through her, a quiver he felt.

Regan's trembles went through her and into him causing the vampire to wrap his arms about her, holding her tightly as his kiss deepened. So passionate was his demanding kiss that Regan felt her knees buckle. To her dismay the kiss ended as Daniel released her, allowing her body to ease away from him. The sensations that spun wildly through Daniel both electrified and burned his insides. He had to release her for his own good, otherwise, the kiss would overpower him. Passion was more of an addiction to him, a very dangerous addiction, so when he felt a familiar tightening within the pit of his stomach and a loud scream within his brain for more, he had to force himself to step back from the human.

With a quivering breath, he reached out to tuck a lock of her hair behind her ear. "If I can kiss you like that again, I would see you every chance I could get."

Regan didn't know what to say in response. She stood staring at him, her cheeks burning red. A bubble of some pleased sound tumbled about within her throat as she stepped away and past the heavy door that she shut behind her till her reflection became hidden by the glass. Half way up the stair, she glanced back to see Daniel's shadowy form disappearing from view, then, with a burst of giggles, she raced up the stairs and to the door of Joyce's flat.

"Joyce!" Regan called once she managed to open the door. Regan dropped her handbag to a chair, took off her shoes then proceeded into the flat. The apartment seemed vacant, dark, and oddly cold so she headed to Joyce's bedroom where she gently knocked upon the door. "Joyce? Are you home?"

"Joyce?" she inquired once again as she pushed the door open.

The bedroom was dark, not a light was on, and silent, too silent. Carefully, Regan stepped further in. When she got to the edge of her cousin's empty, she turned on the bedside lamp. Warm light flooded the room, illuminating a vacant bed, and from the look of it the sheets and cover had gone through a tornado. Regan left the bedroom heading through the small flat with confusion twisting about within her mind. There was no sign of her cousin anywhere.

Maybe Joyce hadn't returned from the club yet. Or maybe she had gone back out. Those possibilities were pushed aside when Regan just happened to glance to the sitting room to see her cousin's purse and keys on the coffee table. Now that was odd. Upon closer inspection Joyce's wallet was gone and so was her mobile phone, only the keys and the purse remained. Maybe she had run out with friends and left her keys thinking that Regan would be back by the time she returned. Maybe she went back to the club, or maybe to the store for some milk, or maybe...

Groaning loudly, Regan bopped herself on the side of the head when her confusing thoughts turned to worrisome paranoia. "Hush up, brain," she muttered in an attempt to stop her mind from filling her with fear.

Pushing the negative thoughts away, she headed to the guest room, pulling pins out of her hair as she went, then began the difficult task of unlacing and unlatching the gown and bodice that she wore. Finally, when she was able to undress, she fell limp upon the bed clad in her chemise.

Left to her thoughts, Regan closed her eyes and allowed herself to drift back to the memories of her evening with Daniel, sighing as she remembered the way his kiss had felt upon her lips. She could still smell the scent from his exotic aftershave and taste his lips. Most of all, she could still hear the smooth accent of his English voice caressing her ears. His touch, his scent, and his voice refused to depart her soul. Unable to move, Regan gave in to the remnants of Daniel Thorn and the allure of her dreams.

~ ~ ~ ~

J oyce was cold - so very cold – and her body ached all over. Slowly, her mind pulled awake to be confronted with throbbing, dull pain. She felt dizzy and nauseated as her stomach lurched when she moved to sit. The last thing she remembered was David waking her from sleep, then everything went black.

Joyce shook her head only to groan as a touch of vertigo sent her back down to the old, worn bed she had woken on. The air around her smelled musty, thick and old, as if she was in a barn or an old castle. Besides the ringing in her ears the constant sound of dripping water, echoing all around her, drowned out any other sounds she tried to pinpoint.

It took a moment for her to get her bearings, but when she finally opened her eyes, Joyce saw darkness. She was in a room, or what she thought could be a room, but with no light she couldn't make out any details or furniture. The dank coldness cuddled her close and seeped through her skin to her bones creating a chill that was unnatural. She had no clothes on, only a blanket that had been wrapped about her. After a few deep breaths, she tried to sit up once again so she could steady herself and analyze her situation.

"Hello?" she called out, her voice sounding raw as it bounced off the walls around her. "Is anybody there?"

Nothing - just silence.

Shivering, Joyce stood up on shaky legs that threatened to collapse beneath her. She shuffled forwards while feeling through the darkness with an outreached hand till her palm came flat on the wall. She squeaked to the sensation of watery dampness and porous stone. Where was she?

"Hello!" she called out once more - louder and stronger than before. "Can anybody hear me?"

No answer came.

She continued to move using her hand to guide her way along the wall. Each step she took was placed carefully before the other. Nothing was around her. She didn't bump into any chairs or tables, and so far every inch of wall her hand moved along was the same as the last inch, that was, till her fingers moved from the grainy stone surface of the wall to the cracked sensation of wood. A door! Delight flooded through Joyce's heart as she fumbled for the knob only to discover that the door was locked. Her heart plummeted into her stomach.

"Please!" she screamed loudly while smacking her palm to the door. "Somebody answer me! Where am I?"

Panic, anxiety, and fear coiled about Joyce's heart like a vice, tightening to the point she felt sick. She banged over and over on the door till her palm burned with raw skin, and when she couldn't hit the door any longer, she turned to jerking and yanking the handle. "Open the door! David, please, answer me!"

Tears began to flow down her cheeks till her skin stung and her eyes swelled. When she couldn't breathe but painful gasps of air, Joyce gave up. She kicked the door violently as a scream tore through her raw throat, but then she jumped back in shock as the door handle clanked to the ground.

"What the hell?"

Bending down, she picked up the handle then leaned down to examine the door. The old knob of oxidized brass had broken in half and the other side of the handle had fallen in the hallway. Joyce nibbled her lips as she quietly and carefully pulled the door open. The old wood and metal hinges creaked and groaned as the structure was opened.

The room was bathed in light from the bright halogen rods suspended from the vaulted, stone ceiling of the hallway, and the bright, flickering lights penetrated the room causing Joyce to hunch back, shielding her eyes. Slowly the brightness and the aching discomfort in her eyes began to dull, and when her sight came back to her, she stepped into the hall.

It was obvious that she wasn't in a modern building for the walls, the floor, and the ceiling were all made of stone work and cracked, colored tiles that seemed to go on in both directions for miles, or at least till the lights faded into foreboding darkness. From what she could see there were a few doors lining the hallway, but for the most part there was no sign of any windows. This had to be some sort of basement or a long cellar, which meant there could be stairs!

As Joyce looked up and down the hallway, her mind began to replace her excitement of finding stairs with the overall creepiness of her surroundings. What if she had been locked in some old sanitarium that had been abandoned by the employees and the patients were left behind? What if there were psychopathic killers locked behind the doors all waiting to get out and run wild? Joyce whimpered, slipping back into her room. Maybe she should just put the handle back together and shut the door. She'd be safer inside. Wait, what was she thinking? This was reality, not some demented video game. Besides, she had to find a way out of this place.

Maybe there was somebody who could help her - somewhere. She took one step then another out of the room, but then she froze at the awful truth that she had no idea which direction to go. Should she go to the left or go to the right? After a moment of thought, she decided to go right, and if she found a dead end, she'd just retrace her steps and head left. There, that was a simple plan.

Joyce ran, and ran, and ran past more and more doors that all looked the same. How long she had been running she couldn't tell, but so far she hadn't come to any elevator or a staircase. The hallways seemed to twist and turn about each other like a snake. There was no way for her to tell where she'd come from and it would be impossible for her to retrace her steps. There were junctions of hallways running into each other, turns and corners, and dead ends. The basement seemed to go on forever.

Somehow Joyce found a staircase. She didn't hesitate as she ran right up the winding stairs and was certainly surprised to exit into massive room. Stretched out before her was a space that seemed endless. The ceiling was at least two stories high and was barely covered in broken tiles of dirty glass that clutched the skeletal structure of iron and steel. It was raining outside, and watery drops trickled down to the cement floor from between the glass fractures to form puddles upon the dirty floor. It was a factory room! She was looking upon an old production line!

Tiptoeing forwards, she stepped carefully so not to walk upon pieces of machinery and debris that scattered the floor while avoiding the puddles that had mixed with old machine oil. There were aged lockers on the sides of the walls, shelves and work spaces, as well as drums rusted to the floor. She walked by large machines that were nothing but ghosts of their former selves linked together with the remnants of production lines left to corrode over time.

Suddenly, a bird launched itself into the air, flapping its wings violently as it flew up and through a missing square of glass high above. Joyce nearly screamed in shock but a quick thought had her covering her mouth with a hand. She swallowed her scream and made the discovery that she was shaking badly due to her building terror and the truth over her predicament. She had to calm herself. If she was in an old factory, there would certainly be a way out, or better yet an old phone she could use to call the police.

When she finally reached the end of the massive room, she pushed through a pair of double doors to discover another hallway. This one was wider, brighter, and looked more to be of functioning service. The walls had once been painted but the color had long ago been dulled by time and dust. The floor had once been tiled but was now missing pieces and was littered with holes, cracks, and random debris. Office equipment, from decades ago, lined the walls from desks to chairs to filing cabinets. In one corner there was a pile of black fabric that ended up being discarded aprons. There were also old paper files scattered carelessly along with old phones and typewriters looking to date back from the 40's. Wherever she was, time had abandoned the place decades ago.

How bizarre and how frightening. The area looked as if those who had been working in the factory dropped everything and vacated the place without a second thought leaving the building and its production lost to time, rotting away to be forgotten.

Joyce slowed her run to a walk as curiosity tugged at her. She had yet to see hide nor hair of another person, and the only sounds that were about her were the scuttle of an animal or the sounds of birds from outside. Besides the ghosts, she seemed to be alone.

The hallway ended into a large, open area that Joyce entered from beneath a set of stairs. This was obviously the reception area of the factory as there was a large, crescent shaped desk rising from the center of the room, broken and bent seats and benches along one wall, and on another wall hung a lopsided picture frame with cracked and stained glass that caused the image behind to be distorted beyond recognition.

Joyce's heart slammed within her chest and a cry of dismay lodged itself in her slender throat when she saw the doors and windows boarded up. To make the sensation of hopelessness worse, there was a massive chain wrapped through the door's handles with a padlock holding it all together. There was no way to get out. Tears began to flow, and with an agonizing howl of grief pouring from her trembling lips, she crumpled to the floor.

From behind her came an unexpected sound of a door opening then closing. Joyce gasped, twisting about to look up towards the second floor. Somebody had just opened a door, and following the sound came footsteps as well as a male voice growing louder. Joyce quickly scrambled to hide behind an old filing cabinet, taking refuge in the deep shadow it offered. She watched and waited…then froze.

It was David!

93

She watched with enwrapped attention as he walked out from a set of swinging doors and across the balcony that groaned beneath his steps. His stride was purposefully and strong yet casual at the same time. The empty room echoed loudly with David's voice even though he was not speaking overly loud, and from the sound of the conversation, Joyce surmised that he was speaking on his mobile. A call of his name pressed against Joyce's closed lips but she swallowed it as David disappeared behind another set of swinging doors and into the hall behind them.

Slinking from her hiding place, Joyce crept towards the stairs. She took each step one by one making sure not a squeak was heard. At the landing, she crouched down to peek out from the railing, glancing in the direction David had gone where a dim light radiated from further down the hall. The closer she moved towards the light, that brightened as she advanced, Joyce could hear David's voice growing in intensity and volume.

"She's sleep'n like a baby," she heard him chuckle as she hunched down against the door she found marked 'Executive Office.'

"I promise ya,' he went on to say, 'ya won' regret this."

Regret? Regret what? And who was he speaking of, her? Joyce felt the touch of a ghostly, cold shiver run down the center of her spine.

"I had her blood tested. She's go' i'," David went on to say. "Bu' there's still a fifty-fifty chance she might no' make tha Creare. No' every lil human with tha trait will survive tha creation. Bu' Joyce can handle i'."

Joyce's trembled as she overheard David's conversation and the mention of her name. A shiver of fear ran her blood cold when he mentioned that he had tested her blood for some sort of trait. What was he talking about? What trait? She knew nothing about any trait in her blood.

New panic began to race through her to send chills down to her soul, freezing her breath in her lungs. She had to get out this place, and fast.

Whatever hope she had for an escape came crashing down when she spun about, meaning to run, only to come face to face with a man. He was so tall she had to crank her head back to look up to his face, a face that turned her blood to ice. He was pale, so very pale, and his deep blue eyes flashed with a metallic color. With his dirty blonde hair greased back his sharp Italian features and narrowed eyes were evident in the thin light.

Joyce's mouth parted wide to emanate a high pitched scream but no sound came forth when the man raised a finger before her. She heard a voice echo within her mind speaking 'silence'. That was it - nothing more. Blackness enveloped her as her body began to tumble. The last thing she saw was the man's face and his wicked sneer as he caught her in his arms.

VI

I *can still feel her warmth, the bodily heat that is produced by a living*
human, so luscious - so seductive. It has been a long time since I have felt this
heavenly heat wrap itself about me - holding me within its luscious arms. I
have almost forgotten how it feels to be within the arms of a woman - a human
woman.

 I can still feel Regan's lips from when we kissed. I can still see her
vision within my mind's eye. She is so tiny compared to me; I dwarf her with
my height. Yet it was me who felt dwarfed within the loving warmth that I felt
radiating from her heart. Her embrace, so gentle and kind, and her kiss, so
supple and tender, provided me a moment of comfort. How I wish - no - how I
hope I can feel her again.

 She wants to see me before she returns home. I should have said no.
I should have, but I could not. My heart spoke before my brain could remind
me that, as a Lamia, there are rules I must adhere to and obey - the Lex. It is
dangerous to masquerade as a human when I am nothing but a cold and empty
body - dead.

 I don't want to feel so cold anymore, so alone. I don't want to be
reminded, night in and night out, that I am nothing more than a 'vampire'.
For one moment, one precious moment, I was reminded what it was like to be
alive. And so help me, I want to feel alive again. I want to feel her warmth
wrap about me, holding me and comforting me.

 I want to be...alive.

-   *Daniel Rhys Thorn*

~ ~ ~ ~

Regan couldn't sleep, and as the clock turned to flash one in the morning she
found herself pacing the apartment back and forth, from window to window
and from door to door. Joyce had yet to return, and now fear had taken a strong
hold within Regan. She knew that something was wrong. Something had
happened to her cousin. With worry spreading through her subconscious,
Regan couldn't help but fantasize every horrific situation that might have
befallen her cousin. And when her imagination had done its duty, Regan was
panicking.

She should have called the police, after all, that was the logical course of action. Then again, if Joyce was just running late, she wouldn't be too happy to return home to find the police waiting for her. Joyce would never forgive Regan if the police showed up at the club looking for her. But she had to call somebody, if not to just talk out her worry. So she picked up her mobile and called the first number that came to her mind - Daniel.

The instant he picked up the phone his name tumbled from her lips in a forceful sob. "Daniel!"

"Regan?" inquired Daniel with a touch of confusion. *"It's one in the morning. What are you doing up? Shouldn't you be resting?"*

"I can't sleep," she whimpered, pacing once again. "Joyce isn't back. I thought she'd be back by now. Her stuff is here, even her keys, but she's not here. She hasn't called"

"Calm down. When was she supposed to be back?"

"She didn't say exactly, but I didn't think she'd stay out all night when we're going out early in the morning." Regan felt tears welling within her eyes. "What if something's happened to her? What if she's hurt or lost? What if she's…"

"Regan,' Daniel's voice whispered, *'listen to my voice. Calm. Down."*

Regan whimpered again, a sob catching in her throat. But somehow Daniel's voice slipped past all of her fear, her worry, and the echoing sound of her pounding heart to caress her soul. There was a tone to his voice that was melodic in nature and was so very soothing to her. Regan felt herself calming and her breath easing within her aching lungs, and with a deep sigh she sat down to the couch.

"Take a few deep breaths, alright?"

She did just that.

"Do you know if she was going to be meeting any one at the Crucible tonight?"

"She had mentioned wanting to meet a guy to have fun with, but I thought at the time she was just upset because I was out with you. I don't think she'd bring some stranger back here or be stupid enough to go anywhere with a stranger." Regan groaned, sinking into the couch. "At least, I hope not."

"Are you sure she was only going to the Crucible and no other club or party?"

"I don't know."

"Alright, I'll put a call to Rhain and see if he knows of anything. Would that help any?"

Regan sat bolt right on the couch. She smiled brightly as tears began to stream down her features. "Yes! It would. Thank you, Daniel!"

"Let me call my brother and then I'll call you right back. Just stay calm and wait for my call. If Joyce returns home before you hear from me, then call me and let me know. Understand?"

Regan nodded again. "Of course."

"I'll speak to you soon."

"Thank you, Daniel."

"You're welcome."

The phone call ended.

Regan sniffled as she gently wiped at her tears. She hoped that Daniel would be able to find some information from Rhain about Joyce's whereabouts, and with any luck she would still be at the club and would come right home when told that her cousin was worried. And so Regan sat quietly staring at the phone in her hands. All she could do was wait for Daniel's call.

The moment Daniel ended the call with Regan he dialed the number to Rhain's mobile. Depending upon where Rhain was in his club he may not be able to hear his phone ringing. Upon the fourth try Rhain's voice answered along with the thumping sounds of the club.

"Rhain!" Daniel had to scream into his phone. "Go to your office! I need to speak to you!"

"Go where?" Rhain's voice called back loudly.

"Your office, you fool. This is important!"

"Go to the post-office? Why the hell would I go there? The place is closed!"

Daniel rolled his eyes. He howled, "Your office!"

From the phone came the sound of Rhain cursing. Eventually, the blasting music began to dissipate over the sound of Rhain's steps climbing the iron stairs to the catwalk that circled the top of the old cathedral. Daniel heard the music of the band loud and clear then the sound of a door closing.

"Okay, I can hear you a lot better. What do you want, my twin?"

"I need some information, Rhain."

"The condom goes on first."

"You're such a charmer, brother." Daniel groaned. "This is rather important, Rhain, so please pay attention."

"Wow,' Rhain Thorn's voice sounded with a whistle, *'aren't you Mister grumpy pants."*

"Really, Frater, I'm in no mood for your childish banter tonight. Regan has called me. She's very worried about her cousin Joyce who has yet to return to her flat."

"Wait. Regan. Isn't that the girl you were out with tonight?"

"Yes. I dropped her off at her cousin's flat a few hours ago. Joyce was to return soon after, however, she has yet to make an appearance."

"And how does this involve me, or you for that matter?"

"According to Regan, Joyce was at your club tonight."

"So? There're a lot of people here."

"Yes. I'm sure of that," Daniel muttered as he stood from one of the leather sofas in the sitting room of the condominium. He headed towards the kitchen. "I need to know if she is still at the club or if she has left."

Rhain snorted a laugh through the phone. *"Are you insane, Frater? Do you know how many people have come and gone through the doors of my club tonight? Countless."*

"And every single one had their I.D.s scanned at the door." Daniel walked to a cupboard where he took out a glass, and with the phone cupped between his ear and shoulder, removed from the fridge a bottle of dark glass much like a bottle of wine. The content in this bottle, however, was nothing close to being wine. He poured into the glass a substance that was thick and red. "You can check your registry for the name Joyce Scott."

He heard Rhain mutter and grunt in protests and in excuses. "Rhain, this is important. Could you tell me if she was at the club and if you know of any activity she may have been involved in?"

"Fine," grunted the other Lamia.

Daniel leaned to the counter top, crossing his feet out before him, as he began to sip from the glass. Each sip stained his pale lips with a shine of crimson that was licked slowly away. He could hear Rhain sit to his creaky office chair then the echoes of a computer turning on followed by the clicking of keys. After a few quiet moments he heard his twin muttering Joyce's name over and over.

"Here we go. At nine fifty-six Joyce Scott had her I.D. scanned at the door. She ordered,' Rhain whistled, *'six different mixed drinks and three beers within a two hour span of time. Then that's it."*

"What do you mean?"

"There has been no more activity or purchases from her. If she's still here, she hasn't had anything at the bar."

"Has she left?"

"Hold on, let me check." Rhain's voice soon came back over the phone. *"Well, the log shows that Joyce left the club at twelve ten. She never logged back in."*

"Did anybody else leave at that time?"

Rhain snorted again. *"Frater, you should know that answer."*

Daniel frowned, his lips curling about the edge of his glass. "Rhain, I have a very frightened and worried young woman who is expecting me to call her soon with some information pertaining to the whereabouts of her cousin. Is there anything else you can do to help me?"

"Why should some pointless Humanus be a concern to you? She's just a little human. Who cares what's happened to her sister?"

"Cousin."

"Whatever."

"I care, to a degree. If Joyce has foolishly gotten herself into a dangerous situation, that is her issue to deal with. I will not see Regan suffer for that foolish decision."

"You always were too soft. Let me see what the security cameras can tell me. I'll also check with the staff."

Daniel ignored his twin's jibe. "Make sure to ask your undead guests if they have seen her."

"Are you saying that some bloody Lamia has been using my club to find dinner dates?"

"I would hope not."

"And you should know your twin well enough to know that I don't let any Sucker break the laws anywhere near this club. If there was any altercation or fight, I'd know about it, and so far there hasn't been shite."

Daniel finished his drink and licked his lips clear of the crimson fluid that remained. "I know how dedicated you are to your club and our laws, Rhain. I wasn't questioning that."

Rhain cut in with a snip to his voice, *"Give me a few minutes, Daniel."*

Daniel sighed as he ran his free hand through the long strands of his hair that fell free down to his back. He didn't mean any insult to his twin in any way. Rhain, as immature as he seemed to act, was nothing more than hardcore when it came to upholding the Lex that kept their society hidden and protected.

As Rhain turned his attention from the call to his security, Daniel headed from the kitchen to his bedroom. If need be, he would return to the apartment and wait with Regan for any news about Joyce. He hated the guilt stirring within his chest, knowing that she was alone. Wonderful. Now his own mind started to spin with the 'what if' questions. What if Joyce had been the victim of a crime? What if Joyce had been taken from her apartment against her will? What if Regan was in similar danger?

That last question had a dry breath lurching within his lungs.

"Blood Hell…"

The slow curse stopped Daniel cold when his brother's voice came back over the phone. He shivered as the hand of dread tightened about his throat like a vice. "What is it, Rhain?"

"I found your missing cousin, Daniel. You're not going to like this."

"Tell me, Rhain. What did you discover?"

"She left with a Lamia."

"Who?"

"David Servilii."

~ ~ ~ ~

Daniel stared at his phone.

After the call with his twin ended he wandered into his room, sitting heavily to the edge of his bed and contemplating how to tell Regan the situation with Joyce, that she had left the Crucible with an 'unknown' guest.

Damn it! Why did David need to become involved with Joyce? The man was not safe! More to the point, he was insane. David was a Proscriptus, a Proscriptus who had been labeled an outlaw. Though Proscriptus Lamia were not considered banished or even worse, exiled, they were frowned upon by many Familia and Lamia within the Republica of England. Proscriptus Lamia could be dangerous - very dangerous - to Lamia and Human alike, and the idea that Joyce had connected with David, and was now late to return home, had Daniel's worry increasing.

If David had Joyce….

No. He couldn't let his worry start to twist and fill him with irrational thinking. He had to call Regan with some form of information that wouldn't send her frantically calling the police, so he needed his mind to be calm and thinking clearly. He had no other choice, he had to lie to her in order to keep her ignorant of the truth - to keep her safe.

Forcing a lump down his throat, a hard and cold lump, Daniel called Regan. The phone rang only twice when his call was answered. *"Daniel?"*

The Lamia frowned heavily to her anxious voice. "Yes, Regan, it's me."

"*Did you find anything out? Did your brother find Joyce?*"

Daniel breathed in a stale pull of air. "Yes,' he said softly, tasting acid in his own words, 'he found your cousin on the security recordings at the club."

Regan sighed in relief over the phone. "*Is she alright? Has Rhain spoken to her?*"

"No, Rhain hasn't spoken to her."

"*Why not?*"

"She's not at the club."

"*I don't understand,*' Regan whimpered with confusion tainting her voice, '*she has to be there.*"

"She was there, Regan, but she left with a man who was also at the club."

"*Who?*"

Daniel frowned softly at the question and felt bile rise up within his slender throat. "I'm not sure. Rhain's still looking into his identity. There are a lot of guests at the club tonight. It'll take some time."

Regan whimpered, teetering on the edge of tears. Her voice shook. "*Wait, we had our I.D.s scanned at the door! Can't Rhain find his name from his I.D.?*"

"Yes, sweetheart, he can," said Daniel, hanging his head with a lock of his hair falling before his view. "Trust me, Regan, Rhain is doing all he can but he needs time to go through tonight's guest log. He'll have more luck when the doors close."

"*But it's past one in the morning, and the club doesn't close for another hour.*"

Daniel's heart twisted when she began to cry. The first sob that came over the phone twisted his gut. He sighed heavily, dragging a hand through his hair. "Everything will be fine," he whispered. "I promise you, that in the end, everything will work out."

"*How do you know?*" Regan accused through a choked sob.

How the hell did he know? Damn it, he wasn't an Oraculum. Daniel didn't have psychic visions of the future. Tightening his eyes shut, he pressed a palm to his forehead. She was crying even harder now, and Daniel could hear the hitching of her breath as she tried to breathe in between her sobs and her tears.

"I'll find her, Regan," he heard himself say before his mind could catch up to his words. "I promise, I'll do all I can to make sure Joyce is returned to you safely."

"*What should I do? Should I call her parents, the police?*"

"Not yet. It could be that she's gone home with this guy for the night,"

"*She wouldn't do that!*"

"But you did tell me that Joyce was going to the club with intentions of meeting a gentleman for the evening."

Regan sniffled. *"I..."*

"It could be that she did find a companion for the night. If she was upset, as you said she was earlier, than it could be that Joyce does not want to return just yet. If she is enjoying herself, then so be it. Besides,' Daniel whispered softly, 'if I had invited you back to my bed, would you have been able to say no?"

Regan sniffled again as a little whimper trickled fluidly past her lips. *"But this is different."*

Daniel heard Regan take a breath to speak so he quickly added, "However, we cannot jump to conclusions, Regan. There is no point in allowing our fears and worries to overcome our rational thinking."

Regan fell silent.

"I know how worried you are," he whispered softly in hopes of comforting her. "Let us give Joyce till the morning, alright?"

"But she could be out there - hurt."

"Regan." Daniel spoke her name in a commanding voice and in a tone that was flat yet melodic at the same time. "Listen to my voice and listen well. Calm yourself. Feel your heart beating in your chest - hear it echo. Do you hear it?" He didn't want to use the Vocis Sonus Coercêre, but he had no choice.

"Yes..." Regan mewed in a voice that weaved ever so softly, mixing with the delicate touches of gentle, unrecognizable sounds.

"Good. I will do all I can to help locate your cousin. I want you to relax, take a hot bath and make some tea. I will keep in touch with Rhain. If need be, I will visit the Crucible after it closes to aid in Rhain's search. Do you understand me, Regan?"

Again, she mewed softly. *"Yes..."*

"Alright. Go on and rest."

"Yes..."

Regan hung up the phone and the sound of the dead line buzzed softly; the call ended. Daniel sighed, closed his eyes, and slowly shook his head. He smacked himself, mentally, for forcing his will upon her. For a few thought filled moments he stared at the blank screen of his mobile before he turned the screen back on with a brush of a fingertip.

He called Rhain, and on the forth ring Rhain picked up. "Do you have anything news, Frater?"

"I've spoken to my staff. Nobody remembers seeing Joyce with David. In fact, not a single member of my security team remembers David being in the club at all. His I.D. was never scanned at the door."

"Then she met him outside the club."

"That's my thinking," muttered Rain with a grumbled sigh. *"Just having that bastard near my club pisses me off, makes me itch."*

"Would it comfort you to know that I had to break up a confrontation between him and Regan the other night?"

There was a dead and very long pause on the other end of the line. *"Would you care to run that by me again, Frater?"*

Daniel groaned and fell back upon his bed, running his free hand down his tired features. "I forgot to tell you, but the first night Regan and her cousin were visiting your club she had an encounter with him outside."

"Fuckin' hell! Why didn't you tell me, Daniel?" snarled Rhain angrily, and rightfully so. *"You know that bastard isn't allowed near my club! You should've told me right then and there so I could have personally seen his ass kicked across London!"*

"I know...."

"Like hell you do!"

Daniel heard the malice within his twin's voice and instantly regretted whatever reason he had for not telling Rhain sooner. He thought that he had handled the incident but now, as he thought upon the current situation, he realized that if he had told Rhain about David's encounter with Regan then Joyce's disappearance may not have occurred.

"I'm sorry," he said softly in apology to Rhain.

"David's not allowed on my property. You know that. By law you had to report the incident to me, Daniel. Fuck, you know that!" Before his twin could reply Rhain snapped, *"You couldn't help playing the gallant knight, could you?"*

"David was hurting her, Rhain. I had to step in and diffuse the situation before she was seriously injured. I was already leaving anyway, so I saw no harm in doing so considering none of the staff heard the commotion."

Rhain grunted.

"I simply forgot..."

Rhain cursed under his breath. *"Did he hurt her? I have to report it if he did."*

"A simple bruise, that is all."

"And now David returned and took her cousin."

"No need to remind me of that fact," snarled Daniel through clenched teeth. "I didn't think the prick would come back and do something like this. I only saw a young woman in trouble and offered my assistance when I noticed her assailant was David. I reminded him that he was not to be upon the property and ordered him directly off, which he did obey and departed. If I had known..."

Rhain sighed heavily on the other end of the phone as if he could feel the weight of his twin's guilt. *"You did the right thing, Daniel,"* he stated softly with means to calm his brother's building anxiety and regret. *"I can't fault you for that."*

"No, I guess you can't, but Regan sure can when, and if, she discovers that my actions may have caused her cousin to go missing."

"In the end, it is David who will be held accountable for his actions. He returned to my club after countless warnings and an order from the Concilium. He made the choice to ignore all that and my threats to gut him whole, so now he has to deal with the consequences."

Rhain went on to ask, *"Did you tell her about David?"*

"Of course not."

"Good. Now we wait till either Joyce shows herself or she doesn't - as long as Regan doesn't panic and call the cops."

"She won't."

"How do you know? She's human, and humans run on instinct and bloody emotions."

Daniel sighed as he felt a twist of sickness in his stomach. "I used the vocal Coercére on her and urged her to rest for the evening. She will forget her worries for the rest of the night and sleep."

"Wait..." There was disbelief in Rhain Thorn's voice. *"Did you just say what I think you said? Daniel Thorn used his influence on a human?"*

"I had no choice. She was sobbing. I only wanted her to have a moment's peace."

"You're too soft hearted."

"I would rather be soft hearted than cold hearted."

"It'll be your downfall one day, my brother," Rhain whispered.

"That may be so, but not tonight."

"Look, Solis Ortus will be upon us soon. I have a club to start closing up, but I'll let Mark and Cultor know what's going on. They'll keep an eye out for Joyce."

Daniel nodded. "I'll see you when you return home."

"Sure."

"And Rhain?"

"Yes?"

"Thank you, Frater."

"For you, my brother, anything."

~ ~ ~ ~

What happened?

Horrendous, throbbing pain drilled deep within Joyce's skull. Her head hurt and her body ached. She came to with a thick sense of dizziness swimming throughout her head. The last thing she remembered was a face, then pain and darkness. She moaned, lifting her head only to wince as her neck screamed in agony.

The room she was in twisted and turned with the caress of wicked vertigo as she drew open her eyes. It took a few seconds for her to gain her vision, but when she did, she frowned. Bright lights scorched Joyce's eyes causing her to blink violently. As the room became clearer, Joyce noticed a large chair behind a massive wooden desk. The back was to her and it was slowly swiveling, grinding with each twist. Her body weaved suddenly, and groaning, she fell back upon the couch with a puff of dust and dirt blooming about her.

"I wouldn' move just ye', puppe'. Ya took a nasty bump ta tha head."

"Da - David? What happened?"

The chair turned about and there he was, sitting with his body slightly scrunched down, legs parted, and fingers drumming upon the arms of the chair. David took a breath then tipped his head while watching Joyce with a sly grin upon his lips.

103

"Tha funniest thing," he began to say. "Ya got ou' o' yer room an' ran inta my associate, Cecil. He tells me tha' ya were snooping ou' side my office. Is tha' true?"

Joyce, pressing a hand to her forehead, looked towards him with a confused scowl. "I can't remember."

David faked a concerned wince. "I guess he hit ya too hard."

The chair groaned as he stood to cross the office to her side. His touch wasn't too gentle when he reached out, gripping her chin, to turn her face to the side. Yep, there was a lovely and solid bruise forming on the right side of her temple. Cecil didn't have to strike her for good measure. Then again, the man couldn't help himself. That's why David kept him around, hired muscle at its best.

Joyce sucked in a hiss when David touched her sore temple. She glanced to him. "I'm so confused," she whispered painfully. "How did I get here? We were at my flat..."

The man gave a sarcastic shrug of his shoulders. "I was leaving, bu' then I decided tha' ya could come with me. So here ya are!" He spread his arms out to the old and dilapidated office, paint chipping from cracked walls, boarded up windows, and crumbling office furniture covered in dust and grime.

Joyce looked around, clutching the blanket about her. "Where exactly is here?"

"Odd place this place," David chuckled as he pushed from the sofa to walk about the room as if he was examining the purchase of a fine home. "A long time ago I was ou' fer a walk an' came across this abandoned factory. A lo' o' this place was destroyed during tha war. No' many people know o' i' anymore."

Shivering, Joyce wrapped her arms about herself. "Why'd you bring me here?"

"Seemed like a good idea a' tha time."

"You could've just asked me, you know."

David snorted with a roll of his eyes. "Where's tha fun in tha'?" He came to lean against the desk, crossing his feet while his hands went behind him to tap upon the old wood. "Bu' while yer here I have a proposition fer ya, Joyce."

Another cold and hard shiver dragged down Joyce's spine when she fell beneath his intense and unstable gaze. She pressed back to the couch with her legs pulled up close to her chest, wrapped securely within her arms. "Proposition?"

"Ya see, my boss has a slight issue with Daniel Thorn, an' from wha' I gather, yer no' keen on him either. I bet yer cousin's still fuck'n him. Don't tha' just piss ya off?"

Joyce narrowed her eyes.

"Any way," he laughed, waving away her glare. "How'd ya like ta help me break those two up before they ge' too attached ta each other?"

"Why would I want to do that?" Joyce shook her head, scooting to the far end of the old couch. "Look, I was upset and jealous okay? I'd never do anything to purposefully hurt Regan. She's my cousin, and we've been friends since we were kids."

David frowned and his broad shoulders slumped. "Oh, there is tha', huh? Damn human emotions an' crap."

"I think I should leave."

David narrowed his eyes as Joyce began to move from the sofa. In a flash of movement he was at her side, leaning close till their noses almost touched. The grin he had upon his chiseled features set her back with a squeak. "No' ye', puppe'. Hear me ou'."

Joyce yelped in shock. How could he move so damn fast? She hadn't even stood up when he was at her side, pushing her back with his mere presence. Her body broke out in goose-bumps that spread rapidly along her cold, shivering flesh. She swore she felt an intense sensation of danger seeping out from him directly into her soul. She wanted away from him.

"Please, David, just let me go home, alright? I won't tell anybody about what you've done."

He bobbed his head with his features twisting in thought. "I can' do tha'." Chuckling, he sat beside her and put a muscular arm around her shoulders, yanking her against his side as he crossed one leg over the other. "Yer cousin's really important ta ya. I ge' tha'. We all need somebody close ta us, but ya see, Regan's in danger."

Joyce's eyes snapped wide. "Regan's in danger?"

"Oh, yes, she is."

"She's with Daniel Thorn. I don't think anything is going to happen to her."

"Bu' tha's tha thing." David shook his head, giving a 'tsk'. "Daniel Thorn isn' who he seems ta be. He's like his brother, Rhain; two bastards se' on fuck'n around wit' desperate girls. They're players. They toss one girl ta tha next wit' ou' a care. I've seen how they treat young woman who they mark a' their club."

"What do you mean, mark?"

David shrugged. He tapped his fingers to Joyce's shoulder enjoying the way she flinched to each hard tap. "They find a reason ta give a gift ta tha girl they want. One will give i' an' tha other will move in ta sweep her off her feet. Such a sad game they play, an' a dangerous one."

Joyce frowned in a moment of thought before her eyes snapped open. "Oh, God. The other night, when I took Regan to the club for her birthday, the bar tender gave her a necklace from Rhain. She met Daniel after that."

There - perfect. Yeah, David remembered seeing that damn necklace about Regan's neck. "I've seen a lo' of girls wearing tha' same necklace."

"I don't understand. From what Regan told me, Daniel was very polite and nice to her. He took her out to buy a dress for some fancy art event that they went to earlier tonight. He has spent hundreds of pounds on a dress. Why would he do all that and go through so much trouble if he's just going to use her and then toss her?"

The Lamia gave a shrug and whistled out a deep breath. "How should I know? Tha' might be his game. He's a sly one an' comes off as being such a sweet guy. Makes me sick."

"I can't believe this," sighed Joyce, shaking her head. David's words, when compared to what Regan had told her, were very confusing and contradicting.

"Neither ya or yer cousin know tha real Daniel."

"I don't know you either," she muttered, casting him a glare. "How do I know what you're saying's true? You did kidnap me."

David laughed and raised a finger. "Good point. Yer righ'. Ya don' know me a' all really, an' I did kidnap you. But! Tha point is, I've known Daniel fer a long time, girl. I know wha' he's capable of. I know wha' might happen ta Regan."

"Then I'll call the police."

David shook his head. "Like they give a damn. Daniel an' his family are one o' tha wealthiest families in London. They 'ave connections left an' right. They're untouchable."

"Then I'll go home and ask Regan. She'll tell me the truth."

David shrugged. "Ya could do tha', but i' might be too late."

"Then what do I do? I don't know where she is. I don't know where Daniel lives, nor do I know his phone number!"

David shifted upon the couch. There was a soft, almost sympathetic smile upon his lips. He reached over to touch her cheek with cool fingertips. "Don' worry yerself. I don' want ta see anythin' happen ta yer cousin. I've seen enough o' tha damage Daniel an' Rhain Thorn cause."

"Why are you willing to help me?" She shifted away when his overly cool and unnatural touch grazed her jaw.

David offered a blood chilling smile as he crooked a finger towards her. "Come closer an' I'll tell ya a secret."

Joyce gulped. "A secret?"

He nodded, and his grin darkened. "Yea," he whispered, his breath spilling against Joyce's neck in a cool swirl. This time, when she flinched, he tightened his grip upon her shoulder, locking her in place. He wouldn't let her get away. "Will ya listen ta my secret, Joyce?" he inquired softly, his voice barely a whisper.

Joyce shivered a shiver brought on not just by the coolness of his breath but the danger lacing his words. "I don't know."

"Listen ta me," he purred once again as his lips brushed along her neck as his fingers gently guided her features to him, 'and listen ta my voice."

She heard his voice, a melodic caress of deep vibrations that tickled her mind. She felt her skin go hot and her muscles go weak. 'Listen' - she heard the word repeated within her mind even though David didn't speak. 'Listen' - the word repeated once more, and Joyce swore she could feel his voice caressing her soul. A shuddering groan pooled against her lips when she felt his fingers draw away the blanket to expose a naked breast to his desires.

"Listen ta me."

There again came his melodic and musical whisper, slipping sensually through her mind. His touch caressed her breast, teasing the nipple with his roughened palm. Joyce whimpered and her body shifted upon the sofa desiring more of his touch. When his mouth settled upon hers, kissing her softly - hotly - she moaned and her mind tumbled into a pool of swirling darkness. The only sound that came from her was a gurgled mumble. Her eyes glazed over, hooded by drawn lids, as her vision began to blur.

When David drew back, his smile turned cold and cruel when he saw the irises of her eyes nothing more than a black speck. Good - very good. She was fully under his influence when David felt her last barrier break. "Good girl," he whispered as he bent his head to kiss her lips. "Welcome to my world, Joyce."

Joyce couldn't think. She couldn't move.

No scream came from her, no cry of fear or panic, when she saw him change through the cloudiness of her eyes. She saw his smile turn to ice, and in the next second his face was shadowed like a Demon. His mouth parted wide to expose long, sharp fangs - tipped red. His eyes flashed with a shine of metallic silver, and in a heartbeat, he was upon her, gripping her and pulling her up to him. He dug a hand into her hair, yanking her head to the side, and still she couldn't respond - couldn't move - couldn't scream. Not even when his teeth tore at the soft flesh of her neck did Joyce utter a sound.

Like a lion on a kill, David pressed himself across her body till something within her pliable, mortal frame snapped.

Pain lanced through Joyce when sharp needles pierced her neck. Something, wet and hot, began to trickle down her neck and from around David's parted jaws. Her body jerked, a reaction of pain surging through her muscles. She couldn't breathe! Her lungs tightened beneath the panic that slammed against her heart in wild fear.

Terror gripped Joyce. Then suddenly her body was released from the paralyzing hold and she arched violently off the couch - shaking and seizing. She tried to scream but when she opened her mouth only a watery sound tumbled forth along with a stream of blackening blood. She could taste her blood as it filled her throat, searing her insides as agonizing pain exploded throughout her. Every nerve and every synapse was on fire, over loaded with paralyzing torture.

David drank, and drank, and drank Joyce's sweet blood that flowed so readily through her thinning veins. Like a drug, her blood seeped through him, igniting his wretched soul.

The creation of a Lamia was a delicate event and often, in these modern days, performed under the observation of Lamia medical personal so to ensure that the human going through the Creation had as much of a chance to survive as possible. However, even under such precautions and critical observations a human had a fifty percent chance of survival. But outside the reach of medical care, the survival of the individual could plummet drastically.

When he heard the delicate beating of Joyce's heart slow, David eased the manic pressure of his feeding. The end of the Creare had to be precise. If he stopped too early, Joyce would die. If he continued to feed, draining the last bit of her blood, she would die. There was a very narrow window for the Creare to take hold and for the genetic trait to activate. As the sweetness of her blood turned sour, David drew away from her neck.

Joyce's eyes had turned glassy, staring to the ceiling in a twisted look of surprise and horror, and her body went limp against the couch. Her warm skin turned cold and pale. Death hung close to her, lulling her into its embrace, but not yet, David wouldn't allow death to take her just yet. He felt her pulse within her neck, his fingers slicking over the trail of blood that wept from the holes in her neck. Beat after beat slowed within Joyce's chest till the last pump of her heart pushed against his fingers.

Joyce was dead.

Sweeping back her hair, David tipped her head back and gently parted her mouth. He then raised his right wrist and sliced a deep, narrow line with a fang. Blood, thick and black, began to well out of the wound, spilling free as David held his torn wrist over her mouth to allow drop after thick drop to drip into her throat. Even if she couldn't drink his Sanguis, the blood would slide down her throat and seep throughout her body seeking out her Proprietas to trigger the Key to her awakening. When he figured he had given her all of the blood she would need, David licked his wrist.

The Lamia glanced to his watch then back to Joyce as he stood from the couch, dragging his shirt sleeve over his mouth to wipe away the blood stain that painted his lips. All that was required now was time. How much time was needed was up to Joyce and her body.

Secure in his belief that Joyce would turn, David barked out, "Cecil! Ge' in here!"

The door to the office groaned opened and the Lamia who had caught Joyce out in the hall entered with his nostrils flaring to the heavy stench of death that hung upon the musty air. "Is she dead?" he asked in a voice that held not an ounce of concern.

David flashed his friend a proud smile. "Depends on which 'dead' yer thinkin' o'. Bu' yea,' he purred, sliding his gaze over Joyce's blood coated body, 'she's dead."

Cecil stepped across the room to inspect the woman. He glanced to his 'friend'. "Did the Creare take?"

"We'll find ou' soon enough."

"What do you want to do with her now?"

"First, I need ta ge' this girl lookin' presentable." David turned to his desk where he jotted down an address upon a piece of paper that he then handed to Cecil. "When I'm done, take her ta this address."

Cecil took the paper. "Why?"

"Entertainment my friend!" laughed the Lamia with a devious glint to his eyes. He pointed a finger to Cecil. "Her place is on tha second floor on tha North side o' tha building. Ge' her back inta her bedroom through tha window I left I' unlocked. Do no' be seen or heard, understand?"

Cecil nodded and folded the piece of paper that he tucked into the back pocket of his jeans. "Sure."

David stepped back to Joyce. He released a sigh as he bent to gently kiss her forehead then closed her eyes. "If she comes back ta life, she'll come back ta me."

He turned from her as Cecil moved to pick her up. "Be gentle with her."

VII

This world is a very frightening place. It always has been; it always will be. The monsters that live amongst the shadows, human and supernatural alike, will never allow peace and serenity to take hold. Those of us who want nothing more than a calm existence will be sorely displeased when the truth of life's dark lies come crashing down upon us.

Rhain has a saying that is profoundly useful - shit happens. And it does, in the crudest of ways.

I know David has taken Joyce due to my actions, my interference in his nightly play. He is a Proscriptus, after all. Everything he does is to cause suffering to others. But why must an innocent suffer? Why must Regan suffer? Joyce made her bed, and her bedfellow was David. That cannot be changed. But the fact still remains that Regan's heart is pouring tears of anguish and self-induced guilt.

Who will dry her tears? Who will comfort her? And who will tell her that everything...will not be alright? Joyce will not return. The moment she said her first word to David was the moment her fate was sealed.

-     *Daniel Rhys Thorn.*

~ ~ ~ ~

Hours passed so very slowly while the night continued to grow darker with every passing minute. Regan had taken Daniel's advice to soak in a hot bath, a few lavender bath salts added for soothing comfort, and once out of the bath she dried herself then dressed in a pair of flannel pajamas dotted with colorful smiley faces. Her mind was slowly turning to slumber with Daniel's suggestive words caressing her subconscious, pushing her to sleep. That's when she heard, or thought she heard, the sound of a window slamming shut.

"Joyce?" Regan called, stepping out into the hall and to her cousin's bedroom. "Are you in there?" She gently knocked on the door.

She heard no sound from inside the room and no response to her knocking or calling. Ever so slowly, Regan opened the door, inching it open so the light from the hall could illuminate the darkness within. When the door opened fully, Regan's heart smashed against her chest. She saw Joyce lying face down on the bed with her hair strewn about her.

"Joyce!" she exclaimed, rushing to the bedside and nearly falling atop her cousin in sheer relief and joy. "Where have you been? It's almost three in the morning. I've been so worried about you!"

Regan huffed when her cousin remained silent. Rolling her eyes, she sat to the bedside to scold Joyce. "Don't tell me you've already passed out. Come on, wake up and let me know you're alright." She grinned playfully, poking her cousin on the shoulder. "I'm not mad at you. I was just very worried about you."

When her cousin still didn't answer, Regan frowned and pressed a hand to Joyce's shoulder to give a little shove. "Joyce?"

Nothing.

Panic swelled within her chest when she touched Joyce's arm to find her damp as if she had been out in the rain. She was cold - so cold.

"Hun, you're freezing. Here, you need to warm up or you will catch a cold." She drew the heavy comforter over her cousin's body, and as she did so a sickening sensation of unease began to twist in her gut as she stared down to her cousin. This wasn't right, Joyce being so quiet - so still. Gently, Regan brushed aside her cousin's hair. "I hope you're not sick, Joyce. Come on,' she pleaded, giving Joyce another rough push, 'wake up damn it. Don't make me dump water on you."

Regan frowned, bending down to peek at Joyce's face. Her cousin's eyes were tightly shut and lips parted with a faint wheeze and gurgle sound pushing from her throat. Every dangerous situation began to swirl through Regan's mind, fueled by her panic stricken imagination. Joyce could be sick, she could have alcohol poisoning, or some bastard could've drugged her…or worse!

As Regan went to move off the bed, a lock of Joyce's hair fell from her neck exposing the horrific fact of her condition. What she saw curdled her blood. There upon Joyce's flesh were two pink marks perfectly placed next to each other. The marks were faint but obviously fresh, swollen and irritated.

"What in hell," she muttered, leaning in close to examine the marks.

What she saw reminded her of insect bites - spider bites. How strange. Fearing that Joyce had been assaulted, she pulled back the blanket to look at Joyce's clothing. The corset she was wearing was on backwards and not even laced correctly, her skirt looked as if it had been put on in a rush, and she was missing any shoes. Regan's breath caught in her throat when she saw red ridges zigzagging beneath the loose ties of the corset, and decorating Joyce's arms were dark bruises. Terror swelled within Regan's body sending goosebumps to erupt along her flesh.

"What happened to you?"

Joyce moaned a wet and gurgled moan, "Da…vid…"

David? Regan knew that name! But could it be the same David she had the conflict with outside of the club? Without thinking, and acting only on pure dread, Regan flew from the bed and back to her room. She could hardly function, she was so terrified! Her hands were shaking uncontrollably as she fumbled for her mobile so she could call the first person that came to her.

Daniel!

When finally Regan was able to operate her incompetent 'smart phone', she glanced back across the hall to make sure Joyce was where she had been left, on the bed…face down. "Please answer," she whimpered. When the call was picked up, she yelped frantically, "Daniel!"

110

In the privacy of his bedroom, Daniel had just stepped out of the shower when his phone began to ring, sounding Moonlight Sonata softly from a bedside table. He dropped the towel he was using to dry his hair into a chair as he sat to the bed to answer the call, but before he could speak a polite greeting, his name was howled out with such a ferocity that the Lamia pulled the phone away from his ear.

"Regan?" he asked, recognizing the voice through trembling tones.

"Oh, thank Heaven you answered! Something's wrong, Daniel, really wrong." Regan whimpered through sobs that were already bubbling past her lips.

"What are you doing up? You should be sleeping," he said in slight disbelief. It was a rare occurrence when a mortal could draw themselves from an induced Coercêre.

"I was about to get to bed after a hot bath but then I thought I heard somebody in the apartment."

Daniel frowned. "What do you mean?"

"It's Joyce," she blubbered on the other end of the phone line. *"I thought I heard a window closing, so I went to check her room and she's there! She's on the bed..."* And then her words failed her as panic filled breaths took away her ability to speak.

"Breathe, sweetheart, breathe."

On the other end of the phone Regan sounded as if she was gasping for air with quick, sharp breaths. After a few seconds, she continued on to say, *"Joyce must've come in when I was bathing. One minute she wasn't here, then the next she was. Daniel, something's wrong with her."*

"Explain."

"I thought she had passed out but,' she paused, sucking in a sharp hiccup, *'something's wrong with her. I know it. There are marks all over her, her clothes are all in disarray, and..."* She whimpered with trepidation echoing in her shaking voice. *"I think she was assaulted. There's bruises, like handprints, on her arms. Should I call the police?"*

Only one word registered in Daniel's mind and it send cold spikes to rake down his spine. "Marks? What type of marks?"

"There are scratches all over her as if something clawed her, an animal or maybe branches. I think she was bitten by something."

"Bitten?" Daniel's heart fell into his stomach.

"Yes, there are two marks on her neck. Oh, Daniel,' Regan cried out over the phone, *'what if the guy she was with drugged her? What if she's been raped?"*

Daniel certainly didn't like the direction of this conversation, especially knowing the man Joyce left the club with. Knowing David, he probably fed from Joyce and took the Edĕre a little too far. Swallowing a thickening lump in his throat, Daniel asked quietly, "Can you describe what the marks look like?"

"Like bug bites," she answered shakily, her voice echoing her frustration through the phone. *"They're small and really close together on the side of her neck. I should call an ambulance. She looks really sick."*

111

"Calm down, sweetheart,' he cooed softly, 'keep breathing. You must stay calm. Now listen to me. I need you to trust me. Can you do that for me, Regan?"

"I...I think so," she stuttered through a hiccup.

"Go back into the room and take Joyce's pulse. I need you to tell me anything else you notice that's unusual about her."

"I don't want to..."

"Please, Regan,' he whispered in appeal to her, 'this is very important."

He needed her to go back into that room and tell him exactly of Joyce's condition. There were factors and conditions of the young woman's current status that would tell him what had happened to her. If Regan refused to go, he would have no other choice but to resort to using the Coercêre again. With the simple use of imposing his will upon her mind, Daniel could coerce her back into the room to answer his questions. But doing such again was already making the Lamia's heart ache with guilt from the first time he used that ability upon her.

"Alright..."

Daniel sighed in relief and hung his head causing a stray lock of black to tumble against his cheek. He brushed it aside with an irritated slap. As Regan was heard walking through the apartment, Daniel stood from the bed to dress. He could hear her labored breathing, laced with her fear, and also heard the sound of her apprehensive footsteps padding across carpet then wood then carpet again.

"Joyce? Hun? Can you wake up?" he heard her inquire then sigh softly. *"She's not responding to me, Daniel. Oh, God, she's so cold."*

Cold wasn't a good sign. At the mention of 'cold', Daniel froze. His chest felt tight while shuffling Regan's words about within his mind. "It's been raining," he heard himself mutter as if his voice made up the excuse before his mind could stop him.

"Then she's sick. She has to be." Regan's trembling voice gasped. *"She's making strange noises, Daniel - gurgling. I don't think she can breathe."*

"Feel for her pulse." He heard a rustle of fabric then a few seconds later a terror filled sob that sounded much like his name.

"I... I can't find her pulse!"

Daniel's lips pulled back in a low snarl. "Try her wrist, Regan."

"N...n...nothing. I'm not doing this right. I'm not a nurse!" Regan began to sob once again

"You're doing fine, sweetheart," he said softly to help ease her. With every panic filled cry from Regan, Daniel felt his heart twisting in knots.

Too many facts were adding up in all the wrong ways. Joyce was cold, pale, had been bitten, and now it was discovered that either her pulse was too low to be detected with a simple touch or it was almost nonexistent because it wasn't there.

"Is there anything else?" he asked with a very heavy exhalation.

112

"She mumbled a name. She said David. Daniel,' Regan breathed out into the phone, *'what if she met that guy that had bothered me at the club? What if he did something to her?"*

A low and very angry hiss slid from Daniel's tight throat. "Listen to me, Regan. You must promise to do exactly as I say."

"I think I need to call a doctor."

"No!" Daniel snapped then instantly regretted his harsh tone when he heard a squeak over the phone. "I'm sorry,' he apologized as he swept a hand through his hair, grumbling as his lean fingers snagged in a wet knot, 'I didn't mean to snap at you. No doctors."

"But..." stuttered Regan.

Daniel forced himself to calm, but doing so was so near impossible when his own worry continued building. "Regan, I will be right over."

There a tiny little whimper sounded over the phone followed by, *"Should I make her some tea, if she wakes up? She's cold. I don't want her to catch a chill."*

Daniel smiled to himself as he grabbed his car keys from off a table top. How could he say no to such an innocent request? If making Joyce some hot tea would keep Regan calm and focused while he made his way over to the flat, then so be it.

"Of course you can,' he told her as he finished dressing, swept his hair back from the collar of his shirt then proceeded to leave his room, but not before snatching his wallet from the dresser, 'but listen to me. This is important. After you make the tea, I want you to get out of the apartment. Take all the keys and lock the door behind you. Go to the front door of the building and wait for me. I am on my way. Do you understand? Do not go back into flat."

"I can't leave her alone," she said in protest.

Grumbling, he rushed through the condo but not before grabbing his discarded coat. "Please, do as I ask. Don't question me."

Regan whimpered, and that tear filled whimper fractured the last line of Daniel's heart. *"Fine. But you won't leave me, will you?"*

"Don't worry. I'll stay on the phone with you." He was in the elevator of the condo within a minute. "I'm on my way, sweetheart. Wait for me."

~ ~ ~ ~

Daniel quickly made his way from the condo down to the parking garage. He took to the streets in his Porsche 911 turbo, a beautiful and very expensive machine of black with pewter trim that purred to life with the push of a button. As he drove quickly, but carefully, through the twisting London streets, he listened to Regan crying after he turned the call from his mobile to the car's blue-tooth.

To his dismay, she still hadn't left the apartment.

"But why?" Regan inquired through a sob. *"Why do I have to leave her? I don't understand!"*

"Sweetheart,' he said with his calmness dissipating and while interrupting her blubbering and sniffling, 'if she was given some sort of drug, I do not want her waking up and, in some form of a drug induced state, attack you. I want you safe. How many times must I state that?"

That one lie left a rancid taste in Daniel's mouth and a twist of guilt curling within the pit of his stomach. He hated to lie for any reason, and found no honor in doing so. Even so, he had no choice if he wanted to keep Regan as safe as possible. In a way, he was lying to himself as well. Joyce was either dead or very close to it.

"I don't know," Regan whimpered with reservation in her voice. *"I'm so scared."*

"I know you are,' Daniel breathed out in sympathy to her fear, 'but you don't need to be. I'll be there soon."

"Please don't leave me," pleaded Regan through fresh tears that were laced with the soul wrenching sound of her sobs.

"I won't. Regan?"

After a sniffle and a hiccup, she answered, *"Yes?"*

"Trust in me, sweetheart. I won't let anything happen to you."

"Please hurry."

A soft beep sounded behind Regan's crying, and he cursed under his breath when he saw Rhain's name flashing as an incoming call. Damn it, the last person he wanted to speak to right now was his twin. Knowing Rhain, he wasn't going to stop calling till he got through. Then again, it could be that Rhain was calling with information.

"Regan, Rhain is calling through on the other line. He might have information for us. Can I put you…"

"No! Don't go!"

Again, Daniel's phone began to play. Rhain had hung up, but now Kain's number flashed. What was this? A family inquisition? If Rhain told Kain anything, there was going to be hell to pay. Daniel returned his thoughts to Regan with a grumbled sigh. "I'm not going anywhere. I need to answer this call - *and kill my brothers while I'm at it.* I swear to you, I won't hang up. I'm putting you right in the seat next to me. I'll be right back with you. Alright?"

"Alright…"

Daniel put Regan's call on hold, switching the call so he could answer Kain. "What is it?" he snapped while glaring daggers towards some punk who just ran across the street, narrowly missing the front of the car.

Kain's deep voice came through the call with a touch of concern. *"Where are you? Rhain's been trying to call you. Is everything alright?"*

"I am on my way to see Regan." He muttered under his breath a great dislike for stoplights when one turned red, forcing him to stop.

"You left her not too long ago."

"Yes, I realize that Kain. However, I think we may have a problem."

"What's wrong?" asked Kain, his voice dropping.

"While she and I were out this evening, her cousin Joyce went to the Crucible. Joyce was last seen leaving the property with the Proscriptus David Servilii."

114

There was a long pause on the other end of the phone, so Daniel proceeded with caution. "According to Regan, Joyce has just returned to the flat. She is unresponsive, cold, and pale." He took a dry breath then growled low, "She's been bitten, Kain."

"Get over there. Now."

"I'm half way there."

"Where's Regan? Is she still in the flat?"

"Of course not! I told her to lock the doors and meet me at the front of the building." Daniel turned the agile sports car down another street. He was trying not to speed, but was failing miserably. Time was clicking on by, and every second counted at this point.

"Call Rhain."

"Rhain is busy. I've asked him to investigate David's presence at the club and his involvement with Joyce. I'll be alright, assuming that Joyce has not been turned. If that's the case…"

"You'll have to deal with it - properly."

Daniel shivered to the veracity in his brother's statement. Kain was correct. If Joyce survives the Creare, then Daniel would have no choice but to confront her with the truth of her painful rebirth and the agonizing reality she had to face. Joyce would be given two choices, either leave the mortal world - willingly - and go with him to be assimilated into the Lamia world through the Domare as required by the Lex, or face the possibility of execution by order of the Concilium if she refused assimilation and threatened the sanctity of the Lamia in England.

"Be careful. If she has survived the Creare, her Parens may have followed her to the flat and may be watching her to see if the Creare has taken. If it hasn't…"

"Joyce will die in excruciating agony."

"And if she does change…"

Daniel's black eyes narrowed upon the street that wove before him. He hadn't thought that far. If Joyce survived the Creation, that would mean only one thing, she had the Proprietas. And if that becomes evident, then there could be a strong chance that Regan would also hold the gene.

"I will deal with Joyce," Daniel snarled with a slice of sharpness to his voice.

"Good."

"What about Regan, Kain? If Joyce has indeed survived the Creare…"

"You will bring Regan to the Domus, directly, so her blood can be tested. If she does have the gene, she is ours to protect."

"I understand."

"If you get any scent of David, grab Regan and get the hell out there. Do you understand me, Daniel? Do not get involved with him. He is far past your skill level."

Daniel snarled and his fingers tightened about the steering wheel till his knuckles turned white. "I'll do what I must, Kain," he bit out as he guided his car around another corner and down another street. Regan's building was just a block away. "I've got to go."

"Be safe, both of you. Ave, little brother."

"Ave."

"Daniel? Are you still there?"

Hearing Regan's shaky voice come back on the line once Kain's call had ended drew Daniel's attention away from the conversation with Kain and back to her. "I'm here. Are you outside the apartment?"

"Yes. Are you close?"

"I'm here."

Daniel pulled his car up to the curb outside the building and was out of the car before the engine was silenced. He took one step then stopped to raise his eyes to the ominous surroundings. He could feel a menacing weight surrounding the structure with shadows wrapping hungrily about it. The Lamia tipped his head to the right then to the left, drawing in two deep breaths of polluted air. He could smell the heavy stench of death wafting from the building and scowled as his stomach lurched.

Taking another breath, he searched for David's scent and caught upon the death tainted air a whiff of an unknown Lamia. A vampire had been here, but too much time had passed for there to be any significant source of identification. Stuffing hands into his long coat, he headed towards the front door.

"Regan?" He knocked upon the distorted glass of the door.

A shadow popped up followed by the jingling of keys. She was so petrified that she kept dropping the keys. With a soft smile, he touched a hand to the glass. "Sweetheart, relax. Calm down and opened the door."

His voice soothed her, and finally, she was able to unlock the door. When the door flew open, clanking against the wall, Regan tumbled forwards with her arms wrapping about Daniel's thin shoulders. He pulled her into his embrace with fingers threading into her hair as she buried herself against him, crying and shaking like a leaf.

"It's alright. I'm here," whispered the Lamia as he nuzzled his cool cheek to her.

"I thought you would never show up," she murmured against his shoulder.

"Forgive me." Daniel offered her a bow of his head in apology and a comforting smile. He sighed, closing his eyes, as he tightened his embrace about her, and in return she hugged him fiercely. "I tried to get here as fast as I could." Tipping his head, he pressed a kiss against her soft hair and whispered, "I'm sorry for worrying you."

Past her sniffles, Regan raised her eyes when she felt the press of his lips and slowly released her grip upon the lapels of his fine coat.

He touched her cheek with the roughened pad of his thumb brushing along her wet skin that was red and sore from her salty, hot tears. Her eyes were bloodshot and her eyelids swollen. "Are you alright?"

"I think so. Joyce is still inside."

Daniel nodded with a glance to the stairs. He then turned Regan about, giving her a little push towards his car. "I want you to go sit in my car. I'm going to check on your cousin."

Shock and fear swept over Regan's features and her eyes went wide as she gaped. "No! Don't leave me."

At first a scowl touched his handsome mouth, but then it curled into a deep frown as the Lamia shook his head sending his long hair to skim across his back. "I want you to go sit in the car and wait for me. You'll be safe there."

"Are you kidding?" she snapped angrily. "The bastard who hurt Joyce could come back! I don't want to be in a car alone!"

"The doors will lock, Regan," he hissed with growing agitation. Having a mortal arguing with him never did settle well with his Lamia blood. Lamia had a naturally short fuse when it came to the unstable rational and argumentative tendencies of mortals, ironic considering his own kind had even shorter fuses.

"I don't give a damn if the doors can lock!" Regan pointed about him to the open door of the building. "I want to be with my cousin!"

Really? She was going to start a debate now, at this time of night and in the street no less? The Lamia's lips pulled back with a low and threatening snarl. "Enough!" he barked. "I don't know how dire Joyce's predicament is, and I don't want you to get hurt! We do not have time to argue this."

"Then call a damn ambulance! What's wrong with you? She could be dying and you're not doing a damn thing to help her!"

Regan was wrong. One way or another Daniel was going to help Joyce. He had a duty to perform, a duty he would perform. Then again, she made a solid point. There was the unknown Lamia scent Daniel had picked up, thin as it was. He couldn't leave Regan in the car, not knowing who was in the shadows - waiting. Perhaps keeping Regan with him was the safest course of action even though her presence would make dealing with Joyce more difficult.

He narrowed his eyes to her as he cupped her tear stained face in his hands. "Very well, but you must obey me. When we get back to the apartment, I want you to go to your room and pack a bag. I don't want you anywhere near Joyce. Do you understand me?"

"No, I don't." Regan whined in confusion and her features twisted with brows knitting together.

"Trust me and do as I say." He pressed a kiss to her forehead then took her hand to lead her back up the stairs. "You're going to be staying with me till we figure out what is going on."

"Stay with you? I want to stay with Joyce!"

"Regan, I'm thinking of your safety here," snapped the Lamia with a glare back to her as they went up the stairs. He could feel her gentle tugs of protest upon his hand, yet the moves only caused his fingers to tighten their grip.

"She needs a hospital."

"She will get her care, but you can't stay at the hospital by yourself. Bloody hell, I'm not going to let you stay here by yourself. I want you with me so I can keep you safe."

117

"Keep me safe?" Regan yelped as she stumbled over a few steps. Daniel was nearly running up the stairs making it hard for her to keep up. "You're scaring me, Daniel. You're acting as if I'm the one in danger when it's Joyce who has been attacked!"

What the hell was he to say to that true statement? Joyce had been attacked. No, she had been more than attacked. But he couldn't come right out and tell Regan that, now could he? *'Yes, Regan, your cousin was attacked. But worse, she was fed upon by a Lamia. You know, a vampire? And now I'm worried that David, because he is one of the most sadistic Lamia in London, might come back and do to you what he did to your cousin. So why don't you silence yourself and let me handle this situation so I don't find you dead on a bed?'*

No, that wouldn't help the situation at all. Explaining any of this to Regan, in any detail, would expose his world to her. If he did that without permission from the Rex or the Concilium, it would be his head rolling on the floor.

Daniel reached for the key when they came to the apartment. "She will be taken care of. The key, if you would."

Sighing in heavy agitation, Regan handed over the apartment key. "Joyce's room is down the hall on the right, across from the bathroom."

The instant the apartment door opened he was met with a heavy, decayed scent. Death hung in the air and the smell filled his lungs till he had to cough behind a hand. He scanned the sitting room with his keen sight and listened to every faint sound that his ardent ears could pick up.

Entering first, Daniel kept Regan close to him, urging her forwards so he could shut the door. "Go on,' he told her, guiding her towards the hallway with a gentle press upon her back, 'I won't be long. Pack only what you need right now."

Regan didn't want to leave the safety and security of his side. She wanted to see what was wrong with her cousin, but Daniel would have none of it. He gave her another gentle push towards the hall. Passing by Joyce's room, she stopped with a soft cry tugging her lips, but Daniel gave her a shove.

Daniel knew when he stepped into the bedroom that the young woman upon the bed was no longer alive. Whatever pulse Regan had felt no longer thumped within Joyce's veins. The stench in the air was so overwhelming that it turned his stomach and made him gag. Moving cautiously, he went to the bedside looking with pity to the young woman who lay face down with her legs bent at an awkward angle and her arms thrown out as if her body had been carelessly tossed. The girl's eyes were wide open, glazed over and pale. Daniel brushed back a lock of her hair at her neck and saw the 'bites' that Regan had described. They weren't even close to being insect bites. No, they were most definitely punctures caused by Lamia fangs.

Joyce was pale, so very pale, and her skin was cold and hard to the touch. Daniel couldn't find a pulse when he tried to tune his senses to find any sound of a heartbeat. There was none. Joyce's heart had fallen still. Whatever feeding had taken place earned Joyce an early and horrific death.

118

No innocent life deserved this type of death, especially after sex. And Daniel could tell that Joyce had been intimate this night. He couldn't ignore the tainted scent of sweat and sex that clung to her. A disgusted curl of his lips exposed his fangs and a low snarl pushed past his clenched jaws when his mind registered David's scent mixed with the caress of sexual release.

Daniel stepped back from the bed, frowning with sympathy to the waste of life tossed aside and left without a care to rot. David must have drained Joyce to the very last drop of her blood. Daniel hoped Joyce had not suffered and was at least granted a quick death, but something in his gut told him that David wasn't so nice. The Proscriptus bled the woman dry for the sheer and sick enjoyment of it. Such an act was known as Homini Senquienem Mittĕre, the act of bleeding a human or Lamia dry of their Sanguis for the simple pleasure of doing so. The act was considered socially unacceptable within proper Lamia society and only recently had been made illegal in many Republica.

With a grumbled sigh, Daniel dug his mobile from his pocket to call Kain.

"Yes?"

"I found Joyce." Daniel's heart felt heavy as he walked to the window so he could scan the surrounding buildings; he saw nothing. "She's dead."

"I see. Can you determine any factors to the cause of her death?"

"She's been drained, that's for sure."

"How long has she been dead?"

"I'm not sure at this point. I haven't been able to examine her body, not with Regan hanging close by." Daniel sighed heavily. "My guess? She's been dead only a short while. Regan told me, not but an hour ago, that she was able to find a thin pulse."

Kain cursed on the other end of the call.

"The question remains, how did Joyce get back if she was on the verge of death?"

"There's no way,' Kain answered, *'she had to have had help."*

"That would explain the Lamia scent I caught lingering outside. Somebody brought her back."

"Was it David?"

"No. I don't know who it was."

"What about Regan? Does she know about her cousin?"

"Not yet," Daniel breathed out with a twitch of pain lacerating his slow heart. "I wasn't sure what was going on with Joyce, so I instructed Regan to pack a bag. What are we going to do with her cousin? I can't leave Joyce like this. If Regan finds out that I abandoned Joyce…"

"No,' Kain agreed with a touch of sadness to his voice, *'Joyce is human. She deserves some dignity in her death. After all, it was one of our kind that did this to her."*

"Regan's safety is priority at this point," Kain went on to tell his younger sibling. *"See her safely to the Domus and give Rhain a call. The two of you can figure out a way to handle Joyce properly, respectfully, without upsetting Regan. We need her calm and thinking rationally. The less chance of police involvement in this matter the better."*

"I understand, Frater."

"Are there any signs of the Creare?"

"Not yet."

Kain paused with a dry sigh. *"Have Rhain run a full check on her."*

"I will. I need to see to Regan. We shall return soon."

Without a goodbye to Kain, Daniel closed the call. He then made a quick call to his twin. Rhain was still in his office doing research, contacting his personal contacts, and speaking to his Lamia staff on any and all information he could gather on David. According to Rhain, over the past three years David had disappeared off the Lamia map, showing his face here and there before vanishing into the Underground. The news wasn't exactly what Daniel had hoped for. After thanking his twin whole heartedly for all his aid, Daniel had to inform Rhain of Joyce's situation. When his twin heard about her demise, he wasn't thrilled.

All Rhain said in reply to the news was, *'I'm on my way.'*

Once the call ended, Daniel strode from the room. He found Regan in the other bedroom sitting on the edge of the bed with her head bowed and a photo held within her shaking hands. From where he stood at the doorway, Daniel could see the tears falling from her cheeks even though loose strands of her rosewood hair curtained her features. Seeing Regan shaking and hearing her hiccups echoed deep within his old soul.

Daniel's footsteps fell silent upon the carpet as he crossed the room to her side. He knelt down next to her, reaching up to touch her wet cheek. He tipped her head up so she would look at him, but even then her gaze appeared distant. "I've called an ambulance to take Joyce to the hospital. Rhain is on his way to meet them here."

Regan sniffled. Daniel's words didn't bring any comfort to her, not even a little smile. She only nodded. "How is she?"

"I'm not exactly sure."

"Then I'm staying till the ambulance gets here. I want to go with her to the hospital."

"Regan,' the Lamia said softly as he moved to sit at her side, 'I'm not going to argue with you. My priority is your safety, and I don't want you here in case the one who did this horrific act upon your cousin returns."

Her eyes hardened as a growl slid across her thin pressed lips. "It was David, wasn't it? He did this to her."

"We can't make that assumption."

"I know he did this to her…"

"Which is why,' said the Lamia softly as he brushed fingers along her cheeks to dry away her tears, 'you and I are going to get your bag and go outside to wait for Rhain. Then we will head to my home while Rhain deals with the medics. He'll make sure Joyce is safe…and at rest."

"Do you think David raped her?"

"I cannot tell. I hope not. Let's leave the diagnosis of her condition to the doctors."

"I don't know what to do," Regan whimpered as a little sob caught in her throat. "I feel so helpless."

Daniel, with a heavy sigh, ran his fingers through her hair so he could lean her head to his shoulder. His eyes closed as her warm body rested against him, the contact instantly seeping through his hard exterior. It wasn't often that he truly found comfort from a human, let alone a human who needed him in such a troubling moment. Daniel had not felt 'needed' in a long time. However, right now, Regan was desperate for his support, his comfort, and his strength, but most importantly, whatever bit of humanity he still had within him.

She needed him.

"You're not helpless. There's just nothing you can do for Joyce currently," he said softly as he pressed a kiss to her soft crown then guided her to stand along with him. "Come along. Let's get your things and go meet Rhain. Then we'll head to my home and get you settled for the night. You can take a hot bath and relax."

Regan was trembling, and her features were shadowed in worried exhaustion as the shock of Joyce's situation finally took hold of her in a grip that was relentless in its release.

The poor thing was too tired and too emotionally empty to answer him. Daniel left her side to grab a coat he saw hung on the doorknob, draped it over her shoulders then took the bag she had packed. With his arm about her, he walked her from the apartment leaving Joyce's corpse behind.

Regan found herself walking down the stairs with her body supported and leaning heavily against Daniel as he took each step carefully along with her. He never left her side, and for that she was so very grateful. She didn't know what she would have done if he had not come to her aid. He didn't question her. He didn't ignore her. Instead, he had done all he could to help her, to comfort her and to help Joyce.

The outside air felt dull, cold and lifeless, against her skin. With Daniel at her side they walked across the wet, lightless pavement to the car where she stood vacant and empty as Daniel opened the passenger door to throw her overnight bag into the small car.

Daniel frowned when he stood back and turned to her. She looked detached, almost ill, and that wouldn't do, so he pulled her tightly into his embrace, and on instinct Regan turned into him, burring her face to his chest. She could hardly feel his hands caressing her numb body as she leaned limply against him. How he wished he could say something to her, but Daniel knew there were no words of comfort that could ease her and take away her pain. Over his long life he had learned one valuable lesson - words often held little meaning when a touch, a kiss, or an embrace could mean more.

So he tightened his arms about her, kissed the soft crown of hair atop her head, and let her cry out her pain.

That was all he could do.

~ ~ ~ ~

Rhain made good time racing from his club to meet his brother. His black and
metallic red Audi r8 turned down the final street with the blue LED headlights
dimming. The vehicle came to a purring stop across from Daniel's car, and as
Rhain exited the vehicle Daniel could feel Regan press herself against him.
Her body went tight, stiff.

"It's alright,' he said gently, soothingly to her, 'it's only Rhain. He
will not harm you."

She wasn't so sure. The man looked intimidating even from across
the street, and as he came closer, with his handsome features glowing in a draw
of his cigarette, Regan felt her heart wobble. Rhain's eyes were locked upon
her, burrowing past her skin with the unnatural blue of the contact lenses
illuminating his eyes.

So what if he was Daniel's twin? The intensity that emanated from
Rhain brought fear to wrap about her heart and the blood to run thin within her
veins. Where Daniel was clean cut and kind, Rhain was the complete opposite.
He was more punk than model with his black hair cut shorter and stained with
metallic-blue streaks, and the aura radiating from him was violent in nature -
dangerous. Tonight, his hair was swept over to the right to cover part of his
face, shadowing the emptiness that shown within his gaze.

"So,' Rhain mused in his smooth, accented voice with a puff of
tainted smoke blowing from his lips, 'this is her, huh? How'd you like the
necklace?"

"Not now, Rhain," Daniel muttered, glowering in annoyance to his
brother. Regan peeked over one of Daniel's arms as her fingers coiled into the
lapels of his coat.

Rhain brushed off his brother's glare. "Where is she?" he asked,
drawing in smoke as his eyes turned towards the apartment building.

"Flat C, second story." Daniel tossed the keys to him. "I've called
for the ambulance. It should be here soon."

Rhain gave his twin a sharp, curious arch of a brow. But when
Daniel turned his eyes down towards the shivering woman in his arms, Rhain
looked away. He didn't need an answer as to why his brother decided to lie flat
out. He really didn't give a shit either.

"Alright then,' he said, flicking the used smoke to the wet ground and
snuffing it out with the toe of his thick boot, 'I'll wait here for them
and...handle...the situation."

"Thank you. I'm taking Regan home."

Rhain gave an absent minded wave. "Whatever."

"Rhain?"

The Lamia paused at the entrance to the building when he heard his
name stuttered quietly from the mortal. He glanced over his shoulder.

"Please, take care of my cousin. I don't want her to die."

What little piece of Daniel's heart still remaining intact shattered upon hearing that pitiful beg from Regan. His arms tightened till he worried he would hurt her. Daniel glanced over the top of her head to look with sympathy to his twin before he turned Regan to the car.

'Shit...' Rhain sighed to himself knowing fully well that all that remained of her cousin was a cold body. He turned away, heading into the apartment and flinching as he swore a piece of his own heart cracked - just a little. Damn women and their tears. They were nothing but trouble, always.

Daniel did not waste much time getting Regan in the passenger seat of his car. Once she was buckled in and he was in his own seat, the car purred to life then moved gracefully in to motion. There was little over an hour, give or take a few minutes, till dawn and Daniel wanted to make sure that Regan was safe within the protective walls of the Thorn Domus as soon as possible.

During the drive, Regan sat pressed against the door and staring out at the passing world. She hadn't said a single word and Daniel had not seen her move, not even an inch. He was worried about her. Just before they drove into the underground garage of the building, Daniel's mobile rang.

"Yes?" He put his cell to his ear so that Regan wouldn't be able to hear his brother's words.

"You need your eyes checked, mate. I've looked all over this apartment. There's no corpse here. I even checked under the bed. Should I check the closet?"

Daniel's features dropped. He looked over to Regan with an attempt to keep the shock off his face. Luckily, she wasn't paying attention. "What do you mean?"

"She's not here. Well, more correctly, she was but not anymore."

"Impossible!" hissed Daniel, turning the wheel sharply.

Regan, at the snap from Daniel, glanced over to him.

"She's not here."

"Damn." Daniel sighed as he drove his Porsche into the secured section of the garage once they arrived back to Thorn Inc. "Look, Regan and I just got back. I need to get her settled. We'll talk more when you get back."

"Alright. I'm going to search some more, then I'll head back home. I'll meet with you and Kain later."

"Daniel? Is something wrong?"

What smile he was able to muster refused to stay upon his lips as he looked to Regan. "No, sweetheart." He looked away so he could park and secure his car. "Thanks, Rhain. I'll see you soon. Be careful." Not waiting for his brother to reply, Daniel closed the call then turned off the car.

He said softly, reaching over to unbuckle her seat belt, "Let's get you in and settled."

She replied with a little nod, and as she got out of the car, Daniel grabbed the bag from behind her seat then walked her through the fenced in section of the garage to an elevator that took them up through the floors of the tall building. They rode the elevator in silence with Regan standing against the back wall with her eyes turned to the floor. Daniel never left her side. He wanted to say something to her but couldn't form any words of comfort knowing that Joyce was now missing. Too many lies had come from him

123

already. He couldn't bring himself to fill Regan with any more lost hope than he already had done.

The guest flat Daniel unlocked looked as if it was more of a honeymoon suite at some fancy hotel in Paris. The apartment had a full kitchen with a dining room attached and a large sitting room with every fancy electronic device for entertainment Regan could possible need. Daniel showed her the bedroom off to the right and the full bath with a deep, free standing bathtub and glass encased shower.

As Daniel took her bag to the bedroom, Regan went about exploring the apartment. When he returned, she stood in the center of the sitting room, and with a sigh, she turned her empty and bloodshot eyes to him. They watched each other for a few seconds before Daniel walked to her so he could wrap his arms about her and draw her against him.

"I am so sorry," he whispered softly, kissing her hair.

Regan felt her body weaken the moment his arms were about her, so she grasped at his coat to keep herself standing. "I feel cold all the way to my bones."

Daniel gently rocked her within his arms as his hands stroked her back in an attempt to warm her. "Are you hungry? I can order some take-out for you."

"I'm not hungry,' Regan mumbled.

"How about a bath?"

Drawing back, she offered him a very faint smile. "Okay..."

Daniel pressed a kiss to her forehead then stepped away.

The bath was prepared for any individual to relax in, offering a selection of scented oils and bath salts. He selected a small bottle of chamomile bubble bath then began to fill the tub. When the bubbles were close to the thick edge of the deep tub and the scented steam filled Daniel's empty lungs, he called out, "It's ready!"

Soon after his call, Regan appeared in the doorway with her arms wrapped tightly about her. At this point, she didn't mind if Daniel saw her naked. She wanted in that tub of Heavenly scented bubbles. She walked to the tub as she began to unbutton the top of her pajamas.

Daniel blinked, realizing that she was ready to drop her shirt, but being the polite gentleman that his mother raised him to be, he stood while reaching out to stop her hands. "I'm going to leave you to your bath, alright? Rhain will be back soon and will want to speak to me. Will you be alright by yourself for a little while?"

"Please stay with me, Daniel," begged Regan, grasping his hands.

He could see a shadowed look of desperation and fear within her eyes. He offered her a smile and a touch to her cheek. "Very well, I'll stay till Rhain returns. Why don't I fix you some tea?" With a nod from Regan, he left her to bathe while he went into the kitchen.

He returned soon after with a cup of steaming mint tea to find Regan deep within the bubbles and hot water, and he smiled to the look of serene peace that was upon her tired features. "I've brought your tea." He stepped to the tub to place the mug to a small, glass top table at the side.

124

Regan's eyes slowly drew open, a drop of moisture clinging to the edge of a thick eyelash. "Thank you," she mewed ever so softly.

With a twist of her body, she shifted in the deep tub so she could lift the mug to her lips for a sip of the warm tea. The minty heat flooded through her body, drawing out a content and breathy mew. "This is wonderful."

"Are you sure you're not hungry?" he inquired from where he stood, a respectful foot or two back from the tub.

Regan nodded her head with her body leaning to the side of the tub. She curled her arms beneath her cheek then breathed a sigh full of confusion and disbelief. "I can't believe this has happened. I can't believe Joyce went back to that club by herself. Why would she leave with David?" She looked up to Daniel. "I thought he wasn't allowed in the club."

The Lamia closed the short distance to the tub, and without a care to his expensive clothing, knelt down before her. "I'm not sure why David was there,' he told her, covering her wet hands with his, 'but Rhain is doing all he can to answer that question for you."

"Do you think David found Joyce on purpose because of the incident the other night? Then again, Joyce has never had good luck with guys. She always picked the bad seed out of the apple. I told her, if she didn't watch herself, that something like this was going to happen to her one day." A little hitch of a whimper caught within Regan's throat. "I didn't want to be right,"

Daniel reached out and wound a wet lock of her hair about a finger. "Regan, what happened to Joyce was probably an accident. You cannot blame her."

Regan frowned and her eyes turned sad as a quiet whisper slipped from her lips. "I don't blame her. I blame myself."

The Lamia blinked and tipped his head. "Why would you blame yourself?"

"For a lot of reasons," she whispered, leaning to the touch that trailed along her cheek. "This all started with me when I bumped into David. He probably found out that Joyce is my cousin and wanted to get some revenge against me. He probably used her jealousy to take advantage of her emotions."

"Why would she feel jealous?"

Regan shrugged. "I don't know. She was so excited for me when I told her about you and our plans, but then today her mood changed. I know she was upset, perhaps a little depressed, and she started to distance herself from me. I thought that maybe I went a little overboard with my excitement and didn't pay attention to her feelings."

"Joyce had no right to get jealous or upset with you."

"It was more than that, Daniel. She was annoyed because I was getting attention from you. She probably felt that she deserved the same. After all,' Regan gave a timid little smile, 'she couldn't stop giggling about how you and your brother are on every teen heartthrob magazine this side of the world."

Daniel snorted. "So she felt jealous over the fact that you got what she had always dreamed of?" Cupping her cheek, he smiled softly to her. "I asked you to accompany me tonight, not her. Her jealousy was her own fault, and none of what has happened tonight is yours. Do you understand me?"

"I feel like I have ruined the beautiful evening we had. I'm sorry I've gotten you involved in this."

Daniel placed a finger to her lips to hush her thoughts. "You did not ruin anything. I will never forget the evening we shared. But most importantly, I'm glad you're not going through this alone. The thought of you sitting alone in some empty and foreign hospital with nobody at your side frightens me. I don't want you to be alone and upset."

The touch of his cool fingers, as they trailed along her cheek, sent waves of comfort through Regan. She had finally stopped shaking, but the deep feeling of remorse and guilt continued to eat away at her soul. Her eyes fluttered closed as she nodded to his words. There was no sense in continuing such a debate when all she could do was wait on word about her cousin.

"Daniel? Will you stay with me tonight? I don't want to be alone."

He wanted to. He wanted to crawl into the tub with her and hold her till she fell asleep in his arms, but he couldn't and for many reasons that Regan would never begin to understand. "I have to speak to my brothers first."

She nodded with a little curl of her lips in a frown. "I understand. You will come back, won't you?"

Slipping a finger beneath her chin, Daniel guided her closer to him. The bubbles sloshed over the edge of the tub to dampen his shirt and coat, but he didn't care. "As soon as I can." Dipping his head, he brushed his lips against hers in a delicate kiss.

Rocking back to stand, he reached down to brush fingers along her damp hair. "Try to rest, alright? I'll come and check on you later."

Regan nodded. "I'll try. Now that I know Joyce will be okay, I think I can sleep."

Daniel winced. Joyce was not going to be okay; there was no way around that hard and cold fact. The woman was dead, and it was his distorted words that lead Regan to think that all of this would turn out right in the end. Perhaps Rhain had been correct in saying that Daniel held too close his humanity, and in doing so would only lead to his demise. But Daniel couldn't release what little bit of his humanity he had left. He didn't want to lose himself to the full darkness that the Lamia world embraced.

He wasn't going to lose the last bit of his soul.

He couldn't lose himself.

VIII

Violence....

    How I detest the gruesome idea of harming an innocent. Ironic that such a thought can come from me considering all the blood that has stained my hands. I've killed many, but only those deserving of death. I've been ordered to take lives and to hunt those suspected of breaking the Lex and endangering those of my race. I come with a name attached to my shadow, a name that still holds weight among the masses - a name that once struck terror in those who walked outside the Lex.

    I still have nightmares of the brutal acts my hands have committed over the decades and the cruelty I have delivered onto my victims. I hear their screams echo within my mind, their begging and their crying. Some deserved their deaths while others simply wanted to be free from what they thought was an oppressive society bent upon controlling their every breath. Either way, they too broke the laws and had to be punished.

    There are times I believe that the ghosts of my victims haunt me. If they cannot be at peace in the afterlife, then why should I be at peace in my undead life? The question does hold some weight to it, doesn't it? I've always questioned myself whether or not I deserve happiness when I have taken happiness from others. Rhain has often chided me on how soft I am. He too stood by me, hunted with me, and killed with me - but he has never fallen prey to the remnants of ghosts and guilt. He holds his head high with pride on the title bestowed upon us and would willing take up the sword again if ordered.

    The only sword I wish to take up is the sword of protection, not of murder and cold terror.

    I will kill to protect those I love.

    I will kill.

-    *Daniel Rhys Thorn*

~ ~ ~ ~

"How is she?" Amber's concerned voice enquired when Daniel stepped through the front door of the rooftop Domus. The stunning Lamia had been sitting in one of the leather chairs in the open sitting-room when the click of the front door drew her attention.

Shrugging off his coat, to be hung upon a coat rack on the wall, Daniel shook his head before he continued further into the room. "She's doing as well as she can."

Amber stood, moving to give him a tight embrace. "I'm so sorry." She drew back when Daniel didn't reciprocate the hug. A frown touched her perfect face that was framed in thick waves of chestnut-red. "Come on, everybody is waiting for you in Kain's office." Taking him by the shoulder, she pushed him down the hall.

Great, the entire family was waiting for him. Right now, he didn't want to deal with an inquisition. He wanted to find out what the hell Rhain meant when saying that Joyce had disappeared, and that was it. But that wouldn't work. Amber pushed him towards the door, and without thinking he snapped his head back with a snarl and a dangerous glare towards her. He wasn't in the mood to be man-handled. At least she backed off with a frown and a soft apology.

His brothers were not the only ones waiting for him when he entered Kain's office. Theodore Servilii was also inside the room, seated in one of the chairs next to Rhain, and the moment the older man saw his associate he asked, "Is she alright? I was dropping by when I was told you were not here. I came to inquire from Kain as to where you had gone. He told me what has happened, including the involvement of my son."

Daniel's eyes narrowed upon his eldest brother who was standing with his back to the room and facing one of the four large windows where a crack in the thick curtains allowed him a view of the city. "I see. Regan is fine, for now."

Theodore sighed in relief with a nod. "That is very good to hear."

Kain drew the curtains closed then turned to face the room with his imposing gaze and aura fluctuating with unease. He was a strong figure of solid muscle standing at six-three and with skin as pale as white chalk, combined with the odd color of his striking red hair, made him appear unnatural. Unlike the twins, his body was built upon core muscles beneath tailored black slacks of silk and a red shirt that was pulled tight along his torso. Narrow, coal black eyes were framed with uneven cuts of blood-red hair that fell along his chiseled features. Power radiated from this man, even when surrounded by family.

He clasped his hands behind his back and looked hard to Daniel. "Rhain has informed us that Joyce was nowhere to be found in her apartment."

Daniel glanced to his twin who was sitting with legs folded before him in one of the deep leather arm chairs. "So I heard."

Rhain muttered, tapping fingers to the chair's arms. "I looked for the girl, but there was no corpse to be found."

"That's impossible. A corpse can't just get up and walk off without the use of magic, and there was no trace of any magical residue within that building. Besides,' Daniel grumbled, 'I'm sure that if Joyce had come walking out of the building, Regan would be in a lot better sorts right now and not exhausted from her emotions and tear burned cheeks."

Rhain turned his eyes away with a slight drone. There wasn't anything he could say in line of his smart remarks to counter that.

128

"Either way,' Kain spoke with his deeply accented voice resonating about the room, 'we need to find Joyce. I agree that a corpse can't get up and walk, so either somebody came back in and got her..."

"No way." Rhain shook his head with a growl. "I found no signs of entry, forced or otherwise. There was only Regan's scent, Joyce's dead stench, and Daniel's fancy cologne."

"There was the faint scent of sexual intercourse on Joyce," said Daniel with a sickening curl of his lips. "She had been intimate with David in that room earlier in the night."

Rhain looked to his brother with a disturbed gaze. "You could smell that? Fuck, what's wrong with your nose?"

Kain grunted, and the urge to wash Rhain's mouth out with soap was nearly overpowering. But he took control of his disciplinary urge with a deep and calm breath. "Then there is one other explanation that we must consider."

Theodore looked to the eldest brother. "Joyce survived the Creare."

Kain nodded.

Rhain and Daniel snapped in tandem, "What?"

"But there were no signs of the Creation taking,' Amber gaped, pointing to the twins, 'they both said so."

Rhain glared towards Kain. "There was no sign, nothing."

"And there was no body to make certain." Kain shook his head with a trail of red caressing his milky white cheeks. "We all know that each human who undergoes the Creare will have a different timeframe that the change will show, either in death or in un-death. It is obvious that Joyce's Creare had not shown itself till after Daniel left the building and before Rhain entered. What other explanation do we have at this point?"

"I find it highly unusual that a human who underwent the Creare showed no signs at all," mused Theodore.

"Besides the bites," sighed Daniel in tired exhalation.

Theodore gave a somber nod then asked, "Can you tell me what her condition was when you saw her?"

Daniel sat heavily to a seat then slumped back with a hand pressing fingers to his forehead. "Cold, pale, and no pulse. The usual. She had the telltale signs of two bites on her neck that were still present. But,' Daniel looked to those around him, 'she was somewhat conscious while I was driving to the apartment. Regan was with her when she called me, not but an hour prior, and said that Joyce muttered David's name. Regan also stated that Joyce was wheezing even though she couldn't find a pulse."

"Unacceptable," snarled Theodore in disgust. The handsomely aged Lamia shook his head of salt and pepper hair before looking to Kain. "Would Joyce have had enough time to recover from the Creation, so quickly?"

"If she had been turned at another location and then brought back to the apartment that might have given her enough time to recover and be able to leave on her own."

"She left the club with David earlier in the night while Regan and I were at Theodore's art exhibit. Would that have been enough time?" Daniel asked the question directly to his elder brother.

Kain narrowed his eyes in thought. "Perhaps."

Rhain snorted and shook his head sending dual colored locks of hair to skitter about his face. "So David went back to Joyce's place, got some tail, and then took her someplace else? Locating his fine place of residence in the Underground will be hard. He has connections throughout Great Britain. He'll vanish into the fog before anybody can spell his name."

"How was David able to get Joyce out of the club, Rhain?" Kain inquired with a slender, red brow arched in curiosity.

Rhain didn't like the question asked to him and returned a dark glare to Kain. "He never got into the club, Kain."

"Then how was he permitted on the property?"

Rhain snarled when he saw Kain's eyes turn an accusatory glare towards him. He pointed a finger back to his brother. "I know what you're thinking. This isn't my fault! I run my club to the fullest of the Lex, and in no fucking way would I let a prick like David..."

He looked to Theodore and said, "All offense meant..."

Theodore chuckled and waved a hand in a form of agreement.

Rhain continued to say, "Crawl his way in. Do you know how many bodies come onto the property every night? Hundreds, if not thousands! My security only have two sets of eyes in their bloody heads, and they're not fucking psychic!"

"So what was the fool doing at the club in the first place if he has been banned?" asked Amber hesitantly and quietly.

Rhain flicked a hand towards his twin. "Ask Daniel. Last week, when he stopped by, David started some trouble in the courtyard but Daniel threatened to rip him a new ass-hole if he didn't leave."

Daniel rolled his eyes. "I wouldn't put my words that colorfully, Rhain."

"But why would he attack Joyce of all people?" asked Amber with confusion knitting her pretty face. "What had she done to him to warrant such a tragic attack?"

Daniel thought back to the night he met Regan and a cold shudder ran his thin frame when he thought of how close Regan could have been to becoming David's victim. With an exasperated sigh, he spoke. "I think I have an answer. The night I met Regan was when she and Joyce were at the Crucible for Regan's birthday. Regan went outside for some fresh air, complaining of a headache, and there was an accidental misunderstanding when Regan was trying to get back into the club. She bumped into David; he thought she had done it on purpose. He was hounding her when I heard her frightened cry, so I stepped in to defuse the situation and ordered him off the property. He backed down then departed without further incident."

He continued on to say, "He was not happy. It may be just coincidence that he and Joyce met this evening. Regan told me earlier that Joyce can be a little unsafe when it comes to meeting men, picking the wrong ones - if you understand my meaning. Joyce was also upset when I picked Regan up for the evening. It could be that all the wrong factors were leading to this tragic event, and David was simply along for the ride. I highly doubt he planned any of this but took a chance when he discovered Joyce's connection to Regan."

"Wrong place; wrong time," mused Theodor with a slow shake of his head. "How sad."

"So,' Amber said, glancing between the men, 'what happened to Joyce then?"

"Well,' Rhain muttered as he stood and went to pour himself a glass of Sanquis tainted wine from a bottle on a side table, 'I can tell you that there was not one single piece of glass out of place, no window open, no sign of struggle - nothing. Either she got up and went out the fire escape, which I might add is directly located outside the bedroom window, or her Parens came back to get her."

"But then we would've noticed, especially you since you were right there." Daniel wasn't so sure Joyce's Parens came back for her, and breathed out, "There was no other scent but hers and David's inside. If her Parens came back for her, that Lamia's scent would have been noticeable - stronger."

Rhain frowned at his brother's use of common damn sense, but then a light came on within Rhain's mind and he pointed his finger towards his twin. "Wait, I think I've figured this out."

When all eyes turned to him, he drained his drink then clapped his hands together. "Alright, follow me on this." He began to pace the room. "David's always had a hard on for our family ever since I banned him from my club, and since then, he's wanted nothing more than to bring all of us down. David must've cracked when Daniel got into his face."

When he saw the looks of mild confusion upon the faces of those around him, Rhain added with a grumble, "He wanted to make a statement. What do you want to bet that David did this just to piss you off, Daniel? He probably figured out, from speaking to Joyce at the club, that she was Regan's cousin. He then realizes, when Joyce slips up that the cousin she is speaking about is the girl you rescued from his suave display of stupidity, that he has a chance to fuck you over. David has probably done this out of some twisted need for revenge. He knows hurting you will end up hurting us all, and we know you are sensitive, Daniel, so seeing Regan go through emotional torment over what he has done to Joyce is an indirect way of getting you back for putting him in his place and probably an attempt to get you to slip up while your emotions are running red hot."

Daniel mumbled under his breath, "I'd rather believe this was all just a coincidence brought on by my actions."

"Is David this smart to create such an elaborate plan on a spur of a moment, Theodore?" Kain inquired to the older Lamia with a flat expression and an inquisitive gaze.

Theodore frowned and shrugged his shoulders. "Not likely. The boy doesn't have much of a head on his shoulders - never did."

"Rhain does have a point," said Kain, ignoring the look of utter shock coming from the 'wild' twin. He came to stand at the edge of the desk. "It comes down to this, David allowed Joyce to return home by some means and for some reason. The answer to the entire question will not be known unless David is questioned. Perhaps she was brought there by the unknown Lamia whom you caught scent of, Daniel, for I doubt David would show his face and a task of risk of getting caught."

"It's possible."

"I am sure we will find out soon. In the meantime, I will need to inform Caius"

"What?" Daniel snapped his dark eyes to Kain. "It's too early to contact him. I haven't even told Regan what has happened to Joyce. She thinks that her cousin is in the hospital!"

All Kain had to do was raise his hand to silence Daniel, and when his younger sibling curled back his lips to release a disgruntled snarl, Kain narrowed his eyes that set Daniel back. "I'm sorry, Daniel," the elder brother hissed. "With David the prime suspect in Joyce's Creare and predicament, it is vital that we have the Rex on our side. He has the resources and the power to launch an investigation and the connections to search down into the depths of the Underground where David is no doubt hiding. Most importantly, Caius has the backing of the Concilium, the Basilica, and almost every Familia Regulus within the Republica. We do not."

Daniel wished the chair would just swallow him up. He didn't want Caius involved even if the man was the Rex of England. The man was a hardcore Lex-lover and ran the Republica with an iron fist. Though Caius often employed the skills of both he and Rhain, Daniel held no love for the Roman.

"I understand your concern for Regan,' Kain continued to say, frowning slightly as he watched Daniel sink into the chair, 'but I have my duty to our Familia, our Regulus, and the Rex - at this point. Besides, I want David dealt with once and for all."

Amber touched a hand to her Socius' shoulder when she heard the snarl coil from deep within him. "We still need to discuss the fact that it is very possible that Regan, like her cousin, has inherited the Proprietas. Do you know their family history, Daniel? Perhaps we can find some information on her and her lineage in the Bibliotheca de Tabularum."

"Not here in London, my dear,' said Theodore with a slight smile, 'the young woman's family is in America. Any records of her human lineage or any record associating her family tree with a Lamia Familia would be in America."

Amber sighed.

"Joyce."

All eyes turned to Daniel whose face was held in a look of thought. He raised a finger, pointing to Kain, and said to all, "Joyce's family are English. If there is a history of the Proprietas within the English side of the Scott family, there would be records. We could try to trace Joyce's family lineage in the Library."

Kain gave a nod, "Agreed. You and Rhain will look into Joyce's blood line."

"Oh man," whined Rhain pitifully. "I hate that stuffy, old library. You know how allergic I am to books. They make me itch."

"I agree with Kain. It is vital that you test Regan's blood if you wish to provide her with Drasus protection, Daniel." Theodore gave his associate a sympathetic smile. "You should know within a day if she does have the Proprietas. Then finding any association to records would be much easier and faster."

"That's a date breaker right there, isn't it?" Rhain chuckled, slapping a palm to his forehead. "Sorry your cousin just bit the bucket, but can I have some blood? Yeah, that'll go over great. I'm sure Regan'll be in your bed in no time, Frater."

Daniel, with a glare to his twin, threw a small pillow from the couch next to him to strike Rhain clean in the side of the face. "Forgive me if I never took notes on your seduction habits, Frater."

With a cheeky grin, Rhain winked in reply.

"Boys,' Kain groaned, drawing both their attentions to him with a snap of fingers, 'behave yourselves. Daniel, find a way to get a drop of Regan's blood. I'll contact Caius and inform him of what is happening."

When Daniel opened his mouth to protest, Kain raised a hand and spoke softly and with sympathy to his brother. "I'll be discrete when speaking of Regan, as gently as I can and with as little detail to the connection between Joyce and Regan. I'll try to leave her out of this developing situation as much as possible."

Daniel nodded. He'd accept that. "I understand, and I appreciate that." He stood, looking to Theodore. "I'm sorry for not meeting you properly, Theodore."

Theodore snorted out a laugh with a dismissive wave of his hand. "Your priority was to see to Miss. Scott's safety."

"Thank you. Now, if you will excuse me, I need to check on Regan before I turn in." Daniel offered a bow to all before departing the room.

Amber frowned as she watched Daniel leave. Tipping her head up, she looked to her Socius. "Why do I have a bad feeling that this is not going to end well?"

Kain shrugged. "Fear, my dear."

"It's all fucked-up if you ask me," Rhain muttered.

Amber sighed.

"Do not worry, dear Amber,' Theodore chuckled, standing from the chair to stretch his arms before he flashed a charming smile to Kain's Socia, 'everything will end on a good note. Daniel's a strong Lamia and a passionate one who will not allow Miss. Scott to fall prey to any harm. I have no doubt that David will meet his end soon, after all, I should have snapped his neck when he was born, if his mother would have let me. If he is to die, then I hope one of you Thorn boys will break his neck for me. He has been a very troublesome child and has caused you and your Familia enough difficulty for one century."

Rhain grinned. "If you want to judge the son, judge the father."

Theodore barked out a heartfelt laugh. "One of these days, Rhain Thorn, your sarcasm is going to be your undoing."

Rhain chuckled darkly as he gave an agreeable solute. "It already is, my friend - it already is."

~ ~ ~ ~

Daniel kept his promise to Regan and returned to her soon after the meeting had concluded. On his way from the condo, he heard Pixie scampering up to him. Regan needed a sense of comfort and companionship while they both rested, so why not let Pixie watch over her? The two would get along perfectly.

"Come on, Pixie,' he called to the little Pomeranian as he opened the front door to the short hall leading to the elevator, 'let's go tuck Regan into bed."

Not long after Daniel left the apartment, Regan left the warmth of the chamomile bath before her fingers turned in to prunes, dried herself off then wrapped herself in the fluffy, white robe that hung upon a peg for guests. When she was all snuggled within the robe, she took her tea to the bedroom where she curled upon the bed to wait for sleep to come her way. Only a few minutes passed when the comforting lull of slumber caressed her eyes, drawing lashes to knit together.

How much time had passed was uncertain when her eyes drifted open, and through her sleepy eyes, she saw a figure seated upon the edge of her bed. It was Daniel, and he was smiling at her. However, he wasn't alone. There was something prancing around on the bed, and with each little pounce and jump there sounded a delicate chime of a little bell.

"Daniel?" she asked through a tight moan as she gently rubbed a hand against her eyes. "What time is it?"

"Too early for you to be up," replied the Lamia in his soothing voice. He reached forwards to brush the back of his hand against her forehead. "I didn't mean to wake you. I wanted to make sure you were alright before I get to bed."

"How long have I been sleeping?" She smiled till a little bundle of fur pounced onto her lap. Regan yelped in surprise when a little dog put its paws upon her chest and began to lick at her face.

"Pixie,' Daniel groaned, rolling his eyes, 'where are your manners? My apologies. Pixie tends to get excited when she meets a new guest."

Regan chuckled, squirming from the energetic and very happy little dog who was neurotically liking her nose. When Pixie finally bound out of her lap to Daniel, Regan sat up with a soft laugh. "She's adorable. Is she yours?"

"Yes." Daniel gave a little pat to the dog's head. "Her name is Pixie. I thought that you might need some company while you sleep. She may not be the best guard dog but she's talented when it comes to cuddling."

Regan scooted closer, reaching out to scratch a tiny ear. There was a slight grin tugging her lips as she looked to Daniel. She never thought that she would hear any man say the word *cuddle*, especially when speaking about his little lap dog. She would pick Daniel as having a sleek Doberman, not a little Pomeranian with bows in her ears and a little pink collar with her name inscribed in silver thread.

"What?" He asked with an uneasy chuckle when he saw the sneaky, little grin upon Regan's features.

134

"Nothing, nothing at all," she mused. "I'd love the company. Are you sure it's alright?"

"I'm sure." He smiled and gave Pixie a little push. The Pomeranian didn't need another offer. She pranced up to the top of the bed then proceeded to burrow herself under the blanket till she was settled. Daniel rolled his eyes with a breathy sigh. "She'll curl up wherever there is a blanket."

Regan chuckled then asked, "Has there been any news about Joyce?"

"Not yet. You know doctors, we all work on their time. Try not to worry." He leaned to press a kiss to Regan's cheek. "I need to rest. However, if you need me, don't hesitate to call me."

Sighing to the kiss, Regan smiled and nodded. Though she was grateful for his thoughtfulness on letting his dog stay with her, she would prefer to have him keep her company. She was afraid, there was no denying that, but she couldn't keep him from his work and the rest he did need.

"I'll be okay," she whispered ever so softly.

"There's plenty of tea and coffee in the kitchen. The company kitchen will be opening in a few hours, so if you're hungry, you can call and place an order through the com system in the kitchen. Dial star, six-eight-nine and you'll be transferred to the kitchen's main office. Order anything your heart desires and it will be brought to you. I've sent a message to the kitchen managers of your name and your stay here, so you don't need to worry about payment."

"You don't have to do so much for me."

"Yes, I do."

He cupped her chin within two deadly fingers then leaned to her to offer her a kiss. This kiss was a gentle embrace that lasted a few seconds longer than their previously shared kisses and played along her lips in a tender and sweet touch.

Was he supposed to be this charming? Regan wasn't so sure. She had never known a man who treated her as if she was important to him, a woman who deserved to be treated properly and cared for. Though they had only known each other for a short time, Daniel Thorn was opening not only his home to her but his comfort and his protection as well. And he offered these without hesitation, without question, and without a second thought.

Regan drew back so she could wrap her arms about his shoulders, hugging him tightly to her. "Thank you for everything," she whispered, pressing her features against the crook of his neck.

The sudden contact flooded his cool body with instant heat, and with a sigh the Lamia had his arms about her, drawing her flush against him. He needed this, the feel of her warmth radiating from her. Feeling the caress of her warm breath spilling along his neck teased a shiver down his spine.

"You don't need to thank me," Daniel whispered in return. He closed his eyes with a cheek pressed against hers as he basked in her mortality. "Get some rest, sweetheart. I'll return by evening."

With a gentle touch, Daniel guided Regan to lie upon the bed. He smiled down to her then leaned to press a kiss to her forehead. With a whisper of 'good night', and a pet to the bump beneath the covers, the Lamia departed the bedroom.

As he left the guest-suite, Daniel noticed a compression in his dysfunctional heart, a tightness he had not felt for almost a century. He frowned and pressed a hand over his heart as he rode the elevator back up to the condo. His chest hurt, or more to the point, his heart hurt. Had leaving Regan behind caused his heart to ache? Or had the overload of emotions he had felt from the gentle Humanus brought on a swell of unmanageable passions? Whatever the answer, Daniel enjoyed the emotions, the warmth, and the sense of being needed.

He had to thank Regan for reminding him that he was not some undead and cold monster, but a being that was still connected to his humanity. She reminded him that he was capable of retaining his heart.

~ ~ ~ ~

David was a man of great patience.

Deep within the ghostly remains of the once grand factory that he now called his home, the Proscriptus sat within his office, staring out a partially boarded up window. Outside, just a hint of light was starting to peek through the cracks in the thick boards heralding the coming sunrise. Hours had clicked on by, and for a little while he wondered if Joyce had survived the Creare. It was only by shear damn luck he had discovered the sweet gene in her, and with that discovery, all the little pieces in his long building plan of revenge were falling into place.

A sly, dark grin coiled his handsome features, and with his elbows bent upon the arms of the old office chair, David tapped fingers to his chin. Would she survive? That was the question that kept pulling through his mind. If she did, great. He could use her to get to Daniel Thorn through the tender emotions of Regan, and then, he would destroy Rhain and topple the great Kain Thorn. He could use Joyce to expose the Lamia world to her cousin, and in doing so, would bring Daniel to the edge of his control and the loyalty he held so deeply to the precious Lex. If she didn't survive, he would dump her body on the doorstep of the Thorn Domus and toy with the little shits inside. Either way, David would win.

Closing his eyes, he basked in the immense feelings of pride and accomplishment at the prospect of bringing the Thorn family down to the dirt. He wanted to see the expression on Kain's face when he burned the flesh right off the bones of his brothers. That expression would be priceless horror and soul wrenching agony - well worth the years of wait.

Behind him, the old door to the room groaned slowly open, creaking with wood and metal that were forced to work against each other. A mixture of fresh scents trickled into the room - the scents of rain, death and woman. There was a faint sound of a heart beating slowly, very slowly, but it was the scent of rain that drew his attention, fresh and clean with a touch of vehicle exhaust that was a stain on London's air.

Wet steps came across the floor to stop at the back of his chair. Only when a set of damp fingers came to tease his cheek did David draw open his eyes.

"Hello, Joyce,' he purred softly with his lips pulling back to show a flash of sharpened fangs, 'so good of you to return to me."

~ ~ ~ ~

A new night started with the sun lowering over the skyline of London in a gentle caress of diminishing light. Daniel watched the darkening horizon as the hazes of blues and yellows began to dissipate with the absence of light. There was no denying the look of exhaustion that gazed back to him from his reflection in the glass doors that lead to the rooftop gardens of the Domus from his bedroom.

Sometime during the day the rain had started once again but now was nothing more than a trickle of watery drops tumbling from the thinning clouds. With luck, the night might just turn out to be a decent one.

With a groan to his raw voice, he turned from the windows, running a hand through his long hair only to mutter and wince when his fingers hooked in the long strands that had twisted during his fitful sleep. His Meditatio had danced from his grasp during the day leaving him tossing and turning, waking and slumbering on and off. He felt truly exhausted, from mind to bones, as he dragged himself to his bathroom to shower.

His mind was so foggy from lack of rest that he passed his mobile without realizing he had a message waiting for him. It was only when he heard the faint sound of repetitive beeps that his brain put two and two together. Quickly, he grabbed his phone, scrolling down, to see who the message was from. It was from Regan, and according to the text message, she was up.

Now both his sleepy mind and body were awake and functioning. He'd never taken such a fast shower in all his life; in and out and still looking presentable in a pair of black slacks, loafers and a snug fitting turtle neck of crimson with slender threads of black knitted within. He was out of the shower, dressed, and in the elevator within twenty minutes but was still grumbling when his fingers hooked within the damp strands of his hair. Maybe Rhain was right. Maybe he should cut his hair.

…maybe…

At the apartment, Daniel gently knocked upon the door. He could hear from within the yippy barking of Pixie combined with the bright laughter that he knew to be Regan's. He chuckled when he heard her squealing inaudible words of play.

"Who is it?" Regan's voice called. Pixie added an excited bark while pawing at the door.

"It's me, Regan," he said, then added, "Pixie, don't scratch the door."

The door unlocked and was pulled open. Before he could say another word, Regan had her arms about him, pulling him into a hug while at the same time tugging him into the suite. Somehow he managed to kick the door closed behind him, and for a moment or two there was a bit of chaos with Pixie bouncing in circles, yipping and barking with her tail wagging happily.

The Lamia sighed, giving in to the embrace, as his arms wrapped about the young woman to draw her tightly against him. He wasn't going to ask why she needed to hug him. He was simply going to enjoy it. Daniel didn't make a habit of allowing people to hug him. He kept others at a distance, for protective reasons of course. Rhain was the playboy of the family who took any woman who winked at him to his bed. Daniel, on the other hand, was more reserved when handling his romantic partners - women or men. But with Regan, he was quickly discovering his reservations and his resolve were slipping from his grasp.

Drawing away from him, Regan blushed and smiled shyly. "Sorry,' she mused, realizing she had hugged him without a solid reason to do so, 'I didn't mean…"

Daniel shook his head with a chuckle. "I don't mind a nice hug when I wake, though usually my hugs come from Pixie, not a beautiful woman."

Regan's blush darkened at his charming compliment. "I hope my text didn't wake you up too early."

Daniel followed her into the sitting room where the scent of roasted coffee still hung in the air. A glance towards the kitchen confirmed that she had found the coffee and the coffee maker. "I'm afraid I didn't notice your text till a short while ago. My mind wasn't cooperating with me tonight. I apologize."

"Don't worry about it." Regan chuckled, waving away his apology as she sat to the couch with a leg tucking beneath her. "Would you like some coffee? I made a pot. I did offer some to Pixie,' she smirked, looking to the Pomeranian who jumped up to sit at her side, 'but she politely declined."

"I try to limit that little one's caffeine intake, for obvious reasons. Thank you, but no. It's too early for coffee for me."

"Do you always work the late shift? I wouldn't think there was such a thing as the night shift in a company like yours. I didn't even think the art community was up so late."

Chuckling, the Lamia shrugged his shoulders as he took a seat next to her. "I've never been able to sleep well. Even as a child I seemed to be more nocturnal. I think I was born with my internal clock running backwards."

Regan gave a soft mew, and in a move that was intimate, she leaned to him with her head resting to his shoulder. Daniel didn't seem to mind and draped an arm about her shoulders with fingers settling to run along her shoulder.

"You must work an awful lot." She peeked up to him with a tiny frown gracing her lips. "Don't you miss daytime life? I can understand your brother being a night owl since he operates a club, but there just seems to be a lot more to do during the day than at night."

"There's a different form of life that comes out at night," said Daniel as he absentmindedly stroked his fingers along her arm.

"Don't you go out, visit the museums, the restaurants, and the shops?"

"I visit the museums often. When you have my background and security clearance to the back rooms and archives, daytime hours do not mean much."

Regan snorted, drawing away to face him. She arched a curious and skeptical brow towards him. "Come on,' she huffed daintily, 'don't you miss going to parks or social events?"

Daniel's black eyes sparkled with mirth when Regan returned such a playful critique on his night life. He too turned his body to face her, leaning against the back of the sofa. He bent an arm atop to brace the side of his head in a deadly palm. "I go to shops when needed. Otherwise, anything I require can be purchased online or ordered for delivery."

Regan barked out a laugh and gave him a push. "You're a shut in!"

Daniel chuckled at her playful shove then flashed her a smile. "I go to parks when I desire to, and I do attend social events that are held by my peers. Come to think of it,' the Lamia mused, clicking his tongue to the roof of his mouth, 'didn't I take you to a shop and to one of my social events? And you, Jamie, and I went to out for curry after a social event."

Regan huffed again. Her cheeks turned a dark red as she crossed her arms then turned her chin up and away in a show of fussy defiance.

"What?" He chuckled while leaning forwards with a dark grin curling his lips. "No answer?" To his complete shock and chagrin, Regan turned back to him and stuck her tongue out. "You cheeky little monkey!" laughed Daniel.

Regan gave a bright yelp when he made a reach for her. She tried to twist away but he was far too dexterous for her, and she found herself being pulled to him with his fingers threading into her hair. Before the next laugh could bubble from her throat, Daniel's lips captured hers. A moan escaped her throat to the sensual and hot caress that fell upon her parted mouth. This kiss was not like the previous kisses. This kiss was demanding, controlling, and sizzling hot. The feeling of his fingers curling against her scalp twisted her stomach in warm knots, however, before she could deepen the kiss, Daniel drew slowly away from her.

He was grinning to her, a smart ass type of grin, as if he meant that kiss to steal away her sassiness. Cocking his head to the side, Daniel ran a finger along her cheek. "What has you so happy this evening? When I left you this morning you were exhausted and depressed. Is everything alright?"

A bright smile touched Regan's features, and she nodded so fast that locks of her dark hair fell away from the binding holding them in a messy bun. "Oh! I can't believe I forgot to tell you, but this morning I got a text message from Joyce!"

All humor, all excitement, and all passion drained from the Lamia. Dry air caught within Daniel's lungs as his heart hitched. "You heard from Joyce? What did she say?"

"Here,' she mewed, pulling her mobile from her jean's pocket, scrolling down to find the message, 'look for yourself."

When he was handed the phone, Daniel cautiously read the message. *'Hey, Regan. I'm okay. Don't worry.'*

"Is this all?" he inquired, looking back up to her with a guarded eye.

"It's not much,' she admitted with a partial smile, 'but I'm glad she is alright. She didn't say anything about being at the hospital."

"She may be busy with doctors." He handed the phone back to her. "When did you get this?"

"Not long ago. I meant to text her back but Pixie kept diverting my attention. I should text her and find out what hospital she's at. Maybe I can visit her later." With hope flashing in her eyes, she looked up to Daniel. "Do you think we can?"

Sighing softly, Daniel gave a soft smile. "I'll put a call to the hospital. Rhain should know which one she's at. Why don't you let me talk to her Doctor and find out how she is and if she can have guests, alright? There's no point heading over there so late only to find out that visiting hours are over. Your cousin needs her rest. She's been through a lot."

Though Regan frowned, she nodded in agreement. "You're right. I'm just excited that she's okay."

"I'm glad you heard from her."

"So am I.

"Are you hungry?" asked the Lamia, giving a pet to Pixie as she rolled into his lap. "You haven't eaten for a while. You have to be hungry."

"I am a little peckish."

"Why don't I order you some dinner."

Regan looked away with a little nibble on her lower lip. "Would it be too much trouble to ask if we could go out for supper?" Before he could respond, she looked back to him with an apologetic smile. "I know you're very busy, but I just thought some fresh air would do me some good. Hearing from Joyce has gotten me too excited to stay inside. I need to get out for a little while, stretch my legs and run in circles."

"I may be busy, but I'm never too busy for an enjoyable outing." Standing from the couch, Daniel drew her to stand. "Get yourself ready, and I will call for my driver."

Regan giggled when she was given a little shove towards the bedroom. "But I am ready. Or are jeans and a t-shirt not acceptable to your Highness?"

Daniel grinned as she gave him a little wiggle of her pert rear clad in snug denim. The sight certainly was a pleasing view. "My dear,' he purred, casting a devious look of dark intent, 'you could be in a potato sack and I would still find you perfectly acceptable and delectable."

Peeking out from behind the bedroom door, Regan cast her own look of devious thoughts along with a sly little wink. "Kinky."

Daniel laughed with a shake of his head then muttered under his breath, "You have no idea…"

IX

I have stayed awake, as the sun climbed up within the sky, many times while thinking about my family, of my brothers and my parents. I have never forgotten the faces of my mother and my father, their smiles or their laughter. Every time I look upon Kain and Rhain, I see my parents. I see their faces reflected within the smiles of my brothers, and I hear their voices within the laughter and the curses of my brothers.

I miss my parents greatly. I will always miss them.

I know that they are watching all three of us, and that they are proud of our accomplishments. I cannot help but wonder if they worry for us or if they are unhappy with us.

None of us, we three brothers, are evil or cruel or murderers by heart. We may be Lamia, but we are all honorable souls who keep close to our humanity and the memories of our mortal life. Our mother taught us to keep close every precious moment; to be humble and to be kind. Our father taught us to take every moment in our hands and to never let go; to protect and to defend.

I have wondered if it is possible for my parents to look upon their children with love in their eyes, or would they turn their backs upon us due to the blood that has stained our hands. If I died, my next breath vanishing from my lungs, would they be waiting for me with arms open and love swelling within their hearts?

I am certain that they would for my parents' hearts knew no bounds when it came to the love they held for their sons. I wish they were here to meet Regan, to meet the woman who has captured my heart. They would have loved her. If they were still alive, they would be happy for us.

We could be such a happy family - all of us - even in death.

-    Daniel Rhys Thorn.

141

~ ~ ~ ~

A few hours later, after sharing one of the most expensive and romantic dinners Regan had ever imagined, she and Daniel walked hand in hand along one of the more popular pathways running the west bank of the Thames River.

When dinner was over, and Regan was mewing in content with a very happy belly, Daniel suggested they take a walk down the Thames to see the magnificent buildings of London's long history and to enjoy the evening air. There was nothing more magical than seeing the glittering lights of the buildings reflecting off the gentle sways of the water. This night the rain had ended early and the sky was clear, not a cloud hung above but the stars sparkling within the dark heavens.

The spring night was unusually warm and scented with the smells of various foods sold by the venders that lined the walkways and the flowers and budding trees lining the paths. Lucky for her there was a vender selling hot cider, teas, and coffee. After a pout, a little whimper, and the most talented set of puppy-eyes Daniel had ever seen, Regan cuddled a hot cup of nutmeg cider as they walked beneath the street lamps.

"You were right. I really needed this walk. It's absolutely beautiful out tonight," mewed Regan while looking up to the star filled night.

"I'm glad you're enjoying yourself," whispered the Lamia with a glance down to where Regan had herself curled to his arm.

To have her so close, acting on intimate embraces, soothed Daniel. This night spent with Regan was a precious moment he would never forget since such pleasing moments were not known to last for his kind. They were fleeting, as were every moment of life that came his way. Sooner or later he would have to let her go, and when that time came, he would be alone again.

"Daniel?"

"Hmm?"

"Do you think I'm over reacting to what happened to Joyce, to everything that's happened?"

"Not at all,' he whispered, stopping their progression to press a kiss to her hair, 'you are reacting the way any loving human being would when the one they care for has been hurt. You are handling all of this very well."

Regan smiled to his support and took the advantage to lean against his solid form. "I hate to bring this up again, but has Rhain discovered anything else?"

"All the evidence suggests that Joyce left the club with David of her own free will. Rhain is still not sure how David got onto the grounds, but when he finds out who made that vital mistake, Hell will be rolling through that church."

"I hope David didn't do this to Joyce because of what I did." Pressing her cheek against his chest to find some comfort, Regan breathed out a held breath of air. Her fingers curled within the fine thread of his turtleneck at the idea that Joyce had been a tool of vengeance. Her voice dropped to a faint mumble, "I apologized to him."

"He knows that, Regan," answered Daniel as he tipped his head to look down to her. "David is a perpetual bastard. He's been a thorn in the backsides of me and my brothers for a number of years. He and Rhain battled over the property of that old church when it was on the market for purchase. Rhain won the bidding, and ever since then David has been doing anything in his power to undermine my family. This tragedy with Joyce was only a card to use in many of his games."

"I just can't get this guilt off of my chest." She drew back and looked away. "I'm sorry. I shouldn't talk about all this right now, not when you've taken time away from your work to spend the evening with me."

"Regan," he whispered, cupping her face and pulling her up close to him. "You can't keep blaming yourself for this. You and I both know that Joyce should take some responsibility for leaving the club with an unknown man. Most of the blame is on David, and when he is found, I shall personally see that he is hung."

"I told her to be careful…"

"You're not psychic. Even you cannot read the future." Letting his fingers caress her jaw, he shook his head. "I don't like to see you beat yourself up over this. At some point in time you're going to have to accept the truth of the situation; accept what has happened and move on so you can help your cousin recover from her trauma, as well as your own guilt."

"I can't help it."

Dipping his head, he kissed her brow with an added whisper, "I know."

"Ah guilt," breathed a deep voice laced with sarcastic enjoyment. "Wha' beautiful bliss ta know tha pain o' internal suffering upon such a sweet soul."

Daniel and Regan turned their gazes to look upon a dark figure walking out from a path behind them. The man stepped past them and to the edge of the path where he leaned to the iron railing. In the darkness, the glow of his cigarette, as the delicate leaves burned when he took a draw, lit the silhouette of his face followed by a swirl of grey smoke. The man looked out of place with a pair of torn jeans, an un-tucked t-shirt, combat boots, and a green bandana about his head. The voice, though, both Daniel and Regan knew.

"David." Daniel's voice hissed like acid, and on instinct placed himself between Regan and the Proscriptus. "What are you doing here?" he snarled, clenching his fists.

"Jus' out enjoying tha night air, mate. Somethin' wrong with tha'?" asked David through a sarcastic and amused chortle. With a flick of his fingers, the cigarette was tossed out to the Thames. He turned to look over his broad shoulders, directly to Regan. "Well, well. We meet again, puppe'."

Regan shuddered and tucked herself closer to Daniel. David's smile sent icy claws down her body, so much so that she turned her eyes away.

Daniel glanced back to her when he felt her fingers grip his shirt, and the fear he saw contorting her face spurred anger through him. He returned his gaze towards the other vampire with a low, threatening growl. "Are you insane, showing your face in public?"

143

A shrug was returned from the Proscriptus. He obviously didn't care. "Oh, I'm as insane as they come!"

Daniel growled, his eyes narrowing.

"You bastard!" Regan yelled, rushing from behind Daniel.

"Regan!" barked Daniel with a sharp bite of his voice as he grabbed her arm to pull her back.

David laughed a cold laugh. "No reason ta yell a' tha girl. You'll frighten tha poor thing."

The darkness that shadowed David's eyes bore through Regan like a hot knife, and she shrank back, bumping into Daniel. When his hands came down upon her shoulders to steady her, she gave a jump and a yelp. The growl she heard come from behind her, deep and primal, had her body trembling.

"Don't even think about i', Sucker,' muttered the outlaw when the Drasus caught the young woman, 'ya know I never travel alone. We're being watched as we speak." He lit another smoke and took a long draw that bloomed red, burning embers to illuminate his face.

Damn him! Was David this foolish to try a confrontation out in public? Was he such a thoughtless fool that he would jeopardize the Lex just for the sick enjoyment of tormenting one human woman? David and his pathetic followers may have no issue tossing the laws to the side, but Daniel was not about to cross the line and end up exiled like David for one quick fuck-up.

Gently, he drew Regan back to his side then snarled, "What do you want?"

"I 'ave a warning fer ya," David muttered back in a puff of smoke. "I know ya an' yer brothers ar' gonna start lookin' fer Joyce, an' I'm sure tha' Kain is prancing his ass off ta tattle on me ta Caius. Though, I'm pretty sure my dear ol' dad is going ta go off ta tha Rex ta bitch abou' me too, tha old prick." David snorted, shook his head, and grumbled. How he loathed Theodore Servilii. If he could only put the man's other foot in the grave and end their decades' worth of bickering, he'd be a happy man.

"You know I cannot do that." Daniel's own voice had dipped to a resonating calmness, and he cautiously slid his eyes to the left then to the right as if he were looking for any individual who was out of place. "You've broken the law, David, so you must face the consequences. You should know the rules by now."

Once again, David shrugged a mindless shrug. "Yer such a little law-kisser,' he chuckled, licking the taste of smoke and tobacco from his lips, 'bu' then you've always been tha' way. I've go' news fer ya, I aint done nothing ya can pin on me."

"You drugged Joyce and assaulted her! She's in the hospital thanks to you!"

Both men glanced to Regan who had just shouted so loudly that a few people around them paused to look in their direction. Daniel pulled her tightly to his side while hissing low to her, "Regan, not now. Be quiet."

Wincing, she snapped her eyes up to him with her features twisting in a look of shock. "Be quiet? Why should I be quiet? He hurt my cousin! She could've died because of him, and I want a damn answer as to why he's done all of this to her!"

"Regan," Daniel snarled past pressing lips. His next words were silenced as David began to cackle.

"Ah! This is great!" David choked out, pointing the glowing cigarette to Daniel. "Ya haven't told her, 'ave ya?"

Daniel snarled, and with Regan looking away, he flashed his fangs.

David continued to laugh. "This is priceless!"

Regan pushed past Daniel, just out of his reach, and raced to David with tears streaming down her cheeks. "You monster!" she screamed, drawing back a hand to slap the man - hard. "Why did you hurt her?"

Daniel's heart froze, and he stood staring in utter disbelief to what had just happened. He saw her strike David hard enough to snap his head to the side, and he clenched his hands at his side as panic arose within him to the great fear that David would snap Regan's neck for what she just did, but the man didn't make a move.

Slowly, David turn his head as a chuckle bubbled up in his broad throat, pushing past the insane smirk forming upon his face. "She's a spunky lil' filly, ain't she?"

"Regan, get back here," hissed Daniel low in his breath and with fingers snapping to the ground next to him. "Now!"

David drew another draw from his cigarette then blew it out as he leaned down close to the Humanus; the smoke made her cough and step away from him. David grinned. How he loved seeing a beautiful, fresh blooded female cower away from him. "Yer cousin,' he purred, 'aint in no hospital, girl. She's with me."

"With…with you?" stuttered Regan past her tears. She stepped away, folding her arms close to her chest. "How can that be? Rhain took her to the hospital. Daniel said so."

"Did he now?" Looking over the woman, David tsked with a shake of his head. "How unlike ya, Daniel Thorn, bull shittin' a lady."

"Give her back!" Regan snapped, narrowing her eyes. "I want her back! If you don't, I'll call the police!"

"I hate ta burst yer bubble, lil girl,' grumbled the Lamia, 'bu' Joyce likes her new home, an' I've taken a liking ta her an' her soft flesh, sassy mouth an' hot temper, especially when she's bucking beneath me, clawing my back as I fuck her like tha slut she is."

Daniel saw the instant look of rage flash across Regan's shocked face. Before she could manage another smack, he was right behind her, locking his arms about her and dragging her roughly against his chest. From over her shoulder he bared his fangs towards David. His control was slowly sinking into the cold dirt.

If David laid one hand on Regan…

145

The flash of fangs brought David's eyes to brighten with a crackle of insanity scorching through his laughter. "Tsk, tsk, tinker boy," he chuckled, wagging a sarcastic finger towards Daniel. "Do control yerself when ou' in public. We would no' wan' ta cause a scene, now would we?"

David was right. What was wrong with him? Forcing his building temper to calm, Daniel eased his grip upon Regan. He didn't need a public spectacle, not with Regan's uncontrolled emotions having sparked some unwanted attention to the three already.

"Regan,' he whispered softly to her, 'I want you to go and sit on the bench. Wait for me there, will you?"

She turned about in his arms, looking to him aghast. "Why?"

He smiled to her. "I am going to speak to David, gentleman to gentleman. I will not be out of your sight. I promise."

"No,' she quickly yelped with a stern shake of her head, 'don't…"

"I must."

"He'll hurt you, like he hurt Joyce."

Her concern for his safety was heartwarming, but he couldn't allow the tender and unnecessary emotions of a frightened and overly sensitive Humanus to stand in the way of his duty to the laws. Daniel's first priority was to keep Regan calm, and easing her fear was simple. He cupped her face and pressed a heated kiss to her lips, a kiss that drew an instant moan from her. And when he felt her begin to relax, he drew his mouth away to see haze shadowing her eyes.

He had no choice. Pressing his lips to her ear, he spoke in a language that was melodic, rhythmic, and warm. Instantly, Regan's body went limp against him, and she mumbled softly against the fine knitting of his turtleneck. Daniel knew when his words had touched her mind, slipping past her defenses to touch her soul, so he gently eased her away from him so she could stand on her own.

"Go,' he whispered to her as he gently pressed his palm to her cheek, 'sit and wait for me."

She couldn't fight the Vocis Sonus. No human will could resist the Coercêre. Without a response from her, Regan turned away from Daniel and walked slowly to the bench where she sat, staring at the ground.

David grinned as he watched the coerced mortal do as she was ordered. He pulled another puff of toxin into his dry lungs then flicked the butt to the cement path. "Was tha' necessary, Drasus, brain numbing yer girl? Wha' a nice lover ya are."

"What I do is of no concern of yours, Proscriptus," replied Daniel as he closed the distance between the two.

"Oh, bu' wha' I do is yer concern? Don' be a hypocritical asshole."

Daniel narrowed his eyes.

"She's a hot piece o' ass. Ta thin fer my taste. Bu' still; I'd fuck her. Ya found yerself a warm, little dumpling ta play with."

The deadly snarl that slid past Daniel's lips drew a rumbling chuckle from the law breaker, a chuckle of sick amusement. David's eyes danced brightly, sparkling with flecks of metallic silver. "I 'ave ta ask, 'ave ya tasted her yet? I wonder if her blood is as sweet an' euphoric as her cousin's. Ya should try her. I'm sure if ya do, ya could taste tha sweetness o' tha trait."

Daniel pulled his lips back, exposing his fangs as yet another animalistic growl pressed forwards. "Tell me what you did to Joyce. I know you were involved, and I know she survived the Creare. But what I don't understand is why you let her go back to her flat to die alone? That was irresponsible, even for you."

"It's really none o' yer business, Drasus toy," muttered David. "Joyce is no' yers or yer girl's concern anymore. Yeah, she survived tha change, an' she came back ta me. She's mine now. I'm her Parens."

"You're wrong," Daniel growled, turning to face the other while his eyes glanced back to Regan and those who walked by. "Joyce is my business. Regan is in torment over the loss of her cousin. She came face to face with her cousin dying and could do nothing to help her. She deserves to…"

"She deserves this, she deserves tha'." David rolled his eyes, flipping a hand, then snapped a harsh and crazed glare to Daniel. "Listen ta me, Lex-lover. She deserves nothin'. She can't 'ave her cousin back, an' ya know tha' ta be true. There's no rule in tha Lex tha' says I 'ave ta give my Filia back."

Daniel frowned when David referred to Joyce as his Filia, a term any Proscriptus should be banned from using. "Regan thinks you've done this out of revenge because of the mishap at the club."

David snorted. "Seriously? No, tha' wasn't tha reason."

"Then why go after her cousin? Why take the chance that Joyce wouldn't survive? When did you discover that Joyce had the trait?"

David shrugged nonchalantly. "Why tha hell no'? Tha girl was damn good in bed, so when I tasted tha trait in her blood, I couldn't help myself. Besides,' he continued to say with a look towards Regan, 'if Joyce survived tha change, tha' means tha' Regan might have tha Proprietas an' might survive. Doesn't tha' strike yer fancy?"

Daniel felt the last bit of his control snap. He turned a murderous glare towards David. He could handle the lewd talk about Joyce, but the moment the other Lamia brought Regan into the conversation was the moment Daniel's protectiveness came to light. "Don't you dare speak Regan's name. I should kill you for what you've done, and given time, I'm sure I will have the pleasure of doing so."

"Play nice," David purred with a finger flicked towards the right then back to the path he came. "Ya 'ave no idea how close yer girl is ta true fear."

David saw Daniel flinch to his words and flashed a charming smile. "Joyce is happy where she is, a' my side, where I'm sure ya want ta keep yer new pet. I won't warn ya again, Daniel, back tha fuck off. Joyce doesn' want ta come back. She's under my protection. If I even smell tha stench o' ya or yer brothers near her,' he paused taking a step closer so he could lean in and whisper harshly, 'I'll rip tha flesh from ya girl's bones…inch…by painful inch after I fuck every sweet hole of her body till she bleeds."

With Daniel staring off into the darkness, David stepped forwards and draped an arm about Daniel's shoulder, purposefully pressing his forearm to the Lamia's throat, as he leaned forwards to hiss darkening, "Do I make myself clear?" He clapped Daniel on the shoulder then walked away.

David's threat held heavy within Daniel's heart as he watched the man turn and walk back into the darkness. If any other Lamia had made such a bold threat, he would've paid little attention. But David's extortions always had weight to them. David was a man of his word; he kept to his threats. The grave promise to harm Regan tore across Daniel's soul, and he found himself releasing an unstable breath of air.

Daniel looked to Regan where she still sat staring to the ground before her. There was no doubt in his mind that he should report this conversation and meeting between he and David to Kain. On the other hand, Daniel wanted to protect Regan, to take her far away from the pain and suffering she has endured. He didn't want to lose her, not now. At this point, it didn't matter if Joyce was content with David or not; a Lex had been broken and punishment had to be delivered. In the end, both David and Joyce would forfeit their lives.

Daniel made his decision as he headed back to Regan. He would inform Kain of this meeting and let him report to Caius what had been said. Then, Daniel would be free to take Regan away, maybe all the way to the Drasus Villa outside of Naples. There, she and her Proprietas would be safe.

"Regan, sweetheart, come back to me," he whispered, taking a seat next to her.

Within her mind, Regan heard his voice. The spell upon her vanished, leaving her blinking her eyes in confusion as the webs of the Coercêre drifted from her. She looked about to see that David was gone and Daniel was next to her. "What happened?"

Daniel smiled and brushed a hand through her hair. "You passed out." Lying to her hurt like hell, but what other choice did he have? "You became so upset at David that you fainted."

"I fainted? I've never done that before."

"It's alright. Everything's fine now. David's gone." He brushed fingers down her cheek only to frown to the coldness of her skin. "You're cold. I think we should be returning now."

Regan frowned but didn't argue as Daniel guided her to stand. They walked in silence back to the car, leaving their romantic evening behind them and David's eyes watching them from the shadows.

~ ~ ~ ~

Regan was asleep within Daniel's arms by the time he carried her back to her guest suite. Unlocking a door with a woman in his arms was rather tricky, but he managed and soon had her reclining upon the bed so he could remove her shoes, tossing them to the floor, then proceeded to pull the blankets over her.

"So, you have finally come back," said Rhain quietly from the doorway where he was leaning casually and watching closely the scene before him. He motioned to the bedside. "Is she okay?"

Daniel glanced over his shoulder. He wasn't surprised that he hadn't heard his twin come into the room. Rhain had always been silent - very silent. "She's fine." He looked back to Regan then said with a mournful sigh, "David found us tonight."

"What? You saw him? When? Where?" Rhain was at his brother's side instantly, frowning heavily and with a critical eye passing over Daniel as if he was searching for any signs of a beating - blood, injuries, or an ass-kicking in general.

"He must've followed us after dinner. The worst is as we've feared. He has Joyce, and according to him, she doesn't want to leave his side. He knows Kain's plans to inform Caius of the illegal Creare. The bastard threatened to harm Regan if I do anything against him or Joyce."

"Fucking hell," cursed Rhain under his breath as he dragged his fingers through his dual colored hair, black sweeping down low over one eye to end in icy blue stripes. "You really think he has Joyce?"

Daniel nodded. "He made a solid point at her being his Filia. I have no doubt that Joyce is with him, but whether or not she wants to stay with him is the question."

"I don't think we should concern ourselves with her right now. Our concern should be focused on David. He's broken too many laws and has shamed our Family name for too long. It's our duty to put that dog down, Daniel."

"He will kill Regan if I go near him or Joyce. He will find her and kill her without a second thought, Rhain. I cannot let that happen."

"That won't happen," his twin muttered. "You know that, Daniel. David blows smoke out his ass 'cause he knows it'll get you riled up enough to make a mistake. So he's using your humanity to start a damn war with our family. You shouldn't let him fuck with your mind...or your heart."

"How can I not?" Daniel asked, snapping his head back to glare towards his twin. "You said it yourself. David's threatened our family for long enough, and I've just sat by and let it happen. You and Kain are the only ones who have tried to stand up to the bastard, and even then your attempts at silencing him have fallen at our feet. If it wasn't for Theodore's influence in the Concilium and Caius standing as Rex...."

"I know where you're going with this,' Rhain snarled, mirroring his twin's angry glare, 'but you're missing one vital point. David's been asking for a beat down for half a century, ever since he screwed up decades ago when he tried to dethrone the last Regulus of this Familia. Not to mention trying to fuck with the Crucible. He won't be getting away with screwing up this time around."

"But this time *is* different." Daniel breathed out a low sigh, turning to look back to Regan. "I have her now."

He didn't need to say anything further. Rhain knew what his twin meant in that short but powerful statement. This time, with David breathing down their necks, there were more important factors that Daniel was holding close to him - protecting. It was one thing for David to threaten the Thorn brothers when they had the backing of the Drasus Familia and the Rex, but it was another issue completely when David was threatening the woman Daniel was falling in love with.

Yeah, Rhain could see it written all over his twin's face. *Love*. He hated the word and the concept as a whole and hoped he never fell for a woman so hard. But Daniel, Rhain sighed at the thought, was forever the romantic. Rhain felt a twinge of pity for his brother. Daniel felt drawn to the need for warm comfort, from either men or women, but there was too much danger in seeking out such intimate affairs, especially within the arms of a Humanus. Rhain had learned to fight the urge to be close to a woman, Lamia or human, for falling in love could mean death, and he didn't like death.

"You're not going to let this go, are you?" he asked in the end, turning his attention to the slumbering girl.

"I can't."

Rhain clasped his brother on the shoulder, a silent offering of understanding. "You know what this means, don't you?"

"Should I?" asked Daniel softly and with an arch of a brow.

"If you want to protect your girl, then we have no choice but to stop David ourselves."

Daniel blinked, taken back by his twin's bold declaration. He leaned back to regard his twin with a speculative eye. "Rhain,' he said, 'we can't go after David on our own, not without permission."

Rhain scoffed. He drew a cigarette pack from the back pocket of his jeans, and with one tap to his palm a white stick of tobacco popped up. "We can, and we will."

"No." Daniel shook his head and leaned forwards till his long hair spilled over his shoulders. "I can't risk your life along with Regan's because of David, because of me."

"Risk my life?" Rhain arched a brow with an amused snort. "You forget, Frater,' chuckled the Lamia as he pulled aside a lock of his twin's long hair to see Daniel glowering at him, 'I lost my life a long time ago. There's nothing to risk."

"Besides!" He laughed, throwing his arms in the air. "This would be the perfect time to grab that prick by the bullocks and neuter him the hard way. I'm talking wooden spoon way."

"Quiet!" Daniel hissed with a snap. "You'll wake Regan."

Rhain gave an impish shrug and a choir boy smile that certainly didn't fit him. He went on to say, "You know that David is never going to give you and Regan any peace. He's going to haunt you by using your damn honor as a dagger to your chest, and he'll haunt Regan with the truth that Joyce is with him, not to mention that you lied to her about Joyce's predicament from the start."

Daniel flinched when his brother clapped him on the shoulder.

"You can't hide your feelings from me. We're more than brothers, you and me. We're twins. We've been able to finish each other's sentences, we've been able to tell when one of us is upset or angered or in trouble, and we've been able to kick ass side-by-side since we were kids." Rhain frowned, pulling a silver lighter from his pocket to strike a flame to his cigarette. He drew in a lungful of scented smoke. "I know this girl has grown on you. I can't, for the undead life of me, figure out why. She's just human."

Rhain took another draw of smoke into his throat, blowing the delicate wisps back out his nostrils. "Humans say that love makes you do stupid shit. Your love for Regan's going to make you do stupid shit, and my love for you, as my twin and blood, would make me do stupid shit. So why don't we let our stupidity protect what we hold precious to us and do stupid shit together - like old times?"

Daniel raised his head with his long hair falling back. He eyed his brother for a short moment, and only when a soft, sleepy moan sounded from behind him did he turn his head to glance to Regan. In her sleep, she had shifted closer to him, reaching out with a blind hand to touch fingertips to his thigh. He smiled to that innocent, yet intimate touch, and covered her hand with his.

Regan smiled in her sleep to his touch and curled herself closer to him.

Rhain, with a brow arched, observed his twin with the slumbering human. The way Daniel comforted her disturbed mind was touching, way too touching. He shuddered. "We don't have much time, Frater. We either strike David now or wait for the fucker to slip away from us. If we do that, Regan will never be safe. What say you?"

The soft smile upon Regan's face brought the answer to Daniel's mind. He swore that Regan's smile would never leave her lips. She would be safe, he would see to it, even if doing so would cost him his life.

"It won't be easy,' he said, 'getting close to David. We won't be welcomed into his territory, and we can't just take Joyce from her Parens. Like it or not, she is David's Filia. He has rights to her."

"Bull shit. The only thing that Lamia has rights to is his own death," murmured Rhain, releasing a lung full of smoke. "And my blade up his ass."

"But what if she is happy with him, Rhain? What if David has found comfort in her and she in him?" Daniel brushed a hand down Regan's cheek. "Do we have a right to rip them apart?"

"David is the leader of the Proscriptus of London, Daniel. By tomorrow morning there will be a warrant out demanding his head on a fucking silver platter courtesy of his own father and our Rex. Besides,' Rhain grinned darkly, sadistically, 'we have our own duty to the Venatio."

Their duty to the Venatio? Daniel smirked as he slid an equally dark look to his twin. He knew exactly what Rhain was speaking of. With a dry breath, he stood from the bed and turned his sleek body to his brother. To protect his heart and the women who captured his heart, he would take up his blade once more and embrace the bloody title that had earned him a cruel reputation upon the streets - the Inquisitor.

"We hunt then?" he asked, offering Rhain his hand.

Flashing a fanged grin, Rhain grasped his twin's hand and pulled him closer to grasp his opposite shoulder. "Tomorrow night, we hunt."

With or without the permission from the Rex, the twins would seek David out…and execute him.

~ ~ ~ ~

Moaning softly, Regan's mind drew her from slumber, and she slowly sat up with a hand rubbing along her tired eyes. She blinked away the heavy haze so she could look about the room. There was a soft glow of light coming from the hall, but the outline of a form walking into the room snuffed it out.

"You're awake," Daniel said with a smile as he crossed the room to the bedside.

Regan smiled sleepily when he sat to her side, offering her a freshly made cup of tea, the brew caressing her senses with a sensual kiss of steam. "You must be psychic. I swear I was dreaming about you bringing me a cup of tea. Sadly though,' she mumbled as she raised the rim to her lips for a warm sip, 'you're still dressed."

"Excuse me?" Daniel chuckled, quickly catching her words that she tried to drown in her mug.

Blinking quickly, she glanced up with a bright chuckle and waved a hand. "Nothing!" Her chuckle ceased when she scrunched her nose, sniffing the air. "Do I smell smoke?"

"I'm sorry about," he sighed with an apologetic frown. "Rhain came to check on you. He had to light up."

"Oh, that was nice of him. I think." She released a deep yawn that tightened her body. "What time is it?"

"It's almost three in the morning," he replied, smirking to her adorable yawn. "How do you feel?" He brushed the back of his hand down her jaw.

"A little better." She mewed to his touch. Leaning back against the headboard of the bed, Regan looked down to the tea in her mug. "Daniel? Do you think David was telling the truth, that Joyce is happy with him?"

"Honestly? I don't know."

"I don't get it," she muttered, twisting her lips in thought. "Why would she leave the hospital and go find him and not return to me? I'm her family. David's just…"

"We'll find out all the answers for you soon, sweetheart. I'll do everything in my power to find Joyce and return her to you, that is, if she wants that."

Regan snapped her gaze to him, her eyes narrowing dangerously. "What do you mean, if she wants that? Joyce is confused. She's obviously scared and doesn't know what she's doing. She's been through a lot of trauma. I know her better than you. She wouldn't stay with David, not after what he did to her and what he put me through."

152

"I understand, but Joyce is the only one who can answer that question." There was more to the situation, obviously, but Daniel couldn't tell Regan the full truth. When she looked away with a frown, Daniel shifted to sit next to her, his arm slipping about her shoulder, and with an idle touch he began to caress his fingers along her shoulder.

"I'll make sure that everything will be alright in the end."

Leaning her head to his shoulder, Regan sighed heavily - a sigh mixed with a whimpered groan of worry. "What do I tell her parents? We were supposed to meet them in Cardiff for the weekend. If Joyce isn't back by then, I'll have to tell them something."

The Lamia cursed within his mind. He hadn't figured that Joyce's parents would become involved in this. Then again, he should've considered there would be parents who would grow worried over the disappearance of their daughter. "Where do her parents live?"

"Newport, in Wales. I need to let them know what's happened."

"In time, Regan."

"In time?" She raised her head from his shoulder, offering a dark glare. "How can you say that? David's kidnapped Joyce. He's brain washed her, and all this time you've kept me from informing the police and now look what's happened!"

Daniel raised his hands before him in a placating and defensive manner. "Sweetheart…"

With a huff, Regan crossed her arms to her chest while casting him a look that radiated the disapproval of the cute term of endearment.

The threat read loud and clear, so he offered her a sympathetic smile. "Regan, we need to use caution in this type of situation. England has different laws than America when it comes to the investigation of criminal affairs. Our society leans more towards respecting personal space and decisions than jumping to conclusions."

Regan opened her mouth to argue but Daniel raised a hand with a polite nod. "Please, listen to me. You must understand the differences in our societies and cultures. An adult woman met a guy at a club whom she willingly departed with, and with no sign of discomfort or force. The police will not see any reason to investigate Joyce's disappearance without warrant."

"But David drugged Joyce. You saw her! She was close to death. How could the police ignore that fact?"

Daniel twisted about to face Regan. She looked close to sobbing so he gently cupped her face within his deadly hands and leaned to touch his forehead to hers. His voice dropped, and he spoke sympathetically and lovingly to her. "I know, Regan. I know. You seem to have forgotten that David says she is happy with him."

"She's not thinking clearly. Have you even considered he may have lied to you?" she snapped back with her features twisting in hot rage. "I can't believe you're siding with David! The police should be handling this. They could at least speak to her and David, find out what is really going on. I'll go and tell them everything that happened. They can get the security cameras from Rhain and find David's address."

"Give me a few days to investigate and see if David's statement has any merit."

"Why?" Regan drew back, shocked that Daniel had ever convenient excuse whenever she mentioned the police. "What can you do that the police can't? I doubt all your money can help in this situation."

"I can do more than the police. All I ask is two days. If I do not stop David within that time, I will drive you all the way to the very doorstep of Joyce's parents' house and call the police myself. You can even dial the number."

Regan's eyes narrowed even more as she studied Daniel's handsome face with speculation. "Why is it that every time my brain tells me to run right to the police, my heart tells me to listen to you?"

The Lamia's lips kicked in to a curl of a smirk, a dashing smirk but one that was touched by wickedry. He shrugged. "I'm not sure, my unending charm?"

"No,' she mused then smiled and leaned closer to him, 'I think it's your sexy accent."

Daniel arched a brow to her answer then snorted, rolling his eyes. "I prefer my charm."

"Well,' Regan purred, touching a kiss to the corner of his lips, 'I prefer your accent, but I'll settle for your charm." When he moved to return the kiss, she drew back and raised a finger between their faces. "Two days. I'll give you two days because you're too damn hot for your own good."

Now he was hot? Daniel always considered his charm and natural tenderness to be the most attractive points to his character, but to Regan he was just damn hot. Well, if being hot would allow him two days to hunt down and rip David limb from limb, then so be it. He'd take it. Grinning, he drew her to him till his mouth claimed hers in a cool, supple, and needed embrace. Regan didn't hesitate to return his kiss. She moaned and leaned even closer to him till her arms were about his shoulders.

Urged on by her embrace, Daniel threaded his fingers into her hair to cup the back of her neck. He slanted his mouth against hers, deepening the kiss with a trail of his tongue to the parting of her lips. With a soft groan, she parted her lips, allowing his tongue to slip forwards into the heated recesses of her mouth. A sharp claw ran down Daniel's spine as he tasted the heat of Regan's mouth, and his fingers curled till nails threatened to cut into her scalp if not for her thick locks of dark hair winding around his fingers.

Her lips were so soft, so tender, as they played and caressed in fleeting brushes against his. The muffled sounds of Regan's mews and moans fell hushed to his pressing lips, and a breathy moan escaped her as the path of his cool mouth trailed down her jawline to her neck. And as his fingers tightened within her hair, a gentle tug was given to urge her throat to arch to his play. A merciless path of sharp, little bites danced across her jugular, pulling a tight and throaty whimper from her.

She was so warm, so soft - so alive.

From within her chest, Daniel heard the soft thumping of her heart, and the sound was music to his desires. His lips parted wider over the hollow of her throat, and before he could stop himself, he gently ran the tip of his fangs over the sensitive skin followed by a slow caress of his tongue.

Regan whined pitifully as her body arched eagerly and in desperation to feel more of his slender but hard frame, the weight of his male body. Daniel felt her fingers spread along his shoulders before trailing down his back, pulling at his turtleneck. A tiny growl forced its way passed Daniel's lips when he felt her warm fingertips skim beneath fabric to trace slowly over the cool flesh at the dip of his back.

Quickly, Daniel's mind swirled as every aspect of her being filled his senses. He wanted to feel more of the warmth that radiated from her body, her touches, and her kisses. He wanted to hear more of her sweet, sensual moans that tumbled past her lips from the caress of his hands and the play of his lips. As he trailed his lips back along her neck, Daniel rose above her, tipping her body back as he took her mouth once more in a heated kiss.

She wanted all of him, his body and his passion, and her desires were spoken within the kiss that pressed against his mouth. His kisses were like fire sweeping desperation through every inch of her body, spreading liquid heat through her veins to pool between her legs. There came a soft mumble of his name pressing against her lips, falling silent when his slick tongue pressed forwards to tease hers. Oh, Heaven! He was perfect, even at kissing! Every move of his mouth against hers was in perfect sync to the teasing of his fingers along the back of her neck.

With every kiss - with every touch - Daniel felt the emptiness within him fill with the anxious need to consume Regan. The Lamia felt pure bliss as her lips trailed down his ashen skin to leave a warm path of flesh. A deep groan forced itself past his parted lips when his throat was brushed by her hot breath, and an even deeper groan resonated in his throat to the pleasure felt when her teeth nibbled a path along his neck, the most sensitive, pleasurable, and erotic part of his body. Daniel curled his fingers against her, nails nipping at her, till she whimpered from the painful nips.

Daniel was faintly aware that she was tugging up his shirt. His lips trembled when her mouth befell them and when the warm wetness of her tongue, skimming along his lower lip in a slow devious motion, diverted his attention from her hands sneakily exposing the tight flesh of his chest. His skin tingled to the track of her fingertips as she moved her touch along his chest then over his shoulders. Daniel skimmed his fingers down the smooth curve of her body till he gripped her rear, and in one fluid motion had her cuddled within his lap; her legs parted about him to embrace his hips.

The delicate weight of her body flooded him with hunger, so he pulled her to him, eliciting a deep moan from both. There was no hiding his desire for her as his shaft could be felt swelling against her core, embraced by her quivering thighs. As the heat between the two continued to stir in wild and wanton pleasure, Daniel tried to keep his gentility in his grasp, but his hands quivered with his fluctuating control. Daniel considered himself a tender lover. A lover, none the less, with a dark, erotic side that often crossed pleasure with

155

pain. If Regan truly wanted him, wanted every part of him, he would grant her access to the depths of his lust.

Regan arched her body as Daniel dragged his fingers along the outside of her denim clothed thighs. With his eyes darkening to black pools, the Lamia drank in the way her muscles moved beneath fabric, and all he could think about was how her smooth, hot skin would feel while flexing and caressing against him. He skimmed his digits along her thighs, over her hips then up her slender belly bringing her shirt along with them. Gripping the collar, he pulled her shirt over her head as she lifted her arms.

With their play progressing quickly, and before Regan knew what was happening, she was on her back with her clothes disappearing from her body. A sly grin coiled her lips when Daniel scooted down her to pull her jeans off. All she could do was laugh and squirm beneath his hungry gaze in hopes of easing her building embarrassment. Regan hadn't been intimate with a guy for years, so to lie beneath Daniel's intensity sent trembles through her and little goose-bumps of insecurity to decorate her flesh.

She was panting by the time he had her panties tossed to the floor, and all she could do was stare at him with eyes full of quivering desperation while pressing her thighs together when she saw Daniel's dark eyes trailing up her naked legs to her hips, over her stomach, and then higher and higher to settle upon her lace covered breasts. It was his devious smile that twisted slick knots of lust in the depths of her belly to blossom heat between her thighs.

Daniel wanted her naked. To see only a portion of her luscious curves clear of fabric was not enough to help ease his frenzied cravings for her. More like a torturous tease. When only one article of clothing remained, he leaned down to kiss her lips and tasted her erotic moans as he played his fingers over the edge of lace before slipping his hands beneath fabric. Her lips quivered with lust that sound in tumbling whimpers and soft squeaks as he toyed with her breasts till her nipples hardened beneath his skilled palms.

Breaking the kiss, Daniel ran his lips along her cheek to whisper, "Lift up…"

Somehow, his command registered within Regan's sexually delirious mind, and she ached forwards with a soft mumble then pouted when Daniel's hands left her aching breasts to remove her bra.

"You're not playing nice," Regan mumbled.

"I'm not?" Daniel couldn't help but laugh as her eager hands groped for him. He caught one of her hands and brought her palm to his lips, and across her wrist his tongue slowly lavished a cool path of slickness.

"You still have clothes on."

"I do, don't I? Forgive me," he purred sensually, dangerously as he leaned back. "How insensitive of me. Allow me to remedy this horrible inconvenience." He took hold of his turtleneck, pulling it up and tossing it away. The moment the fabric was gone, he fell upon her, locking his mouth with hers in a struggle of dominance.

Regan giggled to the gentlemanly words he spoke, but the fall of giggles ended in a throaty moan when she found herself pulled into Daniel's lap. His mouth fell to kiss and nibble her shoulders, tugging and nipping upon her flesh with sharpness to his bites that sent electric shocks through every fiber of her being. Her thighs tightened about his hips, pressing her core against the rough fabric of his slacks, and her fingers clawed at his bare shoulders to leave lines of red against his pale skin.

Groaning through a tight hiss, Daniel shuddered to the feeling of her nails digging into his skin. He moaned against her lips when he felt her body tighten about him, grasping him when their bare flesh touched. The sensation of her hard nipples and plush breasts teasing his chest had him shaking with his dissipating control.

"Oh, God..." breathed Regan through a sinful moan, tipping her head back when she felt the hot, slick trail of his tongue run along her collar bone. He was a master at this sensual game with his tongue flicking, his teeth nipping, and his lips suckling upon her skin.

Daniel wanted nothing more than to tear into Regan's supple body till she was nothing but a trembling mess of beauty upon the bed. Her thighs tightened about his waist as he allowed his hands to skim palms down her body, fingers dipping into every crease and curve of her luscious form. Daniel bowed over her, his lips parting to drag his cool tongue down her sternum till his starving lips surrounded one pert nipple to lick, suckle, and lavish with sensual attention.

Daniel tasted her flesh, nipping and kissing the arch of her breasts then further down to the smooth planes of her slender stomach. He could smell her hot, feminine scent that recklessly flooded his senses, and like a stallion, his nostrils flared as he listened to the sounds of sexual approval that taunted him. The needy moan of his name brought his mouth back to hers where his tongue thrust forwards greedily, hungrily. He was quickly losing his control. The shaking of his hands proved rather annoying when trying to fumble with the button and zipper of his slacks.

But Daniel couldn't help but smirk when both his and Regan's amused chuckles mixed within their kiss as she tugged playfully upon his slacks. Their bodies twisted awkwardly as they tried to free him of the troublesome fabric, but somehow the slacks were pushed down along with his boxer briefs till he was as naked as sin.

Breaking the kiss, Daniel hovered over Regan, smiling down to her as he brushed the back of his fingers along her cheek. "Are you sure you wish to continue?"

Was he seriously asking *that* question now? They were both naked with his body resting between her parted legs, allowing her to feel his throbbing, swollen flesh against the slick folds of her body. The first contact of the swollen tip slicking against her hot entrance sent shocks of erotic heat racing through her body. Regan mewed as she lifted her hips to meet the slow rocking motion of Daniel's body.

To answer his question, Regan tickled her fingers down his spine before she took a solid grip upon his firm buttocks. With a curl of her nails, she pulled his hips against her while giving a slow squeeze to his lean flesh. Regan tipped her head to trail her tongue to the sensitive spot just beneath Daniel's ear as she scrunched her nose when a lock of his long hair tickled the tip of her nose.

She whispered warmly, "I need you right now, Daniel. I need to feel your strength and your comfort."

Daniel's eyes pressed tightly shut when his aching flesh rubbed against her outer folds. He growled to the piercing of her nails, but welcomed the pain with the thrill of life. But it was her words of necessity that melted his heart and warmed his cold soul.

She needed him? Very well, he would give her all of him.

"Then you shall have me," he whispered into a new kiss.

X

I have found her...

    One night, just one night, and everything I have ever believed in has vanished. I once cursed the Fates for playing games with my emotions, and I have often proclaimed how I had no need for a deep relationship, nothing more than a companion for a single night of entertainment, of sex, not love-making. But then, in one night, my own regulations and restrictions on a quick companion broke.

    I couldn't stand by and let her be hurt. I was drawn right to her, and from the first moment I saw her I wanted to embrace her, protect her, and keep her safe - with me. I felt a pull from deep inside me, from a further place than my soul, to consume her entire being.

    I can't explain what I felt and experienced when our eyes locked. I only know one fact - Regan has changed my life. And soon, she will have changed me. The future is unwritten. And I am afraid.

    All I know is that her image burns within my mind and haunts my dreams. If it is true that all of us have a soul-mate, then Regan is mine. She will be mine, that I am sure, and I will protect her from the monsters that wait to feast upon her innocent soul.

    -    *Daniel Rhys Thorn*

~ ~ ~ ~

Regan gazed up to Daniel as he slowly came over her, his naked flesh glowing within the dim light of the room. He hovered over her, and just one touch of his flesh brushing along her sizzled her skin. She reached for him once she had settled upon the bed, shivering in wild anticipation as her new found lover slowly lowered himself, as he inched forwards, to brush his lips over her quivering stomach. A little gasp trickled past her lips to that gentle and sensual kiss. One little kiss scorched her cheeks with a deep blush of red, and she smiled to Daniel, brushing back trails of his long hair so she could watch the way his lips pursed to kiss her flesh. With a soft sigh, Regan closed her dark eyes and rolled her head back, giving herself over to the swirling pleasures of Daniel's sexual administrations.

He moved leisurely, slipping over her body upon hands and knees with his long, lean form rippling with taut muscles beneath his pale flesh. He kissed a trail of coolness along her stomach, nipping gently at her skin before running his lips between her breasts. Not a touch of his lips was felt upon her breasts as Daniel drew away, raising his head till their eyes met and the most handsome of gentle smiles took his lips.

Moving forwards, Daniel loomed over Regan with a touch trailing along her trembling lips. She kissed his fingertips, and the tender expression of passion slammed within his heart a surge of life that sent blood rushing to his strained erection. He claimed her mouth in a burning kiss that guided a deep moan from within him. He could taste her desire by the way her lips played over his and by the way her tongue moved boldly to dance with his.

He threaded fingers into her hair to hold the kiss while easing his tight body down upon her. When their naked bodies touched for the first time, the kiss was paused as a slow, building whimper bubbled up within Regan's throat. Daniel nipped her lower lip before gently tipping her features back so he could skim kisses down the arch of her throat.

When he felt Regan's arms wrap about his shoulders, Daniel tightened his eyes closed to the sensation of being held - truly held. Her embrace was tender as she drew him closer till their bodies were pressed together and she was shifting her legs to accommodate his trim hips. The first contact of Daniel's shaft to the warm folds of Regan's body had tight moans tumbling from each partner.

Regan lifted her hips in anticipation and in desperation to feel one caress of Daniel's throbbing flesh. But he wasn't ready to give her the pleasure she hungered for, not just yet. He moved once more, skimming his flesh along hers causing her to whimper as his chest dragged across her quivering breasts. He mumbled something against her breasts, softly and in a tumble of cool air, before he raised one to his lips that parted about a taut nipple.

A forceful sound echoed from Regan, and she moaned wantonly to Daniel's sensual suckling. Trembles broke out across her body, prickling her skin with goose-bumps, and she gasped to the slick lavishing of Daniel's tongue to her nipple. Her vision blurred as a lustful haze hooded her eyes, yet she managed to glance down to watch him suckling her, veiled in a curtain of his ebony hair. His touch flooded her with pleasure, his fingers caressing her breasts in gentle and precise strokes and squeezes, and when he drew his cool, moist mouth from her, Regan whimpered pitifully - painfully - to the look of hunger shadowing his handsome face.

He openly gazed upon her breast and the slick nipple he had been suckling upon, and before her gaze he began to tease the nipple, twisting and gently pulling upon it till she cried out and arched her body. A grin coiled Daniel's lips as his dark eyes slid within their sockets to observe Regan's shifting expressions of sexual bliss that graced her face, and as he toyed with one breast, he turned his hot attention to the other nipple, dipping his head to capture the bud with his teeth.

160

The bite was tender, meant to mark her flesh, and Regan trembled to the play. She rolled her head upon the bed, her body arching and twisting as Daniel toyed with her. His grip upon her breast tightened, becoming firm and aggressive before softening and turning gentle once more. There was a pattern to his fore-play, guiding Regan to a cliff of absolute pleasure before bringing her back down only to raise her once again.

Within minutes she was a quivering body of slickening flesh, mumbling his name in fevered sounds. And when Daniel's fingers touched her for the first time between her legs, the room was bathed in the most heart wrenching cry of passion he'd ever heard. Regan's fingers curled into Daniel's hair, digging painfully into his scalp, but it didn't seem that he cared. He growled about her breast as if encouraged by her cry and by the pain. He bit her nipple as the heat of her slick flesh spread lust through him like a wildfire, burning his insides with desperate, sexual starvation.

Releasing the nipple held gently within his mouth, Daniel leaned forwards then stretched out along her side, turning his black eyes to see her smiling shyly to him. He pressed the palm of his hand against her and reached up with his other hand to caress fingers against her cheek. "Do you trust me?" he quietly asked as he began to tenderly palm the warm folds of her sex.

"Yes," she replied through a tight lipped whimper, her legs parting so she could feel the flat of his palm.

"Good." Daniel ran his eyes down her body, watching intently the way her sleek muscles moved and danced beneath her fair skin.

There was a perverse sense of pride that swelled within him as he watched his hand tease her sex, and her warm scent - female and sexual - tormented his senses till he groaned in pleasure. He wanted to taste her, to feel her against his lips, but at this moment his first priority was for Regan to experience the pleasure he could grant her.

Tenderly, he parted her outer folds so he could caress his fingers over her slick skin, and when a squeak of pleasure licked his ear, Daniel glanced up to see Regan's beautiful features locked within an expression of pleasure. Her lips parted and her eyes drifted shut, and when her body arched off the bed, the Lamia smiled.

"Oh...oh Daniel," she whimpered sensually as his fingers slicked over her, teasing the hooded bundle of nerves till she was quivering and rocking upon the bed.

Bending his head, Daniel ran his lips along her jaw, kissing the corner of her mouth as his name tumbled from her once again. Kisses were placed to her chin then down her throat as his caress grew bolder, harder, and faster. With one easy push, a lean digit slid into Regan's body.

Regan's mind swirled with passion to the flood of hot sensations that coursed from her head to her toes. Daniel's fingers worked magic as they stroked in and out of her slick core. He had parted her - opened her - making sure that each stroke of his fingers had Regan's body trembling with utter need as she clawed him and thrust herself wildly upon the bed.

"You're so hot, so wet," groaned Daniel in a painful hiss as he pressed his naked hips against her thigh allowing her a feel of his painful erection as it strained between their bodies.

161

Regan whimpered, reaching for him as her hooded eyes drew open, lashes forced to separate so her eyes could focus.

Daniel moved closer so she could embrace him, and she slid her hands into his hair, cupping the back of his neck and guiding his mouth to hers. The kiss was hot, deep, and mimicked the motions and the thrusting of his fingers. Sliding a lean leg over hers, Daniel parted her thighs wider so he could twist his wrist and slide another finger forwards to join the first two. Regan swallowed a throaty whimper, and the Lamia smiled against her lips.

When neither could contain themselves, when their lust overpowered their thoughts and their desires ran hot through their veins, Daniel drew his fingers from her flesh then raised his hand to his lips so he could lick away her juices. Their eyes locked, and slowly he positioned himself between her parted legs. With a wily smile gracing his lips, he loomed over her and trailed fingertips over her cheek.

"Are you ready? If you don't want…" His words were silenced by a single finger pressed against his lips.

Regan smiled to him and arched upwards so she could kiss the corner of his lips. "Please don't stop, Daniel. I couldn't bear it if you did."

Those words electrified Daniel's heart and sent warmth seeping through his body, and he gazed upon her with tenderness in his dark eyes. He kissed her finger, took her wrist in his gentle hold then ran his lips along her palm. "Don't say such poetic and passionate words."

Regan chuckled softly, mewing as she watched him kiss and nip her palm. "Why not?"

He released her wrist, gently taking hold of her chin as he lowered his lips to hers. "I may just fall in love with you."

Regan's heart skipped a few beats and a trembling gasp fluttered from her lips, but that gasp was snuffed out when Daniel took her lips in yet another breath taking kiss. And as he did so, he reached between their bodies with her hand held in his and gently pressed her palm to his throbbing shaft.

In that suave voice of his, he whispered against her lips, "Claim this moment, Regan. Guide me."

When Regan's delicate fingers came about him, Daniel felt a hard shudder course through his body and he groaned deeply. In one motion, slow and precise, Daniel pressed the tip of his shaft against her opening then slide himself into her hot, moist, and mortal body. The sensation of her slick channel grasping him and tightening about him as he entered her washed through him a feeling that was unexplainable.

Regan reached for him with a look of shadowed passion, embracing Daniel with her body. And when he came to lean down, sheathing himself fully within her, Daniel dipped his head to kiss her lips. A deep moan tumbled into the kiss as the last inches of his thick shaft lodged within Regan's tight channel. The rhythm was set, Daniel's lean body drawing back then surging forwards, pulling mumbled sounds of erotic bliss from the mortal beneath him.

Regan felt a flame scorch her, wrapping itself about her flesh as he began to move within her, caressing her from within and stroking her with the lengthy inches of his shaft. And soon, Regan matched Daniel's pace, arching and rocking her hips up to meet every thrust.

Daniel had often cursed himself for not embracing a true lover over his lifetime. Though he had taken pleasure in a few mortals who would forever hold a part of his heart, he often thought himself selfish for not seeking the pleasure of a true relationship. Yet as he moved and stroked himself within Regan's pulsating core, he knew fully well why he had withheld himself from taking a long-term lover. No woman or man could make him smile or laugh the way Regan could, and no other woman or man had a touch that soothed his troubled soul or an embrace that offered him honest comfort.

The truth was simple and did not surprise him at all.

He was in love with her.

~ ~ ~ ~

As Daniel released his defenses and allowed Regan to envelope him with her innocent, human passion, he realized that the want to consume her was slowly encroaching upon his control. He wanted to hold her, he wanted to love her, and most of all he wanted to taste her.

Lacing his fingers with hers, Daniel raised Regan's arms above her head, pinning them to the bed at her head, and when her fingers tightened in response, he smiled softly to her before dipping his head. His lips fell to tease her neck, nipping and suckling her flesh, as he continued to thrust smoothly in and out of her quivering flesh with building intensity. His strokes were deep and hard then shallow and gentle before becoming rough and grinding. The bed beneath them groaned and creaked in protest to the motions that forced the metal frame to shift.

"Put your legs…about me," he panted against her neck in a spill of cool, delayed breath.

Whimpering, Regan obeyed and slid her quivering, slick thighs about Daniel's flanks, drawing her body closer. Her momentary lover growled harshly against her throat to the feeling of her tight channel sucking his shaft deeper into her body and at an angel that sent shudders down his spine. His thrusts turned aggressive, impaling himself again and again, till he withdrew himself from her moist flesh only to embed himself once again. Soon the room danced with the echoing sounds of their pleasure, erotic moans and groans mixing with desperate whimpers and sighs, as dampening flesh met in slapping caresses.

With their bodies entwined, Regan tossed her head back, releasing begging cries, as Daniel heightened his erotic torment upon her body. The bestial snarl that fled from his lips when she turned her hungry mouth to his throat, feasting upon his pale skin, swept sensual pride through Regan, and she began to rock herself up to meet the motions of his hips. The need, the desperate necessity, to feel the contact of their bodies overwhelmed her with the desire for Daniel's groin to rub and tease her sensitive sex.

The feeling of her mouth indulging upon his throat threatened to push the Lamia over the edge of ecstasy. His lips parted, flashing his fangs that throbbed with hunger. Fear tugged at Daniel as the urgent desire to dig his fangs into her neck floored him. He released one of her hands to curl his fingers into her hair, yanking her head to the side, and before he could stop himself, he pressed his parted jaw against the taut flesh of her neck. He snarled in hunger and lapped at her skin with his tongue, and just as the tip of his fangs grazed her flesh, Regan whimpered his name.

The Lamia clamped his jaws shut with a click of bone and pressed his eyes closed as he fought for control. With their shifting moans dancing the room and the amatory sensation of Regan's folds clamping about his throbbing member, the vampire could barely keep himself from sinking his teeth past her flesh.

Regan felt as if she was about to explode! Daniel felt so good - so right! His movements were violent, driving her back and forth upon the bed, and to steady herself, Regan dug her free hand into the bed-sheets, crinkling the pressed fabric. Her flesh felt hot and wet with sexual hunger the more he played her like a violin, stroking her higher and higher till she was screaming in ecstasy. Her thighs hurt, pulsating painfully, as they struggled to hold onto Daniel's slickening hips just so she could feel the devious caress of their quivering, swollen flesh as he danced in and out of her.

Regan's head lulled back upon a pillow of her dark hair, and the pit of her belly twisted and turned in sensual, swirling knots of desperation. Instincts ordered her to grind her weeping sex harder to the swollen base of Daniel's shaft in order to achieve the final strokes that would send her into erotic, sexual oblivion. She wanted to keep this sensation forever, never to forget the way Daniel felt as he made frantic love to her. Her breathing grew rapid and her heart began to race within her chest till she screamed out in pleasured release!

Daniel's blood boiled hot within his veins, the cold fluid turning hotter the harder and harder his old heart had to pump. His teeth hurt, aching to the core within his gums, as he grew closer and closer to his own release! His jaws hurt, parting wide through the fight Daniel had with himself to keep from piercing Regan's throat for just one taste of her sweet blood that his soul craved. He was willing to throw caution to the wind and break the Lex for just one drop of her crimson Sanquis.

The sound of Regan's release plummeting from her lips in a shattered cry of pleasure was one of the purest sounds he had ever heard. Without missing a beat, Daniel continued to bore into her quivering body as her orgasm rushed like liquid fire along his buried flesh. A few more thrusts and Daniel met his own release, tearing his mouth away from her tantalizing flesh to howl like a beast over a kill! Then, as pleasure came crashing down upon him, Daniel's body rolled forwards, dropping atop Regan. Not wanting to weigh her down, he began to shift away from her, slowly sliding his jerking shaft from her clutch. That was, till he felt her arms tighten about him. Blinking, he rose up over her trembling body to see a soft, dreamy smile upon Regan's lips - bruised and swollen from his kisses.

"I'm too heavy for you," whispered Daniel, bending low to brush his lips to her damp brow.

"No you're not," Regan breathed out with a soft and contented sigh. "You're perfect."

"Am I?" He chuckled softly, trailing a line of lazy kisses down along her cheek and neck.

"Yes. And I can't move."

The Lamia's chuckle vibrated from deep within his slender build. He rose up on his elbows to gaze down to her, brushing a lock of her hair from her temple.

"Besides,' Regan purred, shifting her hips as a grin spread her lips to the groan she heard from Daniel, 'I think you feel way too good to move right now."

"I agree." He groaned when he felt her hot channel tighten sensually about his buried shaft. In fact, he wasn't sure he'd be able to move. Regan was far too comfortable, inside and out. Then again, he could content himself with nibbling upon her neck while listening to the musical thumping of her heart.

Ecstasy and pure bliss kissed Regan as her body came down from her orgasmic high. Daniel seemed to weigh nothing as he rested upon her with his head nestled to the crook of her shoulder. She could feel a tiny hint of cool air caressing her skin from his shallow breaths. She kissed the shell of his ear as her fingers combed through his long hair that fell in thin, inky strands here and there about their naked, damp bodies.

With a low mumbling curse, Daniel drew his flesh from Regan's moist heat. He rolled from her, moving to rest upon his back and welcoming her into his arms. Cuddling was not an act he often participated in with his previous lovers, yet here he was holding Regan against his naked side with one of her bare legs draped over his lap while lazily caressing her sleek thigh with a deadly hand.

Daniel wanted nothing more than to experience every inch of Regan's body in every erotic way till she went horse from screaming his name. Such pleasure is all that he wanted, but he was happy to have her curled in his arms, basing in the warm afterglow of sex. What a pity the night was going to end far too quickly.

"Regan' he whispered as reality tapped him upon the shoulder, 'I have something of great importance that I must do. I may be gone for a short while, perhaps a few days, but I will return as soon as I can."

The mortal frowned, lifting her head till her chin rested to the fold of his arm. "What about finding Joyce?"

He pressed a kiss to her forehead as she looked up to him. "I will not stop investigating Joyce's location, but this is a promise I made to Rhain, sweetheart. A previous engagement."

When her frown deepened and she moaned, he added, "I truly am sorry. You can stay here as long as you need. Anything you desire will be given to you, and I'll give you Amber and Kain's numbers. If you need anything or you have an emergency, you can call them directly, and you can always call me. All I ask is that you stay inside the building for your own safety, please. You'll be safe here and away from David."

Pouting, she leaned up to prop herself up with an elbow.
"What if I hear something from Joyce?" she asked, looking down to him past falling locks of rosewood.

165

"Then you let Kain know and he'll do what needs to be done." Before she could reply, her lips parting to speak, Daniel raised his head to kiss her silent. "I'll keep in touch with the police while I'm gone. If I find out any new information on your cousin, I will contact you directly. You have my word, sweetheart."

When she gave him a curiously arched eye, Daniel drew a cross over the naked flesh where his heart beat ever so slowly beneath. "Cross my heart."

A frown took Regan's soft features and her lips twisted as she pouted, sighed, and nodded. "Alright. When do you leave?"

"Soon."

"How long do I have with you tonight?"

Daniel took a quick glance to the clock on the bedside table that flashed a warning to him that time was quickly running away, however, there was still an hour or so on his side. A sly grin spread his lips as he turned back to her, cupping the side of her face with a deadly hand. "I have more than enough time to enjoy you once again, my dear Regan."

"Oh?" she purred sensually, deviously as her eyes softened beneath a cuddle of thick lashes.

Daniel's eyes narrowed as Regan slid her naked body over him to straddle his hips. He could still smell their sexualized scent upon their flesh, the scent so very enticing that it made his stomach convulse. To feel her soft, slickened folds settle about his semi-swollen erection brought his eyes to flutter closed. And when she ran a tender touch along his sides, the Lamia found that he was putty to her sinful seduction.

Spurred on by her sense of sensual pride and new found confidence, Regan took hold of his hands to press his palms to her proud, quivering breasts. She nibbled her lower lip then moaned sweetly when he began to roll the firm mounds, teasing the pert buds as he watched the reaction of pleasure dance across her face.

She looked down to him with a breathy sigh, and her lips parted as she let the tip of her tongue skim along them. "Are you sure?" she purred, raising one of his hands so her tongue could caress against his lean digits, licking and suckling the tip of one finger.

Daniel swallowed a lump within his throat. He found it hard to concentrate as he watched the wicked twisting of her body above him as she began to tease him with her hips. His eyes transfixed on the delicate sweeping of her slick tongue across each fingertip before her succulent lips parted to encase his middle finger. The moist heat enwrapping his finger had his body responding eagerly to her, and he growled as his swelling shaft rubbed against the folds of her apex.

"Yes,' he tightly breathed out, 'quite sure."

Regan took his hands and ran the flat of his palms down her body, over her shuddering breasts, her trembling belly then lower to press his fingers against her slick sex.

Daniel groaned as he pressed two digits past the swollen petals of her sex and into her trembling passage. She was hot and so very wet, ready for him already. Her body rocked, pushing against his digits till he left her vacant. Only then did he wrap his hands about her slender waist, and in one quick

166

movement, lifted her then brought her down with such brutal force that he impaled her fully and with a collision of flesh. Regan's beautiful body arched violently as a sharp cry of pleasure tore from her parted lips.

Without much care to being gentle, Daniel began to thrust himself into her, over and over with little abandonment. His hands, gripping her hips, never allowed her hot sex to depart his swollen shaft. He wanted her locked to him, accepting his control and his quick dominance over her.

"There will always be time for you," he snarled tightly as he drank in her moans. He threaded fingers into her hair, pulling her to him to claim her cries of ecstasy with a kiss that tore through his soul.

~ ~ ~ ~

Through her hazy sleep, Regan's hand slid across the bed, moving gently to touch cool sheets. When she woke, eyes fluttering open, she stared across the arm's reach to see the naked indent where Daniel's body had rested. But he wasn't there. A frown tucked her lips then drifted to a curious smirk when she saw a note resting upon the bedside table.

How romantic of him to write her a note. She picked up the small fold of paper then reclined upon the disrupted pillows to read.

Regan,

> *Forgive me for having to leave without saying goodbye, but I did not want to wake you. I couldn't wake you. I hope to return as soon as I can. While I am away, please humor me and stay within the building unless you notify Kain or Amber. If you must leave, take my car. I left the number for my driver by the coffeemaker along with all other numbers you may need. If you have any questions, feel free to contact Amber or Kain. You can also text me if you need me. I may not be in calling range, however.*

> *Till I return, be safe.*

> \-   *Daniel Rhys Thorn.*

Though she didn't like Daniel being away, she couldn't demand he stop his life. Such a demand would be selfish of her. He was doing all he could to locate Joyce. What more could she ask for? Well, there was no reason to lie about in bed till Daniel returned. She could at least try and divert her mind from all that has happened. She was, after all, visiting one of the most magnificent cities in the world. There were museums to explore and beautiful parks to stroll about in, not to mention countless cafés, coffee shops, and restaurants to indulge her stomach.

Quickly, she showered then contacted Daniel's driver with a tentative schedule for her day, and soon she was waiting down in the magnificent lobby of the massive building. She didn't have to wait long for Patrick, the driver, to bring the car around, and within a short amount of time she was standing outside the entry to Harrods. Patrick informed her to take her time, and when she was ready to be picked up to call him and let him know where she was. She agreed, then rushed into the historical department store.

Close to four hours passed before Regan came out of Harrods. She gave a thought to calling for the car, yet opted for a short walk before the heavens decided to open and release its wet hold. The hours were slipping away as Regan wandered the city. Though she didn't directly know her direction, she was rather crafty at hunting down the closest coffee shop and found one not too far away. As she sat sipping her coffee and watching the street outside the glass windows, the sky opened up and rain cascaded down from the clouds.

People scattered, seeking refuge from the rain in shops and doorways. She wasn't surprised when Patrick texted her, requesting an update on her schedule. After informing her that the weather was to turn rather unpleasant, they agreed for a quick pick-up. She only had to wait ten minutes while he maneuvered through the wet streets.

While she waited, Regan turned back to sipping her latte and flipping through the pages of her new book. She was completely unaware of a shadowy figure standing across the street within the torrential rain while watching her amongst the pedestrians. Nor did she notice the wicked sneer that coiled the shadowy features just before it seeped into the welcoming darkness of an alleyway.

It wasn't long till Patrick drove up to the curb of the street and honked for Regan's attention. Gathering her belongings, she rushed from the shop and out into the pounding rain. A laugh echoed from her throat as she darted past people and their umbrellas and sloshed through the deepening puddles. Patrick climbed out of the car and scurried around the side to open her door with a heavy umbrella covering most of his face. The driver motioned her quickly in; she didn't think twice to the offer.

Regan slid into the backseat, laughing as she swept water from her clothes and hair. "Can you believe this rain? Teach me to bring an umbrella with me next time I go out." When there came no answer, she glanced up only to frown upon seeing the security glass was up and blocking her view of the front of the car and Patrick.

Twenty minutes into the drive and Regan became aware that the drive was taking longer than it had when traveling to Harrods earlier in the day. And though the rain was building into a storm, the streets were not hampered in any way, nor was the car forced to divert its direction for an alternate route. Yet she couldn't ignore the prickling sensation that something wasn't right.

Unease twisted within her stomach, and so she leaned forwards to call to Patrick. "Where are we going? I don't remember seeing these buildings on our way here."

Regan frowned when silence was her only answer. "Patrick?" she called, stretching forwards so she could tap upon the window.

Suddenly, the window whispered as it began to slide down. The relieved smile on her lips disappeared the moment the end of a gun was pointed right at her. She sucked in a quick breath and pressed tightly to the seatback. "Patrick?" she squeaked. "What's going on? What are you doing?"

It wasn't Patrick who answered. The face that appeared sent terrified shivers down her spine. "You…"

"'ello, puppe'."

~ ~ ~ ~

When the sun finally set, Daniel and Rhain departed into the rainy night.

Their goal was to find information on David, his plans and his location. Their connections ran deep and so did those who feared them. When they were walking the streets, the streets emptied and fear filled the air.

When working together the brothers were a formidable team of killers. Known as the Inquisitors, their reputation had spread so vast over the past three decades that the current Rex of England had bestowed upon them the title of Legatus, assassins working under Caius for secret killings. Under the order of Caius, both Daniel and Rhain had completed over five hundred assigned missions ending in the deaths of unaccountable Lamia and Humanus. With their impeccable and unquestionable skills at tracking and hunting, the twins were skilled at finding their quarry quickly and doing all that was required to obtain their goals.

After visiting with a few of their closest, and most trusted, contacts, Lamia embedded within the Proscriptus population of London, they learned various bits and pieces of distorted intel on David's whereabouts and activities. Word through the Law-Breaker grapevine spoke of odd changes in David's already usual behavior. Over the past three years the man had become more volatile in nature and unstable in his actions and decisions, becoming dangerous to the safety of many Proscriptus living and operating in the London Underground.

One bit of information, however, was repeated by all of their contacts. It seemed that many high ranking Proscriptus among the population were starting to worry that David was becoming a vulnerability to their hidden society. Most of the Proscriptus population wanted nothing to do with causing problems with the Lex abiding Lamia, especially the Rex. They simply wanted to live free from the laws that bound them under the rule of the Rex and the Concilium. However, there were groups within the sub-culture that wanted to revolt in revolution and destroy those bindings that controlled their lives. They wanted nothing more than to stand up and execute the Rex and bring down the power of the Concilium. While many of the younger Proscriptus hungered for such excitement, seasoned and aged Lamia within their society viewed the deviant plan as nothing but suicide - to all of them.

Over the past decade, David had risen in rank among the Proscriptus, becoming a sort of self-proclaimed leader to the more violent 'free-thinkers'. His goals centered on war and chaos, starting with the undermining of the powerful Lamia Familia who controlled London - including the Drasus. It seemed that David was not just a tack in the backside of the Thorn brothers but a budding concern among the Lamia across the Republica.

The feeling amongst their contacts was that David, and his little happy band of moronic Proscriptus, had disappeared from the Underground almost nine months ago, vanishing into areas of the Underground that only the most desperate or insane would dare to venture. His activities and his thinking had become so unstable that the Proscriptus leaders of the London Underground had considered their own Venatio for him and his followers. They couldn't risk their safety and the safety of others because one criminally insane Proscriptus ran rabid.

Word was it that David was birthing a tragedy. But what that plan was couldn't be determined. Secrecy ran deep within the Lamia world, even deeper within the Underground. The twin's influence and contacts reached only a short distance into that dark and twisted sub-world. It was suggested, by several of their contracts, that to find empirical evidence on David's campaigns the twins should search out an outlaw Lamia by the name of Angus McFarland. According to their contacts, this Lamia was known as one of David's most avid supporters and was also known to having a flapping tongue and would often drop hints of David's plans over a pint, or three, or a well-rounded death threat.

With information and location in hand, the twins set out to find Angus McFarland. They arrived at their destination as a distant whistle of a barge slowing trudging up the Thames blew to sound midnight. Daniel scanned the area from his rooftop perch high above the dark and vacant dockyard bellow. He turned his scrutinizing gaze towards Rhain who was signaling his other half by pointing down to the street. Following his brother's indication, Daniel saw the Proscriptus they were hunting heading into an abandoned building. They would need to move quickly if they were to catch their prey before he disappeared.

With deadly grace the twins rose up in the dark sky, standing tall and straight before walking right off the ledge of their posts. They descended in a controlled fall right to the alley bellow, one landing in perfect step followed by the other and with such precision that they stepped forwards upon determined strides without a single wince or sting of discomfort.

Stalking was certainly a talent inborn in the brothers. Through silent communication, using hand signals, the twins split with Rhain moving to the right and Daniel slipping off to the shadows at their left. As their quarry walked by, the two hunters moved into action, attacking quickly. They descended upon their victim before the Proscriptus released one sound of alarm.

Before Angus could react, his body hit the ground with violent spasms as powerful jolts of electricity exploded through his system by the stun gun pressed to the base of his neck. Due to the Lamia's hypersensitive nervous system, their bodies could not handle large volts of electricity without falling victim to paralysis. Their bodies and their systems would shut down, leaving them frozen for a period of time, time that could be used to the advantage of others. Within seconds, Angus lay limp upon the slime covered pavement, his eyes staring at a hooded figure standing behind him and fully aware of all that was being said.

Rhain hunched down to wave the stun gun before Angus' face. "Sucks to be shocked, huh?"

"We must move quickly," said Daniel in a chipped yet quiet tone of voice.

Grumbling, Rhain stood. "Fine. Let's get out of here. I'm tired of the air smelling of fish."

Angus didn't even grunt as the two grabbed his limp body, yanking him up from the dank ground to drag him into the shadows.

~ ~ ~ ~

"**W**ake him up."

"With pleasure," purred Rhain as he cracked his knuckles.

One brutal blow shattered the captured Lamia's jaw - splintering bone, cracking teeth, and tearing flesh. The Proscriptus' body jerked as pain flooded every fiber in his being, sparking his systems back to life. A gurgled cry of anguish pushed up from his throat as he came back to his un-life.

Slowly, Angus blinked his pale brown eyes as his mind flicked on. He looked about the thick darkness making out his surroundings to be a small room with only a single light swaying from a hanging wire directly above him. Water dripped off to one side and the smell of dank mold filled his lungs when he took his first draw of rotten air.

A low snarl pressed his thin lips till his hazy vision locked upon two shadowy figures standing a few feet away. He couldn't make out any direct details to the individuals, but they were the same who attacked him.

"Wha' 'ha hell ha'e yew done tew me?" snarled the man in a voice that was tainted with bloody and broken bones. Something cracked when he spoke, and a glob of thick blood dribbled down from the corner of his torn lips.

No answer came to him, so he snarled once more then leaned forwards. His eyes flashed a hint of silver when he discovered that his body was tied to a chair. His arms were wrapped behind the back and locked with a chain and his ankles were tethered to the legs of the chair.

He growled, "Yer gonna pway fer this..."

"I do not think so," Daniel said with a shake of his head as he stepped forwards and into the swaying light. He drew down his dark hood to expose his pale yet feminine features lined with long strands of ebony and an aura that radiated controlled and steady anger.

Angus narrowed his eyes. "Who are yew?"

"You don't need to know who we are at this time. You simply need to know that, as of this moment, your life is in our hands. I would suggest that you cooperate if you wish to see another night."

A snide curl of a lip was given as Angus ran his eyes over the Lamia speaking before looking to the other.

Rhain stepped forwards, tapping a large, leathery object he held within a hand against a slender, leather coated thigh. "We have some questions for you, Proscriptus scum."

Angus chuckled then spat out a wad of bloody phlegm. "I aint got no answers." He snarled when his words brought pain to flood his broken jaw. "Fwuck off..."

171

"I don't think he's taking us seriously, Frater."

Daniel narrowed his black eyes. "So it seems. What a shame. Why don't you give him an incentive?"

Pulling back his thick hood, Rhain offered Angus a cruel sneer. Only a sinister chuckle was given in the form of an answer as he leaned forwards to attach a thick collar about the neck of the Proscriptus. Angus twisted, trying in vain to avoid the fitting, but it did no good as the collar was latched and synched up tightly.

His lips opened to release a string of curses, but then he heard a series of metal snaps locking into place. Angus froze. His eyes went wide, watching the Lamia before him step back to join the other.

"Angus McFarland,' spoke Daniel in a clear voice, 'you are a known associate of David Servilii, the Proscriptus leader here in London. My brother and I require information as to his whereabouts. Your name was passed along to us as having the answer." He stepped forwards, raising his chin in judgment.

Angus snarled. "I dun know a Dwavid. I aint answering…"

Daniel gave a nod to his brother.

Rhain stepped forwards, bending as he raised a gloved hand to wag the leather leash. "Look,' he said with a sly grin to his cruel lips and a wicked shine of excitement in his bright blue eyes, 'don't be stupid with your life. We're not here to waste time playing with your pathetic ass. Don't play the martyr for David. He doesn't give a shit about you, and neither do I. I won't hesitate to pull this cord and end your sniveling little existence, and when I do, fifty dull blades are going to slice into your neck, one after the other, till they sever your head from your shoulders. It'll be a very painful and slow death. A death you will be aware of till the last blade cuts the final strand of skin."

Angus locked a breath within his lungs when his eyes glanced to the leather cord. "Yew bullshitt'n me."

Rhain jingled the cord. "Try me."

Daniel stepped behind his twin, gently touching him on the shoulder. "Is David worth your life?" he inquired to the Proscriptus as he took a seat upon another chair, his long legs crossing as he gracefully folded his hands in his lap. He sat straight and proper and with dark eyes narrowing.

Angus narrowed his vision, watching the Lamia with the short, metallic blue and black hair standing before him, grinning and swaying the cord back and forth.

"Now,' said Daniel with a slow building grin, 'let us begin."

~ ~ ~ ~

Rhain slowly circled the tethered vampire with icy, predatory eyes that never wavered, watching every draw of stale breath and drip of blood. "I'll ask you one last time. Where is David?" He flexed his fingers, flicking drops of blood to the dusty floor, and his eyes trailed over Angus as the man shook from pain. The exact number of blows Rhain pounded into the man's skull was no longer being counted. Daniel stopped at thirty-two.

172

Neither twin was surprised that Angus was still hanging on to consciousness. After all, not only had his jaw been broken but his cheek bones, an orbital socket, and no doubt a few sections of his skull were pieces of bony shrapnel. His face was swollen to the point where he would no longer be recognized. Rhain's brutality rarely left any looking close to being 'human'.

When Angus didn't reply, or couldn't, Rhain stalked forwards to grab a fist full of his hair, yanking his head back till some joint went pop. Angus winced from another flash of pain then groaned as the thick edges of the collar pressed into the base of his skull.

"I may not be getting tired of beating you into a pile of broken bones, but I'm sure getting bored of your silence." Rhain tightened his grip. "Answer me and this will all be over."

"Fuck yew," Angus spat out with a liquid hiss and a mouth full of bloody phlegm. He was panting now, his energy vanishing as Sanquis oozed from his wounds.

"I would be very careful if I were you. This is not the time for you to be acting on the stubbornness of our race," stated Daniel calmly as he slipped on a pair of thick leather gloves. "If you continue to speak, you'll bleed yourself dry."

Angus, after taking a few deep breaths of air, grumbled to Daniel, "Why dew yew wan' Davwid?"

"He has recently come into being a Parens," replied Daniel as he cleared his voice with a slight cough. "The woman, his Filia, is of interest to us."

Angus closed his eyes as a tremble rocked his body. A gurgled chuckle bubbled up in his throat. "I dun know any woman."

"Her name is Joyce Scott."

"Oh yea,' purred Angus with a chortle as he shifted his jaw, bones and tissue already healing and his speech returning, 'I heard of her. Rumor is she's a good fuck." A sharp curse fled his lips when his head was snapped to the side due to the force of the backhand that came across his face. "Fuck!"

Rhain stepped back, snarling. "I'm getting tired of this, Daniel."

Daniel? Angus rolled his head forwards as he licked blood from his lips. He stared at the two, his mind shifting and working behind the shine of his eyes. "Wait,' he panted, 'I know you two. Yeah, you're the two brothers David's had a hard-on for." Angus chuckled. "Why are you two interested in his new bird?"

Daniel narrowed his eyes. "That is none of your concern."

Angus smirked. "You won't be able to find her."

"Yes,' said Daniel coolly, 'we will."

Angus snorted. "You can't get close to David. You don't know who you're dealing with."

"No,' said Daniel as he slowly stood from the chair, his fingers cracking at his sides, 'you don't know who you are dealing with."

He crossed the small space to stop before the Proscriptus. Reaching out, Daniel grasped the man's chin, tightening his fingers till Angus cried out in pain as a leather covered finger slipped into his healing jaw to snap a section of bone. The healing of Angus' jaw gave way and once again the jawbone fractured, piercing through flesh between Daniel's gloved fingers.

Leaning close, Daniel spoke in a slow and deep voice, "My brother prefers his questioning tactics to be quick and brutal. I, on the other hand, prefer my tactics to be slow, precise, and merciless. Allow me to introduce ourselves."

Daniel calmly and gently took hold of the protruding sliver of bone, and in one quick snap, broke the section off. The Proscriptus howled as shards of broken bone tore across his flesh. "Our born names are not important to you, however, the name entitled to us by our reputation will no doubt register both fear and respect within your deplorable brain."

Taking that slivered section of bone and tightening his grip, Daniel leaned Angus' head back. Without a flinch, without a hint of concern within his eyes, Daniel managed to secure the flesh beneath the man's right eye with a gloved thumb and slowly pulled down the bottom lid. He then brought the sharp end of the shard to the edge of the quivering eye.

Angus' eyes went wide. He shook in the chair. "What - what are you doing?"

"Making it clear as to who you are fucking with," Daniel answered smoothly as he pressed the jagged end of the bone into the corner of the eye-socket.

Angus bellowed in panic, jerking and struggling against his bindings, as the bone slid forwards, slicing through tissue and along the back of the delicate orb while carving through the optic nerve till the full length of the bone was buried within in a stream of red blood.

"We are Venati,' hissed Daniel through clenched jaws as he twisted the bone behind the quivering eye, 'we are the Inquisitors. And you will answer our questions as to the location of David Servilii and the condition of Joyce Scott, Filia to David Servilii. If you do not, you will experience pain beyond your worst nightmare - a nightmare I am more than willing to birth." One flick is all it took to dislodge the eye from the socket. The orb popped out with a sickening gush of blood and flew across the room to splatter against the farthest wall.

Rhain didn't even flinch as the orb flew by his cheek, teasing a kiss of blood as it went by. The high pitched howls of agonizing torment that echoed off the damp stone walls of the cellar brought a twisted grin of pleasure to slide across his handsome features, and he gently wiped the back of a hand across his bloody cheek.

Angus spasmed wildly within the chair, jerking so hard that the chains binding him rattled against the wood. Blood gushed from the eye-socket, seeping down his face and Daniel's hand as Daniel wound fingers into the Angus' hair. "So help me I will shove this bone into your brain and dig out!" Daniel howled with a flash of his fangs.

Twenty-two minutes later and Daniel was wiping blood from his hands. Rhain shook his head while clicking his pierced tongue to the roof of his mouth. "Too bad he answered. This was just getting entertaining."

174

Daniel, looking with disgust upon Angus' brutalized body, snorted and stuffed a bloodstained handkerchief into his coat pocket. "Time is not on our side right now, Rhain. At least we have our answers."

"And how do we know this ass told us the exact location of David and Joyce?"

"I'll run it by my contacts."

Rhain blew out a whistle as he pulled out a pack of smokes from his pocket. He popped one up, lit it then offered the pack to his twin.

Daniel waved away the offering. "We should head back. I need to make sure Regan is alright."

"Fine," grunted Rhain as he blew out a lung full of toxic smoke. "What about him?" he asked as he jerked his chin towards Angus. "He's still alive."

"He'll heal, given time." Daniel swept his hands through his hair, gathering the long strands into a binding at the base of his neck. "We'll leave him here. We can't take the chance of him reaching David and informing him that we're on his trail. If he catches scent that we're snooping about, David will take to the wind with Joyce and dig himself deeper into his sewage hole."

"Come, Frater. We have what we have come for." Daniel turned away, heading to the door.

Rhain smirked. "Yeah, I'm coming."

Suddenly a click was heard, a mechanism in the leather collar becoming activated. Daniel froze where he stood, his eyes going wide as he slowly looked over his shoulder to Rhain who was staring hard at the Proscriptus. Angus was far too enveloped in his pain to realize what just occurred, but Daniel knew.

One blade at a time was released, each sounding with another hinging click. The first blade that slid through Angus' flesh with a dull kiss caused the Lamia's eyes to draw wide. His body bowed forwards as a second and then a third blade, each longer than the previous, met the first, taking another inch of flesh. The Proscriptus released an animalistic bellow of agony as the next blade, and then the next, and the next was triggered, splitting flesh and spilling blood.

Angus tried to fight his bindings, tearing and twisting as he continued to screech out in burning pain. His body began to spasm, his legs twitching and his hands fisting and pounding against the back of the chair. Soon his cries morphed into wet gurgles as blood pooled up within his throat, spilling out of his mouth in thick waves. As the remaining blades were triggered, the man's head tipped to the right a little further with each slice.

Daniel winced when the remaining blades completed the objective of the collar. His stomach twisted into a sickening knot as a slick sound, like a wet, fleshy zipper curdled his hearing. He looked away just as Angus' head tore from his neck to fall to the floor with a wet 'plop', rolling a few times till catching upon a broken divot in the cement.

It took a few steady breaths for Daniel to calm himself before he looked back to Rhain with a brow arched and a questionable gaze within his eyes. "Was that necessary?"

"You said it yourself,' muttered Rhain with a cut to his voice, 'we can't take a chance of him getting back to David. Would you rather take a chance of this shit getting free and telling David or act to keep Regan safe?"

Daniel turned to face his twin. His lips parted as if he were to speak but only a sigh came forth. He gave a nod of his head, conceding that Regan's safety was the greater concern.

Rhain dropped the cord without a care so he could light up another smoke. He walked up to his twin, clasping Daniel on the shoulder. "Let's go."

Once out of the tunnels, buried deep beneath the ground and even deeper within Drasus territory, Daniel raised his head to the delicate trickling of rain. He drew in a deep breath of clean air, free of the taint of pollution considering they were twenty miles outside of London.

"Now what?" Rhain asked through a puff of smoke.

"We should…" Daniel's words were cut off as his mobile began to sound. Text message after text message, voice mail after voice mail began to slam the smart phone. He cursed under his breath. "Damn,' he muttered as he started to run through the call list, 'we were so deep in the tunnels that I had lost signal. Looks like Kain and Amber have been trying to call me."

Rhain pulled his mobile form his pocket as it too began to scream of unread texts and messages. "Bloody hell."

Stepping aside, Daniel began to listen to the first message. It turned his blood to ice.

"Daniel? It's Kain. I don't know where you and your brother are right now, but you need to get back to the Domus right away. Amber's been trying to reach Rhain, but he isn't answering his phone. Pull your twin from whatever bed he's in and out of the arms of whatever whore he's bedded and get home. Now!"

From where he stood, Rhain winced to the shout that came from Daniel's phone. "What was that all about?" he inquired.

"I'm not exactly sure, but according to Kain, you're in bed with a whore."

Rhain snickered and shrugged his shoulders as he casually strolled forwards. "Maybe something's happened," he said out of thought. The moment his words drifted to the wind was the moment Rhain stopped and looked to Daniel. His twin had gone pale and his eyes were as wide as saucers.

"Regan," they both said in unison.

XI

I *can't get her out of my mind.*

> *Regan Scott...*
> *Every thought is focused upon her. Every dream flashes her image to me. She is haunting me in my sleep. She has consumed me.*
> *I never thought I would care about another, in the idea of intimacy, as much as I find myself caring for her. Her laughter warms my heart; her kisses warm my soul. I can't get her out of my head.*
> *Whether or not that is truly a bad thing, well, I'm not sure.*
> *My mother had hopes that I would meet a proud, young woman of upper society and marry the girl, but I find myself falling in love with a girl raised in the country and taught to ride horses before learning to walk. I would have her no other way. She has taken my heart, and soon she will have my soul.*
> *I have not loved another for a very long time. With Regan, I hope I never have to love another. I wish to be with her - only her.*
> *I would give her everything her heart could ever desire - even my life - if she would have me.*

> -   *Daniel Rhys Thorn*

~ ~ ~ ~

Amber was waiting for the twins when they returned, her beautiful face decorated with a trail of bloody tears. She stood from her seat, trembling to keep herself in control as she went to greet the twins. Her voice quivered and another watery tear trailed down her cheek to further paint her skin. "I'm so sorry, Daniel."

"Where is she?" Daniel snapped, rushing up to grasp Amber roughly by her arms, giving her a few sharp shakes. "Where's Regan?"

"Daniel!" Rhain barked, moving to pull his twin's hands from Kain's Socia. "Stop it!"

With hands shaking, Daniel drew back, cradling his arms to his chest. "I'm sorry, Amber. Please, where's Regan?"

"You should speak to Kain, Daniel. He's in his office," she answered with a heavy frown turning down her lips. "And Daniel, the Rex is here."

177

"Caius? He's here?" Rhain asked then snarled as he threw his arms up in the air. "Fuck! Well, there goes the fun of the night."

Amber offered Daniel a gentle touch to his arm. "They're waiting for you. Best not keep them waiting."

The twins followed Amber down the wide hall till the three entered Kain's large office. Waiting within was Kain and Caius Scipio, a man who never liked to be kept waiting. Though his appearance was calm as he reclined comfortably within one of the leather chairs, one lean leg crossed over the other, there was always an aura of promised danger dancing around him. Behind him stood his ever present shadow and personal assistant Constantine, a young man many believed to be more than just the assistant to the Rex but the man's deadly Lieutenant. Kain stood in his usual position, standing before his desk with his powerful arms crossed to his chest and listening quietly to Caius.

The moment the office door opened the conversation between the two commanding men stopped and all eyes slid to the twins and Amber. The atmosphere within weighed heavily upon the room, and the silence that fell was thick enough to be cut with a knife - a dull knife.

"Salve, Rex," proclaimed Rhain, using the traditional and proper Lamia greeting added with a slight touch of droll sarcasm. "What do we owe this honor?"

The current Rex of England turned to regard the two youngest brothers in the Thorn family with his green eyes filled with intensity, and made note to ignore Rhain's usual annoyance for Rhain had always proclaimed an allergy to formal business meetings. He bid them enter with a wave of his hand. "I wish I was visiting upon a less urgent matter, but it seems that tragedy has struck this family that has prompted my involvement."

"I paid all those parking tickets," Rhain muttered under his breath, but when he saw Kain arch a red brow to him, he chuckled innocently and recovered himself by saying, "Anybody want a drink? I do. Long night and all." As he walked across the office to the mini-bar, he could feel Kain's unamused eyes digging into his back.

Ignoring Rhain, Daniel stepped further into the room, locking his eyes to the Rex. "What has happened?"

Caius looked to Kain with a nodded, so Kain took a deep breath then spoke with his deep voice vibrating, "I'm very sorry, Daniel, but Patrick is dead. His body was found in an alley not far from Harrods."

Daniel paled. "What? When?"

Caius lifted a hand and flicked a finger over his shoulder.

From behind the Rex, Constantine stepped forwards with controlled and dangerous grace. His blue eyes, distant and empty, turned to Daniel as he drew from the breast pocket of his crisp blazer a small wallet that he offered in an outstretched hand. "One hour and twelve minutes ago an unknown Lamia reported the discovery of your driver, deceased. This was found in the alley with his body."

Daniel took the wallet and sighed in recognition. The driver's license within verified the wallet to being Patrick's. He looked to Constantine and asked, "What happened to him?"

Constantine's emotionless eyes shifted to Caius who gave a slight nod. Clearing his smooth voice, Constantine answered Daniel. "The cause of his death has not been determined. The details will be left to the medical examiner who will prepare a report once the autopsy is completed. The report will be delivered to Caius, and when thoroughly investigated, will be forwarded on to you and your brothers."

Daniel's lips moved as if to form another question when suddenly his eyes went wide and he turned his gaze to Kain. "Was Regan with Patrick?"

Kain slowly shook his head. "If she was, there were no signs of her. The car is still missing."

"The car is missing?"

"It appears that Patrick arrived this morning to pick Regan up and then drove her to Harrods,' answered Kain, 'at least, that's what his log indicates. The last log of his within the system was a notice that he was returning to Harrods to retrieve her. Neither returned."

Taking a step back, Daniel fell into a chair. He was shaking, and his already pale skin turned white. Amber was at his side, offering him a cup of water and cooing gently to him. He took the water, frowning as the shaking of his hand caused the liquid to spill over the edge. "What about Regan?"

Caius gently cleared his voice and motioned Constantine back to his position, and the tall, black haired Lamia obeyed and returned to his spot behind the Rex. Caius laced his hands within his lap as he watched Daniel shaking. "The Urbanae Seniatatis Cara has been notified of the situation. Kain has provided me with a description of Miss. Scott, and an alert has been sent to all Familia and all owners of Negotium within the Terreotorium. An investigation has started on Patrick's death and the kidnapping of Miss. Scott."

Daniel's eyes went wide. "Kidnapping?"

Caius nodded a somberly then drew a deep breath of air into his lungs. "We must speak of this woman, Daniel, and the fact that her cousin has been missing, reportedly taken from her own flat by David Servilii."

Daniel twitched and ran his empty eyes to Kain who stared at him with a hard eye. "You reported Joyce's disappearance?"

"Of course," said Kain with a curt nod. "I told you that I would."

"You should have informed me, yourself, of Miss. Scott's connection with Joyce Scott and the fact that you and your brother had knowledge of the woman's illegal Creare. It was your duty to the Lex and to me, as your Rex, to have reported the incident at Joyce Scott's flat."

Daniel slid his eyes to Caius who had spoken and flinched when he fell beneath the Roman's imposing and intense eyes. He then looked to Rhain who was standing at the bar and who shrugged his shoulders ever so slightly. Gulping, Daniel looked back to the Rex. "My apologies, sir, but my direct concern was for Regan's safety."

"Which could have been dealt with correctly if you had bothered to inform me."

Daniel turned his eyes away and sighed heavily. The chair he sat in groaned as he leaned forwards, hunching his back, to stare into the cup of water. "I understand, and that is my fault. I knew at the time the situation was of a delicate nature and needed to be handled with the utmost care, however, I also knew that Regan could not be allowed to discover the deteriorating condition of her cousin once Joyce mysteriously appeared. It was my duty to see to Regan as she was adamant about contacting the police. If I had not acted promptly, she would have contacted the emergency service, and then the situation would have escalated. I could not allow that."

Caius narrowed his green eyes, regarding Daniel carefully, as he listened to every word the Filias was saying. "Explain to me what occurred the night Miss. Scott returned to the flat after your evening with her at Theodore Servilii's art exhibit."

He raised a hand, indicating a solid point that was mirrored with the underline threat within his next statement, "And I warn you, do not leave out a single detail, no matter how small it is. With Joyce unaccounted for, obviously having survived the Creare, and now her cousin having been taken, it is imperative that I know all that has occurred."

"Do you understand me?" he went on to ask.

Daniel gave a gloomy nod then closed his eyes as he prepared himself to relive the past few days, making sure every detail was given. He started with telling Caius of Regan's worried call when Joyce had not returned till late in the evening. He told the Rex that he tried his best to set Regan's worries aside and indicated that he had contacted Rhain for any information of the young woman's whereabouts at the Crucible. That is when he went on to explain that Joyce had last been seen at Rhain's club before leaving the property with David of her own free will.

Rhain confirmed that with a nod before draining his glass of whiskey, drowning the muttered curse that was on the tip of his tongue.

Daniel went on to explain that Regan had called him not long after, full of panic that Joyce had returned, however, in dire need of medical attention. Daniel knew from Regan's quick exam of her cousin that she had been fed on, and unfortunately left to die. Regan had wanted to contact the police and call for an ambulance, but Daniel couldn't allow that so he rushed over to the apartment to see Joyce's condition for himself and to make sure Regan was safe.

He told Caius that he had informed Kain of what was going on and that he had seen Joyce, and sadly the young woman was deceased. Kain confirmed this and told Caius that he had ordered Daniel to return with Regan, to protect the Proprietas they had suspicions that she carried. Rhain was to see to Joyce - dispatching the woman if need be.

Daniel informed Caius that he brought Regan directly to a secure apartment within Thorn Inc., met with his brothers and Theodore to explain the situation, and then returned to see to Regan before he turned in for the day. However, the heaviness of the room pressed down upon his shoulders when he mentioned his impromptu meeting with David. He didn't want to look towards Kain, but his eyes slid across the room any way and he winced when he saw Kain's lips twitching with rage and disappointment. He didn't bother to inform those within the room that he spent the previous night making love to her, but did inform them that he told her that he would be leaving for a short while with Rhain and would return as soon as he could. When finished, he hung his head so a few strands of his hair could grant him shelter from his brother's murderous glare. Beneath his breath, he muttered an apology.

Caius listened to Daniel and every word that was spoken. When Rhain and Kain were mentioned, the eldest speaking, he looked to the other Lamia before turning his attention back to Daniel. He didn't speak or stop the young Lamia from his explanation of the previous events. Though he did turn a curious glance to Rhain as the other, more dynamic, twin crossed the room to take a seat when Daniel told of his and Rhain's venture this night.

He wasn't pleased that the twins had taken such a delicate matter into their own hands as there were important guidelines to follow with such a situation. However, he did understand Daniel's need to protect Regan. If she did hold the Proprietas within her blood, it was vital that she be protected by Daniel - by all of them

When Daniel was finished, Caius slowly rose from the chair, his taut body moving beneath his fine suit of storm grey that accented his green eyes and his black hair. The handsome man, of proud Roman lineage, crossed the room in determined strides to stand before one of the windows. He laced his hands behind his back and took a deep breath that expanded his taut chest before looking out to the reflection of London spread out before him, lights glittering in the darkness of night.

"Has it been confirmed that Miss. Scott does have the Proprietas?" he inquired smoothly, his voice a mixture of Italian and English accent.

Daniel gave a frown and a slight shake of his head. "Not yet. But I am sure that the trait is in her blood."

Caius regarded Daniel through the reflective glass of the window. "Oh? Have you tasted her Sanguis?" Daniel's black eyes snapped up, wide with shock as if the very idea was taboo to him. Caius' lips turned to a slight smile. "I see. Then you make this assumption on the simple fact that David told you that Joyce Scott had, in fact, survived and is currently residing with him?"

Daniel gave a slow nod.

"And you believe his word?"

"We also have confirmation from a Proscriptus by the name of Angus McFarland," said Rhain.

Caius turned to regard Rhain with an impassive brow raised. "And who is this particular Proscriptus?"

"An associate of David's," replied Rhain with a lick to his dry lips.

"And how did his name come to your attention?"

Rhain glanced to Daniel and felt his heart crack upon seeing a thin line of red trailing down over his twin's pale cheek. When Daniel looked away, Rhain turned his hard gaze to the Rex. "Daniel and I went out to hunt for information on David's whereabouts, as well as any information on Joyce. Many of our contacts mentioned Angus, so we searched him out."

"I see." Caius turned around, raising his chin as his jaw tightened and his voice pressed thin. "So you and brother not only withheld important information pertaining to an illegal Creare, but you both took it upon yourselves to seek information on David Servilii. I take it this Angus McFarland is not available for questioning?"

A sly and twisted grin graced Rhain's lips. "Unfortunately, he's indisposed."

Caius' hard eyes narrowed and a flash of anger could be seen within the silver speckles. "You mean he has been disposed of."

Rhain shrugged and snorted. "What can I say? I have butter fingers."

A curl of displeasure touched Caius' handsome lips and he scowled to Rhain's admission that the Proscriptus had been killed. "I see that my Inquisitors have been rather busy." Shaking his head, the Rex tsked and stated, "I am not pleased, not pleased at all. In fact, I'm greatly disappointed in both of you. If either of you had bothered to inform me of what was happening, I could have taken steps to secure Miss. Scott in a safe residence till Joyce and David were located."

"You mean lock Regan away and scare her to death?" Rhain barked out a laugh. "Yeah, that would've been a great postcard home. Hi mum and dad. Guess what? Joyce was kidnapped and I was taken into custody by some guy pretending to be a King! I have a selfie with Joyce's bloody corpse. Hugs and kisses!" Rhain threw up his arms in disgust. "Bloody brilliant!"

"Rhain!" barked Kain, moving to stand from the desk, and when he did, the room froze. "Watch your tongue, boy."

Rhain snarled, pulling back his lips to flash his fangs in a show of dislike to his brother's authority and command.

Caius raised a hand to Kain that had the elder brother retreating a step. He took a step towards Rhain with his chin lifting and a critical glare shadowing his Roman features. From Rhain, Caius looked to Daniel who had finally raised his head, and the rigid Rex sighed when he saw a bloody streak staining Daniel's rather beautiful face. "Tell me,' he said, 'what do you plan to do now?"

Daniel shook his head. "I have no choice. I must find Regan. I made a promise to her that I would keep her safe." He lowered his head and whispered pitifully, "I have failed her. And now my failure has taken the life of my Servus, my friend."

A soft whimper came from Amber as she draped an arm about him, dabbing at his bloody tear with a soft tissue. "No,' she cooed, 'you have not failed her, Daniel. And you are certainly not responsible for Patrick's death. You have tried your best to protect Regan, but David took advantage of the situation."

"David warned me to stay away from him and to leave Joyce alone. He told me that she was happy with him and didn't want leave him." He raised his red touched eyes, looking from Kain to Caius. "He knew already that you were going to be notified, sir, and he had his suspicions that both Kain and Theodore would speak with you. He must have learned that Kain had spoken to you somehow."

Caius bristled and growled low within his throat. "Are you insinuating that David has a spy in my confidence?"

Daniel gave a faint and helpless shrug.

"I highly doubt that." Finally, Constantine spoke, and his warm and melodic voice, a mixture of Welsh and Italian, caressed across the tense atmosphere of the room. He took a few steps forwards, pausing at the side of a table as he looked to Caius for permission to continue to speak, and with a nod from the Rex, he cleared his voice. "Only three were in the office when discussing this matter - myself, Caius and Kain. It is more than likely that David assumed that Caius would eventually discover his involvement, so he took the initiative by abducting Miss. Scott. He took her to deliver a message to not only Daniel but the entire Thorn family that he has the power to do as he wishes and that if any of you pursue this matter, he will carry out his threat."

Caius nodded, agreeing with his Lieutenant. Turning his gaze back to Daniel, he inquired, "I ask again. What do you plan to do?"

"What can he do?" Amber asked back, sitting now upon the arm of Daniel's chair, comforting him more like a coddling mother to a child than an adult to a heart-broken and worried man. "David is a very powerful Lamia, not only in battle skill but in the numbers of his followers. It's common knowledge that he has strong and influential Lamia, Proscriptus and Lex abiding alike, on his side. If he wishes to disappear or gather allies to his side, he has no trouble doing so. Daniel can't fight against him and his followers by himself."

Daniel eased from Amber's embrace, gently drawing her arm from about him. "I don't care how many followers he has. He has Regan. I will go into David's personal Hell to find her and bring her home before David touches a hair on her head." He narrowed his eyes and the blackness within flared as his voice lowered to a venomous hiss. "I will hunt him down and silence him for good. I will spread through the Underground and the Proscriptus masses a solid warning that no soul should dare mess with my family or those important to me."

Caius crossed the room to Daniel, and when he came to stand before the Filias, Daniel leaned back so their eyes could lock. Reaching forwards, the Rex took hold of Daniel's chin within a three finger grasp. "You swear to this?"

Daniel flashed his fangs as the metallic flecks in his eyes stirred. "On my life."

"On your life?" Caius tipped his head, his grip tightening till a slight flinch creased Daniel's brow. "That is a potent declaration. Most men would not swear upon their life, the cost is far too great for their pitiful ego to accept. What spurs your heart, Daniel Thorn? What is it about Miss Regan Scott that has you so hot for David's blood?"

"She is my Socia, and I am in love with her."

All eyes turned to regard Daniel with a level of shock, that is, till Rhain howled out, "Fuck!"

The room fell silent once again till Caius and Kain sighed heavily and in unison.

The Rex clapped Daniel on the shoulder, speaking softly and oddly comfortingly. "I understand you want to run off and skin David for taking this young woman, but I cannot let you go rushing off blindly to your death. Though I understand that it is your right to protect your Socia and keep her close to you, killing David would not look good on you within the Concilium."

"That's bullshit," snapped Rhain with a bite to his voice. "The Concilium should give Daniel a damn medal for sucking up his balls and going after this prick. David's been a pain in the ass of the English Concilium and Basilica for three or four decades now. The Senators and Ieudi have been foaming at the mouths for David's blood. Though Regan's involvement in this entire mess is a fucked up tragedy, this situation is the perfect scenario needed for David to finally be hunted down and dealt with. Hell, it shouldn't have taken this long to deal with the bastard. It's almost as if somebody is protecting his ass from the fire of judgment."

Caius returned to his chair, taking a seat. He crossed one knee over the other then brushed a hand down a pant let as if sweeping away a speck of dust. "I agree with you, Rhain."

"What?" Kain and Daniel asked at the same time, stunned that anybody would agree with Rhain's well-known rants of dislike of the political and legal system of the English Republica.

Even Rhain was shocked. "You…do?"

Caius nodded as he squared his broad shoulders. "David has been a scourge upon this city and the Lamia of this Republica for half a century, if not longer. He is a threat, and you are correct in saying that his trial for his crimes is long overdue."

Rhain arched a brow. "What are you saying?"

"You and Daniel are two of the most feared Legati working directly under my order. I have given you both lenience to perform your duties without the concern of the Concilium, and for decades you have followed my orders and carried out your duties impeccably. And in the wake of your battles, you both have excelled and have become legend, gaining a bloody and feared reputation as being the Inquisitors, my Inquisitors. Amber is correct in saying that Daniel cannot face David and his associates on his own. However, with his twin at his side, I believe David can be defeated and Daniel can be victorious in his vendetta."

The twins passed a cautious eye to each other before looking back to Caius. "What are you getting at?" asked Rhain.

Caius, brushing back a lock of his black hair, turned his cold eyes to the twins. "I am ordering you both to dust off your blades and take up your title of Inquisitor once again. I want you two to hunt David by any means, across any borders, and into any domain and cut him down!"

Rhain's lips pulled back to show a smile of fangs. "Is that an order?"

Caius leaned forwards in the chair with a groan of leather. He locked Rhain and Daniel with a cruel smile that pulled back his handsome mouth. "Indeed it is, and all within this room can bear witness to this formal Venatio called down upon David Servilii. This Venatio is to be carried out from the shadows and in silence. Is that understood?"

Rhain nodded with a devious chuckle. "What's not to understand?" He looked to Daniel and asked, "What say you brother?"

Daniel's dark eyes narrowed on their Rex, and though he heard his brother, he was solely focused upon Caius. "Do you want him dead or alive?"

The chuckle that came from Caius was both pleasing and disturbing; pleased that the twins would follow his commands and destroy David, and disturbing simply because he found the notion exiting. "Alive. However, if his death cannot avoided, I will have no complaints."

Breathing out a slow breath, Daniel nodded then raised his chin as a low snarl danced from his lips. "To bring Regan back to me safely, I will carry out your orders and bring David's dead heart back upon a silver platter."

"Good,' Caius purred softly, leaning back within his chair, 'very good. Flush him out of the hole he has dug himself in and tear him apart. I will give you forty-eight hours. No one must know of this Venatio. Use whatever means you must to carry out this hunt. Do you understand?"

The twins replied in unison, "Yes, sir."

Caius nodded then waved a dismissive hand. "Good. Now go. Report to me when your order has been completed."

Without hesitation, Rhain and Daniel offered a nod to their King before they departed the office, and when the door closed, Kain slid his expressionless eyes to Caius. "Are you sure about this, Caius? Rhain and Daniel may be strong and imposing fighters, but David is much stronger than them."

Caius chuckled, flashing an amused smile to his associate. "You do not give them enough credit, my friend," said the Rex. "Have confidence in their abilities for they have the blood of the Drasus Familia within them, and that blood breeds warriors. Your siblings are formidable killers, which is one reason I employ them in my service."

"Besides,' he went on to say, 'never underestimate the power of a man who is in love and whose lover is in danger. Daniel has the hunger and the drive to find David and eliminate him."

"I suppose you are right." Kain nodded his head and silenced any more concerns. He glanced towards the office door, frowning heavily as he muttered under his breath, "Be safe…both of you."

~ ~ ~ ~

"So, what are you going to do when you get Regan back? Have you thought about that?"

Daniel glanced to his brother as the two walked through the Domus. "Honestly? I haven't thought that far ahead yet. All of this is happening so quickly. I haven't had any time to sit down and figure this all out. Regan's been the sole focus in my mind since I met her, increasing by the hour, and now, I can't help but feel my Daemon howling her name."

He shook his head, and his voice dropped. "This is all my fault. If I had not asked her to join me at Theodor's place, then she would have been at the flat the night Joyce disappeared and Joyce would not have departed for the Crucible. They would have been together. Joyce would not have met David."

"Then you would not have Regan."

Daniel glanced to Rhain only to frown and look away. "I would rather have her safe than have her in danger. If having my life vacant of her presence would keep her safe, then so be it."

"Bull shit," said Rhain with a snort and a roll of his eyes. "You're in love with her. You'd never be able to let her walk out of your life. Doing that would drive you insane. What Joyce did was the catalyst of all this. It's her own fault, not yours and not Regan's. I still believe this was all a damn good swing of coincidence."

"How can you say that?" asked Daniel as the two walked down the small hallway to the elevator.

"How can you not? Bloody hell, Daniel. Will you put your humanity aside and stop thinking you're the cause of everybody's problems? We're only responsible for our own shit. Even if our actions or thoughts or words produces a negative effect from the behavior of others, we're not responsible for them."

"That's not true. You're responsible for the safety of your patrons. If a guest at your club is served too much alcohol at the bar, it's your and your staffs' responsibility to not allow that individual to get behind the wheel of their car and drive off. If they do, and end up killing somebody or themselves, you're liable since you let them walk out piss drunk."

"You're damn right about that. That's why I have strict safety rules in my establishment. But that's something completely different."

"How so?" Daniel asked as he pressed the button for the elevator.

"You and Regan went out for a nice evening, and that night Regan's safety was your responsibility. Joyce let her petty, human jealousy cloud her judgment. So to comfort her own negativity she went out looking for a guy to fuck for the night, and I highly doubt she ran a background check on the bloke. She didn't have to leave with David, but she did anyway. And that's her own damn fault."

"Besides,' he went on to say with a smirk, 'our entire race circles around the Fates and their damn games. Who knows? Maybe that night it wasn't just you and Regan who were walking the lines of your destiny, but Joyce and David. If we go along with the Fates, all of this was meant to happen. And on that thought the outcome is supposed to happen as well. Did you ever think of that?"

The elevator arrived, the doors silently opening, and the two brothers entered - Rhain leaning to one wall and Daniel to another. The doors closed behind them, and Rhain pressed the button to send them down into the belly of the building.

Daniel leaned his head back to the shiny wall and turned his eyes up to the Venetian glass ceiling. "No."

"You should, especially if you've taken Regan as your Socia. You're going to have a lot of explaining to do when this is all over. You might want to start thinking on what you're going to tell her."

Daniel didn't respond. He closed his eyes and placed his hands behind his back, fingers tapping to the wall.

"She's taken over your soul."

186

Daniel mumbled something past his scowl. Not in the mood to discuss his personal feelings for Regan, Daniel chose to be silent.

Rhain pulled a packet of cigarettes from a back pocket, popped up a stick then proceeded to light it. If Daniel was going to comment on him smoking in the elevator, well, he could go fuck himself. While watching his brother's face, Rhain drew in a drag from the cigarette then blew the smoke from his lungs through his nostrils. "Why don't you ever talk to me?"

Daniel's eyes looked forwards, yet still he said nothing.

Rhain jabbed the cigarette in Daniel's direction. "We're brothers, you and me. We're blood! Yet you still keep yourself distant from me. Why?"

"Whatever do you mean, Frater? We talk all the time."

Rhain's eyes narrowed. "Don't get passive fucking aggressive with me, you git. I'm talking real talk, you know? I'm talking about what's going on inside your head and inside your heart. You don't need to hide your emotions from me just because you think I'm not capable of having the same feelings or understanding them."

Rhain sighed while running a hand through his spikey hair. "It's like you don't trust me with your secrets anymore."

Daniel raised his eyes then sighed heavily. "Forgive me, Rhain. I know you mean well, but my private life is just that, private."

"You should've told me you were in love with her the other night, after your run in with David. Then again, I figured you had fallen for her before you slept with her." Rhain drew in another pull of smoke, held it in his lungs for a few moments, allowing the luscious heat to swirl about, then slowly released the cloud.

Daniel raised his eyes, stunned that Rhain had discovered that he had slept with Regan. He shouldn't be surprised, considering they could nearly read each other's thoughts - twin powers and all. But he suspected, that in passing, Rhain had smelled Regan's sexualized scent upon him.

"You haven't been in love for over seven decades, though I think you came close with that guy in Japan. What was his name?"

"Yuu."

Rhain nodded and blew out another puff of smoke. "Yeah, that's the guy. So tell me, what's so special about her?"

Daniel groaned as he closed his eyes, bowed his head and crossed his arms to his thin chest. "I don't know."

"Yes, Daniel, you do."

"No, Rhain, I don't. There are too many reasons; I can't think of just one or even two."

"Don't fuck with me, Daniel," Rhain groaned, pointing his glowing cigarette towards his twin. "I can read you like a book. I saw that look you had on your face when Caius ordered the Venatio. That was the look of a man lost to love and filled with relief. The only reason you're so hot for David's death is because he's carried out his threat and has your girl, and now you have permission to hunt him down and carry out his execution. You're not going to stop till you pull every bone from his body."

187

Rhain licked the smoky taste from his lips as he leveled his twin with a steady and sturdy eye. "You won't rest till you have your Socia back."

Daniel's black eyes darkened as he glared across the elevator. Suddenly, all of his emotions, his worry and his fear, came rushing out from him in one harsh snap. "You're damn right! I'm going to massacre that Proscriptus! He has no right to threaten Regan, nor does he have the right to take her from me. I won't let him hurt her!"

Daniel pressed his hand over his heart. His voice dropped as he snarled, "She's mine, Rhain. Regan is all I think about. Ever since I met her, she's found a way to burrow into my heart and bring it back to life with her innocence and her human spirit. You don't know what it's like to have light fill your darkness only to have that light snatched away. I've been in the dark for too long. I want my light back. I want her back."

Daniel turned to face the wall where he pressed his forehead against the glossy wood. "The reason why I didn't tell you is, in truth, because I thought you wouldn't understand. You've had many lovers since your Nasei, and even now you're with two or three different women a night. You don't open yourself up to your women. Most of the time you don't even ask them their names so you don't form any sort of emotional attachments to them. You wouldn't know the fear of losing one of them, the fear I have that Regan may not survive her captivity with David. You wouldn't understand the torment I am going through thinking that bastard might try and change her! I can't begin to imagine her going through the pain of the Creare alone, and I doubt David would do the humane thing and put her out of her pain if the Creare doesn't take effect. I don't want that! I don't want her suffering for his insanity!"

"I,' Daniel paused taking a shuddering, shallow breath, '…I can't lose her."

Rhain, who drew another pull from his cigarette, let his brother rant and point a judgmental finger to him. After all, they were brothers, and time after time again they turned on each other when in their own battles of pain and stress. Daniel's heart came pouring out along with his words, fear and love over powering him.

"You're right,' said Rhain softly, looking down to the floor, 'I don't know what you're feeling. In fact, you're right on all of it. I don't want to get to know one woman and experience all the crap that comes with an intimate relationship. I don't want to put my heart out there on the line for some trollop to come and use to her desire. I won't become a play thing to anybody."

Daniel chuckled, glancing slightly over his shoulder. "But you're willing to play women to your needs."

Rhain shrugged. "I never said I didn't. Women come to me for one thing and one thing only, sex. They might have hope that afterwards they'll weasel their way into my life and my heart, but that won't ever happen. So you're right, I don't know what it would be like if the woman I fell in love with was taken away from me, but I do know what it would feel like if somebody tried to fuck with the Crucible. I would lay down a path of pain on their soul that they never could have imagined. I might not have a woman like Regan, but I have something of great importance to me, my brothers. And for you and Kain, I would fight against the entire world."

Daniel closed his eyes, giving a slight smile. "I pity the fool who vomits on the floors of your club."

Rhain's lips curled in to a smirk and he chuckled. "Don't pity Alasdair. He only gets drunk enough to get sick on the floors every few months."

Daniel chuckled softly.

Rhain flashed his twin a grin. "You're a fool in love."

Daniel turned back around to slump against the wall. "Yeah, I am."

"I'm glad you found her, Daniel. So you need to give some thought on how you're going to proceed with this, not just our hunt but in dealing with Regan after."

"First thing's first, Frater,' said Daniel as he leveled his brother with a dark expression of hunger, 'we find David, we kill him, and then we burn his world to cinders."

The elevator glided to a stop and the doors swept open.

Rhain clapped his twin on the shoulder as he pushed from the wall, stepping into the center of the elevator. "Then we'll figure that out when we get there."

With a smile, he walked out into the short hall, pausing to glance back and call, "Are you coming? Or am I going to have all the fun on my own?"

Daniel pushed from the wall, following his brother into the garage. "Let's go."

XII

He's taken her. David has her, my Regan. I will not permit him to harm her. I will not allow it! I will hunt him down and rip his soul apart. This world has had enough of David Servilii and the insanity that his twisted mind has created - the corruption of his soul. Regan's spirit is far too gentle and her humanity far too serene to be tortured by his darkness. She is mine; my responsibility and mine to protect. I will dust off my title, raise my sword, and drive my blade through David's black heart - over and over again - till the organ is nothing more than a slab of rotten meat.

Heed my warning, David. I am coming for you, and there is no corner on this planet where you can hide, no shadow dark enough to sink into. Your life will be mine. I promise you that.

- *Daniel Rhys Thorn*

~ ~ ~ ~

"*N*o, you can't! David, you promised!"

Regan woke up cold and curled up on the hard floor of a dark room that smelled heavily of dust and mildew. Her head hurt, throbbing in agony, and her throat felt raw as if there was a layer of stagnant dust coating the insides. How long had she been unconscious? All she remembered was David's cruel face looking at her from behind a gun. She would never forget the murderous look within his eyes before pain turned into blackness.

At that thought, she gingerly touched a hand to her forehead only to wince to the sensitive nerves firing beneath her skin. He must have struck her with the gun, knocking her unconscious.

When the haze cleared behind her eyes, Regan sat up with a painful wince from the hard floor pressing against her aching bones. After collecting her dizziness, she looked about her - confused as to her location. Where was she? There was only one light within the room, shining brightly from the ceiling. She couldn't make out any specific details to the room besides the coldness seeping from the cement floor and the old stone walls. There was, however, a door shadowed within a corner.

Shortly, it became clear that Regan was not alone. There were voices dancing through the timeworn door from out in the hallway, muffled but close by. The closer she scooted to the door, the clearer the voices became.

"Daniel Thorn was warned."

It was David's voice, and the tone sent a quiver through her from the snarl she heard echoing his words. "I told him ta fuck off an' keep his nose ou' o' my business, bu' wha' happens? My own father calls ta try an' talk some sense inta me. Then Daniel an' his bastard brother tortured one o' my best men an' tore his head from his body! Tha' is unforgivable!"

"But David, Regan didn't have anything to do with that!"

"I warned Daniel. I told tha' little dick tha' I would take his girl if he didn't crawl home an' play nice."

"But why did you have to hurt her? You could've let me talk to her. She would've come with me if you'd just given me a chance to convince her. You don't have to keep her locked up!"

"She is my trump card. I will use her ta ge' wha' I want," replied David with a harsher snap to his voice. "I won't 'ave any more o' my men killed by any Lex lovin' Lamia! Yer new ta this world, Joyce. You would be wise no' ta question me. This is my territory. I do wha' I please!"

"Are you going to do to her what you did to me? Are you going to turn her in to another monster? Are you going to kill her too?"

"Is tha' wha' I am ta ya, Joyce? Yer killer?" he asked calmly. "Am I nothing more than a monster ta ya?"

"Of course not, David,' she said softly, almost too soft for Regan to understand, 'but I swear, if you hurt my cousin, you'll regret it."

In the next second a painful yelp was heard echoing the hallway followed by a loud howl. "Ne'er threaten me! Do ya hear me, Joyce? I am yer Parens. I gave ya life!"

"You took my life!"

Within her cell, Regan had her ear pressed against the grimy door to hear as clearly as she could the conversation going on out in the hall. Joyce sounded enraged that David had kidnapped her cousin. But what did Joyce mean when David called himself her Parens and that he gave her life while she accused him of killing her? Joyce sounded scared and upset!

"Joyce!" Regan howled, banging her fists to the door. "It's me! Joyce, let me out!"

Outside in the hall, the pounding on the door silenced both David and Joyce. They looked a few doors down, and from the corner of his eyes, David saw Joyce's features twist with a look of painful guilt. She was crying; her beautiful alabaster cheeks painted with thin lines of watery blood. It tore him apart. She was his first and only Filia. No - she was more to him than that. She was his Socia.

"Ah, Joyce,' he sighed, pulling her body into his embrace, 'don' cry. She is only here ta bring Daniel ta me. After I 'ave dealt with him, I'll le' her go."

Joyce shook her head against his chest. "I am not an idiot, David. I've been paying attention to everything over the past few days, learning as much as I can about the Lamia world. I'm getting a sense of what you do and how you do it. I know Regan's not safe here. You promised me that you'd keep her safe and treat her right. I don't want her to get hurt. She's my best friend."

191

Joyce whimpered. "Promise me that once this is over she can stay with us. Maybe you can change her if she wants to. You can do that, can't you?"

David breathed out a stale sigh as he stroked Joyce's hair. What she was asking him wasn't too far off his true course. He'd use Regan to draw Daniel to him, kill the fucker, and then declare war on the Thorn family, the Drasus Familia, and the damn Rex of England. He'd see all of them burn for the humiliation they brought upon him. If using Regan would secure his goals, then so be it. If she had the Proprietas, then, when all his enemies were nothing more than dust, he would see that she too faced the Creare. Regan would make a lovely edition to his new Familia. By agreeing to the desperate pleading from his Filia, David would have the pleasures of both women.

"Alright,' he told her softly and with a gentle kiss to the top of her head, 'I promise tha' I will see yer cousin safe. Once I deal with Daniel I will take yer cousin under my wing. Ya won' 'ave ta live with ou' her - ever."

David would enjoy Daniel's demise a hell of a lot more if he captured Daniel, drove the bastard insane by the use of Regan, and then sit back to watch the Thorn boy go mad by his own Daemon.

The slow, twisting smile that coiled David's lips had a brow arching upon Joyce's features. She tipped her head and asked, "What are you thinking?"

David leaned down, brushing his lips against hers. "Regan will do me well." He touched her chilled cheek. "Ya two will stand by my side an' serve me well."

Joyce's eyes slowly narrowed. She didn't like hearing that Regan would also be at David's side, her rightful side. That wasn't fair. David didn't need anyone but Joyce at his side. "I don't understand…"

The Lamia chuckled as he stroked her cheek. "Regan will serve me long after I rip Daniel's body ta pieces. She'll share my bed along with ya."

A slow growl slid past Joyce's pressed lips. "Over my dead body!" she snapped. "She abandoned me for Daniel! There's no way I'm letting her take you, and to hell if I'll let you abandon me!"

David cocked his head to the side. The fuming anger that burned from within Joyce's eyes brought a chuckle from him. "Yer no' pretty when covered in a layer o' jealousy, my dear." He leaned to whisper to her ear, "Ya belong ta me, Joyce. Ya don' question me. Regan, in tha end, will be mine, an' I will use her ta fill my desires just like I used ya." Lifting a finger, he dragged a nail along her cheek with enough pressure to part her skin.

Joyce winced, leaning away from the stinging cut.

"I'm putting ya in charge o' Regan, Joyce. I' is up ta ya ta keep her calm an' make her understand wha' is going on. I' is in her best interest ta cooperate at all times. Bu' understand this,' he told her, raising a finger before her eyes, 'ya can't say one word about our kind ta her. Understand? No' a word on Daniel. Nothin'."

When he saw the shadow of defiance in her eyes, David coiled fingers about the back of her neck and pulled her against him. He crushed his mouth to hers with his tongue thrusting deeply in a kiss that violated her sweet mouth with intensity and power. He bit her lip hard enough to draw some blood, but when he heard his lover moan, David drew away.

His kiss had Joyce purring and leaning up to meet him. The taste of her own blood had her licking his lips, spreading instant warmth to coil and flex within her belly as her arms slipped about his shoulders to hold herself close to her Socius. She was completely under his thumb, she knew it but didn't care. In her mind David was hers as much as he thought she was his.

She whispered adoringly, "Of course, David. I will do all that you ask of me."

Control - David loved it. The power he had over Joyce, her mind, her wants, and her body was all within the palm of his hand. He kissed her forehead then released her. "Go ta her. Tell her tha' her life depends on her being a good girl." He gave a swat to her backside, sending her to stumble forwards. The giggle that came from her brought him to grin before he turned down the hall.

When the voices stopped, Regan heard footsteps coming closer, and when the metal lock of the door clicked, she scooted away in panic till her back hit a wall. It did not take long for the door to open, casting light into the small room. Regan recoiled as the bright light tore through her eyes, rendering her unable to see the person who came walking in before the door closed. The dim darkness eased the pain as her eyes fluttered open, but it took a few seconds for the spots and stars to dissipate.

When she could see clearly, she gasped and stumbled forwards to hug her cousin tightly. "Joyce! It's you! I thought you were dead!"

"You're finally awake," Joyce said flatly, stiffening to the embrace.

The delight in Regan turned to horror when Joyce stepped away, and Regan saw that her cousin's flesh was sickly pale and her eyes were dull and empty. Regan shivered to the coldness seeping from her cousin. She backed away. "Joyce? Are you alright?"

Joyce squared Regan with a hard glare. "What's wrong? Don't you recognize me?"

Regan mumbled behind a hand, "What has happened to you? You look..."

"Dead?" A cackled laugh slipped from the young Filia's lips. "If you only knew."

"I don't understand. Where am I? What am I doing here?"

"You're in David's house; my house,' she added with a proud smile, 'and he brought you here."

"This place is your house?"

Joyce chuckled. "Of course it is."

Anger and hurt crossed within Regan's eyes. "How can you stay here with him? He kidnapped you! He kidnapped me." Pushing from the wall, she grabbed at her cousin's hands, pleading with her, "Let's get out of here, Joyce! Daniel's waiting for me. I have to get back to him. We'll get you to a hospital."

Joyce pulled her hands from Regan's grasp with a hard snarl and a snap of teeth. "I'm not going anywhere with you or that bastard Thorn boy you've thrown yourself at! I'm staying here with David."

Regan recoiled as if she had been struck, and a look of horror mixed with complete shock shadowed her features. "What? How can you say that after all that he's done?" She began to step away till her back hit the cool, damp wall. "I don't understand."

"He's done nothing but given me everything I have ever wanted. I am a queen in his eyes! There's no way I'm leaving the man I love."

"Love? That man couldn't even spell love if he tried! Don't be blind!" She pushed from the wall, rushing to grasp Joyce's shoulders. "Listen to me! He's brainwashed you, Joyce! Snap out of this. Come on, let's go home. We'll go to Daniel. He'll take care of you. We'll find out what..."

"No!" Joyce howled as she jumped back and backhanded her beloved cousin so hard that the blow sent Regan down to the floor. A look of electric rage danced through Joyce's green eyes. She growled at her cousin, "I am a part of him, and he's a part of me!"

Pressing a hand to her chest, Joyce's features twisted in to a sickening expression of dark and irrational narcissism. "He is my will, and I am his devotion."

Tears of fear and bewilderment tumbled down Regan's cheeks. She scooted away when her cousin took a step closer. "What has happened to you? What has he done?"

Joyce chose to ignore her cousin's questions with a little scoff. She then smiled the most chilling smile one could ever produce as she squatted down before Regan with her arms across her knees. "David says he has plans for you. He wants you to behave yourself and do what he says so he can finally get his revenge on Daniel and his family. So listen to me, Regan. If you don't behave yourself and do exactly as David tells you, well, you won't be happy with the results. David doesn't like to be disobeyed."

Joyce chuckled with a wicked grin and mewed as she stood, "He promised me that he wouldn't hurt you."

Regan slowly shook her head as hot tears trickled down her face. "Why would you do this to me? You're my cousin."

"I am doing all of this because David has asked me to. I want to make him happy," Joyce purred in disillusion.

Regan gulped. "What does he want with Daniel and me?"

Joyce shrugged with a wave of a flippant hand. "Honestly? I could care less. I just know that killing Daniel would make him very happy, and that would make me happy. I wish you could understand that when you're in love you would do anything to see the man you love happy."

Shivering, Regan shook her head in complete disbelief. She was no longer feeling shock but some other emotion she couldn't completely understand, disgust was one part of that complete emotion. "I don't think I want to understand anymore. You're not the same Joyce I've known since we were kids. I don't know what David's done to you..."

The look of disturbing pride that Regan saw flutter within Joyce's eyes brought a shudder to race through her. She whispered in horror, "David's insane."

"No, my dear cousin, he is a God." Joyce laughed out loud as she spun about in a drug like state. "He is my God! You'll see!" With those last words, she skipped from the room.

The door slamming shut and locking caused Regan's body to flinch. Joyce was gone and Regan was left to stare through the empty room as confusion grew and grew within her. Pressing herself back to a corner of the cold cell, Regan huddled in her own embrace. In the darkness, she tugged her knees up to her chest, wrapping her arms about them. Bowing her head, she silently began to cry and prayed that Daniel would find her.

~ ~ ~ ~

Rhain narrowed his eyes and swept another wet lock of his drenched hair from his face, the tenth to stick to his forehead. He took a deep breath, drawing into his lungs the mixed scent of nature, pollutants, and rain. Through the pelting rain and the darkness, Rhain drew aside a branch of the thick hedge-line that shielded his view of the massive factory looming not too far away. His fine nose twitched as a trail of water slid down the slope, pooling at the tip before dripping down and catching upon his handsome mouth.

He licked away the drop as his eyes shifted beneath damp lashes to look in the direction he knew Daniel to be hiding. While a mortal may see only shadows, Rhain could see the illuminating outline of Daniel's body with his keen eyes; his twin's aura an unsteady wave of blue with touches of flexing red.

Overhead, howling thunder was followed by crackling lightening, and the mating of the two elements of natural destruction drew his electric blue eyes skyward, causing his eyelids to flutter as the rain struck his eyes. Rhain looked to the factory and scrunched his nose before releasing the heavily leafed branch as he slipped back into the thick shadows. His steps were quiet, precise, as he crept over to his twin's side.

He spoke softly, in an almost inaudible whisper, "Well? What do you think?"

"I'll give it to David. He's found himself a solid structure to take root in. There's probably a dozen or so entrances and exits to the building, probably all locked and secured with alarms. We cannot spend any spare time checking each entry, door or window. We would be here till sunrise."

Rhain's lips curled and he snarled softly, "No telling how many sentries he's got posted around the place."

Daniel's snarl mimicked Rhain's, and he slowly sat back upon the balls of his heels. "Did you bring the schematics?"

With a nod, Rhain drew from the back pocket of his leather pants his smart phone, and with a few swipes of a naked finger, peeking out from a leather glove tipped with spikes along the knuckles, he brought up the blueprints to the building. He inched closer so Daniel could see; the soft glow of the screen tickled their identical features.

"This building was an old World War II factory where parts for the tanks' stirring systems and wheels were manufactured. It housed some administrative offices on the first and second floors as well. There are four floors plus an expansive cellar and basement, two assembly rooms on both the north and the south sides of the building, delivery garages to the east, and the main entry to the west."

"What's this?" asked Daniel as he pointed to a small section on the prints in the north-east corner of the building.

Rhain leaned closer as he scanned the image. "I'm not sure. It looks like an entrance going down into the basement level, a drop of some sort."

Daniel glanced back to the small opening in the brush so he could scan the area. His lips parted to speak, but he shut his mouth quickly as his lips curled with a wave of disgust. The Lamia raised his head, nostrils flaring as if catching a scent that caused him to cover his nose in revulsion. "Do you smell that?"

Rhain arched a slender brow, curiously watching his brother's sudden change in demeanor. To Daniel's inquiry he sniffed the air, not once but three times, before his face twisted in a look of disgust. "Damn, au de Flesh-Eaters."

"Zombies," Daniel nodded in agreement and sighed in annoyance.

"I hate this smell,' muttered Rhain, 'a combo of spoiled meat, soiled earth, rotten eggs, stinky tofu and polluted death."

"The question is,' added Daniel as he leaned forwards, 'where are they? The stench is strong, meaning they are close by. Otherwise, the scent would have been diluted due to the rain."

True to Daniel's comment, the most deadly undead of all undead came stalking from around the building. Five zombies in total, flesh rotten and hanging from their bones, slowly meandered and limped along the outside perimeter of the factory, slinking from around an obscure corner. All five had been men at one time. And from the looks of their tattered clothing they dated over one hundred years prior, maybe older. How the creatures managed their mobility when most of their muscular and bone structures were nothing but string cheese and dog chewies was beyond Rhain. Hell, a few of them were walking upon broken feet that cracked with each step.

Zombies, in the world of the Lamia, were not like those shown in modern computer games or movies. These were created through magic and by very powerful Venefici who had stepped over the line of decency to embrace the immoral and chaotic powers of the Ars Magica of death- Necromancy. Those sorcerers who proclaimed themselves to be Necromancers were either sought for their abilities to harness and control the powers of death, or shunned for their disturbing skills that many believed was used to abuse the souls of the dead.

Playing with the souls of the deceased, Lamia or Humanus, was considered highly taboo within the Lamia world. Though there were ancient cultures around the Lamia world who praised the necromantic arts and would do anything to have a strong Necromancer in their midst. Rumor had it there were a few Familia within the United Kingdom that bred their Proprietas with intent to harness Necromantic Venefici. And here it seemed that David was one of those Lamia willing to pay a Necromancer for his or her service.

Rhain felt a cold shiver run through his body as one of the Flesh-Eaters lumbered past him. The 'thing' paused with a sloppy jerk of its body, tipping it's torn skull to one side with a wet click of vertebrae as if it was trying to hear with the one fleshy knob of ear that still clung to its head. The creature's eyes were nothing but milky white globs with one orb sunken in the skull while the other seemed to protrude from the orbital socket with a sickening bulge. With no lips over broken teeth, the zombie released a low, watery groan that sent a tremble through its distorted corpse.

Rhain growled from deep within his throat when the creature turned towards him and raised its head to take another watery sniff of the air. Whoever had raised these zombies had done so with the sole purpose of using them as guardians, heightening their magical senses for tracking and hunting. Considering them to be hounds, the creator had implanted in his or her creations all senses needed to hunt through the aid of magic. Though a few of the creatures did not have eyes or ears, or even a nose, their ability to sense out their pray came from a slew of magical sensors that extended a good amount of feet in diameter around them.

Rhain had to hold back the reflexive need to vomit as the smell of ancient decay washed over him. His instincts told him to lash out and kill the creature for it was nothing but a stain upon the world, but his rational mind commanded him to remain still. Killing, let alone touching one of these creatures, would alert the Master not only of the creature's location but what had happened. Rhain cursed within his mind. Necromancy was not a magic he could ever appreciate or respect, so he had to hold himself completely still, force his anger to subside, and slow his heart in order for the Flesh-Eater not to detect his heartbeat. With the rain cascading down from above, he had a better chance of his scent being diluted with the polluted water as even a Lamia's body released a slight smell of death that, though undetectable to humans, was detectable to creatures of the undead.

From the corner of his eyes, Rhain saw Daniel flick a few fingers towards him, indicating to Rhain to calm down. The cautious gaze in Daniel's intense eyes was not one Rhain was unaccustomed to seeing. It meant that Daniel knew that Rhain was itching to fight, but a battle was not necessary and would only draw unwanted attention to their position. With a deep breath, releasing the breath in a puff of chilled air, Rhain nodded before sliding his eyes back to the zombie and its fellow undead who were creeping closer. The creature was looking right to Rhain, but luckily the thick brush and the darkness kept his form hidden from view. However, if the thing took one more step, Rhain would be smack-dab in the detection zone of the zombie's radar - and caught.

Rhain forced a dry, hard lump down his throat as the Flesh-Eater leaned forwards, sniffing. His fingers twitched just above the holster to the Tantō strapped to his right thigh. He stole a glance to Daniel to see his twin focused upon the other two zombies as if he was quickly running through a plan of attack within his mind. Good. Daniel had a fine talent for creating a plan on the whim, but damn, Rhain wasn't in the mood to mess with this many guardians. The fuckers were fast and deadly and their bites could decay Lamia flesh like an acidic infection. He certainly didn't feel like having his flesh molted off his body this night, or any night for that fact.

Suddenly, a high pitched whistle raced through the air, piercing the night. The keen hearing of both Lamia and the zombies picked up the sound, and they all turned their attentions to the direction of the whistle - the factory. The twins released sighs in harmony as the zombies forced their dilapidated bodies to turn about, lumbering and limping back the direction they came. Their master had called for them, and they had obeyed.

When the creatures disappeared around the corner, Rhain shook his head and whispered, "I'm going hard turkey off zombie movies from now on."

Daniel smirked as he stood, his lean frame coming to rise up in the darkness, and the paleness of his alabaster skin shined past the outline of his black clothing. "Now that we know these creatures are here, we must face the fact that there is a powerful Necromancer within these walls."

"Fucking Necros," Rhain spat.

"We'll need to find a more secure entry into the building. Let's take another look at those plans."

Rhain stood, stepped closer, and presented his phone once more. "The delivery shoot into the basement would be our best bet. There are stairs and elevators heading up to the main floors of the building. My guess is that the elevators no longer work."

"We won't know which way to go and how to get to the upper floors till we get into the building." Daniel shook his head with a disgruntled grumble. "The structure's old and could have collapsed halls and other damage we won't know about till we face the obstacles. Not to mention that David probably has every soldier and creature in his arsenal wandering the hallways and grounds. He has Regan. That means he's expecting us."

He cast his brother a look of mild concern. "We could be facing a lot of combatants once inside."

Rhain nodded as he slid his phone back into his pocket. "Sounds like we'll have a lot of fun then."

"We're here to find Regan, get her to safety, and secure David - dead or alive. Any others that get in our way…"

"Are expendable."

Daniel nodded, and this time his own lips echoed his twin's dark grin. "Indeed. Shall we go, Frater? There is an entrance to be discovered, and we only have a few hours of darkness left."

"Then let's not keep your damsel waiting."

With inhumane speed the Inquisitors descended upon the building. They moved from shadow to shadow, forming from the darkness itself, till they rounded the structure and came to find the service entrance that had long been forgotten. The cellar rose up from the dank earth and was nearly undetectable if one didn't know it was there. Daniel shivered as he looked at the entrance and the wall of the building for it seemed as if Mother Nature was trying to snuff out the existence of the structure, wrapping vines and limbs so tight that the bricks and mortar were punctured and broken. The cellar doors themselves were nothing more than rusted pieces of contorted metal locked together with a thick industrial strength chain. He and Rhain worked quickly, yet diligently, to remove the tangled brush and vines. And with one pull, Daniel was able to snap the copious chain from the doors.

But before Rhain could pull open the doors, Daniel stopped him with an arm stretched out and a finger to his lips. "Not yet,' he explained, 'allow me to check for any alarm system. We cannot afford any mistakes."

"You say this after yanking the chain off?" Rhain gave his twin a very unamused and droll stare. Daniel returned the same look, so Rhain gave in with a sigh. "Fine."

With a conceding nod, Rhain stepped back and Daniel moved forwards, carefully moving his hands over the connection of the cellar entrance to the structure. He wanted to make sure there were no wires running the surface or any signs of magic. Though he was not as talented as Alasdair at detecting magical signatures, he had sensitive enough fingertips to get a tickle if there was any magical residue lingering around. After a moment, he stepped back and gave Rhain the all clear with a sharp nod.

The smell of dank mildew and stale air slapped them hard when the doors were opened. They instantly backed away, shielding their mouths and noses while releasing equal grunts of irritation. When the air settled, Rhain leaned forwards to take a careful look down the pitch-black tunnel. His features scrunched and he looked back over his shoulder to mutter, "There's a ramp going down. My guess? This was used for barrels to be rolled into the basement. There're no steps, just a nasty slope."

"Then we should proceed with caution."

Rhain tsked. "That's a shame."

"Why is that?" asked Daniel with a brow arched.

"I'm allergic to that word!"

"Rhain!" Daniel barked as his twin took a leap forwards into the tunnel, disappearing into the darkness. He made a grab for his brother's jacket but his gloved fingers missed Rhain's jacket collar by a hair's breath. "Damn it," he snarled dangerously, glaring into the tunnel. "When we get home, I'm going to beat some common sense into him, even if he's allergic to that word as well!"

With the shaft being the only clear entry to the building and with time wasting, Daniel could not dawdle on the outside. Unlike Rhain, he carefully proceeded into the tunnel, taking care to close the metal doors behind him. The descent down the cement slope was not an easy one as decades of moisture, dripping down from the ceiling and walls, had coated the cement with a slick skin of slime and mold. Daniel had to carefully maneuver his body so his footing did not slip out from under him. It was tricky, but he managed.

"Well, that was one of the most disgusting things I've ever done." Daniel shuddered as he came to stand at the bottom of the ramp. He dusted his coat off only to wince seeing a watery layer of mucus on his gloved fingertips.

"We've got to get one of those," chuckled Rhain, cracking his back with a number of loud pops.

"Good luck convincing Kain of that." Clapping his brother on the shoulder, Daniel gave him a shove. "Let's move on."

Rhain, with another chuckle, raised his hands in defense as he stumbled forwards from his twin's push. "Shall we be quiet about it, or shall we blow through this building like a maelstrom?"

"One way is your way. The other is mine. Let's just get ourselves out of this basement and to the upper levels first. When I find Regan, we'll burn this building, and any left within, to the ground."

Rhain flashed his brother a fanged grin and said with a twisted purr of delight, "I love the way you think, my twin."

"Our two minds think alike."

"Damn straight."

"Sometimes."

Rhain chuckled darkly, catching his twin's meaning.

The two searched the expanse of the basement for the closest stairs leading up. The task was much harder than they had originally thought. Luckily, they weren't hindered by any of David's followers as they worked their way through the labyrinth of twisting halls, crumbling walls, fallen beams, and false corridors. A few times, however, they were forced to back-track, rounding a corner then proceeding down another dark and empty hall. The underground cellars stank of mildew and rancid sewer water no doubt from a line beneath the structure having ruptured. And with the building being long abandoned, the city of London chose to either ignore the condition of the property or one too many a concerned eye went missing when peeking through the broken windows.

Finally, they came upon a section of crumbling and distorted stairs leading up to an open door, broken in many parts but manageable to negotiate. Daniel paused at the top to look out and survey the first floor hall. He saw and felt no presence - living, dead, or even undead. He gave a quick motion to his twin, and the flicking of fingers sent Rhain rushing across the empty hall to slip into the shadows of a door's shadowy alcove. Rhain looked one way while Daniel looked the other, and when they were both reassured that they were alone, they advanced.

They found the first floor hallways littered with old barrels, tools, office equipment, papers, rusted sections of machinery, and other odd and random factory debris. Old doors were off their hinges with some having given in to their deaths, fallen and rotting upon the floor where they lay in an outline of dust and dirty. The brick walls and cement floor were spotted with char marks from a fire that had swept through the building over a decade prior, and the very air smelled of ancient smoke and old water. Due to the open holes in the ceiling and the damage to the building's plumbing, water still continued to drip down to gather in small, standing puddles. Some of the corridors that Rhain had pointed out on the blueprints were inaccessible for one reason or another, and to their dismay, they found the main elevator had long ago fallen to the basement to break apart in a pile of rusted and twisted metal and cords.

When they had searched the first floor thoroughly, the twins crouched in a dark and empty room to look over the map to pinpoint the safest route to the next floor. "Where do you think David's dug in?" Rhain asked.

"My guess would be somewhere in the center of the building on the second floor. Here," Daniel replied, pointing to a room on the map that was in the center of the second floor with no windows and two doors, one leading from the hallway and the second leading to a small hallway between two walls that ended in another corridor. "This small hall here looks like a private entrance, perfect for a quick escape if needed."

"Yeah, it looks like it runs through the wall."

"I would think that Regan is being held in a secure area of the building, away from any parts that may be crumbling."

Rhain turned his head with a slight frown. "You think she's back in the basement?"

Daniel continued to scan the map by using his fingertips to move the image. After a few moments of examining the blueprints, he shook his head. "I can't say for sure. There were sections of the basement we couldn't access. She could be down there, but I would have to break down walls to locate her. I might have to search room by room, if need be."

"That could take a long time; time that we don't have." Rhain glanced to his watch. "A couple hours at the least, maybe three at the most."

"Perhaps it is best that we split up. We can cover more ground that way."

Rhain tipped his head to the side sending a lock of metallic blue along one cheek. "Are you sure? You want to find both Regan and David, yourself."

"I trust that if you find Regan you will keep her safe, and I trust that if you find David you will leave him to me to dispatch." Daniel stood as he tightened black leather over a set of fingers. He glanced down to his brother. "We can cover more ground this way, considering our time is clicking on by."

With a groan of leather, Rhain stood and dusted his hands off. "We'll keep in touch, yeah?"

Smirking, Daniel offered his hand. "We're twins, Rhain. We're always in touch. If I find Regan or David, I will let you know directly."

Rhain clasped Daniel's hand. "I'll do the same."

"God speed, Frater."

"Good killing."

~ ~ ~ ~

The silence in Regan's cell was broken by the sudden echo of the heavy bolt unlocking followed by the rickety door grinding open.

The sound jolted Regan from the fitful sleep she had fallen into after her body could take no more sobbing. An emotional breakdown put her into a numb coma, but the shocking light coming from the hallway caused her eyes to flinch and her mind to jolt. She pressed herself to the jagged wall behind her with a hand coming up to shield her eyes.

Somebody was in the cell with her as heavy footsteps clomped across the cement floor towards her. A yelp tore from her raw throat when a hand grabbed her arm, yanking her from the hard floor.

"Get up," commanded a gruff voice.

"Let go!" she screamed, fighting against the hold.

"Shut ya mouth, bitch," growled a second voice. "David's called fer ya, and we are to escort you to him."

Pain laced through her as she was pulled towards the door. Regan stumbled as her feet tried to find their footing, but the man's grip was too strong for her to fight, but fight she tried. "Let me go! You're hurting me!"

If the man cared, he didn't show it. He didn't even look in her direction as he shoved her from the cell, out into the hall, and into the arms of his comrade. "She's a lively one," he chuckled with his eyes dragging lewdly down her shivering body.

The second man grinned down to Regan with a grin so dark it sent a shudder of ice through her body. His eyes were sunken back into his skull and held a sickly, yellow-green color to the irises. He looked ill with skin that was ashen grey, but with the strength he used to hold onto her wrists there was no way the man was ill at all. The grip caused Regan's body to buckle as she released a cry of discomfort.

"Don't hurt her too much, ya idiot, or David won't be too damn happy," said the first man as he jerked a thumb down the hall. "Let's go. We don't want to be late. David don't like to be kept waiting."

The two men weren't gentle as they dragged her down hallways then up some rickety old stairs. The three moved from the basement level up to two more floors before moving down a few more hallways that were littered with debris and old office supplies. Regan saw no other living soul around, and there were no signs of life within the crumbling building that was nothing more than a ghostly whisper of its former self. Windows that they passed were either boarded up, covered in newspaper, or shattered.

When she stumbled, she was pushed forwards with a bark of, "Move it!"

They stopped at an office door where the speckled glass had been painted black. Before she could squeak, Regan was pushed through the door. She landed hard on the carpeted floor sending up a cloud of dust, dirt, and mold to the air. With a violent cough tearing through her body, Regan pushed herself to sit up, waving a hand before her face.

"That wasn't very nice!" she snapped through a loud and painful hack.

"Behave yourself, or you'll be sorry," growled one of the men. He jabbed a threatening finger towards her then shoved his comrade, who was cackling with laughter, back out the door.

Regan waved the pillow of dust away from her as she continued to cough. When the cloud settled, she slowly looked around her new surroundings. The room she was in did little to soften her fear. It was small, an office, with a few windows boarded up tight. The wallpaper upon the walls was peeling away, exposing damages brought on by time, cracks in the wall and holes in the plaster. There was a painting of a hunting scene upon one wall, but it too looked like it had given up on life as it leaned far to one side. Even the old sofa appeared unsafe with the fabric torn, springs puncturing the seats, and one side that had fallen in. She shivered till a low, wooden groan was heard, and it was then she realized that she was not alone. The chair behind the wooden desk was turning back and forth with the low squeak of rusted, protesting gears. As her skin prickled with icy chills, Regan slowly turned to face the desk.

And when the chair turned about, a whimper tugged hard at her lips when she saw none other than David seated casually; his hands were laced to his lap. With a sly grin upon his lips, the man gazed to her with amusement dancing in his eyes, and a silver sparkle caught in the dim light provided by a desk-lamp. The way David appeared eerily calm sent another claw of ice down Regan's spine. Her spine wouldn't be able to take much more fear.

"Don' mind them two," he said with a flat voice riddled with cruel sarcasm. "They were raised in a barn. I've tried ta teach them proper behavior an' etiquette, bu' some men will be nothing more than animals."

Regan slowly sat up to her knees. Now that she was cold with fear, she wrapped her arms about her upper body as if to protect herself. "What do you want with me? Why am I here?" She couldn't help the fresh tears that began to tumble down her dust covered cheeks.

"Come now,' David purred, standing from his chair with a creek of leather to cross the room to her, 'there is no need ta cry." He sounded sincere as he bent to one knee before her, offering her a tissue. "Dry yer tears. Ye'r safe, fer now."

Safe? She doubted that David knew the meaning of the word. She wanted to recoil away from his touch but found herself frozen to the floor. "What have you done to Joyce?"

"Joyce,' he mused, pleased in the way Regan's body responded in tremors of panic to his very presence, 'she is ma finest lov'r an' tha most delightful treat I 'ave ever indulged in. She's made a fine edition ta ma growing family."

Regan's eyes narrowed, and her brows furrowed in confusion. "You're a monster. I don't know what you've done to her but she's not the same Joyce I knew."

"No' any more. Joyce has become somethin' more than tha simple human ya once knew as yer cousin."

"Why have you done all of this?" Regan asked, looking about the dirt covered room.

"So many questions. Are ya sure ya wan' ta know tha answers? They are frightening an' far beyond ye're mortal understanding." The Proscriptus reached a cold hand out to brush fingers over her tear slickened face. Her beautiful flesh was warm, and he sighed to the comfort the soft heat offered him. And though he could feel the warmth of her blood rushing through her veins, it was the pounding of her fear filled heart that called to him.

Regan flinched to the touch that brought bile to rise within her throat. She leaned back with her head turning away from his reach.

David chuckled as she turned away. He could've forced her to look back at him, but he wasn't interested in scaring her with the use of brute force. She wasn't like Joyce. Whereas Joyce enjoyed and encouraged David's dominance, Regan was much softer, more timid than her assertive cousin. He couldn't gain Regan's trust and favor through threats, nor could he persuade her with sexualized promises. No. If he was to lure Regan to his side and away from Daniel, he would need to do so with tenderness and gentility - as long as his patience lasted.

"Yer a guest in my home," he told her.

"Do you always keep your guests locked in a room? Do you always kidnap family members of your guest and drug them? Do you always send jerks to bring your guest to you? If so, I don't want to stay in your house anymore. If you don't mind, would you please show me the way out? I'd like to go home now."

David chuckled to her demands and to the stern look upon Regan's face, her lower lip pouting out and her beautiful eyes narrowing behind thick lashes. "I canno' le' ya go just yet, no' till ya play yer role in my game an' bring Daniel Thorn ta me. Tha's all I'm asking o' ya, Regan. If ya can do tha' fer me, be quiet an' do as I say, I promise tha' ya will no' be hurt, an' in tha end ya will be home."

"Joyce said you want to destroy Daniel and his family. I won't help you. I refuse to! Hell will freeze over before I help you hurt a hair on Daniel's head!"

Her little outburst brought a harsh laugh from the Lamia. "Ya don' seem ta understand tha situation yer in, girl." David leaned closer to her with a curl of his lips showing a wicked sneer. "I'm sure Joyce explained tha' if ya don' do wha' I want then yer no' going ta like tha outcome o' my displeasure."

"I can be a very reasonable man,' he told her softly, gently - coldly, 'bu' if ya cross me, I can make yer life hell." This time when he touched her, his grip was tight upon her chin. He felt muscles wince beneath his fingers as he drew her towards him till her head was bent back and pain crossed her pretty face. "Ya will help me, Regan. Ya 'ave no choice bu' ta follow ma command, if ya want ta live."

She flinched with a sharp whimper to the nip of pain his fingers bit into her skin. Regan tried to shake her head but David's grip held her chin steadily. "Go to hell," she whispered heatedly.

Though Regan wanted to protest and fight, there was no way she could fight him. And if she managed to free herself, where would she go? How far would she get in an unknown area, considering she didn't even know where she was? What would happen if David or one of his men caught her?

"Ya can' fight me, Regan," he purred darkly as he brushed the back of fingers along her neck.

He closed his eyes to savor the feeling of her pulse thumping wildly against his caress. When he opened his eyes, David leaned closer till his lips brushed the shell of her ear as he whispered, "I will 'ave ya, sweet human. Just ya wait. One way or another, ya will welcome me inta yer arms as ya 'ave welcomed Daniel."

Hot tears flowed down her dirt stained cheeks. His touch had her stomach twisting and his vile breath had a hard lump building within her throat. Regan whimpered through the soft cries that tumbled past her quivering lips. With nowhere to go, with no power to fight, Regan's psyche broke. She began to sob, uncontrollably. Her body quivered and jerked with each heart wrenching sound that tore from her petite frame.

"Why? Why are you doing this?" she sobbed, her body trembling within his grasp.

"Revenge. Power. Mostly entertainment. There are many reasons ta my actions," he said against her cheek. David drew a deep lungful of her scent, a delicate combination of innocence, flowers, dirt and.... What he smelled upon her skin brought a growl from his throat. "I smell him on ya," he snarled with his nose pressed to her skin and his grip tightening upon her chin. "Ya went ta 'is bed, didn't ya?"

Regan whimpered.

"Wha' a shame."

Sighing, David drew back, looking to her with disappointment. "I had hoped tha' tha bastard hadn' touched ya yet. Bu' it seems tha' I'm a bit too late. Oh, well." He shrugged with a shake of his head. "Ya will still serve yer purpose. If ya do as I say, I will give ta ya tha same gift I gave ta Joyce. Ya will stand a' my side, an' in my bed."

"Don't make me sick," hissed Regan once he let his grip upon her chin go. She narrowed her eyes to him. "I'll never give in to you. I'll never do as you say, and to hell if I ever end up in your bed. You may have seduced and tricked Joyce to think you're some God, but I know you're nothing but a Demon!"

A deep, animalistic growl slid from David's thin pressed lips, and his eyes flashed a murderous warning to the human just before a wide hand wrapped about her slender throat. "My men told ya ta be nice, Regan. Tha' was no' being nice. Do ya enjoying being tha whore ta tha' Lex lov'n Drasus prick?" To feel her tremble, to hear her breath hitch, and to hear her heart skip a few wild beats he tightened his fingers about her throat, one at a time.

With emotions enraged, encouraged by the image of this beautiful human enwrapped within twisted passion in Daniel's arms dancing within his mind, David's Daemon came roaring with life. His Daemon was easily excited and easy to turn to rage. In one quick motion, the Lamia had Regan on the floor. Her sudden cry of terror echoed deep within his body, stroking more and more of his Daemon's lust and hunger. David took hold of her shirt and tore it open. Only her scream of horror drowned out the sound of ripping fabric.

"No!" Regan screamed as she twisted about, her hands flying and nails clawing against David's chest. "Stop it! Let go of me!"

In one move he flattened her to the filth covered floor. Then he was on her, his heavy body pressing against her as he parted her thighs with a thrust of his knee. Crying to the feeling of that hard thrust against her pelvic, Regan closed her eyes in an attempt to hide the image of David's proud and psychotic smile.

"Shut yer damn mouth, Drasus whore!" David howled in a voice that trembled with ire. He dug a hand into her hair to yank her features back to him then growled lowly, "I will do as I wan' with ya. Ya were warned ta behave. Ya chose ta ignore tha' request, an' now ya 'ave ta pay tha price."

Regan whimpered then cried out in pain as her hair was pulled and her neck was wrenched to the side. Tears spilled down her cheeks to burn against her skin, and when she opened her tear blistered eyes, she found herself looking into the eyes of a monster. There was a look written on David's face that had her paling with fright.

"What…are you?" Regan heard her fear coated voice press out with a tight whimper.

David swooned with the sound of her fear, enjoying the power he had to induce terror. He chuckled darkly as he leaned to press himself down atop of her, giving her a feel of his physical prowess laced within every inch of his male body. "I am a God," he answered with a delusional smile parting his lips to show, with twisted pride, the mark of the Lamia - fangs.

The cry of Daniel's name died in her throat as David's mouth descended upon her.

XIII

~

I can still hear her. Her soft cries echo within my mind. And the image of her tears rips my soul apart.

I can't begin to imagine the horror she must have felt when David took her. I don't want to imagine what he has done to her now that Regan is his captive. I can only guess as to the cruelty he is pressing down upon her and the terror she must be going through.

I will do all I can to find her, to save her, and to bring her back to me. I can feel her agony desperately trying to reach out to me, calling me to her like a beacon through the darkness. There is no structure secure enough, no hole in the ground deep enough where David can find shelter that I will not demolish. I will find him and drag him out to burn within the rays of the sun.

He will know pain.

He will know suffering.

This I swear.

I don't know what will happen Regan is returned to me. Her world has been turned inside out. I want to keep her with me and embrace her into my world where I can keep her safe. I owe her that much, now that I have failed her.

Will she hate me when the time comes that I must tell her the truth? Or will she fear me - the monster that I am? I can't have her hate me, nor can I have her fear me. Both would be my undoing; both would destroy me. I already know that I cannot be without her. My Daemon will not allow it. I must take her. I must claim her. I must kill for her.

Forgive me, Regan, for bringing you into this tainted world that I was unfortunate to be born into.

Forgive me for thrusting you into the pain and agony that follows me like a cursed shadow.

Forgive me...

-   Daniel Rhys Thorn

~ ~ ~ ~

With Rhain heading up to the third floor, Daniel proceeded to search the first floor as he made his way towards the north stairs that would lead down into a section of the basement that, according to the blueprints, was inaccessible from the rest of the basement. He hoped Rhain had not encountered any of David's associates. Daniel, on the other hand, was not so lucky.

Another victim to his blade crumpled to the floor in a gurgled cry of pain as inch after inch of his flesh began to decay till there was nothing left but a disjointed skeleton. With a snarl, Daniel turned his deadly gaze towards the Lamia who remained. Two of David's men had rounded a corner and were caught by surprise when a blade swept out from the shadows of a corridor to slice clear through the first Lamia's stomach. When Daniel stepped out into the hallway, he faced the second Lamia, the blade of his katana dripping with a thin line of thick black blood.

"Who the fuck are you?" demanded the Lamia as he fumbled for his weapon, a gun held in the back pocket of his jeans.

Daniel narrowed his dark eyes as his lips pulled back with a showing of fangs. Gloved fingers tightened about the decorative hilt of the katana that was of beautiful carved ebony leading to a guard of etched pewter. He gently caressed the two-hundred year hilt as he began to advance upon the younger vampire.

The Lamia, with his weapon now drawn and shaking, began to retreat as Daniel advanced.

Daniel growled, the katana raised at his side, as he continued to advance while speaking clearly, "Run. I dare you."

"I don't run from no mother fucker!" barked the Filias in a show of stupid defiance and young immaturity.

Daniel snorted in disgust. "Don't be a fool. Are you willing to die for David and his worthless ideals? Is your life that meaningless to you?"

"Shut up!" The Lamia took another step back and then another with a quick look to his left then to his right. "Don't come any closer! I'll shoot!"

"If you had any pride in you, Lamia, you would have done so already."

He continued to advance, pushing the other Lamia further away with his determined strides. The young looking man, with gun still quivering in hand, retreated till his back thumped against the wall behind him. With no other place to go, he leveled the gun with a surge of fresh resolve - or pitiful instinct.

He never had the chance to pull the trigger.

Daniel moved with unnatural speed, and with perfect precision stopped with his blade pressing a deadly kiss to the Lamia's thin throat. A trickle of fresh, dark blood danced down the silver blade from the delicate slice that parted the vampire's neck. "I warned you." One quick draw of his hand had the blade slipping delicately over skin, parting flesh wide to expose lines of muscle.

With a gurgled and wet jumble of words, the young Lamia crumpled to the floor, lifeless, then began to convulse violently as his body, like the other, began to rot away. Daniel didn't bat an eye or offer an expression of pity as he swept his katana through the air to fling away the remaining blood before sliding the weapon into the sheath strapped at his back.

'DANIEL!'

He was only a few steps away when he stopped to the call of his name. "Regan," he breathed out as a cold chill flowed across his skin. Her voice echoed within his head, screaming out in panic and pain. She was close. He could feel her desperation reaching out to him. Forcing his heart to calm, he closed his eyes and centered his soul. Cocking his head left then right, Daniel tried to hone in on her location. He had to concentrate, but maybe…just maybe…

There! Above him! Daniel opened his eyes as a twisted grin coiled his lips, and with a surge of strength and speed, he rushed forwards, a booted foot coming down to crush the distorted skull of the young Lamia he had just killed.

~ ~ ~ ~

Regan twisted and fought against the powerful man who pinned her down upon the floor. David's touch revolted her and his kisses made her swallow her screams within her throat. She knew that he was going to rape her, and by doing so, he was going to obtain his revenge on Daniel by tainting her.

David's foul, cold breath froze the flesh of her neck as he suckled wetly upon her skin. He groaned as his hands began to molest the soft flesh of her youthful breasts after having torn her bra off, exposing her to his hungry gaze. David was more than pleased with what he saw. Regan's body was much softer and desirable than Joyce's less ample physique that was now chilled by the Creare. There was a perverse and disturbing delight he felt upon seeing the tears pour down the mortal's face when he forced her legs apart with his knees then began to unzip and unbutton her jeans.

The realization of what was about to happen slammed her heart against her slender chest in terror. 'Daniel,' Regan whimpered within her mind as her sight began to blur from the burning of her tears.

Coming to her rescue was a loud buzzer that began to wail within the dilapidated office.

"Fucking hell," David snapped. His voice shook on the verge of lost control.

Through her tear reddened vision, Regan noticed a red light flashing above the door. That was just before the door burst open and a young man came storming in with a look of mild alarm upon his face

"David,' he barked, 'the trigger alarm at the main stairs has been set off." Though he looked to Regan, he showed no care to what David was doing to her. He looked away without a passing glance of concern.

"Wha' tha hell do ya mean? Who is i?'" David growled through clenched jaws, obviously annoyed at the disturbance and the damn timing of the buzzer.

"I'm not exactly sure, but it seems we have two intruders who have infiltrated the building. Security team A has found Adams and McGregor dead on the third floor."

"Adams an' McGregor?" David blanched then twisted his features into a look of pure fury. Those Lamia were two of his best! He had known them personally for over a century! To know they had met their Denique Nex, their final death, had him straining with rage.

"Just them two?" he snarled between grinding jaws.

The other Lamia nodded his head then answered, "As far as security can tell. The two intruders are keeping their attacks to a minimum. Security team B has been dispatched to locate the intruders, but so far the security system is unable to track their movements."

David snorted with a roll of his eyes. He glanced quickly to Regan as he said absent mindedly, "Ya won' be able ta, no' with tha Inquisitors in our mist."

"Inquisitors?" asked the man with a bewildered look to his features.

"They were before yer time, Blake. Tha Thorn twins were once two of tha most feared Legati who went abou' performing private assassinations fer tha Rex by order. I thought they had retired, bu' obviously Daniel is willing ta dust off his sword ta come ge' wha' is his." With a chuckle to his lips, David flashed Regan a sharp grin.

"What are your orders?"

"No one is ta face them," David answered as he looked back to Blake. "I won't lose any more o' my men ta their blades. None o' ya can face them an' survive."

Blake gave a pensive look then asked, "What about the Flesh-Eaters?"

David gave a nod. "They're expendable. Ge' Grayson an' his pets ou' on tha trail o' our guests. Le' tha zombies deal with them."

Blake gave a smirk and a nod before he departed.

Regan winced when the door slammed shut, and fear took an icy hold on her once more. She didn't want to see the other man go because the moment he was gone David turned his rage upon her. Confusion ran through her mind to what she had overheard, yet also hope to the knowledge that Daniel and Rhain were here - for her! Daniel was risking his life to rescue her. Yes, she had hope now.

When David looked back to her, she narrowed her eyes dangerously, and through the tight hold on her throat rasped, "Daniel's here....for me..."

David began to chuckle then laughed harshly. Gripping Regan's throat, he hauled her up close to him. "He's savin' me a trip ta find him," he told her with a sneer. "This way, he can say his final farewell ta ya before I le' him burn."

"However,' David went on to say as he brushed a hand slowly down the smooth column of his captive's neck to press fingers to the pounding pulse running beneath her thin skin, 'this could be a good time ta tell ya just wha' yer sweet Daniel Thorn truly is. So listen closely."

With a destructive and cruel grin, David drew Regan closer till an ear touched his lips. "He's a monster."

Regan shuddered to his touch, and she tried to turn her head away but found his other hand balling in her hair. Snarling, she took a short-lived touch of strength and narrowed her eyes to him. "He's no monster,' she growled, 'you're the monster."

David chuckled, his lips curling in to a sneer before he licked them, slowly and to expose a hint of his sharp fangs. "Girl,' he purred with a devious chortle, 'ya 'ave no idea wha' type o' monster yer new boyfriend really is."

The blood in Regan's face drained leaving her ghostly pale at the sight of sharp fangs.

The look of shock and fear within her eyes had a brow arching upon the Lamia's features. He stared at her for a short moment before chuckling softly, "Ya don' know tha truth about him and his brothers, do ya?"

She shook her head with a faint whimpered.

Under the Lamia Lex, no Lamia was to disclose their world to a mortal without going through the proper channels and then the proper stages of training, the Domare, for the Humanus intending to integrate into the Lamia world. And that was only allowed once a human was brought under the tutelage and protection of a Familia. A Lamia could not regurgitate the truth of their existence and their world on a coffee date with some fling picked up on the side of the street - or at a club.

Even David had to admit that there were a number of Lamia who didn't give a shit about the Lex - including him. Though he held no love for the laws, he wasn't about to expose their world to just anybody that would result in any of his brethren going to their deaths from human ignorance and distress. Under his control, if any of his Proscriptus let one little secret slip their lips, those lips were sealed. Permanently.

How hypocritical of him, considering his own intentions.

Daniel was a good boy under the laws - a Lex Lover. The pompous bastard ate the laws, brushed his fangs with the laws, and slept with the damn Lex books next to his bed! There was no way the Drasus boy told Regan one ounce of truth about him, his world or his family. Regan knew nothing. Not a damn thing.

David composed himself with frightening ease and gently released her throat. He even caressed the irritated mark on her flesh that outlined his hand. "Le' me give ya some advice, girl," he told her with his eyes locked to hers. "This world ain' wha' ya think. There are monsters in tha shadows just waiting ta pluck away yer life. There are powers tha' yer mortal mind canno' come ta imagine. Yer Daniel is righ' in tha middle o' them monsters. Ya 'ave no idea wha' he's capable of."

Regan's dark eyes scanned David's face. She gulped as he spoke of monsters, of powers, and of Daniel. She shook her head in disbelief. "You don't know the Daniel I know. He's one of the kindest and most generous men I have ever met."

"Maybe ta ya,' he chuckled, 'bu' ta tha rest o' us, he's tha worst of tha worst. Yer boy ain' no angel." Rocking back on his heels, the Lamia stood in his proud glory. "Ya may want ta dress yerself fer meetin' him,' he smirked to the disarray of her clothing then added, 'as well as ya can."

David didn't give her much time to dress, and with her shaking hands, Regan had a hard time trying to clasp her bra. There was no hope for her shirt, so she tried as well as she could to tie the torn fabric together to hide what dignity David had left her. When she was finished, he grabbed her by the back of her neck and shoved her forwards and out of the room. But just as they reached the hall, he stopped her with a rough jerk and growled low in her ear.

"I expect ya ta behave yerself. One wrong word…one wrong move…an' I will gut yer precious Daniel before yer eyes, an' ya will 'ave nothin' left o' him ta fuck bu' a skeleton. Do ya understand me?"

The painful squeeze upon her neck drew a whimper from Regan. She nodded her head in silent understanding.

"His life rests in yer hands, so don' be stupid."

Regan felt her heart spiral in agony. Was David capable of killing Daniel? And if so, why couldn't somebody call the damn police? What the hell was going on?

As David walked her down the empty halls of the complex, Regan couldn't help but feel the claws of dread reaching out for her. She was shaking so badly that she tripped over broken tiles on the floor only to have David roughly grab her and shove her onwards. She silently prayed that Daniel, and Rhain, were alive. They had to be.

~ ~ ~ ~

Rounding a dark corridor, Regan fell back against David as a cry of horrific terror escaped her throat as she came face to face, and inches, from a creature she thought only existed in movies and in books. She quickly turned her face against David's chest when the stench of filthy, rancid breath struck her.

The 'thing' before her reached out with a gnarled and fleshless hand that was nothing more than rotten bits of wet skin and tendons hanging from long, bony fingers. A low, hungered sound bubbled up from the creature's torn throat to be released from a parted mouth that had been savagely ripped open to expose teeth. Drool, a mixture of mucus and phlegm, dribbled past the opening, and its eyes, one protruding from the socket more than the other, were nothing but milky white globs that jiggled with every lurching move. Though there was clothing, torn and dirty, upon the creature's body, one could see the remains of brutal injuries no doubt caused by the attack that killed the once living man.

"Fuck! Grayson!" David barked as he held Regan against him in some form of a protective embrace. He stepped back a few paces as his own features scrunched to the smell of decay that came wafting from the mobile corpse.

Somebody spoke off in the darkness, but Regan couldn't hear clearly the mumbled words. They made no sense to her and sounded more to be throaty syllables than anything constructive. However, as the voice grew in sound and in commands, she felt a frightening intensity of weight settle upon her. Before she could stop herself, she had her fingers curling into David's shirt.

The Lamia tightened his hold on her when Grayson's melodic words began to formulate the magical command that had the zombie slowly drawing away.

"Forgive me," spoke a refined English voice from a man who stepped forth from the distant shadows. He gracefully strode past his zombie with no reservation or repulsion and even touched the creature on its hairless head to shove it away. "Kevin smelled fresh meat - living meat." Red eyes, blood-red within the entire socket, locked upon the young mortal cowering against David. The handsome man arched a delicate brow of white before looking to his leader. "You have a guest?"

"Yeah,' David muttered with a snarl, 'an' ya scared tha shit ou' o' her."

Grayson Harding Baird frowned as he ran his eyes over the appearance of the woman, taking note of the torn garments, dark bruises, and tear stained cheeks. He gave the Proscriptus leader a critical glare that radiated his displeasure at the woman's maltreatment. Though Grayson was also a Proscriptus, considering he was thought to be dead, he continued to hold himself to his own standards of ethics and perverse morals. And one moral point he held dear to his heart was the distaste of any abuse towards women. He didn't know what had occurred that earned the woman her current state, but he had an inkling that the cause was one in the same - David.

Grayson offered a polite bow of his head. "My apologies," he said in his smooth accent, not only for the Zombie at his side - his pet - but also in apology for David's behavior. "Kevin here seems to take a fancy to pretty girls."

He popped the Flesh-Eater on the head causing the creature to give a wet whine. "He can be such a flirt at times. A shame really. There's never a chance for a second date. He has a nasty habit of devouring his dates."

Regan opened her eyes to glance behind her. The zombie was still there with its torn head raised and its empty nostrils flaring as if it was catching a scent. But then she turned her shivering gaze to the man next to it and drew in a quick hitch of air. The man David called Grayson was extremely handsome in face - tall and lean. His porcelain flesh glowed within the darkness, and the long strands of his stark white hair seemed to flutter about him in a dance of a ghostly breeze. He was almost too beautiful for a man, and would be considered perfection dressed in his fine leather pants, boots, and a silk shirt of white if not for his eyes.

213

Regan trembled when the weight of the man's solid red eyes settled upon her. The intensity of his gaze sent trembles right through Regan's soul, leaving her with an empty and cold feeling in her stomach. No man, no living man, should have an aura so black - like an empty abyss.

"'ave ya spread ou' yer pets in tha compound?" asked David.

Grayson gave a nod. "Of course. I have four out in the yard and have placed a dozen more within the walls."

"'ave they caught a scent?"

The Necromancer gave a slight nod of his head. "Three of my children have caught the scent of two unknown individuals in the basement near the delivery shoot. From there your uninvited guests parted ways. The last communication indicated that they ascended the upper stories of the compound, one taking the third level and the other the first floor."

David scowled. "I need tha intruders found, Grayson. They are 'ere, somewhere. Flush them ou'."

Grayson tipped his head, amused that David would cast commands that he knew would be seen to. "Do you have any suspicion as to the identities of your guests, David?"

The Proscriptus gave a snort of amusement. "Yeah, yer brother's boyfriend an' the bitch's prissy ass twin."

Brother's boyfriend? Grayson's handsome lips tucked down in thought. "As far as I know, Alasdair's not gay. However, you may be referring to his business associate Rhain Thorn."

"Who else would I be yacki'n abou'?" David raised a hand with a finger pointed to his most powerful Sorcerer. "Daniel Thorn is ta be brought ta me alive. Understand?"

Grayson raised a questionable brow but agreed to the request with a nod.

Regan swore she heard 'Kevin' groan in protest to the order.

"What about Rhain?"

With a sly and cruel grin of pleasure caressing his features, David replied, "Slaughter him."

Grayson gave a chuckle and a sadistic grin of anticipation. He offered a bow of his lean body. "Understood." Turning upon the heels of his fine boots, he slapped Kevin on the shoulder. "Feeding time, Kevin. Let us go."

The two disappeared into the shadows whence they came, and the slick dragging of the Zombie's steps could be heard echoing the tumbling walls.

Regan's eyes went wide. She gave her own protest to the order as she began to struggle against David. "No! You can't do this!"

David didn't listen to her cries of protest or her begging pleas as he pulled her off into the depths of his domain.

~ ~ ~ ~

Rhain was the first to come in contact with one of David's prized, undead soldiers. Two were right before him in the hall, blocking his path and his destination. Behind them rested the stairs that lead up to the third floor. Damn it! Sighing, the Lamia ducked back into a dark corridor so he could come up with a plan on how to deal with the zombies. Fucking hell - he hated zombies. Even zombie movies made his skin crawl. The real things made his stomach sick.

The dead were to remain dead and to be living out an honorable existence in the afterlife. They were not meant to be brought back in to some pitiful and mindless reality where their rotting corpses were used as fodder and machines for killing.

Rhain curled his fingers to the hilt of his Tantō. How was he going to kill two zombies at once? These fuckers could be fast, like hunting hounds with senses on steroids. If he was lucky, they wouldn't have caught the smell of his body already. He needed time to think. If there were two, there were more. They were like rats in a wall, and somewhere in this old building was their Master - the Necromancer behind the magic.

He would have a better chance at putting these two down as quickly as possible in order to get past them and move on. He couldn't waste his time fucking around with them. With a slow and cautious movement he slid his weapon into the sheath strapped at his right calf. He took a glance out into the hall to double check the position of the creatures as he planned each move he would make in advance, each strike he would land and to where his attacks would fall to ensure the perfect kill. The one on the left would fall first; the one on the right a second later.

He would need to act quickly in order to exterminate them before either could alert their fellow Flesh-Eaters and their master to his position. With one twist of his right wrist, a compact and well hidden crossbow slid from his sleeve, preloaded with six silver bolts and four exploding darts. Rhain would have no problem disconnecting the creatures from the one who controlled them. Then, he would seek out the Necromancer and put an end to his disgusting and disturbing practices.

On the count of three, Rhain spun into the hallway - exploding into action. He raised his arm, and before the zombies could set their blank eyes upon him, he had fired two of the silver bolts. The first bolt impacted through the right eye of one zombie and through what little brain matter was left to impale to the wall. That zombie collapsed with arms and legs twitching. The second bolt struck the other zombie through the neck, putting it down to the floor but not incapacitating the creature.

Grumbling, Rhain stalked up to the Flesh-Eater. It was already rising from the floor as he came up and kicked it in the head, causing a sickening snap to echo the empty hall. He broke the creature's neck with that violent kick, then Rhain's heavy boot slammed down atop the hairless head to hold the corpse down as it flailed aimlessly. He then fired another bolt right through its head. The creature stilled. He took no comfort in knowing that no matter how many undead he put down, the Master could reanimate and use them again and again till there was nothing left of the corpse but a pile of shredded bones.

Glancing behind him, Rhain pulled the bolts from the pair and hoped that Daniel was making better time. But then a piercing alarm erupted all around him. He cursed, covering his ears with his hands. Great! Fucking great! An alarm had been tripped. "Well,' he muttered to himself as he flicked the crossbow back into his sleeve, 'looks like the party's started. No use being polite and quiet now."

Grinning, he looked down to the zombie at his feet. One stomp of a heavily booted foot had the head flattened with pieces of skull, tissue, and brain splattering all over the floor. "That should do it." He wiped his boot along the dusty floor.

With the alarm sounding, Rhain figured that the Necromancer would send more zombies to investigate the floor, especially now that two suddenly vanished from the collective connection. So why not make as much noise as possible with as much destruction as he could in order to flush the fucker and its pets out? Then, he could kill the freak. No other souls needed to be tortured under the Necro's spells. That was just inhumane.

Up the flight of stairs he ran, moving speedily through the halls with eyes and his ears open for any signs of Regan or David. Rhain hoped he would find Regan so David could be left to Daniel. His brother needed to claim vengeance for what the Proscriptus had done to the woman Daniel claimed as his Socia. David's death was Daniel's right.

So where could she be?

If not in the basement then where? Rhain thought for a moment he had caught her scent as he moved down a hallway, but the scent was fleeting and disappeared as he came across another zombie. Just like the first two, this female fell to a bolt shot through her open mouth, cutting her spinal cord.

However, just as Rhain turned another corner something sharp sliced through the air. He jumped to the side with his body rotating into a flip that landed him a good ten feet away and in a safe crouch. He narrowed his eyes to see his assailant standing ready and flanked by four more zombies, all of which had their greedy eyes locked on him. But it wasn't the zombies that had Rhain's attention. No, it was their Master.

"Impossible," he breathed in pure shock. "You're dead..."

Rhain slowly stood with a hand reaching to release his Tantō. He eyed the figure before him with a gaze of suspicion and caution. "What the hell are you doing here, Grayson? You're supposed to be dead."

Grayson tipped his head, offering Rhain a polite smile of greeting. "It's a pleasure to see you again, Rhain Thorn. It's been a while, hasn't it?"

"Yeah, I'd say so." Flexing his fingers about the delicate hilt, Rhain eyed Alasdair's older brother with a very worried eye. "It's been over a decade since you died. I never thought I'd find you in David's stronghold. Then again, I never thought I'd see you alive."

Rhain cocked his head with his cunning eyes running over Grayson's body. He shivered to the visible aura of blackness that wrapped and caressed about the Necromancer's body. The blank, red eyes ran a cold shiver through Rhain's heart.

216

The Necromancer shrugged his thin shoulders, shifting silk across his flesh. With an attitude of indifference, Grayson glanced to his pets then back to his brother's longtime friend. "Should it surprise you?"

"Of course,' replied Rhain. "You were the prize of the Augur Familia, the top of your class and the damn apple of your father's bloody eye. You were your Pater's Successor! What the fuck have you done, Grayson? Do you have any idea…"

"Please,' Grayson chuckled with a delicate hand raised, 'spare me your warmth. I'm not here for a happy reunion, Rhain Thorn."

"Oh? Then why don't you step aside and let me pass. I have a schedule to keep."

Grayson shook his head and slender strands of white kissed his alabaster cheeks. "Unfortunately, I cannot permit you to go any further."

"Let me guess. You're going to try and kill me. Am I right?"

Grayson's slender lips curved into a devious and sadistic grin.

"Yeah, I figured. You never did like me." Rhain growled then slid his disgusted gaze over the looming undead that weaved where they stood, their hands flexing and their jaws opening and closing with slick strands of drool and phlegm dripping down to the floor. "I take it these little pedigree pets are yours?"

"They are." Grayson looked right then left, casting a proud smile to the creatures that stood at his side before looking back to Rhain. "Beautiful, aren't they?"

The Drasus shook his head. "Honestly? I find them disturbing and completely repulsive."

"You would, of course, but that matters little to me."

"What happened to you?" Rhain asked as he took a few cautious steps forwards. "How is it that you could come back from the dead?"

"Simple. Power, Rhain!" Grayson called out with his arms opening wide and his features twisting in to a look of perverted pride and immense delusion. "I have gained ultimate power by mastering the necromantic magic banned to us Venefici! Long ago I placed upon myself a powerful spell of reanimation and regeneration. If killed, which did happen, my body would rebuild itself, repair itself, and restore itself so that I may return to life!"

Rhain grimaced. "So, you're beyond undead?" Confused and thoroughly disturbed, Rhain slowly shook his head as he spoke in sympathy, "There's a reason that magic is illegal to use and practice, Grayson! It corrupts all that it touches and will consume the user's heart and soul till there is nothing left but a corrupt monster!"

The Necromancer snorted with a roll of his eyes.

Grayson truly didn't care, and Rhain, in his shocked disappointment, snarled. "I can't believe you would be willing to risk everything you've ever had, Grayson. I've known you since I befriended Alasdair."

Rhain took another step forwards, his fingers tightening. "What about Alasdair? Hmm? What about your brother? You're not only his Frater through the Augur name but you're his blood! You were born from the same mother. Alasdair's never stopped mourning your loss!"

It was all true. For decades, Grayson had been the shining star of all the Sorcerers and magic users in the United Kingdom. In fact, his name had spread across the channel to central Europe, bringing him and his Familia fame. But none expected any less from the Successor and first born son to Maximus Baird, the Regulus of the Augur Familia in England. Grayson was born to master the world of the Venefici.

Yet fame came with stress and demand, and Grayson soon found himself being commanded by both his Familia and the Consanguine Rex to handle many a delicate and magical affair. He had served Caius Scipio for several decades before being elevated to Instructor of his Familia, a position that brought with it great respect and power. He carried out his duties without fail and without question and with a coldness that grew in to a hunger for death and destruction gained from raw power.

Then, one day, he was sent on a mission of the greatest of importance and secrecy by Caius only to return in a casket to his Familia. His death left his father and his brother devastated. It was obvious, however, that Grayson showed little interest to the feelings of his family.

"Should I care about my little Frater's feelings?" he inquired smoothly and in a voice that was flat and removed.

Rhain's jaw went rigid. He stared at his old friend in complete disbelief. He muttered sadly, "You were everything to Alasdair. He mourned your death. He and your father gave you a proper Funus in your Familia's Sepulcorem. For fuck's sake, Alasdair still visits your tomb!"

Rhain released a sigh of stale air. "When did you stop caring? Tell me,' he hissed with fangs glistening, 'when did you stop loving your brother?"

Grayson's hard features seemed to soften beneath that heart aching question, but only for a moment as the image of Alasdair visiting a dark tomb with his name inscribed in cold rock warped a knot of guilt within his stomach. He quickly shook away the momentary emotion with a smirk. "I escaped, Rhain. Through my death I ran away from the corruption that has taken hold within this Republica and many Familia within, your Familia and mine included. The rules, those damn Lex, are nothing but tools of suffocation and tyranny!"

"The Lex are for all of us to follow, to ensure our world is controlled and unexposed! The Lex are what keep us safe." Rhain pointed his short blade towards Grayson only to have the zombies react with snarls and lashes of their clawed hands. "At one time you were an advocate for the Lex!"

Grayson narrowed his eyes with a flash of anger. His lips curled till he flashed his fangs with a snap of his jaws. "No longer am I a puppet of the laws! I am my own Rex. I have created my own Lex; the rules that bring me immortalized power!"

Grayson's declaration made Rhain physically sick. "I'm sorry, mate," he said with a frown upon his lips and a dismayed gaze in his eyes. "I had prayed that your soul had found rest in the Caelum, but I guess you couldn't handle heaven so you've returned to hell."

Grayson snorted, undeterred from Rhain's heart filled statement. With a flick of his fingers, the zombies surrounding their Master slowly backed away. He dismissed their assistance without a thought then began to carefully unbutton the long sleeves of silk that adorned his slender arms - rolling up the expensive fabric.

"Are we to fight with blades?" he inquired as he raised his arms, exposing the intricate glyphs of magical symbols that had been physically carved into his body before death. He began to mumble unheard words, calling forth a touch of dark magic that caused the glyphs upon his forearms to glow red. Slowly, the power of his spells began to form, coiling and spreading from glyph to glyph till black energy lapped at the fingertips of his right hand. And upon his fingers were born unholy blades, dripping with the power of the dead. He then raised his other hand and the same energy coiled wildly about his palm to form a raging orb of red and black crackling energy.

"Or magic?"

Rhain snorted as he flipped his Tantō, the sound of silk and leather caressing against one another whispered through the air. "Magic's not really my thing."

The grin on the Necromancer's pale face fell; he was unamused. "No kidding."

Rhain shrugged his shoulders then laughed. "Yeah, the Drasus missed the magic gene. But that's fine. I'll just rip your heart out with my bare hands!" He released a howl as he rushed in to motion, moving in a blur towards the other Lamia.

Grayson snarled when Rhain launched his attack - blade raised. The orb of power burst in to black flames as he waved his arms in an intricate and delicate circle, calling forth more of his demonic magic. Black lines followed the motion till he had written the syllables of his spell, glowing, before him. Immense energy erupted all around him causing the floor of the basement to rumble violently and the walls and ceiling to fracture.

The symbols hovering in mid-air began to turn, forming sections of magic as Greyson swept his hand outwards. When his bladed hand connected with the symbols, ravaging power detonated outwards and towards Rhain, swimming through the air and tearing at the walls and the floor to rip apart the very structure of the building.

"DIE!"

~ ~ ~ ~

Rhain never could stand the feel of his own bloody tears. He didn't like to show himself as weak or emotional, but at times he couldn't help it. He felt as if the slow beating heart in his chest had ruptured, overly flowing with pain and sadness. He didn't know what to feel as he stared down at Grayson who lay dying upon the floor. Rhain hadn't wanted to kill him, but he was given no other choice. He had hoped that he could convince Grayson to return to Alasdair and their Familia, but the Veneficus refused with his continual bull shitted propaganda on how David would free the closed minded Lamia of England.

Yet now, as he stood over Grayson's fallen body while watching the last drops of blood drip from the gash within his side, Rhain could only think that there could have been a better way for their fight to have ended. Grayson had always been a stubborn one, sticking to his beliefs with little to no want to ever deviate from them. Just once, couldn't he have listened instead of arguing?

Grayson took his last breath.

"You never could listen to reason," muttered Rhain under his breath as the heavy thought of how to tell Alasdair weighed upon his heart. He bent down to gently close Grayson's eyes yet paused as he saw the red blood in his eyes, the mark of the Necromancer, recede to be replaced by solid black. He gently closed Grayson's eyes then stood as his friend's body began to rot.

"I promise you, Grayson, that when all of this is over I'll come back for you and return you to Alasdair. You won't be lost to rot in this fuck hole." With a dry sigh, Rhain turned away. No more thoughts were put towards his friend's second death; Rhain turned away.

He moved from room to room, hallway to hallway, and stairs to stairs. With the Master dead, the remaining zombies in the factory began to crumble into the dust that had given them animation to begin with. For the most part, he didn't stumble across any other member of David's welcoming party. It seemed that the entire building fell eerily silent, that form of silence that seeps into the soul. The air still smelled of death, fresh and fading alike, but no more battles came his way.

Or so he thought...

Those who dared to threaten his determination were met by his blade. Most were young and ignorant of their skills and proclaimed that they would climb the ranks of their comrades by taking him down. Well, fuck them and the damn donkey their ignorance and arrogance rode in on. Unlike his brother, Rhain operated without a level of honor and ethics to his destructive battles. He preferred to get his hands dirty, to taste flesh and blood. He wanted to see the look of terror upon the faces of those who battled him as if their expressions were a prize for his memory to savor.

Another young Proscriptus fell before him with a large hole torn into his face from where Rhain's blade had penetrated through the right eye socket before slicing clean through the skull. The others in the small group fell back in either fear or awe of his skill. Then came the shouts of anger and the promises of death and vengeance all fueled by young stupidity. They rushed Rhain, drawing their weapons; blades glistened and guns fired. Throats were slashed, bullets were dodged, and flesh was torn till only one Lamia remained facing him.

Rhain, being the distorted individual that he so proudly was, drew up his blood soaked hand that had just torn through a throat and licked the thick liquid from his fingertips all the while locking eyes to the Lamia before him who shook ever so slightly. "Do you know who I am, boy?" he asked, delighting in the horror that took over the Filias' face.

When the Lamia didn't reply, or couldn't find the strength to do so, Rhain laughed then bound forwards with such speed that the other had no time to react. Blood spattered against Rhain's pale face as he drove his hand up through the bottom jaw of the Filias and into his brain. The sensation of soft tissue and brain matter squishing past his fingertips ran a shudder of sadistic pleasure through Rhain's body. One yank and he pulled the front of the youth's face away, sending a spray of brain, blood, tissue, and bone across the hall to paint the wall besides him.

Looking back at the trail of rotting corpses, Rhain sighed as he shook body matter from his hands, grunting as he tried to wipe wetness from his face. He scowled as he looked down to his coat. "Damn it. This was one of my favorite coats."

He hadn't tasted fresh Sanguis from the heat of battle for over three decades, at least not in a true fight. In all honesty, Rhain had wanted to put his murderous past away after carrying out countless assassinations and hunts under the guise of the Inquisitor. The thrill of the hunt, of the battle, and of the taste of hot blood would never leave him no matter how hard he tried to bury the desire and the cravings.

He wondered how his brother was fairing in his search for Regan. Surely Daniel was winning any and all battles he came against, knowing his skill. Smirking, Rhain returned to his hunt for David. He raced further on, moving from one winding corridor to another. Fucking hell, the blaring alarm never ceased and was now giving Rhain a damn headache. And why hadn't David shown himself instead of sending out useless fodder? Rhain shook his head in disgust.

How could David have manipulated so many young Lamia who swore allegiance to him so readily? They were young and ignorant of the truth of their world and the dark operations that waited to ensnare them. All they knew was the propaganda spread to them in lies upon the cold streets that they were tossed out into.

Rhain doubted if many of the Proscriptus who sided with David had any Familia to support and protect them. Maybe their own Parens had been the ones to abandon them. The reasons were endless, but the truth of the matter was that David was using each and every one of them for his own needs and his own goals. To sacrifice the young was a crime that could sentence a Lamia to the Basilica to be tried for the wrongdoings against their brethren and their race. David deserved to be sentenced to the harshest of executions, Crucis Supplicium - crucifixion.

That is, if Daniel didn't gut the bastard first. Honestly, Rhain would prefer to see David hanging from a wooden beam with crows feasting on his eyeballs. Then again, he knew that the horror awaiting David at the end of Daniel's blade would be a far more painful and slow death. Yeah, let Daniel deliver the final blow. David deserved agony.

221

XIV

I have never liked killing without a purpose.

I have never enjoyed the idea of torture for the use of gaining information, nor do I enjoy the use of pain and terror to gain respect. Yet I have done both - without hesitation and with eagerness.

I am not a pacifist.
I have killed.
And I will kill again.

When I find David, I shall kill him. I will enjoy every moment of his death. I will watch his blood spread upon the very ground he has stained with his presence. And I will savor the last drop of his blood as it drains from his lifeless body.

- *Daniel Rhys Thorn*

~ ~ ~ ~

"Tell me where she is!" howled Daniel at the writhing Lamia he held by the throat. He pushed the blade of his katana a few more inches into the man's gut, making sure to rotate the blade to cause the blade to slice into organ meat.

The Proscriptus, dangling off the ground, whimpered through the agony of the sharp tip slipping between his ribs to run metal against bone in a deadly kiss. "I…I don't know!" The feel of the blade sliding against his bones sent scrapping sensations through every fiber of his being! It was agony! Pure agony!

"You're lying to me," hissed Daniel as he leaned closer to flash his fangs. "I don't like liars."

Indeed, the pathetic law-breaker was lying. Every Lamia under David's orders knew of Joyce, his 'guest'. They had all been given orders to leave her alone unless they wanted to face the wrath of their commander. This sad shit had even seen her the night David arrived with her, but he wasn't going to admit that.

As the blade ruptured a lung, the young Lamia released a blood churning cry of suffering and tightened his hold on Daniel's wrist in a last attempt to free himself. He tried to kick out at his assailant but to no affect as his injuries continued to leak vital Sanguis from his body leaving him deprived of the energy needed to fight.

"I will give you till the count of three to tell me the truth or I shall gut you where you stand." To prove his threat valid, Daniel gripped the hilt of his katana tighter then slowly began to saw it back and forth within the Lamia's body.

With his eyes bulging from their sockets and blood bubbling up from his throat, the Proscriptus cried out in a desperate plea, "Fuck! She is in the basement cellars in a holding cell!"

Daniel snarled, leaning forwards. "Pathetic filth! I warned you not to lie to me! I have already searched the basement level, including the cellars, and found no recent scent of hers remaining!"

"David must've moved her!"

Daniel narrowed his black eyes to slits. He snarled softly, "Where would he take her?"

"His...office."

"Where is David's office?"

It was hard for the Lamia to answer when he could barely keep from drowning in the blood and fluids that pooled in his throat. He may be a vampire, an undead creature and for the most part immortal, but he could still drown in his own blood. "Room...fifteen..."

"What floor?"

It was too late. The Lamia in his grip jerked as his body began to spasm. More blood began to spill from his mouth, splattering against Daniel's face. He dropped the Lamia to the floor. The Proscriptus jerked wildly before falling still and starting to rot. Pulling his blade from the corpse, Daniel shook his head.

Damn it...

So, David's office was room fifteen. He glanced around to read above the closest door, thirty-eight. Room fifteen was behind him then. Very well, he would search for the office, and with luck he would find Regan and David together, and soon.

Daniel moved quickly from room to room, meeting little resistance. He came to one corridor, following the descending room numbers, only to find that room fifteen was being guarded by a lone Lamia. He didn't look too strong or intelligent, for that matter, not that either characteristic was of importance in a true fight. One Lamia guarding a room would pose no threat to Daniel. David was a fool to leave just one Proscriptus outside his office.

No doubt this Lamia, as with many who sided with David, was not more than half a century old. David didn't seem to be the type of leader to surround himself with qualified and thoughtful minions. Only the stupid, the ignorant, and the soulless took sides with David and allowed the fool to control them. Then again, Daniel had to thank David for employing such weak and untrained Lamia. Compared to them, Daniel was unstoppable.

Inching forwards, he closed the distance on the office and caught the faint remnants of Regan's dissipating scent as it lingered upon the stale air. Regan's scent came to him from two different directions. One was fainter than the other, indicating that Regan had recently left the office. However, her scent wasn't alone. David's scent was there too. Daniel sniffed the air, drawing deep into his dry lungs the mixed smell of female, sweat, and blood. Her blood! Daniel's nostrils flared, and he growled low in his throat before stepping out into the hall.

With intense speed, he lunged at the Lamia who stood guard at the door. Before the guard could draw his weapon, Daniel was on him with a hand in the Lamia's blonde hair. Howling, Daniel swung the vampire into the air, throwing him across the hall with enough force that the wall crumbled upon impact.

"Where is she? Where's the Humanus, Proscriptus?" he snarled.

In four easy steps he advanced upon the stunned Lamia, gripping him by the shirt and throwing him back across the hall to crash through the office door. Daniel stalked after him with his body trembling with rage, rage strong enough and intense enough to entice his Daemon into play.

For one second, one long second, Daniel stopped at the entry to the office. His eyes went wide, shifting quickly within slender sockets, as he was overwhelmed with Regan and David's scents. She had been inside in the room, but the two mixed smells were not all that struck him. He could feel the terror that she had experienced, and the intensity brought an animalistic snarl to rip past his lips as he turned his murderous gaze to the Lamia who was slowly shaking off the attack.

Daniel was on the law-breaker in a heartbeat, grasping him by the front of his shirt and wrenching his body upwards. "Answer me! Now!"

The Lamia chuckled while licking away a trickle of blood dribbling down from his cracked lip. "You just missed her."

Daniel's lips pulled back. He snapped his fangs. "Where is she?"

The Spaniard grinned and replied with a dark purr, "Last time I saw her, David was enjoying her. I can still hear her screams, and the look of sweet horror on her pretty face was something to savor as he took her on the cold floor."

Daniel released a howl that echoed the anger and pain he felt stabbing at his heart. With his control lost and his Daemon craving blood, Daniel let his mind flood with images of Regan's body bruised and broken and covered in a sheen of her own hot, mortal blood. He saw Regan upon the office floor, unmoving, and with her blank eyes staring to him. Above her, David pounded violently in and out of her naked and exposed body, tearing her flesh with his fangs till the dusty floor was covered in steaming blood. With every drop shed, a flicker of light died within Regan's terrified and silent eyes.

Daniel tried to scream her name. He tried to reach out to her but the image vanished. When his mind snapped awake, he saw a flash of silver in the form of a dagger cutting at his throat. He leapt away just as the blade nipped his flesh.

"You should give up, Drasus fool," said the Spaniard as he flipped himself up to his feet. "You'll never find her. David will have you and your brother skinned by morning!"

Daniel narrowed his eyes at the threat. "Enough," he hissed as he sprang forwards with such enraged speed that the other vampire had no time to react. Steel flashed, clashing loudly as the two broke into a series of attacks. This Proscriptus was good, good enough to put Daniel on the defense a few times - but only a few times.

The Spaniard pushed hard, driving Daniel back with strike after strike after strong strike. Daniel's back hit the wall with a crack. He winced, but had no time to react from the pain as the Spaniard drove forwards. He landed a solid kick to Daniel's stomach, drawing a grunt of air, and a trail of blood shot from Daniel's parted mouth.

Snarling, Daniel forced his body to duck as another attack came down upon him. He blocked with an arm then swung his blade back so he could arch it forwards in an attempt to land an accurate slice across the Lamia's midsection. Try as he might, his sword missed contact only to slice through fabric instead of body. Narrowing his eyes, Daniel snarled and pushed from the wall, leaping towards the other Lamia who hurried backwards to avoid the longer weapon. He pressed hard, slashing forwards with such force that his bones vibrated when steel met steel.

Finally, he was able to bury his blade in the Spaniard's stomach. Grabbing him by the shirt, Daniel pulled him forwards thus allowing his body to slide further up the blade.

"I'll ask one more time. Where has David taken my Socia?" He wasn't thinking clearly as his blood pounded wildly within his head. It wasn't often that his heart was forced to work, but at this moment there was little that could keep his Daemon under control.

Wincing, the Spanish Lamia whistled to the feel of the sharp blade parting his insides. He grimaced to the feeling of fluid leaking as some organ was ruptured. "Son...of a ...bitch," he snarled through agonizing pain.

"Is that your answer?"

"Go to hell, Lex-lover."

"So be it." With a growl and a snap of his wrist, Daniel yanked the sword from the Lamia's belly and at the same time shoved him backwards to fall upon the dusty floor of the office. Daniel stalked forwards, blade dripping with dark, thick blood.

Left to bleed out on the floor, the Spaniard curled his lips in a momentary sense of pride as his attacker came closer. The wound on his side throbbed as blood continued to seep from the open hole. "You'll never...find her,' he coughed through the pain then licked away the blood that spat from his lips, 'David will turn her as he did the other."

Daniel stopped in his tracks. "Other? What other?"

More blood gurgled up from his throat as his arrogant chuckles turned to violent heaving. "Joyce..."

Joyce? Daniel's eyes flashed. He flipped his katana to press the tip to the Lamia's throat. "Talk..."

The feel of skin being parted ever so slightly by the kiss of metal had the Lamia flinching. He snarled towards the Drasus. "Joyce's one of us now," he began to say with a cold hearted sneer. "David changed her and she welcomed it, just as her little cousin will. There's nothing you can do, Sucker."

Daniel's lips pressed thin to the insult. What he heard made his stomach twist with the very thought of David turning Regan. Regan belonged to Daniel. His Lamia mind had already decided that she was his lover, his Socia, and he would go to the ends of the world to see her happy and to have her safe.

225

He would have her forever.

Forever.

The word rang out within his mind, spurring a flare of hot determination through his heart. Gathering his thoughts, he inquired, "Is Joyce loyal to David?"

Snorting and rolling his eyes, the Spaniard replied, "The girl is delusional. She lives in a fantasy illusion thinking she is David's soulmate and that he will desire her above all other women for the rest of their undead life. She doesn't understand that David is more interested in your Socia at this moment."

"Explain."

"Joyce he used for sex and as a reason to draw your girl to him,' he swallowed a wad of blood and saliva that formed a wet ball in his throat, 'and he will use your precious human for her body after he has uses her to destroy you."

Daniel frowned. From the short conversations he had with Regan in discussing Joyce, he had been told that Joyce could be very jealous. She had supported his and Regan's budding relationship, but then her attitude towards them changed within a few days, turning from excitement to seething hatred. It was that hatred added with her jealousy that had her at the Crucible the fateful evening that lead to her falling into David's waiting grasp.

Was Joyce capable of hurting Regan just to ease her own depression? Would she sell her cousin to the devil in order to buy David's love? He didn't want to think about the answer for he already knew it.

"I'll let you live if, and I mean if, you tell me what David's plans are. Do I make myself clear?"

"Fuck you," the Spaniard hissed through the burning pain in his side as he arched up so his throat opened a bit more against the blade's sharpened tip. "My loyalty will always be to David and his objectives. Face the truth. You have already failed in your mission. By now, Grayson's children have hunted your brother down and torn him apart. You're alone."

Grayson? Daniel hadn't heard that name for almost a decade. "Grayson Baird? That's impossible. The man is dead."

"Shows what you know," chortled the Spaniard.

To know that Grayson was somehow alive greatly disturbed Daniel. However, he quickly set aside Grayson as more pressing matters requested his attention. Regan was more important than a Lamia supposedly buried within a cement vault. Pity and contentment shadowed his black eyes as he looked down to the wounded Lamia. .

"Why do you hesitate, Drasus?" asked the Spaniard when he noticed Daniel hesitating. "You're weak. You're too pathetic to carry the Drasus Familia name." His eyes narrowed as a sly, dark grin of pleasure took his lips. "Your woman doesn't want you anymore. I heard her say it. She laughed at your name…"

Daniel's eyes thinned, and he flashed his fangs along with a warning snarl for the other to think twice before continuing to speak.

Obviously, the Spaniard had no intention of stopping his verbal attack. He paid no attention to the danger threaded within Daniel's gaze. "And you know what?" he purred. "She begged for David to fuck her. I heard her cry out his name in pleasure as she came for him. Yeah, she was begging for it, hard and deep, screaming like a whore. I've never heard a woman make such sounds like she did. So face it, Sucker, she doesn't want you. You're wasting your time. That human will never be warm for you. You'll just be seconds to David."

Daniel snarled once again. His fingers tightened about the hilt of his katana.

"Tell me the truth. Do you really want to be seconds? Are you really going to be able to look at her with hot desire? Will you ever be able to put yourself inside her body knowing that David fucked her? Will she open her arms to you as she did for David? Will she cry out your name in the same way and beg for you like she did him? Or will she be nothing to you but a used fuck toy that's run out of batteries?"

Enough was enough. The sound that erupted from Daniel's throat was a sound no human or animal could make. He lunged at the other, piercing the man through at the shoulder till the blade dug into the cement floor beneath him. The Spaniard had no time to react before Daniel's fangs penetrated his neck. He jerked and spasmed to the pain that tore through his body the moment he felt his Sanguis being sucked from his veins with such ferocity that a few surely collapsed.

Daniel's feeding was violent, aggressive and painful. So ravenous was the act that blood spilled from the edges of his mouth, dripping down to paint both bodies red. Nails dug into the man's throat, digging out deep grooves in both flesh and muscle, to make sure that the Proscriptus wouldn't shake him loose - like a lion on a kill.

Weakness took over the Spaniard with every ounce of his blood that flowed down Daniel's throat. Be as it may, he couldn't push Daniel off of him as the Drasus fed in frenzied fever. With the realization striking him cold that his blood was being drained he began to fight back, pushing and shoving and bucking in futile attempts to get away. Horror grabbed him, squeezing tight, as the last threads of his life were slowly frayed.

When Daniel felt the last inch of the Lamia's life pulsating against his lips, he released his bite but not with tenderness. No. He tore his fangs from the man's neck leaving torn and ripped flesh parted wide thus allowing the last pint of blood to flow from the wound and spread about the body in a pool of dark red. Wiping blood stained lips upon the sleeve of his coat, Daniel rocked back to stand. He watched in sick awe the Lamia twitch before the last glint of light faded from his eyes. He yanked the katana free, wiped the blade clean on the leg of his pants then sheathed the blade.

There was nothing else he needed to say. The Lamia would die and with his death Daniel would gain some satisfaction in the anger he felt towards David. Without delay, he turned to depart the room, leaving the vampire's body to rot like the factory around it.

227

Back in the hall, Daniel followed Regan's fading scent. He hoped his twin was having an easier time moving through the factory, but with Grayson and his 'children' hanging in the shadows he had a sinking feeling that Rhain might be in more trouble than he could handle. Daniel could search out his twin and offer aid, but he had little time remaining to find Regan or David, or both together, before the sun crested. When time ran out, he and Rhain would be fresh out of their own luck.

~ ~ ~ ~

After clearing the first and second floor, Rhain decided to give the basement a second look. An inkling told him that he wasn't finished down there. There were more rooms and nooks and crannies that he and his twin had missed when they first descended into the depths of the old factory, plus there were areas that he couldn't enter but from other points on the first floor.

Cautiously, he stepped down the main stairs and into the belly of the beast. He looked past corners and through shadows till he found a corridor that looked more like the solitary confinement cells of a long-lost asylum with paint chipping and falling from the ceiling and walls. The place smelled of dank sewer filth from standing water covered in a slick of mildew, oil, and rotten death. The stench was so foul that Rhain had to cover his nose and mouth.

Through the stagnant air, Regan's scent still lingered. The further he walked down the corridor the stronger it became. He easily picked out the remnants of sweat and perfume, the same perfume he had smelled on Daniel when his twin had returned from visiting her. There was one cell in particular where her scent was the strongest. To Rhain's luck and surprise the door was open, but there was no sign of her inside. The cell was empty and dark, and the warm scent of mortality lingered upon a dissipating puff of air.

Damn, another dead end. The good news? When she had left the cell she had been alive.

click

Rhain froze to the feeling of cold metal pressing to the back of his neck, just beneath the base of his skull. He froze, his eyes slowly shifting within their narrowing sockets in an attempt to glance over his shoulder. Fuck! He had been caught off guard, surprised from behind, as his attention had been focused on the task at hand.

"Don't fucking move," demanded the voice of a young woman from close behind him.

Slowly, Rhain lifted his arms to offer a view of his blood tainted hands and red stained Tantō. He grinned as he peeked over his shoulder. "I don't mind the fucking part, but it's rather hard without moving. Don't you think?"

Intense eyes, sparkling with reflective silver, met his playful gaze. "Who are you?" the woman snapped.

Rhain narrowed his eyes. Wait, he knew this girl. Blonde hair - green eyes - looked a little like Regan. "Joyce?"

The answer came with the young woman pushing the gun against the back of his neck with a jerking hand. "Answer my question or I'll blow your head off."

"Alright," he cleared his voice and nodded. "I'll make you a deal. I'll answer your question if you answer mine - first. I just want a name to confirm your identity."

"Why?"

"So I don't kill you."

The young woman narrowed her eyes. After a thoughtful moment she replied, "Joyce Scott."

"You are Regan's cousin. Yes?"

"I answered your question. Now answer mine," Joyce ordered. "Who are you?"

"Rhain Thorn."

Joyce remembered that name and the name of his twin brother, Daniel. After all, Joyce had been a fan of theirs for many years. David had also been bitching about the two twins and their family for days now. She shouldn't be surprised that they had found their way into David's stronghold. He had Regan after all, and Daniel wanted Regan. It was only time that Daniel would come looking for Regan.

"What the hell are you doing here?" she asked even though she knew the answer.

Rhain arched a slender brow and slowly began to lower his arms. "To find you and your cousin."

"Liar," she muttered. "You're here to kill David and take Regan away from me."

The gun shook in her unsteady hands with such force that the metal rattled. Rhain smirked to himself. She had no intention of pulling the trigger. She was too afraid - or so he thought.

"Look,' he breathed out keeping his icy eyes upon her from over his shoulder, 'Daniel and I are here to locate you and Regan. I swear this to you. We're here to take you both to safety, ordered to do so by the Rex. We know you've gone through the Creare, and we know what David's planning to do with Regan. We have been ordered to retrieve you both from David so we can protect you two."

Joyce's lips pulled back in a slow grin as she gripped the hilt of the gun tighter. "You're mistaken. I have no intention of leaving David. He needs me, and I need him."

Rhain's eyes narrowed. What type of fucked up logic was she using? How could she be so blind to everything going on around her, to her and to her cousin? Then again, her Parens was David. That man was capable of spinning any fucked up web of lies he thought up, and Joyce was too delusional to see the webbing.

"When did he change you?" he asked as his keen nose caught the delicate, yet tainted, smell of death upon her. "Oh, wait, I remember. He took you from my club, and you two went back to your flat where you fucked like rabbits. But then something went horribly wrong, didn't it? He showed you

229

the monster in him and attacked you. He left you for dead that night, bleeding dry on your bed."

"Shut up!" Joyce snapped. "What the hell do you know about it, anyway? Hmm?"

"A lot actually. I was the one Daniel called when Regan found you that night. I was the one who investigated what had happened to you. But what I never understood is why David took you out of the apartment to perform the Creare in the first place only to toss you back when he was done with you. Why not let you stay in this pleasant shit-hole to recover properly? Letting you leave was stupid, very stupid."

Joyce narrowed her eyes. "He didn't want to leave me. He knew Regan was going to come home with Daniel and wasn't sure if your brother was going to outstay his welcome. He brought me here and welcomed me into his life and into his arms. I don't remember how I ended up at the apartment after that, but I do remember finding my way back to him."

An arrogant grin teased her lips. "I will always find my way back to him."

"You've got a fucking screw loose. You know that? How could you leave Regan like that? Do you know how scared she was when she found you? She called my brother in tears when she found you bleeding on your bed. If you had stayed, Daniel would have found you and you two would have been brought safely to our Domus where you could have recovered correctly. You didn't deserve to be thrown into your new life like a screaming baby ripped from a womb. Nobody deserves to be treated that way after being reborn."

Rhain sighed with a sympathetic shake of his head. "Regan misses you. She's gone through a lot of shit. She doesn't need to go through David's insanity because you won't come to your damn senses."

Joyce snorted. "Regan'll get over it."

Rhain snarled. "You're a coldhearted bitch."

An amused snort sounded softly from Joyce. "I'm not leaving him."

"Because of one night with David you're willing to put your cousin through hell?" Rhain scoffed as his eyes darkened behind the ice blue contact lenses. "Fuck it. You're not worth recovering, and you're not worth Regan's pity or her love."

"You've got it wrong. I'm being very considerate of Regan, considering what she did to me."

"What the hell did she do to you to deserve all this shit?"

"She betrayed me for your brother, a stupid guy. I was tossed to the side that night my bitch of a cousin abandoned me for her supposed knight in shining armor." Joyce growled then gave a distorted chuckle. "Well, I found my knight too. I found David."

Rhain shook his head. "You foolish girl. Do you even know what type of monster you're feeding your cousin to?"

"Of course I do," snorted Joyce. "I know everything. David's never kept any secrets from me. I know that you Thorn twins are even worse monsters than him. Does Regan know that Daniel's a vampire? I doubt it. I know all about the rules you Lex-Lovers follow, so I'm pretty sure Daniel hasn't spilled the beans to her. Yet."

She went on to growl, "Daniel has taken my cousin from me, and I won't allow that. There's no way I'll let you take David from me too. So, I am going to take my own vengeance on Daniel for taking Regan from me by killing you. I'll do anything to make David happy."

"You're fucking daft." Rhain grinned with a chuckle. "You're mad at Regan for finding love in my brother? You should be happy for her, not wanting to destroy her."

"You don't understand!" Joyce snapped.

"Sure I do. You're a woman, and I understand your sex better than you do," replied Rhain. "You're jealous and using Regan as a scapegoat for your pathetic inability to find somebody to love. But why are you still hooked on her and Daniel when you have David? Isn't he everything you want, your knight in shining armor? Or does he not count anymore? He mustn't be that great in bed if a one night fuck isn't good enough to earn him a spot in your heart."

The echo of the gun discharging rang throughout the tunnels the instant it was fired. Rhain ducked his head in time for the bullet to whiz by his skull, impaling itself in the south wall of the cell behind him. He howled in discomfort to the sudden disappearance of his hearing in his right ear.

"Jesus, Mary, and Joseph!" he barked, turning to face not only her but the gun that was pointed right at his face.

Okay, so maybe she would fire the gun. The urge to reach out and snap her neck was so strong that he could taste her blood, but he forced himself to calm. Time to change his tactic and try a little sympathy before he strangled the girl.

"Look,' he said through a tight snarl, 'I can understand how you feel. Daniel has always been able to get girls to love him. He is the charmer while I just get girls who want to fuck me. Not that I mind, considering I do the same to them. But that's not really the point. Do you think I've never been jealous of my brother and his loving heart? We're twins for fuck's sake. But he is still my blood. He was born right alongside me, and he will always be right beside me till the end of time. I have followed him into this death trap so he can find the woman he's fallen in love with. She is your blood, and family blood flows the deepest."

He shook his head while running a look of hot disgust over Joyce. "You're her cousin, her blood! How could you let David kidnap her? Do you have any idea what he could be doing to her right now? Can you even begin to comprehend what his plans are for her? Do you? Do you even care?"

The weapon quivered, and Rhain noticed the falter in Joyce determination as her features twisted in a look of pain. Yeah, she knew what David was doing to Regan and what he planned on using her for, and that made Rhain both sick and enraged.

"I am his will," she began to whimper as if trying to convince herself that her delusions were her reality. "He's told me that I am what makes him live. He's promised me that Regan will join us so we can be a happy family once Daniel is out of the way."

Rhain swallowed a sarcastic breath as he rubbed at his right ear in an attempt to bring back his hearing. Oh the lies Lamia could tell. He should know, after all, he has used the same tactics on women and his enemies. But Joyce? The poor girl was living in a world far beyond reality. She was really fucked in the head. She truly believed in what David had told her, and now she acted on his word as if it was a creed.

"He's using you for his own purpose just as he has used the other Proscriptus in this piss-hole. All he's wanted this entire time was Regan, not you. He's never wanted you." Rhain's icy blue eyes narrowed and he hissed darkly, "And he used you to get her."

"Shut up!" Joyce screamed in rage that distorted her face into an expression of insanity. The gun went off again, purposefully this time, and the bullet caught Rhain right in the jaw, ripping apart flesh and breaking bone as it tore across his face.

Rhain cried out as he stumbled back against an unhinged door, the old slab of wood buckling under his stumbling weight and sending him to the floor. Holding his broken jaw, that spilled blood past his fingers, he cast Joyce a set of murderous and bestial eyes. Rhain wanted to rip her apart right then and there.

"You fucking bitch!" he howled in a blood gurgled curse. "I'll rip out your damn heart!"

A look of horror crossed Joyce's face when she saw the flash of fatal hunger in Rhain's eyes. She raised the shaking gun before her one more time as a surge of stupid encouragement rushed through her.

"I won't listen to your lies!" she snapped. "David's told me that Regan's only bait for your brother. After he has Daniel, he will turn Regan in to one of us." She gave an insane smile of self-delusion. "The three of us will be a family. I will have David..."

Rhain released an agonizing cry as he stomped a foot to a rake of sharp pain that tore down his spine. "David will have Regan, not you. Get it through your thick head, Joyce. He's only wanted Regan. He used you to get her and Daniel. You were just a damn pawn in one of his sick plans, and you just happened to be too desperate and fucking foolish so you fell right into your part." Damn, it was so hard to talk correctly when blood was pooling in his throat.

"Use your damn brain, woman!" he went on to snarl as he pushed himself from the floor. "If he was so in love with you, then why is Regan even here?"

"She's here so we can be together!"

"Yeah,' scoffed Rhain while spitting a wad of blood past his lips, 'keep telling yourself that. Shit! Enough of this. I can't waste my time on you."

Joyce's eyes widened as the other Lamia went into motion.

Before she could counter him, he grabbed the gun right out of her hands, spun it about, and pointed it right back at her. "Here's the plan,' he snarled, 'you're going to behave yourself and stay here while I go find my brother and Regan. When we're done castrating David's head from his body, we'll come back for you. If you have moved one inch, I will break every bone in your legs and drag you out of this place."

He watched her recoil and back away. "You're young, Filia, and you're living in your ignorance and arrogance. This might come as a fucking shock, but David's not the strongest Lamia out there. There are those of us who are much stronger than him, much colder and much more psychotic. I could kill you with just one touch. In fact, I'm very tempted to do just that."

Rhain's voice dropped to an icy whisper. "Trust me. I'll make you suffer in the end."

He snorted and sneered to her as he wiped blood from his face. "Daniel and I came here to save you and Regan. We were willing to offer you safety in our Familia where we can provide you with the proper education that is required by our laws. You need to go through the Domare, Joyce. Otherwise, you're nothing but fodder for David and other Proscriptus who don't give a fuck about our laws. Don't you see that?"

"Lies…" She gave a slow shake of her head. "It's all lies…"

Rhain flexed his aching jaw back and forth, splintered bone creaking. "David's really skull fucked you, huh?" He grimaced as something sounded in a soft crack. "I can't waste any more time on you. If you no longer care for the safety of your cousin, then I no longer care for your safety. Regan is more important than you right now. She'll just have to learn to live without you, and with Daniel at her side, I'm sure she'll have a very easy time doing that."

Before she could let out a scream, Rhain slammed the butt of the gun against the side of her temple. Blackness engulfed Joyce as searing pain ripped through her head. She tumbled to the cold floor. Though he wanted to kill her for harming him, Rhain couldn't bring himself to do it. He could, in a way, blame her death on David or some other asshole of a Proscriptus. However, to lie to his own brother while Regan cried on Daniel's shoulder wasn't a comforting thought.

With Joyce unconscious and bleeding on the floor, Rhain turned his attention to more pressing matters. He needed to find Daniel. Time was running out and so was his strength. Too much loss of blood would leave him vulnerable and weak to further attacks. Rhain looked one last time to the unconscious female slumped on the floor.

"May Regan forgive you, 'cause I won't."

XV

If I die, will she mourn me? Will she remember who I am if she survives?

Will she shed a tear for the man known as Daniel Thorn - a glint of a memory in her mortal life?

    I cannot fail her.

    I must do all I can to make sure she survives, even if that means sacrificing my existence, all that I have, for her. I will not allow Regan's gentle humanity to be snuffed out, wiped away, because of David's insistent and insane need to destroy me and my brothers.

    Her life is more important than mine. Why? Because she is an innocent, while I - technically - am nothing more than a stain of darkness upon this beautiful world.

    I will give my life so she may live.

    Then, I will not have failed her.

    I will have saved her.

    -   *Daniel Rhys Thorn*

~ ~ ~ ~

Daniel continued on with his search as the minutes continued to tick on by.

With each room he broke into, he came no closer to finding Regan. He discovered only rooms that held nothing more than the ghosts of the past, memories left by those who had brought the factory to life. Still, there was no sign of his Socia, and he was quickly allowing his panic to fuel his mind. He was forced to turn back when a timer chimed on his watch that kindly informed him that dawn was but an hour or so away. Damn, time was slipping through his fingers.

    For all he knew David may have moved Regan out of the building. No. David wanted Daniel to find her. He wanted to use her torture to break Daniel. David was in control. Leaving would prove no use to him. Regan was still here. Daniel could feel her, and knowing she was waiting for him and in need of his protection spurred him in to a flat run.

Daniel cleared the second floor, and as he came around a corner to sprint across the second story balcony that over looked the administration entry, his steps skidded to a stop with such strength that he stumbled. The Lamia's eyes went wide, and he took a cautious step backwards as his dark gaze set upon two figures who were waiting for him across the way.

When she saw him, Regan cried out in desperate tears, "Daniel!"

Elation tore through the Lamia leaving prickles dancing across his skin. Relief flooded through him upon seeing her, and his heart skipped a few beats. "Regan!" Daniel called back. Seeing her within David's arms defused her name in a hiss. What had he done to her? Her shirt was ripped apart, exposing her flesh beneath, and he noticed that her jeans were unbuttoned and altered. "David, you bastard! What have you done to her?"

David finally croaked a laugh; it was a laugh of cruel amusement. "Isn't this sweet?" he chuckled as he drew a sharp nail down Regan's right cheek, slicing deep enough to allow a trail of blood to flow. He sighed in pleasure to the feeling her body trembling against him from the nipping pain. "Such a beautiful reunion," exclaimed the Proscriptus with his free hand brushing fingers up the smooth flesh of her belly to grope a lace covered breast.

The touch gagged Regan causing her to fuss and cry out in protest. But Daniel reacted with a harsh and threatening growl and took a step forwards with his katana flipping behind him, ready to strike. "Take your hands off of her!"

"An' wha' will ya do, Drasus?" he chortled with an amused snort before dipping his head to brush his lips along Regan's cheek, his tongue slipping forwards to lap up the fresh line of mortal blood. "Come on, Mista Thorn. I know ya an' yer clean cut ways. Ya like yer suits tailored an' steamed an' yer women virgins an' sweet. Wha' will ya do with a tainted whore like her?"

"I warn you," Daniel growled, taking a calculated step.

"You'll warn me? Who tha hell do ya think ya are?" David snorted with his eyes darkening with mirth.

"If you've laid one hand on her…"

David's smile twisted into a sadistic sneer and he laughed before barking, "Oh, yes, I did! I took her. Her body, like a flower, opened up ta me, an' she trembled beneath me while screaming my name."

"Don't listen, Daniel! He's lying," screamed Regan past her heart wrenching sobs.

David gave her a rough jerk meant to silence her words. "Shu' i', bitch!"

One thing Daniel could not stomach were lies. Especially those lies created for no reason but to cause the most damage to a person's emotions. And that was exactly what the Proscriptus leader was trying to accomplish; fuck with Daniel's self-control and his trust in Regan. Daniel would not fall for that old trick. He wouldn't walk away, abandoning her to David, just because of a twisted lie. He could never reject Regan. Never.

Daniel raised a placating hand, motioning for Regan to calm herself. "Calm down, sweetheart. I believe you."

David scoffed. "Don' tell me ya believe this whore!"

"Of course I do."

David snorted. "Why? Don' trust my word as an honest gent?"

Daniel grinned. "I wouldn't trust you with a pet rock, David. But if you must know, it is a simple fact, you primate. I can still smell myself on her. If you had sex with her, it would be your stench wafting off of her flesh, not mine. Besides, I would always trust her over you." He took another step, flipping the decorative hilt of his Katana within his skilled hand. The blade kissed the air with a delicate hiss of metal.

"Back off!" barked David with a nasty snap as Daniel began to stalk onwards with weapon raised. To make his own threat a true reality, he raised his other hand across Regan's throat to tease a long dagger against her skin. "I'll saw her pretty, little head from her pretty, little shoulders!"

The glint of metal stopped Daniel in his tracks. His black eyes narrowed.

Regan's reaction was a sharp cry of fear. She began to squirm within David's grasp in an attempt to break free. With a cruel chuckle, David dipped his head to whisper against her ear, "Keep tha' up an' ya will cut i' off yerself." She stilled - frozen in fear.

"What are you going to do, David?" inquired Daniel with his eyes burrowing into the Proscriptus and drawing David's attention from Regan. "Rhain and I have slaughtered every soul inside this building. And from what I've seen, he's taken care of the Necromancer in your service. You harm her and you have nothing left to aid you, no leverage and no allies to use against us. You are all alone."

"Are ya sure ya killed everybody? Even Joyce?" David inquired cunningly and with a wicked grin. "'ave ya killed her too?"

Regan turned her eyes to Daniel, wide and frightened. "Daniel?"

"I have not found Joyce, but I can promise you that neither Rhain nor I will harm her like you have done, David. Now let Regan go." Daniel swept a few fingers before him. "Lower your blade and I might consider letting you and Joyce leave once you hand Regan over to me. The Rex knows of your location. He'll be here soon. You can't run from his hounds. I am offering a gift of good-will by allowing you a head start."

"Lower my blade? Now why would I do tha'?" asked the Proscriptus leader as he looked down to the terrified face he tipped up close. She was crying again, and her tears made her so much more beautiful and innocent to him. Yes, a flower that would open to him any time he so wished. Once Daniel and Rhain were disposed of.

"You've lost all your cards in this game," said Daniel. "It's time to fold your hand."

"Oh,' David chuckled dryly, 'I have one more card to play." With a twisted grin, he glanced to Regan and took a deep, stale breath of air. "I am going ta tell ya a secret now, puppe'. Something tha' Daniel here would kill ta protect."

Daniel froze to what David said. "David," he warned with a quick suck in of a breath as he tightened his grip upon the hilt of his sword. "Don't."

236

The Proscriptus slowly slid his arrogant grin back towards his rival. He didn't need to say anything more for his threat to take hold, but continued on just to take pleasure in seeing Daniel crumble. "Yer boyfriend's been lyin' ta ya, Regan. He's been keeping a secret from ya, a secret tha' he's promised to keep by any means possible. Even takin' tha life of an innocent human."

Clearing his voice, he draped an arm about Regan's shoulders as he swirled and swayed the dagger before her. "An' I don' think tha's very nice o' him. Relationships are formed on trust an' honesty. Don' ya agree?"

Regan whimpered, leaning back from the dancing blade.

"Do ya know tha' once I spill Daniel's dirty little secret ta ya tha' ya will be marked fer death?"

Regan looked terrified as she turned her quivering gaze to Daniel whose features had fallen to a cold and distant line.

David went on to say, "Or maybe I should le' her figure i' all ou' fer herself. Tell me, Regan, 'ave ya ever known Daniel ta be ou' during tha day, struttin' around in tha sunlight?" Leaning down to her, he drew his tongue slowly across her jaw, enjoying how her body tightened beneath the lick. "I bet he's no' one fer eatin' a lo', is he?"

Regan tried to turn her face away from him but David's grip tightened and he forced her to look back to him till their eyes met. "Tell me somethin'. Does yer lover feel as warm as yer own flesh does or does his skin feel cold?"

Regan's confusion turned to a layer of thick fog that began to coat her rational cognition. She shook so badly that her teeth rattled as she looked between Daniel and David with only the sliding of her eyes. She whimpered, "I don't understand."

"Ya 'ave been in his bed, havn' ya?" When Regan bit her tongue and swallowed her answer, David took her silence as truth and barked out a laugh with a judgmental sneer tossed to Daniel. "Ya go' ta be kidding me! A swee' thing like her an' ya haven' fucked her ye'? Somethin' wrong with ya, mate?"

Daniel snarled with his lips pulling back. "Do not be a fool to think you should be privileged to the intimate details of hers and mine relationship."

David shook his head in disbelief. He then tightened his arm about her shoulders and purred darkly, "Tell me tha' he's held yer hand or kissed yer cheek?" She nodded. "Good! So he ain' no fuckin' eunuch. I bet his hand was cold ta tha touch an' his lips felt chilly against yer cheek. 'ave ya felt his heart beating ye'?"

"David, stop this," insisted Daniel with a touch of unease to his tone of voice.

The deviant grin that slid David's lips was truly psychotic. He chuckled. "See? I still 'ave one last card ta play - tha truth."

He had Daniel right where he wanted him. The Drasus would do anything to protect the laws, even if it meant tossing Regan to the wolves. "Look how afraid he is," purred the Proscriptus with a flick of his blade towards the other Lamia. "He knows tha' if ya find ou' wha' he truly is, then ya will be lost ta him forever. Tha Concilium will no' allow ya ta know o' their world an' survive."

237

"That's not true!" Daniel snapped. "The Consanguine Rex..."

"Wha' would he do? Huh?" laughed David with a healthy dose o' sarcasm. "Ya know tha harshness of his rules."

"Rules are there to be broken. I should know. I do it more often than I should."

All heads turned to the stairs and the lone figure appearing from the depths of the building. Rhain stepped forwards, cursing low through incoherent mutters while holding his bleeding jaw where the skin was already starting to knit itself back together over bone that was progressing through a self-induced bone graph. He smeared blood coated fingers over the wound then spat a wad of ugly, black phlegm to the dusty floor.

"Regan! Your cousin's a fucking bitch! I don't like her very much," he retorted, then winced and cursed as something in his jaw went pop.

David's face fell with an annoyed groan.

Daniel breathed out a heavy sigh of relief upon seeing his twin, but the bloody wound torn across Rhain's face made the happiness short lived. "What happened to you?"

"She fucking shot me!"

"Who shot you?" Daniel inquired.

"Joyce,' Rhain shouted back then added under a breath, 'the fucking bitch."

"Rhain!" Regan smiled brightly.

Rhain looked forwards, and when he saw Regan, he offered her a sly grin and a salute. "Good to see that Daniel finally found you. I apologize for my attire. I usually don't come covered in blood to a party."

David gave a heavy, hearty laugh at the mention of Joyce. "Ha! So she did do something useful after all. Took her long enough."

"I'm sending you my damn cleaning bill!" Rhain shook his head as if he were still trying to shake way the ringing in his ears. He even tapped his right ear with a palm.

After a sarcastic scoff, David pulled Regan against his chest with the blade poised between her breasts. Both Rhain and Daniel snarled at the same time, expressing the exact same face of wrath. "I'm getting' bored wit' yer games, Drasus dogs. I'll give ya two minutes ta get yer asses ou' o' my home before I gu' her like a squealin' pig."

A wince ran Regan's face, stained with tears, when she felt the sharp tip of the short blade part flesh. When it slid further, puncturing her right breast, she screamed in a surge of fright filled tears.

Daniel roared when the first drop of crimson kissed Regan's flesh. As the warm drop caressed her skin, his self-control fractured and he rushed forwards with katana raised and ready to strike. No longer was he thinking, only reacting. With his emotions now twisting with the murderous demands of his Daemon there was little chance for him to regain his control. That was, till his brother appeared before him, grabbing him by the shoulder and pushing him back.

"No!" shouted Rhain with a sharp growl to his voice.

"Let me go, Rhain," snarled Daniel with a deadly glare slipping to his twin. His nostrils flared as he drew in another scent of his Socia's hot blood tainting the dusty air. "I want his life."

Rhain sympathized with his brother, could understand Daniel's want to kill David, but there was a way to go about it that wouldn't end with Daniel succumbing to his Daemon. For once, Rhain stepped in as the mediator of rational thinking while his levelheaded brother acted without thought.

He saw Daniel's Daemon simmering behind Daniel's onyx eyes, and he felt his twin shaking with rage. Leaning close, unnerved by Daniel's threatening snarl, Rhain whispered hotly, "I know you do. Trust me. I want to see David splayed open on a spike too, but you need to get a hold of yourself. If you attack him with your Daemon clawing at you, you could catch Regan in the cross-fire. You wouldn't be able to live with yourself if you ended up harming her."

Daniel's lips parted as he released an animalistic snarl, trying to force his brother back by intimidation.

Rhain didn't back down. He gripped Daniel's shoulder tighter and glanced back to see David smirking at them from over Regan. Seeing her fear and her tears tore through Rhain's heart, so he turned away. "Look at her,' he told Daniel softly, 'because I can't. Look how frightened she is. This isn't the time to scare her away from you by exposing the truth of our race. We need to think clearly if we're going to get her away from him. We need to separate David from her. As long as he's using her as a shield we can't attack him. You want him dead and her alive. Right?"

Daniel's rage flared within his darkening eyes as he released a demonic rumble, "I *want* her."

Rhain acknowledged his brother's spoken claim over Regan with a curt nod. "And you'll have her, Frater, but first we need to have a plan. So do me a fucking favor and put your Daemon back into its little box so we can go kick some ass and save your girl."

Taking a deep breath, Daniel wrapped a mental hand about his vanishing control. He closed his eyes and took a number of deep breaths to focus his mind in order to force his Daemon back into the pit of his psyche that it had emerged from. When he felt his ravaging rage lower to a rumbling simmer, he opened his eyes.

Seeing the regained control within his brother's eyes, Rhain gave a sly smirk and clapped his brother on the shoulder. "There we go. Feel better?"

A slight smirk etched Daniel's lips till a voice whispered to his and Rhain's keen ears a single word that brought the entire world to an eerie stillness.

"Vampires…"

Both twins winced as a cold claw of reality dug through their hearts, and at the same time they turned their attentions back to David to see Regan looking at them with horrified eyes. David sat his chin upon one of her slim shoulders and sneered wickedly towards the twins.

"Shit," muttered Rhain as he turned about with a whistle sounding past his lips.

Daniel growled low in his throat and tightened his hand about the hilt of his weapon. "He told her," he hissed to his brother. "David told her what we are, Rhain."

It was true. The disbelief shadowed in the horror reflected in Regan's eyes said it all. David had spilled the dirty little secret of their identity and was proud of doing so.

The Proscriptus chuckled a dry chuckle of amusement as he pressed his lips to Regan's tear streaked cheek. "Now ya know tha' truth. I'm no' tha only monster here, Regan." Flipping the blade, David pointed the dagger towards the twins. "An' they're tha worst o' us all. Yer boyfriend an' his pussy brother 'ave killed a lo' o' people by order o' their precious Rex. An' they do so ta protect tha laws tha' we're all suppose ta bow down ta."

David chuckled and added, "Bu' I don' bow ta any Lex-Lover. I'm no' a lap dog o' tha fuck'n Rex."

Regan slowly shook her head; a lock of her dirty hair stuck against a wet cheek. "Impossible…"

"Regan,' said Daniel with desperation lacing his voice, 'don't listen to him, sweetheart. Nothing he says can be trusted."

She whimpered.

Rhain snarled.

David cackled as he wrapped an arm about her chest, pressing down the remains of lace to expose a soft breast so he could spread and curl the hand about her throat. The human in his arms cried out through a throaty whimper when he jerked her head to the side to expose her lovely, tight neck.

"Yeah,' he chided with his lips moving against her flesh, 'don' listen ta me. Le' me show ya tha truth."

"David!" Daniel shouted when the Proscriptus parted his jaws, exposing his fangs that he then pressed against Regan's neck. To Daniel's horror, David sank the sharp tips of his fangs into Regan's flesh, puncturing her skin with a slow entrance. The expression of discomfort and terror that washed over Regan's face fractured what minimal self-control Daniel had managed to regain.

In a split second the dam of his control fractured, spilling forth the rage of his Daemon. Throwing back his head, a chilling and enraged howl erupted from deep within him as he spread his arms with the explosion of his erratic and overwhelming aura.

Time fell still as if the very concept was afraid to act.

David had just enough time to shove Regan out of the way, his fangs tearing across her neck to leave jagged lesions in her flesh when Daniel bore down upon him with his blade raised. They clashed in a sweep of steel that radiated sparks of power. Regan didn't have time to scream when she found herself hitting the floor, and after a moment, she shook clear her shock and looked up to see Daniel and David caught in a clash of blades. Slowly, she pushed up to stand on shaky and unstable legs only to crumble back to the floor as dizziness wrapped about her mind.

Power radiated from the violent and aggressive attacks that rained down by the two combatants. Even though their weapons were different in size, the two managed to strike blows that forced the other to stumble and falter while trying to block and parry well enough to defend their assaults. The explosive force tore across the balcony, pushing Regan back upon the floor and up to a standing position. But with the shockwave juddering the floor, she fell on to her rump with a sharp screech of pain when an ankle twisted out from beneath her.

"Regan!" She looked up to see Rhain sliding to his knees at her side. He grabbed her, fussing as he tipped her head to the side to check the wounds upon her neck.

"Fuck," snarled the Lamia as he tore a piece of his shirt into a strip of fabric that he gently tied about her neck. "Hold this tight against your neck, alright? You're bleeding rather badly. We've got to stop this bleeding before the scent of your blood fills the air. This won't help Daniel's situation."

With a trembling, blood coated hand she did what Rhain commanded and gingerly pressed the cloth to her neck. Daniel? Her heart tripped as she watched David hacking and slashing at Daniel. Sparks flew up from the kissing blades causing her to flinch away.

A cool hand was suddenly felt against her cheek, drawing her attention away from the frightening scene playing out before her. "Don't look,' she heard Rhain tell her, 'focus on me. Alright?"

"What's going on?" she asked through a quivering voice as she raised her eyes to him. Seeing the horrific wound of his broken jaw swept new fear through her. A wound like that should have left a person dead. Yet Rhain looked as if he was recovering rather quickly. Just what were they? David had said one word - vampire. But that was impossible.

Right?

"I'll explain later," Rhain told her as he scanned her for further injuries. "Where else are you hurt? What has David done to you?"

Regan, feeling dizzy and now disoriented, shook her head and shrugged her shoulders. She couldn't even find the strength or the clarity to answer.

Rhain cursed as he brushed back a lock of her hair. A shout from behind him stole his attention. He snapped his head over his shoulder. Daniel had finally pushed David back, putting the Proscriptus down to his back, but then, before Rhain's eyes, David kicked up to land a solid strike to Daniel's chest. Daniel grunted to the strong impact that sent him across the floor to hit a wall. The weakened wall crumbled.

"Daniel!" Rhain howled as his brother stumbled to the floor, blood dripping from his lips. Panic flew into Rhain as he saw David rush forwards, disallowing Daniel any chance to recover himself. "Get up, you idiot. Move!"

"Help him!"

The cry brought Rhain to look back to Regan. She was pleading with him, tears trickling down her cheeks, as she gripped his shirt, jerking helplessly.

"Don't let him die, Rhain." She sniffled, "Please. Don't let my Daniel die."

Rhain stared into Regan's terrified yet beautiful brown eyes and felt his heart fall within his chest as she began to shake. She didn't have to say the words, but he saw reflected within those tears her love for Daniel. Smirking, Rhain touched her cheek to wipe away the dirty, bloody tears that stained her flesh. "I won't let him get hurt. Stay here. Do not move from this spot. Understand?"

Regan nodded numbly.

"Good." After pressing a quick kiss atop her matted hair, Rhain stood and offered her one last smile before he drew his Tantō from the scabbard. With one potent push-off, Rhain bound forwards to join the fight with a wild smile upon his lips.

~ ~ ~ ~

This couldn't be happening.

This was insane.

Regan sat against the old wall in shock, staring at the fierce battle raging before her. Three forms twisted and turned in a dance of deadly precision with blades jarring. She felt numb from head to toe - unable to move and unable to scream, even though she wanted to. She wanted to scream for Daniel with all of her fear bundled into one cry of his name. Yet any noise that came from her throat was nothing more than a bubbly squeak.

This had to be a dream - a really bad dream. Swords were used in movies, not everyday life. And there were no such things as vampires. David just wanted to scare her. Didn't he? This was all a joke. Right? A sick joke?

But what she was watching had no explanation as to the impossibilities to being reality. Both Rhain and Daniel were fighting against David, both moving in perfect unison and driving David back across the balcony. So intense were their attacks that their fierce movements kicked up an unseen gust of wind. When violent blades met in a dance of driving metal, even Regan felt the overwhelming pressure of their devastating blows.

When a wave of power and wind struck her, Regan ducked away, covering her face with an arm as her body was hit by flying debris. Scooting further away, she tried to hide behind a corner of the wall. Uncertainty and dread coiled hotly within her as she touched fingers to the cloth tied about her neck. David had bitten her. She remembered the sharp, stinging pain that pierced her neck when his teeth punctured her flesh.

Vampire…

A tight knot lodged itself within her slender throat as she envisioned a contorted creature stabbing her neck with long fangs. Whimpering, Regan closed her eyes tight then buried her face into her knees as she pulled them against her chest. The echoing sound of war cries and scraping metal rang loud in her ears so she pressed her hands over her ears to try and block out the disturbing sounds. The sounds, however, were not only deafening but unbelievably horrifying, and they reached down to her very soul.

Both Daniel and Rhain were panting, and panting hard. A momentary cease had fallen upon the three fighters as they analyzed one another; evaluating conditions, positions, wounds, and blood loss.

"Who would've thought the prick's this strong?" muttered Rhain as he dragged his arm across his bleeding mouth. He had taken a hard slug to the mouth when he got between David and his brother.

Daniel, licking away a drop of blood from his own lips, glowered to the Proscriptus who was snickering and weaving slightly where he stood. Rhain's statement brought a scowl to Daniel's handsome features. "He's had some training, that's for sure." Shaking his head, he took a breath. Without glancing to his Socia, he inquired of his brother, "How is she?"

"Regan?"

Daniel nodded.

"She's not too good. David put a serious gash in her neck. I'd say she's going to need some therapy after all this shit."

"I'll ask Kain for the number of the therapist he's been trying to get us all to see for the last decade."

Rhain chuckled. He flipped his short blade and muttered somberly, "She knows what we are, Daniel. She's not a stupid girl."

Daniel winced then stole a quick glance to Regan. He could see just the outline of an elbow sticking out from behind a section of wall. "We need to finish this, Frater. I need to see to her wound."

"I couldn't agree more." Rhain shifted his intense gaze, calculating David's weaving stance. The man wasn't weak, just stupid, and kept egging the twins on by dancing where he stood and tossing his dagger back and forth between hands. He was acting like a pompous, wannabe role-player and that pissed Rhain off - even if David was rather handy at using his weapon.

He went on to ask, "Do you have a plan?"

Daniel scoffed then coughed out a breath of heavy dust. "I haven't had time to think of one. Regan can't stay here. It's too dangerous. I don't want David dragging her into the fight again."

Daniel went on to ask, "Can you take her to a safer area, Rhain?"

Rhain frowned heavily. "Are you fucking me? I'm not going to leave your side, idiot."

"I'm asking you to make sure my Socia is safe, Rhain."

"Socia, huh?" Scoffing, Rhain clicked his tongue to the roof of his mouth. "Fine." He took a step away then pointed to his brother. "Don't have too much fun without me. I'll be right back."

"Wouldn't think about it." Daniel tossed his brother a flick of a wrist, dismissing the other's cheeky attitude. With the knowledge that Rhain would keep Regan safe, Daniel could now turn his focus back to David. He began to stride forwards on a determined path as he swept his blade to the side, taking hold of the hilt with both hands in a gentle yet steady grip.

"We're ending this now, David."

The Proscriptus barked out a laugh. "Yer fuck'n insane ta take me on by yerself." With a cock of his head, he watched Rhain jog towards Regan. David would let her go, for now. Once he dealt with Daniel, he would skin Rhain then kill the girl. She'd only cause him problems with Daniel's death.

David wasn't wanting to be surrounded by a sobbing bitch. He already had to deal with Joyce's unhealthy attachment to him - fucking slut.

Chuckling, David turned his gaze to Daniel, grinned then rushed forwards, leaping into the air with blade slashing downwards. "Fine! Bu' first, ya die!"

~ ~ ~ ~

"Hey." Rhain knelt next to Regan, speaking softly, as he gently pulled her hands from her matted hair at her ears. Her skin was ashen grey from blood loss, and her eyes bloodshot from her tears. "I'm going to get you out of here."

Regan blinked, looking dumbfounded at Daniel's twin. She looked past him and around the corner to see Daniel and David once again facing each other in battle. A broken hitch of breath sound from her throat when Daniel stumbled back as David punched him hard in the jaw. But he recovered quickly, spun to avoid another strike then landed a downward blow of his sword against David's hip. The other man howled in pain as blood shot from the torn wound; he rolled off to the side. Without pausing for a breath, Daniel followed, lashing out at David with unbound rage.

A gentle grip took Regan's chin, turning her face back to Rhain. He snapped his fingers before her eyes. "Don't phase out on me, Regan. Stay with me. Can you stand?"

She nodded with a very faint 'mhm'.

"Good." Shifting closer, Rhain hooked an arm about her torso, lifting her easily to her feet. "I'm going to take you to one of the rooms down the hall and you're going to stay there till one of us comes to get you. Understand?"

She nodded again, whimpering as she glanced over her shoulder.

"Don't worry about him," said Rhain in mention of his twin. "He'll be fine. And David will soon be dead."

"But Daniel's hurt."

"He'll heal."

Rhain started to walk Regan towards the hall as quickly as her wobbly legs would move, which meant he was mostly dragging her along. They were half way to the opening of the hall and away from the battle when a loud explosion echoed from deep within the building. The entire structure shook violently, groaning in structural sickness.

Regan screamed, clutching Rhain as he fell backwards against a wall with her cradled protectively in his arms. A piece of debris from the ceiling fell upon them, and he covered her head with a hand, tucking her close to his shoulder. Both David and Daniel stopped in their tracks, shifting and stumbling as the balcony trembled, the walls flexed, and the ceiling fractured. Even David took a quick step back as he scanned the ceiling when a piece of tile crashed to the floor at his feet.

"Regan!"

Raising his head, Rhain looked towards his brother when he heard her name. He barked back, "She's fine! I'm okay too, just in case you're worried."

A second quake shook the building, this one less violent.

"What the bloody hell is going on?"

At Rhain's question, all eyes turned to David. He cast the other two Lamia and the Humanus an arrogant sneer. Another explosion rumbled throughout, shaking the structure more violently than the first time. There was a vehement jerk of the balcony then a loud, wooden groan. This time all four were thrown off balance. Both David and Daniel stumbled back to fall, blades clattering to the floor.

The air suddenly erupted in a high pitched alarm that blared so loudly that everybody winced and covered their ears.

"What's going on, David?" Daniel shouted.

David, who had pushed himself up against a wall, laughed a rather insane laugh as he looked about. "Fire! There's a fire in tha buildin'."

"A fire? From where?"

"Tha fuck I know!" He laughed again as he lumbered to get his dagger.

Rhain steadied himself and Regan as he cursed. "When I was fighting Grayson, he was using a lot of wicked magic. The shit was powerful enough that I bet it did some heavy damage to the structural integrity of the lower levels. Grayson's spells must've done more damage than what I saw."

David laughed in revelation. "Grayson! Tha' fuck'n Necro! Tha boilers are in tha basement level!"

"Boilers?" Rhain and Daniel inquired at the same time.

Throwing his arms up into the air, David turned a slow circle with his head raised to the ceiling. He was laughing uncontrollably as pieces of the ceiling continued to fall all about him.

Regan raised her terrified eyes as another rumble rattled the balcony. "What's going on?"

Rhain glanced down to her, trying to give her a steady smile - which was hard considering the minor aftershocks that vibrated the building. "I'm not sure, but I think Grayson's magic must have done some damage to the boilers, possibly causing one to explode. According to shit-head over there, there's a fire in the building."

Regan's eyes went so wide that they nearly slid from their sockets. "A fire? There's a fire? We need to leave!"

Feeling her start to struggle within his hold as her panic surged, Rhain gently pressed her face back to his blood stained shoulder and whispered to her while she pushed against him, "Listen to me, Regan. Calm yourself down. Calm. Down. Now."

A glassy shadow filled Regan's eyes as Rhain's warm voice slipped past the echoing of the alarm that radiated within her ears. One moment she was standing, the next she was limp within Rhain's arms.

"There we go. All better."

"Rhain!"

The deviant twin winced to the angry bellow of his name. He glanced to Daniel.

"What did you do to my Socia?"

David laughed, pointing his dagger towards Rhain and the human in his arms. "He fuck'n brain-raped yer girl!"

"I had no choice," snapped Rhain to Daniel and the questionable expression of anger within his twin's black eyes. "She was starting to panic!"

Up from the staircase coiled thick, black smoke, sweeping up and out into the open air of the balcony with a crazed desire to be free from the confining hallways. Daniel instantly covered his face with an arm as the suffocating smoke filled his lungs. Even David stepped back, coughing and sputtering.

Beneath them, in the lower floors, the fire was spreading quickly through the dry, ancient building that provided plenty of kindling for the inferno to grow. And with no sprinkler system, the flames would certainly spread till they were out of control. Close by, another explosion was heard followed by the repeated sounds of gunfire.

David's face coiled in to a look of pure rage. "Fuck!" The fire had reached his armory and now the collection of weapons and ammunition were exploding.

This time when the upper floor shook, it quaked with such ferocity that the tiles of the floor cracked and the plastered walls splintered. Like a canyon ripping through the earth, thick cracks began to spread and separate as the shaking continued, increasing in aggression. Before any could react, the balcony jerked with such strength that it bowed upwards then collapsed downwards causing everybody to bounce before losing their footing and falling to the dirty ground. One more vibration tore through the structure, and the left side of the balcony broke away from the wall, twisting as it groaned loudly.

Rhain gave a shout as the ground beneath him and Regan buckled; his footing slipped. He desperately tried to grab onto anything that he could use to stabilize himself, yet with Regan within his hold doing so was impossible. In fact, he had to let his weapon fall from his free hand, clattering to the floor before falling over the edge, so he could keep his hold upon her body. A curse flew from his lips when he landed roughly on his tailbone, no doubt fracturing the damn thing.

The shaking increased as if a tremor opened a hole to hell right beneath the building. To Rhain's horror a section of wall off to his right broke apart sending a large chunk of plaster and wood to tumble down towards him and Regan. In a split second he made the choice to release Regan. With the wall collapsing down upon them, she wouldn't survive without serious injury. He, on the other hand, would fare much better beneath the weight of the crumbling structure.

"Rhain! No!" Daniel's slowly beating heart slammed within his thin chest as he saw his twin push Regan away, sending her across the leaning balcony just before his brother's body disappeared beneath a dense cloud of falling material and dust.

Regan rolled as the balcony's connection to the far wall parted due to a jagged crack racing between the joints. She hit the old railing causing the molded wood to break against her back. Daniel rushed forwards, and though he glanced to the pile of debris covering his brother, he was more focused upon saving his Socia. So close. He was so close to her when the balcony bowed.

246

He lost his footing, falling to his side, as the balcony twisted then swayed, and before his horrified eyes the railing broke apart and sections of wood began to fall to the floor below. It was deteriorating, crumbling beneath his very feet and taking Regan with it!

No! He wouldn't lose her! He couldn't! Scrambling over the rocking floor, Daniel pushed forwards in panic filled desperation to get to Regan.

Pain. Stabbing pain pulled Regan from the hold of the Recodari - the vocal Coercère. Her head hurt and her back felt as if it had been torn apart. Disoriented, she raised her head and her eyes to see a layer of smoke and debris rolling about in the air. Her ears were ringing, yet through her vertigo she could hear her name being called.

Daniel was calling her.

The floor trembled causing her to bounce, and upon discovering that there was no floor to provide safety beneath her legs, she began to frantically kick behind her, seeking leverage to try and push herself up the angled floor. By accident she kicked through one of the balusters, and her body slid out a little further into the open air over the first floor. The move caused her leg to scrape open flesh against broken sections of sharp wood. She screamed to the pain and the sudden horror of finding herself without support as her body slid another inch. The impact of her weight caused two more balusters to break.

Desperately, Regan clawed at the floor, scraping fingertips and nails against broken sections of tile. One nail caught on a raised section of the floor, ripping clear from her finger. Agonizing pain ricocheted through her body causing her to release her hold on the floor.

One more shake and she lost her grip upon one baluster that was still stable. "Daniel!" The cry of his name ended in a scream of terror as Regan vanished over the edge, dangling over the pile of rubble bellow. Her body began to slither the last foot over the edge, but then a jerk was felt and she stopped her descent. Through fear shaking eyes, she looked up to see Daniel. He had fallen to his belly with an arm stretched out and a hand balled into the tethered remains of her shirt. Somehow, he had managed to stabilize himself by using his katana to secure himself to the floor; the tip stabbed deeply into the floor.

"Don't let go!"

Daniel tried to smile, yet his own fear did little to hide itself. "I won't, sweetheart. Just…don't move…" He grunted as he tried to wrap his fingers about her arm.

Regan whimpered. "I'll try not to, but it's a little hard right now."

Tightening his grip, Daniel began to slowly haul Regan back on to the balcony. With one hand working to pull her up, pain surged through him from a stab wound he had suffered in the shoulder, the same shoulder forced to secure her slim weight. His arm was weak, and the unnatural angle of his reach twisted some muscle to the point that he felt fibers tearing.

He didn't care about the pain. He had to save her.

"Almost...there," he snorted as he wrenched her back to the floor. However, the celebration was snuffed out as Regan released a cry of warning. The next thing Daniel felt was unimaginable agony ripping through his torso. His body bowed and his head threw back as a tormented echo exploded from his mouth.

"Stupid, Lex-Lover!" David laughed as he looked down to Daniel as he wedged the blade of his dagger deeper into the soft flesh located right beneath the shoulder blade of the same arm Daniel was using to secure the human. "Why won' ya fuck'n die?"

Balling a fist, David slammed his hand atop the pommel to wedge the blade all the way through Daniel's body till the guard pressed to the Lamia's back. He laughed as Daniel howled in agony. The psychotic Lamia cackled wildly as he squatted over Daniel's back, grabbing hold of the hilt of his blade that he began to saw back and forth, digging the blade across bone and tearing through soft tissue.

The torture that flashed across Daniel's features brought screams from Regan. "Stop it! You're killing him!"

"Tha's my intention!" Pulling the blade free spread an arch of blood through the air. David didn't stop then. He began to stab his dagger over and over into Daniel's back, from shoulders to waist.

Daniel cried out, his face distorting in pure suffering as the blows pounded brutally into him. Blood began to spread from the penetrating wounds the blade punctured through his back and stomach, coating the floor with its red slickness. Daniel jerked and blood pooled from his lips to snake down the angled floor to drip onto Regan's terrified face.

The pain. It was too much. Daniel couldn't move as David continued his assault. How many times the blade had been driven through his body couldn't be counted any longer. With blood seeping from him, Daniel felt not only his strength slipping away but his life. He could no longer fight against David. Daniel could only lie on the floor, looking blankly into Regan's horrified face as he felt his final death tickling his heart.

With what felt to be his last breath, he whispered, "I love you..."

"Daniel!" Regan's cry faded the further down her body plummeted. Only when the room resonated with the sound of loud smashing and cracking of wood did her cry end.

Daniel could do nothing but watch her disappear into the smoke. His body jerked as the blade was forcefully wrenched from him. He didn't have enough strength to raise his head when two shadows fell before his view, tumbling over the balcony. He only saw a flash of blue streaked hair plummet before him. "Rh...ai...n..."

Then everything went dark.

248

XVI

If we survive this coming battle, I will acquisition Rhain the most expensive bottle of aged brandy money can buy. Then again, there is nothing I could give to Rhain that would be enough to express my thanks for setting aside his own safety and his own concerns for his life to stand at my side in this hunt for David - to save Regan.

Rhain is more than just my Lamia brother, another Filias to Kain; he is my twin. The blood that flows within our veins was shared between us when we were being formed within our mother's womb. Since our creation, our conception into human life, we shared each other's heart beats and vital nutrients. We shared each other's souls. We grew up together, and we went through the Creare together. We have shared our dreams, our nightmares, our hopes, and our fears together. The bond between us is greater than the bond with Kain - our Frater - our Pater.

I would never ask Rhain to risk his life for me. Then again, I would have no need to do so because he would willing do so without question and without hesitation. I once thought I would do the same for him, but I know now that I cannot risk my life any more, not with Regan depending upon me. How can I risk my life when she is my life? I am sure that Rhain understands this. And though I would run into battle at his side, he would stop me from laying down my life to protect him. He would never admit it, but Rhain is truly an honorable man. And though he is often the center of aggravation within our family, our family would be nothing without him.

He is Rhain Thorn - my brother - my blood.
I love him.

-   Daniel Rhys Thorn

~ ~ ~ ~

Rhain groaned as his lungs flared to life with a deep draw of stale breath. Icy blue eyes snapped open when his mind pulled itself from the momentary black-out that left him unconscious. Shaking away the tight grip of painful disorientation, Rhain slowly pushed himself up. His arms hurt and something in his back cracked. Muscles quivered when they were forced to act as he tried to regain his mobility.

"Danny?" Daniel's childhood name broke from Rhain's dry mouth as he coughed with such intensity that drops of blood flicked from the corner of his torn lips.

Rhain's ears buzzed and his vision swam with distorted, cloudy images. One thing was for sure, the body he put a hand upon was very real and not part of his screwy vision. Looking down, he sat his eyes on David. Poor bastard had landed on his back, and protruding from his side was a pipe and some thin shards of wood. At this point, Rhain couldn't tell if David was dead or alive - hopefully very dead.

The horrific realization came to him that one more inch and the pipe would have pierced his body as well. But then his eyes went wide and he snapped his attention to the second floor to see nothing more of the balcony but warped metal and fractured wood. The entire balcony looked like it had been struck by a missile. The damage was that great. And there, lying limp at the bend, was Daniel. Alarm flooded Rhain as he scrambled away from David and to the pile of broken remains that had collapsed to the lobby.

"Daniel!" he called before coughing again. "Speak to me!"

Nothing.

"Say something, you bloody git!"

Nothing.

Looking about, Rhain scanned the debris field only to have his heart fracture when he saw Regan. She had fallen onto the lobby desk of wood and marble. With his mind fogging from the overpowering stench of hot, fresh blood from his brother, Regan, and David, Rhain stumbled over to the desk where he reached out with a shaking hand to gently touch Regan's cheek.

She was bent awkwardly, strewn on her back with a leg broken just below the knee and twisted at an awkward angle. From what he could see she also had a dislocated shoulder and a nasty break in her right arm that contorted the wrist beneath. Blood pooled beneath her turned head from the gash received from the landing.

Rhain's features fell to a look of pity and sadness as he touched her cold cheek then pressed fingertips to the pulse-line in her neck. At first he couldn't find any rhythm of life, but then a faint kick was felt against his fingertip and the Lamia chuckled with a slight smile.

"You're alive," Rhain breathed in a sigh. "Do me a favor and stay alive. Daniel won't forgive me,' he took in a shattering breath, '...if you die."

Daniel. Rhain's brother needed him. Pushing from the desk, he stumbled back to the balcony, climbing up the pile of wreckage with great discomfort. "Wake your sorry ass up, Frater. Your girl's in bad shape, and I've got a splitting headache! You can't die on me. If you do, Kain will fucking ground me for life! And that's a God-damn long time!"

He stumbled, sliding down a board that shoved splinters into his palm. A high pitched bellow of sharp pain fell from his grimacing lips as he flailed his arm around then began to blow on the cuts like a child. "Bloody hell! That fucking hurt!"

"Daniel!" He snapped his eyes upwards then grabbed a chunk of broken wood that he lobbed up to the balcony. It missed its target. Fortunately, the next piece of wood struck his intended target - his twin's head. "I know you're not dead, so wake the fuck up!"

Rhain scowled when his brother remained stationary. Through a low snarl that had his lips tucking down, he barked out, "If you're dead, I'm snagging your Socia!"

That threat brought a tiny twitch of Daniel's hand that was hanging off the remains of the floor. Rhain chuckled when he heard a faint curse slide past his twin's lips.

"There we go. Come on. Move your ass!" Rhain glanced over his shoulders to the boarded windows and saw through a faint break in one of the boards a hint of delicate light. "We don't have much time left, Frater! If we don't get out of here soon, we're going to be barbeque and your girl is going to die!"

Another groan came from Daniel followed by shaking movement. "I...hurt..."

"I know you do, but so do I and so does Regan. But you have to fight through the pain and get your ass down here."

Daniel raised his head, strands of his long ebony hair falling forwards to curtain his blood painted face. The taste of iron staining his palate churned his stomach and wrenched a sick knot in his throat.

"Rhain?" His brother's name tumbled in a deep pant pushed through a wave of nausea as his body spasmed and his head spun. Snarling, Daniel closed his eyes to try and swallow the urge to vomit. "Regan? Where..."

Rhain cursed as he plucked another splinter from his palm. "She's not going to last long. We need to get her to a hospital and fast. But that will require you to get your ass down here. Now! Fuck!" He swore once more as he pulled a thick shard of glass from a finger.

Daniel grunted. "I...can't move."

"Yes, you can! Come on, brother. You've got to get up! If you can't do it to save your own life, then do it to save Regan's!"

Daniel put all of his remaining strength to pushing himself up, but he collapsed when every fiber of his soul screamed in anguish. The sensation of his own blood squishing against his cheek, when his face fell into the standing pool beneath him, made his skin crawl.

Rhain winced as he watched his brother collapse. The scene destroyed Rhain's heart that was already nothing more than a pile of pity. He wasn't sure if he liked the feel of the sympathetic tears threatening to spill from his eyes. Seeing his brother in such a weakened state was something that Rhain never wanted to see, let alone witness outside of his nightmares.

Since they were children Daniel was the one who always came to his aid, helping him when Rhain hurt himself in some foolish fashion. Daniel had always been there to defend him against Kain and other powerful Lamia when he had dug his grave a little too deep. To this day he fought away the nightmares that often plagued his dreams, replaying various situations when Daniel had been injured due to one of Rhain's wild plans that had gone terribly awry.

Time was wasting, and Rhain was now left to make sure that two lives, besides his, remained just that - alive. That was far too much pressure for him to handle. The feel of desperation setting in surged his adrenal in to gear causing the muscles in his right arm to start to shake.

"Look. I know you're very, very weak right now, Frater, but you've got to catch your strength and move." Fucking hell, was that his voice shaking? "Regan needs you, Daniel. You can't give up when you've finally found the woman you've been searching for your entire life. You've dreamt of her, Frater, for so long. You can't give up on her, and you can't give up on me!"

Swallowing a lump of determination and anger, Rhain inched his way directly beneath his twin and shouted, "Get up, you fucking bastard! You've got to get up! Live for your Socia!"

His...

Socia...

Daniel's vision, faded and colored red from blood, wavered as he looked out over the expanse of the lobby, searching for any sign of Regan. The desk. There she was, contorted like a rag doll. A howl of heart felt suffering erupted form the Lamia as he saw his Socia's aura flittering out of existence.

Turning his gaze, he saw Rhain looking up to him with anguish shadowed features that were painted with colorful bruises and splotches of dry blood. Rhain was right. He had to move. He had to. Daniel could feel the calling of Solis Ortus, and the building weight of the cursed sunrise called his Lamia body to sleep. With dawn encroaching on night, Daniel's instincts were starting to kick in, ordering him to seek shelter and to survive.

Tightening his resolve, Daniel pressed his torn palms on the floor to raise his torso. The wounds dotting his body tore open even more since his limited blood supply had yet to endorse proper healing. And with the wounds opening what vital remnants of his remaining Sanguis began to leak from the multitude of holes littering his body.

Snarling, Daniel echoed a painful cry through clenched jaws as he tried to move his legs. Only one obeyed, but even then a dislocated knee refused to operate fully. "I don't have enough strength to stand!"

"Then don't stand. Roll off the balcony. I'll catch you!"

"Are you insane?"

Rhain cracked a wicked grin. "Kain thinks I am. After tonight, I'm pretty sure I am!" He raised his arms and braced his feet under a large beam to secure his balance. "Now fall before I drag my hurting ass up there and push you over just for the hell of it!"

Grinning through his pain, Daniel reached to his side to dislodge his katana from the floor. He tossed it carelessly over only to hear Rhain mutter a violent curse, then he rolled forwards and off the balcony. He expected to feel himself break upon the rubble below, but instead, he felt his brother's arms secure a tight hold about him.

Rhain grunted from the impact, then he fell to one knee, striking it on a brick. He fell backwards, dropping Daniel as he swallowed a cry of scraping pain. "That's it,' he barked as he tried to regain his balance, 'I want a vacation, and it better be fully paid for!"

Blowing out an annoyed breath of air, Rhain turned his fuzzy eyes to his brother then groaned under another annoyed breath. After securing Daniel's katana into the sheath strapped to his brother's back, he shifted to gather Daniel into his arms then cursed upon seeing his brother's shirt bathed in blood, torn from the violent stabbing and stuck to his brutalized back.

"Bloody hell, Daniel," Rhain mused through a hopeless whisper. "What am I to do? Tell me." As gently as he could, he brushed aside a long lock of matted, black hair - sticky with clotted blood, dirt, and sweat. "Damn it. Why'd you have to go and get hurt, Danny? I don't know what to do. You're injured, Regan's not going to last much longer, and David's already stepping over into hell. You're the smart one, not me."

"Tell me,' he insisted as a slick of blood trickled down his cheeks, 'what do I do, Frater?"

Daniel's eyes slowly drew open, forcing ebony lashes that had stuck together apart. He turned his hazed eyes to Rhain then lifted a weak hand to lay limply to Rhain's cheek. "Save...her..."

Rhain shook his head. "No. You know I don't play the gallant knight very well. Besides, I'm not going to put up with her tears when she finds out you're dead." Rhain didn't pause for a second thought before he raised a wrist and dug his fangs into his own flesh.

Blood seeped past his lips as he pulled his fangs away then shoved the bleeding wounds against his brother's mouth. At first Daniel refused his brother's offering. Feeding from another Lamia was considered rather taboo, even under such a delicate and life-threatening situation. But this wasn't the first time one had offered the other lifesaving Sanguis in order to save the other. Daniel winced as Rhain roughly wedged his wrist past his lips, allowing blood to spread against his teeth. The taste of Rhain's potent Sanguis both disgusted and thrilled Daniel.

"Don't be a nob, Daniel. Don't fight me. I've got enough to spare and you're running on empty. Regan will need some Sanguis in order to sustain what remains of her life if she's going to have any chance of survival. I'd rather it be your blood she sucks on than mine." He pushed again, his snarl darkening. "Drink before I pull your mouth open and shove my hand down your throat."

There was no use fighting the urge or the offering. Rhain was right, Regan would need strong blood in order to survive, and to hell if Daniel would let any other Lamia donate their Sanguis to her. She was his Socia - his responsibility. Daniel felt his brother's blood wash down his throat, spreading through and encouraging his body to produce more of his own blood and then mixing together to restore much of his needed strength.

With the urge to see to Regan's safety burning hot within his body, the ferocity in Daniel's feeding grew. He grasped his brother's wrist with a weak grip at first, but as his strength began to return he bit into Rhain's arm with his nails till fresh drops of blood welled about his dirty and cut fingers.

Rhain hissed, closing his eyes, as his twin's desperate feeding bloomed heat throughout his cool body. There was no use preventing the sensation of sensuality that the Edēre naturally produced, which is why the act was labeled as taboo unless under extreme circumstances. In more delicate situations, and with a Lamia pushing the edges of the Morbus, the Edĕre could lead to intimate acts - even between siblings.

Yet Rhain couldn't think about that downside to the Edĕre. He had to help his brother recover so that Regan could recover and the three could get the hell out of this shit-hole - to recover. And in truth, the last thing he needed was Daniel to cross over to the dark-side and release his Daemon - again. If that happened, if Daniel allowed himself to become embraced by the Desiderium, then Rhain would have no choice but to...

He shook his head and the thought away. He bent over Daniel and whispered. "Drink, damn it. Drink."

And so Daniel drank, and drank...and drank.

~ ~ ~ ~

Daniel's first step was slightly off the mark, twisting and stumbling as his dislocated knee worked itself back into place, as he tried to descend the pile of rubble to the lobby floor. He slid a few times, cursed more than once, and almost tore his expensive slacks on a contorted beam. Once he gained his footing, he limped to Regan while wiping a line of blood from his lips. The lingering taste of Rhain's blood churned his stomach even though the power spurred strength through him.

"You're welcome," barked Rhain as he cast his brother a wave as he carefully slid back down the pile of rubble, taking expert care to keep his hands away from broken timber. He really didn't need any more splinters, really.

"Sweetheart?" Daniel whispered the endearing pet-name as he came to lean over Regan. Reaching out to her, Daniel ran his eyes and a hand over her, feeling for wounds, searching out injuries, and checking her pulse. When he felt the faint pulse beneath her flesh, he smiled and glanced back to his twin, calling, "She still has a pulse! It's very weak, but she's alive."

"I told you!" Rhain, being his ass-of-a-self, raised his brother a single digit as he went to investigate David's condition. He just happened to glance up to the same crack in the window boards to check the gauge of sunrise. "We're cutting it close, Daniel!"

"I know!" Leaning away from his lover, Daniel unbuttoned the cuff of his fine shirt so he could roll the sleeve up. "I won't need long." He wiped away any remains of blood, dirt, and sweat then delicately bit into his wrist, without a wince, to free vital blood that would provide Regan's dying body with enough rejuvenating properties for survival - but only just.

Afraid to move her, Daniel gingerly parted her mouth so the drops of thin blood could drip from his wrist and past her lips. All that was needed was enough of his Sanguis to seep past the thin, fleshy lining of the inside of her cheeks. With Regan's genetic code already holding the Proprietas, Daniel's blood would act as a catalyst causing the Proprietas within her to respond. His blood would also trigger whatever hidden key-traits were within her; one being the ability to heal.

As he forced his bleeding wrist to her mouth, he leaned to press a kiss to her dirt stained and sweat slickened forehead while gently stroking her matted hair. "Everything's okay now, my Socia. I'm here. You're safe. Come now, you have to drink. Drink as much as you can."

He pressed a kiss to her temple. "I won't lose you, Regan. I can't. Not now. I've only just found you."

Closing his eyes, he pressed a dirty and cold cheek to hers and whispered, "Come back to me."

A faint gurgle sounded from deep within Regan's throat causing Daniel to draw back with a smile of relief caressing his handsome mouth. She moved slightly as her head rolled on the desk, but she didn't open her eyes or speak. A move, however, was a good sign - for now. It meant that her body was repairing itself as the healing properties of his Sanguis spread through her cells.

"A little more. Can you drink a little more for me, sweetheart?" A mousey mew was her response, and Daniel smiled once again as he closed his eyes and set his forehead to hers. "Good girl."

Rhain stared down at David while his brother saw to Regan. He swore the bastard had moved. "You don't look dead." Rhain prodded David's side with the tip of his boot. When the Proscriptus didn't move, Rhain jabbed him a little harder, then harder still till a rib cracked. That tiny injury brought a grunt from David. A sadistic smile broke across Rhain's face as he looked over his shoulder to his twin and called, "Hey! David's alive. Want me to end his suffering or do you want to..."

"Leave him to me!"

The dangerous snarl in Daniel's voice brought a slender, black brow to arch over one of Rhain's contacted covered eyes.

Daniel looked over his shoulder and inquired in a softer voice, "Is he awake?"

"Let me ask him." Rhain looked back to David. "Hey, ball-less prick. Are you awake?" When David didn't reply to the vocal question, Rhain kicked the pipe sticking out of the man's side. The vibrations would send enough pain through David's system to wake him from his unconscious state. And it worked. David groaned, and a bubble of blood popped from within his mouth.

"Yeah,' he called to his twin, 'he's awake!"

"Good!" Daniel looked back to his lover, stroking her bruised cheeks as he added, "I'll make him suffer for what he has done to my Socia." He kissed Regan's bloody lips, tasting his own Sanguis. He touched her face one more time before he turned, walking to Rhain.

When Daniel saw his brother's questionable gaze, Daniel jerked his chin towards Regan. "Stay with her."

Rhain didn't question his brother. In fact, when they passed by each other on their determined paths, Rhain flashed Daniel a twisted grin as he saw his brother's black eyes burning with the want to kill. It had been a long time since Rhain had seen that hellish shadow within his twin's gentle eyes. Once to the desk, he turned about and leaned back to the hard structure, kicking out his ankles to cross one to the other then folded his arms about his chest.

"Good thing you're unconscious right now, Regan," he said the mortal. "You don't need to witness what Daniel's about to do."

~ ~ ~ ~

For a short time Daniel simply stared down at David. The Lamia wasn't moving much, but every few seconds his body would jerk. Yeah, he was alive. But not for long. Daniel wouldn't permit David to live. His and Rhain's orders were clear - David was to die by any means possible - and Daniel would carry out his orders with the greatest of pleasures. Such a pity that he couldn't keep David alive long enough to make the man's death a slow and violent end.

Moving, Daniel came to stand over the broken vampire then slowly knelt to a knee as he reached out to grab a handful of David's hair. He wrenched the man's head up while leaning down before he snarled through a dark and demented voice. "I know you're awake, David, so listen well to what I have to say. By the order of the Consanguine Rex you are hereby detained for crimes against the Lamia of the Republica of England, the unauthorized and unnecessary Creare of Joyce Scott, and the kidnapping, attempted rape, and attempted murder of Regan Scott, my Socia. Do you understand these charges?"

Daniel raked David with a cruel and murderous glare before pulling his lips back to a twisted, yet pleased, grin. "By demand of the Consanguine Rex, you are to be executed on location once detained. Do you understand this, Proscriptus?"

David groaned. The man could barely hear past the loud buzzing ravaging his brain. Putting words together was rather difficult considering he was barely alive and holding on to the last string of his life.

But Daniel didn't care. He had orders, and he would follow through with them. Snarling, Daniel pressed a hand over the metal pipe sticking from David's side then slowly, methodically, pushed it down while grinding it against the man's ground-up insides. The pain brought a reaction from David. His body shook from both agony and shock, and a low, blood filled gurgle of torment bubbled up from his throat to pool at his lips.

"Tell me,' Daniel muttered as he leaned closer, 'tell me why you have spent decades hunting my brothers and me. What did we do to you to deserve your hatred?" When David didn't respond, Daniel struck the pipe with a fast jab of a hand sending horrific vibrations of torment through the other Lamia.

David's eyes jerked open as the pain ricocheted within him, bouncing against every bone in his aching body. Through hazed eyes, he looked to Daniel then coughed up a wad of blood and saliva. He panted to gain his breath then growled, "Ya took my father ..."

Daniel arched a brow with a cock of his head. "We took your father?" Theodore - he must mean Theodore. The man was David's biological father as Theodore had been changed two decades after David's birth, and when David reached the age of thirty-four, Theodore was forced to change his own son.

256

"How do you figure that?"

David groaned, his eyes closing and his head leaning back.

"Hey!" Daniel barked, striking the pipe once again. "Wake up!"

David snarled, his eyes parting open.

"We're not finished. Explain yourself."

"My bastard father,' David went on to say through hitching breaths, 'loves ya. He never…loved me."

"You're saying all this destruction, all this pain, and all these years spent trying to destroy my family is all because of Theodore not loving you enough?" Daniel couldn't believe what he was hearing. Sure, Theodore held deep resentment for David due to the fool's constant humiliation towards him and their Familia with his Proscriptus activities over the past centuries, but the old Lamia never once stopped loving his son.

"Rhain thinks all of this is because he was able to win the bidding for the Crucible."

David tried to laugh - tried and failed.

Daniel shook his head, wincing as reminders of his brutalized body struck him with nips of healing discomfort. "You're an idiot, David. Theodore has never stopped loving you. He's always held hope that you would rescind your Proscriptus title and return to him and your Familia. He's never given up his love for you. It's you who turned your back on him and cut all ties with him."

David snarled then panted as he leaned his head back to the debris pillowed beneath him. "Yer tha fool, Drasus dog." He coughed once more then offered Daniel one of the most sadistic and psychotic smiles Daniel had ever seen. "Go on. Kill me. Ge' i' over with. Ya 'ave yer orders, just like I had mine."

Orders? Daniel's brow knitted in confusion. "Orders? What orders? You mean all of this was done by another's orders?" When David didn't reply, Daniel slammed his hand down on the pipe.

David's broken body spasmed as he cried out in a blood curdling echo of anguish!

"Tell me!" howled Daniel as he yanked David closer by his hair, bending the man's body around the embedded pipe. "Who told you to take my Socia from me? WHO?"

David tried to chuckle, but the sound bubbled forth with a dribble of blood. "Yer family 'ave many enemies, Daniel. Ya an' yer twin 'ave left a trail o' blood across Europe tha' has drawn tha hatred o' many a Lamia. There ar' powers just waiting ta take ya down. I am only a solider. Nothin' more."

Rage began to swim once more within Daniel, licking at his Daemon. David's words ran cold claws down his spine, building unease within him that there could be others waiting in the shadows to do not only him harm but his brothers and his lover.

"You willingly put my Socia at risk, assaulting her and nearly taking her life, all because of an order?"

David chuckled.

"She was an innocent in all of this!"

257

"Her innocence vanished tha moment ya brough' her inta our fucked up world. I' is yer fault she's in this mess." David sneered. "Ge' down off yer high horse, Drasus. Ya would've done tha same given tha order. How many innocent Humani 'ave ya used in tha pass ta see yer orders through? Hundreds I be'."

He chuckled then licked his lips clear of blood. "I'd watch ou' fer ya girl. A sweet thing like her will draw a lo' o' attention. They'll come fer her. When yer back's turned, they'll ge' her."

"Why?" Daniel snarled through thin lips. "Regan doesn't need to be involved in our wars of hatred."

David chuckle, locking Daniel with a look of disdain. "Ya fuck'n Sucker. Ta destroy ya. Why else?"

From across the wide room, Rhain's voice echoed, "Control yourself, Daniel!"

Control? Daniel scoffed. His grip shook as he wadded his fingers into David's hair, ripping strands from the man's scalp. The wince he saw sweep across the Proscriptus' face eased some of his building rage, but not enough to stop it.

Through a voice that quivered with thinning ice, he growled, "Do you have anything else to say before I carry out your execution?"

David chuckled then spat a wad of bloody phlegm at Daniel. It struck the other Lamia's pale cheek to slide down, leaving a slick trail of goo. "Yeah, I go' somethin' ta say." He slowly turned his head to flash Regan's unmoving image a wicked grin of desire. "She would've been a good fuck."

Those were the proverbial words that broke Daniel's back. Every point that had fueled Daniel's anger from David's cruel schemes bombarded his psyche in one massive explosion. He threw back his head releasing a tormented baying of rage while at the same time his aura surged forth in a wild vortex of insanity.

The power was so strong that it struck Rhain within seconds causing him to shield his face with an arm then twisted about to cover Regan with his body. They fared better than David. He took the brunt of Daniel's Daemon that cried out for blood. With Daniel's eyes flashing red and fangs bared, the Drasus tore into David's broken body with animalistic ferocity!

Daniel raked David's chest with his nails, scraping away fabric then digging into soft flesh to spill warm blood and tissue. He was snarling like a rabid beast, snapping his fangs as he tore chunks of meat and organs and bone from the cavity that became David's abdomen. The man beneath him screamed out in unimaginable anguish as his chest was turned in to an empty, gaping hole. Unable to move, David could do nothing but lie upon the floor and be torn apart by Daniel's bare hands.

When there was nothing more of David's gut, Daniel turned his savagery to David's head. Gripping a fist full of hair, Daniel began to slam the man's head over and over and over again to the broken rubble beneath. The brutality of the strikes echoed the room in sickening crackling. David's skull did not last beneath the brutal violence, and soon the cracking turned in to wet squishing when brain met the floor.

Hot blood pooled out beneath the Proscriptus' body, spreading out to drip through the wreckage of the balcony and stain both bodies. With the intensity of Daniel's assault, blood sprayed back to splatter his handsome features, painting him a gruesome coloration of dying life.

When the ferocity of Daniel's aura retreated back into his body, Rhain slowly drew away from Regan only to have his eyes go wide with the horrific sight of Daniel's Daemon. There had only been one time in the past when Daniel's resolve had fractured and a taste of his immense and hellish Daemon slipped forth. Rhain had almost paid with his life in order to bring Daniel back to his senses, and he swore he would never again come face to face with the devastating power that his twin kept locked within him.

Cold fear reached deep within Rhain, coiling icy claws about his soul. He wasn't one to experience fear, but at this moment he knew fear.

~ ~ ~ ~

Daniel didn't stop. He couldn't. Now that his Daemon had come forth all he could do was watch the destruction of David's body from behind his own eyes. He screamed for his Daemon to stop from within his mind, but his dark essence refused to listen.

In one final show of enraged power, Daniel balled a fist then brought his hand down into David's face. The Lamia was already dead, there was no question on that, but Daniel wanted to erase every last remains of the man's existence. With a nauseating crack of bone David's face broke, caving in around Daniel's fist. When he tore his hand from the cavity, he pulled compounds of creation from David's face: bone, brain, tissue, and muscle. Blood sored through the air along with remnants of what used to be David.

Heaving breaths ploughed through Daniel causing his body to quake as his red eyes observed, with disturbed pride, his handy work. After a tense moment of eerie calmness, he began to stand - righting himself with a roll of his body till he stood straight. He cocked his head to the side while raising a blood and tissue coated hand to be licked by his tongue. But as he turned with a sadistic grin spreading his lips, his head snapped to the side and he was sent skidding across the floor to crash into a column, snapping it in half.

"That's enough!" bellowed Rhain as he cradled his hand to his chest. The blow he landed to Daniel's face not only dislocated his brother's jaw but shattered a few of his fingers. Taking a breath, he muttered, "Enough, Daniel. He's dead. David's dead."

When Daniel moved, Rhain took a step back, preparing for an attack. "Don't make me fight you, Frater."

Daniel rose from the floor like a demon - a creature born to thrive in hell. His back rounded in a graceful arch, disks of his spine popping audibly back into place, and his blood coated hands flexed - clawing at the air at his side in grotesque strokes. His head bowed down causing a layer of his long hair to curtain his pale, blood spattered face. A ghostly visage was presented with a single eye of onyx rage and burning red peeking out from inky strands of hair, and with a soft click he moved his jaw back into place. When his eyes locked to Rhain, they flashed red as he bared his fangs towards his own blood and a low rumble of animalistic excitement purred from his throat. He took one threatening step then paused as the most beautiful voice echoed within his mind.

"Dan...iel..."

Snarling, he slid his gaze to the desk when Regan's tiny voice spoke to him. A gentle rumbling of a moaning purr trickled past Daniel's throat as his eyes softened and the red glow within faded. He began to walk towards her, and as he did, his Daemon began to disappear along with the redness in his black eyes. As he stepped by Rhain, he reached out a trembling hand to clap his brother on the shoulder.

No words were spoken as Rhain turned about to watch Daniel walk to Regan's side. It seemed that the battle was over, and a heavy weight of exhaustion settled onto Rhain's shoulders. With a groan, he walked over to an old chair and collapsed onto it only to wince when some bruised and broken part of his body met the structure. It was then he realized he was missing his Tantō. Damn. There it was, back on that cursed pile of debris.

"How is she?" he called out to his brother after a moment of gathering his strength. And when he could move again, he stood from the chair and head off to retrieve his favorite weapon.

Daniel, at Regan's side, gently stroked her face with his blood soaked fingers. "I'm not sure. I thought I heard her call my name, but she's not responding to me." He pressed fingertips to her neck, and a slight smile broke his lips. "Her pulse is stronger."

"Good."

Both Rhain and Daniel turned their eyes to the sound of a deeply agitated voice. Standing at a door in the corner of the large lobby were three silhouettes seeping forth from the shadows. The twins felt both relief and hesitation upon seeing Kain standing with both Caius and Constantine. On reflex, Daniel snarled and slid his arms about his Socia's body as well as he could without causing her any more damage.

"Well, party's over." Rhain grunted as he slid his Tantō into the scabbard then descended the debris pile for the last time.

Kain's coal black eyes narrowed on his brothers. He didn't know whether or not he wanted to murder them himself or hug them. They looked as if they had just survived a war of devastating proportions, and from the wreckage around them, he was pretty sure they had. They looked utterly and completely broken, and their condition confused Kain while at the same time slapping him cold with fright. He wanted to yell at them and embrace them.

Clearing his voice, the Rex stepped forwards with a presence and a stride that radiated his powerful and his important position. The man known as Caius Scipio, Rex of England, strolled forwards with the air of both an aristocrat and a warrior. In truth, he was both. Born in a time when the Roman Empire had swept across the known world, Caius became a tool and a hand of the Empire's conquering desires. He was, and still claimed to be, a son of Rome. He not only demanded respected but obtained it from Lex followers to Proscriptus alike.

He stepped to the unrecognizable remains of David and stared hard at the gory sight. Then he raised his eyes to the twins, analyzing their conditions and their appearance. From obvious blood splattered clothing and body, it was clear that Daniel was the culprit of David's death. With a slight scoff, he glanced back to the floor only to gingerly take a step back so his shined loafers of expensive, Italian leather were not dirtied by bodily debris.

The handsome Roman, as he would be referred to as nothing else, raised his steady eyes towards the twins once more and spoke in a calm and controlled voice. "I see that you two have completed your objective."

"Yeah," groaned Rhain as he pushed up from the chair; a muscle in his right leg quivered and strained. "Can we go home now?"

"Soon."

"Soon?" snapped Daniel with his eyes narrowing. "We need to go now. Regan needs emergency care right away or she won't survive much longer."

Caius turned his eyes to the woman within Daniel's arms. He sighed softly with a slow nod of his head. "Of course." With a snap and a crook of a finger, Constantine walked forwards in his ever stoic presence. "Constantine will see to Miss. Scott."

Daniel's eyes flashed. His Daemon disagreed with the very idea and in a sense so did he. "No," he snarled with a flash of his fangs. "She is my Socia. She is my responsibility. I will see to her care."

Kain's low and vibrating voice snarled in caution, "Daniel, watch your tone."

Caius, upon hearing the warning, raised a hand to dismiss Kain's disapproval. "I understand Miss. Scott's delicate situation. However, if you intend to argue with my command, you must understand that you will be placing her in greater jeopardy. I am sure the last thing you wish to know is that you aided in her declining condition."

Constantine ignored the dangerous glare that came from the Thorn twin as he stepped to the desk, waiting patiently for his next order while he stared hard at Daniel. The handsome Lieutenant squared his sharp jaw that did little to harden his already impassive and beautiful features. He narrowed his sky-blue eyes behind a stray lock of thin, glossy black hair, yet said nothing in argument towards Daniel.

Refusing to flinch beneath Constantine's dangerous eye, Daniel glared to the Lieutenant. Let him try to touch Regan. Daniel had killed already this night, he wouldn't think twice in pommelling Constantine into the ground. In fact, there had been times when he and Rhain had discussed all the torturous ways to rid the world of the little known, but greatly feared, Constantine. When the other Lamia refused to retreat, Daniel looked back to the Rex.

"She is my Socia," he reaffirmed.

Caius nodded. "Yes. I appreciate that fact,' he said in a softened voice and sympathetic eye, 'believe me, I do. I have had my share of Socia, and a wife, through my long life, so I understand your desire to protect Miss. Scott. However, you must think of her safety first and foremost."

"I am," he bit back. "We're wasting time. We can get her…"

"With those injuries?" Caius tipped his head to the side sending a dark lock of his tight queue of dark hair along a shoulder. "What mortal hospital could you take her to where the medical staff would not be phoning the police within two seconds of your arrival? There would be much explaining to do regarding her condition. And as you have said, our time is growing short."

Snarling, Daniel glanced down to Regan. He didn't like to hear the rational thinking of the Rex right now. He couldn't even think. He just wanted to be with her, to see her safe.

Kain spoke next, stepping forwards while taking care not to overstep the authority of the Rex. At the same time, he needed to make sure Daniel didn't draw Caius' displeasure by being a deviant child. "Listen to your Rex, Daniel. His word is absolute. There is no hospital where you can take Regan and not draw attention to the both of you and the circumstances of her predicament."

"Then where should I take her?" Daniel sent his dark eyes over each Lamia. "Do you expect me to dump her in the street and let some kindhearted pedestrian handle her care?"

Rhain frowned with a shake of his head. "Don't be stupid, Frater. Nobody would ask you that."

Daniel snarled at his twin, and Rhain glared back.

"Rhain is correct," said Caius with a slight smile playing his handsome mouth. "That is not an option. Constantine and I will return with her to my Domus where she can rest for the evening and receive emergency care. I will call ahead and have all that she requires waiting for us. She will be seen by my personal physicians. Would that be acceptable? It is the least I can do to compensate her for becoming a needless victim in David's illegal and cruel games."

"Sir,' Constantine spoke up in a voice that was smooth, musical and cold, 'she will need a blood transfusion, and quickly."

Caius opened his mouth to comment on his Lieutenant's observation when Daniel snapped, "No!" The Rex arched a brow, and a flash of disapproval at the younger Lamia's defiance shined within his eyes. "I beg your pardon?"

Daniel tightened his arms about Regan. "I won't let you pump her full of another's blood. She is my Socia. She has fed from me already. It is my Sanguis that is keeping her alive."

"I see," Caius mused under his breath.

Suddenly the room shook with Kain's commanding and deep voice. "Daniel! That is enough!"

All eyes turned to Kain, except for Caius, who continued to stare in pity at Regan.

"Stop being a disobedient child!" Kain went on to shout. "I expect this insubordinate behavior from Rhain but not from you."

Rhain gaped. "The hell?"

"Do not argue with your Rex! We cannot risk exposing your involvement in Regan's condition to a public hospital. Let Constantine take her."

When his younger sibling dared to part his lips as if to respond, Kain took a threatening step forwards. His hands, balled at his sides, shook with the fading sense of his own self-control. "Do not make me take her from you!" Snarling, he snapped his deadly glare towards Rhain while pointing at Daniel, "Handle *your* brother."

Even Rhain flinched beneath Kain's immense rage when his brother's fiery glare landed on him. This wasn't the time to argue with Kain. Without question, or a sarcastic retort, Rhain limped to Daniel's side. He bent low to speak then paused with a glance to Constantine. "Do you mind? This is private." He flashed a cheeky glare.

The only show of a response was a narrowing of Constantine's blue eyes before he took a few steps back.

Rhain continued to glare at Constantine till, in a show of childish attitude, he placed his back to the Lieutenant. He then leaned close to his brother's ear, whispering softly so that none other could hear. Whatever Rhain was saying obviously made some rational argument for agreeing to Caius' command as Daniel's features softened and a wash of heart-wrenching pain swept across his stained face.

"Do this for Regan," Rhain stated as he stepped back.

With fresh stains of thin, bloody tears slipping down his face, Daniel carefully stood from the desk. He gathered Regan in his arms before turning to Constantine, to which he leveled the Lieutenant with a deadly gaze of promised pain before growling, "If you harm her…"

"No harm will come to Miss. Scott," said Constantine as he moved forwards to take the human.

There was a moment of hesitation when Constantine reached for Regan, but a gentle prod from Rhain encouraged Daniel to release his Socia to the care of the Rex. Daniel's heart shredded in to pieces as he felt Regan's dead weight drift from his arms. Seeing her cradled within Constantine's cold and unknown embrace brought a pull of anger within him, but he held back his want to strike out. Rhain was right. He had to let her go so she could be saved.

The humiliating truth that he could do nothing to protect his Socia bore through Daniel like a wave of overwhelming weakness and shame. Here he was known as one of the feared Inquisitors, and he could not even keep his own Socia safe. What type of man was he if he could not see to her care? Turning his head away, Daniel closed his eyes as he forced himself to stop crying.

"She'll be fine,' Rhain told his twin softly as he clasped Daniel on the shoulder, 'you know she will."

"It is time for us to leave this place." Caius' voice resonated through the room. "We have little time remaining till Solis Ortus."

"What about this mess?" Rhain called out as he pointed towards the destruction around them. "David wasn't the only Proscriptus here. Daniel and I faced a lot of his grubby friends in the halls. I slayed at least ten or more, can't say for sure about Daniel."

Caius nodded while scanning the debris. "I have already assigned a recovery team to arrive as soon as possible. They will handle the disposal of all remains."

"What about Joyce?" Daniel's question brought Rhain to curse. "Shit! I can't leave yet. I told Regan's cousin to stay in the basement till I came to retrieve her. I've got to go get her!"

"No!" Kain shook his head, sending jaw length strands of thick, blood-red hair to kiss his alabaster cheeks. "You're not going anywhere but home."

"The hell I am! We can't leave her. If she gets out, she'll take all of David's dirty secrets with her. She survived the Creare, Kain. She's David's Filia. She holds vital information about David's activities and plans!"

Before Kain could argue, Caius spoke out. "I agree completely. I will call for a member of my Regis Tutela to see to her recovery." With a curt nod, Caius motioned Constantine forwards. "I assume there are no other points of interest you or Daniel need to inform us?"

Rhain shook his head. Daniel couldn't take his eyes from Regan. "Very well," Caius went on to say. "Let us leave. Miss. Scott cannot wait any longer, and neither will the Sol."

As the group departed the building, Rhain pulled his smart phone from a back pocket. He cast a glare to the backsides of Kain and Caius, adding daggers to Constantine.

At his side, Daniel glanced to him and frowned seeing Rhain thumbing through his phone. "What are you doing?" he inquired softly so no other could overhear him.

"Contacting an associate of mine."

"Why?"

Rhain glanced to Daniel, his voice dropping. "I promised Grayson I wouldn't leave him in this shit-hole to be found by Caius' cleaning crew. Alasdair would never forgive me."

A crease of concern formed upon Daniel's brow. "Rhain..."

"Don't jump on me, Daniel. I know what I'm doing, so let me do what I need to do. Grayson should be with his brother. End of story."

Daniel sighed but did not question Rhain. He looked the other way so he wouldn't be privy to the contact Rhain was texting. Right now, he had more important worries to focus on - his Socia.

XVII

I can still feel his hot blood coating my skin. I can still see the redness of his blood slipping through my fingers. And I can still see the remnants of his life painting my vision.

David is dead.

I took his life by bashing in his skull. I can't remember how many times I slammed the back of his head into the concrete, but it was enough to turn his skull into a jigsaw puzzle of bone and his brain into a hot slick of pudding. I couldn't stop, not when he was alive and not when he was dead. All I wanted was his life - every - last - drop. He made my Regan suffer, so I made him suffer. I made him bleed.

Do I regret the ferocity of my attack considering I abhor violence? No. I do not. I will never tell Rhain this, but I let my Daemon slip on purpose. I released that dark creature to seek vengeance for my Socia's pain. I only wish I could have tortured David the way he deserved to be tortured - slowly and with as much agony as possible.

Even now I want to find David's rotting corpse, revive his soul, and tear the very fibers of his being apart with my own hands.

Bodies die, but a soul is forever.

David better pray that he wakes in hell. For when I die, I will haunt him to the ends of existence, find him in whatever corner of hell he will hide in, and rip his soul apart.

- *Daniel Rhys Thorn*

~ ~ ~ ~

Outside the factory the sky was starting to brighten, heralding the coming sunrise. The small group of Lamia exited the building from a side entrance, they had broken to enter, and out into the circular drive at the front of the building. Waiting for them there were two vehicles and one very worried Amber.

The instant she saw the group her eyes fixated on Regan lying limp in Constantine's hold. A cry of shock tore past her lips that had Kain moving quickly to her side, and with tears sliding down her cheeks, she reached for her Socius. "What happened to her, Kain?"

"I don't know yet," he told her gently.

265

"Where is Constantine taking her?" she inquired when the Lieutenant walked past her to the car he and Caius arrived in. Rhain followed to help secure Regan into the back seat of the black Audie q7 while Daniel held back, staring at them with unblinking and empty black eyes.

"I'll explain in the car, Amber,' Kain told her as he gently he could without losing his stern authority, 'but we must leave."

Another gasp of shock tore through her when Daniel came closer. She didn't even recognize him with his black hair stuck to skin coated in layers of dried blood and flesh. "Daniel!" Rushing to him, she dragged him into her arms only to yelp when he flinched, hissing in pain. "I'm sorry!"

He tried to give her a smile, but the sign of affection wavered to a heavy scowl.

"Kain?"

The eldest brother stared hard at his lover when she turned her horrified attention to him. Before she could strike up a battle of words, he opened the front passenger door of his black BMW x5. "I'll explain on the way."

While helping Daniel into one of the backseats, Amber leveled her Socius with a critical and worried eye. "Where are we going? We're cutting sunrise close."

"I know," Kain told her in a low voice as he raised his intense eyes to the horizon. "We'll go to Theodore's place. He's not too far away, and he has the appropriate medical facility to take care of Rhain and Daniel's injuries since his home is a Templum."

Amber nodded in agreement. "Alright."

"Can we go? I need a bloody nap."

Upon hearing Rhain's voice, Amber turned about and smiled to the other twin who was lumbering towards the car. She could see him shaking from blood loss and weakness. "Rhain!" With a cry of happiness, she threw her arms about him.

"Fuck!" He didn't want to push Amber away, but her hug racked his broken body with pain. "Not so tight, woman!"

She winced, giving him a gentle smile of apology. "I'm sorry, Rhain."

"I hope you know what you're doing." Rhain's chipped voice growled to Kain as his eyes bore into his brother's skull. "Daniel's not going to forgive you for this."

Kain sighed. "I can live with his anger for a while. However, turning Regan's care over to the Rex was the precise course of action given the circumstances. We can do little for her at this point, and she cannot be seen by humans at some unknown hospital."

"I know that,' Rhain grunted with a roll of his eyes, 'and I'm sure Daniel knows that - but still. The way you treated him, Kain, was cold and it was harsh."

Kain narrowed his eyes yet said nothing.

266

Rhain stepped past, purposefully shoving Kain out of the way with his shoulder while speaking in a low and hostile tone, "If you ever use me to control my twin like that again, I'll rip out your cold heart myself. I don't care if you are my blood. I've had enough of your overbearing authority and neurotic control."

Kain didn't respond, didn't even move as his sibling walked around the car to enter the vehicle at Daniel's side. Amber stared at her lover in astonishment to the blatant charge from Rhain. They stared at each for a short moment before Caius walked up, clearing his voice.

"You will not make the chase to your Domus, Kain."

"No. We'll be paying a visit to Theodore's Domus."

Caius nodded in agreement. "Very well. I will call you by the evening and update you and Daniel on Regan's condition. Good luck, my friend. Ave." With a curt nod, the Rex returned to his vehicle, saying something to Constantine as he got into the driver's seat, turned on his car then drove off.

"Let's go." That's all Kain said as he opened the driver's door and slid effortlessly into the driver's seat.

Amber frowned as he slammed the door, jerking just slightly. Giving a nod, she hurried about the car, scrambling into the front passenger seat. Amber nodded and once she and Kain were settled, the vehicle hummed to life and sped off.

~ ~ ~ ~

Caius raised his eyes to the rearview mirror to see Constantine's stoic reflection within the thin glass. Since entering the car, the silence had grown so thick that the Rex felt it weighing down upon him. Constantine was always silent unless spoken to or interjecting a well-placed opinion. However, Caius could not help but feel that his Lieutenant was being unusually quiet.

"How is she?" inquired the Rex as he turned his attention to the streets. He wasn't one for breaking mortal laws, but with the coming sunrise cresting, retaining the proper speed was the last thing on his mind. Luckily, his London Domus was not too far away.

Constantine replied with his frighteningly calm voice, "She is steady, for now."

"Good. Let us keep her that way. Miss. Scott is a very important human. I cannot lose her."

"Yes, sir." Constantine turned his vacant and seemingly empty eyes down to the mortal stretched out upon the seat with her head in his lap. He brushed a lock of her matted hair from her blood covered and bruised face. The smell of her mortal blood filled the inside of the car, circulating through the air and filling his lungs and causing his nostrils to flare.

A quick scan of her body showed many signs of the brutality she had suffered while in David's control. To cover her decency, Constantine had covered her exposed breasts as well as he could with her torn shirt. With all that she had gone through, she should not be exposed in such a delicate state. Regan deserved some remnants of her feminine virtue.

Constantine never felt pity. He never felt sympathy or guilt. He was estranged from the very concepts of care or tenderness. Yet he couldn't help but feel some unknown emotion kick his heart as he stared to her innocent face. To him, there was an eerie beauty to her blood splattered visage.

Turning his gaze away, Constantine focused his attention to the passing city outside the window with a finger pressed diligently upon her smooth neck where her unsteady and faint pulse licked his finger.

~ ~ ~ ~

"What the bloody hell is going on?" barked Theodore Servilii from the second story mezzanine of his Victorian brown-stone. He leaned over the thick railing while flailing an arm out to the open. "It's almost sunrise! Who the hell is at my door?"

Greg, his Puer, casually stepped across the wide entry hall towards the door while blatantly ignoring his employer's complaints. Having been serving Theodore for more than forty years, the Servus held no reservation to rolling his eyes at the barking of the Lamia. Theodore was a barker not a biter, pun intended.

"If it's those unscrupulous school girls selling their bloody cookies again, threaten them with the dogs!"

"We do not have any dogs," muttered Greg with another roll of his aged eyes.

"Don't talk back to me!" Theodore hissed. The closer the sun came to caressing the horizon, the more agitated the old Lamia became.

Greg opened the door then quickly stepped aside with shock showing upon his face. He turned to call, "Sir! It's the Thorn family at your doorstep."

Theodore, blinking his eyes in disbelief, quickly began the trek down the winding stair case. "The family?" he pondered, and indeed he saw all four members. "Kain! What do I owe the pleasure of you banging on my door right before sunrise?"

"Twenty seven minutes," the Servus spoke to all, closing the door once the group had entered. He then locked the many bolts and lowered the security shutter over the door before setting the alarm to activate.

Servilii muttered a curse towards his Servus. All irritation drained from Theodore's aged features, along with whatever color remained on his skin, when he sat his eyes upon the state of the twins. Both Rhain and Daniel were coated in dried blood, bruises, cuts, and other injuries that riddled their weak bodies. As weak as Rhain was, he was supporting Daniel who was paler than a ghost and so frail that his aura was nearly nonexistent.

Theodore turned a critical and surprised eye to Kain. "What the devil has happened to them?"

268

Kain raised a hand and offered his friend an apologetic smile. "I apologize for intruding on you, Theodore. However, it is imperative that Daniel and Rhain receive some medical attention here at your Templum."

The Elder didn't hesitate on urging his friends inside. "Of course! You and your family are always welcome here. You know that. I will see to your brothers' treatments." He pointed fingers towards the twins with a devious grin. "After I find out what is wrong with those two."

Kain groaned, "Do we have time for this?"

Theodore jabbed a finger towards Kain. "If I am going to provide these two with medical care, I need to know what has happened to them. Plus, I would really appreciate knowing if, by the evening, I will have some very disgruntled victims of whatever cat fight these two got into at my doorstep." He pointed to Rhain. "Rhain looks like his jaw was put through a sausage grinder!"

Rhain's eyes went wide. "Seriously?" He released Daniel to tumble into Amber's embrace, causing her to yelp, as he rushed to one of the large Venetian mirrors to prod and examine his injury.

The image reflected back to him was nauseating. Flesh hung from the torn sections of his exposed jaw where teeth and bone peeked through muscle that did, in fact, look as if it was put through a meat grinder, or at least an infestation of flesh-eaters. But he was sure none of the zombies he had battled laid a hand upon him.

Moaning pitifully, he prodded at the injury trying to put flesh back together. The piece didn't stick and fell limply against his jaw. "Son of a bitch..."

"War wounds, my dear boy!" Theodore laughed brightly. "Just what have you boys been up to, covered in blood and dirt with the fresh smell of life lingering upon you? Have you two been hunting?" He asked his question with a sly and devious grin coiling his lips as his eyes slid from one twin to the other.

Kain set a hand to his friend's shoulder and said in reassurance, "I will tell you everything you desire to know, Servilii. But please, Daniel and Rhain need to rest and recover as much Sanguis as possible."

"These two need more than just rest, Kain." Servilii blew out a critical whistle with a slow shake of his head. He turned towards his butler. "Greg, I want you to set these boys up with whatever medical aid they will need, and they will need a lot. There are a few bags of Elder Sanguis in the cellar. Get these two in the REC room before they bleed to death on my floor!"

Greg gave a nod then motioned the twins to follow him. Once again Rhain took up supporting Daniel. "This way."

When the three departed the hall through a small door beneath the winding stairs, Theodore turned his attention to Kain. "I take it you would prefer to stay here for the day? You won't make it back to your home."

"If possible, yes."

The older Lamia gave a chuckle and a nod of his head. "Of course." Then he turned his charm to Kain's stunning Socia. "And you, my dear? Would you care to spend the evening with *me* as well?" He flashed her a devious grin and a waggle of his brows as he stepped to her side with an arm offered.

Catching the elder's hint, Amber chuckled while offering a kiss to his cheek. "Not in this life time, Servilii."

"What about the next life time?" he asked her teasingly as she stepped past him. "There's always a next time!"

"Theodore,' Kain rumbled to the older Lamia to try and draw his pampering eyes away from Amber, '....sunrise?"

"Oh, yes. See what happens when you get to my age and a beautiful woman walks past you?" He chuckled. "Come! I want to hear what dragged the twins through the barn yard and the slaughter house too."

Theodore guided Kain and Amber into his private office where he prepared them a fresh cup of tea, loaded with a healthy dose of Sanguis at the simple bar. "Now,' he insisted once they were all settled, 'tell me what has happened to your brothers, Kain. I'm interested to know what they've been up to."

"Caius ordered them out on a hunt."

"Oh?" asked the elder Servilii as he raised his teacup to his lips. "May I inquire as to the identity of their quarry?"

Amber passed a cautious eye to Kain. Her Socius sighed as he leaned back in his chair then cautiously answered, "David."

Theodore's eyes narrowed at the name. "I see." He lowered his gaze to his teacup then said softly, "So, my bastard son finally crossed the line and pissed off old Caius, has he?"

Kain nodded. "You know as well as all do that David's dangerous behavior would finally push Caius to act."

Theodore looked up to Kain and nodded. He agreed completely with what Kain said, even though he didn't want to hear the truth. "I know, and I understand. The boy has always been a stain on my Familia and on my family name. I did all I could to try and convince him to return to me and face the Basilica for his crimes. I knew there was no hope for any point of honor or rationality to reach him."

"But there has never been any hope for him," Theodore went on to say as he set aside his cup to a table at the side of his chair. "I'm surprised he's lived this long." Servilii raised his eyes that reflected a touch of sympathy for his son. "Tell me, Kain. What did David do to finally have a Venatio called out on him?"

Amber frowned as she buried her eyes into her teacup, nibbling her lower lip.

When neither she nor Kain responded directly, Theodore cleared his voice. "Kain, answer me."

After collecting his thoughts through a fall of closed eyes, Kain drew open his charcoal eyes to regard his old friend with a look of sadness. "He kidnapped Regan Scott outside of my building, kept her held hostage within an old factory he and his fellow Proscriptus were hiding in, and performed an illegal Creare upon Regan's cousin, Joyce Scott."

Clearing his voice, Theodore calmly crossed one of his legs to the other. He asked, "What else?"

Kain arched a brow to which Theodore added, "I know my son, Kain. That is not all he did."

"I'm not exactly sure of Regan's condition, but I am sure that Caius will add an attempted rape charge to the list, multiple charges of assault, the attempted murder of Rhain and Daniel, as well as a book of Proscriptus activities and crimes against the Crown."

Theodore shook his head sending a few strands of pepper and salt against his brow. "Where is Miss. Scott now?"

"Caius has taken her to be seen by his personal medical staff at his Domus. I should be hearing from him tonight."

"I see. I'm very sorry for all the trouble my son has caused you and your siblings, Kain." Theodore shook his head then released a sigh of shame. "I should have put a stop to his insanity a long time ago. I knew when he was born that he would be nothing but terror to me and my wife. I thought he would grow out of his deviant behavior, but it seems that I was very wrong."

"Theodore,' Amber mewed softly, 'you cannot blame yourself for David's actions. He made his bed of choices on his own, and for many decades. We all know you did what you could do to try and regain control over him and to keep him out of Caius' line of sight. I'm sure even Caius understands that fact."

Theodore mustered a soft yet uncomfortable smile that he offered to the beautiful woman. "The sins of the son are the sins of the father. Is that not the saying?"

Amber frowned heavily, stealing a peek to her lover who watched the elder Lamia with intense yet sympathetic eyes.

Taking a deep breath of air, the Servilii Elder rose from his chair, moving to the fire that crackled within the fireplace.

Kain frowned. "I am truly sorry, Theodore."

The Elder waved a dismissive hand. "I stopped being sorry for that boy a long time ago. He never held any love for me, so I stopped holding love for him."

He turned back to the room, looking to Kain with his dark eyes narrowing and holding hard. "Did they kill him?"

Kain gave a sincere nod. "Yes."

"Which one exactly?"

"Daniel."

Theodore breathed a saddened sigh. "That would explain the severity of their injuries considering the focus of David's cruel attention was upon Daniel's woman. However, it looks like both of your brothers had battled David. If I had to compliment my son on one of his talents, fighting would be that one. However, combined with his insane Daemon, he could certainly be a very dangerous foe. David should have died centuries ago. His insanity had been roaming this world for far too long."

Licking his lips, Theodore went on to ask, "What are Miss. Scott's injuries?"

"We're not sure,' answered Kain with a slight shrug of his broad shoulders, 'though I know Daniel had to give her some of his blood in order to sustain her. She is in bad shape, but will survive."

"Poor dear." Theodore gave a sympathetic frown. "She is a vibrant young woman. A shame she had to meet our world in such a way."

"Well,' he went on to say, 'it's getting early. I'm sure you and Amber would like to retire for the day. I'll show you to a guest room. Is there anything either of you two need?"

Both Kain and Amber shook their heads.

"Very well. Amber, you know your way around the house and the kitchens. If you need anything, help yourselves. I will have some fresh clothes sent to your room."

"Thank you, Theodore."

Kain rose from his chair, his tall and powerful frame uncoiling muscle after tight muscle. "I would like to see my brothers first."

"Of course. You know where the REC room is."

With a nod of his head, Kain departed the room. Amber stood from her chair, watching her lover depart before stepping to one of the kindest Lamia she had ever known. She smiled to Theodore, reaching out to gently caress a hand along his arm. "I am very sorry for your loss, Theodore."

The older Lamia smiled warmly to her. "You, Kain, and the boys have nothing to be sorry for."

Looping her arm to his, she walked him from the room. "Come, let's have a quick drink and make a toast to a new day."

~ ~ ~ ~

$\textbf{D}$own in the recovery ward, a large medical room of white washed walls,

expensive medical beds, and even more expensive equipment, the Thorn twins were slowly going about ridding themselves of the dirt, grime, and blood that they had been bathed in during their brutal battles.

Already the pieces of blood coated clothing were starting to harden and stink. And truthfully, Daniel couldn't stomach the smell of Regan's blood any longer as it was now dry and cracking. Greg had shown them to the REC then departed, informing them that he would return directly with IVs of Elder Sanguis. He encouraged them to shower. A shower was just what Daniel needed.

"How's your back?" Daniel heard Rhain ask as he grunted when he bent down to remove his boots. "Very stiff,' Daniel replied then sucked in a painful breath of air when some muscle in his back went tight, 'and painful."

Rhain, who was sitting upon one of the beds after he had stripped off his soiled shoes and shirt, stepped up to his brother to touch Daniel's back, sweeping aside Daniel's long hair that was nothing more than a bloody mess of knotted strands. He frowned seeing the stab wounds marring his twin's slender back and pale flesh.

"Damn,' he muttered under his breath, 'there has to be at least fifty or more wounds here, Daniel."

Daniel glanced down to his chest, gingerly brushing his fingertips over the exit wounds where the blade David had used to stab him penetrated all the way through his body. "How bad are they?"

"They could look better, but they could look worse. They're healing, but you've lost so much blood that it'll take at least a few weeks for all of these to heal. They'll need to be stitched."

"I figured."

"All I want is a nice shower, some fresh blood, and a bottle of Jack!" Rhain groaned as he ran a hand through his hair only to curse when a finger twisted into a nasty knot. "What about you, Frater? Care to share a bottle with me?"

When Daniel didn't respond, Rhain glanced over his shoulder to see that Daniel had seated himself on the edge of his bed, staring to the floor and the wrist he had fed Regan from. Casually, Daniel ran his fingers over the two bite wounds and did so while in deep thought.

"She'll be fine."

Daniel raised his dirty face to the sound of his brother's voice. Rhain spoke of Regan, and the mention of Daniel's Socia twisted the guilty knife further into his heart. "I shouldn't have let her go, Rhain," he began to say with a heavy, dry sigh. "She's my Socia, but I've turned my back on her when she's needed me the most."

"She needed medical care the most, Daniel. You did the right thing by letting her go with Caius. You know the Rex will see to her care and give her the best treatment. Better than what she would've had at any human hospital, at least."

When Daniel wouldn't raise his head to look at him, Rhain stepped forwards to grip his twin's chin to lift his gaze. "You can't beat yourself up over this, Danny. You've done that too many times. When are you going to except the fact that you're limited like the rest of us when it comes to trying to save those we care about?"

"I don't just care for her,' Daniel grumbled, ignoring the fact Rhain had used his childhood nickname in a way to appease the tension simmering between the two, 'I love her."

"Yeah, I got that." Rhain sat to the bed across from his twin, leaning forwards and with his arms coming to fold across his legs. "You scared the shit out of me tonight, Daniel," he said in all seriousness as he locked his black eyes to his brother as the first thing he did once in the REC was remove his contacts. "I haven't seen your Daemon come out in a long time. I didn't think I'd ever see it again."

Daniel flinched, looking away. He stared down at his hands. No matter how hard he tried to wipe the stains away, his flesh still remained red. He needed a shower and a hard loofa scrub to get rid of all the filth that tarnished him.

"I'm sorry,' Daniel heard his trembling voice mumble as he threaded fingers into his matted hair then bowed his head forwards, 'I didn't... I couldn't control it. I don't remember what happened. One minute I was in control of myself and the next..."

"Nobody would blame you."

"That's not the point, Rhain." Daniel raised his eyes to his twin, feeling thick tears swelling within his eyes. "I pride myself on my internal balance. I've spent decades learning the many forms of meditation from Masters all over the world, and in one second all of that training vanished."

"What triggered it?"

Daniel licked his dry lips then replied in a low mumble, "David said that Regan would've been a good fuck."

Rhain blew out a whistle. Now he knew why his brother snapped and didn't blame him one damn bit.

"That was the last thing I remember. But I knew what I was doing, Rhain. I saw what I was doing to David from behind my eyes. But I couldn't stop my Daemon, not till I heard Regan call my name."

"Call your name?" Rhain shook his head. "Sorry, mate, she didn't say anything."

"I heard her."

Rhain sighed then pointed to his own jaw. "By the way, how's your jaw?"

Daniel touched his cheek then shrugged as he touched a very sensitive spot. He knew Rhain was talking about having to strike him. It wasn't the first time one twin had to assault the other for one reason or another. "You did what you had to do. I thank you for that. If you hadn't of brought me back to reality, I could've..."

Rhain narrowed his eyes and snarled, "Don't even finish that thought, Danny. I don't want to hear it. It didn't happen. You didn't attack me or Regan. So let's just forget your momentary slip of control and move on."

Daniel gave a solemn nod in agreement. After a quivering breath that expanded a painful lung, he went on to ask, "What now?" When Rhain looked to him expectantly, he added, "What do I do now, Rhain? What do I do with Regan? What will happen to her when she wakes up and I'm not there to comfort her? She's going to be scared and confused and surrounded by strangers."

He went on to say in a jumble of quivering words, "I don't want her to be afraid of me. I don't want her to run away from me. I can't lose her."

"You won't lose her. She loves you."

Daniel turned away.

"When you were fighting, she told me to help you. I know she loves you because I saw it in her eyes. You've just got to handle this with care. Give her time and see how things unfold once she's healed and you two can hook up and discuss what happened."

Daniel scoffed with a shake of his head. "If Caius lets me see her again. She knows of us now, Rhain, and he won't be happy."

"She has the Proprietas, Daniel. She'll be given the chance to be welcomed into our family and go through the Domare."

"If she chooses to."

"She will. That girl will walk through the pits of hell for you."

"How do you know?"

Rhain smirked. "I saw it in her eyes."

Daniel lowered his face into his hands. His voice quivered as he whispered, "I'm scared, Rhain. What if she doesn't survive?"

"She'll survive. You gave her enough of your blood to trigger the healing trait of the Proprietas. And now that she's in Caius' care she'll be given the best treatment that can be provided to a human - anywhere."

"Hey,' Rhain said, drawing his brother's gaze back to him, 'we'll figure this out. We always do."

Daniel's lips parted to respond when suddenly the door to the medical room slid open. Expecting to see Greg returning with their Sanguis, the twins were rather startled to see Kain walking in. Daniel and Rhain cast each other a quick glance of concern before setting their attention to their elder brother. Neither said a word as Kain walked into the room to stand at the foot of the beds.

He scanned them with his unblinking and unreadable eyes. Neither looked to be healing well and were still dangerously pale. Daniel was shaking ever so slightly, and Rhain looked sick. Kain took an unsteady breath when he saw the wounds dotting Daniel's chest. Just what the hell had his brothers gone through?

With that question floating within his mind, Kain suddenly became aware of how close he came to the true possibility that he could have lost his brothers in battle to David. Though he knew how strong the twins were and how valued their battle talents were to Caius as the Inquisitors, he had to admit that he had never seen the two looking as if they had one foot in the grave. Never before had they looked like death.

Kain's stomach contorted, and his cold heart froze within his chest. He wasn't one for expressing his emotions, at least those emotions that came with sensitivity and compassion. He had always been hard and cold, almost distant, when dealing with his brothers since they were children. He had to in order to raise them, protect them, and care for them after the deaths of their parents. Even after their Creare, Kain was still the only one able to protect his brothers and keep their tight family safe.

There had been too many days Kain spent being tormented with nightmares during his Meditatio, all centered about his fears of his family falling apart and his brothers returning home to him in body bags - nothing but rotting corpses. He jerked as if his mind slapped him awake from his private thoughts. Daniel and Rhain were staring at him, expecting some sort of lecture that would be typical of this type of situation. But this time around Kain couldn't bring himself to berating his siblings.

Instead, he motioned them to him with a beckoning of two fingers. "Come here."

275

Daniel slowly stood from his bed. Rhain on the other hand fell back upon the bed with a groan. "Oh, hell. Just get on with it already so we can get cleaned up and get some damn rest."

"Rhain." Kain said his brother's name in a tone of voice that was flat and that shook ever so slightly.

Something wasn't right. The twins looked at each other, passing uncomfortable glances, as Rhain stood from his bed. Like children caught beneath their parents' wagging fingers they stepped up to their older sibling.

In fact, Daniel spoke first with the need to quickly defend both he and Rhain's actions. "Kain…let me explain."

What happened next took both twins by surprise. In fact, they were stunned. Kain threw his arms about their shoulders, drawing them into his embrace as he threaded his fingers into their hair, cradling their heads against him. "If you two ever do anything so senseless again as to recklessly risk your lives, I will never forgive you. Do you know how close I came to being an only child?"

He buried his face into their hair and drew in the mixed scent of theirs, David's, and Regan's blood. The smell tore through him like a wild fire, flaming his panic and his fears. Curling fingers into their scalps, he hugged them tighter. "I will not lose either of you. Do you understand me? I cannot lose you. You are all that I have. We are all that's left of our family. Mother and father would never forgive me if I let anything happen to either of you."

The twins didn't know what to do or what to say. Kain had never hugged them before. Never. Not even when they were children did he dare to embrace them. He had always been in control of them. He was the stone that held up their family pillar and the one soul that saw to their survival after the death of their parents. All that the twins had and had become were due to Kain and his never ending pursuit of care and support.

For Kain to show his emotions was almost unheard of besides expressing his anger and disappointment, which was quite often. This was a very uncommon event, and it left both Daniel and Rhain speechless. In fact, they often swore that Kain was born without the ability to feel positive emotions. They often passed snide teases to Amber, questioning whether or not their brother could even feel pleasure. But this? This was almost disturbing.

Kain stepped back, releasing his hold while ignoring the gaping stares of his brothers. "You both will be quests of Theodore till he discharges you from his care. Caius will be phoning me this evening to update me on Regan's condition and the clean-up of David's stronghold. I want you both to focus on healing for today. Neither of you are permitted to leave until you're given a clean bill of health. Do you understand me?"

When the twins failed to answer, just stared at him, he added in a softer tone of voice, "Do this for me. Please?"

He dragged his eyes over the twins only to pause once again upon the wounds to Daniel's chest. Gently, he took hold of Daniel's shoulders to turn him about. Kain's strong, stoic face pulled back to show sympathetic pain for the brutal marring of Daniel's back. "I don't want you two to give Greg or Theodore any problems with your care. Do as you are told. I'll come check on you in the evening."

"Rest well," he told them then turned and strolled out of the room leaving the twins staring at his departing back.

"What…just happened?"

Daniel shrugged his thin shoulders to his brother's question. "I'm not exactly sure."

"That was creepy."

"I agree."

Giving a gentle clap to his brother's shoulder, Rhain pushed Daniel towards the showers. "Come on. Let's get a shower before Greg comes back. I'm going to get my damn nap even if it kills me."

~ ~ ~ ~

*N*ot long after Kain left, both Daniel and Rhain had showered and dressed in the pajamas provided for them and were just turning to rest when the door opened. Greg strolled in carrying two bags of Elder Sanquis to a table between their beds.

"Here we go, lads," he proclaimed as he began the diligent task of setting up the bags for transfusion. "My apologies for this being late. If you are ready, I can begin the transfusion."

"What's on the menu, my good man?" Rhain groaned as he eased back onto the posh medical bed, stretching out his sore legs.

"Elder Sanguis. Eight-hundred and forty-two years." After the bags were hooked up to the IV lines, Greg turned to Rhain to engage the needle, yet Rhain stopped him by pointing to Daniel and saying, "Hook him up first. He's in worse condition than I am."

The Servus frowned yet nodded as he turned to Daniel. The man's frown deepened as he scanned the wounds on the Lamia's chest. He gently leaned Daniel forwards so he could examine his back. Tsking, he shook his head. "These will need to be stitched so they can heal properly. Without care, they could become infected."

Daniel muttered tiredly, "Do what you need to do."

Greg nodded. When he finished hooking Daniel to his bag of Sanguis, he turned to aid Rhain.

Rhain touched his throbbing jaw only to wince to the stinging pain.

"I would ask that you stop touching your wound," Greg said with his eyes narrowed. "I'll stitch it up when I am finished with your brother."

"Sure. It's not like I'm going anywhere."

It was a slow process, stitching up the multitude of individual stab wounds that tore through Daniel's body. At least Greg was very careful, tending to the stitching with a gentle and mild touch. He was an expert, finishing each stitched wound with a tiny little knot of the thread before turning to the next. When he was finished, he cleaned the wounds with an antiseptic that would aid in the quick healing of Daniel's wounds.

Rhain tipped his head, looking to his twin. "Hey? Are you okay?"

Daniel nodded and replied, "Yes, Rhain. I'm fine."

When Greg had finished with him, Daniel laid back upon the bed, closing his eyes as he took a deep breath. Finally, the air smelled of cleanly washed flesh and clean linen, no longer of blood and death. He couldn't stop himself from yawning. Now that his body was able to ease, Daniel felt wave after wave of exhaustion wash over him; the type of exhaustion that could leave an individual nauseated. He had to close his eyes to keep his sight from swimming around in pool of vertigo. Through his hazed mind he heard Rhain hiss and curse slightly at Greg, to which the Servus replied that Rhain was whining like a child.

"There we go." Greg stood after he clipped away the last thread after knotting it tight. "I would try to limit your speech till evening. You could easily tear the stitches and do more damage to the healing flesh." The snapping of his medical cloves echoed the crisp room. "You will be able to rest soon."

"I don't think I'm going to be able to sleep," grumbled Daniel.

"Of course you will. The Sanguis will aid in your Meditatio."

Rhain blinked and Daniel arched a brow. "Excuse me?" asked Daniel.

Greg went about cleaning up. He answered straight forwards and clearly, "There was a moderate dose of sedatives added to your Sanguis. You'll be asleep within a few minutes."

Rhain charged through a tight lipped snarl, "You've drugged us?"

"Of course," answered the Servus without a flinch to the glares and the snarls. "Such was the request of your brother and why I took so long preparing the infusions."

"Kain told you to sedate us?"

"That bastard!"

Greg looked between the two with an aged brow raised. "Have you two looked at yourselves in a mirror? Even I would question what you two got into. I wouldn't be surprised if neither of you slept due to bad dreams and pain, which neither of you need at this moment. You need rest and a very deep Meditatio to aid in the healing of your wounds."

The man smirked then added, "If you wish to argue with your brother, feel free to do so. Though, I would not suggest it. He and his Socia have retired to a guest room. He doesn't look willing to discuss anything at this moment."

Both of the twins groaned. If Kain gave the order, why fight it? In truth, they both knew that a deep, meditative sleep was needed and that neither one would obtain it without some outside influence. In secret, Daniel was rather appreciative of Kain for the instructions as the sedatives would help calm his mind and the twisting worry building over Regan and her condition. His heart eased, knowing he would wake up and be able to speak to Regan. He really needed to hear her voice.

Rhain watched his brother slowly slip into the Meditatio. He almost looked peaceful, but Rhain knew his brother well enough to know Daniel was hurting inside. Closing his eyes, Rhain laid his head back to his pillow, gingerly touching the fresh stitches.

"I will be turning in for the evening soon,' Greg went on to say while Rhain's mind began to drift away, 'so another Servus will check in on you both during the day. By nightfall, I will come in and..." He turned about to see both of the twins having succumbed to the lull of the sedatives.

A chuckle fell his lips, and he nodded. "Rest well."

~ ~ ~ ~

Regan could hardly move. Her body felt heavy and drained of all energy to the point she had to fight to keep her eyes even partially open. With her throat feeling dry, she couldn't call out as her foggy mind drew her from a heavy slumber. It took some time for her to fully open her eyes, blinking rapidly, so she could look around. The room she was in shifted when her vision swam. She could barely make out the decorations, the paintings or the overall expensive taste that surrounded her.

Groaning, she tried to sit up but none of her muscles would obey her command. She was left exhausted and panting. When she tried to move her left leg, the limb refused. Slipping a hand beneath the covers, she felt a metal and fabric brace circling the center of her leg. The next move drew her wonky attention to her right wrist and to the brace secured about it. Grunting, she tried once more to move. After a few more tries, she pushed and squirmed till she was sitting and leaning against a high tower of fluffy pillows. A soft beep sounded to her side, drawing her attention to a medical monitor that showed all her vital signs dancing across the dark screen. Her eyes ran an IV line that was attached to a thin needled taped to the top of her hand and leading to a bag of red fluid above her bed. A little wave of dizziness washed over her causing her to buckle for a moment.

At least the room felt warm and eased her with dim light. Sharp crackling of a burning fire tickled Regan's ears, and she noticed, off in the distance of the large room, a healthy fire burning in a deep set fireplace. Taking a breath to steady her wooziness, she looked about the room in hopes of forcing her vision back into place.

There were heavy curtains drawn shut over five separate windows that seemed to grow from the floor to the tall ceiling, keeping the room in shadow. A few lights were on from their brass holders screwed into the wall at each side of the fireplace. As her eyes grew more and more accustomed to the dimness through her wonky vision, Regan saw more detail of the room, or what could be presumed as a museum art gallery.

Moaning, she swallowed a lump that had grown within her throat only to wince as a wave of shakiness struck her stronger than the last. With a breathy sigh, she settled back to the large and comfortable bed. Wherever she was certainly wasn't the cold and desolate factory where David had held her.

David!

Regan whimpered as her entire body shuddered with pain as memories flooded into her mind. She closed her eyes and gripped her hair as she folded over onto her side. So many memories! So much pain! Her ears suddenly exploded with her own voice screaming out in pure alarm as she saw a glint of silver, flashing above her then driving down - over and over and over again. Then there was blood, so much blood, and it sprayed against her in hot splotches till her own vision saw nothing but crimson.

A cry ran from her throat as she curled tighter till she was pressed into a ball and the needle embedded in her hand began to slide out as the medical tape gave way. The blood she saw was Daniel's! Through her vision she saw David's shadowy figure hunched over Daniel as he tried desperately to hold onto her while David stabbed him over…and over…and over again.

Suddenly, she was falling. Agony tore through her causing her to buck upon the bed, yanking the needle from her hand to drip a line of red liquid down her arm and across the bed as the IV line fell away. A torturous cry of anguish echoed the room as she cried out Daniel's name. The next thing Regan knew she was being lifted within a set of strong arms. She came against a hard chest, and through her ringing ears she heard the rustle of fabric. The bed shifted as the person who held her reached for the IV line while pressing a cloth to her bleeding hand.

Regan didn't move. She only cried.

Faintly aware that she was moving, Regan opened her eyes to see a shadowy form looming over her. Dressed in a finely pressed suit of black, the young man laid her back to the bed then began to wipe blood from her hand.

"You must try to remain still, Miss. Scott. You must not pull this needle out again," stated the man in a collected, tight, and flat tone to his fine accent, a mix of Italian and Welsh.

He sounded agitated, annoyed at her really, but Regan was too exhausted, too emotionally destroyed to care about who the man was and why he sounded annoyed. Through foggy eyes, eyes filled with tears, she watched him stand and walk about the bed to fuss with the IV and the monitor.

"Where…am I?" she managed to mumble after a hitching breath and a whimper.

The man, seemingly young, didn't even glance to her. He only turned back to her when ready to replace the IV with a new needle. "Safe," he told her - simple as that.

Regan winced when the new needle slid into her flesh to puncture a swollen vein. At least he was gentle. Once the needle was secured in place with another piece of tape, Regan took a deep, steadying breath and licked her dry lips.

She went on to ask through a dry throat, "What's happened to me?"

"All of your questions will be answered in time, Miss. Scott,' said the young man, 'but for now you must rest."

Slowly, she rolled her head to see him injecting a clear liquid through a side tube into the fluid bag. "Wait. What are you doing?"

He didn't answer her, just focused on pushing the entire contents of the syringe into the IV bag.

Regan's heart began to pound within her chest as fear wrapped its cold fingers about her. She went to reach for him, intent on stopping him, yet he easily avoided her reach. But when she went to pull out the infusion needle in her hand, his grip snapped out faster than she saw and he wrapped lean fingers about her hand, stopping her.

She was crying now and begging through noisy whimpers for him not to hurt her, to stop whatever it was he was doing. But her vision was starting to blur, and her body felt heavy and her mind was quickly giving in to the lull of slumber.

The last thing she saw was the man turning to face her with his handsome and youthful face set in tight lines and caressed by a lock of thin black hair that had fallen from a tight queue at the back of his neck. His eyes were almost crystal blue - brighter than the contact lenses Rhain wore. And though his eyes were like the eyes of an angel, they were shadowed by the darkness of a demon.

Regan's arm went limp within his grip, so he gently placed it to the bed at her side. Within a few heartbeats she was asleep. Once Constantine had settled her back down to sleep, he made sure she was secure and that her vital signs were stable. Just as he stepped away from the bed, intent upon departing the room, he paused to take one last glance at the human.

He calmly picked up the phone upon the table and pressed a button. "She's ready." Just as he hung up, the doors opened and a team of medical personal entered. They moved to the bedside, and Constantine backed away as the Lamia went about preparing Regan for transfer.

"Remember to send a sample of her blood to be tested. Inform me directly when she is out of surgery."

The white coated doctor gave a curt nod of his head. "Yes, sir."

Constantine watched as Regan was transferred to a medical bed along with the IV and fluid bags. He didn't speak as she was wheeled from her room. He followed at a distance then turned down a separate hall, leaving the human to the care of the doctors. After all, she was just a human - nothing special and nothing to be concerned for. So why was Caius so curious about her? What was it that made Regan Scott important to the man? Narrowing his eyes, Constantine looked upon her sleeping form with an eye of cold loathing. What made *her* so unusual?

She was nothing.

She was expendable.

And so she would remain.

XVIII

*A*m I in love?

Am I even capable of feeling such an intense emotion? If so, then I am sure that I am no longer falling in love with Regan. I am in love with her. I must be. What other explanation is there for what I have done? I blindly risked my life to save her, and not once did I consider the grave danger I was facing. In fact, I was willing to sacrifice myself to see to her safety.

I must be in love with her.

After all, she consumes my thoughts. Yet not in an obsessive way, but in a way that has wrapped my soul and my heart in unimaginable warmth. It's the same type of feeling that you experience when you miss a person who has been away for a very long time, so much that all you think about is that person returning to you. You earn for them, and their return brings you happiness and comfort - love.

This is what I am feeling with Regan, the want for her to return to me so we can be happy. So we can love each other without fear of being torn away. But will she love me as I love her? What if she rejects me? What if she fears me?

Is she capable of loving a monster like me?

No one can love a monster.

- *Daniel Rhys Thorn*

~ ~ ~ ~

"**Y**ou're awake. Good."

Regan's attention was drawn from staring at a painted portrait hanging upon the wall to a voice that spoke from the open doors of her temporary bedroom. A slight scowl formed upon her lips as she stared at the young man who had sedated her the night before.

"Oh, it's you," she grumbled in pure distaste. She looked down to her injured leg and gently ran her fingers over the stitched skin. She sighed heavily as her eyes also looked to the brace upon her wrist, and then she looked to Constantine. "Are you here to drag me off to some more secret surgeries and tests?" She followed him with her eyes as he walked towards her.

"The surgeries and the tests have all been necessary to see to your recovery."

"But you still refuse to tell me why." She huffed, slumping back. "I doubt the quacks performing the surgeries have a single medical degree to share amongst them."

"I can assure you that the medical staff under Caius' employment are above the ranks of the simple minded doctors at any hospital within London."

Regan snorted. "I don't like being kept in secret."

"Would you have preferred to live with your injuries?"

"I would have preferred to go to a hospital."

"You have been treated, free of charge I might add. You should not complain. You should be grateful."

Regan sighed. His statement had her swallowing a lump of humility, and she looked back to the brace upon her arm.

The man didn't react to the coldness in her voice as he crossed the room carrying a silver tray that held a pitcher of water and a glass. "Would you care for some water?" he asked as he sat the tray to the bedside table then began to pour the cup full of ice water; the cubes clinked against the fine crystal.

Regan nodded and licked her dry lips as she eyed the water with throaty hunger.

He helped her to sit up against the pile of soft but thick pillows. "Drink slowly," he instructed her as he raised the glass to her lips.

Regan didn't complain about the assistance he offered, even so, a few drops slipped down her chin. Greedily, she drank the entire cup before coughing as the last sip of icy, refreshing water trickled down her parched throat.

"Easy,' he said flatly, softly, as he gently eased her back to the pillows then sat the cup down, 'don't move too quickly or you'll pull your IV out - again."

To make the point, he looked down to make sure the needle was still in her hand and the tape secure. He then raised his sky-blue eyes to Regan as he reached out to gently lift her arm, placing a device over a finger that would read her heartrate.

"How are you feeling?" he inquired as he observed the monitor.

"Much better."

"What is the level of your dizziness?"

Regan shook her head sending a few thick waves of luscious rosewood against a pale, scared cheek. "It's gone."

"And your pain level?"

"Moderate."

"One to ten."

Regan shrugged. "Four."

"Good. Would you like an aspirin?"

"No. I think I can handle it."

He nodded again then turned his attention to the monitor where he pressed a button. The annoying beeping ceased.

"Are you going to answer my questions now? I'd like to know the severity of my injuries that required operations."

"I am not the one to answer your questions, Miss. Scott."

Regan frowned. "Why not?"

"It's not my duty."

She tipped her head, eyeing him curiously. "I don't understand. You're holding me against my will and not answering my questions."

"You are not here against your will."

"Oh? I don't remember asking to come here. And I don't even know where I am. You won't tell me."

"All your questions will be answered in time, once you have rested and recovered some more."

Regan frowned even more as the young man stepped to one of the large windows where the darkness of the night seeped through a split in the fabric.

"Would you like some fresh air? It's rather chilly out tonight."

She nodded to his question and replied, "I would appreciate that."

He was right. When the thick window was opened a gust of crisp, clean air danced into the room and across to kiss Regan's cool cheek.

"Are you hungry?"

"Not really."

"You should eat something to help regain your strength."

"Yeah, I'll do that once I don't have the fear of you drugging me again."

The young man stepped to the end of the bed to stare blankly at her. "Sedating you was necessary to keep you calm so you would do no further damage to your systems than what had been done during your attack."

Her attack? Regan frowned and curled further into the thick blanket that she had pulled up to her neck. She remembered the attack, that brutal and violent attack.

"I'll have some food delivered to you soon. You will need to get up and walk soon to help keep a blood clot from forming in your leg."

"Oh, wonderful! I have a barn dance I need to get to by Monday."

"I will return later." With that said, he turned towards the door.

Before he could get too far, she called out to him, "I would like a shower, or a bath." Though somebody had washed off her body while she was unconscious, Regan needed to feel clean from within - not just on the outside.

The man paused at the door, glancing back to her from over a thin shoulder. "If you are able to stand and walk with moderate stability in a few hours, we can see about a shower, after you eat of course."

The scowl that crossed Regan's lips went unnoticed as the man disappeared into the hallway. She was left alone once more. With a sigh, she closed her eyes and leaned towards the continuous breeze that kissed her.

When next the man appeared, at least two hours later, he was not alone. A young woman was with him, holding in her arms a few towels, a bathrobe, and a change of clothes. Regan had just finished a simple dinner of fruit and yogurt when they entered. She was feeling rather rejuvenated. But when she saw the towels, her dark eyes went wide and she mewed in delight.

With a motion of a finger, a silent order from the handsomely tall man, the woman went off to a side door, disappearing into an adjacent bathroom. Within a few seconds the caressing sound of water falling danced the room.

"Were you able to eat?" asked the black haired man as he stepped to the bed.

As usual, his presence was ever stoic, ever passive and ever expressionless. His eyes, as they ran along her body, left Regan feeling cold and unwanted. She nodded to him, and he glanced to the tray to confirm her agreement.

"Good." He went to the side of the bed and carefully removed the IV and then proceeded to removing the braces from her arm and her leg. Reaching out his arm, he said, "Come. Let's see if you can stand."

"I want some answers first."

"Soon."

Regan grumbled then twisted to offer him her hand. As cold as he could be, he was very gentle and observant when helping her move. And now that the IV had been removed, Regan was able to move with more mobility and less discomfort. One foot touched the floor first to feel carpet beneath her toes, but when she stood, her feet began to quiver and that quiver began to travel up her legs. She went instantly weak, leaning back to the bed, only to be caught by a strong arm coming to press against her back.

She was amazed that she was able to work her injured leg so soon after surgery, yet it seemed that her leg was strong enough to support her. Regan stood with his aid and took a few tentative steps forwards. With a few more steps she was able to strengthen her strides even though there was a limp to her steps.

Concentrating on her next step, she inquired carefully, "Can I ask you something?"

"If you wish."

"I've seen you almost every night since I woke up, yet I still don't know your name. You've never introduced yourself. What's your name?"

"Constantine."

"Constantine what?"

"Just…Constantine."

"Nice to meet you, Just Constantine. I'm Regan."

"Yes,' he told her as he walked her towards the bathroom, allowing her to guide their movement and their pace, 'Daniel Thorn mentioned your name."

At the mention of Daniel's name, Regan stopped with her attention snapping to Constantine. "You know Daniel?"

The young man, pale as a ghost, tipped his head and nodded. "Yes."

A leap of relief flashed through Regan and shined within her dark eyes. She smiled brightly, excitedly. "Where is he? Is he here? I want to see him."

"No. He is not here."

"Where is he?"

"Recovering."

"Does he know that I'm here?"

"He does."

"Has he come to see me?"

"No."

Frowning, Regan turned her eyes away. What excitement she felt quickly dissipated. Why hadn't Daniel come to see her? Was he mad at her? Had something happened to him? All those questions and more began to twist and turn, rekindling her panic.

"Is he okay?" she heard herself inquire in a very timid and quiet voice.

"Of that I am not sure. I have yet to hear an update on his and his brother's condition."

"I hope he's not seriously injured."

"I assure you, Miss. Scott, that he is fine."

"Sir? Her bath is ready."

Constantine nodded to the pretty blonde woman that stepped from the bathroom. He offered Regan's arm to her then stepped aside. "Take care of her, Janine."

The woman nodded, smiled, and gently walked Regan into the bathroom. Constantine turned on his heels, striding from the room.

When she finished, an hour and a half later, Regan wasn't surprised to find Constantine waiting for her when she stepped from the bathroom with Janine aiding her. The two were chatting quietly with Janine carefully guiding Regan's every step. When Janine noticed Constantine, her chirpiness vanished and her presence stiffened.

Constantine stared at Janine with his flat eyes, and like before, she quickly departed Regan's side when he flicked a finger towards the door.

Regan frowned but said nothing as she sat down to a large, thick back chair. She adjusted the black t-shirt she was given to wear then smoothed down the seams of the pink and black plaid pajama bottoms. She jerked when she felt fingers grip her chin, turning her face up to him then to the right and then the left. She wasn't sure exactly what he was looking at, or for, and his touch felt cold, making her instantly uncomfortable.

Whatever it was he searched for must have been found for he gave a curt nod and released her chin. The bath had done her well. She looked refreshed and more alive than when he had left her. "Are you feeling better?" he asked as he laced his hands behind his back.

Regan nodded, a thick clump of her wet hair slapping against her cheek that she pulled away. "Yes."

"Good. Caius wishes to speak with you."

"You mentioned him before. Who exactly is he?"

"The man responsible for your care. This is his private home. You are his guest, and he is very interested in the progress of your recovery. When you are ready, I will take you to see him."

Regan narrowed her eyes and raised her chin. "I'm ready."

Constantine arched a slender brow, his lips parting to speak, but Regan raised a hand and cut off his words. She told him sharply, "Now." Giving a slight sigh of agitation, Constantine gave a nod. "Very well. I will help you put your braces back on. However, if you take one wrong step, I will put you back in this bed. Do you understand me?"

Regan smiled to him. "I promise not to fall on my face, but I can't promise not to walk like a drunk."

The Lamia's face tightened, and it almost seemed that he was going to roll his eyes - almost.

~ ~ ~ ~

David…was dead?

Regan blinked her eyes in disbelief to what she had just heard. She sat in a deep chair, feet flat on the floor with toes twisting within her soft socks. She stared at the carpet while rubbing at the brace over her wrist. She didn't want to believe it, but Caius assured her that David was, in fact, dead. And what was worse, Daniel had killed him. So many terrifying emotions started to swim about within her, and she began to shake ever so slightly with her confusion.

Caius frowned when he saw her petite body shake subtly. Glancing to Constantine, he spoke softly, "Call for some tea, would you Constantine?"

Constantine gave a curt nod then stepped to a finely crafted desk where he did just that via a com-link.

"I know what I have said must sound very confusing to you, Miss. Scott, but I assure you that everything I have disclosed to you is the honest truth."

"I don't understand," mumbled Regan with a slight shake of her head. "How could Daniel have killed him?"

Caius cleared his voice as he cast a sly glance to Constantine. His lieutenant responded with a blank expression and a slight nod. "How much do you remember of your ordeal with David?"

She tried to think, really tried, but nothing came to the front of her memory but twisting blackness. "I don't remember much. After all, I don't even remember being injured as badly as I was. Then again, I obviously suffered some severe trauma if I was unconscious."

"I apologize for not keeping you informed of your operations. You must understand,' Caius said softly and with a tender smile, 'when you arrived here, your condition was very serious. My medical staff had to see to the multiple breaks in your leg and wrist as quickly as possible. Your health and recovery was of the greatest priority."

Regan frowned and her lips twisted. "It blows my mind that some random guy would have an entire medical staff and surgical room available to him."

Caius' handsome face brightened with an amused smile at her comment. "All will be revealed to you in time. Tell me. How are you sleeping?"

287

"Besides being sedated every night?" Regan glared to Constantine.

"Constantine informed me that you had a nightmare earlier. You called out Daniel's name."

Wincing, Regan looked away and slumped back into her chair wishing the deep structure would suck her in. "I've had many."

"What are the themes of your nightmares?"

"I remember seeing David stabbing Daniel, and not just once but many times. There was so much blood. Daniel tried to hold on to me when I was hanging over the balcony. He really tried. But I think I fell when his grip gave way. That's all I remember till I woke up here. Even then, what I did remember were just broken bits and pieces."

Caius gave a nod as he shifted within his chair, and his long legs, clothed in pressed slacks of beige, crossed over one another at the knee. "You went through quite the ordeal. I'm not surprised that you are having memory issues after your fall. Your psyche is needing to heal, not just your body. You took a decent knocking to the back of the head, and you were unconscious for a while. Your doctor is confident that your memory will return in time."

Regan stared at the extremely handsome man with bright green eyes and crisp features. He didn't look over fifty even though there was an air of wisdom and age about him mixed with a hint of danger. Something in his eyes, some dark and twisted shadow, made her skin crawl. Shivering, Regan pressed back into the chair. The man frightened her, but she wasn't sure why.

"Are there any more questions I can answer for you?"

"Yes,' she replied, 'why am I here? Why hasn't anybody called the police about David? Also, where is my cousin Joyce?"

Caius glanced to Constantine who came to his side, bending close to whisper into his ear. Regan narrowed her eyes, watching the two men comment quietly before Caius turned his eyes back to her.

"You are here so you can heal properly. The police have been notified and are doing their duty to their fullest, investigating David's involvement in a home-grown terrorist ring based here in London. Scotland Yard has been searching for him for over a decade now. Your cousin, I'm afraid, is still missing."

A heavy frown fell upon her lips. "I don't understand. How could Joyce be missing? I saw her there. She spoke to me, and I heard her voice outside the cell David had kept me in. She was pleading with him not to hurt me and said something about making us a family. She wanted David to make me like her, whatever that meant."

Caius' eyes narrowed and his face seemed to draw tight. "There is evidence that she had been in the factory,' replied Caius in a smooth transition with an equally smooth voice, 'but when the police went to locate her, she was nowhere to be found. Her location at this moment is unknown."

Regan went on to speak once again, her lips parting, but then falling quiet when the man raised a hand. "I know you have a plethora of questions, but this is not the time to delve in to all of them. In time, and when you are a little more stable, we shall speak some more."

Caius smiled to her, and Regan felt a sliver of ice pierce her heart. "I have one more question." The man nodded and she inquired, "When can I see Daniel? I need to know that he's okay, that he's alive."

Once again, Constantine leaned to whisper to Caius. Regan wasn't sure what was going on, but she had the sudden feeling that she was on the outside of a very large secret and that secret was her. She frowned upon feeling her heart plummet into her stomach.

"Daniel Thorn is doing well. I can assure you. In fact, I have spoken to Kain Thorn of your recovery. He has assured me that he will pass on your progress to Daniel."

"That's not good enough. I want to speak to Daniel."

The fine man dressed in a tailored suit smiled to the mortal. "Regan,' he said softly, sympathetically, 'Daniel did not end his battle with David without his own injuries. He and Rhain will need time to recover and heal."

"So they're in a hospital?"

"Not exactly."

Regan scowled, her forehead furrowing into fine lines of deep confusion. "If they're hurt, they need a hospital."

"They are at a private clinic, not a hospital."

"I just want to know he's alright."

"And you will. Soon."

There came a knock upon the door. "Enter!" called Caius, and on his order the doors opened and an elderly man dressed as if he was a butler came in carrying a silver tray and a tea-set.

The older gentleman said not a word as he stepped to a table where the tray was place. With a nod to Caius, he turned and left the room.

"I've had some tea brought for you," he motioned Regan to the tray that also held a plate of simple pastries. "Please stay and enjoy the pastries. If you'll excuse me, I must see to some private business."

Regan didn't want any tea. She wanted answers and she wanted Daniel. But it seemed that she had little choice on the matter when Caius and Constantine both departed the room without a single word to her, and when the door closed behind them, she closed her eyes and curled up in the chair.

Out in the hall, with the door closed, Constantine turned to Caius to level the Rex with a guarded eye and said with a bite of judgment to his voice, "Was it wise to tell her of Daniel's condition? She is a smart girl, for a Humanus. She knows that we are keeping information from her."

Caius snorted, ignoring the glare from his Lieutenant - for now. "I gave her enough information to answer her questions at this time. She must stay in her confusion so I can handle this situation correctly without her human curiosity getting the better of her. It is all about controlling her, thus controlling this state of affairs."

"What did you tell Kain Thorn?"

"I told him what he needed to hear and what will keep Daniel at bay."

Constantine slid his glance to the closed door. "And the human? What is so special about her that she must be here?"

Caius arched a slender brow as he regarded his Lieutenant curiously as if there was more to Constantine's questions than just his own interest for the girl. "She is none of your concern, Constantine. Your job is to make sure she is kept in line, safe and compliant, till I can confirm my suspicions with the bloodwork sent to my Consiliator."

A tick formed in a sleek muscle of Constantine's slender mouth. Before he could speak again, Caius added an explanation that Constantine did not need to have. "The genetic profile of her Proprietas has disclosed a very unique Maiores."

Constantine stared at Caius as if he wasn't sure of what he had just heard. What link was there in Regan's Proprietas that would perk Caius' interested, especially in a possible genetic lineage to any Lamia or Lamia Familia.

"Keep an eye on her," said Caius. "And Constantine?"

The cold Lamia tipped his head when Caius glanced back to him.

"Make sure she has some tea. She looks…tired."

Constantine crossed a slender arm across his chest and pressed a closed fist over his heart as he offered a curt bow to his General and replied proudly, "Hail, Rex."

~ ~ ~ ~

"Regan is doing well then?" asked Kain the next night and from the privacy of Theodore's personal office. Daniel and Rhain had yet to awaken from their sedative induced Meditatio, so he was allowed some time to speak to Caius again on Regan's condition without the twins hounding him, especially Daniel.

"Yes. She has been doing very well, actually, and is responding to treatment. She has been receiving Elder Sanguis, and the infusions have helped her recover quickly from the surgeries she has had to endure in order to repair the multiple breaks she suffered."

Kain released a held breath, and his heart fell into his stomach. "Surgeries? Daniel will not be pleased."

"Perhaps not, but the surgeries were required. No exceptions."

"I understand. Thank you for your care. When will you be releasing her, Caius?"

"There are a few more tests that my doctors need to run as soon as she wakes. She is sleeping now."

"Has she said anything? Remembered anything?"

"Not yet. It seems that she has been having difficulty collecting her memories due to the concussion she suffered as a result of her fall. However, she was reliving distorted sections of her traumatic captivity through her dreams. Due to these night terrors, she has been lightly sedated during her sleep."

"Sedated?" A frown formed on Kain's lips as he sat heavily to the desk chair. "Her nightmares are so bad that she must be sedated? Daniel will not approve, and I wouldn't blame him as I'm not comfortable with this. The poor girl doesn't need to be doped-up."

"Unfortunately, her emotional and mental states are not as strong as her body. My physicians are monitoring her and treating her as needed."

Kain cursed under his breath as he ran a hand through his blood-red hair. Daniel wasn't going to be happy with this news - not one damn bit - and would no doubt voice his opinions in the form of intense rage. "My brother will want to see his Socia as soon as possible."

"Of course. When she is doing better, I will arrange for a visit. Regan has inquired as to Daniel's injuries. Are your brothers doing well?"

"Yes,' said Kain, 'they're healing, surprisingly. They both took a beating. Daniel mostly."

Caius was heard blowing out a whistling sigh. *"I am very sorry for what David put you and your family through, Kain. I hope his death by your brother's hand has brought you a taste of revenge."*

"I care little for revenge. I want my brothers to heal and Regan to be safe and returned to us." There was a moment on the phone when silence fell. Silence that Kain wasn't too sure he was comfortable with. Caius going silent was never a good thing, and it made Kain very uncomfortable. "Caius?"

"Forgive me. It seems that I found myself lost in my thoughts."

Kain's coal-black eyes narrowed. Caius never lost his thoughts. The man lived in his own world of self-control. "When will Regan be permitted to leave?"

"Within the coming days. I will contact you when she is ready to depart my home and my care."

"I would appreciate that. I will come to retrieve her myself."

"That is not necessary. I will have Constantine see to her return when she is able to. I do not want to take any chances that David's followers may be watching for her."

Kai nodded in agreement. "Very well."

"By the way. You need to instruct your brothers to remain at Theodore's till they hear from me. Word on the wind is that a few of David's supporters have discovered the identities of his killers and have launched their own Venatio on your brothers. They should remain in seclusion till I have handled this situation publically."

"I'm not surprised. How long?"

"I meet with the Concilium today to inform them of David's demise, if they have not heard already. There are many Senators who have been baying for David's life for decades, centuries truthfully. I would expect the Concilium to deliver medals to your brothers."

Kain snorted.

"I must go. Thank your brothers on my behalf for dispatching David. We will speak later. Ave."

"Ave." The word slipped from Kain's lips in a disconnected mumble when the call ended. Something, he wasn't quite sure what, dragged ice through his body in the form of a cold warning. He wasn't sure what he was sensing, but he had the sinking feeling that there was trouble brewing and that Caius wasn't telling him the full truth.

Regan belonged with Daniel. She was his Socia, and it was his duty to protect her and the Proprietas she carried. Caius was sly, very sly, and as the Consanguine Rex, he was always planning and scheming. Nothing the Rex did ever came without consequences or compensation, even acts of kindness. Just what was Caius playing at? What secrets was he keeping?

Shaking his head, Kain pushed from the chair and left the room. He had to speak to Daniel, and with each step he took, he prepared himself for his brother's anger.

~ ~ ~ ~

"No." Daniel shook his head once again as he turned to pace the same line he had tracked across the living room carpet eight times now. "I want her back. Now."

Kain sighed while watching his brother walking back and forth from shuttered window to couch then back again. Daniel was agitated, and rightfully so, but he was growing even more agitated with every passing minute. Though his body had healed well with the aid of Greg, enhanced Sanguis, and the repair to his wounds, Daniel's mental state was not recovering as quickly as Kain had hoped, or liked for that matter.

Rhain had reported that Daniel was still experiencing some troubles during the Meditatio and had woken Rhain a few times with his mumbles and disoriented sleep-talk. Both Kain and Rhain were very worried that Daniel's emotional state, the unease in knowing Regan's condition and the dramatic violence he endured beneath David's assault, were all leading him closer and closer to the Desiderium, a condition where a Lamia became dangerously out of control due to the overburden of ailments on the body and the psyche.

Rhain, reclining in a chair by the crackling fire, looked from Daniel then to Kain then back to his twin. He could feel, no, he could taste the anger radiating from Daniel and it made his skin prickle with nervousness.

"I know you want Regan with you,' Kain said in his calm and collected voice, 'but Caius is right. She needs as much recovery as possible. His doctors are still running a more few tests and are monitoring her after her surgeries."

Daniel snarled and jabbed a finger to his brother. "They had no right to operate on her without my consent!"

Kain arched a brow. "They had every right, Daniel. She needed the surgeries, and the Rex does not need your permission to treat any within his care." When Daniel curled his lips and began his pacing once again, Kain sighed and shrugged his shoulders. "Honestly, I would rather her cleared of all ailments and injuries before she returns to us. Wouldn't you be? She needs to be of sound mind when she is faced with the knowledge of what has truly happened to her and what will become of her."

Kain leveled Daniel with a dark glare. "Have you even considered the fact that if she does stay with you and go through the Domare that the Concilium might want to speak to her on this matter?"

292

"Why should they? You told me Caius will handle the Concilium."

"Yes,' Kain said with a nod, 'but that doesn't mean there will not be questions on their mind. They have a right to an official inquiry even if Caius shakes their political hands. The Senators will want to secure their own hands in this matter. If there is any investigation in the future, we will need Regan to have a clear head."

"Are you trying to tell me that Regan is having a psychotic break?"

"Caius is concerned that her psyche may be more damaged than she is letting on, given her nightmares."

Daniel's eyes narrowed and a low rumble sounded as he turned his back.

"Speaking of mental health,' muttered Rhain with a jerk of his head nonchalantly to his twin, 'somebody's walking the edge."

Daniel stopped, eyeing both his siblings. "Piss off," he snapped then began to pace again.

Rhain whistled with a skeptical look to Kain who had squared his shoulders and his jaw.

"Daniel," grunted the eldest brother. "Tell me you have control over yourself."

Daniel flipped a hand, dismissing Kain's concern with the flash of a single finger.

That wasn't the answer Kain wanted. With corded muscles shifting beneath black jeans and a decorative t-shirt of silver, he stood then reached out to grab Daniel by the sleeve as he stalked by him. "I'm talking to you, Daniel Rhys Thorn."

With a sharp snarl and a flash of fangs, Daniel spun on Kain, slapping away his hand and striking out with a balled fist. "Give me Regan!"

In one smooth move, Kain twisted Daniel about then slammed him down onto the table behind them. The wood cracked when Kain slammed him down once again with a quick jerk. "Control yourself!"

Giving a shout, Kain leaned down to Daniel, snapping his own fangs, and barking, "Do not make me restrain you, Daniel! I will not have you walking the edge right now. Not now!"

Rhain was on his feet and slowly approaching the two with cautious, calculated steps. He stopped when a voice coughed. The room went still, very still, and all three men turned their eyes to the door. Theodore didn't look too pleased at the mishandling of his table as he eyed the three brothers with a warning glare.

Kain drew back from Daniel, hissing and turning his back so Rhain could step forwards, grabbing his twin by the arm to pull him up. Daniel looked disoriented, confused and shaken.

"Is this a good time to remind you three of whose house you are taking refuge in?" asked Theodore as he stepped forwards, lacing his hands behind his lean back. The man's handsomely aged face curved in to set lines of annoyance. "That table is over two hundred years old." He flicked fingers to the twins. "Older than you two. I would ask that you take care of my furniture."

It was Rhain who gave a lopsided grin and muttered, "Sorry. Kain doesn't know his own strength."

Kain snorted, and Theodore didn't seem too sure on the statement either. "Kain, your Socia is looking for you. And Rhain, your mobile's been ringing nonstop for the last two hours. Would you mind answering it before I toss it in the garbage disposal? Your ringtone is rather offensive to my ears."

"Fine,' Rhain threw up a hand as he strolled casually to the door, casting Theodore a snarky grin, 'but there's nothing wrong with a little Dark Waters. It enlightens the soul." He clapped the Elder on the shoulder as he stepped into the hall.

Theodore shook his head, turning his attention to the remaining brothers. "Kain, Amber is insistent on speaking to you."

The eldest brother curled his lips with a dangerous glare tossed to Daniel. Without a word, he turned on his heels and stalked from the room.

When Kain departed, Theodore slowly shut the office door. Daniel wouldn't look at him, just kept staring at the floor. He looked like a child caught with his hand in the cookie jar. One arm was wrapped about his torso to hold a hand to his other arm and strands of his long hair curtained his face that Theodore was sure looking very troubled.

Clearing his voice, the Elder crossed the room to a small bar where he fixed a whiskey on the rocks, extra Sanguis. "Daniel,' he stated when he turned about, 'take a seat. Let's talk."

Raising his black eyes, streaked with red lines, Daniel gave a slight nod then quietly moved to a chair to sit.

"Here. Drink this."

Daniel took the offered glass in silence, and Theodore frowned upon seeing the glass shake just enough to cause the small cubes of ice to clink. Taking a breath, the Elder sat to a chair. "I take it that Kain had a good reason to lay you flat?"

Frowning, Daniel leaned forwards with elbows resting to his parted knees. The ice clinked again.

"Drink up and tell me what the bloody hell is happening to you."

Minutes later and Theodore was chuckling under his breath. Daniel looked even more confused than earlier. He wasn't sure whether the other man's laughter was positive or negative.

"My dear boy,' laughed Theodore with a shake of his head, 'you're not going mad with the Desiderium - not yet. Your confusion is based upon one simple fact."

Daniel blinked with brows furrowed.

"You're in love. You're infatuated with this young woman. You're immobilized by her." When the other Lamia looked away, Theodore inquired gently, "Have you ever been in true love, Daniel?"

Daniel looked as if he would answer but the words never came out. His frown only deepened. He looked down to give a shake of his head.

"No wonder you're bloody confused. Love is a difficult emotion for us men to understand, even more so since we are Lamia." Theodore smirked as he glanced to an old portrait of his wife, David's mother that hung upon the wall of his office. "As men, we are already cursed in trying to discover the key

294

to being in love with a woman, or a man, if that is your preference. Making the painful discovery that we truly are in love can be very hard for us to handle, almost shocking. In the end, we can become confused and unsure of ourselves, even frightened."

After taking a long draw of his whiskey, Daniel licked his lips and said softly, "I didn't expect to fall in love with her, Theodore. One moment I was asking her for coffee and then next I was picking up my sword again in the name of Venatio. When I was told of David taking her, I felt nothing but boiling rage. It calmed when Rhain and I went on the Venatio - all for her."

Daniel bowed his head and ran a single hand through his hair. "It's my fault she's in the condition that she is in. It's my fault that she experienced such brutality at the hands of David. And it's my fault that she almost met her death. If I had just turned away from her that night at the club, she would not have been involved in David's desire to destroy my family. And maybe Joyce would not have been changed. They both would be safe and happy."

"Is that what you think?" asked Theodore with a tip of his head. "You think that if you had not intervened when my son first approached Regan that she would be safe and her cousin still human?" The man snorted with a shake of his head. "One thing about my son, the bastard was stubborn. Whether he used Regan or another human or another tactic against you, David would have found his tool of battle against you and your brothers."

"But why Regan?" asked Daniel as he turned his eyes to the Elder. "Why did David have to choose her as his tool?"

"Fate."

Daniel's black eyes blinked as his handsome, almost feminine features knitted. "Fate? I don't think I understand."

"Our society, our race, our traditions, and our history are based upon the reasoning that the old Fates cursed the Familia of the Prima Lamia. With that known, do you think that in our everyday relationships that Fate does not play a part?"

"I've never thought about it all that way."

"You and Regan have been Fated to be together. You two are your Destiny. That is why all of this has fallen into perfect progression. You were Fated to be at the club that night as was Regan and her cousin, even David. You three were Fated to come together. Every decision you've made and every choice she has made have all been made because they were to be made."

Theodore chuckled. "You cannot blame yourself for the results of Fate."

Daniel looked away. "Is that why I love Regan to such a degree that every moment I think of her, every second I see her face or hear her voice my Daemon stirs, and I feel my control slipping? Again?"

"Kain told me of the violence that David suffered under your hands. I don't blame you for letting your Daemon come out to play and end David's destructive ways. David pushed you. He forced you into a corner, hoping that you would react the way you did. His mistake was thinking he could battle you, bring out your Daemon, and survive."

The man snorted in disgust. "He was always a fool."

"So what now?" Daniel asked. "I don't even know what to do now. I want to speak to her. I want to see her. She's probably scared. She doesn't know where she is or who is around her. I want Regan to know that everything is alright and that I'm sorry I can't be there for her right now. I want to be. I want to be at her side so badly, but I can't."

"That is understandable, Daniel,' said Theodore with a comforting smile upon his aged face, 'and I am sure that Regan would be thrilled to hear from you. Now doubt she needs to hear from you." He raised a placating hand and spoke clearly with his next words so that Daniel would not misinterpret the underlined importance of caution. "But you must remember that she is human and has no knowledge of your true self or our race. You must be extremely careful how you proceed with this matter from now on."

"I just need to know she's safe and that she doesn't hate me, doesn't fear me."

"She loves you, boy. She'll never hate you. She'll never fear you as long as you are honest with her once you find the specific moment when you're able to reveal your true self, safely and with no repercussions."

Daniel looked hopeless. "When will I know that time?"

Theodore shrugged his shoulder. "You'll know."

"What if my Daemon comes back and I can't control it? I swung at Kain. I've never swung at him unprovoked. Rhain's the one who throws punches without a care." Fear crept through Daniel's soft eyes; a glance of panic tossed to Theodore. "I can feel it pawing at me, and I can hear its cackling laughter echoing within my mind with pride over what it had done to David. It wants more. More violence. More blood."

Theodore sympathized with his friend - he truly did. He also didn't want to see Daniel's Daemon raise its ugly head in his own home. "Would speaking to Regan give you strength enough to control your Daemon till you are able to see her again?"

Daniel's eyes went bright. "Yes,' he gave a quick nod, 'most certainly, Theodore."

The Elder gave a nod and rose from the chair, clapping Daniel on the shoulder as he walked to a small table. "I'll make a call to Caius, pull some strings."

"You would do this for me?"

"Love is a precious commodity to our kind, Daniel," said Theodore as he glanced back to the younger Lamia. "It should never be squandered. Besides, who am I to walk all over Fate?" He cast Daniel a wink then swept a hand to the door. "Now get out and go apologize to your brother before you three revolt in my home! I'll come find you after I speak to Caius."

Daniel chuckled, tossed back the rest of his Sanguis tainted whiskey then stood from the chair. He offered the Elder a respectful bow, and without a word he rushed from the room.

Theodore chuckled then sighed as he looked up to the portrait of his wife. "Well, my dear, it looks as if this life of mine is not over yet. Do me a favor. Find our son and take care of him. He never knew what it felt like to be loved, maybe now he can find some peace in your love. Tell him I'm sorry for not being there for him, and tell him…"

He paused with a dry sigh as a single drop of crimson skimmed down his cheek. "Tell David that I never stopped loving him."

~ ~ ~ ~

*N*ight had once again settled across London and thirty-seven hours had passed since her arrival at Caius' home. Regan had just finished a simple dinner of miso soup and sautéed tofu when Constantine walked into her room. At least he knocked this time, yet still he refused to await permission to enter. He strolled forwards as if he owned the room. He acted like it, commanding attention with his very presence.

Setting down her glass of water, she looked away from the window she was seated at so she could regard the ever formal and ever stoic man. "At least you learned to knock," she muttered.

Constantine, with his eyes locked upon Regan, crossed the room to stand at the table showing no hint of amusement at her jibe. He ran his eyes over the young woman then to the empty bowl and plate. "You have eaten I see."

"Yes."

Reaching out, he took hold of her chin, turning her features back to him. Regan had grown used to him doing so every time he showed up, and no longer fussed or complained. "How are you feeling tonight?"

"A little tired. I'm feeling stronger than this morning."

He nodded curtly then motioned to the phone on the desk. "You have a call waiting for you."

"A call?" Regan perked, her eyes going wide as she scooted back her chair and hobbled over to the phone. With her weakness slowly dissipating, she no longer needed the support of another to move. The leg brace aided her on its own. Constantine glanced over his shoulder, watching her approach the desk where she fumbled for the phone's receiver.

The moment Regan picked up the phone a voice came over the line inquiring, *"How may I direct your call?"* She replied, "I'm Regan Scott. I was told there is a call for me."

"Please hold."

Soon after, the most beautiful voice came across the line, instantly soothing Regan's heart. *"Sweetheart?"*

"Daniel!" Mewing, Regan sat heavily to the desk chair. "Is it really you?"

"Yes. It's me."

"I'm so relieved to hear from you. I've been so worried about you. Caius told me you were in a medical clinic, you and Rhain. He said you two were injured." Her voice dropped and she whimpered, "Are you okay, Daniel?"

"I'm doing much better, Sweetheart. I've healed from much worse." Daniel's voice paused before speaking once again. *"Kain spoke with Caius earlier. He mentioned that you were having difficulty recuperating and that you've been having nightmares."*

297

Regan frowned, her eyes darting to Constantine to see him standing next to the table and looking as if he wasn't paying attention, but she knew he was. She knew he was listening to every little word she was saying and was memorizing it all. She turned her back to him and covered her mouth with a hand, trying to act sneaky. She swore she saw him glare.

"I've been very frightened, Daniel, and very confused. I keep reliving little bits and pieces of what happened to me. I don't remember much, but what I do remember is shadowy at best." Drawing in a deep breath, she leaned down in her chair. "The last thing I remember was David stabbing you. I remember you saying something to me then letting me fall, but that's it. I guess my dreams were getting so bad that I've given a few sedatives in my tea."

Regan glared towards Constantine, but the man just ignored her truthful accusation.

"You've been sedated?" Daniel snapped on the other end of the phone and sounded as if the admission was news to him, *"Who sedated you, Regan? Tell me."*

"I don't know who exactly,' she grumbled to Constantine, 'but I have a pretty good guess."

Constantine narrowed his sky-blue eyes but said nothing.

"I'm sorry, Regan. I'm sorry for all of this. It's all my fault. Everything that's happened to you and your cousin has been my fault."

Regan frowned and shook her head. "No, Daniel. Please don't say that. David acted on his own. He made his own choices for his own reasons. You can't be held responsible for his actions."

Daniel was heard sighing on the other end. *"There's so much I want to tell you, so much I need to say to you. However, I'm unable to do so at this time. I know you must have many questions that need answering, but you'll have to wait a little bit longer before I can answer them. I need to handle a few important matters on my end. Can you do that for me? Can you wait a few days?"*

"Wait? No,' Regan whimpered as fresh tears prickled her eyes, 'I want to leave this place, and I want to be with you. I don't want to be here anymore. I don't like it here, Daniel. This place frightens me."

"You're in a very safe place, sweetheart. I know that Caius can be very overwhelming and Constantine is no doubt being a prat, but you must get better before you can be released. Caius will not release you from his care till he is certain you have recovered well enough that you won't be stumbling into a backwashed street hospital."

Regan sighed, and Daniel went on to say softly, *"I know this isn't easy on you. None of this has been easy on you. You've gone through so much. All I want to do is be there with you, hold you in my arms, and tell that everything will be alright. You must forgive me, Regan. I meant for none of this to happen. You mean so much to me, and I can't bear the thought of you being upset with me, even hating me. Though I would understand..."*

"Don't be an idiot, Daniel. You came, risking your own life, to save me. You and Rhain both put yourselves in harm's way for a girl you hardly know. How can I be mad at you? How can I hate you?"

"Because my actions put you in grave danger. My actions alone brought David into your life, and in doing so, took your cousin from you. Knowing I had a hand in that..."

"Miss. Scott."

Regan raised her eyes when Constantine spoke her name. He had walked closer to her and was now standing a few feet away, staring at her with his impassive eyes.

"You have a medical appointment in a few minutes. We must be going."

She sighed softly, cursing under her breath. "Daniel? Constantine is reminding me that I have a medical appointment I need to get to."

"A medical appointment? What type of appointment? Are you sick? Are you hurt?"

"I think it's just a checkup for the surgeries,' she replied with a slow shake of her head, 'but I'm always having more and more blood drawn, and nobody's telling me why. I'm feeling much better today and slowly getting my stomach back. I'm not as weak or off balance as I had been, but I'm being poked and prodded left and right. I'm not sure what's going on, but I know I don't like it."

"Only a few more days, sweetheart. Then you're coming to my home where I can see to your safety. I'll take care of you. Can you wait a few more days?"

Regan smiled softly and nodded. "Yes. I think I can. If you'll call me tomorrow and the next day and the next day."

Daniel chuckled warmly on the other end of the line. *"I'll do that, on the dot. You just rest, and if Constantine gives you any trouble, tell him he'll have to deal with me."*

A devious grin was offered to Constantine from Regan. She liked the idea of Daniel coming to her aid and putting the pompous man in his place. "I'll certainly do that. I need to go. Daniel? Could you do me a favor?"

"Of course. Anything."

"Tell Rhain thank you for me. I know he did his best to find Joyce. But please tell him, from the bottom of my heart, that I appreciate everything he's done. I know he was hurt, badly. I didn't want that to happen."

"No one wanted to be hurt, sweetheart. I'll make sure to tell him."

"Thanks. One last thing."

"What's that?"

"I love you, Daniel."

"I love you too."

XIX

I can't sleep. I can't eat. I can't even think. I can't do anything without her.

Knowing she's away from me, even though she is safe, is driving me into a darkening circle of depression. I cannot help but worry for her. Caius is seeing to her safety and to the healing process that Regan will need to go through in order for her body to heal due to severity of her injuries. I want to be there with her so she need not be alone and with strangers.

I also want to tell her that David is dead, and that he can no longer torment her, haunt her dreams, or terrorizer her.

I can't imagine what she is going through, physically, emotionally, and mentally. Her soul must be teetering on the edge of sorrow and there is no one there she knows to catch her when she finally falls. I should be there. I should be the one to catch her. I should be the one to hold her and comfort her. I should be the one who tells her that all will be fine and that she is safe and never again would she have to leave my side.

She is my Socia, my lover. I am all she has in London now - at least till Joyce is found. If Joyce is found. I am the only one who can watch over her till she decides on the path of her future - our future.

Protecting my Socia falls upon me as my sworn duty. I've already failed Regan once. I cannot fail her again, not when she needs me the most.

She is my fate.
She is my destiny.
She is my soul, my very breath, and my heart.
Regan is everything.

-   *Daniel Rhys Thorn*

~ ~ ~ ~

Two nights had passed before the Rex gave Rhain and Daniel permission to leave the Servilii Templum, however, only after the discovery was made that a few of David's associates had put out a 'hit' on the Thorn twins. There had also been a threat on the Thorn Domus that was investigated and handled. The Rex made a public statement of David's death at the hands the Rex's personal Legati after a Venatio had been granted by the Concilium of England, and with him as the Rex and many Senators hungering for David's destruction, none argued or questioned the truth to his words. With the statement given attention was drawn away from Daniel and Rhain, but it would take a few months for the ripple of disturbance to calm within the Underground.

During his stay at Theodore's, Daniel had only been able to speak to Regan once. Though he had tried to reach her, each time his call was thwarted by Constantine and some excuse as to why Regan was indisposed of. More and more tests were being run on Regan, and that began to worry Daniel. It wasn't long till Daniel figured out that the Lieutenant was giving him the run-around, purposefully blocking Daniel's every attempt at contacting his Socia. Eventually, his calls went unanswered.

Once he and Rhain were permitted to leave the Templum, Daniel was relieved to be able to recover Regan, but Caius thwarted him once again by claiming that Regan was not yet ready to leave his care. There was no further explanation, only a direct order for the Twins to return to their Domus and await further communication from him. The notice stated that Regan was doing better, that she wished Daniel not to worry about her, and that she would be returning to the flat owned by Joyce in a few days.

Daniel's return home felt nothing like the joyous occasion it should have been. Though Rhain was thankful to be back, Daniel felt as if he was stepping into a prison. He wanted nothing to do with anybody, family or employee. He went directly to his room where he locked the door and turned off the lights.

All he wanted to do was see her. He wanted to rush off to the Royal Domus, crash through the doors, and demand he be allowed to see his Socia. Screw Caius and Constantine and their rules. It was his right to see to Regan's needs and be there for her care. What was wrong with that? Caius could still have his medical staff continue their treatment at Daniel's home. They shouldn't mind as it would offer Regan comfort and a sense of familiarity to remove her distress. To be denied access to his Socia angered not only him but his simmering Daemon as well.

Nothing could be said, or done, to ease the internal pain Daniel was feeling as the minutes turned to hours and the hours turned to days. He refused to speak to his brothers or to Amber and took Pixie into his room as his own source of comfort. He was called to meals, offered food and drink and Sanguis, but he refused all offerings. Worry spread through the family members, and soon Kain was demanding Daniel open the door to his room. Even with the threat from Kain, Daniel remained in seclusion, waiting with growing impatience for Regan to call him.

Eventually, three days after returning home, his family had enough of his sulking and increasingly depressive mood. Neither Amber nor Kain could get through to Daniel, so it was Rhain who stepped up to bring his twin back to reality. With a bottle of Sanguis in one hand and a plate with two slices of Amber's home-made veggie pizza in the other, Rhain knocked on the door of Daniel's room with a foot. When a few seconds passed without any response, he 'knocked' again, kicking a little louder.

"I know you're in there," he called, nudging the door once again. "Open up, Frater. You're hungry and I have food."

"Go away!"

301

Rhain scowled to the bark from within the room and shrugged. "I can't do that, Daniel. I've been given an order to check on you, so you better open this door before the big bad wolf of a big bad brother comes and blows your door in."

"Piss off."

"This pizza is getting cold, you git. You haven't eaten in days, nor have you had any Sanguis. I know you're hungry. Hell, my stomach's having sympathy growls to yours. You don't have to eat the pizza, just let it sit there and stare at you. Come on, be a good brother and open the door."

A few more seconds passed when the soft click of the door's lock was heard unlatching. Rhain frowned when he saw nothing but darkness from within, thick and unwelcoming, and with the darkness came the stench of unwashed body. "Fuck," he muttered as he nudged the door open so he could enter then kicked it shut. "Have you showered lately?"

Though the room was pitch black, Rhain could make out Daniel's form inching back onto his large, antique bed. There was not a single light on and the security shutters were down making the room appear to be completely cut off from the outside world. Rhain sighed as he sat the plate and bottle down to a table he could see at his side. He turned on the small table lamp that sent a dull but sufficient light to penetrate the darkness.

Daniel hissed when the light struck him, so he curled to his side to hide his eyes in a pillow. Pixie sat up, wagging her un-brushed tail to Rhain as he stepped to the bedside. Shaking his head, Rhain looked about the disorderly room, frowning to the dirtiness that was strewn about. "What the hell happened in here? This isn't like you, Daniel." He grumbled as he picked up a shirt that had been tossed haphazardly to the floor. "My room isn't this bad, and that's saying something."

When Daniel didn't reply, Rhain scratched his head before he sat upon the bed, facing his twin. For a few minutes of silence he stared at his identical twin. "I can't imagine what you must be feeling,' he said softly, smiling as Pixie crawled into his lap, 'unable to see your Socia, even talk to her. You've got to be worried for her."

Daniel still didn't respond.

Stroking the Pomeranian's soft head, Rhain went on to talk to his twin as if Daniel was actually paying attention. If Daniel wanted to ignore him, that was fine, but he'd keep on talking. He was good at that, talking when nobody gave a shit to what he was saying.

"You know that she's safe and that she's being taken care of. Caius wouldn't be foolish enough to let her suffer after all she's gone through, that would put a damper on his next election. She has the Proprietas after all, and that makes her important, not only to him but to you and me and this family. She's a strong girl, for a human." Rhain chuckled as the tiny dog rolled over onto her back and kicked her front legs at his hand for a belly rub.

"I've never been in love," he went on to say, softer and with a touch of reflection to his voice. "I thought I was once, but I think that was heartburn. Kain thinks I'm incapable of feeling love or knowing what love is, but I know what it is. If I didn't, I couldn't love you or Kain as my brothers. So I know what you're going through, the fear and confusion. I've felt that a few times in

302

my life, most certainly the first time your Daemon showed. I almost lost you that night, and I vowed to never let another person I love be lost to me. That's why I would follow you into any battle, into any hole in hell, and into any cloud in heaven to make sure you were safe. And if I'm able to feel that, I know you're feeling the same for Regan right now."

"I would go through hell for her." Even Daniel's voice sounded dusty and raw.

Rhain lifted his black eyes, void of contact lenses, to regard his brother's coiled form. "I know," said Rhain softly and with a somber nod. "And I'm sure she'd go through hell for you too. In fact, I'm pretty sure she just did. You can't give up on her, not after all you two have gone through."

Daniel shifted just enough to look over his shoulder and past a few locks of stale hair. "Who said I was giving up on her?"

"Nobody." Rhain gave a shrug, watching Pixie wiggle about within his lap. "But it sure looks like you are, locking yourself away, taking no food, water, or Sanguis. At least you've remembered to feed your dog." Rhain picked Pixie up, her little back legs kicking out as she yipped. "He is feeding you, isn't he?"

The Pomeranian squirmed to try and lick his cheek.

Daniel scowled, tightened his arms against his chest then rolled away to stare angrily at a dark corner of his room.

"Come on, Danny." Rhain looked back to his twin, reaching out to touch a calf only to frown when he felt how cold Daniel was. "This isn't right, getting all depressed. It sure isn't healthy. The longer you go without taking any food or blood the closer you'll get to succumbing to your Daemon again. It's waiting," grumbled Rhain. "Even I can feel its distant presence dancing about with excitement. You can't let yourself fall into the abyss when you're so close, when you've come so far."

Giving a sigh when Daniel didn't respond, Rhain kicked off his shoes then stretched out on his back next to his brother. Locking his hands behind his head, he stared up at the ceiling. "I'm not leaving till you talk to me, or at least eat some damn pizza."

From next to him, Rain heard a disapproving grunt and the sound spread a grin to his lips. "I've got all night, Frater. And the next night, and the night after that. I'm not leaving your bed till you respond to me and give me what I want."

Rhain blinked then barked out a laugh as he glanced to his brother's back. "Wanna fuck?"

A faint snort of a laugh was heard then Daniel's cracked voice responded, "You always could break tension with some inappropriate and ill-timed joke."

Rhain shrugged, uncoiled an arm and poked his twin in the shoulder. "You're so cute when you're sulking."

"Bite me."

"Kinky."

Daniel sighed a deep and breathy sigh that raised and lowered his shoulders.

"By the way," stated Rhain as he poked his twin again for good measure. "Regan's back to the flat. Kain got the call not too long ago. So why do don't you suck it up, get your head out of your Daemon's ass, shower, and go see her."

"And say what?"

Rhain snorted a chuckle. "I don't know. You could always start with something simple like 'is everything okay?' or maybe 'would you like some tea?' You've waited almost a week to see her. Now's your chance, but you're going to squander the moment by staying here." Rhain turned his eyes back to the ceiling, his lips forming a scowl. "Some boyfriend you turned out to be."

"I'm not her boyfriend."

"You're right." Rhain raised himself up on his elbows, glaring at his twin's back. "You're her Socius, you moron. That makes you more important than some boyfriend. That makes you her protector, her lover, her confidant, and her provider. That makes you her life, Danny. That makes her yours and you hers."

Daniel narrowed his eyes then sighed as the heavy lids of his eyes closed beneath thick, black lashes. "What use am I to her when I can't even protect her?"

Snarling, Rhain reached over and slapped his brother upside the head. When Daniel cursed, holding his head and rolling to his side to glare, Rhain was right there in his face and glaring back. Daniel blinked in surprise when Rhain grabbed him by the collar of his shirt and hauled him closer. "You listen to me, you git. If you don't break out of this depression, I'm going to beat it out of you. I've done it before, so I have no reservation in doing it again. Mind you, I've gotten damn good at clobbering some sense into you just as you're good at beating some commonsense into me."

Rhain snorted as he ran his annoyed gaze over Daniel's pale and unshaven face, a few days-worth of stubble shadowing his handsome lines. "I never thought you'd be this pathetic, this weak because, of some girl. Maybe you're right. Maybe Regan doesn't deserve you because you can't handle being her Socius, you can't handle the responsibilities and you can't handle stepping up and taking control of the situation."

He shoved Daniel back, raking his twin with a calculating and judgmental eye. "Regan's expected a lot more from you. Have you bothered to think what she's going through right now, after being tossed back to the same flat where her cousin died, alone and with nobody to comfort her? Who knows what lies Caius has told her to warp her memories of what's happened to her. What if she's lost in her own fears, crying and begging you to come to her and make all this shit disappear? And all you can do is sulk in your fucking bed and feel sorry for yourself! Well done, mate. Well done."

Daniel narrowed his eyes and pulled back his lips to snarl. "I don't need your sarcasm right now."

"You're right," said Rhain, softer now as he reached out to wrap his brother in his arms, hugging him tightly. "You need your Socia, and she needs you. You need each other right now. You need to go to her and secure your place in her heart. Your Fate is waiting for you, but she won't wait long if she thinks you've abandoned her. What then, Danny? What will you do then?"

Daniel wasn't expecting his twin to hug him. Rhain wasn't the hugging type, neither was Kain, but there were times in the past when Rhain had embraced his brother when the need was there, when he knew Daniel desperately needed him, needed the familiar contact and stability that Rhain could offer. Sighing, Daniel leaned against Rhain's strength.

"I'm scared," he stated and in a voice that quivered ever so slightly. "I've never been scared like this before."

Rhain winced when he felt something wet slide down his neck. A tear. His brother was crying, and that single tear broke his heart. "Go to her. Go talk to her. Go listen to her. Go embrace her and tell her that you love her."

Shaking his head, Daniel drew back and wiped his hand across a stained cheek. "What if she thinks me a monster? I can't explain to her what happened with David, but she'll have questions. She'll want to know why she wasn't taken to a hospital and why you and I were not taken to a clinic. She'll want to know how one man like Caius can provide her all the care she has needed."

Daniel covered his face in his hands as a muffled groan was heard as he fell back upon the bed. "How am I to explain to her that vampires exist and that I am one? David already let fly the open book of truth, and now it's up to me to turn the pages for her. I've never had to do this before."

Rhain shrugged. "Make shit up as you go along. Sooner or later you're just going to have to deal with this and get it over with. Whether or not she believes you and trusts you is up to her. But think of it this way, with all she's seen and gone through, Regan would be daft to think you're crazy. So get a damn shower."

Rhain slid from the bed, stretching as he did so then bent to grab his shoes. "I'll drive you to the flat. I'll give you an hour. If you're not out of this room in an hour, I'm going to drag your ass over to Regan looking like you smell." He paused at the door, tossing his brother a serious look. "I'll do it. I will deliver you to her, unconscious if need be." He opened the door and raised a hand to present a single finger. "One hour."

Daniel frowned, feeling very uncomfortable that this matter was being forced upon him and that he had no choice in the speed of the progression. When the door shut, he looked to Pixie who stood up with her paws tapping against his arm. "I don't smell that bad, do I?"

The Pomeranian tipped her head then yipped.

Daniel sighed then forced his body to stand, pushing up from the bed upon unsteady legs. A wave of dizziness rocked his body and he sat back down with a thump. He was weak, and in his weakened state his stomach growled to the faint scent of vegetarian pizza that tickled his fancy. If he was going to confront Regan and all her questions, an event that might last all night, he would need a full stomach and a great deal of energy. The shower could wait, right now he needed his stomach filled and the warmth of fresh Sanguis coursing through his veins.

Within an hour, he was ready to face the woman he loved.

~ ~ ~ ~

It wasn't easy for Regan to step back into Joyce's apartment, not after all that had happened to her cousin and to her. Knowing that Joyce was still missing both worried and frightened Regan. She was worried that her cousin would never be found and frightened that Joyce might come back and still be wrapped up in David's control. If Joyce did come back, what would happen? If she did return, Regan hoped that Joyce would be better, to some degree, and that her obsession with David would have vanished.

The apartment was cold and dark when she walked in after unlocking the door, and a hard shiver ran her spine as the stale air rushed into her lungs. With a whimper, she stepped back only to yelp when a strong, yet gentle, hand came to rest upon her shoulder.

"It's alright. Take your time."

Regan wasn't so sure. Gulping, she glanced over her shoulder and to the imposing man who had followed her into the apartment. Caius Scipio had insisted on accompanying her to the flat, stating that he wanted to make sure she arrived safely and that he would not feel comfortable till she settled in. Though she was grateful for his offer, the presence of the man only added tension to the situation. She still wasn't sure what to think of him. Then again, she still didn't know anything about him besides the facts he was extremely wealthy and managed to hold a lot of power - whatever that power was exactly was still unknown to her.

Licking her lips, Regan stepped away from the tall man, fumbling off to the side to turn on the light to the sitting room. Once the apartment was bathed in light, she looked about as if the place was foreign and unwelcoming to her. Hugging her arms about her, she walked forwards till she saw Joyce's purse and phone still upon the table, where they had been left. A tight lipped whimper pushed up from her throat along with a trickle of tears slipping down her cheeks.

Caius, though he wasn't frowning, sympathized with her. After all, her cousin had died in the apartment and still the Filia's memories remained. The ghost of Joyce's humanity haunted the flat; Caius was certain about that. The handsome man, dressed in his tailored suit of black and red pin-stripes, stepped forwards and about the living room and kitchen, taking his time to observe the quaint surroundings that were, in his opinion, too modest. With his fine senses he could smell the last remains of Joyce's mortal blood clinging to the air.

Glancing to the side, he spoke to Regan in a tone of gentleness. "You still have the option of staying at my home till it is time for you to return to the States."

Regan looked up and shook her head. "No. I need to be here incase Joyce returns. She'll need me to look after her till she recovers from her ordeal with David."

Caius arched a brow. He had insisted that she stay with him, but Regan fought him at every turn. She swore that Joyce was out in London, lost and confused, but would eventually return to the flat. Regan wanted to be ready for Joyce's return, and if needed, Daniel had told her that she could stay with him. And though Caius wasn't pleased that Daniel had extended the offering to her, Caius couldn't force the human to stay with him, not till Regan was welcomed into the Lamia world - one way or another - for she had a very unique lineage to her Proprietas.

"Very well." The Lamia gave a polite nod of his head. "You have my number, correct?" Regan nodded and he smiled to her. "Good. Do not hesitate to call me if you need anything."

"I still don't understand what is going on. It's like I'm living in a dream and none of what's happened was real, one of those dreams that feels real but it is only a dream." She looked to Caius with a frown. "But it was real, all of it, wasn't it?"

"All of your questions will be answered in time, Miss. Scott."

"I wish Daniel was here. I don't understand why he hasn't called me. He said he would, every day, but he hasn't."

"I am sure he has his reasons. Now,' Caius stepped up to her, reaching out to tip up her face with a finger beneath her chin, 'why don't you get a hot bath, fix yourself some tea, and rest for the evening. It is late, and you are still recovering from your own ordeal."

As tempting as a bath was, Regan wanted to see Daniel more. Yet sadly, she knew trying to contact him would be useless. He wouldn't answer his phone. Obviously, if he couldn't keep to his word and call her to check up on her, then why would he bother answering his own phone? Such depressing thoughts only tightened Regan's sadness, her loneliness, and her apprehension that something was wrong with him. She hadn't done anything, had she? Or had he really believed David's lies? Did Daniel really think she would let scum like David do anything more than just touch her?

"I will call you tomorrow evening to check on you."

Snapping out of her darkening thoughts, Regan watched Caius walk to the door. He stopped and offered her a polite smile. "The offer is still upon the table, Miss. Scott. If you need a place to stay, you need only call me."

"Thank you,' she said honestly and with a little nod, 'but I don't think I could stomach any more of Constantine's lack of give-a-shit. I was close to throttling him with a pillow."

Caius chuckled, his handsome face tightening with amusement. "A solid pillow throttling might do him some good. Good evening."

When the door closed behind Caius, Regan didn't hesitate to lock it. The apartment felt cold, so cold, and distant as if she was a stranger within. Without Joyce, her attitude and her laughter, the apartment felt empty. Caius was right, Regan simply needed to warm herself up. He had told her in the car on their way over that she would feel this loneliness and that it was perfectly understandable, but it was up to her to push her distress away and find a focal point to calm herself.

That focal point was Daniel, or it had been. But now as the days passed and no word came from him, she was questioning if he had even been real or just a figment of her imagination.

Scowling, Regan stepped further into the apartment, stopping at the guest room to prepare a change of clothes. She paused at Joyce's room to shut the curtains while making a note to strip and wash the bed linen on the next day, then she progressed to the bathroom where she went about filling the tub with hot water. The bath was wonderful, the hot water coiling steam into the cool room as Regan sank down into the deep tub. Minutes passed, and soon Regan discovered her fingers were starting to prune, and though she didn't want to leave the soaking comfort of the lavender scented bubbles, she didn't want to shrink.

And so she forced herself from the tub, draining the water and drying herself off. After dressing in a fresh set of pajamas, a matching bottom and top of swirling pinks and blue colors, she shuffled into the kitchen to make herself a cup of tea. While the water was boiling about within the kettle, Regan dug into the freezer and pulled out a frozen dinner of macaroni and cheese, nothing special but it was something. While the stove warmed up, Regan made her tea then settled on the sofa to watch some TV drama. Her phone never left her reach, incase Daniel called. Within an hour the warmth of her dinner had replaced the vanishing warmth of her bath, and she was slowly drifting into sleep upon the couch.

Across the city, Daniel and Rhain rode in silence through the dark London streets, passing beneath flashing street lights and through a slight mist that drifted across the cooling streets. A faint rain had tumbled down from the dispersing clouds, not too long ago, and now left the heated cement to cool. With the clouds drifting away the sky was left to brighten and sparkle with the millions of stars that shown down from above.

Rhain, as he drove carefully through the streets, passed quick glances to his brother who sat staring out the window, chin resting atop a fisted hand. They hadn't spoken to each other when Daniel arrived in the garage to meet Rhain by his car. The silence grew heavier and heavier with each mile that passed by. But it wasn't long till they arrived at the flat, and Rhain slowed his expensive spots car the closer they drove to the building. After parking, he glanced out the window, leaning forwards just enough to look up in the direction of Joyce's flat.

"The lights are on. That's a good sign."

Daniel responded with a deep sigh as the leather of the seat groaned when he moved. He reached for the handle of the door but hesitated as the tight grip of dread coiled about his gut. "I don't think I can do this," he muttered, drawing his hand back to his lap.

Rhain groaned heavily, his forehead falling to the steering wheel. Without looking to his twin, he raised a hand and pointed at the passenger door while muttering, "If you don't get your ass out of this car, I will drag you by your hair to the front door of the flat."

Frowning, Daniel glanced to his twin with worry knitting his handsome face. His retort was at the tip of his tongue but Daniel selected to hold his tongue, and with a deep breath he exited the car. Rhain followed and stepped about to stand at his side.

The twins stared up at the apartment windows for a few seconds before Rhain drew in a breath of the street tainted air. "I don't think I smell anybody in the area."

"The rain would've washed away any lingering scents."

"Not directly." Rhain kicked at a piece of gravel on the street. "It doesn't look like this area got too much rain. Come on, let's go before Regan turns in for bed." He gave his brother a push forwards, walking behind him a step just to make sure that if Daniel made a break for it he'd be able to catch his twin quickly. Behind him, his car beeped.

Daniel felt sick, very sick, the closer he walked to the flat. A knot, large and vile, twisted within his throat till it lodged at the back of his mouth. Once he was at the front door of the building whatever internal strength of willpower he had disappeared. He stepped back only to collide with Rhain who pushed a hand to his back.

"Don't even think about it," muttered Rhain at Daniel's back as he pushed his brother forwards while reaching about to point at the call box on the panel by the door. "Push the button. If you don't, I will."

Daniel's throat felt both dry and tight, so very tight. But to Rhain's threat he swallowed the lump down his throat then gathered his courage to push the button beneath Joyce Scott's name. The buzzer rang…and rang…and rang. Nobody picked up, and for some reason Daniel felt his heart fall into his chest. He glanced behind his shoulder to Rhain and asked quietly, "Are you sure she returned here tonight?"

Rhain nodded. "Push the button again."

Daniel did as suggested and again the buzzer rang.

Upstairs, Regan was deep in her sleep when the doorbell sounded for the first time. It rang three times and not once did the soft bell wake her. However, upon the forth ring Regan snapped wide awake, twisting about on the couch and nearly falling to the floor. She rapidly stood up, stumbling over the coffee table with a yelp and hopping then to the door. A grunt pulled from her lips as she fell against the door and slapped her palm to the button on the call box.

She could hardly catch her breath. "Don't go!" Those were her words screaming past her lips as a panic laced breath tore from her lungs. "Please, don't go. I'll be right down!"

Keys! She needed keys to open the door downstairs, and for a moment she forgot where she put them. Scrambling, Regan located the keys then rushed out of the apartment. Hobbling down the stairs proved tricky as her legs were moving faster than her mind could place her steps, but she made it to the door safely. However, unlocking the door was not so easy. She fumbled for the keys, dropping them a few times before her fingers could grasp the right one.

From outside the door there came a soft, almost pitiful, chuckle followed by Daniel's voice speaking loud enough to be heard but gentle enough to sound sympathetic. "Slow down, sweetheart. Take a breath."

Regan paused, her eyes snapping upwards at the sound of Daniel's voice. Fresh tears shined within her warm eyes and goose-bumps exploded across her skin. "Daniel?" She stepped closer to the door and pressed a palm over the distorted glass. "Is that you?"

A shadowy hand appeared and touched the glass opposite of her own. Regan smiled as relief and happiness flooded her. "It's me. Rhain's here with me. We'd like to come in and speak to you, if that's alright," she heard Daniel say.

When she finally managed to unlock the door, she threw it open and in one move had her arms about Daniel's neck. The force of her embrace had him stumbling back, grasping her in order to steady himself. When he found his footing, he tightened his embrace - pulling her as close as he could.

Daniel curled his fingers against his Socia, one hand disappearing into her damp hair, as he nuzzled her hair with a cheek. He pressed kisses across her brow. "I'm so sorry," he muttered over and over again and in between the fluttering kisses.

A quiet cough from the side drew the lovers' attentions. Rhain was trying hard not to smirk, but his lips couldn't help form a devious grin. "Do you both mind we go inside? Public displays of affections aren't my thing." He jerked his thumb over his shoulder to the open door.

Drawing back, Regan chuckled and blushed when she saw Daniel's beautiful smile and his dark eyes glistening with amusement. She reached a hand up to touch her palm to his cheek, and when he closed his eyes and nuzzled her palm, she released a soft whimper. So many words were right there against her lips to be said but not a single one was formed.

Hearing her worried whimper and seeing her wet cheeks, Daniel drew her back into his arms and kissed the top of her head. "Let's go inside, shall we? We have a lot to discuss." He eased Regan back, laced a hand with hers then walked her into the building.

Rhain was the last to enter, and just as he closed the door a soft breeze brought to his attention a faint scent. He narrowed his eyes and drew back his lips with a slight hiss. So, a Lamia had been close by and not too long ago. Damn. The scent wasn't one Rhain had wanted to catch. Scanning the area, Rhain growled low in his throat, a growl that was both deadly and greatly displeased. "Caius…"

~ ~ ~ ~

Daniel couldn't let go of Regan, not even after the door to the apartment was closed. He clung to her as if his very breath depended upon it, and it seemed that Regan was not quick to let him go either. As they stood in the living room, embracing each other, Rhain declared he would make some tea just so he could get away from the sickeningly sweet reunion. Time seemed to slow, offering the reunited lovers some time before they were forced to pull apart. Regan couldn't stop crying, and even Daniel couldn't keep a thin tear of tainted red to slide down an alabaster cheek.

Frowning in confusion, Regan gently wiped away that tear. She stared at the red drop that stained her finger before looking up to Daniel. "What's going on, Daniel?"

He took her hand and wiped away the tear before sighing and motioning her to the sofa. "There's a lot to explain, Regan. Are you tired? I hope not because the answers that I have to offer you may take all night to tell."

Regan sat and Daniel came to sit at her side once he pulled his coat from his arms. He twisted to face her, offering her what comforting smile he was able to muster. "I'm going to let you guide this conversation, sweetheart. Ask one question at a time and I will answer appropriately. Start with the most important question to you."

Regan nodded and took a breath then asked, "Do you love me?"

Daniel blinked. He wasn't expecting that question to be the most important, not when he considered he had just cried a tear of blood and David reported him to be a vampire. But he didn't deny that such a question soothed his worry and warmed his heart. Reaching out with his deadly hands, Daniel cupped her face and leaned to kiss the corner of her lips.

Against her soft mouth he mumbled, "With all my heart. I love you, Regan."

Regan offered a kiss in return then gently pushed him back. And though he looked confused at the move, she smiled lovingly to him. "Then I can trust that you won't lie to me."

Daniel shook his head, his frown creasing even more that she would think he could lie to her. "Of course you can trust me. I wouldn't lie to you."

"He's too much of a moral prick to lie, Regan!"

Both turned their eyes to the kitchen to see Rhain biting into a cookie he had dug out of a package, no doubt discovered in a cupboard. He shrugged as he shoved the cookie into his mouth. Regan chuckled when Daniel hung his head in a look that was almost shameful, but she smiled again and brushed away a long lock of his black hair. The tender move brought his onyx eyes to lift, along with a lopsided grin.

Regan ran both her eyes and a fingertip over the gentle contours of Daniel's features. She inquired softly, "Why didn't you call me? I've been waiting for you to call me. Did you forget about me?"

Daniel's heart broke, and the actual break could be seen flashing across his face. "No,' he said as he shook his head, 'I could never forget you. I tried to call. I called as often as I could, but every time I reached through Constantine would tell me that you were indisposed with another medical appointment. After the fourteenth call, my calls went unanswered."

Regan's brows furrowed. "That's odd. Constantine told me that you had never called." She huffed and grumbled under her breath, "I knew there was a reason I didn't like him. He was lying to me, probably the entire time."

"Prick," mumbled Rhain in a cookie muffled grunt from the kitchen.

Regan smiled to Daniel, yet her smile wavered before turning to a little frown. "At least you tried."

"I would've come to see you, but I wasn't allowed to leave Theodore's home till I was properly healed."

Regan tipped her head, glancing to Rhain who shrugged his shoulders again. "I don't understand. Why weren't you able to leave?"

"It took longer for me to heal from my injuries. I wanted to see you so badly, but I could only call you and that was with the aid of Theodore Servilii. If it wasn't for him speaking to Caius on my behalf, I doubt the Rex would have permitted that single call."

"The Rex?"

Daniel slid his hands from his face, looking to Regan with a frown. "That's part of the 'lots to explain' part."

"Oh, I see." She shifted with a deep breath and nodded. "I really thought you had forgotten me. Constantine kept saying that you wouldn't care what happens to a little human. Why would he care what you feel towards me?"

From the kitchen came a loud and disgruntled snort. "Because the prick's an emotionally disturbed bastard who needs a swift kick up the ass!"

Ignoring his twin's shout, Daniel reached up a hand to thread fingers through her luscious hair. "Constantine should not be a concern to you right now."

"You're my only concern," she whispered through a breathy sigh and as she nuzzled her cheek to his shoulder. "You look sick and thin. Have you been eating?" Frowning, she poked at his thin chest with a finger.

Daniel caught her hand, lifting her fingers to his lips. "Not as much as I should be. I couldn't bring myself to doing much of anything. I was spiraling into a dangerous depression."

Depression? Regan shifted back, her hands falling to her lap. "Why were you depressed?"

"Because I couldn't do anything to help you. I couldn't see you, I couldn't speak to you, and I couldn't leave the clinic I was at to visit you. I felt useless and weak." Groaning, Daniel leaned to the back of the couch with his head tipping back and his hands setting over his face.

Regan's lips curled down to a frown and she grumbled with a slow shake of her head as she drew away, looking to him with eyes full of sympathetic sadness. "I'm sorry for doubting you."

"No one would blame you. I made a promise to you, but due to outside factors I wasn't able to follow through with my promise. However, I'm here now,' he stated as he reached for her, pulling her to him once more, 'and I won't leave till you have all your answers. So ask your next question."

She didn't fight him and curled intimately to his side with her head resting to his shoulder and a hand pressed against his chest. "I saw David stab you, over and over again. I saw the pain on your face, and I felt your blood against my skin. How can you be alive after what he did to you?"

Rhain blew a whistle as he walked about the couch, cookie package in hand, to take a seat in a chair across from them. He looked to his twin and gave a curt nod before gnawing on another cookie.

"I healed."

"How?"

312

"With some needed rest, some stitching, and a good amount of Sanguis."

Regan tipped her head. "What is Sanguis?"

"Blood."

She turned her gaze to Rhain with eyes slowly went wide. "Blood?"

"Yes."

The answer drew Regan's eyes to Daniel who was offering her an uneasy smile. "Are you serious?" He nodded and she groaned. "Show me."

"Excuse me?"

Regan reached for Daniel's shirt, untucking the dark material and lifting it up along his taut stomach. He shifted, giving a laugh as her fingertips brushed a ticklish spot.

"Maybe I should leave!" Rhain laughed and flashed a grin.

While fussing to keep his shirt down, Daniel glared to his twin before snagging Regan's hands. She grunted and glared but he smiled as he inquired, "You want to see some proof?" She nodded, and so he gently released his grip upon her hands so he could stand, then he began to unbutton his dress-shirt. It wasn't but a second after the material drifted from his shoulders that he heard Regan's sharp cry of alarm. Even Rhain winced as he looked upon his brother's mangled chest with a twist of compassion.

Daniel went to turn around, but his action was stopped when a delicately shaking hand pressed against his back. "Oh, my God," the Lamia heard Regan breathe out. "There must be more than fifteen wounds."

"Twenty eight to be exact," correct Daniel then sighed when Regan turned him about to face her. She gasped once again, quickly covering her mouth with her hands when she saw the twelve exit wounds stitched closed. He winced when she gingerly ran her touch on the outside of one of the wounds.

"How did you survive this?" she asked and with all seriousness tainted her question.

"A special blood-infusion. Probably the same concoction that was given to you."

"And peroxide. Lots and lots of peroxide," chirped Rhain with a laugh then a cough when Daniel glared at him.

"All of these...' Regan whispered, lowering her hands, 'were because of me."

Shaking his head, Daniel brushed the back of his hand across her cheek only to feel the caress of fresh tears against his skin. "No. Nothing that happened was because of you. As I said the other day in the guest suite, David is responsible for his actions, nobody else - especially you. If anything, you should blame me for getting you involved in all of this from the start. But that is water under the bridge, what we do now to move forwards is our responsibility. And that's why I am here, to find out how you want to move forwards."

Regan gulped and slowly slid her arms about his waist, pressing a cheek to his bare chest. Through the thin layer of his cool skin she heard the slow beating of his heart and found the retarded rhythm to be rather soothing. "Tell me everything. Don't leave out a single detail."

"Everything?" he asked and she nodded her head in confirmation. Licking his suddenly dry lips, Daniel glanced over his shoulder to his twin.

Rhain finished another cookie then set the package to the table. With a grunt he stood and said, "Maybe I should leave. Three's a crowd anyways, right?"

Regan drew from Daniel, looking to Rhain with a soft frown. "You don't have to leave, Rhain."

Giving a handsomely sly grin, Rhain ran a hand through his multi-colored hair and shook his head as he waved a hand. "I'm only the designated driver." He pointed to his brother and added with a chortle, "I only came along to make sure he didn't dick-out on you."

Daniel scowled to the choice of words Rhain used to describe his hesitation, but in the end, he had to thank Rhain for helping him see the light in the matter. When Regan eased from his arms, he frowned as she stepped to Rhain to kiss his cheek.

"Thank you," she said with a warm smile. "I know you went through a lot of trouble, both of you, so I want you to know that I will never take your bravery or your sacrifices light-heartedly. I'm not sure if there's any way I can repay you."

Rhain smirked to the kiss then leaned closer to her to whisper in her ear. "Just love him, alright? Trust everything he says, and trust in him. He'll never lead you astray. He'll never break your love or your faith. If you can do all that, he'll make sure you are the happiest woman in the world. He would give you anything to see you smile."

Regan's dark eyes softened, and she smiled earnestly to Rhain when he winked at her. "I will."

Rhain stepped to the door, tossing his twin a quick wave. "Call me when you want to be picked up."

Regan had stepped back to Daniel and he wrapped her in his arms once again. The feeling of her warm, mortal heat seeped through his chilled flesh, so he hugged her tighter. "Stay with me," he heard her whisper, and her delicate plea caused his heart to skip a few beats. Glancing to Rhain, Daniel smiled and shook his head. "Thank you, Frater, but I think I'll be here for a little while."

Rhain flicked him a few fingers as he opened the door. "Have it your way, just don't stay up too early."

Daniel caught the warning within his brother's words and nodded. "I'll be careful. Goodnight, Rhain."

Rhain bid the two a goodbye then departed the flat with the door clicking closed behind him. In the silence that fell, Daniel and Regan held each other, comfortable to be within each other's arms once more. Neither wanted to speak. Neither wanted to move. But there were questions that needed answers and answers that needed explanations. So with a regretful and breathy sigh, Daniel removed his arms from about Regan.

"I believe Rhain was supposed to be making tea, however, I think he forgot." He gave a slight chuckle, a nervous chuckle. "Why don't I make us some?"

Regan shook her head and gently urged him back to the sofa with her hands against his bare shoulders, careful not to touch any of the stitched wounds. "No, you sit here and don't move. I'll make the tea. I can do that." Leaning to him, once he had sat, she gently tipped up his head and kissed his forehead. A lock of his black hair tickled her lips as she did so.

Beneath her kiss, Daniel's eyes fluttered closed and he drew in a deep pull of her scent - lavender. He then watched her walk into the kitchen with a turn of his head. Daniel smiled to himself as Regan went about preparing their tea. Observing her swept longing throughout his heart, longing for some form of place in his life, substance that had been long missing - a partner to share his life, go on adventures with, celebrate holidays with, and enjoy daily activities with.

Regan was more than just a possible partner for him, a focal point of his love and his attention. She was his Socia after all - she was his life.

Once the kettle boiled and the high-pitched whistle sounded, Regan quickly prepared their mugs then walked back to the couch, sitting down as she offered him his mug. "I hope I did this tea correctly. Joyce said you English drink black tea with a lemon wedge, so I cut up a lemon." She gave Daniel a timid little frown and a worry knitted brow. "Is that right?"

He chuckled and smiled, amused and elated at her ignorance of his culture. "It's fine. Thank you."

"I wouldn't want to embarrass you with my ignorant American ways." She gave a chuckle, playfully of course and with a little snicker caressing her lips.

Daniel's chuckle was warm and vibrating as he raised the rim of his tea mug to his lips. The warm brew swam through his chilled insides to spread luscious heat from the delicately crafted leaves, and he sighed as he took a second sip. His body must still be healing if he felt this cold and had not even realized it, so he took another sip before settling back to relax.

"So, mister vampire,' he heard Regan say softly - quietly – after she took a sip of her tea, 'tell me what makes you, you. And remember, spare no detail."

Daniel flinched inwardly as he raised his black eyes to the human sitting across from him. He expected to see her eyes full of shock, resentment, judgment, and fear, but instead he saw her eyes sparkling with amusement and a sly little grin decorating her lips. "You remember that fact, do you?"

She nodded. "Oh, yes. These past few days spent at Caius' home allowed me time to reflect on everything that has happened, form the moment I met you, to Joyce's disappearance and my time spent at Hotel Del Ass-Hole. I remember everything David said when you showed up on the balcony before your fight with him. His questions, though bizarre, made sense when I sat back and looked at everything happening around and what 'people' were saying to me. Oddly enough, it seems a lot of confusion has dissipated."

"I hope this doesn't make you uncomfortable. I mean,' she shrugged glancing down to her tea, 'maybe I should be freaking out a little more, you know, like all the girls do in the movies."

315

Daniel felt sick to his stomach, and he groaned leaning his head back with his eyes closing. "This isn't going to be easy for me. I've never had to explain myself to a human before. I don't even know where to begin." The softest of touches pressed against his cheek, close to his mouth, in the form of a subtle kiss. He opened his eyes, glancing to the side to see that Regan had scooted closer.

"Start at the beginning."

"The beginning?"

Regan nodded, smiling, and reached out to twist a lock of his silky black hair about a finger. "Yes, the moment when Daniel the vampire was born."

"The beginning," mused Daniel with a lick to his lips while watching, from the corner of his eyes, the way she twiddled his hair. The soothing caress swept a touch of exhaustion through him. "Well, my kind do not refer to our race as vampires."

"Oh? Then what do you call yourselves?"

"We are…Lamia."

XX

To be loved is a beautiful thing, but to be loved by a human is something that even I cannot explain.

Regan loves me. I can see her love within her eyes and hear her love within her voice. When she looks at me with her dark eyes sparkling and a smile upon her lips, the world becomes much smaller and all my worries disappear. I used to fear being alone, yet I kept myself locked away from any who offered their love to me. Instead, I went to those who opened their beds to me. I thought that love was pleasure. And though I did care for some whom I took as lovers, none of them seized such a deep hold upon my soul as Regan. Two of my past lovers will always hold a part of my heart, but Regan will be my heart.

I no longer fear being alone for I will never be alone again.

Her mortality humbles me and reminds me of what I strive daily to protect - the last inches of my own mortality. I refuse to allow the last threads of my humanity to be tainted by the darkness of my world. Her laughter softens the hardness of my exterior, and her warmth heats the coldness of my blood. I will do anything and everything in my power to protect her mortality and her humanity, the kindness of her heart and the gentility of her human nature. My life will be her life, my blood - her blood.

As my Socia, she will be my heaven - my all and my life.

As her Socius, I will be a demon to those who would do her harm.

Heed my warning. Hurt her, make one tear slide down her soft skin, and I will release hell upon your soul. The pain you feel will be felt in your next incarnation.

This I swear.

*-	Daniel Rhys Thorn.*

"**W**e are...Lamia."

There was no going back once those words left Daniel's mouth. The truth was out, and it was up to Regan to accept all that he had to tell her. He had to trust her explicitly with the delicacy of his identity and his race. And though he knew he could trust her, there was fear dancing about within his stomach like wild butterflies drunk on the purest of nectar, or Rhain's secret stash of vodka.

317

They stared at each other while silence hung in the air. He could tell she was weighing his words by the deep gaze that pressed heavily upon him. Only when Regan sighed and took a sip of her tea did the tension break as a little smile tugged her lips. Daniel took that tiny smile with relief and let the breath he held flutter past his lips.

"When were you born?"

"That depends on which birthdate you are inquiring about. There was my human birthdate and the date I was born into the Lamia world, what is known as the Nasei."

Regan shrugged. "Give me both dates."

"I am one-hundred and ten years old, and I was born February fourth in the year nineteen-four. I was fifteen when I went through the Creare, the act that changes a human to a Lamia. My Creare did not finalize the transition till nineteen-thirty when I was twenty-six."

"That's why you look so young?"

"Yes. Though my race does age, a natural progression of sorts, it is a very slow process that can take thousands of years."

"I see. This change is not instant?"

Daniel shook his head. "No. The time of maturity into a Lamia can differ. Kain's Creare took thirty years. I believe Rhain's Creare took about the same as mine, give or take a year or so."

"How do you know when the change is complete?"

"Again, that varies depending upon the Lamia. Mostly it is signaled by the heightening of our natural abilities."

"And those are?"

Daniel chuckled softly. "I'll explain those in time, right now we should stick to the basics to help ease you into all of this."

Regan gave her agreement with a nod. "How old is Kain?"

"Kain was born September twenty-second, eighteen ninety-four. He was changed in nineteen-sixteen at the age of twenty-two. He was twenty-five when Rhain and I were changed."

"What about your parents? Did they know what happened to you and your brothers?"

A shadow of discomfort fell across Daniel's handsome features. He sighed, and his voice dropped when he replied to her. "No. They never knew what happened to us because they were not alive."

"They passed away?" Daniel nodded in answering of her question, and so she pressed on by asking, "What happened to them?"

"They died on a voyage to America. April fifteenth, Nineteen-twelve."

A tiny gasp pressed up from Regan's throat and a sympathetic frown pressed her lips down. "The Titanic."

Daniel nodded.

"I'm so sorry."

"Their deaths were a long time ago." Taking a dry breath, Daniel drowned his frown with another long sip of his tea.

"Tell me what happened, the reason you and your brothers were changed."

Daniel's next pull of air tightened his lungs, and an expression of pain etched his face. He looked away and muttered, "That's not an easy topic to discuss. I don't like to speak of my death."

His death. A cold shiver ran along Regan's spine to the reality of that word - death. Daniel had died. It was as simple as that. Seeing the disquiet knitting his features, Regan gently touched his face, guiding his gaze back to her. "I can't imagine how painful it is to talk about this, but you agreed to spare no detail in answering my questions. Please don't renege on your promise to me."

Daniel's black eyes danced across her face, and his shoulders shifted when he sighed. He took her hand from his face and laced their fingers together. "I haven't told many people, Lamia or Humanus, about my death. It's a very personal topic."

"But I'm more to you than other people, right?"

Daniel's eyes brightened, and his chuckle cleared the discomfort on his face. "Yes," he told her, lifting her hand to his lips. "You are mean more to me than other people, of course. So you deserve to know everything about me." He smiled as Regan settled herself closer to him, nestling her head to his shoulder and draping a slender leg over one of his thin thighs - a move that was comfortable and intimate.

Daniel settled a hand over her leg, caressing slowly along the outside of her thigh. "After the death of our parents, Kain stepped forwards to see to mine and Rhain's care. We were still young and Kain was eighteen, just about to enter University to study business and banking. Kain was changed first, but I will leave his story to him to tell. Rhain and I didn't know about his change till our own Creare came about."

"You and Rhain were changed at the same time?"

He nodded. "Yes. An illness swept through our small village causing many children to fall fatally ill. In modern terms the illness is known as whooping cough, deadly to children. Kain was immune due to him being a Lamia already, but Rhain and I were not so lucky. Like you and your cousin, my brothers and I held the Proprietas within us when we were still human."

"The Proprietas?"

"The genetic mutation that is in all humans connected to a Lamia lineage. You have it, and so did Joyce. Otherwise, she would not have been able to complete the Creare. And since you have it, you can become a Lamia if you survive the change."

Regan's features scrunched. "If I survive?"

Daniel tapped a finger to the tip of her nose. "We're getting off track here."

Regan rolled her eyes then grinned. "Fine. Tell on."

"Kain arrived a few minutes after Rhain and I succumbed to our illness. We passed a few minutes apart. To make a long, and uncomfortable, story short, Kain arrived in time to perform the Creare upon us, making him our Parens. We survived, obviously. After that, Rhain and I were sent to live with Kain and go through our Domare."

"Parens? I heard David call himself that when he and Joyce were talking outside the cell that I had been kept in."

"Sadly, David was correct. A Parens is a Lamia's creator, the single Lamia who performed the Creare upon a human. That individual is our parent."

"So Kain is yours and Rhain's parent?"

"Yes. He is also our Frater, which is Lamia for brother."

"So David was Joyce's Parens?"

"Unfortunately, yes."

"You mentioned a Do...mar...e? What is that?"

"Domare. In short, it is a training period that all properly changed Lamia must go through in order to learn of our culture, our traditions, our history, our Familia, and all that makes up the Lamia as a race in general."

"Did Joyce go through one of those?"

Daniel frowned and shook his head. "I doubt it. David was what proper Lamia call a Proscriptus, an outlaw Lamia who has broken away from the traditional Lamia population and laws. He was listed as a rogue and a troublemaker and did not follow the proper laws of our kind, the Lex. Joyce was not put through the Domare. When she is found and accepted into a Familia, she can go through the Domare. Also, any human who is invited into our world must go through a form of the Domare in order to be accepted and permitted to stay."

"I see." Regan licked her lips. She sat up and turned to face Daniel, squaring her eyes with him. "What would you do if I asked you to provide proof to back up your words?"

Daniel tipped his head then smirked. "We can wait till sunrise."

She scoffed playfully. "Oh? Will you burn like the vampires in the movies?"

"In a way, yes. However, we don't burst into flames. The sun does cause us damage, much like an advanced and progressive skin cancer. Our flesh burns away, but the rate of this burning depends upon the exposure to the sun. With less direct exposure to the sun we can heal ourselves given time and care. But most of the time we are less lucky to sleep off the damage done by a sun-burn. Long exposure, more intense, exposure to the sun can kill us."

"So you can't go outside at all during the day?"

"It wouldn't be wise. However, that doesn't mean my kind go crawling off into a coffin to sleep in some comatose status. We are active during the day, though exhausted and slow. Our abilities can also diminish, leaving us vulnerable. We can be outside during sunrise and sunset, as long as the sun is not present above the horizon."

"Then let's not do the sun-test. I bet that makes the long summer days rather difficult."

He chuckled with a nod. "The summer can be depressing to some of us. But as you saw, our world is active in the evening just as the mortal world. We have events and social lives that keep us active in the evening. There are restaurants and pubs to visit that are open during the evening hours, many that are owned by Lamia."

320

Regan's eyes went wide, and she snapped her fingers. "Oh! You can eat. I saw you eat at the restaurant we went to with Jamie. And I've seen you drink coffee. I thought vampires couldn't eat or drink anything but blood."

"That's a myth. You must understand that what you see in movies or on the telly and what you read in books are all modern interpretations based upon the ancient myth created to cover the truth of my race. Over centuries, different cultures and peoples have created their own versions of the vampiric myth. I'm not sure which myth created the inability of a Lamia to eat or drink, but we can. The food must be simple though, organic and made with as few processed materials as possible. The products must also be low in sugar, unnatural additives, and chemicals. Drinks are much in the same. Too much alcohol or caffeine can cause havoc on our stomachs. We can get sick off of too much bad food and poor drink, but we can recover through a good sleep."

"That must make grocery shopping difficult."

Daniel gave a sheepish shrug. "You get used to it. It's no different than having to live on a strict diet due to a medical condition or the choice to be vegan or vegetarian."

"I suppose so. That explains why you're so thin." Regan gently poked at his chest.

Chuckling, Daniel took her hand and raised her fingers to his lips for a gentle kiss. "Being thin is, for the most part, a genetic condition to all us Lamia. Our diets do not permit our bodies to become over weight."

"What about people who were overweight before becoming a Lamia?"

"Their bodies would adjust and a natural weight loss would occur after the Creare. Unfortunately, this natural thinness and weight loss doesn't mean a Lamia cannot over indulge in food and drink."

"But the person won't become over weight?"

"No, only violently ill."

Regan winced. "So, do you need blood then to live?"

Daniel nodded. "Yes. But we're not going around the dark streets dragging victims into alleyways and sucking their blood dry."

"But if you can eat food, why would you need blood?"

"Our digestive systems are very delicate. And though we can handle foods, we do not properly process many nutrients out of the digestion process as a human would. Because of this malfunction, we need to ingest the nutrients that have already been processed to replace these missing vitamins and minerals through the consumption of blood - Sanguis."

"Human blood?" Regan asked the question with a heavy scowl.

Daniel nodded. "Human blood holds the purest nutrients needed to support our continual survival. We can live off of animal blood, but not for long. There are also Lamia made supplements."

Regan pursed her lips and nodded, accepting his words. "What about Rhain's smoking? Does that bother him?"

"Not directly. It just makes his clothes smell like he rolled about on the floors of his club."

"What about your race being immune to illnesses and diseases? Do you catch colds?"

"We can become sick and ill, but not to the degree that a human can. However, we can fall prey to an illness called the Desiderium if we ingest blood that is tainted by human drugs or medications, or if we have not fed for a long time. It is a sickness of both the mind and the body that makes a Lamia experience an intense period of mental instability and violent hunger. A Lamia who gives in to the Desiderium, quite literally, goes insane and must be quarantined for treatment, if possible."

"If possible?"

"There are times when a Lamia in this state has been…humanely put down to save the Lamia from suffering or attacking others in his or her delirious state."

"Oh,' breathed Regan with a little whimper, 'that doesn't sound pleasant."

"It isn't." To his statement, which Regan felt to hold a touch of personal experience, she raised her eyes and frowned. Daniel, noticing her look of concern, tucked back a lock of her hair behind her ear and gave her a reassuring smile. "That's another story for another night."

"I get the feeling that there will be plenty of stories to be told."

"I've been alive for a while now, there are a lot of stories."

Daniel's smile vanished, exchanged for a perplexed expression when Regan slid into his lap. His body tightened and a slight groan fell from his lips as her delicate, human weight settled upon him. His throat went tight when she leaned close to him, eying him as she pressed the tip of her nose to his.

"Prove all of this. Show me, somehow, that you are what you claim to be."

He smirked a lopsided smirk. "I would give you my birth certificate and driver's license but those are both fake."

Leaning back, Regan presented her right wrist. Daniel blinked, looking from her hand to her face. She pressed her wrist closer to him. "Bite me."

"Excuse me?" Daniel asked with a snorted chuckle.

"You heard me. Bite me."

A heavy scowl crossed his face, and he gently brushed aside her hand. "No."

"Yes." She pressed her hand to him again.

Daniel's face fell and so did his voice. "No."

"Why not?"

"I don't like,' he paused to swallow the lump that had formed in his throat then continued to say, 'I'm not comfortable with biting people."

"But you have in the past, right? I mean, to feed?"

"In the old days, yes, but in modern times we have more polite methods."

"So why not bite me? If you have fangs, you can bite me."

"I have fangs," he muttered, almost embarrassed that she would think otherwise. "I just don't like to show them off."

"Daniel,' Regan muttered with an exasperated sigh, 'you're being difficult."

He arched a slender brow, shocked she would make such a claim considering her request. "Regan, sweetheart, this isn't easy for me. I can't just go around proclaiming what I am on the sleeve of my shirt. There are rules and regulations that must be followed, strict traditions and guidelines. There are laws I have sworn to uphold. Which, I might point out, I'm breaking right now."

Groaning, Daniel reclined his head and covered his face with his hands. He grumbled something when he felt Regan's grip about his wrists, attempting to pull his hands away, but he fought against her. He wanted to hide so he could think on what his next course of action would be.

But Regan wasn't going to let him hide, and eventually she was able to pull his hands from his face. He was glaring at her, but she wouldn't back down. "There must be something you can do to prove to me that what you're saying is true and that you're not just screwing about with my head like everybody else has done."

For some reason anger coiled within Daniel, licking at his heart, when she tossed him in the same sinking boat as David, Caius, and Constantine. He would be the last one to lie to her, and it hurt his pride and his love that she would question him. "You want proof?" he asked with a growl to his voice.

Regan nodded.

"Fine," he muttered while pulling his hands rather forcefully from her grip. He raised his right wrist to his mouth. "Here's your proof."

What happened next seemed to freeze time for Regan. She not only saw Daniel's teeth elongate into sharp fangs but heard the instant when the sharp tips pierced the tender flesh of his upturned wrist. The sound was unexplainable, sounding of something fleshy and wet being punctured and pulled apart as he scored his flesh. Blood, thick and dark red, welled up from the corners of his lips to slide down beneath the sleeve of his shirt and drip to his lap.

With a sharp cry of alarm, Regan went to grab at his hand, meaning to pull his mouth from his wrist, but Daniel pushed her back, drawing away enough to snarl at her. "This is what you wanted, isn't it? Proof?"

She covered her mouth with her hands but couldn't take her eyes away from the redness that stained his mouth, his lips and his teeth. When he drew back, he presented his wrist to her with the two gaping holes leaking vital blood. She couldn't look, so she turned away only to wince when Daniel grabbed her chin to force her eyes back.

"Don't turn away," he growled fluidly. "This is the reality of my world, Regan."

A whimper formed within her throat, lacing her words with fear. "You're going to bleed to death. You need a bandage or stitches, a doctor."

"No." Daniel's handsome face skewed up into a look of distorted cruelty. "I do not need doctor nor a bandage. This wound will heal. So look at it." He growled sharply when she didn't, "Look at me, Regan. Look at the vampire that I am."

She whimpered again and closed her eyes.

"Look at me!"

The snap to his voice drew Regan's eyes open. She was crying again, and her watery tears slid between Daniel's fingers that held her chin. He raised his bleeding wrist closer and she saw that the bleeding was already slowing.

"Is this not enough proof for you? I can give you another example of what I am if you wish."

"Daniel, you're scaring me."

He scrunched his nose and growled softly, "That is not my intention. Unfortunately, my world is scary. So am I." Licking his lips, he held out his blood coated hand. "Give me your wrist."

Regan paled and clutched her wrist tightly to her chest. "Why?"

Daniel leveled her with a dark look, his lips pulling back into a devious grin. "You said that as long as I love you that you will trust me. Are you questioning your trust in me? My love for you?"

Regan gulped and slowly offered him her hand. "Are you going to hurt me?"

"No," he told her as he took her hand and raised her wrist to his lips. "You want me to bite you. So you shall have your bite."

Regan tried to pull her wrist away, fear gripping her heart, but Daniel's grasp was iron-clad and refused to release her. Watching his bloody mouth part open, exposing his fangs, swept fresh panic through her, and before her eyes she saw a flash of David's cruel smile. A whimper lodged itself within her throat while she struggled, but Daniel wrapped his free arm about her body, jerking her and pinning her against him.

Then the bite came. Regan expected pain and prepared herself to cry out but the bite was soft - almost tender. There was a nip of discomfort when the sharpness of his teeth pierced her flesh. Regan felt a quick wave of discomfort, but then Daniel sealed his mouth about her wrist and began to feed. The soft pressure of his suckling replaced her fear with luscious heat. Before she could stop herself a little moan bubbled up within her throat, and she closed her eyes when she felt his hand urge her closer by pressing against the dip of her back.

Releasing a soft sigh, Regan felt her body relax and soften as she shifted closer to him. She placed her other palm against his naked chest and curled fingers against his cool flesh as he increased the pressure of his feeding. Another moan fell from her lips, this one louder and deeper than the first.

The Edère did not last long, and soon Daniel was drawing his mouth from her wrist with a slow trail of his tongue along the small wounds. The bleeding was not overly aggressive and slowly began to cease while Daniel lapped at the remains of the blood that painted the underside of her arm. Before she realized what was happening, Daniel was kissing her and she was returning his kiss feverishly.

Regan moaned, pressing into him, as Daniel sealed his mouth to hers. The thought of blood coating his mouth never crossed her mind as the raging heat blooming within her stomach commanded her attention. She couldn't explain the sudden explosion of sexual need that rushed through her, but she could explain that the desire was solely focused upon Daniel. Regan wanted to feel him touching her, caressing and kissing her, and she wanted to feel him filling her to completion.

Daniel, on the other hand, came to his senses and quickly calmed the kiss, but not without a playful nip to her lips. He looked at her with shock in his eyes, then he sighed as he began to wipe blood away from her mouth. "I'm sorry," he muttered in a tone of voice that was laced with awkwardness.

He expected Regan to pull away in horror to their mixed blood painting her lips. Instead, she chuckled with a shrug of her shoulders. "I guess I should be sort of disturbed that I kissed you with blood on your mouth, but for some reason it sort of excites me." The shrug of her shoulders was accompanied by the caress of a delicate blush across her cheek.

Daniel flashed a devious grin as he licked his lips. "Oh? The Edĕre can be rather pleasurable."

Regan draped her arms about his shoulders, threading fingers into the long strands of his hair. Leaning closer, she brushed her lips to his and whispered softly, "Your bite is very sensual. The caress of your tongue and the pressure of your suckling was so tender and erotic."

A deep groan reverberated through Daniel, rising up within his throat, as his lips parted as if awaiting another kiss. But the kiss never came. Instead, he felt Regan slipping off his lap, and through the haze of his eyes he saw her standing before him with a hand offered to him. Suddenly, Daniel felt his nerves crackle and a wave of unease coursed through him. Ever so slowly, he raised his hand then paused as he arched a brow to her.

"Come with me," she told him when he hesitated.

As he placed his hand in hers and stood, Daniel inquired, "Where?"

"To the bedroom."

Daniel slid his gaze to the hallway. "Why?" He blinked his onyx eyes as she guided his eyes back to her. She was smiling to him, and he found himself lost within the warmth of her eyes.

"To make love to me."

~ ~ ~ ~

Regan's glistening body writhed beneath the precise assault of Daniel's fingers. The smooth motion of his lean digits, gliding in and out of her, rocked her body in sensual motion - back and forth - back and forth - upon the crumpled bed sheets. Sharp gasps and high pitched cries tumbled from her parted and trembling lips with each thrust of his talented fingers that twisted and pushed within her. She clutched his back, curling her fingers into his flexing shoulders while he nibbled and suckled the hollow of her throat.

The trail of his slick tongue, lapping and caressing, brought shivers to decorate Regan's flesh. She tipped her chin up, rolling her head to the side so Daniel could have access to her throat. And when he nipped at her jugular, dragging his teeth across the sensitive spot, Regan released a pitiful whine of pleasure. She arched her back, undulating her hips in a silent and greedy beg for more of his attention.

Not to displease her, never to displease her, Daniel began to move his body down hers while running kisses over the curves of her petite physique. He paused at her chest, unable to ignore the succulent call of her breasts, and parting his lips he raised one to his mouth. The instant his cool lips enclosed about a swelling nipple Regan beneath him gave a squeal of delight. A groan fell past his lips, vibrating the hard bud he suckled, as he felt Regan's hot passage tighten about his fingers.

She tasted and felt divine, and the cries that echoed the room flooded Daniel with uncontrollable desire. The previous feeding still swirled within his thin veins bringing with her blood the bubbling hunger for sex - raw and hot sex. He wanted her, badly, and there was little he could do to keep himself under control. The Possessio was something he had never experienced before, the unnatural and uncontrollable urge to possess one of his lovers in all ways possible. But with Regan, he quickly found himself tasting the Possessio as his blood heated and his body swelled with desire. It was hard to think; hard to hear past the violent throbbing of his blood coursing through his head.

One thing was for sure, every desperate and decadent cry that fled from Regan's mouth was music to his ears and spurred lust through every fiber of Daniel's being. Drawing away, he let slide the hard nipple from his mouth but not before he lavished the bud with the tip of his tongue one last time. He glanced up to see his Socia's beautiful features warped in a shadow of lust; her warm eyes hooded and her soft lips parted. They stared at each other before Daniel moved further down her body, grinning all the way as he allowed his free hand to skim fingers along her belly.

He guided her legs further apart, caressing his hands along the insides of her naked thighs, and sat back to gaze upon the femininity of Regan's human beauty. She tried to close her legs but Daniel gently stopped the motion. "No," he whispered huskily and through a tight breath. "Don't be shy in front of me. I want to look at you."

"Every time I close my eyes I see you falling away from me. I see you crumpled upon that hard desk, unmoving and staring up at me with emptiness in your eyes." He reached to splay his palm over her stomach, and his eyes closed as he felt the rise and fall of her abdomen just an inch or two above. "I want to know, no, I need to know that you are alive."

A shiver danced through Regan as she stared with wide eyes to the vampire knelt between her parted legs. His words were so romantic and touched a part of her heart that prickled with passion and love. "Daniel," the whisper of his name drew his eyes, and Regan smiled to him. "I am alive. You saved me."

He saved her.

That single statement broke an internal dam of emotions that Daniel had been fighting back, and a bloody tear welled within his eyes. He released a quivering and dipped his head to press a kiss to her stomach. Anticipation clawed at Regan, raking her insides with hot nails when he finally moved. Every shift of muscle beneath his pale skin was graceful while moving his lean form to settle between her thighs. Daniel slid a hand over her flesh then beneath her quivering buttocks in order to lift her off the bed.

The first caress of his tongue sent erotic shockwaves to bombard Regan's body. She arched off the bed, whimpering, when the second lick lavished her sensitive folds. Then the third and the fourth came to tease her and she gasped and danced upon the bed, trying in vain to feel more. Daniel drank in the pleasurable sounds that echoed about them as he tormented her luscious folds. He licked and lapped at her, swirling the tip of his tongue against her before pressing his tongue forwards into the heat of her body.

To hear more of her luscious sounds Daniel eased his fingers back into her body without missing a lick against her folds. He thrust his fingers, pushing and grinding, twisting and curling and all the while his tongue caressed and moved against her. The lovely music that filled his ears sent his heart to soar and he moaned to the slickness that met his lips. Harder and faster he moved his fingers as he ground the palm of his hand against her.

It wasn't long till Regan's body shook, and she panted a tight warning that she was close to release. Yet Daniel didn't stop, he kept pushing her closer and closer to the edge of pleasure till he felt her hands fist into his hair, pulling till he hissed in pain. Reluctantly, he drew his mouth from her, rising up so she could see him licking her slickness from his lips. His motions ceased when his fingers slipped sloppily from her, earning him a cute pout and a pitiful whine.

But still she kept a hold of his hair, letting the silky strands slide through her fingers as he sat back till the ends wrapped about her wrists. Pouting, Regan panted as she shifted upon the bed in a pitiful attempt at easing the throbbing tightness between her legs. She reached for him, and Daniel smiled as he loomed over her.

"Please don't keep me waiting, Daniel," she whispered painfully as she ran her hands over his bare shoulders, tracing muscles along his corded arms.

Daniel's smile turned to a questionable frown. "Are you sure you want this, Regan? Want me? Now that you know that I am a monster and what I am capable of, do you really want to invite me into your body to make love to you?"

With a breath released in a fluttered sigh, Regan moved to her knees and saw that Daniel's dark eyes had followed every flex of her muscles. When she was knelt before him, she timidly cupped his face with her hands. Their eyes met, and she leaned to kiss his lips in a soft and chaste kiss.

"You are not a monster," she said in a tumbled whisper. "You are the man that I love; the man who captured my heart and saved my life. You could never be a monster with your kindness, your love, and your protective nature. You are my savior, Daniel Thorn. My savior."

Daniel didn't move. He watched her with hawk-like eyes, taking in and observing every motion. When she leaned close to him, he closed his eyes and dipped his head so he could draw in a deep breath of her sexualized scent. He brushed back her hair and ran his lips over her slender throat. So entranced was he by the taste of her skin and the scent of her lust, that he was blind to her devious fingers working to free his body from confining fabric.

327

A slow hiss bubbled up in his throat as she threaded one hand into his hair, at the base of his skull, then wrapped her other hand about his aching erection. The feeling of her warm fingers closing one at a time about his flesh flooded Daniel's nerves with pleasure, and he growled against her throat while rocking his hips wantonly into her grip.

"I love your touch," he murmured hotly against her flesh in a spill of cool breath as he wrapped his arms about her, coiling fingers within her hair. "Don't stop," he groaned hungrily. "Please, don't stop."

Stop? Regan was past the ability to stop. Even if she wanted to, her body would not allow her. Then again, she couldn't think past the sensation of Daniel's body rocking against her, his chest brushing against hers as his arms tightened about her. Never before, with any of her past relationships, had a lover so brazenly demanded sex from her. But Daniel was demanding her attention by the simple motions of his body, by the soft mumbles of her name, and by the deep groans of his pleasure. Even the scraping of his nails against the back of her neck surged sexualized excitement through her body. She wanted more, so much more, that she felt the last slivers of control fracture.

Though he was enjoying her lovely caress, Daniel finally had enough of her gentle stroking. His body wanted, no, it demanded to be inside of her. His soul wanted to make her his once again and to claim her finally as his Socia - properly. The Possessio wanted to be finalized, and the call of the bonding echoed wildly from within his soul.

In one, smooth motion Daniel had her lifted and pinned against him by a hand cradling her bottom. She weighed nothing as she was lifted, and as he moved Regan found herself upon her back. Daniel was quickly upon her, pressing frenzied kisses to her throat and neck. He was all raw power, muscles coiling and rippling beneath his pale flesh as he strained for control. Snarling, he ground himself against his lover, sliding his throbbing flesh over her wet folds while drawing out desperate whimpers from Regan's quivering lips.

There was no more need for words of encouragement to be passed between the two, for their moans, their groans, and their motions spoke of their desperation to be united in physical pleasure. The Daemon inside Daniel snarled in rapture when Regan's nails bit into Daniel's flexing buttocks while at the same time arching herself to him. It took one thrust for Daniel to embed himself within her, fully and completely. The Lamia's entire body shook to the sudden sensation of her hot walls clutching his erection as the thick flesh slid flush within her. Regan uttered a gurgled cry that fell silent when Daniel snarled and captured her mouth in a sizzling kiss.

They kissed hungrily, urgently, with lips moving and caressing and tongues thrusting in a wicked dance of ecstasy. Daniel had never felt such a drastic need to have pure sex with somebody before, not just to make love to another but to fulfill a hunger for animalistic mating. But with Regan moving beneath him, arching and thrusting to meet the pumping of his body, he couldn't help but relinquish some control to his Daemon so he could feel the lust filled passion that he greedily feasted upon with every kiss they shared. Every thrust was precise, made to bring both partners the greatest of pleasure with the caressing of sensitive flesh.

Daniel prided himself on being a gentle, slow building lover who took his time pleasuring his partner. A wave of hot shame washed over him that he was acting like an animal with one intention to accomplish - to mate and mate well. He was snarling, growling and thrusting violently, and the thought he might hurt Regan swam around his mind. However, the human beneath him encouraged him to thrust harder and deeper as she bucked to him and cried out in pure rapture. There was no stopping the heightening of their pleasure. He could smell her lust as the air in the room grew heavy with the saltiness of the sweat that danced their flesh.

He swore he could feel the ravaged beating of her heart as their chests met in the rubbing motions of their moving bodies. And when Regan slid her slick thighs higher over his flanks, to lock her ankles against his lower back, Daniel felt as if he would die from the sensations of his shaft gliding at a deeper angle. Regan's body threatened to push him over the edge far too early, so Daniel had to clench his jaws in order to focus his mind. But he couldn't slow his actions. Instead, he drew back then drove harder and harder till the bed creaked and groaned beneath the intensity of his thrusts. When their bodies set the perfect rhythm, both lost themselves in the moment that sealed their love.

Regan was the first to reach the pinnacle of pleasure, grinding herself shamefully against Daniel's hard form till her petite frame arched violently off the bed and a loud cry echoed from her parted lips, mingling with the erotic symphony of slapping flesh. The Daemon inside of Daniel howled out its pleasure when Regan's quaking body vibrated against him, and when the feel of her wet release swirled about his throbbing shaft, Daniel had to bite his tongue to keep himself from his own release. He wasn't ready, even though he was so close!

With pleasure ringing in his ears, and his body begging for release, Daniel coiled his arms about Regan as he drove as deeply as he could inside of her. He wanted to push her into another release, so he continued to caress her shaking channel with brutal, quick thrusts. Grunting and snarling, he buried his face against her neck, breathing in her luscious scent of sexual release, and licked the salty sweaty from her skin. When she tipped her head, offering her neck to him as she cradled his head to her, Daniel felt his heart burst within his chest.

"Please..." he heard her whisper breathlessly, urgently.

Daniel knew what she was requesting, and truthfully he wasn't sure he could stop himself even if he tried. The Daemon inside of him purred and clawed from within, urging him to part his jaws. Before Daniel could catch himself, his mouth opened and his fangs elongated against the smooth column of her neck.

In one press Daniel pierced her neck and Regan released a trembling cry of pleasure! Her body shook violently, and so he tightened his arms about her while driving himself as fast as the muscles in his hips could flex, stroking them both to a more powerful and sadistic release. With hot blood slithering down his throat, Daniel felt himself disappear, falling into the precipice of orgasmic pleasure. He drank and drank and drank till the taste of Regan's irony blood filled his senses. When enough was enough, and their bodies

329

slowed from their unified release, Daniel eased his teeth from her flesh and gently licked away the blood that stained her skin.

He hurt, physically hurt, as his lungs had been forced to expand and contract in order to fuel his body with the needed oxygen to complete the intense coupling. Now, as the moment was cooling, his body began to retreat and his systems relaxed as he eased his trembling form atop the comfortable body that shook beneath him.

He groaned and moved as if to remove himself from Regan's body only to find her arms locking him against her. "Don't," he heard her mumble, and that little mumble brought his shadowy eyes to lift. He raised himself to his elbows, curtains of his long hair falling about their features, as he leaned over her so he could look upon her pleasure washed features.

"I'm too heavy."

Regan smiled and shifted upon the bed as a luxurious sigh tumbled from her lips. "I've told you before that you're not heavy." Arching up, she kissed his blood painted lips.

A chuckle mixed with that kiss before Daniel drew back to wipe a finger along her neck. "I didn't hurt you, did I?"

Regan shook her head, a pleased little mew sounding from within her throat.

Daniel kissed her neck where the marks of his bite, the Modĕre, lingered. With a tight groan he withdrew from her body, shifting to sit upon the bed with a hand sweeping back his hair that had tangled from Regan's grip. They laughed as his fingers caught in the black strands.

Regan sat to his side to help unwind the tangles. "How long can you stay?"

"That depends,' he replied softly, 'on you and on the sun. I'm afraid I can't stay here once the sun crests. There is no place that I could take refuge where the sun's rays could not reach me."

"Not even with the curtains closed?

"I can't take any risk." He frowned when she grumbled, but then a smile graced his lips as he cupped her face with a set of lean fingers. "Come with me, Regan. You can stay at my Domus, with me, till it is time for you to return home."

Return? How that word stung and brought a shadow of sadness across both of their faces.

"I don't want to leave," she said softly as her hands fell to her lap. "I want to stay with you." Groaning, Regan let her forehead fall to his naked shoulder and pitifully whimpered, "I'm sorry. That sounded extremely stalker-ish, didn't it?"

Daniel chuckled and eased her into his arms. "There's a lot we need to talk about, Regan. Now that you know about my world there are important protocols that need to be followed."

"Like what? Am I not allowed to leave now?"

"You can leave,' he replied and felt his heart lurch at the idea, 'but it will be difficult. If it is ever discovered that you breathed a word of this reality to anyone, even your own family, you will face the ugly side of the laws that I abide by."

A shiver ran along Regan's spine and she flinched to the truth of his words. She couldn't begin to imagine what could befall her if she broke his confidence. "I would never do anything to hurt you or any other in your secret world, Daniel."

"I know that,' he said with a whisper as he tucked her head against his neck, 'but those who control the Lamia population here in England don't know that, and the Concilium is operated by paranoid bastards who haven't left their homes in the last five-hundred years. They don't trust humans and greatly dislike the human world all together. If our laws were fully up to them, there would be laws blocking all interaction and communication with the mortal world."

He went on to say, "Let's not worry about that right now. We need to take our relationship one step at a time."

Regan mewed and stated the obvious, "I think you telling me you're a Lamia is taking a huge step in our relationship, don't you?"

When Daniel smirked, Regan nodded and eased back. "I understand what you mean. However, I still want to stay. I need to know what has happened to Joyce. I couldn't live with myself if I left and she was alone. I will always feel some responsibility for what happened to her."

She quickly raised a finger to press to his lips when they parted with intentions to speak. "I know what you're going to say. You've said it before that I'm not responsible and you're right, but I'm going to feel guilty for a little while."

Taking her finger gently, Daniel cocked his head to the side to kiss the underside of her wrist. "Then stay,' he told her passionately and with his black eyes searching her features. "Stay with me so we can be together. We'll look for Joyce together, and we'll find her. I promise you that."

"Are you sure? I mean, what will your brothers think?"

"They won't be distrusting of you, if that is what you're thinking. In fact, with Joyce still unaccounted for and David's associates and allies still wanting revenge, both Rhain and Kain would want you staying with us, especially Kain. He will want to personally see to your safety as the head of our little family."

Regan frowned heavily and a shadow of worry creased her brow. "Am I still in danger?"

"Yes,' said Daniel as he tucked back a lock of her hair behind a little ear, 'you are. Till Caius settles the unstable waters of the Underground, David's associates will be wanting blood. They will be looking for you and for Rhain and me with a need for revenge. But with you under the protection of my family and my Familia, they will not be foolish enough to try and harm you. Rhain and I took down David, their leader and a very strong Lamia at that, and they will remember that."

"You are that powerful and influential to keep me safe?"

Daniel nodded with a sly grin pulling his lips. "Yes, sweetheart, I am. My Familia is known for creating a very powerful and skilled warrior class of Lamia. We Drasus bring fear with us wherever we go."

"Drasus?"

"Lamia are,' he paused to arrange his answer in a way that would not confuse her, 'categorized by a family surname all derived from the Prima Lamia, a group of Lamia who were the original families cursed by the Fates with the Proprietas - or so the legend goes. Over time, these families spread their Proprietas across nations and then across the globe. We are all protected by our Familia, supported both financially and socially in any way that we need. Some Familia are more powerful and active in politics while others have their hands in every financial market that exists. Any human changed by a Lamia of a certain Familia will take on the surname of that Familia and harbor the singular traits and talents contained in the key traits of the Proprietas. "

"Like your Familia creates strong warriors?"

Daniel nodded and smiled. "Yes. There are Familia who produce powerful magic users, Lamia we call Venefici. Alasdair belongs to one such Familia. Others produce Lamia who are psychic while other Familia produce Lamia talented in strength or speed."

Regan drew in a breath that she blew out in a puff. "This is all very confusing."

"I know, but that is why you can go through the Domare, that is, if you really do want to stay with me."

Arching a brow, Regan shifted to face him as she pressed a palm over his slowly beating heart. "If I stay, what will I mean to you? Will I become just some quick fling in a relationship that will be unstable and become pointless to you in a few years?"

Daniel snorted a disgruntled snort and Regan chuckled, "It's an honest question!"

He tapped the tip of her nose with a finger. "One thing you must understand when it comes to my race is that we Lamia are very passionate in almost everything we do, in every act and in every relationship, whether negative or positive. And I don't enter a relationship without being dedicated to the other partner."

Regan narrowed one eye and gave him a skeptical look. "I bet you say that to all the girls to sound more romantic."

He balked and laughed softly. "Honest! And I would have you know that I have not had as many lovers or partners as you may think. I've only had one other serious relationship and that was decades ago. Lovers I have had, yes, but they have been rare and few between. My work is important to me and often demands more of my time than I have to spare."

"So you're married to your work?"

"Partially because I have not found another who can take its place." Smiling, he leaned to kiss her cheek. "For far too long I've hidden myself away in my office, tirelessly scraping away dust and grime from history just so I could find my place."

When he looked away and sighed, Regan dipped her head so she could see his eyes past a long lock of his hair that she pulled aside. "So, what you're telling me is that for a long time you've only taken a few lovers, married yourself off to your work, and locked yourself away in your office? That's a shame."

Daniel chuckled. "Why is that?"

"Not to sound cliché,' she said with a shrug and then a wry grin, 'but you are hot as hell. No woman could resist you."

"Or man," muttered Daniel under his breath.

Up shot a cautious brow and Regan inquired quietly, "Excuse me?"

Daniel sighed. "You would find out sooner or later. I'm bisexual." A wince ran his handsome face the moment the social label that he hated passed forth from his lips.

Regan stared at him. "And that means…?"

"I've had both male and female lovers in the past."

Huffing, Regan sat back with her arms crossing against her naked breasts. Her lips twisted as she grumbled, "I'm going to have a lot of people to fight, aren't I? Good thing I brought my stupid stick with me so I can beat people back with it."

Daniel asked with a look of bewilderment, "Fight?"

Balling a fist, Regan's gentle face tucked into a look of dramatic pride. "Defend your honor against sluts and man-whores who want to take you away from me!"

Daniel blinked, staring at her before he broke in to overjoyed laughter. Reaching out, he cupped her face within his hands and drew her mouth to his for a kiss. "Ah, my Socia. You would have no need to battle others for my attention."

Giggling beneath the kiss, Regan asked, "Why's that?"

"Because I love you, my Socia, not them."

Regan nodded. "Good. I'd hate to become a violent person. I only get the urge to draw blood when somebody cuts in line at the coffee shop. And you don't want to see what happens when somebody else gets the last cookie in the cookie jar."

Chuckling, Daniel pulled her into his arms and sighed as she curled her mortal body to him.

"Daniel?"

"Hmm?"

"What does Socia mean?"

"It means a female lover in Latin. It is a term used to signify the importance of a lover in our world. It is also a highly respectable title that is not given to just any partner in a relationship. The person must be truly special to a Lamia, and deeply loved. It also grants you protection within my Familia and a status with the Lamia society. You are more than just Regan Scott, the human. You are Regan Scott, Daniel Thorn's Socia and with that title comes respect and fear that if anyone harms you in any way I will rain terror down upon them that they never imagined possible."

"We protect those we love as life is a precious commodity to us," he went on to say with his luscious voice dropping in tone as he closed his eyes and nestled a cheek atop her hair. "I have lost many whom I have loved, even coming close to losing my own brothers, so I do not give my love easily. But know this. I will protect you with the last drop of my blood if I must."

A whimper trickled past Regan's lips and she tightened her arms about him. "Don't say that," she muttered with a slight hiss. "I don't want to ever see you go through so much pain as David put you through, not for me or for anybody else. I don't want you to suffer again. I want to love you, if you'll let me, and I want to make you happy."

She pulled back so she could look to him. "What can I do to make you happy?"

Daniel's heart shattered to the gentle hitches in her words that heralded the tears that he soon felt slithering down his cool flesh. "Oh, sweetheart,' he breathed softly as he tightened his hold about her, 'you've already made me very happy. You've accepted me as the man that I am and have declared your love to me. All you could do now is openly accept me as your Socius and come back with me to my home."

Taking her wet face within his hands, Daniel pressed his lips to her forehead. "Say you'll come home with me, Regan. Become a part of my life. Be my Socia. Let me be your Socius. In return, I will give you my life, my loyalty, and all the love that my heart is capable of giving."

She couldn't stop crying silent tears that reflected the unimaginable love that swelled her heart. Whimpering, Regan leaned to him and offered her lips for another kiss. "What can I say to such a beautiful declaration?"

"Say yes."

XXI

What will the future bring me? What is my Destiny?

Those two questions haunt my thoughts, but in a good way. I've never been one to care about the future as I always built my future day by day. If I wished to do something, I did it. If I wished to buy something, I bought it. If I wished to go someplace, I traveled. I never had to consider another person, beyond my brothers, and those two never had enough weight that I would base a choice or a future decision upon their needs or their desires. But now I have Regan, and I must incorporate her into my daily activities, my thoughts, and my choices.

I don't have much of an ego, so doing so won't be difficult. In fact, I like the idea of having to ask myself if I should do this or do that based upon the fact that she is in my life, whether or not she will agree with me. I'm looking forwards to arguments with her, moments of laughter, and even the tears that will come. Any decision I make could upset her or please her. I'm not a selfish man. I have never had another to consider or to please to such a degree that a life-partner deserves. However, I think I will enjoy asking her if she would like to go someplace or see something or travel somewhere. Doing so makes me feel important, and it makes her important.

She's in my life now.

The future is unknown, for both of us. We'll make our own Destiny and walk the path we want to walk, not the path the Fates have set for us. I don't know what life holds for us, but I hope Regan will stay a secure point in my life for a long time to come. I've only just found her. I can't have her taken away from me too early.

Will I ever change her? Could I, if there was ever a situation where her life became forfeit?

After saving her life, would I ever be able to take it even if doing so meant saving her?

- *Daniel Rhys Thorn*

~ ~ ~ ~

Ꮖt was late into the night, with just a few hours before sunrise, by the time Daniel and Regan returned to the Thorn Domus. Thorn Inc. was quiet; a massive building that was utterly silent. They arrived via taxi to the main entrance, and with the use of a security badge, Daniel was able to open the doors. He walked Regan through the three story, open-air lobby, pausing to wave to the two Lamia security guards at the front desk as they waited for a single security elevator at the side of the large entry. It didn't take long for the two to ascend the building, gliding past floors, only to have the elevator stop at the top floor where the rooftop condo of the Thorn family rested.

Their return was met by the other two Thorn brothers and Amber, all waiting for them in the sitting room. Regan hesitated at the door to the condo, but with a gentle whisper in her ear Daniel urged her into the immaculate home. She noted right away that one sibling looked amused while the other looked eerily calm. Amber stood by Kain, smiling warmly with friendly eyes. Rhain was smirking dangerously from his seat, and Kain stood in the center of the sitting room with hands clasped behind his back and his dark eyes settled upon Regan. She shuddered and slipped behind Daniel to peek past his arm.

Her lover passed a smiling glance at her when he felt her fingers curl against his back. "Don't mind Kain. That's his happy face."

Regan glowered. "Great."

"Regan,' Kain said in a heavy English tone, 'please come in."

Daniel moved forwards to take a seat upon a couch, leaving Regan frozen where she stood. "Regan," he called, snapping her gaze to him. She didn't have to be told twice, so she darted over to the couch and sat next to him. Her eyes, though, never left the imposing elder brother who was built as if he lived on the rugby field when compared to the thinner framed twins.

Rhain watched the way the mortal curled against Daniel then chuckled softly as he shook his head. "I told you, Kain,' he smirked, casting a wicked glance to his elder sibling, 'you can scare a kitten."

Amber sashayed behind Rhain and copped him on the back of his head. Kain smirked. "I can also tame kittens."

"I think that one needs some work," muttered Rhain as he rubbed the back of his head. "Like a shock collar."

Amber's lovely face twisted into a sarcastic smirk, a smirk that Rhain then returned.

"Regan, this pathetic lot is my family," Daniel said softly. He pointed to each respectively. "Pay no mind to them. You will only bring yourself a headache."

Regan shrank next to him as an intense sense of intimidation coiled within her from the gazes of the three other Lamia.

"Daniel has informed us of your situation, Regan," said Kain, and though there was a forming smile upon his lips, there was coldness to the expression. "You have gone through a lot on behalf of this family and our extended history with David. Though I am saddened to the pain that you

336

experience and the suffering of your cousin, I am pleased that you have had the strength to cope as well as you have with all that has happened."

"I have heard from Caius," he went on to say - his smile vanishing. "He will be visiting tomorrow evening to see how you are recovering and to explain your options now that you know of our world."

He leveled Regan with a dark gaze, intense and powerful. "Your knowledge of our world is a serious matter, Regan, so steps and great caution must be taken as we move forwards with your assimilation. Our family cannot take a chance that you may expose us."

Regan eyes narrowed and she sat straight. "I would never expose Daniel, or any of you, not after all that you have done for me."

Kain raised a hand with a slight smile tucking his lips. "I have no doubt that you believe your words, but one little slip of your tongue can bring great harm to not only Daniel but to the rest of us. And from that one little slip our entire world, our race, our traditions, and our lives could be put into jeopardy."

"I have gotten you in trouble, haven't I? All of you." She frowned with her body sinking back into the couch.

"No,' said Kain, drawing attention back to him, 'this is all David's creation. He brought down his own destruction, which was overdue. None of what has happened is your fault. You must understand that. However, now that you are a part of our lives the Rex wishes to invite you formally into our world. That is, if that is your wish."

"We have discussed the option," said Daniel as he cast his Socia a tender smile.

"The decision is not to be taken lightly, Regan."

Regan licked her lips and nodded to the statement given by Kain. "I understand that."

"Are you willing to walk away from your mortal family if need be, Regan? Are you willing to turn your back on everything you have known, everything you have worked hard to achieve, and all of your goals and dreams?"

Regan's smile softened and she sat straight while taking Daniel's hand. She looked to him and her smile warmed. "You only find a love so powerful that it would risk everything, even life, for you once in a lifetime. Daniel has shown me that he has that love for me." She looked to Kain and her smile was replaced by a look of determination and strength. "I will find a way to adapt my old life to my new life without risking anything that is precious to me."

Kain narrowed his coal-black eyes and nodded to her, a tender smile shaping his sharp mouth. "Daniel,' he looked right to his Frater and Filias, 'I am sure you two would like to rest for the day. I would suggest you spend the remaining hours before sunrise explaining a few of the most important and primary rules to Regan. If you will excuse me, Amber and I have some paperwork to see to." He offered his Socia a nod and the two stepped off down a hallway.

Rhain looked to his twin and licked his dry lips. "Well, I would love to stay and chat about pointless crap but tomorrow is going to be a busy evening at the club. I have a new band to break in, and sadly, I have to inform Alasdair about Grayson." He sighed with a slow shake of his head. "He won't be happy."

"Take care of yourself," said Daniel to his twin.

Regan chimed, "Good night, Rhain. Thank you for all that you've done for me."

He cast a wink to Regan before he stood with a wave over his shoulder. "Have a good rest."

Daniel groaned as he stood, and somewhere in his body a joint popped. "It is late. But Kain is right. I do have a few things I need to explain to you before I rest." He smiled with a hand offered to his Socia.

"Where are we going?" she asked, allowing him to tug her up.

"Where else? To my bed." He flashed a devious grin as he raised her fingers to his lips.

~ ~ ~ ~

The moment the bedroom door opened, Regan heard bright and excited yips rush towards her along with the pitter patter of scampering feet. She was greeted by Pixie who danced a little circle while wagging her feathered tail with her little front feet patting against the floor.

"Oh, Pixie!" Scooping the little dog up in her arms, Regan laughed while nuzzling the Pomeranian that was frantically licking at her cheeks.

Daniel rolled his eyes as he stepped past Regan to turn on a light switch that bathed the room in gentle light from two classically designed Tiffany lamps, one upon each night stand next to a beautiful Victorian poster bed. He left her to walk to a marble fire place where he bent down to turn on the gas flames.

With Pixie in her embrace, Regan walked into the beautiful and ornate room, looking up on the three walls painted in a rich two-tone of deep copper beneath a wall divider of rosewood. There was a heavy bookcase of ebony along one wall that held upon its shelves both old and new leather-bound books. Hanging upon the walls were a few Japanese wall scrolls and woodblock prints depicting feudal battles and scenes of nature. There were also several glass display-cases holding fragments of history, a vast collection of pottery and pieces of archeological discoveries. But upon closer inspection Regan discovered there were pieces of Roman or Greek fresco works, a chunk of stone that looked like it had come from a tomb mural in Egypt, a beautiful jar with the top looking to be that of Anubis, as well as a large oval object painted with a man's face who was either Roman or Greek. There were a few other items in the cases that she had never seen before. One, though, made her stomach churn.

She slowly looked behind her. "Daniel?"

"Hmm?" He looked up from the bed where her bags had been set. "What's this?"

Smirking, he stepped to her side to look at the object she was pointing to. "Oh, that. It is the mummified hand that once belonged to the priest whose stomach is in that canopic jar."

Regan paled. "You have a mummified hand and a stomach in a jar?" She whimpered and looked to the double-door closet. "You don't have zombies in your closet, do you? I've had enough of those things."

"No, sweetheart. No more zombies." Laughing, he kissed her cheek again. "Long ago, I was invited on an expedition to Egypt when the Valley of the Kings was discovered. My curiosity brought back the hand and the jar when mummies and artifacts were being sold on the streets of Cairo. These days, I fight to preserve the history and the artifacts of many ancient cultures. Inside these cases are some of my most precious and long held possessions that I personally birthed from history at dig-sites across Egypt and the Mediterranean."

Regan scrunched her nose, making a sour face. "I thought Anubis was the God of the underworld in the Egyptian pantheon. What is he doing on a jar?"

"He was actually the God who oversaw mummification and is said to have guarded tombs. He and his army would hunt down any who dared to desecrate a tomb. I'm sure I'm on his list for a heart to heart considering, in my early years of archeology, I entered a few tombs without knocking first, or without invitation." Daniel chuckled and added, "The canopic jars are in the images of the four sons of Horus. The one who looks like Anubis is named Daumutef. His jar holds the stomach of the individual who has been mummified."

Regan glanced to him. "You know a lot, don't you?"

"I've been around for a while and have never stopped gaining knowledge."

He kissed her softly then went back to unpacking the items Regan had shoved into her travel bags. "Would you like me to hang these up for you?"

"I can unpack, just show me where."

"There are plenty of hangers in the walk-in closet. Tomorrow, I'll move some items and clear some drawers for you in the dresser. Would that be alright?"

Regan nodded then continued her examination of Daniel's room. Every item of convenience had been granted to him from the expensive music system to the impressive iMac computer upon a wooden desk. What was missing, however, was a television. "You don't have a television in here?"

Daniel looked up to her with a shake of his head. "No. I prefer my room to be a sanctuary of quietude where the end of the night can be released without the annoyance of television dramas. There is a television in the main sitting room and in the movie room where you can find almost every movie ever created digitally saved onto our entertainment system. However, if you want one, I can look into getting one."

"No. Solitude. I like that." Moving to the two glass doors, Regan glanced out to the expanse of the building's roof that had been turned into a beautiful Roman garden complete with a center fountain, a runway pond, gazebo and a patio under a covering. The house bordered the garden to the north, south, and east with the west side walled off with a magnificent stone wall complete with four massive gargoyles. There were garden lights strung up through the small trees and solar lamps glowing among the bushes.

"Your home is absolutely stunning, Daniel."

Smiling softly, he stepped to her to look over her shoulder to the dark world outside the glass doors. He placed his hands to her shoulders then drew her against his chest as his arms moved to embrace her. "This is your home too, if you so wish it."

With a contented sigh, Regan closed her eyes and leaned back against him. She thought back to all that had happened since she met the vampire - the adventure, the passion, and the danger. Before that fateful night at the club, she had a regular life full of stress from school, family issues, and relationship problems. She had been working at her simple retail job, battling between managers and customers, to earn just over eight bucks an hour. The job was nothing fancy and certainly nothing to write home about.

Daniel had everything, or so it seemed, and though his world was filled with danger and regulations, he seemed rather content and happy with his life. But could she really fit into his life? Would she be welcomed? Could she toss her reality aside and run off with the perfect prince who was offering her a bounty and his kingdom?

"Do you think I'll fit in with your family? What if they don't like me? What if we don't get along? What if I annoy everybody?" She asked, canting her head to the side as he rested his chin to her shoulder.

"The fact that you are here, with me, tonight means that you have already been accepted by my family. Everything will work out. But it won't be easy, sweetheart. You'll be tested, but I will be at your side no matter what. We Lamia take loyalty and dedication far above the ideals that humans often appreciate. To us, life is precious since we cannot produce life on our own. Our numbers are small and the world massive, so we protect that which is dear to us; our lovers, our Fili, and our Familia."

Loyalty and dedication were concepts Regan prized next to virtue and ethics. If Daniel embraced all those concepts, and more, she would be happy with him.

"Would you like a bath before bed? Though, I'm sure you're exhausted." He nuzzled her cheek.

"That does sound lovely."

"The bath is across the room with a shower and a Jacuzzi tub. There are fresh towels in the closet. I don't have any feminine body wash. We can get you some tomorrow."

"No smelly girlie stuff?" Regan chuckled with a pout. "I guess I'll have to smell like a boy for a night."

Daniel snorted. "Think you can manage?"

"Sure. I won't take too long." She offered him Pixie then kissed his cheek before heading into the bathroom.

"Would you like some tea? I might make myself a cup before bed."

Regan called out over the sound of tumbling water, "Well, if you are going to, I wouldn't mind a cup!"

Tea wouldn't be too hard to make. Pixie followed Daniel out of the room and to the kitchen where he went about preparing the tea. He picked a lovely chamomile to brew with some fresh agave nectar for sweetening. When he was finished, and had returned to the bedroom, he discovered that Regan was still in the bath.

He peeked into the room and smiled when he saw her shoulder deep in the tub with a few of the jets running and her hair floating about her shoulders. Good, she needed the comforting soak. "I brought your tea," he told her, drawing her sleepy eyes to him. "Would you like your tea here or at the bed?"

"I'm not sure," Regan mewed. She pitifully tried to lift an arm only to grunt dramatically. "I don't think I can move. I have a bubble jet massaging my butt."

Daniel smirked. "Lucky jet. I'll put your tea by the bedside."

"Thank you. I'll be out soon."

"Take your time." He nodded then disappeared into the bedroom.

Regan didn't take too much longer. When she was done, her flesh scented of hazelnut body wash, she stepped out of the tub, turned off the water to be drained then wrapped herself in a thick, fluffy towel. Her hair was damp and stuck to her face as she rubbed the thick and coiling strands with another towel. When she walked from the bathroom, she saw Daniel resting upon the large bed with Pixie half way off of his chest on her back. He had changed into a pair of Steward plaid flannel pajama set and looked as if he was ready to drop off to sleep.

When he saw her, he offered her a smile and patted the side of the bed next to him. "How was your soak?"

"Warm, very warm," she purred. Daniel had found a pair of her pajamas in her bag and had them waiting for her, so she quickly changed then slipped up to the bed and coiled into his awaiting arms.

He chuckled deeply as he caressed fingers down her neck. "The sun will be up shortly. I can feel it deep in my bones."

"I take it that I'll have to get used to sleeping during the day and being up at night?"

"Not really. Like I said earlier, I can function during the day if need be. However, I shouldn't make a habit of it. I have days when I can't sleep and end up working down in the lab."

"Do I have to be inside if I'm up and you're resting?"

"Of course not. You can come and go as you please. I will get you a cardkey to the main doors of the building and to the garage that will also give you access to the private elevator. I'll also pass a message to security that you'll be staying with me. Perhaps soon I can show you the building, where you can go and what areas are off-limits, and what is in the area that you may enjoy seeing. We can go out when we want to for dinner or movies and so forth. If you do need to travel when I cannot leave the building, I can make arrangements with a driver."

"This will take some getting used to." She sighed with a tiny yawn slipping past her lips.

"I know. It's overwhelming." Daniel smiled and pulled the comforter about them. He then grumbled. "I forgot that I was to tell you the rules."

Regan yawned again, tucking herself to him as Pixie came trotting up her side to curl up above her head upon her pillow. She giggled to the feather soft touch of the dog's tail against her nose. "Kain did say that, didn't he?"

"Think we can put off the discussion till tomorrow?" The Lamia bit back a deep yawn as his mind grew cloudy with the call of the Meditatio.

"I think that'll work."

"Don't tell Kain."

"Your secrets are safe with me - all of them."

"I know, sweetheart. I know."

~ ~ ~ ~

Regan slept on and off during the day. The events of the last few nights, her recovery and the fright of Daniel's self-inflicted wounds, had left her physically, emotionally, and mentally exhausted. A few times she woke to make sure Daniel was still slumbering next to her, then she drifted back to sleep with her body curled tightly against him.

When darkness settled, Daniel woke. Through his groggy mind he smiled upon seeing Regan's sweet features still held within the embrace of sleep. He reached out to touch fingers to her cheek and contemplated on the strangeness of waking up with a warm mortal in his bed. He liked this, waking up with Regan next to him safe and sound.

Regan stirred as he unwound himself from her limbs, and with a sweet little moan, she snuggled closer to him with her features pressed against the crook of his arm. Daniel had not the cruel heart to wake her, so he left her sleeping upon the bed while he got a shower and dressed to meet the Rex who was scheduled to arrive in a few hours. He took Pixie out to the garden to potty then placed her back upon the bed. In a few hours he would return to wake Regan, thus giving her time to dress before Caius' arrival.

It seemed that most members of his family were already up. Rhain was at the Crucible, Amber was seated in the kitchen, drinking her morning mixture of blood infused cappuccino while reading the daily paper, and Kain was in his office - as usual. With enough time on his side, Daniel descended down into the belly of the Thorn Inc. building to check upon the weekly schedules and work load. While he was gone Regan woke, and upon finding the bed empty, she rose and headed from the room. The smell of coffee directed her to the kitchen with a yawn and a set of closed fingers rubbing at her sleep filled eyes.

Amber looked up when she heard Regan enter. She smirked and licked her lips clean of red tainted foam. "Evening, sleepyhead," said the Lamia with a sweet grin to the tousled and sleepy girl.

Regan yawned and smiled to Kain's lover. "Please tell me where I can find some coffee. I can smell it," she murmured, slipping up to a stool at the middle island of the massive, modern kitchen.

"Well, you wouldn't want a sip of mine. But,' Amber motioned towards the single cup brewer, 'there's a nice selection of coffee pods in the cabinet over the coffee maker. There are some flavored creamers in the fridge - a nice selection - the mugs are in the cupboard above and the sweeteners next to the mugs. Help yourself."

"Oh, sweet lover of coffee," Regan mewed as she laid her head down to the counter top, then she slowly extended her arm in the direction of the coffee maker.

Amber arched a brow and chuckled. "Is everything alright, kiddo?"

"It takes me a little while to wake up," mumbled Regan while wiggling her fingers pathetically. "Come to me coffee." She sighed dramatically, "Why can't they make a transforming coffee maker that will come to you and make coffee?"

"They do, it's called a lover." Amber winked playfully.

"Well, mine seems to have disappeared and something tells me that Pixie won't be any good at making coffee. No opposable thumbs."

Amber snorted a laugh. "Daniel's downstairs. He went to quickly check on the lab to make sure his staff have not thrown a 'boss is gone' party."

"Oh..." Pushing herself from the seat, Regan made the choice to make her coffee.

"Did you rest well?"

"Very well. I don't think I've slept so late in a very long time."

"The Rex should be here soon. He's coming early, as usual."

"I hope everything will be okay," mused Regan through a guilt ridden sigh.

Amber offered the mortal a supportive smile. "I wouldn't worry about it. After all, Caius took you into his care. That's very unusual for him, but him doing that for a Humanus is a good sign that he likes you and offers him a little boost in the next election. The Rex may be a jerk at times and a Leviticus, which makes him a double jerk in my book, but he is fair and good hearted. He's going to want to speak to you, so I would get your coffee and drink up. I doubt drool and pajamas will make you look good."

Regan gave a nod. "You're right. I should find some breakfast before he shows up."

"Already taken care of." Amber chuckled and added, "Daniel would not let you starve. He sent out to the bakery down the block. There's a box in the fridge filled with pastries for you."

Regan scuttled to the fridge where she pulled the door open with a jerk, and there before her eyes rested a white pastry box. Her stomach grumbled with hunger when she pulled out the box and took a peek inside. It was not a second later that she was sitting with her coffee, a strawberry-cream filled pastry, and the open box before her, calling her name like an evil, little bakery demon.

"I'm in love," she moaned sweetly as she devoured the pastry and her coffee.

Amber laughed. "Poor Daniel, needing to compete with pastries and sweets. Speaking of him, did he explain to you the basic Lex, the rules and laws?"

Regan squeaked, her cheeks full of pastry, as she looked to the other woman with the largest 'oopsie' eyes possible.

"Of course he didn't. I'm sure you two were discussing more adventurous and pleasing topics."

With a sly, devious grin tucking against the rim to her coffee mug, Regan shrugged. "A lady never kisses and tells."

"Is that so?" Amber asked with a dark smile upon her lips. "What do you think, Daniel?"

Regan's next bite paused over the pastry as she slowly looked over her shoulder. There was Daniel stepping into the room with a slight grin settling his handsome face. Regan's heart slapped her as she stared at him. Oh, how handsome he was! His long hair of onyx was pulled back into a long braid and he wore a pair of simple black slacks with a fine polo-shirt of checkered black and red tucked into the slacks. Good thing her mouth was already gaping over the pastry. Without the pastry, she would look rather foolish.

Gathering herself back under control, Regan licked her lips and crossed a finger over heart. She said with a devious grin and a playful voice, "I told her nothing."

Stepping up to her, Daniel chuckled then bent to press a kiss to her cheek. "I see you found your breakfast. Are the pastries acceptable to you?"

"They're wonderful,' Regan mewed, 'and very delicious. Thank you."

"Good." He touched a second kiss to her cheek then stepped to the counter to fix himself a cup of coffee, only he added some thick red liquid he poured from a black bottle.

"Amber reminded me that we forgot to discuss the rules this morning."

Daniel made a nod. "That's right. I couldn't wake you, so I checked up on my staff. But the rules are rather simple," he began to explain once he had his coffee and was seated across from the women, and to each point he raised a finger. "The first is to never expose our world. If you do, there are deadly consequences, more so because you are a mortal. That one rule is forbidden to break. The second rule is very important because of David's followers being upset over his demise. It is to be aware that you are more prone to being targeted by other Lamia and those who serve them. Stay close to me, to my brothers, and to Amber. Do not go anywhere without informing me where you are going."

Regan frowned. She didn't like the idea that she was going to be on lockdown. "All the time? You said I could come and go as I please."

"This is true. Till you are formally inducted into the Familia, you are like a small fish out of the stream with bears circling you. You are a young, mortal woman who aided in the destruction of David and his happy, demented family. You are also justifiably ignorant of our Lex and a stranger in England, a country that is not your own. This is just for your protection, Regan, that's all."

344

She looked down to her coffee. "I don't like the idea of being locked away."

"You're not being locked away, sweetheart," Daniel assured her gently. "I don't want David's associates coming for you. I want the waters to calm and for you to be formally welcomed into our Familia for your protection before you are released away from my reach."

The mortal blanched and slowly looked away.

"Hey,' Amber said softly as she touched the girl's shoulder, 'don't get down. We all had to go through a time of uncertainty when we were first introduced to this world. And we all had to go through the Domare so we could learn the rules, be processed through training, and experience a short house arrest."

Regan looked between Amber and Daniel with a hopeless frown. "But that means I can't even tell my father why I'm going to stay in London, drop out of college, and bunk up with one of the hottest bachelors in the business world. Right?"

Daniel arched a brow. "Who said I was one of the hottest bachelors in the business world?"

Regan passed him a little grin. "You need to get out more. Joyce had a collection of magazines with you and Rhain on the covers."

Daniel shuddered and dipped his head to mutter over the rim of his mug, "I was blackmailed into those interviews."

"All things in good time," Amber said as she finished her coffee. "We'll figure out how to tell your father when the moment is right."

"Also, you don't have to drop out of college," Daniel added. "There are plenty of schools here that you can look into and send your transfer applications to. The option is always available to you."

"I'm already stretched on funds as it is, and I'm running on scholarships with a lick, stick, and a promise."

Both Amber and Daniel arched brows at her.

"Sweetheart,' he chuckled, leaning forwards while looking to her, 'whatever funds you need I will provide. If you wish to continue your education to the degree level you desire, I will support you in any way. Just say the word."

Regan's heart sank in her chest. His words made her feel elated and guilty at the same time for her humbleness hardly permitted her to take handouts, especially a handout offering financial security for her college.

"We have time to discuss all of your concerns later. The Rex will be here soon, if he's not here already."

Suddenly a com speaker upon the island beeped and Amber reached across to push a button. "Yes?"

"Are Daniel and Regan with you?" It was Kain inquiring.

"Yes. They're here being all lovie dovie with each other."

"Tell them to get their hands off each other. Caius is ready to speak to them. Send them to my office."

The speaker went quiet so Amber turned to the two. "You heard big brother. Get going."

Regan pouted and looked to the box of pastries longingly. "Can I take a scone?"

"They will be here when we're through," Daniel told her with a grin.

"Can I bring my coffee at least?" She asked, hugging her mug protectively to her chest.

Smirking, the Lamia gave her a gentle tug. "Yes, you can bring your precious coffee. Let's not keep Kain and Caius waiting."

Regan looked down to her pink and white pajama set. Daniel followed her gaze and smiled. "They make you look innocent. A gold star for you. Come."

He took her hand and pulled her from the stool. With a glance back to Amber, who waved a few fingers to her, Regan followed her Socius with her bare feet padding along the floor. The two walked down the south hall, just a few doors down, when they arrived at a set of tall, oak doors. Daniel opened one door, allowing her to step into Kain's large office were two men stood before the fireplace in conversation. One Regan noticed as Kain. The other was Caius.

Dressed in a fine suit of white and black, the Rex of England turned when Daniel and Regan entered. His smile was genuine and his deep green eyes seemed to sparkle. "Ah, Daniel, good to see you again. You look well," he said in warm welcome before turning his smile to Regan then grinned to Regan. "It is a pleasure to see you once again, Miss. Scott. How are you feeling?"

"Salve, Rex," said Daniel in polite Lamia greeting. Having closed the doors behind him, he guided Regan over to one of the leather couches. Daniel took a position upon the back of the sofa right behind her. To ease her fear he caressed a few fingers down the back of her neck through the curtain of thick locks.

Regan smiled to Caius, a timid smile. "Much better. Thank you."

Caius took a seat across from the two, crossing one leg over the other. Kain stayed where he was to watch over the group with his intense presence. "That's good to hear. I'm sure you and Daniel have a lot to discuss, so I will not keep you two long. I wanted to come by and see how you were doing after leaving my care."

"I'm doing well, now that I'm here. Daniel's keeping an eye on me."

Caius gave a nod to Daniel and a slight grin. "I would expect nothing less from him. Kain has informed me that you are considering staying with his family. Do you have intentions of assimilating as an Advena Humanus to our world and going through the Domare?"

Regan licked her lips and found a tight knot lodging itself within her throat. "I...I would like to," she said ever so quietly while passing a cautious gaze to Kain. "If...it would be alright."

"Have you given the matter some thought? Deciding to become a member of our mortal brethren is an important decision, not to be taken lightly. The Domare is not easy. Has Daniel explained the details of the Domare to you?"

Regan nodded. "Just a little. We haven't had a lot of time to discuss everything."

Caius nodded and a lock of his black hair kissed his cheek. He casually brushed the thin strand back into place. "Of course. I am sure that when you make your choice Kain and Daniel will see to the arrangements."

"Arrangements?"

"Yes. The Domare is a long process involving training, education, and testing. You may be sent away to another location for an unknown period of time where you will be tutored by an Elder of the Drasus Familia, or an Elder close to the Thorn family."

Regan's eyes blinked and a quick breath was sucked into her lungs. "I could be sent away? For how long?"

Caius offered a shrug of his tight shoulders. "That would be unknown till the Domare is in progress. The time you spend on your studies depends upon how well you study. Once the Elder assigned to your tutelage has decided you are ready, you will be offered three chances to pass a series of intense assessments. If you can pass the exams, then you are formally inducted into our Society and accepted openly as a member of the Drasus Familia."

A tiny whimper escaped Regan's lips, and she looked down to her hands that tightened to her pajama bottoms. A gentle touch fell upon her shoulders, squeezing reassuringly. "When must I make my choice?"

"The sooner the better. Right now, the Proscriptus Lamia of the Underground are in riot over the so called murder of David Servilii. They viewed him as a leader to their twisted sub-society. It will take some time for the right strings to be pulled to calm their anger and settle their demand for vengeance. The sooner you enter the Domare, the quicker the target on your back is removed."

Regan flinched and looked over her shoulder to Daniel. There was a look of sadness to his eyes, but still a soft smile rested upon his lips. With a sigh, she looked back to Caius and Kain. "Daniel's told me that David's death has caused a great disturbance among his associates. He's warned me to be careful and not leave without informing him where I'm going."

"Yes," said the Rex with a faint nod. "Unfortunately, David had a deep running network of associates, powerful across the board, who will continue to support his ideals, even after his death. Some may try and seek vengeance against Daniel and Rhain by using you as a target. It would be best that you stay close to Daniel and his brothers for a short while."

Regan felt her stomach tighten. She sighed with a little nod of her head, but the butterflies within her belly continued to race about. She felt ill to the prospect that she could go through all the terror she had endured under David's control again but with an entirely different vampire, one who may be stronger than him, and be taken further away from those who wished to protect her.

A faint chuckle and a smirk touched the Rex's handsome features. "Don't worry, Miss. Scott. You have more allies than you realize. Trust in Daniel and his family. Trust in me. We will not let any harm come to you. After all, it was one of our kind who forced you into this world. And force is not the way I would prefer to see a young woman of mortal blood enter the Lamia world."

347

The Roman cast the two lovers a thoughtful smile. "I am glad that you are considering staying with Daniel, Regan. He is a strong man, kind and generous. His family will see to your safety, and with their guidance you will have no problem passing the Domare."

Regan blushed and glanced back to Daniel. His smile broadened and a slight wink was tossed her way.

Unlacing his hands, Caius clapped them together as he looked to Kain. "Well, what is the first step to this new and budding relationship, Kain?"

"We need to assimilate Regan into our Familia and introduce her to our Regulus."

"Ah, yes, Divon." Caius nodded his head. "Nice fellow. I'm sure he will adore her. Has her blood been officially tested for the Proprietas?"

"Not yet. With Joyce being able to survive the Creare it was only speculation, till this point, that Regan had the trait as well," answered the eldest Thorn brother.

"More than a speculation. I've tasted her blood," Daniel spoke up, and in doing so drew the eyes of the other two Lamia. "The Proprietas is there. I can guarantee it."

Caius turned his eyes to Regan. "Then the first step is to have your blood officially tested, Miss. Scott, to confirm Daniel's suspicion. Without official documentation that you do have the Proprietas the Domare cannot go forwards."

She looked to the Rex with a nervous frown. "What if my blood doesn't have the trait? Then what happens? Will I have to leave Daniel?"

Daniel leaned close to speak softly, "No, sweetheart, you're not going anywhere. I'm certain you have the trait. The test is only a formality that will register you within the archives of our Familia."

She sighed again, so Daniel gently touched her cheek. "Don't worry."

"This is all very intimidating," she grumbled.

Caius chuckled. "You won't be thrown into our world without a handbook, my dear. However, we do have a situation to handle at this point. When you were under my care you mentioned that you have a father back in the States, and since your visit I have done some research into Joyce's family tree here in England. Her parents will have to be watched if they inquire with the police as to her disappearance or if she tries to contact them. We cannot let any expose us, not even Joyce. If she exposes us, she and any who listened to her words will be dealt with accordingly. This applies to you as well. Any further communication outside these walls, including to your father, will need to be handled with extreme care. Do you understand what I am saying?"

Regan nodded slowly. "Yes. I do. I wouldn't dream of causing any more difficulty. I wouldn't forgive myself if something happened to Daniel or any of his family because of me. I've already caused Daniel and Rhain a lot of physical suffering." She shook her head then bowed her head as a little sniffle tumbled form her voice. "I couldn't live with myself if Daniel suffered any more than he already has."

"Then what of your father, Regan?"

348

Kain's question drew her eyes and she frowned heavily. "I don't know. That's on the list of topics to discuss. My father is really the only one I have left. My mother passed away a few years back. My dad and I are the black sheep of the family. Besides Joyce and her parents, most of the family have distanced themselves from us."

"I'll find some way of explaining to him why I'm staying here," she added after a heavy sigh.

Daniel looked up to his brother and the Rex. "You have my word that she and I will consider every option. I will walk her through the Domare and answer any of her questions." He leveled Caius with a stern and strong eye. "I will take full responsibility for her."

"Daniel," Regan gasped softly with a look of shock tossed back to him.

He smiled to her then leaned to kiss the top of her head before looking back to the other two Lamia. "As my Socia, she is my duty."

Caius nodded his agreement. "Agreed. Now we must discuss Joyce."

Regan perked. "Did you find her?"

The man shook his head. "Not yet. I had my men search the entire factory to find her, but it seems she has disappeared. To where,' he shrugged, 'I do not know. But neither I nor my men will stop till we find her. All Templum and Negotium in this Republica have been notified of Joyce's situation, as have all the English Familia. My contacts in the Proscriptus ranks are on the lookout for her. Trust me, they wish no part in the corruption that David started, nor do they want one of his pets causing problems. If she surfaces, I shall know about it.

He locked Regan with a harsh gaze. "This means that you must keep your own eyes and ears open, Regan. There is a strong chance that Joyce will try to find you or contact you, for either revenge or sanctuary. She is alone now and without her Parens to watch out for her, and that means she has no sanctuary or partners to see to her care. And with every passing minute fewer of David's supporters will want to deal with her."

"What will you do with her if you find her?"

"It is not a question of if,' Kain answered in a tone of voice void of any care or concern for Joyce's wellbeing, 'but when. When she is found, she will be brought to justice for her role in your kidnapping and as David's accomplice."

Regan sank back as her stomach twisted to the thought of what justice meant in the Lamia world. She frowned while thinking of her cousin outside and alone in this new world, with no help from a family like Daniel's. A gentle touch upon her cheek drew her attention to her Socius; Daniel was smiling to her.

"Don't worry,' he told her gently, 'everything will be done to see her safe, but she does need to face the consequences of her actions. I can't lie to you, sweetheart. Her punishment may be severe."

"I'm curious, Regan," Caius spoke up with a slight smirk upon his handsome mouth. "What do you think of all of this?"

349

She gave a timid shrug. "I think I'm still processing everything well enough. The more I see the easier it is to believe everything I've been told. And trust me, what I've seen in the past few days is enough for a few months."

The Rex chuckled with a slight nod. "Do you have any questions for me?"

"I think most of my questions will be for Daniel since they're more personal." After a moment of thought, she did add, "However, I guess I do have a question."

Caius bid her to continue with a motion of his hand.

"What happens to me if I'm shown I have this trait? Joyce was turned, wasn't she? Will that happen to me as well?"

"Why don't you answer her question, Daniel?" The Rex insisted with a nod towards the younger Lamia.

"Regan,' Daniel began, 'just because it is proven that you have the trait doesn't mean you will be turned. There is no automatic switch that's turned on at one point or another, or during some magical circumstances. When you think of the movies and books, you think of the transference of blood from the human to the vampire till the human is nearly drained. That is the point when the vampire feeds the human his or her blood. It's that exchange that turns the human to a vampire. That's not exactly how it works with us Lamia. Not just any human can be changed."

"Then what happens?"

"Remember when I told you last night that the trait is triggered by the blood of a Lamia?"

Regan nodded.

"The gene within you must be triggered by an outside influence, the blood of a Lamia. The process is very exact and very delicate. What would happen is that most of your blood would be drained till only the blood containing the Proprietas remains. That is the moment when you are closest to death. The Lamia would then feed you his or her blood, but the amount needed to trigger the Creare varies depending upon the human. Sometimes it is a large amount, sometimes only a small amount."

Daniel smiled to her as he brushed his fingers through her hair. "At that point the gene will be triggered and you go through the Creare, the change. Now,' Daniel moved off the back of the sofa so he could sit next to her with his eyes looking into hers, 'this part is the downside to the change, and the most frightening. There is a fifty-fifty chance that a human who is going through the Creare may or may not survive."

Regan blanched. She leaned back from him just a bit with a look of complete disbelief and shock. "The person might not survive?"

Daniel nodded sadly. "Correct. There is no perfect change. The change can be a very painful event because the human body does physically alter on a molecular level. That alteration leads to trauma on the body and the human psyche. Your eyes will change due to increased vision. Your hearing will sharpen. Your skin will thin, your veins become dry, your senses heightened, and your body will become stronger so the density of your bones will increase. Your muscles will become much more flexible leaving you to feel as if your muscles are being torn apart at that time."

"There is no romantic explanation of the Creare." He touched her cheek lovingly and whispered, "I wish there was. Some say this percentage is to weed out those who are not strong enough to handle our world."

"That's horrible." She looked quickly to Caius and Kain. "Do I have a choice in going through the Creare or is it required, like with Joyce?"

"My dear,' Caius said, offering her a soft smile, 'going through the Creare is your choice as ordered under the Lex. No human is to be forced through the change, as was the unfortunate situation pertaining to your cousin."

"In other words,' Daniel went on to say, 'whether or not you want to go through the change is up to you. You must know what you want due to the risk. Deciding too quickly is not a wise choice. Often, if you have not passed the Domare, the Concilium of England and even the Regulus of your Familia may not permit you to attempt the Creare. Every precaution is taken when a human desires to go through the Creare. If you wish to go through with the Creare, then the decision is made solely by you."

"That's good to know. So how did Joyce go through it?"

Caius cursed under his breath then sighed with two fingers pinching the bridge of his nose. "The Proscriptus, such as David, desire to be free of the Lex. They no longer wish to be ruled or controlled, as they call civil obedience. So they operate outside the Lex with exception to the rule of exposing our world. The terror they know I would bring down upon them keeps them at bay, at least those with half a damn brain in their heads."

"Joyce,' he went on to say, 'was no doubt changed without her consent once David discovered she had the trait. The Proscriptus community needs more members, so it is easier for them to create new ones rather than try to recruit due to the disillusions and the threats that they bring upon other Lamia. They live and operate on the edge of our laws, and many of the new Fili care little for upholding the Lex. In regards to your cousin, David most likely used her Creare as a tool to lure you to him, and in consequence brought Daniel to your rescue."

Regan frowned. "What do you mean?"

"I think what the Rex is saying,' Daniel began to tell her as he gently combed fingers through her long locks of dark silk, 'is that David changed Joyce with intentions of returning her to the flat where you would be able to find her. He knew I was with you that night because Joyce probably told him. He probably hoped that our possible discovery of her would push me over the edge and land me in trouble. However, he didn't count on the chance that Joyce would come to beforehand. It is by instinct that a newly changed Lamia seeks out his or her Parens. That is why, when Rhain went to check on Joyce, she had vanished."

"Oh,' Regan frowned with her eyes turning downward, 'poor Joyce. So she was lured in by David and then put through all that agony only to be left alone? If she had just waited, you could've helped her before she got back to David. Right?"

Daniel gave a solemn nod.

Sighing, she leaned to her lover. "I feel horrible. Now she's lost again."

351

"We'll find her," he whispered against her soft hair. "I promise you."

"I am sure you are feeling overwhelmed with all of this," Caius spoke with a chuckle and a knowing smirk to his lips just as he leaned to look to Kain. "Then again, I can't remember when I went through the change. Am I getting too old, my friend?"

Kain snorted with a roll of his dark eyes, his snort drawing a grin from the Rex. "Even you refuse to answer my question. Smart man." Chuckling, Caius looked back to Regan and Daniel with. "I have one more question for you, Miss. Scott. Does it not scare you to know that our kind,' he stated sweeping an arm out to Daniel and Kain, 'have been upon this world for thousands of years and you never knew we were this close to you?"

"Honestly? It is a little frightening."

"Would it scare you even more to know that I am older than two thousand years and that I was born during the early development of Rome, before the great Empire was born?"

"Oh," She breathed with a little uneasy chuckle. "You look good for your age."

Caius barked out a laugh, a laugh that rumbled through his powerful form. He winked playfully to her then slowly stood from the chair. "With that being said, I shall entrust Miss. Scott to you and your family, Daniel. Kain, am I to understand that you and Divon will be at the Concilium meeting this coming week?"

"Of course." Kain offered a bow.

"Grand! Miss. Scott,' Caius offered her a polite incline of his head, 'it was a pleasure seeing you again. You are in good hands. Daniel, watch out for her. Don't lose this one. Kain, would you see me to the door? Or should I call your lovely Amber to see me to my car?"

Kain narrowed his eyes towards Caius knowing full well that the man was only jesting about his Socia. "Not on your undead life."

Caius laughed while clapping Kain on the back as the two departed the office. They left Regan and Daniel sitting together, his arms about her and her head resting to his shoulder. "Are you okay?" he asked softly.

"I think so," was her reply in a tender, little mew. She tipped her head so she could look up to him. "Honestly? I'm a little scared."

"If you weren't, I'd be worried." The Lamia pressed a kiss to his Socia's forehead.

"What now?" she asked as she slipped her arms about Daniel's slender frame. Feeling him so close gave her strength and comfort in this new world where uncertainty seemed to rule.

"How about we talk about our future over a pastry and another cup of coffee?"

Regan nodded her head. "Pastries are good."

"Then, I thought I could show you around the building, perhaps my lab."

She twisted a bit to look up to him. "Do you have a mummy down there?"

Daniel grinned. "Yes, I do."

She clapped him on the thigh as she sat up. "Then what are we waiting for? Those pastries won't eat themselves." She stood then looked down to her slender belly while rubbing a hand over fabric. "Yes, my precious, we shall feast."

Daniel laughed, and laughed well.

XXII

*U*pon *my word, upon my blood, and upon my life I swear to you my loyalty and my dedication.*

I will love you, Regan Scott, till the end of my long life - my final death. And even then, I will love you forever... beyond the rays of the sun and beyond the clouds of heaven.

-    *Daniel Rhys Thorn*

~ ~ ~ ~

T hree months later...

"I swear, if I see one more date, one more name, or one more term, I'm going to scream!"

"I told you that the Domare could kill!" laughed Philomena with a finger wagging towards Regan. "But nobody would listen to me!"

Regan sneezed. "I think I'm allergic!"

Rhain laughed and gave his brother a nudge. "You certainly snagged a smart one, Daniel."

"Shut up," muttered Daniel. He called lovingly to his Socia, "Stay strong, Regan. Theodore wants you to finish reading that book..."

"Dictionary!"

"Text book of Lamia terms and history,' Daniel corrected when she snapped to him, 'by next Thursday. You have an entire evening of tutoring with him tomorrow."

"I'm not surprised Theodore offered his support to help Regan through the Domare. He's taken a liking to her," said Rhain as he looked down to his tablet to run over the liquor inventory.

"He treats her as if she were his own blood daughter." Daniel shrugged. "I can't blame him. She has a captivating personality. Besides, I think he feels a bit responsible for what David put her through."

Rhain arched a brow and shifted his eyes to his brother. "So he lost his Lamia son and adopted a human daughter? The man's insane."

Alasdair chuckled. "Is Rhain jealous? Here I thought he only had Pixie to compete with." The Sorcerer chortled then yelped when he was kicked in the shin. "Hey! Watch it. I bruise easily," he muttered with a glare sent to his business partner.

Rhain glared right back, undaunted to the true threats that Alasdair was able to magically create. "Like a bloody banana, you fruit cake."

"When is Regan scheduled to take the Domare?" Alasdair asked as he reclined within his bar seat. He swept a lock of tainted orange from his sharp features that gave herald to his Italian decent.

"In a month and a half, maybe two."

Rhain whistled. "Isn't that a bit early?" He looked down the bar where he saw Philomena trying to explain something to Regan in finger gestures. He was pretty sure he saw the middle finger presented a few times.

"That's what I thought, but Theodore assures me that Regan is more than ready. He said that her mind is like a sponge, soaking up everything she studies and all that he tells her. They will be reviewing her books over the next few weeks, then they will run through a few practice tests." Daniel also saw those gestures and was tempted to call Regan away from the crazy Lamia, but he didn't have the heart to label Phil as being 'crazy'. The sound of the women's laughter brought a smile to his lips.

"I'm sure she's excited."

"I'm not sure if she's excited or petrified," Daniel clarified to Alasdair's comment.

"She'll be fine," Rhain muttered, waving a hand before grumbling. "What the hell is wrong with the numbers from last night, Lazer? Is an employee handing out free shots again?" He shoved the tablet to Alasdair who frowned upon seeing the data.

"I would hope not," grumbled the Sorcerer. "If they're smart, they wouldn't pull any more of that shit, not after the last time."

"Alasdair,' said Daniel softly and with a touch of trepidation to his voice, 'I've been meaning to inquire as to your Familia's preparations for Grayson's reburial."

Alasdair raised his eyes that had suddenly filled with a shadow of sadness. "I wish that the situation with Grayson's burial was that simple. Unfortunately, I must keep the information a secret from everybody, including my father." He gave an absent minded shrug. "Everybody thinks he's dead."

Alasdair reached for a shot glass of copper liquid. "Even if I told my father what happened, Grayson would be labeled a traitor and would be banned from being buried anywhere near the Familia Sepulcorem. I can't have my brother labeled as a traitor, so I'm going to risk my father's wrath and keep what happened a secret."

Daniel and Rhain both frowned, sympathizing with their friend. "I'm truly sorry," said Daniel softly.

Alasdair waved a gloved hand and shook his head. "You have nothing to be sorry for. I'm not happy with what my brother did to you and Rhain, especially towards Regan. I still can't wrap my mind about what happened. He was given a bloody funeral." He paused as a confusing thought twisted about in his mind. "Damn. If he's not buried in his tomb, then who is? There's a damn body in there!" Alasdair groaned and tossed back the shot, grimacing as the powerful liquor tore down his throat then scowled heavily.

He licked his lips then went on to say through a breathy sigh, "I never thought that the bastard walked the dark arts, Necromancy. Like my father, Grayson had always been an honorable Lamia, one who followed the Lex and did what he was told. He had pride for our Familia and our friends. He was my father's Successor."

Alasdair dragged a hand through his unruly hair. "This is just...a shock. I don't even know how he died - again."

Daniel blinked, his eyes snapping to his twin. "You don't know?"

Alasdair shook his head in a silent 'no'. He didn't see the look Daniel passed to Rhain or the glare Rhain passed back to Daniel.

"I see," sighed Daniel as he tossed his brother a very displeased expression. Rhain had blatantly lied to Alasdair, keeping the truth of Grayson's death hidden. That was certainly unacceptable in Daniel's book, but the friendship between Alasdair and Rhain was their business, not his. If Rhain wanted to put their friendship and business partnership on the line to keep such devastating news of his involvement in Grayson's demise a secret, then that was his decision to make and the consequences to accept.

"What will you do then, if you don't mind me asking?" Daniel inquired as he turned his attention back to the Warlock.

"My brother deserves a peaceful rest and a final burial. Even if he followed the dark arts and fell in line with a Proscriptus scum like David, he deserves some respect. And I will grant that to him. However, I only have a short period of time to contain him before his body starts to regenerate."

Daniel tipped his head. "Contain him?"

"Yes. A Necromancer's body can regenerate over time, so I will need to find a place where I can secure him and keep an eye on his rebirth. I can't just let him rebuild himself then go walking off to fuck up somebody else's life."

"I see. Then where will you bury him?"

Alasdair's slender eyes slid a glance to Rhain.

Daniel's gaze followed. "Rhain?"

The other twin groaned, glaring to his brother. "What?"

Daniel narrowed his eyes as his mind quickly twisted on every possibility that could occur and involve Rhain and the need for a protected tomb. After a second of contemplation, his features curled into a shaken expression. "No." He looked back to Alasdair who gave a nod then back to his twin. "No! You can't. Do you know how foolish it would be to bury Grayson here? You would be putting your club and your lives in jeopardy! Not to mention the fact that you two would be breaking about ten Lex."

"For fuck's sake, Daniel!" Rhain threw up his arms. "It's our club and our property, so we can do whatever the hell we want!"

"No, you can't. The Crucible and the cemetery are registered as a Templum, and that means you must abide by certain laws or you will lose your license."

"Actually, we can." Rhain flashed a grin. "Alasdair and I have studied the laws and there's nothing in them about burying somebody who is already buried. You forget, my smart twin, that Greyson is said to be buried in a tomb in the Augur Villa. Nobody will know that there's going to be a burial, so nobody's going to question who is being buried anyway."

Daniel groaned. "What happened to Grayson's body anyway?"

"You remember when we were leaving the factory you asked me who I was texting? I contacted a Proscriptus associate of mine who is a rather tricky son-of-a-bitch. He owed me a good favor, so he didn't mind slipping behind Caius' cleaning crew to locate Grayson's body before the factory was torn apart."

A Proscriptus? Daniel hung his head. "This is getting better and better."

"Relax," chuckled Rhain as he clapped his brother on the shoulder. "Alasdair and I have this completely under control."

"I still don't like this," muttered Daniel, tossing the other Lamia a very critical and judgmental eye.

"Well, too bad," huffed Rhain, sticking his pierced tongue out to his brother. "There's nothing you can do about it. So, pppffttthh." He flipped his twin off.

Daniel's features turned sour. "You two are unbelievable." He shot his brother and his friend a stern glare. "Have you taken any precautions to preventing Grayson's regeneration from happening too quickly?"

Rhain rolled his eyes. "Of course we have! We're not completely daft, are we?"

"Oh? Do tell?" Daniel grumbled under his breath as he crossed his arms to his chest with a speculative brow arching. Yes, let them explain. Daniel's ears were wide open and his lecture was right on the tip of his tongue.

"Relax, Daniel," said Alasdair with a charming and confident smile. "I know plenty of spells that will help prevent Greyson from regenerating too quickly, as well as a few that will keep him bound not only to the tomb but to the cemetery."

Daniel turned his cautious gaze to the Veneficus. "And your spells are strong enough to keep Greyson contained?"

Alasdair nodded. "Of course. Are you doubting my skills, Daniel?"

"I would never doubt your skills," muttered Daniel with a dry sigh. "I doubt the sanity of this idea."

The Veneficus chuckled. He understood Daniel's concern and the need to protect Rhain from himself. But Rhain was right, the two had done enough research to find the loop holes in the Lex that would allow them to do as they needed and quietly, outside the gaze of any prying eye that is. "I will bind Grayson to the tomb, setting up a barrier that he cannot cross and that will also keep his powers limited. Though I can't prevent him from regenerating, I can slow down the progression well enough. What might take just a few months could be drawn out a few years, maybe a decade at best."

"What if he gets out? He was an extremely powerful Veneficus, and as we have seen, has taken on the talents of Necromancy with great adaptation. What if he is able to break through the barrier?"

357

Alasdair began to explain, "*If* that happens, and I stress the 'if' part, I will also place a boundary line around the cemetery. No matter how quickly he regenerates and what level of power he is able to regain, he will still be very weak and won't be able to push past two barriers. And hopefully, by then, I'd have figured out a way to explain all of this to my father without drawing the attention of the Rex."

Alasdair gave a sigh as he leaned forwards with a long arm reaching for a bottle of whiskey. "I would like it if Grayson's death has destroyed whatever connection he had formed with the demons that granted him the powers of Necromancy. The dark souls that he bound to him will only grant him their power as long as they are…fed. Once they realize their associate is no longer able to fulfill his or her contract, they will remove their powers and go find somebody else's soul to play about in. Maybe then I can talk to him, figure out what went wrong and why he crossed the line."

Alasdair slid his eyes to Daniel and stated firmly, "If I can find a way to save him, I'll do it. I won't give up on him."

Daniel nodded and offered his friend a gentle touch to the shoulder. "I can't fault you for that. I would do anything for my brothers as well, and I would do anything to protect them, even if they had crossed the lines of honor."

"It's much quieter in here without the music and the crazy people." Regan suddenly appeared at the edge of the small group, her voice chiming with a soft chuckle. She stepped to her lover's side and smiling to him as he raised one of her hands to his lips.

Rhain snorted, "Wait an hour and you'll change your mind."

"Regan,' Alasdair spoke up with a charming smile upon his features, 'if you have any more questions on Ars Magica, you let me know. Alright?"

She nodded gratefully. "I will. Thank you." Looking about the club, Regan mused, "I like the club like this. It's rather homey."

Rhain shuddered, sulking down in his bar seat.

"Did you hear that, Rhain?" Alasdair chuckled, nudging his business partner. "Our club's homey. We should have some doilies knitted for coasters." He began to look about the stained-glass windows with a scrutinizing and motherly eye. "Maybe some lace curtains…"

Regan stuck her tongue out.

Philomena, who had just walked up on the conversation, broke into a bright laugh.

Daniel smirked as he stirred his drink, a true bloody Mary. "This is the only time I prefer to visit. Otherwise, this place is loud, obnoxious, and full of hormonally raging mortals, which is right up Rhain's alley."

His twin growled from his seat.

"So, it was a fluke that you came in the night I was here?" With a sassy huff, Regan crossed her arms and tapped a foot against the barstool she now sat upon. "Wonderful. I'm just an oopsie blip in your life."

From next to Daniel, Rhain leaned to his twin and whispered in Daniel's ear. "Dig yourself out of that one, smart ass."

Was that a challenge? A side glance was offered to his twin along with a sly smirk before Daniel turned to his lover and reached a slender finger out to trail along Regan's smooth chin. Her eyes narrowed, but he would not be deterred. "Not a fluke, sweetheart," he murmured as he leaned close to her. "Fate," he corrected. "Why else would I come here unless it was Destiny that called me?"

Regan's delicate lips twisted as she weighed the truth and the romance of his statement. Leaning forwards, she offered him a kiss to the corner of his lips where the tip of her tongue swept out to gather a little drop of his tainted drink that grasped the edge of his lower lip. She no longer held any concerns or discomfort in knowing that most of the food and drink Daniel partook in, privately, was created with Sanguis as an ingredient.

"That's better," she purred sweetly.

"Ah, young love," sighed Philomena dreamily.

Alasdair leaned forwards, tapping her nose. "Bored with me already, luv?"

"You're such a freak, Alasdair." Phil huffed and gave him a shove. The hopeful brightness in her eyes that was passed to Rhain was promptly ignored as he looked down to his empty glass, which had held fresh blood not too long ago.

"But a freak in many fun ways," Alasdair added with a wink to both girls, and both girls rolled their eyes.

Regan took a sip of her diet soda with a twist of lime and cherry syrup; four cherries added for taste. "So,' she smiled, looking to Phil, 'are we still going to the all night movie marathon of Alfred Hitchcock?"

Philomena's eyes went wide and she giggled excitedly. "Are you kidding? Of course!"

"What?" Asked Daniel and Alasdair at the same time. Yet the Sorcerer muttered with a pout, "I want to go."

Daniel frowned to Regan. "When did you two decide this?"

"A few nights ago," answered Regan as she mindlessly twiddled a lock of his long hair about a finger. "You're going to be gone this weekend with Kain, so Philomena invited me out for movies on Friday night since Rhain will be here and Amber is going to be gone as well. I don't want to be alone, and Rhain shouldn't have to babysit me."

"Amen to that!" chimed Rhain as he raised his empty glass in a toast to her logic.

"Rhain should have a sense of loyalty when a favor from his brother is requested of him," mumbled Daniel with a hard glare and an even harsher tone to his voice.

Clearing his voice, Daniel looked back to Regan. He could insist that she stay in the Domus for her own safety, or even spend the weekend at Theodore's. The Elder would be delighted to have her over considering she was the only one who listened to his old war stories and could make homemade, organic butterscotch brownies with a touch of Sanguis. "Perhaps you should wait…"

Instantly, Regan raised a finger before Daniel's eyes that had the man's onyx orbs crossing. "Don't start," she muttered playfully. "I'll be fine. Phil will be with me, and she won't let anybody hurt me. Will you Phil?"

Phil smiled brightly and nodded. "I'll bring my Taser."

"See?" Smiling, Regan looked back to Daniel to ease his concern with a touch to his arm and a kiss to his cheek. "We'll be fine. I'll keep in touch and text you between movies. Alright? Please let me go."

"You have your tests," he stated in argument and displeasure.

"Yes,' she nodded in agreement, 'and you've told me that I'm more than ready to take, and pass, the Domare. One night won't do me any harm. It's not like I'm going to become suddenly stupid."

"Are you sure you don't need more time to study?"

Regan shook her head.

"Damn, brother," Rhain groaned. "Her tests are in a few months. One night out is not going to kill her. Regan will come with me to the club, then she and Phil will leave to the movies. The cinema is not but two blocks away, and they promised to be back here so I can take Regan home when the night is done. She can stay up in the office, searching through porn sites if she wants, till the club closes. Stop being a stuffy, old vampire and let the girl have some fun."

Encouraged by Rhain's support, Regan passed her Socius the largest set of puppy dog eyes she could muster. Her lower lip even quivered.

Daniel sighed. He couldn't fight that little lip quiver or his twin's supportive logic, minus the porn sites. "Then perhaps I should see if the Domare can be moved forwards a few weeks just so you can get the tests over and done with."

Regan smiled with a quick nod. "That would be great!"

"Very well," Daniel pointed an accusing finger towards Phil. "I don't want any of your shenanigans, Phil. Do you understand me? You two go to the movies and that's it. You bring her back here without any detours."

"Shenanigans?" Rhain asked with a cheeky grin upon his features. "Who the hell still says shenanigans? You're getting old, Frater."

"If I am, then so are you…my twin," muttered Daniel, flashing the same grin in return. He then stood and offered his arm to Regan. "Shall we go?"

"Are we still on for our movie date tonight?" She asked as she slipped her arm to his, hugging his arm close.

"Actually, I have something else in mind."

Regan blinked and tipped her head. "But we had planned on some movies. We were going to pick up some Chinese take-out on the way home."

"Are you complaining?" Daniel chuckled then gave a cheeky shrug. "Very well. I had something very romantic in mind, but if you want to pass up a lovely evening for Chinese take-out and a B-rated movie at home, then we can do that."

Regan narrowed one eye and arched the brow over the other. "How romantic are we talking about?"

"The definition of romance." Daniel locked his eyes with her from over the rim of his glass as he took the final sip of his drink.

Regan's lips formed the perfect o-shape and her eyes glistened with delight. The grin that curled Daniel's lips as they drifted from the glass sent a shiver down her spine. Licking her lips, she turned to Rhain and offered him a hug. "Sorry to dash, but we must be going." She gave him a quick 'smooch' on the cheek, which he grumbled to.

Alasdair gaped and pointed to his cheek. "Where's my kiss?"

Smirking, Regan kissed his cheek. She then waved to fill and called, "Phil! I'll see you soon!"

Daniel couldn't retain the chuckle that bubbled up within his throat. He sat down his glass then gathered his and Regan's thin coats from the backs of their chairs.

Regan took his hand, giving a frantic tug. "Come on, darling. Let's go be romantic!"

Daniel leaned to kiss her forehead but then he blinked as she grabbed her coat and darted away. "I'll go get the car!" she chimed as she danced away, heading quickly to the door. Daniel snorted and dug out the keys to his expensive car from his pants' pocket. "You don't have the keys! Can you even drive a manual?"

Regan turned about, stepping backwards while calling to him, "Don't question me!" She offered an overly sweet smile then turned about and stalked off to the doors.

Daniel sighed, turning his attention to the group with a devious grin, or a lop-sided smile of wickedry. "Well, I must be going. It was a pleasure. Rhain, I'll see you back at the Domus."

Rhain flipped a wave over his shoulder. "Yeah, sure."

"Have a good night," said Alasdair.

Philomena cooed, fluttering her lashes. "You two have fun."

Daniel winked, "We most certainly will.

~ ~ ~ ~

"So? Where are you taking me?" Regan asked the question as she watched the scenery pass them by. They drove along the Thames with the building lights glistening off the moving water. Even with the hour growing late, the streets and the sidewalks were heavy with vehicles and pedestrians.

When Daniel didn't answer, she glanced to him and reached over the consul to poke at his slender thigh. "Are you going to tell me or are you going to be sneaky about our destination?"

Daniel thought on that question, and in the end he answered with a grin. "Sneaky."

Regan huffed, curled her nose, and looked back out the window.

He looked to her, quickly, before looking back to the road. "What's wrong? Don't you trust me?"

"Of course I do," she chuckled. "But I also know how devious and cunning you can be."

He nodded with a proud smile. "Yes. I can be rather devious and cunning, can't I?"

Regan chuckled, and they finished the short drive in silence. However, as they rounded the last corner their destination became blatantly obvious. There was no way Regan could ignore the massive structure of circular design that rose high into the night sky. Rising up before her view was the world famous Ferris wheel called the London Eye; a massive construction of steel that created a modern engineering feat of man.

Regan snapped her attention to Daniel as the car pulled to a stop in the car park. "Oh, no. You're not serious."

"Of course I am." He shut off the car and was about to exit when he noticed Regan hadn't budged. She had pressed herself against the seat and looked pale - frightened. Daniel frowned. "What's wrong?"

Gulping, Regan slowly turned her eyes to him and whimpered. "Is this a bad time to tell you that I'm really scared of heights?"

Daniel blinked his eyes, stunned at the news. "Honestly? Yes. After all, you flew over here."

She whimpered again and looked back out the window. "But that's different."

The Lamia leaned back in his seat, an arm draped over the steering wheel. "How so?"

"Planes are magical constructs flown by wizards," she answered with a deep breath then motioned to the construct. "That thing is a concept of Satan and made by his demonic herd of Chihuahuas."

Daniel laughed softly, deeply, as he shook his head. He then slipped from the car, shut the door behind him, and walked about the car to open her door. "Come now," he said with a soft and gentle chuckle as he offered her his hand. "You can't visit London and not take a ride on the London Eye."

Regan grabbed the door and made a move to close it but Daniel caught the door and held it open as he arched a brow. He looked to the London Eye then back to Regan as he leaned slightly to the car. "It's perfectly safe, Regan."

"Sure, that's what everybody says. Then they get on one of those things and it breaks and goes rolling all over the town!"

That arched brow upon Daniel's features lifted even higher as he listened to her. "What do you watch on the television that would give you that impression?"

"Those made for SyFy channel movies." She was dead set on believing any Ferris wheel was a death trap.

Smiling, Daniel shook his head at her innocent, yet paranoid, words. "Just like Rhain. If you don't come out of that car, I'll come in there and get you."

Regan narrowed her eyes at him. "You really want me to go on that thing?"

"Yes."

"Why?"

"Because I have paid a nice sum of money in donation to the upkeep of this wonderful creation of mankind so we can take a private ride."

The answer brought Regan's fear to weaken and a wave of guilt to cross her heart. Her body eased as she shifted forwards to regard her handsome lover with a look of disbelief. "You did?"

Daniel nodded.

"Why?"

He smiled and motioned her out of the vehicle with a set of fingers. "Do I need a reason to bestow a romantic evening upon my Socia? If you want to know, I realized that your trip here to England has been stunted by a lot of pain, emotionally and physically. You have far too many bad memories of the last few months than good. You shouldn't harbor any negative memories. They'll haunt your soul. So I've done this to help create new memories, happier memories. Also, I would like to spend a beautiful evening with the woman I love, if that's not too much trouble."

Looking to him, Regan whimpered and nibbled her lower lip. "You're a dream, aren't you? Tomorrow I'm going to wake up and you're going to be a pumpkin. Right?"

The Lamia chuckled and rolled his black eyes in amusement. "Yes. Tomorrow night I will be a pumpkin and Rhain will be a professor at Oxford. Now please, humor me?" He pressed his hand further. "I won't let anything happen to you. I swear that upon my life."

Regan's delicately painted lips turned down to a fragile frown, and she stared up to his dark eyes and warm, inviting smile. His words held a promise of safety and wonder that caressed away her fears. With a little sigh she gave him her hand allowing him to guide her from the car.

"You didn't have to go to this much trouble, Daniel," she said.

"Yes, I did," he told her as he guided her arm through the hook of his elbow. They walked forwards as he continued to speak, "I told you that life is very precious to us Lamia, especially to me. Life can be short, too short, so I want to experience every moment I can with you."

"But this is too much."

"Is it?" He tipped his head then shrugged. "Perhaps it is, but that's not the point. The point is, I have the money to pay for such an evening as this with intentions of spending a wonderful evening with you. I promised you a romantic evening, so accept this as what it is - a romantic moment spent with me."

Taking a deep breath, Regan eyed the massive structure cautiously, curiously, and with a breathy sigh. "The butterflies in my stomach have butterflies in their stomachs and they're all practicing for the circus."

Daniel squeezed her hand as they walked closer to the wheel. "If you are afraid of heights, then this is the perfect opportunity to put your trust in me, if saving you from David wasn't a trustworthy event already."

Just love him, alright? Trust everything he says, and trust in him. He'll never lead you astray, and he'll never break your love or your faith in him. If you can do that, he'll make sure you are the happiest woman in the world.

As they walked, Regan stared at him while letting Rhain's words tumble about within her mind. She smiled and gently hugged his arm. "You're right. I'm being silly, aren't I?"

363

"You're being yourself," he said, glancing down to her. "We all have our fears and our worries. However, we can't let them control us or we'll never experience life. It's up to us to battle our demon of fear, take control and face life head on. You have nothing to fear because I will always be ready to aid you in your battles."

"Then I have nothing to worry about."

Once they were at the Ferris wheel Regan's fear of heights crept back about her. It was one thing to let her ego give a swing at her pride, but convincing her brain not to be afraid was a different matter altogether. She tried to take little steps backwards, laughing nervously as she twisted about in Daniel's arms when he tried to stop her, but she couldn't get away from him. They laughed, their bodies coiling about each other as they wrestled while walking the last few feet to the gate where a Lamia attendant was waiting for them. He kept on, gently, urging her with soft whispers and pleading looks till she pouted, and with hesitation, finally agreed as long as she could keep her eyes closed.

But when she was standing at the base of the structure with her head craned all the way back to look up, she felt vertigo kiss her. Never before had Regan dared to give up her trust and go on faith to ride one of these, not even at the Illinois State fair. The Merry-Go-Round was good enough for her! Even going on an airplane had her popping a few anti-anxiety pills, but this took the cake.

She was shaking. Daniel could feel her trembling as he stood behind her with his hands upon her shoulders. A part of him felt guilty for trying to pressure her, then again, there was a stronger part of him that kept pushing him to get what he desired. And what he wanted was to have Regan with him as they slowly circled the sky over London. He gently pressed his fingers to her shoulders as he leaned in closer to her with his chest pressing to her back.

"You'll be fine," he whispered. "Do you want me to help ease you?" He kissed the shell of her ear.

Help ease her. She knew what he was speaking of, a special ability of the Lamia called the Coercêre. Every Lamia held the ability to coerce a weaker Lamia or a human by the use of three different techniques; the Recodari, the Vocis Sonus, and the Attingêre. Daniel had explained to her that he was rather handy at the Vocis Sonus, the vocal Coercêre that allowed him to coercer another with the use of his voice. In fact, he had admitted to her that he had used it once before on her when David had cornered them along the Thames. Regan had been upset with him, not for long, then realized that he had used the ability in order to protect both of them.

"Just a little?" She asked the question while looking back to him as she pinched two fingers close together. "Tiny bit?"

"Tiny bit." Smiling softly, Daniel bowed his head to her then tightened his hold about her. He drew her back to his chest and ran his lips along her neck. "Listen to my voice,' he whispered softly - seductively, 'listen to the beating of my heart. Close your eyes and listen."

She did just that, taking a deep breath and closing her eyes as she focused her mind on the feel of Daniel's body against her. The coolness of his breath and the gentleness of his voice quickly swept through her with a trickle of warmth. A weight was lifted from her shoulders as her Socius continued to speak in a dialect that was both mysterious and unknown. Regan doubted she would ever come to understand the true language of the Lamia. The words were more than seductive as they played against her ear with gentle presses of his lips. They were sensual and commanding and made her soul feel heavy and weak. She moaned as the caress of the succulent words warmed her blood while creating a haze across her mind.

"Open your eyes."

She obeyed his command with a little mew then gasped with her dark eyes going wide. With a squeak, she jumped back only to find herself wrapped within her lover's arm, secured tightly. Before her was the skyline of London glittering within the darkness. They were high above the ground, rotating in a smooth motion as the massive wheel turned slowly. One minute Regan was upon the ground, the lovely solid ground, and the next she was in an oval compartment surrounded by glass - lots and lots of glass.

The wheel suddenly stopped with a gentle jerk.

"How did I get up here?"

"You walked, with my guidance." Daniel hugged her as he leaned down a few inches to set his chin upon her shoulder.

"You sure you didn't just toss me over your shoulder or something?"

His reflection in the glass echoed his wide smirk. "No. I thought I would save that for later."

When he saw Regan close her eyes and felt her tense up, he laced their hands and pressed her palms over her stomach. "Don't close your eyes. If you want to live in a world filled with excitement, adventure, and pleasure, you'll need to keep your eyes open. Otherwise, you'll miss many chances to enjoy events that are a once in a lifetime opportunity."

Though she didn't feel any fear due to the Coercêre still whispering about within her head, she felt trepidation to the motion of the wheel that told her she was getting further and further from the safety of the ground. Her fingers tightened about his till her knuckles turned white. However, Regan couldn't deny the beauty that was stretched out before her. She could see through the clear night a landscape of buildings and a blanket of stars stretching through the heavens where the lights of the city glowed within the sky. As her body eased, her fear drifting away, her grip upon Daniel's fingers softened and she leaned back to him for more comfort than support.

"Wow," she mewed softly and with a timid smile forming upon her lips.

Daniel chuckled. "Is that all you can say? Wow?"

"Give me a moment. I'll come up with something."

Smiling, Daniel closed his eyes and pressed his lips to her temple. "There are so many wonders I want to show you, Regan. So many places I want to take you. We can explore this world and our life together, but not if you keep your eyes closed."

365

"As long as we don't have to climb a mountain, I think I'll be good."

"What about the Eiffel Tower?"

"I'll bring a parachute."

"You do realize that the Domus is on top of a tall building, correct? Are you going to stay inside and not enjoy evenings with me in the garden?"

"You can lure me out with cookies."

Daniel snorted a chuckle then pressed his features into her luscious hair while groaning pitifully, "I give in."

Smirking, Regan brought his hands up to her lips to kiss his fingers before tightening his arms about her.

"Try to keep your eyes open. There's more." Raising one of their laced hands, he pointed to the right. Her eyes followed his motion and Regan was heard sucking in a quick gasp.

"Oh…my," she breathed.

Off to the side of the car was a table lit with standing candles and decorated with a tray of chocolate covered sweets from strawberries and banana slices to marshmallows and pretzels. Next to the tray was an ice bucket containing a bottle of champagne and two glasses.

Whatever words were on the tip of her tongue failed to be spoken, and only a soft breath was released. Regan mewed, twisting slightly to look back to her Socius. He kissed her forehead then released his hold upon her hands so he could walk to the table. Regan held back so she could watch his tall form move gracefully and enjoy the beauty that was his handsomeness. Daniel always dressed in style, from finely tailored slacks and shirts to brand-name jeans and sweaters. Tonight, his slacks and turtleneck were covered in a long coat of maroon and black and the ensemble was topped with a cashmere scarf of silvery black. With his onyx hair falling down his back, free this night, Regan was sure there was no other man in the world as striking, or as romantic, as her Daniel.

Daniel uncorked the bottle then carefully poured two glasses as Regan moved to his side. Smiling to her, he offered her one of the glasses and raised his in a salute. "Here's to the end of a charming evening and the beginning of a blessed relationship."

They sipped their drinks to acknowledge the toast then turned to their serene surroundings. "I don't know how to thank you for all that you've done, Daniel." Regan couldn't look at him as a warm blush took her cheeks. It seemed that when their eyes met she felt her heart tightened and her breath hitch. She turned from him, and in grasping her will power, walked to the wide window.

Daniel cocked his head as she stepped away. He placed his glass down then walked up behind her, his hands setting to her shoulders. "Sure you do."

She turned about in his grasp, raising her eyes to him as a curious line etched her brow. "How?"

Smiling, he looked out over her shoulder to the scene before them. With a finger beneath her chin, he dipped his head while guiding her mouth to meet his in a soft kiss. "Say you love me. That is all the thanks that I need," he said in a whisper as their lips met.

A hot shiver ran down Regan's spine, and she leaned to him with her arms wrapping about his shoulders and her lips offered up to his kiss. Yes, she loved him. She loved him with all of her heart and with all of her soul. There were no words that could describe the immense sensation of adoration she felt for him. No words had been created to describe the euphoria she felt for him. Love was the only word she could use; love filled with passion and pride, loyalty and dedication.

With fingers curling through his hair at the back of his neck, Regan arched herself to him. Her eyes closed and her lips brushed against his as her words mixed with a tearful declaration, "I love you, Daniel Thorn - my Lamia."

"My vampire."

Thorn Trilogy Glossary of Terms
~ ~ ~ ~

A
~

Adoptio: This is the term used when one Lamia of another Familia or Libre status is adopted by another Familia to become a full member of the new Familia.

-   In this instance the adopted Lamia may change their Familia surname and take the surname of his/her new Familia.
-   When this occurs, the Lamia's records must be changed within the Library of Records and also filed with both the Concilium and Basilica in order to update any legal /criminal paperwork that the Lamia's name may be associated with.

Adoptivus: This is the term for a Lamia who has been adopted into a new Familia.

Adultus: This is an 'adult' Lamia.

-   These Lamia are older than 300 years and beneath the age of 1,000 years.

Advena Humanus: A human who is welcomed into a Familia, also known as a "newcomer."

-   This is usually by a Lamia taking a Humanus as a Socius or Socia.
-   Most of the time, the Advena has been proven to hold the Proprietas and who is brought into the Familia not only due to a romantic connection a Lamia within that Familia but also for protection and care.

Aestas: The summer season

Ancilla: The title given to the head female Servus to a Familia or individual Lamia.

Ars Magica: Sorcery and other magical abilities inherited through the Proprietas.

-   Not every Lamia will present a talent in Ars Magica.
-   There are many different forms of Ars Magica: elemental control, sorcery, healing, etc. Some Lamia excel at becoming Warlocks, Veneficus who specialize in very rare form of battle magic.
-   Necromancy is a form of Ars Magica that is frowned upon due to the skill of harnessing magic based upon the powers of life and death, and the ability to create death and manipulate the dead. Those who cross into this skill of Ars Magica are either revered for their skills, or shunned.
-   Some Familia are stronger in producing Lamia with great skills in Ars Magica while some Familia do not have the genetic alteration within their Proprietas that will produce magic users.

368

Attingere: The touch Coercêre.
- This is the ability for a Lamia to influence or control a weaker Lamia or Humanus through physical touch / contact.

Auctor Generis: A Lamia's direct 'vampiric' ancestors.
- This is traced through their Lamia lineage passed down from their Parens.

Ave: The official farewell spoken in the Lamia world.

B
~

Basilica: The official Lamia court where judges, Iudex, representing each Territorium in a Republica decide upon the punishments for crimes against the Lex and Humanus laws.
- There is only one Basilica in each Republica.
- Judges are selected by the Senators in the Republica's Concilium and are voted into office.
- Judges are voted upon every forty years and can only hold four terms in office.
  - This can be done in succession or over a Lamia's extended lifetime.

Bibliotheca de Tabularum: Ever Republica will have a 'Library of Records' where all the written records are kept.
- For the most part, these records are open to 'public' view. However, more sensitive documents (degrading and fragile documents) are kept in an underground facility that is monitored and controlled for the survival and the care of these documents.
  - Lamia 'births' and 'deaths'.
  - Lamia marriages and divorces.
  - Familia adoptions.
  - Both Lamia and Humanus genealogies and Familia trees.
  - Public complaints.
  - Basilica and Concilium records open to the public.
  - Nobilis titles given and removed.
  - Histories and traditions of all the Familia who have settled in that Republica.
  - Lists of all Familia members, Reguli and Successors.
  - Social Traditions found within the Republica.
  - The Republica, Terretoriums and Regio histories.

Bloody: A modern term for a Lamia who is addicted to blood or feeding.

Bruma: The Winter Solstice.
- This marks the 'New Year' to Lamia as the sun rises later and sets earlier, giving Lamia a longer time out within the world.

C
~

Caelum: The Lamia version of the afterlife.
- There is both a 'Heaven' and a 'Hell' understood within Lamia societies.
- Beings from both realms walk upon the mortal plane and can be summoned for magical needs by a Familia's Venefica / Veneficus.

Castigatio: The act of being formally punished.
- There are many forms of punishment that can be bestowed upon a Lamia or Human, living within the Lamia world, by the Basilica.
- These punishments range from different forms of verbal warnings to physical punishment; the most severe being execution such as Crucis Supplicium.

Coercêre: A Lamia's natural ability to coerce a Humanus or a younger / weaker Lamia through three different techniques: **Recodari** (mental), **Vocis Sonus** (voice) or **Attingĕre** (touch).
- Most often a Lamia is talented with just one of these three abilities; though, there are records indicating that some Lamia have been gifted with the ability to use two or all three of these Coercêre, such is rumored to only be if the Lamia contains some level of great psychic ability(s).

Conciliator: The "match-maker" in a Familia.
- These are Lamia Geneticist whose job it is to test a Humanus for the Proprietas, the vampiric genetic trait.
- These individual Lamia are protected and are often considered 'sacred' to many Familia.

Concilium: A Republica's counsel of elected Lamia.
- The number of seats in a Concilium depends upon the population of Lamia in each Territorium within a Republica.
- The Concilium meets to discuss the operations of the designated Republica and also settle disputes, questions, concerns and other every day issues.

Coniungi: The act of 'mating' that will seal a Lamia marriage.
- This also seals the Possessio.

Consanguine Rex: The "King" who presides over a Republica. The short term for this title is simply 'Rex'.
- The influence of this individual is great throughout the Republica with the ability to influence the activities and decisions of not only individual Lamia, but also Familia.

- There is no true way a Lamia becomes entitled with Consanguine Rex as each Republica has their own set of rules for the crowning such as: election, Familia entitlement, battle…death…etc.
- The Rex holds sole power in dissolving both the Basilica and the Concilium, calling upon new voting for both.
- The Rex also has the ability to strip noble titles from Lamia and can also grant titles of nobility to Lamia whom she or he deems worth.

Constituere: The Lamia assigned by upper level Lamia within a Familia, Concilium or Republica to deliver formal notices of discipline, punishment or other vital notifications of business throughout the Lamia world.
- There is a strict understanding that these individuals are not to be harmed under any circumstances.

Creare: The "Creation" of a new Lamia from a Humanus proven to have the Proprietas.
- There is a 50 / 50 chance that the Humanus will survive this transformation.
- The amount of time taken for a Humanus to go through the Creare varies depending upon the health of the Humanus and the strength of the Proprietas.
- If a Humanus does not survive, they can experience a very painful death and often times will be 'euthanized' to save horrific agony.

Crepasculum: The traditional term for the 'Time of Dusk'.
- At this time the Lamia's body shows physical changes as their internal systems begin to prepare automatically for slumber.
- Lamia can venture outside during this time, once the rays of the sun have diminished.

Cresta: A Lamia Familia crest.

Crucis Supplicium: The highest level of Castigatio that can be ordered by a Rex or the Basilica - Crucifixion.
- The only way a judgment of crucifixion can be halted is by order of the Rex.
- This specific form of execution is handed down to those who have committed the greatest of sins against the Lamia world, exposing the Lamia or an assassination attempt upon a Rex or Reguli.

D

Daemon: This term is used in reference to every Lamia's inner 'demon', a representation of the brutality, cruelty, blood thirst and power that is the Lamia.
- This is not to be confused with a demon, a being of Hell.

Decora: A Lamia's Familia crest tattoo.

De Origine Scriptus: The original Lex passed down from the first Concilium.

- The exact date is unknown, though it is speculated that the original laws were created soon after the fall of the Roman Empire.
- The location of these documents is only known to a handful of powerful Lamia; all of who are unknown. It is rumored that many Rex around the world hold these documents, but such is just a rumor as many young Lamia believe that the documents do not exist.
- The current Lex are said to have been taken from these laws and modified over time.

Denique Nex: The formal term of a Lamia's honorable death.

- Often times, this will be seen upon an epitaph before the date of a Lamia's death.
- However, this title is not given to any Lamia who have broken laws, who have been exiled or banished and will be removed from documents and epitaphs if required.

Desiderium: A very powerful urge for a Lamia's 'desire' or 'obsession' to possess another.

- When a Lamia desires a Humanus or another Lamia with such intense obsession, the Desiderium can manifest itself in violent or often bizarre behavior that is uncharacteristic of that Lamia.
- Often times the Desiderium can become so great and overwhelming that a Lamia can hardly keep themselves from performing the Creare upon a Humanus, whether or not that human possesses the genetic trait or not, as a delusional need to have the individual of obsession with them, to make that individual like them, is all consuming.
  - o **NOTE:** When a Humanus is killed due to an illegal Creare, the Lamia responsible for the death will be brought before the Basilica under the formal charge of murder and punished accordingly.
- A Lamia, when embraced by the Desiderium and when pushed to the limit, will often times, and unknowingly, release his or her inner Daemon.
- A Lamia who reaches a high-risk level of the Desiderium are often locked away and monitored till the Desiderium passes due to lack of interaction with the individual that the Lamia desires to possess or the object of the Lamia's obsession.
- Madness, insanity, violence and sexual hunger are just a few symptoms associated with the Desiderium that has been allowed to escalate.

Divortium facere cum Familia: The divorce of a Lamia from his / her Familia.

- This act is considered very taboo and is still frowned upon in modern Lamia society.
- Those who divorce their Familia, for the most part, become Proscriptus.
- There are many reasons why a Lamia may choose to divorce the Familia. However, there are not many reasons why a Familia would welcome a Lamia back.

Divortium facere cum Marito: The formal divorce of a Lamia from his/her wife.

Divortium facere cum Uxore: The formal divorce of a Lamia from his/her husband.

Domare: The training of a new Lamia or an Advena Humanus in the rules of the Lamia world.
- Humanus who are integrated into this world do not receive the intense training that a new Lamia receives.
- The Domare is done by an Elder of a Familia and may take months to years to complete, depending upon the abilities of the new Lamia or the difficulties of the progression.
- In order to pass the Domare, the new Lamia or Advena Humanus are given tests by the Concilium.
  - The Lamia must pass the test…if not…there are only two options: The Familia can petition for this Lamia to be accepted (rarely done) or the Lamia can declare Libra (freedom from a Familia) - most of the time there is little to no options depending upon the Concilium.
- A Humanus is given three chances to pass the tests.

Domitas: The official term for the integration of a new Lamia or Advena Humanus into the Lamia world and the Familia that they are to be a part of.
- It is expected for a Lamia or Advena Humanus to be integrated as smoothly as possible and under great care to prevent any complications.
- Great caution must be taken if a new member shows any hesitation in the Domitas.
  - If this individual refuses to integrate properly, 'measures' are taken.

Domus: A Lamia's independent residence.
- A Lamia's main Domus must be within that Lamia's Republica, but not directly in a specific location

E
~

Ecclesia: A Holy place or Church where Elders, Senators, Reguli or the Rex are buried.
- These are automatic Templums, places of safety and of sanctuary.

Edĕre: The act of feeding.
- This act can be both pleasurable and brutal or even both.

Elder: A Lamia that has reached over 1,000 years in age and who has achieved titles through deeds of honor proclaimed by his or her Familia.
- Once this title is given, it cannot be rescinded.
- This title is gifted by the Regulus of individual Familia.

Exsilium: To be banished or exiled.

- Both a Humanus and a Lamia can be exiled or banished from a Familia, Negotium, Territorium or Republica by order of a Rex, Concilium or Regulus.
- Individuals can be banished / exiled from Negotium under the order of the owner of the Lamia business with restrictions set by the owner.
- An order of Exsilium can be revoked, but only by the individual who gave the order.
- A banished / exiled individual is monitored, especially if said individual is a Humanus or a Lamia who proclaims Proscriptus title.
- This is often seen as worse than an execution as there are not many Templum or Familia who will offer protection to these individuals. However, Underground groups of Libre Lamia will take in the banished or exiled. Some Ecclesia will offer sanctuary to the exiled or banished.

Exsul: An exiled Lamia or Humanus.

Exsulare: To be in exile.

F
~

Familia: A Lamia's household or Lamia family that share the same lineage and genealogy back to the surname belonging to the Prima Lamia of their lineage.

- Lamia will hold two surnames, the surname of their human parents as well as the Familia name.
- Proscriptus or Exsul Lamia will often disinherit their Familia surname, and so too will Familia divorce themselves from these Lamia or Humanus
- Familia extend across the globe and into many cultures. It is very important for the Regulus within a Republica to meet with the other Reguli within their Familia every decade or so in order to remain informed of Familia events and happenings.
- Many Familia still practice traditions that have been passed down through their Lamia lineage and their cultural inheritance.
- Some Familia are known to produce Lamia who excel or demonstrate certain abilities in Ars Magica.
- There are Familia known as Rogues who will act outside of the Lex and often stretch their power and influence into the Underground and into the functions of other Familia.
- There are some traditions where Lamia marry between Familia to extend the political powers or unique abilities of that Familia.

Flesh- Eaters: A slang term for Zombies.

Filia / Filias / Fili (f/m/p): This term is also used in reference to a Lamia being the 'child' to a Parens.

Funus / Funeris (s/p): The formal and traditional term for a Lamia funeral(s).

374

Frater: The formal and traditional term for a Lamia's brother(s).
-   This can be a Lamia's birth brother, a Familia brother or both.

G
~

Genus: A Familia's ancestral tree showing every Humanus and Lamia as well as splintered blood lines and other Familia that have connections to the Familia's Prima Lamia.
-   Through these extensive collections, protected in secret vaults in each Familia's villa, the Proprietas of a Humanus can be traced directly.

H
~

Homini Senquienem Mittĕre: The act of bleeding a Humanus or Lamia dry of their Sanguis.
-   This is mostly seen during the Inediă Vitam Finire, the Starvation, or the Desiderium when the Lamia is ignorant of his or her actions.
-   To do this to a Lamia is subject to extreme punishment or even execution depending upon the status of the victim and the victim's Familia.
-   There are traditions documented throughout Lamia cultures where this practice was once a ritual performed upon Humans and is now treated as a Taboo. However, there are Lamia who will pay a great deal of money to indulge in such an act within the safety of the Underground Laniena, a slaughter house.
-   Some Underground Horti provide mortals and Lamia for Lamia to enjoy this act.
-

Hominum Genus: The Human Race as a whole.
-   Many Lamia look down upon the human race as an inferior and weaker race meant for nothing more than stock for feeding, a means for survival.

Humanum: Mankind.

Humanus: Human / Humans.

Horti: A house of pleasure where Lamia go seeking warmth, comfort or sexual favors by humans or desperate Lamia who are employed at the business.
-   Humans who work within these houses are registered with the Concilium and are aware of the world that they work in. They are also monitored. They belong to the Horti and the owner of the Horti.
-   These houses can be run by Lamia or by Humanus who are a part of the Lamia world.

- These houses must follow strict codes and rules set down by the Concilium.
- Horti operating within the Underground are not registered and do not follow the rules set upon them by the Concilium.

$$\underset{\sim}{\mathbf{I}}$$

Immanitas: The brutality of a Lamia's inborn strength and power.
- This can be physical, mental or magical.

Infans: A newly created Lamia who is not of the age of 100 years.
- In some Lamia cultures and Familia, this age can vary. The most accepted amount of years is listed as two hundred.

In Manu Homisis: A pardon for an execution given down by the Rex only.
- In order to be granted such a pardon, there must be overwhelming evidence against the Basilica's order of execution.
- This can be granted even after an execution in order to clear both a Lamia's name and the Lamia's Familia name from being tarnished.

Instituĕre: A formal, low level punishment that is mostly handed down by the Regulus of a Familia for disobedience or petty crime / law breaking.

Iudex: A single judge seated on a Republica's Basilica.

Iudicium: A Basilica's judgment handed down during trial.

$$\underset{\sim}{\mathbf{L}}$$

Lamia: A Vampire.
- The Lamia began as a rumored curse brought down by the Fates in order to punish citizens of ancient Rome when they began to question and mock the Gods.
  - According to this rumor, this curse invaded the population, sweeping through in the guise of a plague. The plague either killed individuals through a quick, yet very painful death, or altered victims by:
    - Slowing down organ functions.
    - Suffering serious burns from daylight.
    - Ability to digest only the finest and most delicate of foods and drinks.

- Needing to feed from the living, humans or animals, and digesting fresh blood that helps to regulate bodily functions.
- Turning victims into carriers of the plague.
- Victims who remained 'human' were said to carry the plague, infecting others through breeding.
- Lamia were soon rounded up all across the Roman Empire and placed within secured military forts where they were monitored and left to expire.
  - These encampments were in some of the harshest of regions throughout Europe and were meant to kill off those who were weak.
  - Within these camps those who were carriers of the Proprietas mated and over time the Lamia populations began to expand.
    - Within half a century the camps were overrun by the Lamia within
    - The Roman Empire often sent out small military battalions to retake the camps, but many times these skirmishes ended in complete slaughter with the Lamia winning.
  - As the skills and talents of the Lamia began to take hold and to increase, the Senate of Rome began to secretly hire skilled Lamia to act as enforcers and regulate the Lamia populations and hunt down those Lamia who threatened the great Empire of Rome.
    - This marks the date within Lamia history where Lamia were beginning to become integrated within human society.
- As history progresses, so too does the Lamia world, cultures, societies and Familia – expanding and adapting as the human world deteriorates.

Laniena: A 'slaughter house' where both humans and animals are harvested for Sanguis or for body parts.
- The term originates from ancient times where blood was harvested within slaughter houses on the outskirts of cities and towns.
- These are often shadowed as veterinarian services, funeral homes or blood banks run by Lamia or a Familia.
- Most Laniena operate within the rules and restrictions of the Concilium, but there are Laniena that are run in the Underground and are cruel and violent places that allow live 'victims' to be tortured and brutally murdered.
- There are documents indicating that high level humans from all over the world pay an outrageous amount of money for the privilege of the torturing and killing of the animals and humans that are being harvested within the Underground Laniena.

Larva Genus: The tradition term for the Lamia race.

Legatas: These are Lamia within a Familia who act as the official Ambassadors.
- These Lamia act in the stead of Reguli on minor official Familia business.

Legatus / Legati (s/P): These are powerful and skilled Lamia who are selected to operate as assassins under the control of the Concilium, Rex or a Regulus.

- These individual Lamia are often ordered to perform the Venatio, a requested and legalized hunt.
- The identity of these individuals are unknown but to those who often hire them, and even then, they are mostly known through a 'nick-name'.

Legis Violator. A Lamia law-breaker.

- Depending upon the Lex broken and the severity of the crime, a Lamia may be punished or executed.
- Law-breakers can request sanctuary from a Familia or seek refuge within a Templum or an Ecclesia.
- A Lamia who has broken the law will receive a formal notice to present himself or herself before their Regulus, Concilium or Basilica (depending on severity of crime) for proper disciplinary procedures.
  - If the Lamia does not turn himself or herself over within ten days, the Regulus must report them to the Concilium. At that point a Venation may be called upon the offender.

Letum: The concept of death.

Lex: The current, modern and or updated Lamia laws based off of the De Origine Scriptus that are said to have been written close to the fall of the Roman Empire.

- Every Republica has their own interpretation of these laws.
- It is vital that Lamia traveling between Countries know the Lex of other Republica.

Lex Lover. A slang term for a Lamia who follows the Lex.

- This is often used by Proscriptus and other out-laws.

Libre: A Lamia who proclaims 'freedom' from the Lex.

- This does not make the Lamia a law-breaker as many of these Lamia still hold the separation of the human and Lamia worlds sacred.

Lustra: A degrading institution where Lamia sell themselves to other vampires or even humans in order to obtain finances, protection and such.

- These are run in the Underground outside the laws of the Concilium and are inhabited mostly by Lamia registered as Libre, Exiled or Banished.
- Most of these are operating Horti.

M
~

Maior: This is the formal and traditional term for a Familia's Elder or the oldest living Lamia within a Familia.
- This title comes with the ultimate form of respect.
- The age of a Maior is from 1000 years and older, but the age does vary depending upon the Familia and the Familia traditions.

Maiores: A Lamia's vampiric ancestors.
- These are individuals whom have the same genetic coding of the Proprietas.
- Each Familia contains libraries full of these recorded genealogies.

Mancipium: In the old Lamia traditions, this is the term for a Lamia's household slave.
- In most modern-day Lamia societies, human slaves are not kept and this tradition is no longer practiced. However, in old world Lamia Republicas and Familia bound to old traditions this practice is said to continue and is often considered a status symbol of Lamia high society.

Marita: Wife.

Maritus: Husband.

Martyr: A Lamia who believes and acts as if both the human and Lamia world can coexist.
- This thinking is considered the most dangerous form of 'free-thinking' that exists within the Lamia world as the fear of these Martyr's exposing the Lamia can endanger every Lamia in the world.
- There are groups of Martyr Lamia working in the Underground, and those who are discovered are reported and monitored by the Concilium of their Republica.
- Many Republica consider these 'free-thinking' Lamia to be so dangerous that they are listed as Legis Violatas.
  - These Lamia can face criminal charges in the Basilica and can often face sever punishments and or execution.

Mater: This is the term for both a Lamia's human birth mother and a female Parens.
- To many Lamia, their human birth mother is of great importance. Birthdays are a day of great celebrations that honor mothers as the "Life Giver" to all Lamia.

Matrona: The title given to the female mate of a male Regulus.

Meditatio: This is what Lamia call 'sleep'; however, this is more of a form of deep meditation.
- This 'sleep' can aid in the recovery of energy as well as aid in the healing of light to moderate injuries.
- Lamia do not like being woken from the Meditatio too quickly and can often experience a few seconds of disassociation or confusion.

Militaris: The military fraction serving directly under the Concilium.

Morbus: The 'sickness'.
- Lamia can become very ill, sick, and delirious often succumbing to a form of dementia when their systems become overloaded by the effects of feeding on too many humans who have ingested drugs, alcohol or synthetic medications.
- If the symptoms of the 'sickness' are caught early, the Morbus is easily treated with a deep Meditatio or blood transfusion.
- Symptoms will differ from Lamia to Lamia and can manifest as a singular symptom or a multitude of different symptoms.
- Advanced symptoms are harder to cure, and if there is no attempt to help cure these symptoms, they can progress into the Starvation, a dangerous scenario that can create a rabid and dangerous Lamia who is out of control and on the verge of releasing their internal Daemon.

Mordĕre: The actual Lamia 'bite'.
- This is not the same as feeding as many Lamia consider biting to be a sign of passion - an erotic experience.
- There is a social understanding that one Lamia does not 'bite' the lover of another Lamia as this act is a very intimate act.

Mortalis: The concept of mortality.

N

Nasei: This is the traditional term for the 'birth' of a new Lamia into the Lamia world.
- This is also celebrated as the concept of a Lamia's Birthday.

Nature et Ingenium: Lamia are born with one or more 'natural gifts' that are specific to that Familia and are passed down through the bloodline.
- These can be any assortment of magical abilities such as shape changing, intense strength, healing abilities, psychic abilities, summoning abilities, elemental control...etc.

Natura Humana: Human nature.
- This understanding is not lost upon Lamia and is often honored as a part of every Lamia and their behavior, choices, ideals and beliefs.

Natura Lamia: Lamia nature.
- This nature is darker, crueler, stronger and colder than a Lamia's gentler 'Natura Humana'.

Negotium: The formal term for a Lamia owned business that operates inside both the Lamia world and the human world.
- These must be registered and regulated by a Republica's Concilium.
- Those Negotium that are operated by banished, Underground or Libre Lamia have a harder time getting a license to operate and may have difficulty finding a location within a Territorium.
- Owners of these businesses hold the right to banish any Lamia from their business.

Nobilibus: Lamia nobility.
- These Lamia often are born from human nobility or royalty.
- Any Fili 'born' from these Lamia are automatically Nobilis.
- A Rex can remove or give these titles to non-noble born Lamia.

Nobilis: A Lamia who comes from noble mortal stock.
- In order for a Lamia to obtain this title and rank in their society, they must be able to provide their human genealogical tree that can trace their bloodline back to some noble family.

Notis Companguĕre: This is the traditional term for a wide-spread Lamia tradition upon which many Lamia mark their bodies with a tattoo, a Decora that represents their Familia Crest, a Crista.
- This tattoo can be done through magic or through ink.
- This marking is acceptable for both men and women.
- Proscriptus often will have the mark removed as a show of their divorce from their Familia.
- Lamia declared out-laws or criminals will have this mark removed and destroyed.
- For those who have been executed or who have died, this marking is cut away and stored within Familia vaults for record and safe keeping.

Nox: Night.

O
~

Oraculum / Oraculi (s/p): Every Familia has a Lamia with strong psychic or medium abilities.
- These Lamia are prized and are to be protected at all cost.
- The skills and extent of the abilities will vary from Familia to Familia with some Familia producing more powerful Oraculi than other Familia.
- It is not uncommon for these Lamia who have turned Proscriptus to hire out their abilities, though this is considered very taboo as Lamia can be very paranoid creatures who do not want another Lamia to know their most intimate of secrets.

Orator: These Lamia deliver minor messages and invites between other Lamia.

- These were mostly used before the development of technology. However, some Familia, who continue to embrace traditions, still use these services. Some Orators are used to deliver formal messages of personal celebrations and invitations to formal events.

P
~

Pater: This title is given to a Lamia's human father or their male Parens.

- There is a 'father's day' that is celebrated, but this day is not as grand in celebration as the 'mother's day' concept.

Parens: A Lamia's 'Creator'.

- This is the Lamia who performs the Creare upon a Humanus.

Possessio: The intense desire to possess another, Lamia or Humanus, sexually.

- The intensity of the Possessio varies depending upon the will power of the Lamia, the object of the sexual desire, the reason for the Possessio and the physical, mental and emotional condition of the Lamia.
- The Possessio can become dangerous when the Lamia has embraced his / her Daemon or the Desiderium.
- Many Lamia who are involved in a passionate, romantic relationship or a marriage view the Possessio as a very important symbol to their dedication to their relationship and or their significant other.

Praeses: The male lover to a Regulus.

Praetor: The Lamia in charge of the Legatus.

- This individual is the 'best of the best', and their identity is usually altered when they take this position.
- Many Lamia who take this position will formally leave their Familia, family and friends in order to accept the new identity given them.
- This is a title of great honor, respect, status and responsibility.

Prima Lamia: These are the Lamia founders of the original Familia.

- Many of the Familia still in operation are from the original families who fell victim to the plague and who all Lamia are said to have been born from.
- Some of these Prima Lamia are known through detailed records kept over time. However, many of their names and their histories have been lost to time.

Prima Oraculum: The most powerful oracle Lamia who shadows the Rex at all times.

Procreare: The traditional term for the mating or marriage of a Lamia to another.

- This refers mostly to two Lamia; however, it is not unheard of for a Lamia to mate or marry a Humanus connected to their world, though it is frowned upon.

Proprietas: The genetic trait that is passed through human lineage and that can be traced back to those original Lamia afflicted by the plague and thus the genetic mutation.

- The genetic trait can be traced through the blood of a Humanus and or a Lamia to determine which strain the individual has.
- A tracing of the strain may not determine a directly Familia lineage, but can give hints to the Familia connections Lamia and other Familia may share.
- Specific abilities, talents and skills can be triggered through an enzyme within fluid transfer from the Parens to their newly created child.
    - o   Over time, these genetic 'abilities' have become a form of Familia inheritance, meaning, many Lamia within that Familia show these abilities.

Proscriptus: This is a Lamia who has divorced his / her Familia and has declared freedom from the Republica and the Lex.

- Oftentimes, these Lamia join groups within the Underground and live out of the reach of the Concilium, the Basilica and the Lex.
- Many Proscriptus simply want to be free from their Familia and pose no harm to the Lamia society as a whole as they continue to live by the Lex, yet there are more Proscriptus who fight against the control of the Lex and who pose great threats to the safety of the Lamia, the societies and the Lex.
    - o   These Lamia who become dangerous often find themselves with a Venatio order signed for their deaths in order to maintain the 'peace'.

Puer: The title given to the head male Servus, servant, of a Familia or a single Lamia.

Q

Quasitor: The presiding Iudex of the Basilica.

R

Recens Natus: A 'new-born' Lamia up to 60 years of age.

- These Lamia are monitored for proper behavior and are often restricted to their movements within certain governmental buildings within a Republica.

Receptaculum: A refuge or sanctuary within a Territorium.
- There are no more than 100 of these within a single Republica.
- These must be licensed and registered with the Concilium.
- They are monitored strictly and can have their licenses revoked if too many laws are broken or incidences involving negative / criminal Lamia behavior within their borders.
- By law, there is to be no violence, murder, feeding, bleeding or any other illegal or inappropriate activities or behavior happening within their borders.
- Any Lamia or Humanus, no matter who they are, cannot be harmed or removed from the property if they proclaim sanctuary within a Receptaculum.
- Failure to obey these laws will mean a Receptaculum's license to be revoked.

Recodari: The mental Coercère.
- This is the ability for a Lamia to influence or control another weaker Lamia or Humanus through their mind.

Reipublicae: Lamia politicians who help promote Senators and Iudex for positions.
- It is not uncommon for these Lamia to influence the directions and decisions of the Concilium and the Basilica.

Republica: The formal name for a country.

Regio: These are major cities within a Republica that contain a set population amount.
- Each Regio is controlled by a Familia.
- Permission to operate a Negotium within a Regio is required in order for the business to be licensed by the Concilium.

Regio Familia: The Familia who claims dominance in a Regio.
- There are many ways this title can be taken, given or taken away.

Regis Tutela: The Lamia 'royal guards' who operate under the direct order of the Rex.
- It is a known fact that many of these Lamia are trained assassins.
- The number of these guards varies.
- These Lamia guards are fiercely loyal to their Rex.

Regulus: "Chieftan" or the head of a Familia.
- Each Familia has their own traditions and rules regarding the giving and removal of this position and the responsibilities and duties of this position.
- These titles can be given to a male or female Lamia, but must be 500 years or older.

S

Salve: The official greeting in the Lamia world.

Sanguinarius: Blood thirsty.
- If a Lamia's need to feed is not sated, the Lamia may slip into a desperate hunger that, if ignored, can lead to Starvation.

Sanguis: Blood

Sanguis Tradĕre: The addiction to blood or to feeding.

Senator: A Concilium member.
- This Lamia is voted in by the Reguli of the Familia within a Territorium.

Sepulcorem / Sepulcra (s/ p): These are cemeteries / graveyards where Lamia are entombed.
- These are always Templums and can be located within churches of both Humanus and Lamia operation.
- Many Familia have private Sepulcra located within Villas.

Servus: A human servant to a Familia or individual Lamia.
- Due to regulations and laws, these individuals must be paid and registered.

Socius / Socia (m/f): The lover or consort to a Lamia.

Sol: Sun or Sunshine.

Solis Lux: Sunlight

Solis Occasus: Sunset.

Solis Ortus: Sunrise.

Solstitium: The summer solstice.
- This is the official end of the year for the Lamia due to the fact that as summer approaches the amount of darkness decreases, meaning Lamia have less time to be active within the mortal world.

Sub Noctem: Nightfall.

Successor: The Lamia declared to inherit the Regulus or Rex title.

Sucker: A slang term used in place of Lamia or vampire.

Supplicum: Capital Punishment.

Surculus: This is a vulgar and degrading insult used by 'unsophisticated' Lamia.

T
~

Templum: A Familia run sanctuary for members or friends of that Familia.
- These do not need to be registered, licensed or monitored outside of the Familia.

Territorium: These are the same as Counties, States, and Provinces within a Republica.

Trueidare: A Lamia who is given the title of 'butcher'.
- These Lamia are in charge of "butchering" animals and humans in Laniena.

U
~

Ultor: The official Lamia who carries out execution orders.

Underground: A modern term for a Lamia society that has developed over the past two hundred years where the rules and the laws of the Concilium, the Basilica, Rex and Reguli have little reach or control.

Urbanae Seniatatis Cara: The law enforcement department under the control of the Concilium who watch the behavior of Lamia in public, and who ensure that the laws are being followed.
- These Lamia are authorized to make arrests and give out citations.

V
~

Venalicius: A trader in illegal goods, mostly operating in the Underground.
- There is a large black-market throughout the Lamia world that buy, trade and sell human and Lamia slaves, weaponry, magical devices, blood, money…etc.

Venatio: A declared hunt for a wanted Lamia.
- This can be declared with request by the Rex, a Regulus, a Senator, an Iudex, a Negotium owner or a Successor.
- Lamia who are not in title standing can request a Venatio through a formal process with their Senator Representative who will then take the request to the Basilica. If the request is authorized, a Venator will be assigned the hunt.

Venator / Venati (s/p): These are Lamia who shadow as hunters and who are assigned a Venatio.
- These Lamia are employed by the Concilium, Basilica, a Familia or even the Rex.
- Many of these Lamia have achieved celebrity status for their abilities to be cruel, cold, calculating, skillful and masterful.
- Many of these Lamia are known by 'nick-names'.

Venefica / Veneficus / Venefici (f/m/p): A Lamia sorcerer.
- These Lamia can specialize in many different schools of magic.
- The most difficult and powerful level of magic would be achieving Warlock status.
- Necromancy is a school of magic that can be learned through underground teachers, but this school is looked down upon within Lamia society due to the manipulation of the dead and of death.

Venustas: A Lamia's inherent charming ability.

Villa: These are Familia estates where the Reguli are housed.

Vigiles / Vigili (s/p): The individual 'police' within the Urbanae Seniatatis Cara.
- For the most part, these are Lamia. Though it is not uncommon for some Humanus to be employed as Vigili.

Vocis Sonus: The vocal Coercêre.
- This is the ability of a Lamia to influence or control a weaker Lamia or a Humanus through the use of their voice.

Deadly Thorn
~ Book Two in the Thorn Trilogy ~

2016

~ ~ ~ ~

He wasn't alone in the pouring rain, in the darkness, and on the empty street.

In fact, Rhain had not been alone since the previous night. He was being haunted - hunted. His mind was so preoccupied with the luscious memories of Maeve Oldcastle that the once dreaded Inquisitor had not realized that he was being shadowed - stalked.

Following at a distance behind him, Maeve treaded carefully, cautiously, as she slipped from shadow to shadow. Her eyes never left him, sure to submerged herself in the rain to keep her scent from reaching him, for he was a deadly Lamia and one trained from his undead birth to hunt - to kill.

When he got on to a bus, she followed from the rear entry, taking a seat behind him. They rode for what seemed an hour, or more, through the quiet streets of London at the deep hour of the night. And when he departed, so did she. What was he up to, traveling such a long distance on a single bus ride? She wanted answers, so many answers. Rhain was not the only one being haunted. For nights and for days Maeve found her thoughts twisting and turning about the handsome Lamia, and those thoughts came with unknown and frightening emotions. Even as the Meditatio called her into the hold of slumber he invaded her dreams, calling to her desires.

Her mind was troubled and her soul was frightened. Maeve didn't know why she was following him, she just was. Her body acted as if she had no control, waking from her sleep with a deep drive to hunt him down. But why? She didn't know. She knew only that she had to seek him out so that her questions could finally be answered.

He was as deadly as he was dangerous, born to the Drasus Familia and carrier of that Familia's accursed skill of deadly battle and frightening violence. She should not take him lightly. She should not allow the two moments of pleasure shared with him to divert her from her mission - to kill him. Revenge was a powerful urge, a strong taste and a passionate emotion. Maeve wanted to taste his blood. She wanted to have her revenge.

Into the night she disappeared, becoming nothing more than a fading silhouette within the dark rain.

~ ~ ~ ~

An hour later and Rhain found himself back home within the Thorn Domus located on the top floor of Thorn Inc. Unable to keep his mind calm and his depression from wrapping a clawed hand about his throat, he walked through the quiet condo and out into the garden where the pounding rain pelted the flowers and the greenery. He walked down one of the cobble stone paths, past the runway pond and the fountain, to stand at the wall that over looked the London skyline.

He was glad to be back home and standing among the beautiful flowers and the quiet serenity of the night, though off in the distance the siren of an emergency vehicle sounded. The rain no longer mattered, now that his body was too cold to even feel the drops soaking through his heavy jacket and seeking out his old bones. With a breath released a tumble of smoke fled his nostrils and he licked his lips and flicked his used cigarette out into the air; the stick tumbled down to the world below. The handsome Lamia closed his icy blue eyes and raised his pale face to the rain, pleased to feel the cold drops scattering across his flesh and pelting his cheeks.

"What is wrong with me?" He asked himself through a deep groan of annoyance.

"I ask myself that same question every time I close my eyes."

That voice!

Rhain's eyes snapped open and he spun around with his face suddenly intensifying, then he saw Maeve's shadowy form walking towards him through the falling sheets of rain and he relaxed - slightly. He smiled but then noticed how tightly she hugged herself, her shoulders scrunched forwards and her head bowed with locks of her darkening blonde hair curtaining her face.

"Maeve?" He asked, cocking his head to the side so that a thick lock of unevenly metallic blue and black hair slapped against his temple. "How did you get up here?"

How did she get up to the garden, forty or so floors up and past security? Suddenly, Rhain felt ever nerve of his body strike to life in warning. The sound of her voice, quivering ever so slightly, and the tight posture of her body told him that something was wrong - something was very wrong.

She stopped, and Rhain found himself pressing back against the wall.

"What have you done to me?" She inquired as she came to stand a few feet from him, her head still bowed and water slipping off her shoulders "Tell me,' she said as she raised her head, 'what have you done to me?"

"What the hell…" muttered Rhain as he saw streaks of blood coloring her fair face, streaking down from her eyes in a form of watery tears.

Slowly, he pushed away from the wall to take a cautious step forwards and slowly raised a hand out to her. "Damn, woman. What's happened to you? Your aura is almost flat-lined."

It was true, he could see the lines of her delicate aura jerking about her, thin as they were. He narrowed his eyes and took another step to see that she was sparsely dressed, certainly not for walking about in this downpour. In fact, she was clothed in a thin sundress of white that stuck to her body as if it

389

was second skin and the leather boots she wore were covered in mud and dirty. She must freezing, her flesh was stark white! Rhain could hear her teeth chattering through the sound of the thundering rain.

He frowned as he began to methodically walk towards her, judging his steps. When she didn't answer him, just turned her head to the side as a spams tore through her, he motioned her to him. "Come here."

As he stepped closer he could hear little mumbles of incoherent words tumbling past her lips, and her head and body jerked and swayed where she stood. Something definitely was not right. "Let's go inside, alright? I'll make you some tea and you can warm up."

Maeve stepped away and out of his reach. She mumbled something and whimpered, flinching to the rain.

"Are you hurt? Did somebody hurt you?" Rhain gently took hold of her shoulders, gripping her tight as he was afraid she'd collapse. She rocked back and forth, avoiding any contact with his eyes, but Rhain could see the subtle twitching of her muscles as they fought against hypothermia.

"Too many questions," whispered the woman.

"What questions?"

"So confused..."

"Then let me help you."

Whimpering, Maeve finally raised her eyes and offered a short and tight smile. "I have lost my control. I have lost my direction, my will. I only wanted to know, to feel you, just once. But I couldn't help myself. I couldn't stop myself so I went back to you, for more of you." She shook her head and a slick of rain cascaded from her blonde hair. "That wasn't supposed to happen."

"So we had some good times together. What's wrong with that?" Rhain smirked and gave a devious chuckle. "There's nothing wrong with seconds."

"No!" screamed Maeve, sweeping her arms out wildly to knock away his grip. She looked with horror to him and stumbled back away from him.

Rhain's eyes went wide as his grip was slapped away and he instinctively took a step back. "Did I miss something? I thought we were getting along smashingly."

"I do not expect you to understand, Rhain Thorn,' she growled with a hiss to his name and with her gaze dropping to the water logged pebbles of the drowning pathway. "You weren't supposed to..."

Maeve's breath hitched. She then shook her head violently as if the final words of her statement were words she was not about to speak. When her eyes snapped open she sprang forwards with blinding speed and a gleaming dagger of silver raised before her, ready to strike. The pounding of the rain was broken by her banshee scream of rage.

"Fuck!" barked Rhain as he stood shocked at the sudden reversal of her behavior, yet he caught himself and quickly moved to the side as the dagger narrowly missed kissing his belly.

He went to grab at her hand but she moved upon dexterous footing to rake her nails towards his throat. Ducking back, he spun about, flipped himself backwards to avoid her oncoming swings that sliced and slashed through the pouring rain! The blade whistled through the rain as her slices drove Rhain back with such ferocity that he had trouble keeping his footing. Their steps splashed through puddles and through sections of garden and dirt, and as the rain continued to cascade from the heavens so did Maeve's screams.

Every muscle in his body was called into defensive action, blocking and twisting and even flipping away. She was good, damn good, and kept on advancing without pausing to think of her next move or to gain her balance. Not since the assault on David's factory almost six months prior had Rhain needed to use his natural skills of battle. In fact, he was appreciating the lack of fighting so he could focus on more important matters, the Crucible and the beautiful ladies who visited the club.

With another twist of his body in the air, perfectly executed, Rhain skidded across the stone path, ignoring the slicing pain that ran his body when pebbles tore across his pain. He howled in building anger, "Have you gone mad, woman?"

Maeve was panting and trembling as she stopped her pursuit to face the other Lamia. All she saw was red, sheets of bloody red, as her tears stained her vision and fed her rage and her pain. Her eyes narrowed to thin slits as she leveled her dagger.

Rhain's deadly eyes narrowed and his lips parted to show a flash of his elongating fangs. "What the hell are you doing?"

"My duty," she hissed then lunged for him again with a maddening shriek.

Warlock
~ A Thorn Trilogy Novel ~

Out now on Kindle download and paperback on all amazon.com sites.

~ ~ ~ ~

Georgeta whimpered in pure, unadulterated fear.

Trembles threatened to shatter bone with their strength as she looked upon the shadowy tormenter of her dreams. She thought a little nap would be of no concern. She was very wrong.

"I knew it was only a matter of time till you came back to me," said the entity of moving shade as it stood before her, watching her. "Have you missed me, little one?"

Georgeta narrowed her dual colored eyes. A tight knot lodged within her throat, cutting off any words of retort that came from her mind.

"What is wrong? Can you not answer me, child?"

The being stepped forwards, away from the horse that stood patiently on the field. There was no battle taking place in this dream. There were no bloodcurdling sounds of men howling in agony as they were torn apart by blade or by arrow. The air smelled of nothing but smoke, heavy and thick. Silence was all about her, snuffed out by the viscosity of the fog.

Georgeta tried to move. She wanted to run, to flee, as the shade came closer to her, but she couldn't move. The moment she awoke within her dream she fell to the ground, pushed down and held by the fog. The being, her ancestor's memory, controlled the fog. It did as he wished and fed both his power and her fear.

"Leave me in peace!" Georgeta snapped in her native tongue, a last attempt at threatening the entity to dispersing. She knew the threat would not work. Threats never worked.

The shade tipped its head; long strands of inky blackness slid away from its rounded head in the form of hair. Even though the being's body was nothing but dense, moving shadow there was shape and form to it. There were small details of clothing, of armor, and of weapons strapped to its side. However, there were not many details to the features or skin, nor bone or muscle. Only shadow made up the body.

Was it smiling? She couldn't tell, but its voice sounded greatly amused.

"You should know not to command me, little one."

"This is my mind. These are my dreams. You do not belong here!"

Giving a gurgled chuckle of hilarity, the shade stepped forwards till it was but a few inches away from the trembling Lamia. It reached out with a long arm till the back of thin, bony fingers gently skimmed along her cold cheek.

"I am here,' it said with a low purr, 'and I shall always be here. This is my realm. You should know that by now."

Whimpering, Georgeta pulled away from the icy, clammy touch. "Why do you torment me like this? I have done nothing to you!"

"Your Familia curse keeps me here, little one. You know who I am. And you know that I will never leave my cursed ancestors alone. Especially you…"

She looked back to the entity, her eyes filling with bloody tears. "You were the one that cursed your ancestors. We should not be tortured for your actions!"

A gargled chuckle rumbled from the entity! When Georgeta looked away, it grasped her chin to force her to look back to it with a painful grip. When she winced, when she whimpered, it purred in satisfaction. "My curse has given me eternal power, little one. Whether you or any other member of your Familia embrace the gifts that I provide you is your own choice. Thus is my legacy!"

Georgeta understood that there was a positive side to the Tepes curse - immense power that a Lamia of her Familia could harness at any given time. The cost of such a gift was to be tormented by the cell memories that survived within each of them. However, Georgeta didn't understand as to why the memory her mind held became something more than a memory, a frightening reality.

"Why me?" she asked through thin, bloody tears that began to slip down her alabaster cheeks. "Why are you here, inside of me?"

The entity's black face cracked, splitting to show a wide, wild smile. More cracking, more splitting and two eyes tore from the blackness to show glowing red orbs.

"Simple, little one,' whispered the being as it slowly knelt down to one knee before her, 'you are mine."

It leaned closer, torn mouth parting wide to allow long, black tongue to slide forth…reaching out to lick away her bloody tears. The grip upon her chin tightened.

Georgeta gasped through a nip of discomfort as she was roughly pulled forwards till their cheeks touched.

"You will always be mine," snarled the shade.

"I am not yours," whimpered the Lamia. A cold shiver ran her body when she felt the tip of its wet, hot tongue flick against her ear. She tightened her eyes shut and tried to order her body to move. It didn't.

Her proclamation didn't settle well with Vlad. He growled deeply, fingers curling till sharpened nails bit into her flesh. Drawing back, the shade narrowed his glowing eyes. "I am growing weary of your insolence!"

Vlad rocked back to stand, reached down to grab a handful of Georgeta's luscious curls, and in one pull, yanked her body upwards and off the ground. Her cry of alarm and pain brought another cackle of amusement from him. She was pulled against his hard form; her body locked within an arm's embrace.

"You are strong, but you are growing weaker by the night. Soon, I will be free from you, and I will take my place upon the Dracul throne!"

Through the pain, Georgeta managed to open her eyes, locking her gaze to the twisted and cracked face. "I will never allow you to be free...Vlad Dracul..."

The entity's torn lips pulled in to a psychotic smile, enjoying hearing its true identity, its ancient name, spoken from her. "Little one,' Vlad purred, 'you will have no choice. Once the bindings that keep me locked within you are broken, I will rip from your mind and rain chaos down upon our cursed Familia. There will be none to stop me, not even you."

Gathering up a touch of courage, Georgeta leveled her eyes with a slow glare. "I might not be strong enough to stop you, but Alasdair will stop you."

A twitch of annoyance curled the side of the ripped lip at the mention of the Warlock's name. "Ah. You think your precious Alasdair is strong enough to protect you?" The entity chided through a cold chuckle. "How sweet..."

Georgeta hissed, "I do not think. I know."

The pride heard within her hissed words fueled the entity's anger. The grip within her hair tightened as he pulled her head close till their lips were but an inch apart. The cold, stale breath that fell with his words washed over Georgeta causing her to flinch.

Vlad howled when she looked away, "LOOK AT ME!"

She recoiled and whimpered with a wave of panic rippling through her. She slowly looked back to the haunted face of Vlad Tepes.

His glowing red eyes softened in a pleased and distorted sort of way. The entity removed fingers from her soft locks to run a bony digit slowly along her features, gathering the sticky wetness of bloody tears. "Even in your fear, in your terror, you are remarkable."

Now that her head was free from the hold, Georgeta was able to draw away from the icy touch. "Do not touch me," she snarled.

His red eyes flashed in warning. "I shall touch you all I want, little one. You seem to forget that you belong to me."

"I belong to no one." Georgeta whimpered once again. Her resolve weakened as the entity ran his touch between her breasts.

"Is that so? Shall I remind you of the power I have over you when you are in my realm?"

Georgeta's breath hitched in a tight gasp. "Please...don't..."

A shiver of excitement etched through his body, and he pressed a hand over her chest. With a cruel, psychotic laugh, the entity...Dracul...tore the shirt from Georgeta's body. The fabric flew away, dissolving in the fog. The remainder of her clothing began to dissipate as she cried out, twisting and fighting the hold.

"No! Stop!"

He laughed, brightly...insanely as if enjoying Georgeta's new found terror and struggle! "Do you think your precious Sorcerer will still want you once he discovers that I have taken your soul with my ethereal body since my manifestation? Do you really think he will desire you knowing that the inside of your mind is no less innocent and pure as your perverted thoughts of him are? Do you?"

More bloody tears streamed down Georgeta's alabaster cheeks. She tried to pull away. She tried to fight, but Vlad's grip only tightened. Her naked body was pulled roughly to the solid, shadowy form. Pushing and fighting against him seemed to only flood Vlad with pleasure. He laughed, cackling and barking, the more she fought against him.

"Once I am free you will belong to me in all ways. I will first have your mind and then,' with a low, sensual and gurgled purr, the being ran a shadowy digit, touched in blood, down the arch of her throat, 'I will have your body. You *will* be mine again, my love."

"I don't think so."

The amusement upon Vlad's distorted, shadowy face drained away when the fog rippled with unsteady and powerful energy. When a distant voice echoed about, the entity's brow ripped when it was furrowed, and the being looked about.

"Let her go."

Red eyes flashed then narrowed. Vlad snarled then shouted, "Who's there?"

"I said, let her go." At the anger within the echoing voice, the fog rippled, twisting and bending before returning to its solid density.

The entity snarled again, deeper this time, and said in a commanding tone, "Show yourself!"

Georgeta whimpered as the grip about her tightened. She winced in pain to the sudden power that appeared within her dream. There was a familiarity to the sensation, but when the voice spoke, her heart slammed within her chest. *'Alasdair!'*

Hearing the name scream out in delight within Georgeta's thoughts, Vlad's entity slid a cautious gaze back to her. His torn lips pressed tight before curling up and pulsating. A surge of power tore through the fog, splitting the created wall in to an open doorway. His red eyes narrowed as a figure began to step forth from the distorted opening, casually and with an air of superiority.

"So...' chuckled the entity, 'you finally decide to show yourself."

A relieved smile bloomed upon Georgeta's tear streaked and fear riddled face. "Alasdair!"

The Warlock calmly walked forwards; gloved hands stuffed into the pockets of his jeans. His amber eyes locked upon the two forms before him, narrowing dangerously upon seeing the way the shade held on to Georgeta's body. The sight of her beautiful face lined with bloody tears, that had dripped down to paint her now naked chest, ran hot rage right through Alasdair, yet he remained eerily calm as he continued to cross the foggy void.

He stopped before the two, watching them carefully. "Would you mind releasing my fiancée? I'm sure she's getting cold."

Vlad tipped his head, puzzled by the request. "You think your demands shall be met here? This is my world, boy,' the shade hissed, 'you have no say here."

"This is *not* your world," Alasdair corrected with a slow shake of his head. "This world, as you call it, is within Georgeta's mind. She is sovereign here."

"She is weak."

"She is tired and she is afraid."

The torn lips of the being parted allowing a garbled laugh to bubble up from his throat. "She is weak!"

Alasdair narrowed his amber eyes - black flecks shifting. "No, she is not. You keep her locked within her terror so her control over this domain and over you is weakened. Doing such is the only way that you can have control over her. I wasn't able to sense her power before because it was masked by her overwhelming fear of you."

The infectious entity chuckled as he slowly stepped around Georgeta to pin her before him, exposing her bloody nakedness to her fiancé. "She will never have power over me," Vlad said as he leaned over Georgeta's shoulder to run his thick tongue over her flesh. The muscle slowly split with a line of dark mucus before spreading across her neck, the two parts moving separately. "She never has."

Alasdair's gaze never wavered. He stood calm and still - ever observant.

When the Warlock didn't reply, didn't react to the insults and the jibes, Vlad scoffed with a snort. "Do not be so cocky, boy," chided the shade. "Your power is nothing compared to mine. Leave. Now."

Alasdair did not move.

Georgeta whimpered. She was crying, and every little sob that he heard shoved the knife of pain deeper into his heart. He couldn't stand seeing her in such a state, her terror mocking her - touching her.

Once again there came silence from the Veneficus. The being growled low, not pleased with the Warlock's blatant impudence. "You refuse to leave?" Silence. "So be it,' purred Vlad as he reached an arm about Georgeta's shivering body to cup one pert, petite breast to lewdly tease and caress her, 'stay and bear witness to the spoiling of your bride."

Georgeta cried out when sharp claws dug into her breast. Vlad's shadowy form ground against her from behind, giving her the feeling of 'his' hardening 'member' that had been used to humiliate her and torture her body for decades. Past her trembling view, Georgeta stared helplessly at Alasdair. He hadn't moved, but she could see his rage building by the volatile sweeping of his aura. Shame swept through her at being so exposed to him - molested right before his gaze.

"Please...go," she whimpered towards her betrothed in her broken and panic filled voice.

Alasdair finally reacted, but not in the way that the entity had expected. He offered her a warm smile. "I'm not leaving, not without you."

"I would listen to her, boy. You really do not want to see what I am about to do to her. It's not pleasant, even though it is rather enjoyable - for me." To add insult to injury, Vlad blatantly squeezed the breast he held and ran his tongue along Georgeta's neck.

Alasdair's amber eyes narrowed to slits, and the black flecks within began to shift, moving slowly and melting together. "I will *not* repeat myself."

The shade's red eyes flared. An insane chortle broke through the fog. Vlad focused back on the Warlock, and in an instant of self-induced arrogance and irrational pride he said, "Make me."

The smile that coiled Alasdair's lips was one of expectancy and of eagerness, of cruelty and of frightening coldness. "It would be my pleasure."

In the next moment, his body simply disappeared.

Georgeta's eyes went wide. Panic swept through her as she looked wildly about. "Alasdair!"

The entity's eyes flared. He snarled past flashing fangs. "Where did he go?"

"Behind you."

Vlad's eyes went wide to the voice that fell upon him in an icy breath. He slowly turned his head to look over his shoulder. What he saw reflected in the Lamia's face he had never been seen before. Solid black eyes burned from pale flesh. Power, immense and unimaginable, radiated from the Lamia in forms of raging tendrils of magnificent amber. Alasdair had somehow manifested right behind the entity without any signature to his movements being felt.

"You..."

No other word came from Vlad as Alasdair's face contorted in to a look of murderous fury! Black eyes flared, snapping with a flash of amber and silver just as Alasdair reached out to impale his ungloved fingers into the entity's shadowy face. Vlad cried out as the amber wisps burrowed right through his head, ripping and shredding his corporeal face. The entity spasmed, flailing and snapping, as the Veneficus with clawed hands.

Now free, Georgeta stumbled and collapsed upon the foggy ground, shaking violently. When she looked back, expecting to see Alasdair, she was horrified to see not the Alasdair as she knew but the Warlock that he was.

"I will tell you this only once,' Alasdair said in a voice that now wavered and blended in dual tones, 'so listen well. Georgeta does not belong to you. I will find a way to destroy you. Till that times comes, you will know fear and you will know pain. Most of all, you will know my wrath!"

The entity's body convulsed wildly when Alasdair ripped Vlad's face right from his shadowy head. Screaming, Vlad fell backwards as thick, inky fluid spilled forth from the gaping hole that had been his face. Throwing back his head, a bestial and unearthly howl erupted from the being just before Vlad's body exploded in to globs of thick goo.

Georgeta screamed, covering her head as she fell down upon the ground. Alasdair didn't move. The torn face he held within his naked, ink covered fingers began to dissolve and drip down to the ground. All about them the fog began to disperse, moving back and away from the two Lamia as if it was submitting to the Warlock's power.

"Georgeta!" Alasdair rushed to her as the coils of amber power vanished, slipping into his black eyes where the darkness receded. "Are you alright?" he asked softly as he gathered her limp form into his arms.

She was shaking when he came to her side, moving her into his arms. Her golden-brown eyes opened, and with a whimpering Georgeta threw her arms about his neck, hugging him tightly. She couldn't speak through her tear filled sobs.

397

"It's alright," he whispered as he held her and kissed her bloody cheeks. "I've got you. Everything's alright now." Threading fingers into her hair, Alasdair pressed her tightly to him.

"I was so scared…"

"I know, sweetheart. I know." She wouldn't stop shaking, and Alasdair's heart tore in to pieces with every little tremble. Drawing back, he cupped her face in his hands and smiled as warmly as he could to offer her some comfort. "He's gone now."

"No," whimpered Georgeta with a little shake of her head. "He's never gone."

"For now he is. This cannot go on. I will find a way to remove him from you. He won't torment you any longer. I promise you." He kissed her brow then embraced her once more. She crumbled against him, shaking and sobbing.

"Let's go home. You need to wake up now." Raising her face away from his chest, Alasdair brushed sable coils from her blood stained visage. "Wake up, Georgeta."

Swallowing a lump in her throat, she asked, "Will you be with me when I wake?"

"I'm with you now. Listen to my voice, Georgeta." Dipping his head, Alasdair kissed her bloody lips softly…so tenderly. And through a reverse Recodari, he urged her soul to obey him. "Wake…"

Temptations
∼ Book One of Love Stories ∼
Out now on Kindle download and paperback on all amazon.com sites.

∼∼∼∼

Moon Ghost
Story Four
∼

ummer…

The delicate night was broken by a slow creak of wood and metal sounding through the dark bedroom. The balcony door inched open by an unseen hand, sweeping forwards till the dim illumination of the moon gave birth to its child, the Moon Ghost.

Candra stepped forwards, one cloven hoof at a time, to gracefully stride to the large bed within the center of the room where his silvery-blue eyes settled. A coy smile touched his handsome mouth as he tipped his head. A strand of silver licked his cheek as he bent forwards, reaching out with a dangerous and deadly hand.

The object of his attention did not move, did not respond to his presence. They never did, the women he would visit during the night. They would remain unaware of him till he drew them from their deep slumber with promises of sexual seduction.

A gentle touch brushed along a bare shoulder then down a slender and bare arm. Still the slumbering woman did not move. Arching a slim brow, Candra huffed, and with a sly smirk coiling his lips the Yunhai took hold of the thin blanket to draw it away from the slumbering form. With the weather of summer now coming into bloom, the blanket was unnecessary. The bed gave a groan as the powerful, yet trim, creature slid down upon its frame, curling intimately and familiarly to the woman's back.

Candra couldn't help but grin as he dipped his head to run the tip of his nose along a shoulder, breathing in the delicate, womanly scent that tickled his senses - honey and goats milk - a luscious combination that made the silken texture of her feminine skin even silkier. To his delight, there was a touch of dampness to her pale hair, from an earlier bath, that tickled his senses. Moving forwards, he glanced down to her sleeping features from over her shoulder. In the dim light of the room, the delicate crystals of blues and greens that decorated her temples glistened. Pausing in silence, Candra truly thought he was staring down at a living memory.

Laelia was his past. Ríona was his present and, hopefully, his future.

He kissed her shoulder then slowly ran the tips of his forked tongue along her flesh as a deep purr rumbled up from his throat, "Wake…"

The woman didn't move.

Again the Yunhai grunted, his exotic features knitting at his trim brows. He smirked again and licked at her shoulder before running his parted tongue along her scented neck to flick and lap at her ear. "Ríona,' Candra called hotly, 'wake up."

This time he was able to obtain a reaction from her, one that brought his eyes to narrow. She mumbled and twisted about in her sleep with a cheek nuzzling her pillow. Arching up to a bent elbow, the Yunhai cocked his head as he stared down at her in astonishment. He couldn't believe this! She knew he was coming to visit her and yet she was sleeping!

Well, this wasn't going to do.

Releasing a heavy sigh, Candra drew away the remaining layer of blanket to expose Ríona's curvy form and ran his hot eyes over the delicate layer of pale blue silk that adorned her body. Sharp claws danced along her left leg, moving over sleek muscles and smooth skin till Candra's fingertips graced colored silk. The fabric was drawn higher as his touch continued to climb, exposing more and more of her nakedness to his hungry eyes. Once a curvy hip was visible, his hand moved to spread over the hard bump of hipbone and then upwards, dipping and moving with the curves of her body.

Once again, Candra turned his lips back to her flesh, pressing kisses up and down her shoulder and arm. A delicate nip of sharp teeth pinched her skin and drew from Ríona a tiny moan that was mixed with a tight mumble.

"If you do not wake, I will draw you from your sleep by force," said Candra with a devious chuckle of intent. The threat was not really a threat as he knew both would enjoy the outcome. But still, a gentlemanly warning was appropriate.

Another mumble came past Ríona's lips, and she shifted away from the nips and the licks. Candra arched a brow then chuckled as he pressed his palm to her stomach, keeping her from slipping away. He bent his head and whispered, "You are being cheeky tonight, Ríona." He grunted when the woman kicked out with a delicate foot, landing her heel to his shin.

Through a playful glare, Candra tightened his arm about her and his devious fingers, long and lean, began to travel down her stomach, over her pelvis, and into the crisp curls that settled against her mound. Pressing forwards, Candra slipped his hand between her legs, running the pads of two digits over her folds. He began to caress her, slowly at first - back and forth - till her flesh wept for him.

Even in her sleep Ríona's body responded eagerly to her Yunhai lover, and soon she was moaning sweetly for him. She pressed her hips back, seeking more of his touch, and when he slid a finger into her she hissed through her slumber.

Her tightness brought Candra to tense his eyes and groan against her shoulder when he dipped his head to touch his mouth to her flesh. He really should apologize for his lack of attention to her over the past month, but with the spring hunting season allowing hordes of hunters into the woods, he had not wished to leave his home unattended. Candra would certainly need to make up for his indiscretion, and would gladly do so.

Slowly, almost achingly slow, Candra slid his finger in and of her tight, slickening passage. He thrust his finger so deep that his knuckles pressed against her swelling folds. "I love how hot you become,' he moaned against her neck, 'for me."

A tight whimper echoed from Ríona as her fingers curled to the sheets of her bed. Her hips pressed back and her legs parted, eagerly and willingly begging for more of him.

Candra bit back a low snarl when her hips began to move in time with his pumping fingers, pressing and shifting against his own - rubbing against his swelling shaft. He groaned when he heard a breathy whimper fall from the elf's lips in the fumbled formation of his name. And through his gaze he saw Ríona raise a slender arm to drape over him so her fingers could coil into his hair. She pulled him to her, rolling her head back as she moaned again and whimpered, "Oh…Candra…"

"So,' the Yunhai chuckled with his lips gracing the shell of her ear, 'you have decided to wake and join me for tonight's pleasures, I see."

A sleepy, giggled purr sounded form the beauty as she tipped her head, offering her neck to his kisses. "I was dreaming of you," she whispered, though a gasp took the words to flutter away as she felt his fingers give a deep, hard thrust.

"Where you?"

"Oh…yes…"

"What were you dreaming of?" asked Candra as he nibbled her ear and thrust his fingers quicker, deeper, into her. "Tell me."

"You were making love to me,' she replied softly, sweetly and sensually as she wiggled her hips to his fingers, 'thrusting wildly into me, so deep - so hard."

A lusciously erotic sound tumbled form her throat that sent shivers down Candra's spine. The image alone, created by her sexual words, hardened his shaft further and pulled a knot of lust tight within his belly. Growling, he ground his hips against her pert rump so she could feel how aroused and desperate he was for her.

Grinning, Ríona arched back to her mystical lover and purred as she coiled her fingers into his hair. "Shall I tell you more or shall we create our own dream?"

A deep and vibrating chuckle tumbled forth from Candra as he gently bit at her neck. "I always prefer creating my own dreams."

Reaching between her tight thighs, Ríona gently grasped his wrist to draw his touch and his wonderful fingers from her and up to her lips. She kissed his wet fingers, licking them clean. The caress brought a hard shudder to ripple from his body against her and a deep snarl of desire to fall against her flesh. Though she loved to tease her Yunhai lover, Ríona knew that his patience was quick to thin when he was in no mood for her play. Mewing, she raised her leg to drape over his hip then reached between her legs so she could take hold of his hard, throbbing, and lengthy flesh. A tremble broke through her as Ríona pressed back to him while guiding the swollen tip of his shaft against the slick opening of her body.

Candra needed no further instructions as to what the elf wanted. Her words and the hot wetness of her folds was enough to urge him on. With a soft, breathy sigh, he grunted, "Guide me, Mal'ashery."

Both lovers moaned in unison as their bodies became one, joining at the junction of her womb when Candra thrust forwards to bury himself within her trembling core. He wrapped his arms about her as he began to rock his hips, thrusting and grinding against her. The more she whimpered the harder Candra moved, making sure the motions met her rhythm - that she could feel every inch of him.

Candra's heated grunting and deep snarls fell into the silken falls of Ríona's hair as the pillow beneath her head drank in her escalating notes of pleasure. Her soft begs tickled the Yunhai's pointed ears, urging him to drive harder and deeper, to take her and to claim her.

Her body was his pleasure. His hands roamed over her dampening skin to cup and mold her swollen breasts. Though his claws could kill, his fingers were gentle when he took her nipples to twist and to pull - rolling the sensitive buds against the roughened flesh of his palms.

Ríona's release came fast, ricocheting through her body in a flood of violent and erotic pleasure. Her body bucked, thrusting wildly against Candra as he continued to drive into her till his own release tore through him along with a howl that was muffled against her neck.

Weakened and sated, they fell against each other, panting, shaking, and trembling. Candra slowly drew himself from Ríona's wet and quivering channel with an audible slick pop, and instantly missed her wet heat. Hearing her mew in delight spread a grin to his lips, so he lazily ran kisses over her salted skin.

"That was nice,' she purred sweetly as she rolled over to her back, stretching like a kitten lying in the sun.

Candra tipped his head, watching her, then chuckled. "Only nice? Are my talents to such a low level that you mock them?" He dipped his head to nuzzle her neck.

Such a loving and pleased giggle trickled from Ríona's softly smiling lips. A grin touched her features giving her a shadow of deviancy as the Moon Ghost inched over her, hovering and looking down to openly run his gaze over her naked body. Lifting a hand, she brushed back locks of his fallen hair behind a pointed ear before she set her fingers to caressing his damp skin, enjoying the way finely crafted muscles twitched beneath her teases. "Oh no,' she mewed softly - playfully, 'my words are compliments, Mal'ashery. I would never need to mock you for you always are able to please me in all the right ways."

Candra cast his silvery-blue eyes towards her own, a sly and devious sneer curling his lips. He moved forwards, slowly allowing parts of his male body to press down upon her as he settled between her legs and into her welcoming arms. "I would be hurt if you ever did." He lowered his head and took a pert nipple into his moist, warm mouth - lavishing leisurely with swirls of his forked tongue.

Mewing, Ríona cradled her pale lover to her breasts, content to run fingers through his hair and over the curvature of his horns. When he bit the nipple, she moaned and arched herself to him. "I am glad that the spring hunting season is over," she said after a luscious shiver tickled her spine. "I am not sure I could have handled another month without your visits."

Candra not only raised his head but raised his lean, tight torso up by his broad hands that came to press to the bed at her shoulders. Long ends of silver licked and kissed Ríona's pale cheeks, causing a little giggle to bubble up in her throat. "A month was not too much time to be apart."

"Still, it was too long for me." Sighing, she ran fingers over the sculpted muscles of his arms then wound them to his hair at the base of his neck. "I would have come to you if you had sent me a missive."

He shook his head. "No. I would not have you risking your life among the hunters stalking the woods. A few, I am sure, are associates of Byrin's and had attempted to enter Gattaloch."

Ríona's delicate brows furrowed causing the crystals set upon her skin to glisten in the dim light of a moon ray that streamed through the open balcony door. A frown graced her lips and she sighed, "His friends are even more foolish and drunk than he was. They should know better than to hunt ghosts." She looked to him with a concerned and cautious eye. "Did they harm you?"

"There were no confrontations. Those who entered grew bored of wondering the old halls and departed rather quickly." Candra shrugged his shoulders. "Perhaps Byrin's legacy and friendship were not worth much to them in the end, especially at the risk of losing their lives."

Mewing, Ríona drew her lover to her, kissing his lips with an eager building of passion. Candra groaned softly to the feel of her moist tongue caressing over his mouth, seeking to open his lips and deepen the kiss.

Leaning back, Ríona licked her lips as a deviant smile formed dimples at the corners of her pretty mouth. "We should not waste any more time. We have much pleasure to recover." Slithering a hand between their bodies, she gently closed her fingers about Candra's hard shaft and gave a slow, taut stroke. Watching the way his lips parted in a sigh and his eyes flutter close brought a surge of sexual pride within Ríona. She squeezed him once more before arching her hips to press the swollen tip of his length against her.

One more shift of her body had the thick head pressing forwards. The lovers trembled and groaned to the sensation of her body opening to him then slowly tightening about him. Candra slid an arm beneath her head, gripping locks of her hair within deadly fingers so he could pin her body between himself and the soft mattress. Their eyes locked, and in one powerful thrust Candra drove himself into her.

All about them the room echoed in Ríona's feverish cry of unadulterated pleasure!

❧❧❧❧

Later that night, with only a few hours left till dawn, Ríona stood out on the balcony, gazing up to the star scattered night. Candra was still upon the bed, seemingly asleep from hours of endless and tireless love-making. Rest never came to her as her mind twisted and turned the events of the past months over and over till her thoughts ran wild.

Not to disturb the Yunhai, she slipped form the bed, downed a bed-robe then stepped out to the balcony for some fresh air. The night was alive with the delicate chirping of insects, and upon the breeze came the sweet scents of summer flowers. A smile touched her lips as she touched a hand over her heart.

"I miss you, Warren," she said quietly and to herself. "I hope you miss me too." Raising her pale pink eyes, she looked out and over the thick tree-line towards the village. "Summer will be beautiful this year. The weather is not too hot and the rain is cool in the evening. I want you to know that I will never forget you. I will always love you and cherish the time we had together. Please don't worry about me. I have a guardian now who shall watch over me and see me safe. I only ask that you forgive Candra for delving justice down upon Byrin. I do not want you to be upset with him for killing your brother - your murderer. Nor do I want you angry with me for taking Candra to my bed."

She frowned, her lips twisting in tender thoughts as she bowed her head and closed her eyes with a deep breath of crisp air. "Candra still claims that I am the reborn soul of a previous lover. I'm not sure if I believe him, but his feelings for me hold great care and tenderness. There is a part of me, deep down, that believes him and knows that his words are true."

"I don't want to be alone, Warren," she went on to say with a little shake of her head. "I don't want to walk the rest of my life without someone to share the pleasures of life with. I had you for the time we were blessed to have, but I must move on. I know you would not want me mourning you and living confined within this house till my last breath. We knew I would outlive you, but even so you left me prematurely."

Sighing, she looked high up to the stars and to where she believed 'heaven' rested. "Will you wait for me, Warren? When I pass on, will you be there to greet me with your loving arms and your warm smile? Will you accept me even though I have taken another to my bed, to my heart?" Her eyes shined with tears, and with a little sniffle a glittering drop skimmed down her cheek. Bowing her head, she whispered softly, "I will always love you, my love."

After a few moments of silence, a warm and deep voice spoke out ever so softly so not to disturb the Fae'alyn's thoughts, "You are thinking of him."

Ríona drew her eyes open and her mind drew from her contemplations. With a slight tip of her head she asked, "Of who?"

"Your late husband."

She smiled then turned to the side to see Candra standing in the door. The sight of the mythical creature in all his naked glory and moon kissed skin took her breath away. "Would that upset you if I was?"

The Yunhai shook his head. He replied in all honesty, "No."

And so he should not. Candra held no emotional concern that his 'lover', in the context of a sexual partner and one he did care about, was thinking of a man that she truly loved - had been in love with. Candra would never fall in love with her, never offer her marriage or children, and Ríona was comfortable with that understanding. To his answer, she nodded then reached a hand out to him.

Candra crossed the small space to take her hand, and she moved to curl against his naked chest to rest a cheek over his heart. Within darkness they held each other, content to listen to the soft music of chattering insects.

In the quietude Candra spoke in his melodic and exotic voice, "There are only a few hours of night left. Soon, I will need to return to my home."

Ríona no longer frowned when Candra told her that he needed to leave her for she knew they would see each other again come another night. Now she only smiled to him and bid him a farewell with a kiss to his cheek. She knew that Candra would always be with her, and even after her death, she would always be with him - a memory cherished by him. Ríona would never be alone again for Candra was with her and Warren was waiting for her.

Giving him a warm and loving smile, she arched up to kiss his lips and whispered softly, "Then you should return and rest. I have kept you too long as it is."

The Yunhai returned her kiss then cupped her face within his deadly hands as he pressed his lips to her forehead. "I will return," he told her in promise.

"I know. You always do."

Candra ran his fingers along her skin then dipped his head and whispered softly to a delicately pointed ear, "Close your eyes."

Ríona sighed to the way his breath tickled her ear and his words swept warmth through her soul. To his command she closed her eyes and her lips parting in a soft breath.

"Wait for me," Candra whispered softly. "Call for me and I will come to you. Look to the moon and know that I am always with you, watching you - guarding you."

A caress of a breeze wrapped about Ríona, and after a moment, she opened her eyes to find Candra gone. A smirk touched her lips as she looked out to the darkness to find no trace of him. He always left with those words, a Yunhai promise between lovers. Wrapping her arms about her body, she turned her eyes up to the moon that glowed large within the dark sky.

"Till we meet again in the throes of pleasure. Sleep well Moon Ghost and know that you will always be in my heart."

Desires
❧ Book Two of Love Stories ❧
❧❧❧❧

The Abandoned One
Story One
❧

"Hok'ee!"

The dark woods of Taro erupted into action as the sharp scream of horror sounded. Birds that had been nesting and animals that had been resting moved into action, squawking and bolting deeper into the thicket and away from the clearing. The two combatants, facing each other and panting heavily large gulps of broken air, paused as from off to the right two forms came rushing through the thick brush.

Candra's crystal blue eyes narrowed and his lips pulled back so a low rumbling growl could sound forth. At his sides, his hands clenched and unclenched till the knuckles of his fingers turned whiter than the alabaster color of his skin. "Ríona," he snarled angrily when he saw the Fae'alyn stumble over a buried rock.

Hok'ee's torn features scrunched in confusion when he heard his name called out in the form of a panic stricken cry of alarm. His powerful, fawn-like body retracted from the stance of attack he had taken, straightening as he turned towards the source of the cry. A heavy frown pulled his broken lips when he saw Tali scampering towards him, her thick coils of ebony dancing about her and the glowing paleness of her nightgown parting the night.

"Tali?" Hok'ee canted his head as he questioned her identity.

With Hok'ee's attention turned, Candra once again focused upon the task at hand; his battle with Hok'ee. Snarling, he moved into action. With a surge of strength, he pushed across the ground to reach his opponent in four lengthy, yet easy, strides. The blow he delivered to Hok'ee shocked the other Yunhai and snapped Hok'ee's head to the side, with a sickening crack, from the contact delivered to his left temple. Though Hok'ee tumbled to the ground, his balance lost, Candra did not back down. He drove forwards, landing blow after blow of his fists to Hok'ee's body till the forest around them echoed with the nauseating sound of flesh and muscle being softened.

When Hok'ee's mind came back to him, along with the brutal realization of Candra's assault, the Yunhai released an animalistic snarl and twisted his thin body around to face Candra and the other Yunhai's cruel blows without flinching. Though he tried his best to strike back at Candra, Hok'ee could do little but block the raining slashes and punches. He yapped when

Candra's claws dug into the flesh of his shoulders, raking away skin till layers of sleek muscle were exposed. He cried out in pain when Candra dug claws into his neck with the intention of ripping out his throat.

Yet Hok'ee would not allow Candra to win so easily. Gathering his strength and pushing through the agonizing pain, he latched onto Candra's secured arm with his own hands and leaned back to bring Candra off balance just enough so he could bend his knees and drive his cloven hooves into Candra's gut. The blow knocked the air from Candra's lungs causing him to cough violently a spray of crimson blood, and with Candra's attention turned to the pain of muscles ripping within his abdomen, Hok'ee managed to twist Candra off of him, dislodging the grip upon his neck. Nauseating agony swept through Hok'ee as Candra's nails were ripped from his flesh, taking with them chunks of flesh.

As Candra stumbled back, Hok'ee drove a clenched fist into Candra's bruised abdomen to push the other Yunhai back a few strides. While Candra coughed to regain his breath, Hok'ee doubled over and grimaced in discomfort. He looked to his torn shoulder to see blood seeping down from the wound in his neck, painting his silvery-grey flesh in a stream of fresh, steaming blood. He did not have to touch the gaping wound upon his neck to know the damage that had been done. Snarling, he slowly turned his wild eye to Candra, the single functioning orb spasming with fury within the torn socket.

"I will kill you!" he bellowed as he tried to push himself up from the ground only to find himself folding over when the strength in his arm gave way.

Candra, spitting out a wad of bloody phlegm, gave a bloody smile of pride when Hok'ee fell to the ground. Muscles within his stomach twitched and pulled as each breath of air he took riddled his bruised body with pain. Candra's red stained lips parted with a retort pressing the tip of his tongue, yet Ríona's sharp bark of his name drew his attention to her and away from his intended victim.

"Enough, Candra!" Ríona cried out while trying to hold on to Tali. The younger elf twisted and turned, fighting pitifully to be released from Ríona's stronger grip. Ríona could not help tears from spilling down her cheeks as she stared in awe at Candra. "Why are you doing this?" she asked.

Candra curled his lips, and a sadistic gaze of pride shined within his magnificent eyes. "This battle never concluded over a century ago when Hok'ee and I first faced each other. Tonight, I will finish what I began."

"By killing him?"

A slender brow arched over one of Candra's angular eyes, and he tipped his head in bewilderment to Ríona's question. "Of course."

Ríona's eyes softened with a look of contentment and she sighed with a slow shake of her head. "This is insanity,' she muttered, 'this battle."

A slight smile teased Candra's handsome mouth. "This battle does not concern you, Ríona. Take your friend and leave." He pointed a bloody claw towards the woods and said in a low and threatening tone, "I will not hold back, nor will I stop if either of you get in my way."

Ríona's heart tumbled into her stomach and a twist of bile rose up within her throat. Did Candra really mean he would willingly place her and Tali in danger to win a fight? Would he harm them intentionally? A cold shiver ran through her body as she watched a thick strand of bloody goo drip away from Candra's claws that were stuck with small pieces of skin and meat. She gulped. "Hok'ee is lost in his mind. He is a tortured soul due to the wounds his heart has carried all these decades. His need for revenge against you has driven him mad. The monster his pride has become has tortured him, twisting him into a broken creature! What will killing him bring you, Candra? What purpose will his death serve?"

"Honor."

Ríona blinked then grunted when Tali tried to pull away, so she tightened her arms about her friend and cooed softly to ease Tali's sobbing. Then she turned her attention back to Candra and narrowed her eyes. "Honor? What honor is there in this blood sport? Tell me!"

Candra raised his chin and a lock of his silvery-white hair fluttered against a thin cheek, caught by a stray breeze. "I will achieve victory in defeating Hok'ee." He looked to his fellow Yunhai and sneered in disgust at the pathetic sight. "Hok'ee should know when he has been defeated and submit himself to an honorable death. You are correct, Ríona. He has allowed himself to become tainted by the darkness of his own mind. Like a rabid animal, he should be terminated."

"No!" cried Tali as her body buckled within Ríona's grasp. Ríona gasped and softly cuddled her friendly to her. "Leave him with me,' Tali called out through her choking sobs, 'and I will care for him! He does not need to die! He only needs his suffering to end! Allow me to help him! I beg of you!"

Candra licked his lips; his face a shadow of empty expression. "You are correct, child. His suffering needs to end." Flexing a hand of bloody claws, Candra began to stalk towards Hok'ee.

"Candra! Don't!"

"Stop! Please stop!" cried Tali as she brazenly, tossing caution to the wind, ran towards her Yunhai lover once she dislodged herself from Ríona's arms.

"Tali! Come back!" Ríona's cry of alarm died when her name was bellowed in a shout of rage. Stumbling, she halted her steps and slowly turned her fear etched features towards Candra. The look of hot rage contorting his usually handsome face set her back a few steps, and a sharp gasp pushed up from her throat when he turned his keen eyes to follow Tali's motions.

"Hok'ee!"

The beautiful, alarmed sound of Tali's voice eased little of Hok'ee's agony, yet he managed to raise his eye. Confusion, anger and worry, contorted his features when he saw Tali running towards him. Why would she be running towards him? No. She couldn't be trying to stop this battle. Would she? The little fool! Anger coiled within him and he sat back with a hand pressed out to her.

"No, Tali!" called Hok'ee. "Go back!"

Tali wouldn't listen, or she couldn't. The sound of her loud sobbing no doubt drowned out his call of warning. Even so, if she could hear him, she would not stop - could not stop. She stumbled upon broken twigs, branches, and rocks. She fell to the ground, yelping when her bare feet scraped against debris or her knees struck against a rock. Yet she wouldn't give up, and rose up again and again to try and reach her Moon Ghost lover.

The pitiful sight of Tali's petite frame struggling, becoming soiled with both dirt and blood from fresh cuts, tore sympathy through Hok'ee. He felt a part of his black heart twist and felt a grip of agony take his soul. "No,' he heard himself whisper, 'go back."

"Hok'ee. Please get up!" Tali cried pathetically and through her sobs as she pushed up from the forest floor once again. Tears ran down her face, mixing with splotches of dirt to paint her alabaster skin brown. From behind her, Ríona continued to call her name, begging her not to get too close to the Yunhai.

"Tali!" The bellow of Hok'ee's voice, bathed with dominance, stopped Tali's advance. She stumbled then stood still, her thin arms shaking against her chest. She looked to him with bewilderment and slowly took another step forwards, testing her resolve and Hok'ee's patience. "Stop!" Hok'ee barked as he slammed a hand to the ground with such force that the impact created a crater around his knuckles. "Go back! Leave!"

Tali shook her head as a soft whimper bubbled up within her throat. "I won't go,' she called out as loud as her quivering voice could sound, 'not without you!"

Hok'ee's broken face twisted as he snarled dangerously, both of his eyes narrowing. "I do not want you here! You will only get in my way and get hurt, you foolish girl!"

Tali winced as if she had been hit, the harshness to his voice slicing across her heart. "Hok'ee…"

"Go! Get away from here. I do not need you!"

Shaking fingers balled against the thin nightgown that clothed Tali's chest. Beneath her grip she could feel the pounding of her heart and the panic that fueled the unsteady beat. He didn't mean what he said. He didn't want her to go, did he? She couldn't leave him! If she did, Candra would kill him. Looking to him bent to the ground, the muscles of his body subtly shaking in agony, tore Tali's heart to pieces. She wanted to reach for him, comfort him and sooth him, but the look of rage within his single working eye kept her frozen in place.

Hok'ee turned his good eye towards Ríona and commanded in a sharp bite, "Take her and leave! If you do not, I will kill her myself."

The delicate whimper of his name twitched Hok'ee's long, pointed ears. The expression of deep hurt written upon Tali's features fractured what was left of his heart. He didn't want to speak such a violent threat against her, but what choice did he have? Candra would not restrain his violence, and Hok'ee could not put Tali in danger.

When he saw Tali take a step back, Hok'ee felt a wave of relief. His mind softened and the pounding of his heart eased. As he felt his lips pull into a smile, he bowed his head so a few tendrils of his dreadlocks curtained the tender expression. But the moment of comfort was short lived as Tali and Ríona both screamed. Hok'ee had time to raise his head and notice that the two women were looking away from him with eyes full of horror. Time slowed as he twisted about in the direction of Candra, yet the slowness of time did not give him the opportunity to move. His body ached to such a degree that the muscles of his limbs failed him.

Candra was barreling down upon him with such speed that the thundering of Candra's hooves drowned out Tali's cries. Panic struck Hok'ee with such ferocity that his heart went cold when he saw a blur of white fabric off to his right. Ríona cried out Tali's name, and before his gaze he saw his little elf running to him. There was no time to react! No time to warn her to stop. She was already upon him with Candra's claws poised for attack.

Pushing past the brutal suffering of his battered body, Hok'ee forced himself to move. He half fumbled, half pushed from the ground in order to grab Tali as she reached him. She fell into his arms, her ebony coils flapping about him from the momentum of her run and the impact of her body against his. And though Hok'ee was granted a moment's peace, as he felt her soft body press against him and her shaking arms wrap about his shoulders, the unimaginable pain that laced through his back could not be ignored.

Horrendous agony tore through Hok'ee's body the moment he twisted about to cover Tali's body with his own, throwing her down to the earthen floor as Candra descended upon them. If he had waited, a heartbeat later, he would have been bathed in Tali's hot blood when Candra ran her through with a clawed hand. Instead, Hok'ee protected her and took Candra's deadly blow.

By shielding her with his body, Hok'ee gave himself over to death.

Future Publications
✄ ✄ ✄ ✄

Sweet Roselynn ✄ The day had finally come - the Soul Binding. Roselynn couldn't wait to have her destiny sealed and her mate welcomed into her family. She had waited so long to be with him, to have his love and experience his pleasure. They were to be wed and step together into their future - together.

Ashur couldn't wait to make his move and break free from the invisible chains that kept him a prisoner within his lonely and dangerous world - the world of the Drae. A century had passed, and now he was able to see the light to his darkness. There was only one problem that kept his freedom out of his reach - Roselynn. They were to marry, and his duty was to stand at her side as her husband and her guard till his death. However, he couldn't stay one more decade within the darkness and the coldness of the Drae world. He wanted to feel the light and the warmth of the twin suns. He wanted to feel the wind upon his skin, and he wanted to hear the incredible sounds of life that flourished above.

Most of all; he wanted to walk his own path.

Ashur wanted his freedom, and he would have it at any cost.

He didn't realize that his freedom came with a great cost and that his actions would lead to his and Roselynn's destinies being torn asunder. What would happen to them when their world was thrown into chaos?

The Roman ✄ Molly Alexander has always been dedicated to her lifelong passions - archeology and ancient Rome. When her dream of participating in an excavation in Pompeii came to fruition, she thought life had finally gifted her with happiness. However, happiness was always short lived. Molly never expected that the ghosts of Pompeii's destruction would follow her home. She was never one to believe in the paranormal till her uninvited spirit guest began to haunt not only her daily activities but her nightly dreams

When the memories of the past collided with the events of the present, nothing positive becomes the outcome. A secret was to be revealed, and one soul was bent upon making sure that the past stayed in the past. Can the ghost of a Roman Primus Pilas guide Molly's memories to the truth of their demise and the danger lurking in her future? Or will the love of Molly's life finally obtain the goal he has spent centuries trying to accomplish - the conquest of her heart - while silencing the terrible truth of his murderous history?

ﻙ

Forever ﻙ Tekem thought he had finally found his true love - his soul mate - the woman who would hold his heart in both life and in the afterlife. Ava thought her heart would stay within her homeland of Greece. But then she stepped upon the golden sands of Egypt and her destiny unfolded before her eyes. Their love was a love written in the stars yet destined to be tested by the sands of time.

Betrayal and murder tore apart their fledgling marriage by none other than Tekem's father; a powerful Necromancer driven by his cruel desires for Ava. After the murder of Tekem's mother, Tekem fell to his father's sadistic devices. With her world now soaked in the stain of blood, Ava fell to her own blade. However, the lovers did not realize that their souls would be reunited centuries later; one reborn and one locked within the hold of his rotting corpse - a mummy. Then again, they never expected Tekem's grandfather to save their souls so that Tekem could be reborn to rain vengeance down upon his killer. They were destined to be reunited in love, Tekem and Ava, and reborn in a modern world were the demons of ancient times still battled for dominance.

Would Tekem powerful enough to destroy his father and save the woman who was taken from him centuries ago? Or would he fall to his father once more and fail to save the love of his life for a second time? One way or another, Tekem will survive and prevail. After all, he is the grandson to the God Anubis - and Gods do not die.

About the Author

~

Sarahbeth Lazic is a newly published author of dark fantasy, paranormal romance, and erotica. Bloody Thorn: Book One of the Thorn Trilogy 2nd edition was her first novel begun in 2004. This novel was proceeded by Warlock: A Thorn Trilogy Novel and Temptations: Book One of Love Stories - published in 2014.

Sarahbeth lives in Salt Lake City, Utah with Kaede (a Scottish terrier) and Gus (an adopted Chihuahua) - her two beloved dogs. She is also the proprietor of Sakura's Garden: Zen Grooming for Dogs - the first and fully holistic dog grooming salon in SLC since 2010.

Sarahbeth's love for creativity and writing began when she was in high school, spurred on by her love of history, world travel, and the exploration of ancient cultures and societies. Many of her stories center on her travel adventures and her passion for history and archeology and fantasy. She has been a fan of the paranormal and vampires since a child, and during her college years completed a short study program in Wales where she studied the mythology of European vampires. With the influence of years spent involved in the role-playing games World of Darkness and Dungeons and Dragons, there was little stopping her from expanding her love for short story writing by creating her own realms, fantasies, and novels.

Sarahbeth encourages her readers to find her on Facebook.

FaceBook: Sarahbeth Lazic - Thorn Publications

40295924R00237

Made in the USA
Lexington, KY
01 April 2015